Everyman, I will go with thee,
and be thy guide

Émile Zola

GERMINAL

Edited by
DAVID BAGULEY
University of Durham

Based on a translation by
HAVELOCK ELLIS AND EDITH LEES

Consultant Editor for this Volume
THOMAS MATHEWS
University College of London

EVERYMAN
J. M. DENT · LONDON
CHARLES E. TUTTLE
VERMONT

Introduction, notes and other critical apparatus
© J M Dent 1996

First published in Everyman's Library in 1933
This edition first published in Everyman Paperbacks in 1996

J. M. Dent
Orion Publishing Group
Orion House, 5 Upper St Martin's Lane,
London WC2H 9EA
and
Charles E. Tuttle Co., Inc.
28 South Main Street,
Rutland, Vermont 05701 USA

Typeset in Sabon by CentraCet Ltd, Cambridge
Printed in Great Britain by
The Guernsey Press Co. Ltd, Guernsey, C.I.

British Library Cataloguing-in-Publication Data
is available upon request.

ISBN 0 460 87581 7

CONTENTS

NOTE ON THE AUTHOR AND EDITOR

ÉMILE ZOLA, son of an Italian civilian engineer and a French mother, was born on 2 April 1840 in Paris, but spent most of his childhood and youth in Aix-en-Provence, where he enjoyed a close friendship with the artist Paul Cézanne. He moved to Paris in 1858 with his widowed mother and suffered hardship for several years until the late 1860s, when he began to gain recognition as an opposition journalist, as a defender of Manet and other avant-garde artists and as the author of *Thérèse Raquin* (1867), his first significant 'naturalist' novel. In 1870 he married Alexandrine Meley. Influenced by the ideas of Taine and by the example of Balzac, he developed a scientific view of literary realism, which he called 'naturalism', and in 1869 embarked upon the vast enterprise of writing a series of independent novels, *Les Rougon-Macquart*, linked together by following the fortunes of members of a single family in the various sectors and strata of the society of the Second Empire (1852–70). Though he also wrote short stories, plays and criticism, his masterworks, such as *L'Assommoir* (1877), *Nana* (1880), *Germinal* (1885), and *The Earth* (*La Terre*, 1887), form parts of this twenty-volume series which occupied the writer until 1893. Zola became the leader of a loosely constituted school of naturalist writers and his influence spread widely abroad. His later works, notably his trilogy of novels *The Three Cities* (*Les Trois Villes*, 1894–8) and his uncompleted series entitled *The Four Gospels* (*Les Quatre Evangiles*, 1899–1903), are more didactic in manner than his naturalist texts and are inspired by the novelist's reformist zeal, nourished in part by the birth of his two children by Jeanne Rozerot, Denise in 1889 and Jacques in 1891. Zola's famous intervention in the Dreyfus Affair, particularly the publication of 'I Accuse' ('J'accuse') on 13 January 1898, led to his prosecution and persecution, forcing him into a year of voluntary exile in England. Either by accident or, as many suspect, as a result of foul play, Zola died of carbon monoxide poisoning on the night of 28–29 September 1902 from the fumes of a blocked chimney in his Paris apartment.

DAVID BAGULEY has been Professor of French at the University of Western Ontario (London, Canada) and more recently at the University of Durham (UK). He has degrees from the universities of Nottingham, Leicester and Nancy. His publications include books on Zola and literary naturalism as well as bibliographies on nineteenth-century French literature.

CHRONOLOGY OF ZOLA'S LIFE

Year	Age	Life
1840		Born in Paris
1843	3	Moves to Aix-en-Provence
1847	7	Death of father, a week before 7th birthday

CHRONOLOGY OF HIS TIMES

Year	Literary Context	Historical Events
1840	Proudhon, *What Is Property?*	Marriage of Queen Victoria. Napoleon's remains transferred to Les Invalides
1842	Sue, *Les Mystères de Paris* (1842–3). Death of Stendhal	Chartist risings in England
1844	Dumas, *Les Trois Mousquetaires*, *Le Comte de Monte-Cristo* (1844–5)	Factory Act in Britain. French war in Morocco
1845	Engels, *The Condition of the Working Classes in England*. Wagner, *Tannhäuser*	Beginning of the Irish Famine
1846	Balzac, *La Cousine Bette*. Proudhon, *Philosophie de la misère*	US war against Mexico
1847	C. Brontë, *Jane Eyre*. E. Brontë, *Wuthering Heights*	
1848	Thackeray, *Vanity Fair*. Death of Chateaubriand. Marx and	February Revolution in France. Abdication of Louis-Philippe. Declaration of Republic. June Days. Louis Napoleon Bonaparte elected President of the Republic. European Revolutions
1849	Chateaubriand, *Mémoires d'outre-tombe*. Deaths of Chopin and Poe	California gold rush
1850	Dickens, *David Copperfield*. Hawthorne, *The Scarlet Letter*. Death of Balzac	Death of Louis-Philippe
1851	Melville, *Moby Dick*	*Coup d'état* of Louis Napoleon Bonaparte. World Fair in London's Crystal Palace

1852   12   Develops friendship with Paul Cézanne

1858   18   Moves to Paris

1859   19   Fails *baccalauréat* twice. Publishes poems and a short
              story in *La Provence*

1860   20   Takes menial work and lives alone in poverty

1862   22   Job with publishing firm Hachette. Becomes head of
              publicity department. Naturalized French citizen

1863   23   Publishes articles and stories in the press

1864-6 24-5 First book: *Stories for Ninon* (*Contes à Ninon*), then first
              novel: *Claude's Confession* (*La Confession de Claude*).
              Meets and lives with future wife, Gabrielle-Alexandrine
              Meley. Frequents painters such as Cézanne, Manet,
              Pissarro. Leaves Hachette for regular career in journalism

1852	Stowe, *Uncle Tom's Cabin*. Death of Gogol	Proclamation of the Second Empire with Napoleon III as Emperor. Death of Wellington
1853	Hugo, *Les Châtiments*. Verdi, *La Traviata*	Haussmann becomes prefect of Paris and begins reconstruction of the city
1854	Dickens, *Hard Times*	France and England declare war on Russia (Crimean War). Battle of Balaclava
1855	Death of Nerval	Battle of Sebastopol. World Fair in Paris
1856	Births of Freud and G. B. Shaw	End of Crimean War. Birth of Imperial Prince in France
1857	Flaubert, *Madame Bovary*. Baudelaire, *Les Fleurs du mal*	Indian 'Mutiny'
1858		Orsini assassination attempt on Napoleon III
1859	Darwin, *On the Origin of Species*	Execution of John Brown. Beginning of work on the Suez Canal. Italian War
1860	Eliot, *The Mill on the Floss*	Beginning of the 'liberal' Empire in France. Victor Emmanuel hailed by Garibaldi as King of a united Italy. Lincoln becomes President of the United States. French gain Savoie and Nice from Sardinia
1861	Dickens, *Great Expectations*. Eliot, *Silas Marner*	Outbreak of the American Civil War (to 1865). Wilhelm I, King of Prussia. Kingdom of Italy proclaimed. Beginning of the construction of the Paris Opera House (to 1875)
1862	Hugo, *Les Misérables*. Flaubert, *Salammbô*	French–English–Spanish expedition to Mexico. World Fair in London, attended by a delegation of French socialist workers. Bismarck becomes Prime Minister of Prussia
1863	Manet, *Le Déjeuner sur l'herbe*	'Salon des refusés' in Paris
1864	Verne, *Journey to the Centre of the Earth*. Goncourt, *Germinie Lacerteux*. Tolstoy, *War and Peace* (1864–9)	International Working Men's Association founded in London

1867   27   Serial novel *The Mysteries of Marseilles* (*Les Mystères de Marseille*). Defends Manet. First significant novel: *Thérèse Raquin*

1868–9   28–9 First plans for the *Rougon-Macquart* series

1870–1   30–1 Marries. Leaves Paris for the south of France during the war as a political journalist. Publishes *The Fortune of the Rougons* (*La Fortune des Rougon*), first novel of the *Rougon-Macquart* series

1872   32   *The Kill* (*La Curée*). Friendship with Flaubert

1873   33   *Savage Paris* (*Le Ventre de Paris*)

1865	Claude Bernard, *Introduction à l'étude de la médicine expérimentale*	French section of the International founded in Paris. End of American Civil War. Assassination of Lincoln
1866	Dostoievsky, *Crime and Punishment*	Prussia defeats Austria. Battle of Sadowa
1867	Marx, *Das Kapital*, vol. I. Death of Baudelaire	World Fair in Paris. Liberal reforms in France, but French section of the International dissolved. Last French troops leave Mexico. Execution of Emperor Maximilian in Mexico. Canada becomes a Dominion
1868	Dostoievsky, *The Idiot* (1868–9)	Disbanding again of the French section of the International by the government. Bakunin establishes the International Social Democratic Alliance. Gladstone becomes Prime Minister of Britain
1869	Flaubert, *L'Éducation sentimentale*	Opening of the Suez Canal. Opposition of Bakunin against Marx to control the International
1870	Verne, *Twenty Thousand Leagues under the Sea*. Hugo returns from exile to France. Death of Dickens and of Dumas *père*	French section of the International dissolved again. Franco-Prussian War. Fall of the Second Empire. Siege of Paris
1871		Paris Commune. Thiers elected President of the Republic in France. Trade unions legalized in Britain
1872	Nietzsche, *The Birth of Tragedy*. Death of Gautier	Bakunin and his followers expelled by Marx from the International
1873		German troops leave France. Death of Napoleon III at Chislehurst. Mac-Mahon elected president of the Republic in France. World Fair in Vienna

1874	34	*The Conquest of Plassans* (*La Conquête de Plassans*) Also a play, *Les Héritiers Rabourdin*, and *More Stories for Ninon* (*Nouveaux Contes à Ninon*)
1875	35	*The Sin of Father Mouret* (*La Faute de l'abbé Mouret*). Began writing articles for Russian periodical *Vestnik Evropy* (*European Herald*)
1876	36	*His Excellency* (*Son Excellence Eugène Rougon*)
1877	36	*L'Assommoir*
1878	38	*A Love Affair* (*Une Page d'amour*). Buys property in Médan. The 'Médan Group' forms (Alexis, Céard, Hennique, Huysmans, Maupassant)
1880	40	*Nana*. 'Médan Group' publishes *Les Soirées de Médan*. Death of mother. *The Experimental Novel*
1881	41	Publishes 4 volumes of critical studies
1882	42	*Pot-Bouille*
1883	43	*Ladies' Delight* (*Au Bonheur des Dames*)
1884	44	*Zest for Life* (*La Joie de vivre*)
1885	45	*Germinal*

1874	First Impressionist exhibition, in Paris	Disraeli Prime Minister in Britain
1875	Bizet, *Carmen*	
1876	Twain, *The Adventures of Tom Sawyer*. Death of George Sand.	First International dissolved. Bakunin organizes 'Land and Liberty' in Russia
1877	Flaubert, *Trois Contes*. Goncourt, *La Fille Élisa*. Degas, *L'Absinthe*. Manet, Zola	Queen Victoria becomes Empress of India. Republican victory in legislative elections in France. Guesde founds the socialist newspaper *L'Égalité* [*Equality*]
1878		World Fair in Paris
1879	Dostoievsky, *The Brothers Karamazov*	Grévy becomes president of the Republic in France. Formation of a socialist workers' party in France
1880	*Les Soirées de Médan*. Death of Flaubert	Amnesty for the *Communards*. Gladstone Prime Minister. Transvaal Boers declare a Republic
1881	James, *The Portrait of a Lady*. Céard, *Une belle journée*	Ministry of Gambetta after Ferry's resignation. American Federation of Labor founded
1882		Fall from power and death of Gambetta. Crash of the Union Générale bank. Death of Darwin. Brousse founds the Revolutionary Socialist Party in France in opposition to Guesde, who founds the Workers' Party of France
1883	Maupassant, *Une Vie*	Second ministry of Jules Ferry. French war with Madagascar. Russian Marxist party founded. Death of Marx
1884	Huysmans, *À rebours*	Trade unions legalized in France
1885	Maupassant, *Bel-Ami*. Death of Hugo	Grévy re-elected President of France

1886	Rimbaud, *Illuminations*. Stevenson, *Dr Jekyll and Mr Hyde*. Last Impressionist exhibition	Gladstone, then Lord Salisbury elected Prime Minister in Britain
1887		Failure of Boulanger's *coup d'état*. Sadi Carnot President of the French Republic. Golden Jubilee of Queen Victoria.
1888	Maupassant, *Pierre et Jean*. Strindberg, *Miss Julie*	William II Emperor of Germany
1889		First Socialist Congress in Paris. Founding of the Second International. World Fair in Paris. Eiffel Tower completed. Flight of Boulanger. Formation of the Miners' Federation of Great Britain
1890	Wilde, *The Picture of Dorian Gray*. Ibsen, *Hedda Gabler*.	Elimination of the 'livret d'ouvrier'. Fall of Bismarck
1891	Huysmans, *Là-bas*. Death of Rimbaud. Hardy, *Tess of the d'Urbervilles*	Encyclical *Rerum novarum* of Leo XIII
1892	Maeterlinck, *Pelléas et Mélisande*	Anarchist attacks in France (1892–3). Panama scandal. Gladstone re-elected as Prime Minister. California earthquake disaster
1893	Wilde, *Salomé*. Death of Maupassant	Independent Labour Party formed in Britain. World Fair in Chicago
1894	George Moore, *Esther Waters*	Assassination of Sadi Carnot. Casimir-Perier President of the Republic. Arrest and first trial of Dreyfus. Gladstone resigns.
1895	Hardy, *Jude the Obscure*	Félix Faure President of the Republic. Creation of the Confédération Générale du Travail
1896	Jarry, *Ubu roi*	Annexation of Madagascar
1897	Rostand, *Cyrano de Bergerac*. Gide, *Les Nourritures terrestres*	Campaign in favour of Dreyfus

1898	58	'I Accuse' ('J'accuse', 13 January) published in *L'Aurore*. Tried and convicted (February and July). Escapes to England (18 July). *Paris*
1899	59	*Fruitfulness (Fécondité)*, first of *The Four Gospels (Les Quatre Évangiles)* Returns to France (June)
1901	61	*Work (Travail)*. Publishes collection of articles on the Dreyfus Affair: *La Vérité en marche*
1902	62	Death by asphyxiation (28–29 September). Funeral (5 October). National mourning
1903		*Truth (Vérité)*
1908		Remains transferred to the Panthéon

1898	Wells, *The War of the Worlds*. James, *The Turn of the Screw*.	Acquittal of Esterhazy. Fashoda incident
1899	Tolstoy, *Resurrection*	Loubet President of the Republic. Return of Dreyfus from Devil's Island and presidential pardon. Anglo-Boer War (to 1902)
1900	Death of Oscar Wilde	
1901	T. Mann, *Buddenbrooks*	Death of Queen Victoria. Australia becomes a Dominion
1902		End of the Anglo-Boer War
1903		Entente Cordiale
1905		Creation of the unified French Socialist Party

INTRODUCTION

Zola considered no less than twenty-three alternatives before deciding upon the intriguing (and untranslatable) title that *Germinal*
bears. Some of these alternatives, like 'The Rising Storm', 'The
Burning Soil', 'Clean Sweep' or 'The Crumbling House', denote
violent change; others contain the idea of new growth, like 'The
Germinating Seed', or combine the two notions, like 'Red Harvest'
or 'Fruitful Blood'. But, as the novelist himself later explained in a
letter to a Dutch correspondent, J. van Santen Kolff (6 October
1889), *Germinal* best conveys all the essential themes of the novel
and the intentions of its author:

> I was looking for a title to express the rise of a new breed of men, the
> effort of the workers who, even unconsciously, are freeing themselves
> from the cruelly laborious darkness in which they still struggle. And one
> day, by chance, the word 'Germinal' came to my lips. I did not want it
> first of all, finding it too mystical, too symbolic; but it represented
> precisely what I wanted, a revolutionary April, the leap of a ruined
> society into the spring. And, little by little, I became used to it, such that
> I was never able to find another. If it remains obscure for certain readers,
> it has become for me like a ray of sunlight illuminating the whole work.

The title refers back appropriately to a turbulent period of French
history, to an age of violent change and expected renewal. 'Germinal' was the seventh month, denoting the spring and extending
from 21 March to 19 April, of the new calendar which was
established by Fabre d'Églantine and introduced during the French
Revolution. Zola may also have had in mind that, on 12–13
germinal in year III, that is on 1–2 April 1795, starving Parisian
workers, including a majority of women, rose up against the
government of the Convention. But the title also looks forwards, to
the hope of a burgeoning new society of social justice which the
novel, if only implicitly, predicts merging from the industrial evils
of the present that it depicts.

Zola's narrative of the miners' misfortunes, published in 1885, is
the thirteenth of a twenty-volume series of independent novels,

called the 'Rougon-Macquart' series, after the names of the main branches, one legitimate, the other illegitimate, of a single family, complete with genealogical trees, whose members provide one main element linking the novels loosely together. The other link is the novels' historical setting, for all take place in essence during the Second Empire, between 1852 and 1870, when France was ruled by Napoleon's nephew, Louis Napoleon Bonaparte, the self-appointed emperor Napoleon III. Hence the subtitle of the series: 'A Natural and Social History of a Family under the Second Empire'. The composition of this vast literary panorama occupied Zola for twenty-five years, the most productive years of his life, for he first drew up the preliminary plans in 1868 and published the last episode, *Doctor Pascal*, in 1893. Though, at various stages in his career, he wrote eleven other novels, five collections of short stories, a number of plays and libretti, as well as a large body of art, drama and literary criticism, together with numerous articles on political and social issues, including 'J'accuse' and his other interventions in the Dreyfus case, the Rougon-Macquart novels are his main claim to literary fame and have earned him enduring recognition, despite the scorn of the literary establishment, as one of France's greatest writers.

When Zola began to write *Germinal* at the beginning of April 1884, after several weeks of preparatory work conducted in his usual systematic way, he was at the height of his creative powers. Though always tormented by self-doubt, he had by then the assurance of knowing that he was earning recognition as a major writer in France and gaining considerable fame and influence abroad. But it had been a long hard struggle to make his mark, without any advantages but his native talent and his indomitable determination. He had been born in Paris on 2 April 1840, but had spent his formative years, from 1843 to 1858, in Aix-en-Provence. He never entirely lost a sense of nostalgia for the landscapes of Provence, for the friendships he had formed, notably with the artist Paul Cézanne, and for the freedom that he had enjoyed during these years, blighted as they were by the death of his father, a civil engineer of Italian stock, in 1847 and by the ensuing financial difficulties. Driven to live in Paris, more out of necessity than literary ambition, he failed his *baccalauréat* in 1859 and, thereby excluded from the professions, languished in poverty for two years (1860–62), writing Romantic poetry, dreaming Romantic dreams, but living a far from Romantic Bohemian life. A job with the publishing firm Hachette brought reprieve until, by the beginning of 1866, he could take the bold step of living by his pen as a journalist. Though his early literary efforts received little critical attention, he gained a certain notoriety as an opposition journalist and particularly as a defender of Manet and other avant-garde artists of the day. Zola's only work of this early period that is still widely read today is his novel *Thérèse Raquin* (1867), a story of adulterous lovers driven to murder by their passion and to suicide by their remorse. This remarkable text reveals the extent of the author's conversion to realism, under the influence of the novelist Balzac and the critic Taine, who inspired him to apply in his own fiction scientific principles and physiological laws and to begin to elaborate the doctrine of what he called 'naturalism'.

The term 'naturalism' was a convenient label that Zola used to cover a set of principles that he sought not only to apply to his own works but to extend to the whole of the literature of his age. It referred to the natural sciences, to which, like Balzac, Zola looked as a model for the study of human beings in their social environment, concentrating on their physiological actions and reactions and performing on 'living beings', as he put it in the preface to *Thérèse Raquin*, 'the analytical work that surgeons perform on corpses'. In a broader sense, naturalism also referred to the materialist and positivist philosophy that Zola assumed, rejecting the view of 'man' as a spiritual or metaphysical being and presenting characters as products of their hereditary past, their social conditions and their historical circumstances. In naturalist works, the instincts, the passions, the innate compulsions, what Zola called 'the fatalities of the flesh', play a dominant role as motivating factors of human behaviour. No less important a tenet of Zola's naturalism was the aesthetic principle of the exact imitation of life, inspired as much by the practices of the contemporary painters that he knew as by the example of realist novelists. Naturalists sought to present in their works 'slices of life', representations of all aspects of their society uninfluenced by literary conventions, though they were often accused of concentrating exclusively on the seamier sides of life to shock their readers and promote the sales of their books. Zola's theorizing culminated in his famous essay 'The Experimental Novel' (1879), in which, under the influence of the renowned physiologist Claude Bernard and his treatise on experimental medicine, the author argued that novelists should apply the rigorous scientific procedures of the experimental method to their works and even seek to conduct on their characters the fictional equivalent of a scientific experiment.

Zola's contemporaries were not convinced by the theory of the 'experimental novel', but, in the late 1870s and early 1880s, he enjoyed considerable influence over a number of French writers, including Maupassant and Huysmans, who formed with him the 'Médan Group', named after the place of Zola's country house just to the west of Paris. In reality, the group was more loosely constituted than literary historians have often claimed and, in any case, the so-called 'disciples' of Zola were far more swayed by the literary achievements of the author of *L'Assommoir* than by his literary ideas. But they looked to him for guidance and were part of Zola's ever growing sphere of influence, as the century progressed and as the naturalist movement extended to other European countries and to the Americas to become a major international literary force.

Naturalist works, mainly novels and short stories but also theatre – certain of Ibsen's plays, for example, are often included in the naturalist canon – usually present tragic dramas of degeneration and catastrophe caused by such determining factors as hereditary taints, neurotic temperaments, unleashed instincts and passions, adverse social conditions. The main characters, very often women, are shown struggling to maintain a certain order in their lives but submitting eventually and inevitably to the more powerful forces of their 'baser' character or of the corrupting influences of their environment, lapsing into degradation and depravation. Zola's *L'Assommoir* (1877), the story of Gervaise Macquart, the mother of the hero of *Germinal*, is typical: abandoned with her two sons by her rakish lover, Auguste Lantier, Gervaise, who is a laundress in a poor district of Paris, rallies; she is enjoying a brief period of happiness and prosperity when her new husband, the roofer Coupeau, takes to drinking absinthe after a fall and the father of her two sons returns to exploit her; she is dragged down by the weight of her misfortunes and her own indulgences into the gutter eventually to die of starvation in the slum dwelling into which she is driven in her plight. Other naturalist texts, inspired more by Flaubert and by the German pessimist philosopher Schopenhauer, recount the disillusionments and frustrations of usually male characters caught up in the pointless routines of daily existence.

Clearly *Germinal*, in describing the grim realities of the life and the strife of the miners of Montsou, is consistent with the naturalists' programme of depicting the harsh and shameful realities of the contemporary world. Clearly also we see that Zola's miners are very much formed as well as deformed by their environment: by the degrading daily grind in the inhuman working conditions of the pit, by the starvation rations that they frequently can barely afford, by the decades of resignation to their fate, by the physical infirmities that they develop and inherit. One could even suggest that, in a sense, one of the main strains of the novel is an 'experiment' in the relationship between influences and impulsions. 'My subject', as Zola stated in a letter to Céard (22 March 1885) soon after the novel had appeared, 'was the reciprocal action and reaction of the individual and the crowd, the one on the other.' But, like all of the finest works of literature, or of any art, which are always more complex than the categories into which they are confined, *Germinal* does not conform to the usual patterns of the typical naturalist text. In any case, at the time of writing this novel, even Zola himself was reacting against the models that his own theories and practices had put in place. The 'Médan Group' had largely dispersed by 1884 and Zola was looking to broaden the range and impact of his works. This tendency is interestingly evident in the genesis of the novel, particularly in the development of the character of Étienne, who was originally to fulfil the naturalist destiny outlined for him on the family tree: to illustrate a case of homicidal mania caused by the hereditary effects of the drunkenness of his ancestors. Étienne never entirely loses this function, as his fits of rage in his confrontations with Chaval reveal. But he became more of a political figure than a physiological case study, with a more complex inner life, grappling with the demands of his role as a political leader and with his feelings for Catherine. Only in the extreme circumstances of his final confrontation with Chaval down the mine does he revert fully to his original character type, as if, having witnessed Jeanlin's knifing of the soldier, he were compelled to purge his system of the desire to kill.

Thus *Germinal* grew much less out of Zola's earlier naturalist preoccupation with the laws of heredity than out of a more recent interest in the problems of industrial strife, of the growing influence of socialism and anarchism, problems that were not specific to the Second Empire but more germane to the time in which he was writing the novel or even to a future age. As the novelist wrote significantly at the very beginning of what he called his *ébauche*, the preliminary 'sketch' in which, for each of his novels, he tried out his ideas:

The subject of the novel is the revolt of the workers, the nudge given to society which for a moment cracks: in a word the struggle between capital and labour. That is the importance of the book, which I want predicting the future, putting the question that will be the most important question of the twentieth century.

In his original plans for the Rougon-Maquart series and in subsequent versions, Zola had not anticipated writing a novel about industrial action. Even in the early 1880s, he was still considering a second working-class novel, as a kind of complement to *L'Assommoir*, dealing with the political activities of Parisian workers culminating in the Commune. He would, in fact, take up this theme in a later novel, *The Débâcle* (1892), presenting the Commune as a consequence of the Franco-Prussian war. But, in the political climate of the Third Republic in the early 1880s, as memories of the Commune faded into history, the workers' movement came to be a more relevant form of social protest than insurrection and the strike a more topical means of revolt than the barricade.

The workers' movement in France, held very much in check by the repressive regime of Napoleon III and faring little better under the conservative dominance of the early years of the Third Republic, only began to gain impetus in the 1880s. The first French workers' congresses only took place from 1876 onwards and were moderate in spirit. Labour unions, though tolerated earlier, were not authorized until 1884. Under the leadership of Jules Guesde, however, a socialist party was formed in 1879, but, to Guesde's dissatisfaction, was dominated by moderates (or 'possibilists'), opposed to revolution and favouring legislative reforms. In 1882, Paul Brousse and the 'possibilists' split from Guesde and his party, founding the rival Revolutionary Socialist Party, more revolutionary in name than in spirit, which came to be called, the following year, the Federation of French Socialist Workers. Further rifts occurred, particularly amongst the Marxists, the anarchists and the 'possibilists'. These divisions reflected those, on the broader European scale, at the heart of the International Working Men's Association (the 'First International'), founded in London in 1864 and later led by Marx. The International was riven by competing schools of thought and split in 1872 to be formally disbanded by the Marxists in 1876, with the anarchists, inspired by Bakunin, failing to keep it alive beyond 1881. These divisions are also reflected in *Germinal* in the radically different solutions to the social question proposed by the three militants of the novel: Rasseneur the 'possibilist', Étienne (roughly) the Marxist, and Souvarine the anarchist.

The political action by the miners of France was also a topical issue when Zola came to write his second working-class novel. Miners' groups were lobbying the government vigorously between 1882 and 1884. Paul Brousse, the leader of the 'possibilists', and Alfred Giard were particularly active in introducing bills in the Chamber of Deputies to improve the working conditions of miners. During the summer of 1883, while on holiday in Brittany, Zola met Giard and his conversations with the Deputy for Valenciennes may well have determined his choice of setting for his 'socialist' novel. He had already begun collecting materials for the novel when a strike broke out in the Anzin area, which would turn out to be one of the longest and hardest strikes of the century. The Anzin strike, one of several since 1878, was a symptom of the economic crisis that France was then undergoing, with the mining industry particularly affected by overproduction, foreign competition and uncompetitive extraction costs. Giard invited Zola to visit the region, where the novelist spent eight busy days, posing as the deputy's secretary, visiting the miners' houses, attending meetings, discussing the strike in the cafés, going down a mine, taking notes on all that he saw and heard. These notes ('Mes Notes sur Anzin') have been preserved and published along with the whole preparatory dossier of the novel. They reveal the extent to which Zola's visit provided him not only with valuable information but also with the vivid impressions that would lend to the novel its thoroughly authentic atmosphere.

Back in Paris, Zola went to hear Guesde speak, as well as Paul Lafargue and Charles Languet, Marx's sons-in-law. He read articles on strikes during the Second Empire and books on mines, miners and mining, on the accidents and illnesses of the colliers, on socialist ideas and programmes, all during the month of March 1884, before starting to write his novel on 2nd April. This preliminary research was necessary, of course, because, according to the general plan of the Rougon-Macquart series, the novel had to be set during the Second Empire, some twenty years earlier. In the atmosphere of general industrial unrest towards the end of that era, there had been dramatic miners' strikes, brutally repressed. On 16 June 1869, for example, a strike at La Ricamarie in Saint-Étienne had been put down by soldiers who shot thirteen strikers, whilst on 7 October of the same year, at Aubin in the Aveyron region, fourteen miners were killed when troops opened fire on strikers throwing stones at them. The culminating events of the strike in *Germinal* are clearly based on these incidents. But Zola chose to set the action of his novel at a slightly earlier date, in the years 1866–7, a time of severe economic crisis, of widespread unemployment, when many small industries were ruined, a time also when the International was being formed and when, despite the repression and defeats, there was a growing sense of solidarity amongst the workers and a growing public awareness of their plight.

By not indicating precisely in the novel the date at which the action occurs Zola gave himself the latitude to combine what he had seen in 1884 with what he had read about happening in the earlier period. He was scrupulously exact about the historical accuracy of most details of the novel. He made enquiries, for instance, about women and children working at the coalface and discovered that the practice had been abolished in France only in 1874, though in certain pits in the Pas-de-Calais region it went on to 1876. Yet, as commentators have pointed out, there are certain perceived anachronisms in the novel, the most glaring being the presence of a Russian anarchist in a French coalmine during the Second Empire. Anarchist acts of terrorism, notably the assassination of the Tsar of Russia, Alexander II, in 1881, were a fact of the 1880s and anarchist ideas were only then coming to the attention of members of a general public alarmed at the extreme nature of these views, which they associated with socialism, subversion and social disorder. But the author of *Germinal* was not solely concerned with historical accuracy. He wanted to study, as we have seen, the whole question of social protest in his age, which meant taking certain liberties with historical probability and presenting representative figures belonging to the two sides of the struggle between capital and labour.

The novelist does this in both a systematic and a complex way, by setting in significant opposition to one another certain individuals or groups of characters and, at the same time, by avoiding the danger of turning them into pure stereotypes. *Germinal* is a kind of thesis novel (or novel of several theses) without having a definite thesis of its own. On the one side, as we have noted, Zola presents representatives of the three basic shades of left-wing thought. Souvarine, whose ideas derive in large part from the theories of Mikhail Bakunin and Peter Kropotkin, is at one extreme. An anarchist refugee, who becomes a nihilist as he loses his last illusions about humanity, he is of the dissidents the most faithful to his convictions, totally without personal ambition, yet at the same time always alienated from the workers whose cause he espouses, seeking initially the eventual destruction of the present corrupt society to allow a new society to emerge, then resorting to a violent act of sabotage that destroys innocent lives. Rasseneur represents the opposite, moderate stance of the 'possibilists', whilst Étienne, whose position shifts during the novel from advocating violent revolution to an acceptance of the evolutionary forces of history, largely represents the Marxist position, though the narrator insists upon the confusion of his newly acquired ideas. But both Rasseneur and Étienne are shown in their alternating role as leaders of the miners' action in a less than favourable light, locked in a power struggle for the satisfaction of their ambitions. The Maheu family represents the workers, whose consciousness is undoubtedly raised by the ideas of their leaders and by the events of the strike, but whose suffering is shown to stem more from their rebellion than from the circumstances that prompted it.

In the opposing camp, the Grégoire family is set throughout the novel in contrast to the Maheu family. They are the idle rich, living off their dividends, but naïvely unaware of the extent of the suffering around them or of their own part in it, doing what they think is right with their acts of charity. The ménage (à trois) of Hennebeau is shown with problems of its own and the salaried manager himself can do little to alter the course of events. Deneulin, the small-scale mine owner, is as much a casualty of the strike as the miners and his daughters, though far from admirable characters, show courage in adversity. At all of its stages the novel frusrates its readers' attempts to take sides. Distinctions between good and evil, right and wrong, heroism and self-interest, insight and blindness, integrity and iniquity, are constantly subverted by the text. Zola may not have been a subtle psychologist, as has often been stated, but, as a moralist and as a social analyst, the author of Germinal shows rare insights into the complexities and the shifting nature of human behaviour.

For all the interest that Germinal holds for readers of all times as a historical, social and political document, the novel is essentially a creative work of impressive scope and effect. It is a superbly crafted work of fiction, employing techniques that both draw its readers vicariously into the world of the coalfields and of the dramas that are played out in what to most of them is an alien environment and bring them to an awareness of the broader meanings and the symbolic effects that the novel suggests. Critics have been unanimous in admiring, for example, the opening of the novel, in which, through Étienne's eyes, we discover the eerie landscape with the sinister shapes of the mine emerging out of the darkness and, through Bonnemort's words, we acquire essential information about the place and its history. Elsewhere we 'see' the mob of miners, the 'red spectre of revolution', through the terrified but fascinated gaze of the bourgeois characters. There is an intensity and a compelling vividness to the novel which anticipate the visual effectiveness of the cinema in its ability to coerce the spectator's attention and emotions. Yet the novel retains the suggestiveness of verbal art.

The novel begins with an almost leisurely introduction to daily life in the mining community, as, with a precision worthy of Balzac's descriptions, Zola introduces us into this unknown world in its diverse aspects. In fact, the events of almost the first third of the novel (parts I and II) take place in a single day. But *Germinal* is a remarkably well-paced novel, leading the reader painfully through the slow process of prolonged suffering, then excitingly bringing matters to a head in a series of violent confrontations amongst the characters and the forces that are in conflict in the work. Indeed, the whole rhythm of the novel, its temporal and spatial architecture, is structured by a series of carefully manœuvred confrontations, for *Germinal* is a novel of significant parallels and oppositions woven into the massive design of the work. After the preliminary exposition and a long period during which Étienne grows accustomed to his new environment and begins to assert his influence, the decision to strike, as the crucual conflict comes to a head, occurs dramatically and appropriately at the centre of the novel. Thereafter, passages of painstaking description of the miners' agony alternate with scenes of violent action: the rampage of the miners and the death of Maigrat in part V; the confrontation with the troops in part VI. Then the action of the novel accelerates in the final part, culminating in the violent deaths and disruptions above and below ground, before the coda of Étienne's departure in the sun, which frames the work by referring back to his arrival and contrasts significantly in its optimistic tone with the menacing departure of Souvarine in the depths of night in an earlier chapter. In the vertical triptych structure of the work, with its three essential phases: before, during and after the strike, the action evolves horizontally on two planes, frequently describing scenes that take place simultaneously above and below ground. Here the grim daylight world of political struggle, of long periods of hardship and deprivation and of brief bouts of pleasure, of family life and family misfortunes, of the community with its loves and enmities, the world even of dreams; there the dark night below, the hell of brutish toil, the primeval world of nightmares, of fear, of catastrophe, destruction, death, in the bowels of the earth, in the belly of the monster.

Such is the richness of *Germinal* that critics have exhumed a complex network of themes as intricate as the submerged passages of the mine. There is overall the epic of the struggle of a whole people against their oppression, crushed beneath the weight of their social condition, beasts of burden imprisoned in the pit of their misfortune, searching for the light of day, dreaming of a world in which they might attain dignity and humanity. Their history, their daily lives, their culture, are movingly portrayed in this novel where they emerge as the true heroic force of future change. *Germinal* is also the novel of an individual and his relationship with that community and its aspirations, the story of the rise and fall of a leader, whose visions for his people and aspirations for himself are crushed by harsh reality as the limits of his powers are cruelly exposed. Yet, despite his failure, Étienne does succeed in playing a number of traditional 'heroic' roles: the naïve outsider who completes his apprenticeship in the hardest of life's schools and who leaves when his education is complete, having sown the seeds of the future harvest of revolt; the warrior who takes on the insatiable monster of the mine to liberate its victims; the lover, too, in a curiously delicate romance, in which he and Catherine, the 'chaste' object of his quest, the 'virgin' bride whom he finally takes in the very throes of death, love in a way far removed from the easy promiscuity or the brutal possessiveness so common in the mining community. So closely woven is the fabric of themes in this novel that it is paradoxically the death of Maheu, marking the failure of the strike, that provokes the onset of puberty in Catherine, as if a primitive taboo has been lifted on the love of Étienne for his daughter and the flow of germination is finally released, but only in death. *Germinal* is a fable set realistically in the depths of the mine, but metaphorically also in those deep recesses that the psychoanalyst seeks to explore: the world of Jungian quests, of the traumas of birth or rebirth, of the mysterious links between *eros* and *thanatos*. Indeed, Étienne's descent into the underworld of the mine and Zola's aggrandized vision of the mine, along with other episodes of *Germinal*, have been shown to evoke echoes of a whole range of mythical motifs: Theseus descending to battle the Minotaur, the myth of the Great Flood, the Furies or Erinyes castrating Maigrat, Cronus the capitalist God lurking in his lair, the Elysian fields of Catherine's dreams, Dionysus leading the Maenads in their wild fury, le Voreux the Molech of the coalfields, apocalyptic and evangelical visions, even such apparently anodyne fables as Jeanlin leading Étienne, like the White Rabbit, into the netherland or the battle of Tom Thumb with the giant. Zola's novel of the mines suggests, like all great literature, a host of intertextual allusions to the rich deposits of myth, legend, fable that make up the whole universe of literature itself.

Yet, ultimately, the significance of *Germinal* is not as a text on which the critics can exercise their art, but as a memorable work of fiction that has engrossed, thrilled, inspired generations of silent readers who have suffered with the miners of Montsou and have shared, if only for a few hours, their troubles and their hopes. Perhaps on many of them, like the British miners' leader Arthur Scargill, who read *Germinal* twice as a boy (see the *Guardian*, 26 April 1994), it left a lasting impression and prompted some of them to similar action. To some, no doubt, the events of our century will have diminished the impact of the novel, whereas others will continue to see its enduring relevance in different contexts. But the most eloquent tribute to Zola's novel is still the homage of the delegation of miners who walked in Zola's funeral procession on 5 October 1902 and, with their intuitive understanding of its message and its title, uttered the rhythmic chant of 'Germinal, Germinal'.

DAVID BAGULEY

NOTE ON THE TEXT

This translation is essentially the text of the first complete English version of *Germinal*, which was produced by Havelock Ellis and his wife, Edith Lees, in the early months of 1894. Ellis dictated his translation to his wife in the evenings in her little Cornish cottage, after he had worked on other projects in seclusion in a nearby disused mining shed! Edith Lees wrote out the text and offered suggestions. They divided the fee of fifty pounds. The work was published the same year as part of a series of six Zola novels translated by eminent English men of letters that was issued by the Lutetian Society in 1894–5. In the Victorian age, when publishers could only produce drastically bowdlerized versions of Zola's novels, even then at the risk of prosecution for issuing 'pernicious literature', the unexpurgated Lutetian texts were allowed to appear because they were privately printed in limited editions of 300 numbered copies and sold to subscribers at a high price. In subsequent printings of the Ellis–Lees translation, the original text has undergone minor revisions and corrections. For the present edition, more numerous detailed revisions have been made in an attempt to correct mistranslations, to eliminate the most obvious gallicisms and to render certain words and expressions comprehensible for the modern reader without, it is hoped, detracting from the substance and the period flavour of the original translation.

GERMINAL

PART ONE

CHAPTER I

Over the open plain, beneath a starless sky as dark and thick as ink, a man walked alone along the highway from Marchiennes to Montsou,* a straight paved road ten kilometres in length, intersecting the beetroot-fields. He could not even see the black soil before him, and only felt the immense flat horizon by the gusts of the March* wind, squalls as strong as on the sea, and frozen from sweeping across leagues of marsh and naked earth. No tree could be seen against the sky, and the road unrolled as straight as a pier in the midst of the blinding spray of darkness.

The man had set out from Marchiennes about two o'clock. He walked with long strides, shivering beneath his worn cotton jacket and corduroy breeches. A small parcel tied in a check handkerchief troubled him much, and he pressed it against his side, sometimes with one elbow, sometimes with the other, so that he could slip to the bottom of his pockets both the benumbed hands that bled beneath the lashes of the east wind. A single idea occupied his head – the empty head of a workman without work and without lodging – the hope that the cold would be less keen after sunrise. For an hour he went on thus, when on the left, two kilometres from Montsou, he saw red flames, three braziers burning in the open air and apparently suspended. At first he hesitated, half afraid. Then he could not resist the painful need to warm his hands for a moment.

The steep road led downwards, and everything disappeared. The man saw on his right a paling, a wall of coarse planks shutting in a line of rails, while a grassy slope rose on the left surmounted by confused gables, a vision of a village with low uniform roofs. He went on some two hundred paces. Suddenly, at a bend in the road, the fires reappeared close to him, though he could not understand how they burnt so high in the dead sky, like smoky moons. But on the level soil another sight had struck him. It was a heavy mass, a low pile of buildings from which rose the silhouette of a factory chimney; occasional gleams appeared from dirty windows, five or six melancholy lanterns were hung outside to frames of blackened wood, which vaguely outlined the profiles of gigantic stages; and from this fantastic apparition, drowned in night and smoke, a single voice arose, the thick, long breathing of an exhaust pipe that could not be seen.

Then the man recognized a pit. His despair returned. What was the good? There would be no work. Instead of turning towards the buildings he decided at last to ascend the pit bank, on which burnt in iron baskets the three coal fires which gave light and warmth for work. The labourers in the cutting must have been working late; they were still throwing out the useless rubbish. Now he heard the landers push the wagons on the stages. He could distinguish living shadows tipping over the trams near each fire.

'Good day,' he said, approaching one of the braziers.

Turning his back to the fire, the carman stood upright. He was an old man, dressed in knitted violet wool with a rabbit-skin cap on his head; while his horse, a great yellow horse, waited with the immobility of stone while they emptied the six trams he drew. The workman employed at the tipping-cradle, a red-haired lean fellow, did not hurry himself; he pressed on the lever with a sleepy hand. And above, the wind grew stronger – an icy wintry wind – and its great, regular breaths passed by like the strokes of a scythe.

'Good day,' replied the old man. There was silence. The man, who felt that he was being looked at suspiciously, at once told his name.

'I am Étienne Lantier.* I am an engine-man. Any work here?'

The flames lit him up. He might be about twenty-one years of age, a very dark, handsome man, who looked strong in spite of his thin limbs.

The carman, thus reassured, shook his head.

'Work for an engine-man? No, no! There were two came yesterday. There's nothing.'

A gust cut short their speech. Then Étienne asked, pointing to the sombre pile of buildings at the foot of the platform:

'A pit, isn't it?'

The old man this time could not reply: he was strangled by a violent cough. At last he spat and his expectoration left a black patch on the purple soil.

'Yes, a pit. The Voreux.* There! The settlement is quite near.'

In his turn, and with extended arm, he pointed out in the night the village of which the young man had vaguely seen the roofs. But the six trams were empty, and he followed them without cracking his whip, his legs stiffened by rheumatism; while the great yellow horse went on of itself, pulling heavily between the rails beneath a new gust which bristled its coat.

The Voreux was now emerging from the gloom. Étienne, who lost himself before the brazier, warming his poor bleeding hands, looked round and could see each part of the pit: the shed tarred with siftings, the pit-frame, the vast chamber of the winding machine, the square turret of the exhaustion pump. This pit, piled up in the bottom of a hollow, with its squat brick buildings, raising its chimney like a threatening horn, seemed to him to have the evil air of a gluttonous beast crouching there to devour the earth. While examining it, he thought of himself, of his vagabond existence these eight days he had been seeking work. He saw himself again at his workshop at the railway, delivering a blow to his foreman, driven from Lille, driven from everywhere. On Saturday he had arrived at Marchiennes, where they said that work was to be had at the Forges, and there was nothing, neither at the Forges nor at Sonneville's. He had been obliged to pass the Sunday hidden beneath the wood of a cartwright's yard, from which the watchman had just turned him out at two o'clock in the morning. He had nothing, not a penny, not even a crust; what should he do, wandering along the roads without aim, not knowing where to shelter himself from the wind? Yes, it was certainly a pit; the occasional lanterns lighted up the square; a door, suddenly opened, had enabled him to catch sight of the furnaces in a clear light. He could explain even the exhaust pump, that thick, long breathing that went on without ceasing, and which seemed to be the monster's congested respiration.

The workman, expanding his back at the tipping-cradle, had not even lifted his eyes on Étienne, and the latter was about to pick up his little bundle, which had fallen to the earth, when a spasm of coughing announced the carman's return. Slowly he emerged from the darkness, followed by the yellow horse drawing six more laden trams.

'Are there factories at Montsou?' asked the young man.

The old man spat, then replied in the wind:

'Oh, there's no lack of factories. Should have seen it three or four years ago. Everything was roaring then. There were not enough men; there never were such wages. And now they are tightening their bellies again. Nothing but misery in the country; every one is being sent away; workshops closing one after the other. It is not the Emperor's fault, perhaps; but why should he go and fight in America? without counting that the beasts are dying from cholera, like the people.'*

Then, in short phrases and with broken breath, the two continued to complain. Étienne narrated his vain wanderings of the past week: must one, then, die of hunger? Soon the roads would be full of beggars.

'Yes,' said the old man, 'this will turn out badly, for you can't just throw so many Christians, by God, out on the street.'

'We don't have meat every day.'

'But if we had bread!'

'True, if we only had bread.'

Their voices were lost, gusts of wind carrying away the words in a melancholy howl.

'Here!' began the carman again very loudly, turning towards the south. 'Montsou is over there.'

And stretching out his hand again he pointed out invisible spots in the darkness as he named them. Over there, at Montsou, the Fauvelle sugar works were still going, but the Hoton sugar works had just been dismissing hands; there were only the Dutilleul flour mill and the Bleuze rope works for mine-cables which kept up. Then, with a large gesture he indicated the north half of the horizon: the Sonneville workshops had not received two-thirds of their usual orders; only two of the three blast furnaces of the Marchiennes Forges were alight; finally, at the Gagebois glass works a strike was threatening, for there was talk of a reduction of wages.

'I know, I know,' replied the young man at each indication. 'I have been there.'

'With us here things are going on at present,' added the carman; 'but the pits have lowered their output. And see opposite, at the Victoire, there are also only two batteries of coke furnaces alight.'

He spat, and set out behind his sleepy horse, after harnessing it to the empty trams.

Now Étienne could see over the entire country. The darkness remained profound, but the old man's hand had, as it were, filled it with great miseries, which the young man unconsciously felt at this moment around him everywhere in the limitless tract. Was it not a cry of famine that the March wind rolled up across this naked plain? The squalls were furious: they seemed to bring the death of labour, a famine which would kill many men. And with wandering eyes he tried to pierce the gloom, tormented at once by the desire and by the fear of seeing. Everything was hidden in the unknown depths of the gloomy night. He only perceived, very far off, the blast furnaces and the coke ovens. The latter, with their hundreds of chimneys, planted obliquely, made lines of red flame; while the two towers, more to the left, burnt blue against the blank sky, like giant torches. It resembled a melancholy conflagration. No other stars rose on the threatening horizon except these nocturnal fires in a land of coal and iron.

'You are from Belgium, perhaps?' began again the carman, who had returned behind Étienne.

This time he only brought three trams. Those at least could be tipped over; an accident which had happened to the cage, a broken screw nut, would stop work for a good quarter of an hour. At the bottom of the pit bank there was silence; the landers no longer shook the stages with a prolonged vibration. One only heard from the pit the distant sound of a hammer tapping on an iron plate.

'No, I come from the South,' replied the young man.

The workman, after having emptied the trams, had seated himself on the earth, glad of the accident, maintaining his savage silence; he had simply lifted his large, dim eyes to the carman, as if annoyed by so many words. The latter, indeed, did not usually talk at such length. The unknown man's face must have pleased him that he should have been taken by one of these itchings for confidence which sometimes make old people talk aloud even when alone.

'I belong to Montsou,' he said, 'I am called Bonnemort.'*

'Is it a nickname?' asked Étienne, astonished.

The old man made a grimace of satisfaction and pointed to the Voreux:

'Yes, yes; they have pulled me three times out of that, torn to pieces, once with all my hair scorched, once with my gizzard full of earth, and another time with my belly swollen with water, like a frog. And then, when they saw that nothing would kill me, they called me Bonnemort for a joke.'

His cheerfulness increased, like the creaking of an ill-greased pulley, and ended by degenerating into a terrible spasm of coughing. The brazier now clearly lit up his large head, with its scanty white hair and flat, livid face, spotted with bluish patches. He was short, with an enormous neck, bandy legs and long arms, with massive hands falling to his knees. For the rest, like his horse, which stood immovable, without suffering from the wind, he seemed to be made of stone; he had no appearance of feeling either the cold or the gusts that whistled at his ears. When he coughed his throat was torn by a deep rasping; he spat at the foot of the basket and the earth was blackened.

Étienne looked at him and at the ground which he had thus stained.

'Have you been working long at the mine?'

Bonnemort flung open both arms.

'Long? I should think so. I was not eight when I went down into the Voreux and I am now fifty-eight. Reckon that up! I have been everything down there; at first trammer, then putter, when I had the strength to wheel, then pikeman for eighteen years. Then, because of my cursed legs, they put me into the earth cutting, to bank up and patch, until they had to bring me up, because the doctor said I would stay there for good. Then, after five years of that, they made me carman. Eh? that's fine – fifty years at the mine, forty-five down below.'

While he was speaking, fragments of burning coal, which now and then fell from the brazier, lit up his pale face with their red reflection.

'They tell me to rest,' he went on, 'but I'm not going to; I'm not such a fool. I can go on for two years longer, to my sixtieth, so as to get the pension of one hundred and eighty francs. If I wished them good evening today they would give me a hundred and fifty at once. They are cunning, the buggers. Besides, I am sound, except my legs. You see, it's the water which has got under my skin through being always wet in the cuttings. There are days when I can't move a paw without screaming.'

A spasm of coughing interrupted him again.

'And that makes you cough so,' said Étienne.

But he vigorously shook his head. Then, when he could speak:

'No, no! I caught a cold a month ago. I never used to cough; now I can't get rid of it. And the queer thing is that I spit, that I spit—'

The rasping was again heard in his throat, followed by the black expectoration.

'Is it blood?' asked Étienne, at last venturing to question him.

Bonnemort slowly wiped his mouth with the back of his hand.

'It's coal. I've got enough in my carcass to warm me till I die. And it's five years since I put a foot down below. I stored it up, it seems, without knowing it; it keeps you alive!

There was silence. The distant hammer struck regular blows in the pit, and the wind passed by with its moan, like a cry of hunger and weariness coming out of the depths of the night. Before the flames which grew wild, the old man went on in lower tones, chewing over again his old recollections. Ah, certainly: it was not yesterday that he and his began hammering at the seam. The family had worked for the Montsou Mining Company since it started, and that was long ago, a hundred and six years already. His grandfather, Guillaume Maheu, an urchin of fifteen then, had found the rich coal at Réquillart, the Company's first pit, an old abandoned pit to-day over there near the Fauvelle sugar works. All the country knew it, and as a proof, the discovered seam was called the Guillaume, after his grandfather. He had not known him – a big fellow, it was said, very strong, who died of old age at sixty. Then his father, Nicolas Maheu, called Le Rouge, when hardly forty years of age had died in the pit, which was being excavated at that time: a land-slip completely flattened him, and the rocks drank his blood and swallowed his bones. Two of his uncles and his three brothers, later on, also left their skins there. He, Vincent Maheu, who had come out almost whole, except that his legs were rather shaky, was looked upon as a knowing fellow. But what could you do? You must work; you worked here from father to son, as you would work at anything else. His son, Toussaint Maheu, was being worked to death there now, and his grandsons, and all his people, who lived opposite in the settlement. A hundred and six years of mining, the youngsters after the old ones, for the same master. Eh? there were many bourgeois that could not give their history so well!

'Anyhow, when one has got enough to eat!' murmured Étienne again.

'That is what I say. As long as one has bread to eat one can live.'

Bonnemort was silent; and his eyes turned towards the settlement, where lights were appearing one by one. Four o'clock struck in the Montsou tower and the cold became keener.

'And is your company rich?' asked Étienne.

The old man shrugged his shoulders, and then let them fall as if overwhelmed beneath an avalanche of gold.

'Ah, yes! Ah, yes! Not perhaps so rich as its neighbours, the Anzin Company. But millions and millions all the same. They can't count it. Nineteen pits, thirteen at work, the Voreux, the Victoire, Crèvecœur, Mirou, Saint Thomas, Madeleine, Feutry-Cantel, and still more, and six for pumping or ventilation, like Réquillart. Ten thousand workers, concessions reaching over sixty-seven com-munes, an output of five thousand tons a day, a railway joining all the pits, and workshops, and factories! Ah, yes! ah, yes! there's money there!'

The rolling of trams on the stages made the big yellow horse prick his ears. The cage was evidently repaired below, and the landers had got to work again. While he was harnessing his beast to go back down, the carman added gently, addressing himself to the horse:

'Won't do to chatter, lazy good-for-nothing! If Monsieur Hennebeau knew how you waste your time!'

Étienne looked thoughtfully into the night. He asked:

'Then Monsieur Hennebeau owns the mine?'

'No,' explained the old man, 'Monsieur Hennebeau is only the
general manager; he is paid just the same as us.'

With a gesture the young man pointed into the vast darkness.

'Who does it all belong to, then?'

But Bonnemort was for a moment so suffocated by a new and
violent spasm that he could not get his breath. Then, when he had
spat and wiped the black froth from his lips, he replied in the rising
wind:

'Eh? all that belongs to? Nobody knows. To people.'

And with his hand he pointed in the darkness to a vague spot, an
unknown and remote place, inhabited by those people for whom
the Maheus had been hammering at the seam for more than a
century. His voice assumed a tone of religious awe; it was as if he
were speaking of an inaccessible tabernacle containing a sated and
crouched god to whom they had given all their flesh and whom
they had never seen.

'At all events, if you can get enough bread to eat,' repeated
Étienne, for the third time, without any apparent transition.

'Indeed, yes; if we could always get bread, it would be too good
to be true.'

The horse had started; the carman, in his turn, disappeared, with
the trailing step of an invalid. Near the tipping-cradle the workman
had not stirred, gathered up in a ball, burying his chin between his
knees, with his great dim eyes fixed on emptiness.

When he had picked up his bundle, Étienne still remained at the
same spot. He felt the gusts freezing his back, while his chest was
burning before the large fire. Perhaps, all the same, it would be as
well to inquire at the pit, the old man might not know. Then he
resigned himself; he would accept any work. Where should he go,
and what was to become of him in this country famished for lack
of work? Must he leave his carcass behind a wall, like a stray dog?
But one doubt troubled him, a fear of the Voreux in the middle of
this flat plain, drowned in so thick a night. At every gust the wind
seemed to rise as if it blew from an ever-broadening horizon. No
dawn whitened the dead sky. The blast furnaces alone flamed up,
and the coke ovens, making the darkness redder without illuminat-
ing the unknown. And the Voreux, at the bottom of its hole, with
its posture as of an evil beast, crouched lower, breathing with a

heavier and slower respiration, troubled by its painful digestion of human flesh.

CHAPTER 2

In the middle of the fields of wheat and beetroot, the Deux-Cent-Quarante settlement slept beneath the black night. One could vaguely distinguish four immense blocks of small houses, back to back like barracks or hospital blocks, geometric and parallel, separated by three large avenues which were divided into gardens of equal size. And over the desert plain one heard only the moan of squalls through the broken fences of the enclosures.

In the Maheus' house, No. 16 in the second block, nothing was stirring. The single room that occupied the first floor was drowned in a thick darkness which seemed to overwhelm with its weight the sleep of the beings whom one felt to be there in a mass, with open mouths, overcome by weariness. In spite of the keen cold outside, there was a living heat in the heavy air, that hot stuffiness of even the best kept bedrooms, the smell of human cattle.

Four o'clock had struck from the cuckoo clock in the room on the ground floor, but nothing yet stirred; one heard the piping of slender respirations, accompanied by two series of sonorous snores. And suddenly Catherine got up. In her weariness she had, as usual, counted the four strokes through the floor without the strength to arouse herself completely. Then, throwing her legs from under the bedclothes, she felt about, at last struck a match and lighted the candle. But she remained seated, her head so heavy that it fell back between her shoulders, seeking to return to the bolster.

Now the candle lighted up the room, a square room with two windows, and filled with three beds. There could be seen a cupboard, a table, and two old walnut chairs, whose smoky tone made hard, dark patches against the walls, which were painted a bright yellow. And nothing else, only clothes hung to nails, a jug placed on the floor, and a red pan which served as a basin. In the bed on the left, Zacharie, the eldest, a youth of one-and-twenty, was asleep with his brother Jeanlin, who had completed his eleventh year; in the right-hand bed two urchins, Lénore and Henri, the first six years old, the second four, slept in each other's arms, while

Catherine shared the third bed with her sister Alzire, so small for her nine years that Catherine would not have felt her near her if it were not for the little invalid's humpback, which pressed into her side. The glass door was open; you could see the lobby of a landing, a sort of recess in which the father and the mother occupied a fourth bed, against which they had been obliged to install the cradle of the latest comer, Estelle, aged scarcely three months.

However, Catherine made a desperate effort. She stretched herself, she fidgeted her two hands in the red hair which covered her forehead and neck. Slender for her fifteen years, all that showed of her limbs outside the narrow sheath of her nightdress were her bluish feet, as if tattooed with coal, and her slight arms, the milky whiteness of which contrasted with the sallow tint of her face, already spoilt by constant washing with black soap. A final yawn opened her rather large mouth with splendid teeth against the chlorotic pallor of her gums; while her grey eyes were crying in her fight with sleep, with a look of painful distress and weariness which seemed to spread over the whole of her naked body.

But a growl came from the landing, and Maheu's thick voice stammered;

'Devil take it! It's time. Is it you lighting up, Catherine?'

'Yes, father; it has just struck downstairs.'

'Quick then, lazy. If you had danced less on Sunday you would have woke us earlier. A fine lazy life!'

And he went on grumbling, but sleep returned to him also. His reproaches became confused, and were extinguished in fresh snoring.

The young girl, in her nightdress, with her naked feet on the tiled floor, moved in the room. As she passed by the bed of Henri and Lénore, she replaced the coverlet which had slipped down. They did not wake, lost in the strong sleep of children. Alzire, with open eyes, had turned to take the warm place of her big sister without speaking.

'I say, now, Zacharie – and you, Jeanlin; I say, now!' repeated Catherine, standing before her two brothers, who were still wallowing with their noses in the bolster.

She had to seize the elder by the shoulder and shake him; then, while he was muttering abuse, it came into her head to uncover them by snatching away the sheet. That seemed funny to her, and she began to laugh when she saw the two boys struggling with naked legs.

'Stupid, leave me alone,' growled Zacharie in ill-temper, sitting up. 'I don't like tricks. Good Lord! Say it's time to get up?'

He was lean and ill-made, with a long face and a chin which showed signs of a sprouting beard, with the yellow hair and the anaemic pallor which belonged to his whole family.

His shirt had rolled up to his belly, and he lowered it, not from modesty but because he was not warm.

'It has struck downstairs,' repeated Catherine; 'come! up! father's angry.

Jeanlin, who had rolled himself up, closed his eyes, saying: 'Go and hang yourself; I'm going to sleep.'

She laughed again, the laugh of a good-natured girl. He was so small, his limbs so thin, with enormous joints, enlarged by scrofula, that she took him up in her arms. But he kicked about, his apish face, pale and wrinkled, with its green eyes and great ears, grew pale with the rage of weakness. He said nothing, he bit her right breast.

'Beastly devil!' she murmured, keeping back a cry and putting him on the floor.

Alzire was silent, with the sheet tucked under her chin, but she had not gone to sleep again. With her intelligent invalid's eyes she followed her sister and her two brothers, who were now dressing. Another quarrel broke out around the pan, the boys hustled the young girl because she was so long washing herself. Shirts flew about: and, while still half-asleep, they relieved themselves without shame, with the tranquil satisfaction of a litter of puppies that have grown up altogether. Catherine was ready first. She put on her miner's breeches, then her canvas jacket, and fastened the blue cap on her knotted hair; in these clean Monday clothes she had the appearance of a little man; nothing remained to indicate her sex except the slight roll of her hips.

'When the old man comes back,' said Zacharie, mischievously, 'he'll like to find the bed unmade. You know I shall tell him it's you.'

The old man was the grandfather, Bonnemort, who, as he worked during the night, slept by day, so that the bed was never cold; there was always someone snoring there. Without replying, Catherine set herself to arrange the bed-clothes and tuck them in. But during the last moments sound had been heard behind the wall in the next house. These brick buildings, economically put up by the Company, were so thin that the least breath could be heard through them. The inmates lived there, elbow to elbow, from one end to the other; and no fact of family life remained hidden, even from the youngsters. A heavy step had tramped up the staircase; then there was a kind of soft fall, followed by a sigh of satisfaction.

'Good!' said Catherine. 'Levaque has gone down, and here is Bouteloup come to join la Levaque.'

Jeanlin grinned; even Alzire's eyes shone. Every morning they made fun of the household of three next door, a pikeman who lodged a worker in the cutting, an arrangement which gave the woman two men, one by night, the other by day.

'Philomène is coughing,' began Catherine again, after listening.

She was speaking of the eldest Levaque, a big girl of nineteen, and the mistress of Zacharie, by whom she had already had two children; her chest was so delicate that she was only a sifter at the pit, never having been able to work below ground.

'Pooh! Philomène!' replied Zacharie, 'she cares a lot, she's asleep. It's hoggish to sleep till six.'

He was putting on his breeches when an idea occurred to him, and he opened the window. Outside in the darkness the settlement was awaking, lights were dawning one by one between the laths of the shutters. And there was another dispute: he leant out to watch if he could not see, coming out of the Pierrons' opposite, the overman of the Voreux, who was accused of sleeping with la Pierronne, while his sister called to him that since the day before the husband had taken day duty at the pit-eye, and that certainly Dansaert could not have slept there that night. Whilst the air entered in icy whiffs, both of them, becoming angry, maintained the truth of their own information, until cries and tears broke out. It was Estelle, in her cradle, vexed by the cold.

Maheu woke up suddenly. What had he got in his bones, then? Here he was going to sleep again like a good-for-nothing. And he swore so vigorously that the children became still. Zacharie and Jeanlin finished washing with slow weariness. Alzire, with her large, open eyes, continually stared. The two youngsters, Lénore and Henri, in each other's arms, had not stirred, breathing in the same quiet way in spite of the noise.

'Catherine, give me the candle,' called out Maheu.

She finished buttoning her jacket, and carried the candle into the closet, leaving her brothers to look for their clothes by what light came through the door. Her father jumped out of bed. She did not stop, but went downstairs in her coarse woollen stockings, feeling her way, and lighted another candle in the parlour, to prepare the coffee. All the clogs of the family were beneath the sideboard.

'Will you be still, vermin?' began Maheu, again, exasperated by Estelle's cries which still went on.

He was short, like old Bonnemort, but broader, and resembled him, with his strong head, his flat, livid face, beneath yellow hair cut very short. The child screamed more than ever, frightened by those great knotted arms which were held above her.

'Leave her alone; you know that she won't be still,' said la Maheude, stretching herself in the middle of the bed.

She also had just awakened and was complaining how disgusting it was never to be able to finish the night. Could they not go away quietly? Buried in the clothes she only showed her long face with large features of a heavy beauty, already disfigured at thirty-nine by her life of wretchedness and the seven children she had borne. With her eyes to the ceiling she spoke slowly, while her man dressed himself. They both ceased to hear the little one, who was strangling herself with screaming.

'Eh? You know I haven't a sou and it's only Monday: still six days before the fortnight's out. This can't go on. You, all of you, only bring in nine francs. How do you expect me to go on? We are ten in the house.'

'Oh! nine francs!' exclaimed Maheu. 'I and Zacharie three: that makes six, Catherine and the father, two: that makes four: four and six, ten, and Jeanlin one, that makes eleven.'

'Yes, eleven, but there are Sundays and the off-days. Never more than nine, you know.'

He did not reply, being occupied in looking on the ground for his leather belt. Then he said, on getting up:

'Mustn't complain. I am sound all the same. There's more than one at forty-two who are put to the patching.'

'Maybe, old man, but that does not give us bread. Where am I to get it from, eh? Have you got nothing?'

'I've got two sous.'

'Keep them for a half-pint. Good Lord! where am I to get it from? Six days! it will never end. We owe sixty francs to Maigrat, who turned me out of doors the day before yesterday. That won't prevent me from going to see him again. But if he goes on refusing—'

And la Maheude continued in her melancholy voice, without moving her head, only closing her eyes now and then beneath the dim light of the candle. She said the cupboard was empty, the little ones asking for bread and butter, even the coffee was done, and the water caused colic, and the long days passed in deceiving hunger

with boiled cabbage leaves. Little by little she had been obliged to
raise her voice, for Estelle's screams drowned her words. These cries
became unbearable. Maheu seemed all at once to hear them, and in
a fury, snatched the little one up from the cradle and threw it on
the mother's bed, stammering with rage:

'Here, take her; I'll do for her! Damn the child! It wants for
nothing: it sucks, and it complains louder then all the rest!'

Estelle began, in fact, to suck. Hidden beneath the clothes and
soothed by the warmth of the bed, her cries subsided into the greedy
little sound of her lips.

'Haven't the Piolaine people told you to go and see them?' asked
the father, after a period of silence.

The mother bit her lip with an air of discouraged doubt.

'Yes, they met me; they were carrying clothes for poor children.
Yes, I'll take Lénore and Henri to them this morning. If they only
give me a hundred sous.'

There was silence again.

Maheu was ready. He remained a moment motionless, then
added, in his hollow voice:

'What is it that you want? Let things be, and see about the soup.
It's no good talking, better be at work down below.'

'True enough,' replied la Maheude. 'Blow out the candle: I don't
need to see the colour of my thoughts.'

He blew out the candle. Zacharie and Jeanlin were already going
down; he followed them, and the wooden staircase creaked beneath
their heavy feet, clad in wool. Behind them the closet and the room
were again dark. The children slept; even Alzire's eyelids were
closed; but the mother now remained with her eyes open in the
darkness, while, pulling at her breast, the pendulous breast of an
exhausted woman, Estelle was purring like a kitten.

Down below, Catherine had at first occupied herself with the fire,
which was burning in the iron grate, flanked by two ovens. The
Company distributed every month, to each family, eight hectolitres
of a hard slaty coal, gathered in the passages. It burnt slowly, and
the young girl, who piled up the fire every night, only had to stir it
in the morning, adding a few fragments of soft coal, carefully picked
out. Then, after having placed a kettle on the grate, she sat down
before the sideboard.

It was a fairly large room, occupying all the ground floor, painted
an apple green, and of Flemish cleanliness, with its flags well
washed and covered with white sand. Besides the sideboard of
varnished deal the furniture consisted of a table and chairs of the

same wood. Stuck on to the walls were some violently-coloured prints, portraits of the Emperor and the Empress,* given by the Company, of soldiers and of saints speckled with gold, contrasting crudely with the simple nudity of the room; and there was no other ornament except a box of rose-coloured pasteboard on the sideboard, and the cuckoo clock with its daubed face and loud tick-tack, which seemed to fill the emptiness of the place. Near the staircase door another door led to the cellar. In spite of the cleanliness, an odour of cooked onion, shut up since the night before, poisoned the hot, heavy air, always laden with an acrid flavour of coal.

Catherine, in front of the sideboard, was reflecting. There only remained the end of a loaf, cheese in fair abundance, but hardly a morsel of butter; and she had to provide bread and butter for four. At last she decided, cut the slices, took one and covered it with cheese, spread another with butter, and stuck them together; that was the 'briquet', the bread-and-butter sandwich taken to the pit every morning. The four briquets were soon on the table, in a row, cut with severe justice, from the big one for the father down to the little one for Jeanlin.

Catherine, who appeared absorbed in her household duties, must, however, have been thinking of the stories told by Zacharie about the overman and la Pierronne, for she half opened the front door and glanced outside. The wind was still whistling. There were numerous spots of light on the low fronts of the settlement, from which arose a vague tremor of awakening. Already doors were being closed, and black files of workers passed into the night. It was stupid of her to get cold, since the lander at the loading bay was certainly asleep, waiting to take his duties at six. Yet she remained and looked at the house on the other side of the gardens. The door opened, and her curiosity was aroused. But it could only be one of the little Pierrons, Lydie, setting out for the pit.

The hissing sound of steam made her turn. She shut the door, and hastened back; the water was boiling over, and putting out the fire. There was no more coffee. She had to be content to add the water to last night's dregs; then she sugared the coffee-pot with brown sugar. At that moment her father and two brothers came downstairs.

'Christ!' exclaimed Zacharie, when he had put his nose into his bowl, 'this here won't blow our brains.'

Maheu shrugged his shoulders with an air of resignation.

'Bah! It's hot! It's good all the same.'

Jeanlin had gathered up the fragments of bread and made a sop of them. After having drunk, Catherine finished by emptying the coffee-pot into the tin flasks. All four, standing up in the smoky light of the candle, swallowed their meal hastily.

'Finished?' said the father; 'one would think we were people of property.'

But a voice came from the staircase, of which they had left the door open. It was la Maheude, who called out:

'Take all the bread: I have some vermicelli for the children.'

'Yes, yes,' replied Catherine.

She had piled up the fire, wedging the pot that held the remains of the soup into a corner of the grate, so that grandfather might find it warm when he came in at six. Each took his clogs from under the sideboard, passed the strings of his tin over his shoulder and placed his sandwich at his back, between shirt and jacket. And they went out, the men first, the girl, who came last, blowing out the candle and turning the key. The house became dark again.

'Ah! we're off together,' said a man who was closing the door of the next house.

It was Levaque, with his son Bébert, an urchin of twelve, a great friend of Jeanlin's. Catherine, in surprise, stifled a laugh in Zacharie's ear:

'Why! Bouteloup didn't even wait until the husband had gone!'

Now the lights in the settlement were extinguished, and the last door banged. All again fell asleep; the women and the little ones resuming their slumber in the midst of wider beds. And from the silent village to the roaring Voreux a slow file of shadows moved beneath the squalls, the departure of the colliers to their work, bending their shoulders and incommoded by their arms folded on their breasts, while the sandwich behind formed a hump on each back. Clothed in their thin jackets they shivered with cold, but without hastening, straggling along the road with the tramp of a herd of beasts.

CHAPTER 3

Étienne had at last descended from the slag-heap and entered the Voreux; he spoke to men whom he met, asking if there was work to be had, but all shook their heads, telling him to wait for the overman. They left him free to roam through the ill-lighted buildings, full of black holes, confusing with their complicated storeys and rooms. After having mounted a dark and half-destroyed staircase, he found himself on a shaky footbridge; then he crossed the screening shed, which was plunged in such profound darkness that he walked with his hands before him for protection. Suddenly two enormous yellow eyes pierced the darkness in front of him. He was beneath the pit-frame in the receiving room, at the very mouth of the shaft.

A foreman, old Richomme, a big man with the face of a good-natured gendarme, and with a straight grey moustache, was at that moment going towards the receiver's office.

'Do they want a hand here for any kind of work?' asked Étienne again.

Richomme was about to say no, but he changed his mind and replied like the others, as he went away:

'Wait for Monsieur Dansaert, the overman.'

Four lanterns were placed there, and the reflectors which threw all the light on to the shaft vividly illuminated the iron rail, the levers of the signals and bars, the joists of the guides along which slid the two cages. The rest of the vast room, like the nave of a church, was obscure, and peopled by great floating shadows. Only the lamp-cabin shone at the far end, while in the receiver's office a small lamp looked like a fading star. Work was about to be resumed, and on the iron pavement there was a continual thunder, trams of coal being wheeled without ceasing, while the landers, with their long, bent backs, could be distinguished amid the movement of all these black and noisy things, in perpetual agitation.

For a moment Étienne stood motionless, deafened and blinded. He felt frozen by the currents of air which entered from every side. Then he moved on a few paces, attracted by the winding engine, of which he could now see the glistening steel and copper. It was twenty-five metres beyond the shaft, in a loftier chamber, and placed so solidly on its brick foundation that though it worked at full speed, with all its four hundred horse power, the movement of its enormous crank, emerging and plunging with oily softness, imparted no quiver to the wall. The engine-man, standing at his post, listened to the ringing of the signals, and his eye never moved from the indicator where the shaft was figured, with its different levels, by a vertical groove traversed by lead weights hanging to strings, which represented the cages; and at each departure, when the machine was put in motion, the drums – two immense wheels, five metres in radius, by means of which the two steel cables were rolled and unrolled – turned with such rapidity that they became like grey powder.

'Look out, there!' cried three landers, who were dragging an immense ladder.

Étienne just escaped being crushed; his eyes were soon more at home, and he watched the cables moving in the air, more than thirty metres of steel ribbon, which flew up into the pit-frame where they passed over pulleys to descend perpendicularly into the shaft, where they were attached to the cages. An iron frame, like the high scaffolding of a belfry, supported the pulleys. It was like the gliding of a bird, noiseless, without a jar, this rapid flight, the continual come and go of a thread of enormous weight, capable of lifting twelve thousand kilograms at the rate of ten metres a second.

'Watch out there, for God's sake!' cried again the landers, pushing the ladder to the other side in order to climb to the left-hand pulley. Slowly Étienne returned to the receiving room. This giant flight over his head took away his breath. Shivering in the currents of air, he watched the movement of the cages, his ears deafened by the rumblings of the trams. Near the shaft the signal was working, a heavy-levered hammer drawn by a cord from below and allowed to strike against a block. One blow to stop, two to go down, three to go up; it was unceasing, like blows of a club dominating the tumult, accompanied by the clear sound of the bell; while the lander, directing the work, increased the noise still more by shouting orders to the engine-man through a trumpet. The cages in the middle of the clear space appeared and disappeared, were filled and emptied, without Étienne being at all able to understand the complicated proceeding.

He only understood one thing well: the shaft swallowed men by mouthfuls of twenty or thirty, and with so easy a gulp that it seemed to feel nothing go down. Since four o'clock the descent of the workmen had been going on. They came to the shed with naked feet and their lamps in their hands, waiting in little groups until a sufficient number had arrived. Without a sound, with the soft bound of a nocturnal beast, the iron cage arose from the night, wedged itself on the bolts with its four decks, each containing two trams full of coal. Landers on different platforms took out the trams and replaced them with others, either empty or already laden with trimmed wooden props; and it was into the empty trams that the workmen crowded, five at a time, up to forty of them in all, when they filled all the compartments. An order came from the trumpet – a hollow indistinct roar – while the signal cord was pulled four times from below, 'ringing for the meat' to give warning of this burden of human flesh. Then, after a slight leap, the cage plunged silently, falling like a stone, only leaving behind it the vibrating flight of a cable.

'Is it deep?' asked Étienne of a miner, who waited near him with a sleepy air.

'Five hundred and fifty-four metres,' replied the man. 'But there are four levels, the first at three hundred and twenty.' Both were silent, with their eyes on the returning cable. Étienne again:

'And if it breaks?'

'Ah! if it breaks—'

The miner ended with a gesture. His turn had arrived; the cage had reappeared with its easy, unfatigued movement. He squatted in it with some comrades; it plunged down, then flew up again in less then four minutes to swallow down another load of men. For half an hour the shaft went on devouring in this fashion, with more or less greedy gulps, according to the depth of the level to which the men went down, but without stopping, always hungry, with its giant intestines capable of digesting a nation. It went on filling and still filling, and the darkness remained dead. The cage mounted from the void with the same voracious silence.

Étienne was at last seized again by the same depression which he had experienced on the pit bank. What was the good of persisting? This overman would send him off like the others. A vague fear suddenly decided him: he went away, only stopping before the building of the engine room. The wide-open door showed seven boilers with two furnaces each. In the midst of the white steam and the whistling of the escapes a stoker was occupied in piling up one of the furnaces, the heat of which could be felt as far as the threshold; and the young man was approaching, glad of the warmth, when he met a new band of colliers who had just arrived at the pit. It was the Maheu and Levaque set. When he saw Catherine at the head, with her gentle boyish air, a superstitious idea caused him to risk another question.

'I say there, mate! Do they want a hand here for any kind of work?'

She looked at him surprised, rather frightened at this sudden voice coming out of the shadow. But Maheu, behind her, had heard and replied, talking with Étienne for a moment. No, no one was wanted. This poor devil of a man who had lost his way here interested him. When he left him he said to the others:

'Eh! you might easily be like that. Mustn't complain: every one hasn't the chance to work himself to death.'

The gang entered and went straight to the shed, a vast hall roughly boarded and surrounded by cupboards shut by padlocks. In the centre an iron fireplace, a sort of closed stove without a door, glowed red and was so stuffed with burning coal that fragments flew out and rolled on to the trodden soil. The hall was only lighted by this stove, from which sanguine reflections danced along the greasy woodwork up to the ceiling, stained with black dust. As the Maheus went into the heat there was a sound of laughter. Some thirty workmen were standing upright with their backs to the fire, roasting themselves with an air of enjoyment. Before going down, they all came here to get a little warmth in their skins, so that they could face the dampness of the pit. But this morning there was much amusement: they were joking at la Mouquette,* a putter girl of eighteen, whose enormous breasts and flanks were bursting through her old jacket and breeches. She lived at Réquillart with her father, old Mouque, a groom, and Mouquet, her brother, a lander; but their hours of work were not the same; she went to the pit by herself, and in the middle of the wheat-fields in summer, or against a wall in winter, she took her pleasure with her lover of the week. All in the mine had their turn; it was a perpetual round of comrades without further consequences. One day, when reproached about a Marchiennes nail-maker, she was furiously angry, exclaiming that she respected herself far too much, that she would cut her arm off if any one could boast that he had seen her with anyone but a collier.

'It isn't that big Chaval now?' said a miner, grinning; 'did that little fellow have you? He must have needed a ladder. I saw you behind Réquillart; truth is he'd perched himself on a boundary-stone.'

'Well,' replied la Mouquette, good-humouredly, 'what's that to do with you? You were not asked to push.'

And this gross good-natured joke increased the laughter of the men, who expanded their shoulders, half cooked by the stove, while she herself, shaken by laughter, was displaying in the midst of them the indecency of her costume, embarrassingly comical, with her masses of flesh exaggerated almost to difformity.

But the gaiety ceased; la Mouquette told Maheu that Fleurance, big Fleurance, would never come again; she had been found the night before still in her bed; some said it was her heart, others that it was a pint of gin she had drunk too quickly. And Maheu was in despair; another piece of ill-luck; one of the best of his putters gone without any chance of replacing her at once. He was working in a set; there were four pikemen associated in his cutting, himself, Zacharie, Levaque, and Chaval. If they had Catherine alone to wheel, the work would suffer.

Suddenly he called out:

'I have it! there was that man looking for work!'

At that moment Dansaert passed before the shed. Maheu told him the story, and asked for his authority to engage the man; he emphasized the desire of the Company to substitute men for women, as at Anzin. The overman smiled at first; for the scheme of excluding women from the pit was not usually well received by the miners, who were troubled about placing their daughters, and not much affected by questions of morality and health. But after some hesitation he gave his permission, reserving its ratification for Monsieur Négrel, the engineer.

'All very well!' exclaimed Zacharie; 'the man must be away by this time.'

'No,' said Catherine. 'I saw him stop at the boilers.'

'After him, then, lazy,' cried Maheu.

The young girl ran forward; while a crowd of miners proceeded to the shaft, yielding the fire to others.

Jeanlin, without waiting for his father, went also to take his lamp, together with Bébert, a big, stupid boy, and Lydie, a small child of ten. La Mouquette, who was in front of them, called out in the black passage they were dirty brats, and threatened to box their ears if they pinched her.

Étienne was, in fact, in the boiler building, talking with a stoker, who was charging the furnaces with coal. He felt very cold at the thought of the night into which he must return. But he was deciding to set out, when he felt a hand placed on his shoulder.

'Come,' said Catherine; 'there's something for you.'

At first he could not understand. Then he felt a spasm of joy, and vigorously squeezed the young girl's hands.

'Thanks, mate. Ah! you're a good chap, you are!'

She began to laugh, looking at him in the red light of the furnaces, which lit them up. It amused her that he should take her for a boy, still slender, with her knot of hair hidden beneath the cap. He also was laughing, with satisfaction, and they remained, for a moment, both laughing in each other's faces with radiant cheeks.

Maheu, squatting down before his box in the shed, was taking off his clogs and his coarse woollen stockings. When Étienne arrived everything was settled in three or four words: thirty sous a day, hard work, but work that he would easily learn. The pikeman advised him to keep his shoes, and lent him an old cap, a leather hat for the protection of his skull, a precaution which the father and his children disdained. The tools were taken out of the chest, where also was found Fleurance's shovel. Then, when Maheu had shut up their clogs, their stockings, as well as Étienne's bundle, he suddenly became impatient.

'What is that lazy Chaval up to? Another girl given a tumble on a pile of stones? We are half an hour late to-day.'

Zacharie and Levaque were quietly roasting their shoulders. The former said at last:

'Is it Chaval you're waiting for? He came before us, and went down at once.'

'What! you knew that, and said nothing? Come, come, look sharp!'

Catherine, who was warming her hands, had to follow the gang. Étienne allowed her to pass, and went behind her. Again he journeyed through a maze of staircases and obscure corridors in which their naked feet produced the soft sound of old slippers. But the lamp-cabin was glittering – a glass house, full of hooks in rows, holding hundreds of Davy lamps, examined and washed the night before, and lighted like candles in a funeral chapel. At the barrier each workman took his own, stamped with his number; then he examined it and shut it himself, while the marker, seated at a table, inscribed on the registers the hour of descent. Maheu had to intervene to obtain a lamp for his new putter, and there was still another precaution: the workers filed in front of an examiner, who assured himself that all the lamps were properly closed.

'Golly! It's not warm here,' murmured Catherine, shivering.

Étienne contented himself with nodding his head. He was in front of the shaft, in the midst of a vast hall swept by currents of air. He certainly considered himself brave, but he felt a disagreeable emotion at his chest amid this thunder of trams, the hollow blows of the signals, the stifled howling of the trumpet, the continual flight of those cables, unrolled and rolled at full speed by the drums of the engine. The cages rose and sank with the gliding movement of a nocturnal beast, always engulfing men, whom the throat of the hole seemed to drink. It was his turn now. He felt very cold, and preserved a nervous silence which made Zacharie and Levaque grin;

for both of them disapproved of the hiring of this unknown man, especially Levaque, who was offended that he had not been consulted. So Catherine was glad to hear her father explain things to the young man.

'Look! above the cage there is a parachute with iron grapnels to catch into the guides in case of breakage. Does it work? Oh, not always. Yes, the shaft is divided into three compartments, closed by planking from top to bottom; in the middle the cages, on the left the passage for the ladders—'

But he interrupted himself to grumble, though taking care not to raise his voice much.

'What are we stuck here for, blast it? What right have they to freeze us in this way?'

The foreman, Richomme, who was going down himself, with his naked lamp fixed by a nail into the leather of his cap, heard him.

'Careful! Look out for ears,' he murmured paternally, as an old miner with a affectionate feeling for comrades. 'Workmen must do what they can. Hold on! here we are; get in with your fellows.'

The cage, provided with iron bands and a small-meshed lattice work, was in fact awaiting them on the bars: Maheu, Zacharie, and Catherine slid into a tram below, and as all five had to enter, Étienne in his turn went in, but the good places were taken; he had to squeeze himself near the young girl, whose elbow pressed into his belly. His lamp embarrassed him; they advised him to fasten it to a button-hole of his jacket. Not hearing, he awkwardly kept it in his hand. The embarkation, above and below, a confused packing of cattle. They did not, however, set out. What, then, was happening? It seemed to him that his impatience lasted for many minutes. At last he felt a shock, and the light grew dim, everything around him seemed to fly, while he experienced the dizzy anxiety of a fall contracting his bowels. This lasted as long as he could see light, through the two reception stories, in the midst of the scaffolding whirling by. Then, having fallen into the blackness of the pit, he became stunned, no longer having any clear perception of his sensations.

'Now we are off,' said Maheu quietly.

They were all at their ease. He asked himself at times if he was going up or down. Now and then, when the cage went straight without touching the guides, there seemed to be no motion, but rough shocks were afterwards produced, a sort of dancing amid the joists, which made him fear a catastrophe. For the rest he could not distinguish the walls of the shaft behind the lattice work, to which he pressed his face. The lamps feebly lighted the mass of bodies at his feet. Only the foreman's naked light, in the neighbouring tram, shone like a lighthouse.

'This is four metres in diameter,' continued Maheu, to instruct him. 'The tubbing wants doing over again, for the water comes in everywhere. Stop! we are reaching the bottom: do you hear?'

Étienne was, in fact, now asking himself the meaning of this noise of falling rain. A few large drops had at first sounded on the roof of the cage, like the beginning of a shower, and now the rain increased, streaming down, becoming at last a deluge. The roof must be full of holes, for a thread of water was flowing on to his shoulder and wetting him to the skin. The cold became icy, and they were buried in black humidity, when they passed through a sudden flash of light, the vision of a cavern in which men were moving. But already they had fallen back into darkness.

Maheu said:

'That is the first main level. We are at three hundred and twenty metres. See the speed.'

Raising his lamp he lighted up a joist of the guides which fled by like a rail beneath a train going at full speed; and beyond, as before, nothing could be seen. They passed three other levels in flashes of light. The deafening rain continued to strike through the darkness.

'How deep it is!' murmured Étienne.

This fall seemed to last for hours. He was suffering from the cramped position he had taken, not daring to move, and especially tortured by Catherine's elbow. She did not speak a word; he only felt her against him and it warmed him. When the cage at last stopped at the bottom, at five hundred and fifty-four metres, he was astonished to learn that the descent had lasted exactly one minute. But the noise of the bolts, the sensation of solidity beneath his feet, suddenly cheered him; and he was joking when he said to Catherine:

'What have you got under your skin to be so warm? I've got your elbow in my belly, sure enough.'

Then she also burst out laughing. Stupid of him, still to take her for a boy! Were his eyes bunged up?

'It's in your eye that you've got my elbow!' she replied, in the midst of a storm of laughter which the astonished young man could not account for.

The cage emptied out the workers, who crossed the loading-bay, a chamber cut in the rock, vaulted with masonry, and lighted up by three large lamps. Over the iron flooring the porters were violently rolling laden trams. A cavernous odour exhaled from the walls, a freshness of saltpetre in which mingled hot breaths from the neighbouring stable. The openings of four galleries yawned here.

'This way,' said Maheu to Étienne. 'You're not there yet. It is still a good two kilometres.'

The workmen separated, and were lost in groups in the depths of these black holes. Some fifteen went off into the one on the left, and Étienne walked last, behind Maheu, who was preceded by Catherine, Zacharie, and Levaque. It was a large gallery for wagons, through a bed of solid rock, which had only needed walling here and there. In single file they still went on without a word, by the tiny flame of the lamps. The young man stumbled at every step, and entangled his feet in the rails. For a moment a hollow sound disturbed him, the sound of a distant storm, the violence of which seemed to increase and to come from the bowels of the earth. Was it the thunder of a landslip bringing on to their heads the enormous mass which separated them from the light? A gleam pierced the night, he felt the rock tremble, and when he had placed himself close to the wall, like his comrades, he saw a large white horse close to his face, harnessed to a train of wagons. On the first, and holding the reins, was seated Bébert, while Jeanlin, with his hands leaning on the edge of the last, was running barefooted behind.

They again began their walk. Farther on they reached crossways, where two new galleries opened, and the band divided again, the workers gradually entering all the stalls of the mine.

Now the wagon-gallery was constructed of wood; props of timber supported the roof, and made for the crumbly rock a screen of scaffolding, behind which one could see the plates of schist glimmering with mica, and the coarse masses of dull, rough sandstone. Trains of tubs, full or empty, continually passed, crossing each other with their thunder, borne into the shadow by vague beasts trotting by like phantoms. On the tracks of a shunting line a long, black serpent slept, a train at standstill, with a snorting horse, whose crupper looked like a block fallen from the roof. Doors for ventilation were slowly opening and shutting. And as they advanced the gallery became more narrow and lower, and the roof irregular, forcing them to bend their backs constantly.

Étienne struck his head hard; without his leather cap he would have broken his skull. However, he attentively followed the slightest gestures of Maheu, whose sombre profile was seen against the glimmer of the lamps. None of the workmen knocked themselves; they evidently knew each protrusion, each knot of wood or swelling in the rock. The young man also suffered from the slippery soil, which became damper and damper. At times he went through actual puddles, only revealed by the muddy splash of his feet. But what especially astonished him were the sudden changes of temperature. At the bottom of the shaft it was very chilly, and in the wagon-gallery, through which all the air of the mine passed, an icy breeze was blowing, with the violence of a tempest, between the narrow walls. Afterwards, as they penetrated more deeply along other passages which only received a meagre share of air, the wind fell and the heat increased, a suffocating heat as heavy as lead.

Maheu had not again opened his mouth. He turned down another gallery to the right, simply saying to Étienne, without looking around:

'The Guillaume seam.'

It was the seam which contained their cutting. At the first few steps, Étienne hurt his head and elbows. The sloping roof descended so low that, for twenty or thirty metres at a time, he had to walk bent double. The water came up to his ankles. After two hundred metres of this, he saw Levaque, Zacharie, and Catherine disappear, as though they had flown through a narrow fissure which was open in front of him.

'We have to climb,' said Maheu. 'Fasten your lamp to a button-hole and hang on to the wood.' He himself disappeared, and Étienne had to follow him. This chimney-passage left in the seam was reserved for miners, and led to all the secondary passages. It was about the thickness of the coal-bed, hardly sixty centimetres. Fortunately the young man was thin, for, as he was still awkward, he hoisted himself up with a useless expense of muscle, flattening his shoulders and hips, advancing by the strength of his wrists, clinging to the planks. Fifteen metres higher they came on the first secondary passage, but they had to continue, as the cutting of Maheu and his mates was in the sixth passage, in hell, as they said; every fifteen metres the passages were placed over each other in never-ending succession through this cleft, which scraped back and chest. Étienne groaned as if the weight of the rocks had pounded his limbs; with torn hands and bruised legs, he also suffered from lack of air, so that he seemed to feel the blood bursting through his skin. He vaguely saw in one passage two squatting beasts, a big one and a little one, pushing trams: they were Lydie and la Mouquette already at work. And he had still to climb the height of two cuttings! He was blinded by sweat, and he despaired of catching up the others, whose agile limbs he heard brushing against the rock with a long gliding movement.

'Cheer up! here we are!' said Catherine's voice.

He had, in fact, arrived, and another voice cried from the bottom of the cutting:

'Well, is this the way to treat people? I have two kilometres to walk from Montsou and I'm here first.'

It was Chaval, a tall, lean, bony fellow of twenty-five, with strongly marked features, who was in a bad humour at having to wait. When he saw Étienne he asked, with contemptuous surprise:

'What's that?'

And when Maheu had told him the story he snarled:

'Now we've got boys that are eating the bread of girls.'

The two men exchanged a look, lighted up by one of those instinctive hatreds which suddenly flame up. Étienne had felt the insult without yet understanding it. There was silence, and they got to work. At last all the seams were gradually filled with workers, and the cuttings were in movement at every level and at the end of every passage. The devouring pit had swallowed its daily ration of men: nearly seven hundred hands, who were now at work in this giant ant-hill, everywhere making holes in the earth, drilling it like an old worm-eaten piece of wood. And in the middle of the heavy silence and crushing weight of the strata one could hear, by placing one's ear to the rock, the movement of these human insects at work, from the flight of the cable which moved the cage up and down, to the biting of the tools cutting out the coal at the end of the stalls. Étienne, on turning round, found himself again pressed close to Catherine. But this time he caught a glimpse of the developing curves of her breast: he suddenly understood the warmth which had penetrated him.

'You are a girl, then!' he exclaimed.

She replied in her cheerful way, without blushing:

'Of course. You've taken your time to find out!'

CHAPTER 4

The four pikemen had spread themselves one above the other over the whole face of the cutting. Separated by planks, hooked on to retain the fallen coal, they each occupied about four metres of the seam, and this seam was so thin, scarcely more than fifty centimetres thick at this spot, that they seemed to be flattened between the roof and the wall, dragging themselves along by their knees and elbows, and unable to turn without crushing their shoulders. In order to attack the coal, they had to lie on their sides with their necks twisted and arms raised, brandishing, in a sloping direction, their short-handled picks.

Below there was, first, Zacharie; Levaque and Chaval were on the stages above, and at the very top was Maheu. Each worked at the slaty bed, which he dug out with blows of the pick; then he made two vertical cuttings in the bed and detached the block by burying an iron wedge in its upper part. The coal was rich; the block broke and rolled in fragments along their bellies and thighs. When these fragments, retained by the plank, had collected round them, the pikemen disappeared, buried in the narrow cleft.

Maheu suffered most. At the top the temperature rose to thirty-five degrees, and the air was stagnant, so that in the long run it became lethal. In order to see, he had been obliged to fix his lamp to a nail near his head, and this lamp, close to his skull, still further heated his blood. But his torment was especially aggravated by the moisture. The rock above him, a few centimetres from his face, streamed with water, which fell in large continuous rapid drops with a sort of obstinate rhythm, always at the same spot. It was vain for him to twist his head or bend back his neck. Water fell on his face, dropping unceasingly. In a quarter of an hour he was soaked, and at the same time covered with sweat, smoking as with the hot steam of a laundry. This morning a drop dripping in his eye made him swear. He would not leave his picking, he dealt great strokes which shook him violently between the two rocks, like a fly caught between two leaves of a book and in danger of being completely flattened.

Not a word was exchanged. They all hammered; one only heard these irregular blows, which seemed veiled and remote. The sounds had a sonorous hoarseness, without any echo in the dead air. And it seemed that the darkness was an unknown blackness, thickened by the floating coal dust, made heavy by the gas which weighed on the eyes. The wicks of the lamps beneath their caps of metallic tissue only showed as reddish points. One could distinguish nothing. The cutting opened out above like a large chimney, flat and oblique, in which the soot of ten years had amassed a profound night. Spectral figures were moving in it, the gleams of light enabled one to catch a glimpse of a rounded hip, a knotty arm, a vigorous head, besmeared as if for a crime. Sometimes, blocks of coal shone suddenly as they became detached, illuminated by a crystalline reflection. Then everything fell back into darkness, pickaxes struck great dull blows; one only heard panting chests, the grunting of discomfort and weariness beneath the weight of the air and the dripping water.

Zacharie, with arms weakened by a spree of the night before, soon left his work on the pretence that more timbering was necessary. This allowed him to forget himself in quiet whistling, his eyes vaguely resting in the shade. Behind the pikemen nearly three metres of the seam were clear, and they had not yet taken the precaution of supporting the rock, having grown careless of danger and miserly of their time.

'Here, you swell,' cried the young man to Étienne, 'hand up some wood.'

Étienne, who was learning from Catherine how to manage his shovel, had to raise the wood in the cutting. A small supply had remained over from yesterday. It was usually sent down every morning ready cut to fit the seam.

'Hurry up there, you!' shouted Zacharie, seeing the new putter hoist himself up awkwardly in the midst of the coal, his arms embarrassed by four pieces of oak.

He made a hole in the roof with his pickaxe, and then another in the wall, and wedged in the two ends of the wood, which thus supported the rock. In the afternoon the workers in the earth cutting took the rubbish left at the bottom of the gallery by the pikemen, and filled up the exhausted section of the seam, in which they buried the wood, being only careful about the lower and upper roads for the haulage.

Maheu ceased to groan. At last he had detached his block, and he wiped his streaming face on his sleeve. He was worried about what Zacharie was doing behind him.

'Let it be,' he said, 'we will see after lunch. Better go on hewing, if we want to make up our share of trams.'

'It's because it's sinking,' replied the young man. 'Look, there's a crack. It may collapse.'

But the father shrugged his shoulders. Ah! nonsense! Collapse! And if it did, it would not be the first time; they would get out of it all right. He grew angry at last, and sent his son to the front of the cutting.

All of them, however, were now stretching themselves. Levaque, remaining on his back, was swearing as he examined his left thumb which had been grazed by the fall of a piece of sandstone. Chaval had taken off his shirt in a fury, and was working with bare chest and back for the sake of coolness. They were already black with coal, soaked in a fine dust diluted with sweat which ran down in streams and pools. Maheu first began again to hammer, lower down, with his head level with the rock. Now the dripping water struck his forehead so obstinately that he seemed to feel it piercing a hole in the bone of his skull.

'You mustn't mind,' explained Catherine to Étienne, 'they are always howling.'

And like a good-natured girl she went on with her lesson. Every laden tram arrived at the top in the same condition as it left the cutting, marked with a special metal token so that the receiver might put it to the reckoning of the stall. It was necessary, therefore, to be very careful to fill it, and only to take clean coal, otherwise it was refused at the receiving office.

The young man, whose eyes were now becoming accustomed to the darkness, looked at her, still white with her chlorotic complexion, and he could not have told her age; he thought she must be twelve, she seemed to him so slight. However, he felt she must be older, with her boyish freedom, a simple audacity which confused him a little; she did not please him: he thought her too roguish with her pale Pierrot head, framed at the temples by the cap. But what astonished him was the strength of this child, a nervous strength which was blended with a good deal of skill. She filled her tram faster than he could, with quick small regular strokes of the shovel; she afterwards pushed it to the inclined way with a single slow push, without a hitch, easily passing under the low rocks. He tore himself to pieces, got off the rails, and was in difficulties.

It was certainly not a convenient road. It was sixty metres from the cutting to the incline, and the passage, which the miners in the earth cutting had not yet enlarged, was a mere tube with a very irregular roof swollen by innumerable bumps; at certain spots the laden tram could only just pass; the putter had to flatten himself, to push on his knees, in order not to break his head, and besides this the wood was already bending and yielding. You could see it broken in the middle in long pale rents like an over-weak crutch. You had to be careful not to graze yourself in these fractures; and beneath the slow crushing, which caused the splitting of billets of oak as large as the thigh, you had to glide almost on your belly with a secret fear of suddenly hearing your back break.

'Again!' said Catherine, laughing.

Étienne's tram had gone off the rails at the most difficult spot.

He could not steer straight on these rails which sank in the damp earth, and he swore, became angry, and fought furiously with the wheels, which he could not get back into place in spite of exaggerated efforts.

'Wait a bit,' said the young girl. 'If you get angry it will never go.' Skilfully she had glided down and thrust her buttocks beneath the tram, and by putting the weight on her lower back she raised it and replaced it. The weight was seven hundred kilograms. Surprised and ashamed, he stammered excuses.

She was obliged to show him how to straddle his legs and brace his feet against the planking on both sides of the gallery, in order to give himself a more solid fulcrum. The body had to be bent, the arms made stiff so as to push with all the muscles of the shoulders and hips. During the journey he followed her and watched her proceed, her backside tensed, her fists so low that she seemed to be trotting on all fours, like one of those dwarf beasts that perform at circuses. She sweated, panted, her joints cracked, but without a complaint, with the indifference of custom, as if it were the common wretchedness of all to live thus bent double. But he could not succeed in doing as much; his shoes troubled him, his body seemed broken by walking in this way with lowered head. At the end of a few minutes the position became a torture, an intolerable anguish, so painful that he got on his knees for a moment to straighten himself and breathe.

Then at the incline there was more labour. She taught him to fill his tram quickly. At the top and bottom of this inclined plane, which served all the cuttings from one level to the other, there was a trammer – the brakesman above, the receiver below. These scamps of twelve to fifteen years shouted abominable words to each other, and to warn them it was necessary to yell still more violently. Then, as soon as there was an empty tram to send back, the receiver gave the signal and the putter embarked her full tram, the weight of which made the other ascend when the brakesman loosened his brake. Below, in the bottom gallery, were formed the trains which the horses drew to the shaft.

'Here, you confounded rascals,' cried Catherine in the inclined way, which was wood-lined, about a hundred metres long, and resounded like a gigantic trumpet.

The trammers must have been resting, for neither of them replied. On all the levels haulage had stopped. A shrill girl's voice said at last:

'One of them must be on top of la Mouquette, sure enough!'

There was a roar of laughter, and the putters of the whole seam held their sides.

'Who is that?' asked Étienne of Catherine.

The latter named little Lydie, a scamp who knew more than she ought, and who pushed her tram as stoutly as a woman in spite of her doll's arms. As to la Mouquette, she was quite capable of being with both the trammers at once.

But the voice of the receiver arose, shouting out to load. Doubtless a foreman was passing beneath. Haulage began again on the nine levels, and one only heard the regular calls of the trammers, and the snorting of the putters arriving at the incline and steaming like overladen mares. There was an element of bestiality which breathed in the pit, the sudden desire of the male, when a miner met one of these girls on all fours, with her flanks in the air and her hips bursting through her boy's breeches.

And on each journey Étienne found again at the bottom the stuffiness of the cutting, the hollow and broken cadence of the picks, the deep painful sighs of the pikemen persisting in their work. All four were naked, mixed up with the coal, soaked with black mud up to the cap. At one moment it had been necessary to free Maheu, who was gasping, and to remove the planks so that the coal could fall into the passage. Zacharie and Levaque became enraged with the seam, which was now hard, they said, and which would make the condition of their account disastrous. Chaval turned, lying for a moment on his back, abusing Étienne, whose presence decidedly exasperated him.

'What a worm! hasn't the strength of a girl! Are you going to fill your tub? It's to spare your arms, eh? Damned if I don't keep back the ten sous if you get us one refused!'

The young man avoided replying, too happy at present to have found this convict's labour and accepting the brutal rule of the worker by master worker. But he could no longer walk, his feet were bleeding, his limbs torn by horrible cramps, his body confined in an iron belt. Fortunately it was ten o'clock and the stall decided to have lunch.

Maheu had a watch, but he did not even look at it. Deep in this starless night he was never five minutes out. All put on their shirts and jackets. Then, descending from the cutting they squatted down, their elbows to their sides, their buttocks on their heels, in that posture so habitual with miners that they keep it even when out of the mine, without feeling the need of a stone or a beam to sit on. And each, having taken out his 'briquet', bit seriously at the thick slice, uttering occasional words on the morning's work. Catherine, who remained standing, at last joined Étienne, who had stretched himself out farther along, across the rails, with his back against the planking. There was a place there almost dry.

'You're not eating?' she said to him, with her mouth full and her sandwich in her hand.

Then she remembered that this youth, wandering about at night without a sou, perhaps had not a bit of bread.

'Will you share with me?'

And as he refused, declaring that he was not hungry, while his voice trembled with the gnawing in his stomach, she went on cheerfully:

'Ah! if you are fussy! But here, I've only bitten on that side. I'll give you this.'

She had already broken the bread and butter into two pieces. The young man, taking his half, restrained himself from devouring it all at once, and placed his arms on his thighs, so that she should not see how he trembled. With her quiet air of good comradeship she lay beside him, at full length on her stomach, with her chin in one hand, slowly eating with the other. Their lamps, placed between them, lit up their faces.

Catherine looked at him a moment in silence. She must have found him handsome, with his delicate face and black moustache. She vaguely smiled with pleasure.

'Then you are an engine-man, and they sent you away from your railway. Why?'

'Because I struck my boss.'

She remained stupefied, overwhelmed, with her hereditary ideas of subordination and passive obedience.

'I ought to say that I had been drinking,' he went on, 'and when I drink I get mad – I could destroy myself, and I could destroy other people. Yes; I can't swallow two small glasses without wanting to kill someone. Then I am ill for two days.'

'You mustn't drink,' she said, seriously.

'Ah, don't be afraid. I know myself.'

And he shook his head. He hated brandy with the hatred of the last child of a race of drunkards, who suffered in his flesh from all those ancestors, soaked and driven mad by alcohol to such a point that the least drop had become poison to him.*

'It is because of mother that I didn't like being turned into the street,' he said, after having swallowed a mouthful. 'Mother is not happy, and I used to send her a five-franc piece now and then.'

'Where is she, then, your mother?'

'In Paris. Laundress, Rue de la Goutte-d'Or.'*

There was silence. When he thought of these things a tremor dimmed his dark eyes, the sudden anguish of the flaw he brooded over in his fine youthful strength. For a moment he remained with his looks buried in the darkness of the mine; and at that depth, beneath the weight and suffocation of the earth, he saw his childhood again, his mother still beautiful and strong, forsaken by his father, then taken up again after having married another man, living with the two men who ruined her, rolling with them in the gutter in drink and ordure. It was down there, he recalled the street, the details came back to him; the dirty linen in the middle of the shop, the drunken carousals that made the house stink, and the jaw-breaking blows.

'Now,' he began again, in a slow voice, 'I haven't even thirty sous to make her presents with. She will die of misery, sure enough.'

He shrugged his shoulders with despair, and again bit at his bread and butter.

'Will you have a drink?' asked Catherine, uncorking her flask. 'Oh, it's coffee, it won't hurt you. You get dry when you eat like that.'

But he refused; it was quite enough to have taken half her bread. However, she insisted good-naturedly, and said at last:

'Well, I will drink before you since you are so polite. Only you can't refuse now, it would be rude.'

She held out her flask to him. She had got on to her knees and he saw her quite close to him, lit up by the two lamps. Why had he found her ugly? Now that she was black, her face powdered with the charcoal, she seemed to him singularly charming. In this face surrounded by shadow, the teeth in the broad mouth shone with whiteness, while the eyes looked large and gleamed with a greenish reflection, like a cat's eyes. A lock of red hair which had escaped from her cap tickled her ear and made her laugh. She no longer seemed so young, she might be quite fourteen.

'To please you,' he said, drinking and giving her back the flask.

She swallowed a second mouthful and forced him to take one too, wishing to share, she said; and that little neck of the flask that went from one mouth to the other amused them. He suddenly asked himself if he should not take her in his arms and kiss her lips. She had large lips of a pale rose colour, made vivid by the coal, which tormented him with increasing desire. But he did not dare, intimidated before her, only having known girls on the streets at Lille of the lowest order, and not realizing how one ought to behave with a work-girl still living with her family.

'You must be about fourteen then?' he asked, after having gone back to his bread.

She was astonished, almost angry.

'What? fourteen! But I am fifteen! It's true I'm not big. Girls don't grow quick with us.'

He went on questioning her and she told everything without boldness or shame. For the rest she was not ignorant concerning man and woman, although he felt that her body was virginal, with the virginity of a child delayed in her sexual maturity by the environment of bad air and weariness in which she lived. When he spoke of la Mouquette, in order to embarrass her, she told some horrible stories in a quiet tone, with much amusement. Ah! she did some fine things! And as he asked if she herself had no lovers, she replied jokingly that she did not wish to vex her mother, but that it must happen some day. Her shoulders were bent. She shivered a little from the coldness of her garments soaked in sweat, with a gentle resigned air, ready to submit to things and men.

'People can find lovers when they all live together, can't they?'

'Sure enough!'

'And then it doesn't hurt anyone. One doesn't tell the priest.'

'Oh! the priest! I don't care for him! But there is the Black Man?'

'What do you mean, the Black Man?'

'The old miner who comes back into the pit and wrings naughty girls' necks.'

He looked at her, afraid that she was making fun of him.

'You believe in those stupid things? Then you don't know anything.'

'Yes, I do. I can read and write. That is useful among us; in father and mother's time they learnt nothing.'

She was certainly very charming. When she had finished her bread and butter, he would take her and kiss her on her large rosy lips. It was the resolution of a timid man, a violent thought which choked his voice. These boy's clothes – this jacket and these breeches – on the girl's flesh excited and troubled him. He had swallowed his last mouthful. He drank from the flask and gave it back for her to empty. Now the moment for action had come, and he cast a restless glance at the miners farther on. But a shadow blocked the gallery.

For a moment Chaval stood and looked at them from afar. He came forward, having assured himself that Maheu could not see him; and as Catherine was seated on the earth he seized her by the shoulders, drew her head back, and tranquilly crushed her mouth beneath a brutal kiss, affecting not to notice Étienne. There was in that kiss an act of possession, a sort of jealous resolution.

However, the young girl was offended.

'Let me go, do you hear?'

He kept hold of her head and looked into her eyes. His moustache and small red beard flamed in his black face with its large eagle nose. He let her go at last, and went away without speaking a word.

A shudder had frozen Étienne. It was stupid to have waited. He could certainly not kiss her now, for she would, perhaps, think that he wished to behave like the other. In his wounded vanity he experienced real despair.

'Why did you lie?' he said, in a low voice. 'He's your lover.'

'But no, I swear,' she cried. 'There is not that between us. Sometimes he likes a joke; he doesn't even belong here; six months ago he came from the Pas-de-Calais.'

Both rose; work was about to be resumed. When she saw him so cold she seemed annoyed. Doubtless she found him handsomer than the other; she would have preferred him perhaps. The idea of some amiable, consoling relationship disturbed her; and when the young man saw with surprise that his lamp was burning blue with a large pale ring, she tried at least to amuse him.

'Come, I will show you something,' she said, in a friendly way.

When she had led him to the bottom of the cutting, she pointed out to him a crevice in the coal. A slight bubbling escaped from it, a little noise like the warbling of a bird.

'Put your hand there; you'll feel the wind. It's fire-damp.'

He was surprised. Was that all? Was that the terrible thing which blew everything up? She laughed, and said there was a good deal of it today to make the flame of the lamps so blue.

'Now, if you've done chattering, lazy louts!' cried Maheu's rough voice.

Catherine and Étienne hastened to fill their trams, and pushed them to the incline with stiffened back, crawling beneath the bumpy roof of the passage. Even after the second journey, the sweat ran off them and their joints began to crack again.

The pikemen had resumed work in the cutting. The men often shortened their lunch to avoid getting cold; and their sandwiches, eaten in this way, far from the sun, with silent voracity, loaded their stomachs with lead. Stretched on their sides they hammered more loudly, with the one fixed idea of filling a large number of trams.

Every thought disappeared in this rage for gain which was so hard
to earn. They no longer felt the water which streamed on them and
swelled their limbs, the cramps of forced postures, the suffocation
of the darkness in which they grew pale, like plants put in a cellar.
Yet, as the day advanced, the air became more poisoned and heated
with the smoke of the lamps, with the pestilence of their breaths,
with the asphyxia of the fire-damp – blinding to the eyes like
spiders' webs – which only the aeration of the night could sweep
away. At the bottom of their mole-hill, beneath the weight of the
earth, with no more breath in their inflamed lungs, they went on
hammering.

CHAPTER 5

Maheu, without looking at his watch which he had left in his jacket,
stopped and said:

'One o'clock soon. Zacharie, is it done?'

The young man had just been at the planking. In the midst of his
labour he had been lying on his back, with dreamy eyes, thinking
over a game of crosse* of the night before. He woke up and replied:

'Yes, it will do; we shall see tomorrow.'

And he came back to take his place at the cutting. Levaque and
Chaval had also dropped their picks. They were all resting. They
wiped their faces on their naked arms and looked at the roof, in
which slaty masses were cracking. They only spoke about their
work.

'Another chance,' murmured Chaval, 'of getting into loose earth.
They didn't take account of that in the bargain.'

'Rogues!' growled Levaque. 'They only want to bury us in it.'

Zacharie began to laugh. He cared little for the work and the
rest, but it amused him to hear the Company abused. In his placid
way Maheu explained that the nature of the soil changed every
twenty metres. One must be fair; they could not foresee everything.
Then, when the two others went on talking against the bosses, he
became restless, and looked around him.

'Hush! that's enough.'

'You're right,' said Levaque, also lowering his voice; 'it isn't
healthy.'

A morbid dread of spies haunted them, even at this depth, as if the shareholders' coal, while still in the seam, might have ears.

'That won't prevent me,' added Chaval loudly, in a defiant manner, 'from lodging a brick in the belly of that damned Dansaert, if he talks to me as he did the other day. I don't prevent him, do I, from buying pretty girls with white skins?'

This time Zacharie burst out laughing. The overman's love for la Pierronne was a constant joke in the pit. Even Catherine rested on her shovel at the bottom of the cutting, holding her sides, and in a few words told Étienne the joke; while Maheu became angry, seized by a fear which he could not conceal.

'Will you hold your tongue, eh? Wait till you're alone if you want to get into trouble.'

He was still speaking when the sound of steps was heard in the upper gallery. Almost immediately the engineer of the mine, little Négrel, as the workmen called him among themselves, appeared at the top of the cutting, accompanied by Dansaert, the overman.

'Didn't I say so?' muttered Maheu. 'There's always someone there, rising out of the ground.'

Paul Négrel, Monsieur Hennebeau's nephew, was a young man of twenty-six, refined and handsome, with curly hair and brown moustache. His pointed nose and sparkling eyes gave him the air of an amiable ferret of sceptical intelligence, which changed into an abrupt authoritative manner in his relations with the workmen. He was dressed like them, and like them smeared with coal; to make them respect him he exhibited a dare-devil courage, passing through the most difficult spots and always first when landslips or fire-damp explosions occurred.

'Here we are, are we not, Dansaert?' he asked.

The overman, a coarse-faced Belgian, with a large sensual nose, replied with exaggerated politeness:

'Yes, Monsieur Négrel. Here is the man who was taken on this morning.'

Both of them had slid down into the middle of the cutting. They made Étienne come up. The engineer raised his lamp and looked at him without asking any questions.

'Good,' he said at last. 'But I don't like unknown men to be picked up from the road. Don't do it again.'

He did not listen to the explanations given to him, the necessities of work, the desire to replace women by men for the haulage. He had begun to examine the roof while the pikemen had taken up their picks again. Suddenly he called out:

'I say there, Maheu; don't you bother about people's lives? By heavens! you will be buried here!'

'Oh! it's solid,' replied the workman tranquilly.

'What! solid! but the rock is giving already, and you are planting props at more than two metres, as if you grudged doing it! Ah! you are all alike. You will let your skull be flattened rather than leave the seam to give the necessary time to the timbering! I must ask you to prop that immediately. Double the timbering – do you understand?'

And in the face of the unwillingness of the miners who disputed the point, saying that they were good judges of their safety, he became angry.

'Go along! when your heads are smashed, is it you who will have to bear the consequences? Not at all! it will be the Company which will have to pay you pensions, you or your wives. I tell you again that we know you; in order to get two extra trams by evening you would sell your skins.'

Maheu, in spite of the anger which was gradually overtaking him, still answered calmly:

'If they paid us enough we would prop it better.'

The engineer shrugged his shoulders without replying. He had descended the cutting, and only said in conclusion, from below:

'You have an hour. Set to work, all of you; and I give you notice that the stall is fined three francs.'

A low growl from the pikemen greeted these words. The force of the system alone restrained them, that military system which, from the trammer to the overman, ground one beneath the other. Chaval and Levaque, however, made a furious gesture, while Maheu restrained them by a glance, and Zacharie shrugged his shoulders mockingly. But Étienne was, perhaps, most affected. Since he had found himself at the bottom of this hell a slow rebellion was rising within him. He looked at the resigned Catherine, with her lowered back. Was it possible to kill oneself at this hard toil, in this deadly darkness, and not even earn the few sous to buy one's daily bread?

However, Négrel went off with Dansaert, who was content to approve by a continual movement of his head. And their voices again rose; they had just stopped once more, and were examining the timbering in the gallery, which the pikemen were obliged to look after for a length of ten metres behind the cutting.

'Didn't I tell you that they care nothing?' cried the engineer. 'And you! why, in the devil's name, don't you watch them?'

'But I do – I do,' stammered the overman. 'One gets tired of repeating things.'

Négrel called loudly:

'Maheu! Maheu!'

They all came down. He went on:

'Do you see that? Will that hold? It's a shoddy construction! Here is a beam which the posts don't support already, it was done so hastily. Heavens above! I understand how it is that the repairs cost us so much. It'll do, won't it? if it lasts as long as you have the care of it; and then it can go to hell and the Company is obliged to have an army of repairers. Look at it down there; it is mere botching!'

Chaval wished to speak, but he silenced him.

'No! I know what you are going to say. Let them pay you more, eh? Very well! I warn you that you will force the managers to do something: they will pay you the planking separately, and proportionately reduce the price of the trams. We shall see if you will gain that way! Meanwhile, prop that over again, at once; I shall pass by tomorrow.'

Amid the dismay caused by this threat he went away. Dansaert, who had been so humble, remained behind a few moments, to say brutally to the men:

'You get me into a row, you here. I'll give you something more than three francs fine, I will. Look out!'

Then, when he had gone, Maheu broke out in his turn:

'By God! what's fair is fair! I like people to be calm, because that's the only way of getting along, but in the end they make you mad. Did you hear? The tram lowered, and the planking separately! Another way of paying us less. By God it is!'

He looked for someone upon whom to vent his anger, and saw Catherine and Étienne swinging their arms.

'Will you just fetch me some wood! What does it matter to you? I'll put my boot somewhere!'

Étienne went to carry it without rancour for this rough speech, so furious himself against the masters that he thought the miners too good-natured. As for the others, Levaque and Chaval had found relief in strong language. All of them, even Zacharie, were timbering furiously. For nearly half an hour one only heard the creaking of wood wedged in by blows of the hammer. They no longer spoke, they snorted, became enraged with the rock, which they would have hustled and driven back by the force of their shoulders if they had been able.

'That's enough,' said Maheu at last, worn out with the anger and fatigue. 'An hour and a half! A fine day's work! We shan't get fifty sous! I'm off. This disgusts me.'

Though there was still half an hour of work left he dressed himself. The others imitated him. The mere sight of the cutting enraged them. As the putter had gone back to the haulage they called her, irritated at her zeal: let the coal take care of itself. And the six, their tools under their arms, set out to walk the two kilometres back, returning to the shaft by the road that they had taken that morning.

At the chimney Catherine and Étienne were delayed while the pikemen slid down. They met little Lydie, who stopped in a gallery to let them pass, and told them of the disappearance of la Mouquette, whose nose had been bleeding so much that she had been away an hour, bathing her face somewhere, no one knew where. Then, when they left her, the child began again to push her tram, weary and muddy, stiffening her insect-like arms and legs like a lean black ant struggling with a load that was too heavy for it. They let themselves down on their backs, flattening their shoulders for fear of taking the skin off their foreheads, and they slipped so fast down the rocky slope, polished by all the rumps of the workers, that they were obliged from time to time to hold on to the woodwork, so that their backsides should not catch fire, as they said jokingly.

Below they found themselves alone. Red stars disappeared afar at a bend in the passage. Their cheerfulness fell, they began to walk with the heavy step of fatigue, she in front, he behind. Their lamps were blackened. He could scarcely see her, drowned in a sort of smoky mist; and the idea that she was a girl disturbed him because he felt that it was stupid not to embrace her, and yet the recollection of the other man prevented him. Certainly she had lied to him: the other was her lover, they lay together on all those heaps of slaty coal, for she had a loose woman's gait. He sulked without reason, as if she had deceived him. She, however, every moment turned round, warned him of obstacles, and seemed to invite him to be affectionate. They were so lost here, it would have been so easy to laugh together like good friends! At last they entered the large haulage gallery; it was a relief to the indecision from which he was suffering; while she once more had a saddened look, full of regret for a happiness which they would not find again.

Now the subterranean life rumbled around them with a continual passing of foremen, the come and go of the trains drawn by trotting horses. Lamps starred the night everywhere. They had to efface themselves against the rock to leave the path free to shadowy men and beasts, whose breath came against their face. Jeanlin, running barefooted behind his train, cried out some naughtiness to them which they could not hear amid the thunder of the wheels. They still went on, she now silent, he not recognizing the turnings and roads of the morning, and fancying that she was leading him deeper and deeper into the earth; and what specially troubled him was the cold, an increasing cold which he had felt on emerging from the cutting, and which caused him to shiver all the more the nearer they approached the shaft. Between the narrow walls the column of air now blew like a tempest. He despaired of ever coming to the end, when suddenly they found themselves in the loading-bay.

Chaval cast a sidelong glance at them, his mouth drawn with suspicion. The others were there, covered with sweat in the icy current, silent like himself, swallowing their grunts of rage. They had arrived too soon and could not be taken to the top for half an hour, more especially since some complicated manœuvres were going on for lowering a horse. The porters were still rolling the trams with the deafening sound of old iron in movement, and the cages were flying up, disappearing in the rain which fell from the black hole. Below, the sump, a cesspool ten metres deep, filled with this streaming water, also exhaled its muddy moisture. Men were constantly moving around the shaft, pulling the signal cords, pressing on the arms of levers, in the midst of this spray in which their garments were soaked. The reddish light of three open lamps cut out great moving shadows and gave to this subterranean hall the air of a villainous cavern, some bandits' lair near a torrent.

Maheu made one last effort. He approached Pierron, who had gone on duty at six o'clock.

'Here! you might as well let us go up.'

But the porter, a handsome fellow with strong limbs and a gentle face, refused with a frightened gesture.

'Impossible: ask the foreman. They would fine me.'

Fresh growls were stifled. Catherine bent forward and said in Étienne's ear:

'Come and see the stable, then. That's a comfortable place!'

And they had to escape without being seen, for it was forbidden to go there. It was on the left, at the end of a short gallery. Twenty-five metres in length and nearly four high, cut in the rock and vaulted with bricks, it could contain twenty horses. It was, in fact, comfortable there. There was a pleasant warmth of living beasts, the good odour of fresh and well-kept litter. The only lamp threw out the calm rays of a night-light. There were horses there, at rest, who turned their heads, with their large infantine eyes, then went back to their hay, without haste, like fat well-kept workers, loved by everybody.

But as Catherine was reading aloud their names, written on zinc plates over the mangers, she uttered a slight cry, seeing something suddenly rise before her. It was la Mouquette, who emerged in fright from a pile of straw in which she was sleeping. On Monday, when she was overtired from her Sunday's spree, she gave herself a violent blow on the nose, and left her cutting under the pretence of seeking water, to bury herself here with the horses in the warm litter. Her father, being weak with her, allowed it, at the risk of getting into trouble.

Just then, Mouque, the father, entered, a short, bald, worn-out looking man, but still stout, which is rare in an old miner of fifty. Since he had been made a groom, he chewed tobacco to such a degree that his gums bled in his black mouth. On seeing the two with his daughter, he became angry.

'What are you up to there, all of you? Come on! The hussies, bringing a man here! It's a fine thing to come and do your dirty tricks in my straw.'

La Mouquette thought it funny, and held her sides. But Étienne, feeling awkward, moved away, while Catherine smiled at him. As all three returned to the loading-bay, Bébert and Jeanlin arrived there also with a train of tubs. There was a stoppage for the manœuvring of the cages, and the young girl approached their horse, caressed it with her hand, and talked about it to her companion. It was Bataille, the *doyen* of the mine, a white horse who had lived below for ten years. These ten years he had lived in this hole, occupying the same corner of the stable, doing the same task along the black galleries without ever seeing daylight. Very fat, with shining coat and a good-natured air, he seemed to lead the existence of a sage, sheltered from the evils of the world above. In this darkness, too, he had become very cunning. The passage in which he worked had grown so familiar to him that he could open the ventilation doors with his head, and he lowered himself to avoid knocks at the narrow spots. Without doubt, also, he counted his turns, for when he had made the regulation number of journeys he refused to do any more, and had to be led back to his manger. Now that old age was coming on, his cat's eyes were sometimes dimmed with melancholy. Perhaps he vaguely saw again, in the depths of his obscure dreams, the mill at which he was born, near Marchiennes, a mill placed on the edge of the Scarpe, surrounded by large fields over which the wind always blew. Something burnt in the air – an enormous lamp, the exact appearance of which escaped his beast's memory – and he stood with lowered head, trembling on his old feet, making useless efforts to recall the sun.

Meanwhile, the manœuvres went on in the shaft, the signal hammer had struck four blows, and the horse was being lowered; there was always excitement at such a time, for it sometimes happened that the beast was seized by such terror that it was landed dead. When put into a net at the top it struggled fiercely; then, when it felt the ground no longer beneath it, it remained as if petrified and disappeared without a quiver of the skin, with wide and fixed eyes. This animal being too big to pass between the guides, it had been necessary, when hooking it beneath the cage, to pull down the head and attach it to the flanks. The descent lasted nearly three minutes, the engine being slowed as a precaution. Below, the excitement was increasing. What then? Was he going to be left on the way down, hanging in the blackness? At last he appeared in his stony immobility, his eye fixed and dilated with terror. It was a bay horse hardly three years of age, called Trompette.

'Watch out!' cried old Mouque, whose duty it was to receive it. 'Bring him here, don't undo him yet.'

Trompette was soon placed on the metal floor in a mass. Still he did not move: he seemed in a nightmare in this obscure infinite hole, this deep hall echoing with tumult. They were beginning to unfasten him when Bataille, who had just been unharnessed, approached and stretched out his neck to smell this companion who lay on the earth. The workmen jokingly made room in the circle. Well! what pleasant odour did he find in him? But Bataille, deaf to mockery, became animated. He probably found in him the good odour of the open air, the forgotten odour of the sun on the grass. And he suddenly broke out into a sonorous neigh, full of musical gladness, in which there seemed to be the emotion of a sob. It was a greeting, the joy of those ancient things of which a whiff had reached him, the melancholy of one more prisoner who would not ascend again until death.

'Ah! that animal Bataille!' shouted the workmen, amused at the antics of their favourite, 'he's talking with his mate.'

Trompette was unbound, but still did not move. He remained on his flank, as if he still felt the net restraining him, garrotted by fear.

At last they got him up with a lash of the whip, dazed and his limbs quivering. And old Mouque led away the two beasts, fraternizing together.

'Here! Is it ready yet?' asked Maheu.

It was necessary to clear the cages, and besides it was yet ten minutes before the hour for ascending. Little by little the stalls emptied, and the miners returned from all the galleries. There were already some fifty men there, damp and shivering, their inflamed chests panting on every side. Pierron, in spite of his mawkish face, struck his daughter Lydie, because she had left the cutting before time. Zacharie slyly pinched la Mouquette, with a joke about warming himself. But the discontent increased; Chaval and Levaque narrated the engineer's threat; the tram to be lowered in price, and the planking paid separately. And exclamations greeted this scheme, a rebellion was germinating in this little corner, nearly six hundred metres beneath the earth. Soon they could not restrain their voices; these men, soiled by coal, and frozen by the delay, accused the Company of killing half their workers at the bottom, and starving the other half to death. Étienne listened, trembling.

'Quick, quick!' repeated the foreman Richomme, to the porters.

He hastened the preparations for the ascent, not wishing to be hard, pretending not to hear. However, the murmurs became so loud that he was obliged to notice them. They were calling out behind him that this would not last forever, and that one fine day the whole business would blow up.

'You're sensible,' he said to Maheu; 'make them hold their tongues. When you don't have power you must have sense.'

But Maheu, who was getting calm, and had at last become anxious, did not interfere. Suddenly the voices fell; Négrel and Dansaert, returning from their inspection, entered from a gallery, both of them sweating. The habit of discipline made the men stand in rows while the engineer passed through the group without a word. He got into one tram, and the overman into another, the signal was sounded five times, ringing for 'the butcher's meat', as they said for the masters; and the cage flew up in the air in the midst of a gloomy silence.

CHAPTER 6

As he ascended in the cage heaped up with four others, Étienne resolved to continue his famished course along the roads. You might as well die at once as go down to the bottom of that hell, where it was not even possible to earn your bread. Catherine, in the tram above him, was no longer at his side with her pleasant enervating warmth; and he preferred to avoid foolish thoughts and to go away, for with his wider education he felt nothing of the resignation of this herd; he would end by strangling one of the bosses.

Suddenly he was blinded. The ascent had been so rapid that he was stunned by the daylight, and his eyelids quivered in the brightness to which he had already grown unaccustomed. It was none the less a relief to him to feel the cage settle on to the bars. A lander opened the door, and a flood of workmen leapt out of the trams.

'Hey, Mouquet,' whispered Zacharie in the lander's ear, 'are we off to the Volcan to-night?'

The Volcan was a café-concert at Montsou. Mouquet winked his left eye with a silent laugh which made his jaws gape. Short and stout like his father, he had the impudent face of a fellow who devours everything without care for the morrow. Just then la Mouquette came out in her turn, and he gave her a formidable smack on the behind by way of fraternal tenderness.

Étienne hardly recognized the lofty nave of the receiving-hall, which had before looked imposing in the ambiguous light of the lanterns. It was simply bare and dirty; a dull light entered through the dusty windows. The engine alone shone at the end with its copper; the well-greased steel cables moved like ribbons soaked in ink, and the pulleys above, the enormous scaffold which supported them, the cages, the trams, all this prodigality of metal made the hall look sombre with their hard grey tones of old iron. Without ceasing, the rumbling of the wheels shook the metal floor; while from the coal thus put in motion there arose a fine charcoal dust which powdered black the soil, the walls, even the joists of the steeple.

But Chaval, after glancing at the table of counters in the receiver's little glass office, came back furious. He had discovered that two of their trams had been rejected, one because it did not contain the regulation amount, the other because the coal was not clean.

'A fine finish to the day,' he cried. 'Twenty sous less again! This is because we take on lazy rascals who use their arms as a pig does his tail!'

And his sidelong look at Étienne completed his thought.

The latter was tempted to reply by a punch. Then he asked himself what would be the use since he was going away. This decided him absolutely.

'It's not possible to do it right the first day,' said Maheu, to restore peace; 'he'll do better tomorrow.'

They were all none the less soured, and disturbed by the need to quarrel. As they passed to the lamp cabin to give up their lamps, Levaque began to abuse the lamp-man, whom he accused of not properly cleaning his lamp. They only slackened down a little in the shed where the fire was still burning. It had even been too heavily piled up, for the stove was red and the vast room, without a window, seemed to be in flames, to such a degree that the reflection turned the walls a bloody red. And there were grunts of joy, all the backs were roasted at a distance till they smoked like soup. When their flanks were burning they cooked their bellies. La Mouquette had tranquilly let down her breeches to dry her chemise. Some lads were making fun of her; they burst out laughing because she suddenly showed them her backside, a gesture which in her was the extreme expression of contempt.

'I'm off,' said Chaval, who had shut up his tools in his box.

No one moved. Only la Mouquette hastened, and went out behind him on the pretext that they were both going back to Montsou. But the others went on joking; they knew that he would have no more to do with her.

Catherine, however, who seemed preoccupied, was speaking in a low voice to her father. The latter was surprised; then he agreed with a nod; and calling Étienne to give him back his bundle:

'Listen,' he said: 'you haven't a sou; you'll starve before the fortnight's out. Shall I try and get you credit somewhere?'

The young man stood for a moment confused. He had been just about to claim his thirty sous and go. But shame restrained him before the young girl. She looked at him fixedly; perhaps she would think he was shirking the work.

'You know I can promise you nothing,' Maheu went on. 'They can but refuse us.'

Then Étienne consented. They would refuse. Besides, it would bind him to nothing, he could still go away after having eaten something. Then he was dissatisfied at not having refused, seeing Catherine's joy, a pretty laugh, a look of friendship, happy at having been useful to him. What was the good of it all?

When they had put on their clogs and shut their boxes, the Maheus left the shed, following their comrades, who were leaving one by one after they had warmed themselves. Étienne went behind. Levaque and his lad joined the gang. But as they crossed the screening place a scene of violence stopped them.

It was in a vast shed, with beams blackened by the dust and large shutters, through which blew a constant current of air. The coal trams arrived straight from the receiving-room, and were then overturned by the tipping-cradles on to hoppers, long iron slides; and to right and to left of these the screeners mounted on steps and armed with shovels and rakes, separated the stone and swept together the clean coal, which afterwards fell through funnels into the railway wagons beneath the shed.

Philomène Levaque was there, thin and pale, with the sheep-like face of a girl with consumption. With her head protected by a fragment of blue wool, and her hands and arms black to the elbows, she was sorting next to an old witch, the mother of la Pierronne, la Brûlé, as she was called, with terrible owl's eyes, and a mouth drawn in like a miser's purse. They were abusing each other, the young one accusing the elder of raking her stones so that she could not get a basketful in ten minutes. They were paid by the basket, and these quarrels were constantly arising. Hair was flying, and hands were making black marks on red faces.

'Give it her bloody well!' cried Zacharie, from above, to his mistress.

All the screeners laughed. But la Brûlé turned snappishly on the young man.

'Now, then, dirty beast! You'd do better to own up to the two kids you have filled her with. Fancy that, a slip of eighteen, who can't stand straight!'

Maheu had to prevent his son from descending to see, as he said, the colour of the old carcass's skin.

A supervisor came up and the rakes again began to move the coal. One could only see, all along the hoppers, the round backs of women squabbling incessantly over the stones.

Outside, the wind had suddenly quieted; a moist cold was falling from a grey sky. The colliers thrust out their shoulders, folded their arms, and set forth irregularly, with a rolling gait which made their large bones stand out beneath their thin garments. In the daylight they looked like a band of negroes thrown into the mud. Some of them had not finished their sandwiches; and the remains of the bread carried between the shirt and the jacket made them humpbacked.

'Hallo! there's Bouteloup,' said Zacherie, sniggering.

Levaque without stopping exchanged two sentences with his lodger, a big dark fellow of thirty-five with a placid, honest air:

'Is the soup ready, Louis?'

'I believe it is.'

'Then the wife is good-humoured today.'

'Yes, I believe she is.'

Other miners bound for the earth-cutting came up, new groups which one by one were engulfed in the pit. It was the three o'clock descent, more men for the pit to devour, the gangs who would replace the sets of the pikemen at the bottom of the passages. The mine never rested; day and night human insects were digging out the rock six hundred metres below the beetroot fields.

However, the youngsters went ahead. Jeanlin confided to Bébert a complicated plan for getting four sous' worth of tobacco on credit, while Lydie followed respectfully at a distance. Catherine came with Zacharie and Étienne. None of them spoke. And it was only in front of the Avantage bar that Maheu and Levaque rejoined them.

'Here we are,' said the former to Étienne; 'will you come in?'

They separated. Catherine had stood a moment motionless, gazing once more at the young man with her large eyes full of greenish limpidity like spring water, the crystal deepened the more by her black face. She smiled and disappeared with the others on the road that led up to the settlement.

The inn was situated between the village and the mine, at the crossing of two roads. It was a two-storied brick house, white-washed from top to bottom, enlivened around the windows by a broad pale-blue border. On a square sign-board nailed above the door, one read in yellow letters: *Avantage, licensed to Rasseneur.* Behind stretched a skittle-ground enclosed by a hedge. The Company, who had done everything to buy up the property placed within its vast territory, was in despair over this inn in the open fields, at the very entrance of the Voreux.

'Go in,' said Maheu to Étienne.

The little parlour was quite bare with its white walls, its three tables and its dozen chairs, its deal counter about the size of a kitchen dresser. There were a dozen glasses at most, three bottles of liqueur, a decanter, a small zinc tank with a pewter tap to hold the beer; and nothing else – not a picture, not a little table, not a game. In the metal fireplace, which was bright and polished, a coal fire was burning quietly. On the flags a thin layer of white sand drank up the constant moisture of this water-soaked land.

'A beer,' ordered Maheu of a big fair girl, a neighbour's daughter who sometimes took charge of the place. 'Is Rasseneur in?'

The girl turned the tap, replying that the boss would soon return. In a long, slow gulp, the miner emptied half his glass to sweep away the dust which filled his throat. He offered nothing to his companion. One other customer, a damp and besmeared miner, was seated before the table, drinking his beer in silence, with an air of deep meditation. A third entered, was served in response to a gesture, paid and went away without uttering a word.

But a stout man of thirty-eight, with a round shaven face and a good-natured smile, now appeared. It was Rasseneur, a former pikeman whom the Company had dismissed three years ago, after a strike. A very good workman, he could speak well, put himself at the head of every opposition, and had at last become the leader of the discontented. His wife already held a licence, like many miners' wives; and when he was thrown on to the street he became an innkeeper himself; having found the money, he placed his inn in front of the Voreux as a provocation to the Company. Now his house had prospered; it had become a centre, and he was enriched by the animosity he had gradually fostered in the hearts of his old comrades.

'This is a lad I hired this morning,' said Maheu at once. 'Have you got one of your two rooms free, and will you give him credit for a fortnight?'

Rasseneur's broad face suddenly expressed great suspicion. He examined Étienne with a glance, and replied, without going to the trouble to express any regret:

'My two rooms are taken. Can't do it.'

The young man expected this refusal; but it hurt him nevertheless, and he was surprised at the sudden grief he experienced in going. No matter; he would go when he had received his thirty sous. The miner who was drinking at a table had left. Others, one by one, continued to come in to clear their throats, then went on their road with the same slouching gait. It was a simple swilling without joy or passion, the silent satisfaction of a need.

'Then, there's no news?' Rasseneur asked in a peculiar tone of Maheu, who was finishing his beer in small gulps.

The latter turned his head, and saw that only Étienne was near.

'There's been more squabbling. Yes, about the timbering.'

He told the story. The innkeeper's face reddened, swelling with emotion, which flamed in his skin and eyes. At last he broke out:

'Well, well! if they decided to lower the price they are done for.'

Étienne's presence constrained him. However he went on, throwing sidelong glances in his direction. And there were reticences, and implications; he was talking of the manager, Monsieur Hennebeau, of his wife, of his nephew, little Négrel, without naming them, repeating that this could not go on, that things were bound to smash up one of these fine days. The misery was too great; and he spoke of the workshops that were closing, the workers who were going away. During the last month he had given more than six pounds of bread a day. He had heard the day before, that Monsieur Deneulin, the owner of a neighbouring pit, could scarcely keep going. He had also received a letter from Lille full of disturbing details.

'You know,' he whispered, 'it comes from that person you saw here one evening.'

But he was interrupted. His wife entered in her turn, a tall woman, lean and keen, with a long nose and violet cheeks. She was a much more radical politician than her husband.

'Pluchart's letter,' she said. 'Ah! if that fellow was in charge things would soon go better.'

Étienne had been listening for a moment; he understood and became excited over these ideas of misery and revenge. This name, suddenly uttered, caused him to start. He said aloud, as if in spite of himself:

'I know him – Pluchart.'

They looked at him. He had to add:

'Yes, I am an engine-man: he was my foreman at Lille, capable man. I have often talked with him.'

Rasseneur examined him afresh; and there was a rapid change on his face, a sudden sympathy. At last he said to his wife;

'Maheu's brought me this gentleman, one of his putters, to see if there is a room for him upstairs, and if we can give him credit for a fortnight.'

Then the matter was settled in a few words. There was a room; the lodger had left that morning. And the innkeeper, who was very excited, talked more freely, repeating that he only asked possibilities from the bosses, without demanding, like so many others, things that were too hard to get. His wife shrugged her shoulders and demanded justice, absolutely.

'Good evening,' interrupted Maheu. 'All that won't prevent men from going down, and as long as they go there will be people working themselves to death. Look how fresh you are, these three years that you've been out of it.'

'Yes, I'm very much better,' declared Rasseneur, complacently.

Étienne went as far as the door, thanking the miner, who was leaving; but the latter nodded his head without adding a word, and the young man watched him painfully climb up the road to the settlement. Madame Rasseneur, occupied with serving customers, asked him to wait a minute, when she would show him his room, where he could wash. Should he remain? He again felt hesitation, a discomfort which made him regret the freedom of the open road, the hunger beneath the sun, endured with the joy of one's own master. It seemed to him that he had lived years from his arrival on the pit-bank, in the midst of squalls, to those hours passed under the earth on his belly in the black passages. And he shrank from beginning again; it was unjust and too hard. His manly pride revolted at the idea of becoming a crushed and blinded beast.

While Étienne was thus debating with himself, his eyes, wandering over the immense plain, gradually began to see it clearly. He was surprised; he had not imagined the horizon was like this, when old Bonnemort had pointed it out to him in the darkness. Before him he plainly saw the Voreux in a fold of the earth, with its wood and brick buildings, the tarred screening shed, the slate-covered steeple, the engine-room and the tall, pale red chimney, all massed together with that evil air. But around these buildings the space extended, and he had not imagined it so large, changed into an inky sea by the ascending waves of coal soot, bristling with high trestles which carried the rails of the foot-bridges, encumbered in one corner with the timber supply, which looked like the harvest of a mown forest. Towards the right the pit-bank hid the view, colossal as a barricade of giants, already covered with grass in its older part, consumed at the other end by an interior fire which had been burning for a year with a thick smoke, leaving at the surface in the midst of the pale grey of the slates and sandstones long trains of bleeding rust. Then the fields unrolled, the endless fields of wheat and beetroot, naked at this season of the year, marshes with scanty vegetation, cut by a few stunted willows, distant meadows separated by slender rows of poplars. Very far away little pale patches indicated towns, Marchiennes to the north, Montsou to the south; while the forest of Vandame to the east bordered the horizon with the violet line of its leafless trees. And beneath the livid sky, in the faint daylight of this winter afternoon, it seemed as if all the blackness of the Voreux, and all its flying coal dust, had fallen upon the plain, powdering the trees, sanding the roads, sowing the earth.

Étienne looked, and what especially surprised him was a canal, the canalized stream of the Scarpe, which he had not seen in the night. From the Voreux to Marchiennes this canal ran straight, like a dull silver ribbon two leagues long, an avenue lined by large trees, raised above the low earth, threading into space with the perspective of its green banks, its pale water into which glided the vermilion of the boats. Near one pit there was a wharf with moored vessels which were laden directly from the trams at the foot-bridges. Afterwards the canal made a curve, sloping by the marshes; and the whole soul of that smooth plain appeared to lie in this geometrical stream, which traversed it like a great road, carting coal and iron.

Étienne's glance looked up from the canal to the settlement built on the height, of which he could only distinguish the red tiles. Then his eyes rested again at the bottom of the clay slope, towards the Voreux, on two enormous masses of bricks made and burnt on the spot. A branch of the Company's railroad passed behind a paling, for the use of the pit. They must be sending down the last miners to the earth-cutting. Only one shrill note came from a truck pushed by a group of men. One felt no longer the unknown darkness, the inexplicable thunder, the flaming of mysterious stars. Afar, the blast furnaces and the coke kilns had paled with the dawn. There only remained, unceasingly, the sound of the pump, always breathing with the same thick, long breath, the ogre's breath of which he could now see the grey steam, and which nothing could satiate.

Then Étienne suddenly made up his mind. Perhaps he seemed to see again Catherine's clear eyes, up there, at the entrance to the settlement. Perhaps, rather, it was the wind of revolt which came from the Voreux. He did not know, but he wished to go down again to the mine, to suffer and to fight. And he thought fiercely of those people Bonnemort had talked of, the crouching and sated god, to whom ten thousand starving men gave their flesh without even knowing who it was.

PART TWO

CHAPTER I

The Grégoires' property, La Piolaine, was situated two kilometres to the east of Montsou, on the Joiselle road. The house was a large square building, without style, dating from the beginning of the last century. Of all the land that once belonged to it there only remained some thirty hectares, enclosed by walls, and easy to keep up. The orchard and kitchen garden especially were everywhere spoken of, being famous for the finest fruit and vegetables in the country. For the rest, there was no park, only a small wood. The avenue of old limes, a vault of foliage three hundred metres long, reaching from the gate to the porch, was one of the curiosities of this bare plain, on which you could count the large trees between Marchiennes and Beaugnies.

On that morning the Grégoires got up at eight o'clock. Usually they never stirred until an hour later, being heavy sleepers; but last night's tempest had disturbed them. And while her husband had gone at once to see if the wind had caused any damage, Madame Grégoire went down to the kitchen in her slippers and flannel dressing-gown. She was short and stout, about fifty-eight years of age, and retained a broad, surprised, dollish face beneath the dazzling whiteness of her hair.

'Mélanie,' she said to the cook, 'suppose you were to make the brioche this morning, since the dough is ready. Mademoiselle will not get up for half an hour yet, and she can eat it with her chocolate. Eh? It will be a surprise.'

The cook, a lean old woman who had served them for thirty years, laughed.

'That's true! It would be a lovely surprise. My stove is lit, and the oven must be hot; and then Honorine will help me a bit.'

Honorine, a girl of some twenty years, who had been taken in as a child and brought up in the house, now acted as housemaid. Besides these two women, the only other servant was the coachman, Francis, who undertook the heavy work. A gardener and his wife were occupied with the vegetables, the fruit, the flowers, and the poultry-yard. And as service here was patriarchal, this little world lived together, like one large family, on very good terms.

Madame Grégoire, who had planned this surprise of the brioche in bed, waited to see the dough put in the oven. The kitchen was very large, and one guessed it was the most important room in the house by its extreme cleanliness and by the arsenal of saucepans, utensils, and pots which filled it. There was a nice smell of good food. Provisions abounded, hanging from hooks or in cupboards.

'And let it be golden brown, won't you?' Madame Grégoire said as she passed into the dining-room.

In spite of the hot-air stove which warmed the whole house, a coal fire enlivened this room. In other respects it exhibited no luxury; a large table, chairs, mahogany sideboard; only two deep easy-chairs betrayed a love of comfort, long happy hours of digestion. They never went into the drawing-room, they remained here in a family circle.

Just then Monsieur Grégoire came back dressed in a thick fustian jacket; he also was ruddy for his sixty years, with large, good-natured, honest features beneath the snow of his curly hair. He had seen the coachman and the gardener; there had been no damage of importance, nothing but a fallen chimney-pot. Every morning he liked to have a look around La Piolaine, which was not large enough to cause him anxiety, and from which he derived all the happiness of ownership.

'And Cécile?' he asked, 'isn't she up yet then?'

'I can't make it out,' replied his wife. 'I thought I heard her moving.'

The table was set; there were three cups on the white cloth. They sent Honorine to see what had become of mademoiselle. But she came back immediately, restraining her laughter, stifling her voice, as if she were still upstairs in the bedroom.

'Oh! if monsieur and madame could see mademoiselle! She's asleep, oh! she sleeps like an angel. You should see her. It's a pleasure to look at her.'

The father and mother exchanged tender looks. He said, smiling:

'Will you come and see?'

'The poor little darling!' she murmured. 'I'll come.'

And they went up together. The room was the only luxurious one in the house. It was draped in blue silk, and the furniture was lacquered white, with blue tracery – a spoilt child's whim, which her parents had gratified. In the vague whiteness of the bed, beneath the half-light which came through a curtain that was drawn back, the young girl was sleeping with her cheek resting on her naked arm. She was not pretty, too healthy, in too vigorous condition, fully developed at eighteen; but she had superb flesh, the freshness of milk, with her chestnut hair, her round face, and her little wilful nose lost between her cheeks. The coverlet had slipped down, and she was breathing so softly that her respiration did not even lift her already well-developed bosom.

'That horrible wind must have prevented her from closing her eyes,' said the mother softly.

The father imposed silence with a gesture. Both of them leant down and gazed with adoration on this girl, in her virgin nakedness, whom they had desired so long, and who had come so late, when they had no longer hoped for her. They found her perfect, not at all too fat, and could never feed her sufficiently. And she went on sleeping, without feeling them near her, with their faces against hers. However, a slight movement disturbed her motionless face. They feared that they would wake her, and went out on tiptoe.

'Hush!' said Monsieur Grégoire, at the door. 'If she has not slept we must leave her sleeping.'

'As long as she likes, the darling!' agreed Madame Grégoire. 'We will wait.'

They went down and seated themselves in the easy-chairs in the dining-room; while the servants, laughing at mademoiselle's sound sleep, kept the chocolate on the stove without grumbling. He took up a newspaper; she knitted at a large woollen quilt. It was very hot, and not a sound was heard in the silent house.

The Grégoires' fortune, about forty thousand francs a year, was entirely invested in a share of the Montsou mines. They would complacently narrate its origin, which dated from the very formation of the Company.

Towards the beginning of the last century, there had been a mad search for coal between Lille and Valenciennes. The success of those who held the concession, which was afterwards to become the Anzin Company, had turned all heads. In every commune the ground was tested; and societies were formed and concessions grew up in a night. But among all the obstinate seekers of that epoch, Baron Desrumaux had certainly left the reputation for the most heroic intelligence. For forty years he had struggled without yielding, in the midst of continual obstacles: early searches unsuccessful, new pits abandoned at the end of long months of work, landslips which filled up borings, sudden inundations which drowned the workmen, hundreds of thousands of francs thrown into the earth; then the squabbles of the management, the panics of the shareholders, the struggle with the landowners, who were resolved not to recognize royal concessions if no treaty was first made with themselves. He had at last founded the association of Desrumaux,

Fauquenoix & Co. to exploit the Montsou concession, and the pits began to yield a small profit when two neighbouring concessions, the Cougny, belonging to the Comte de Cougny, and the Joiselle, belonging to the Cornille and Jenard Company, had nearly over-whelmed him beneath the terrible assault of their competition. Happily, on the 25th of August 1760, a treaty was made between the three concessions, uniting them into a single one. The Montsou Mining Company was created, such as it still exists today. In the distribution they had divided the total property, according to the standard of the money of the time, into twenty-four sous, of which each was subdivided into twelve deniers, which made two hundred and eighty-eight deniers; and as the denier was worth ten thousand francs the capital represented a sum of nearly three millions. Desrumaux, dying but triumphant, received in this division six sous and three deniers.

In those days the baron owned La Piolaine, which had three hundred hectares belonging to it, and he had in his service as steward Honoré Grégoire, a Picardy lad, the great-grandfather of Léon Grégoire, Cécile's father. When the Montsou treaty was made, Honoré, who had laid up savings to the amount of some fifty thousand francs, yielded tremblingly to his master's unshakable faith. He took out ten thousand francs in fine crowns, and took a denier, though with the fear of robbing his children of that sum. His son Eugène, in fact, received very small dividends; and as he had become a bourgeois and had been foolish enough to throw away the other forty thousand francs of the paternal inheritance in a company that came to grief, he lived meanly enough. But the interest of the denier gradually increased. The fortune began with Félicien, who was able to realize a dream with which his grand-father, the old steward, had nourished his childhood – the purchase of La Piolaine, which he acquired as national property for a ludicrous sum. However, bad years followed. It was necessary to await the conclusion of the revolutionary catastrophes, and after-wards Napoleon's bloody fall; and it was Léon Grégoire who profited at a stupefying rate of progress from the timid and uneasy investment of his great-grandfather. Those poor ten thousand francs grew and multiplied with the Company's prosperity. From 1820 they had brought in returns of a hundred per cent, ten thousand francs. In 1844 they had produced twenty thousand; in 1850, forty. During two years the dividend had reached the prodigious figure of fifty thousand francs; the value of the denier, quoted at the Lille bourse at a million, had multiplied a hundredfold in a century.*

Monsieur Grégoire, who had been advised to sell out when this figure of a million was reached, had refused with his smiling paternal air. Six months later an industrial crisis broke out; the denier fell to six hundred thousand francs. But he still smiled; he regretted nothing, for the Grégoires had maintained an obstinate faith in their mine. It would rise again: God Himself was not so solid. Then with his religious faith was mixed profound gratitude towards an investment which for a century had supported the family in doing nothing. It was like a divinity of their own, whom their egoism surrounded with a kind of worship, the benefactor of the hearth, lulling them in their great bed of idleness, fattening them at their gluttonous table. From father to son it had gone on. Why risk displeasing fate by doubting it? And at the heart of their fidelity there was a superstitious terror, a fear lest the million of the denier might suddenly melt away if they were to realize it and to put it in a drawer. It seemed to them more sheltered in the earth, from which a race of miners, generations of starving people, extracted it for them, a little every day, as they needed it.

Moreover, blessings rained on this house. Monsieur Grégoire, when very young, had married the daughter of a Marchiennes druggist, a plain, penniless girl, whom he adored, and who repaid him with happiness. She shut herself up in her household, and worshipped her husband, having no other will but his. No difference of tastes separated them, their desires were mingled in one idea of comfort; and they had thus lived for forty years, in affection and little mutual services. It was a well-regulated existence; the forty thousand francs were spent quietly, and the savings expended on Cécile, whose tardy birth had for a moment disturbed the budget. They still satisfied all her whims – a second horse, two more carriages, toilets sent from Paris. But this gave them one more cause for joy; they thought nothing too good for their daughter, although they had such a horror of display that they had preserved the fashions of their youth. Every unprofitable expense seemed foolish to them.

Suddenly the door opened, and a loud voice called out:

'Hallo! What now? Having breakfast without me!'

It was Cécile, just come from her bed, her eyes heavy with sleep. She had simply put up her hair and flung on a white woollen dressing-gown.

'No, no!' said her mother; 'you see we are all waiting. Eh? the wind must have prevented you from sleeping, poor darling?'

The young girl looked at her in great surprise.

'Has it been windy? I didn't know anything about it. I haven't moved all night.'

Then they thought this funny, and all three began to laugh; the servants who were bringing in the breakfast also broke out laughing, so amused was the household at the idea that mademoiselle had been sleeping for twelve hours right off. The sight of the brioche completed the joy on their faces.

'What! Is it cooked, then?' said Cécile; 'that must be a surprise for me! That'll be good now, hot, with the chocolate!'

They sat down to table at last with the smoking chocolate in their cups, and for a long time talked of nothing but the brioche. Mélanie and Honorine remained to give details about the cooking and watched them stuffing themselves with greasy lips, saying that it was a pleasure to make a cake when you saw the masters enjoying it so much.

But the dogs began to bark loudly; perhaps they announced the arrival of the music mistress, who came from Marchiennes on Mondays and Fridays. A literature teacher also came. All the young girl's education was thus carried on at La Piolaine in happy ignorance, with her childish whims, throwing the book out of the window as soon as anything wearied her.

'It is Monsieur Deneulin,' said Honorine, returning.

Behind her, Deneulin, a cousin of Monsieur Grégoire's, appeared without ceremony; with his loud voice, his quick gestures, he had the appearance of an old cavalry officer. Although over fifty, his short hair and thick moutache were as black as ink.

'Yes! It's me. Good day! Don't let me disturb you.'

He had sat down amid the family's exclamations. They turned back at last to their chocolate.

'Have you anything to tell me?' asked Monsieur Grégoire.

'No! nothing at all,' Deneulin hastened to reply. 'I came out on horseback to rub off the rust a bit, and as I passed your door I thought I would just look in.'

Cécile questioned him about Jeanne and Lucie, his daughters. They were perfectly well, the first was always at her painting, while the other, the elder, was training her voice at the piano from morning till night. And there was a slight quiver in his voice, a disquiet which he concealed beneath bursts of gaiety.

Monsieur Grégoire began again:

'And everything goes well at the pit?'

'Well, I am upset over this rotten crisis. Ah! we are paying for the prosperous years! They have built too many workshops, put down too many railways, invested too much capital with a view to a large return, and today the money is dormant. They can't get any more to make the whole thing work. Luckily things are not desperate; I shall get out of it somehow.'

Like his cousin he had inherited a denier in the Montsou mines. But being an enterprising engineer, tormented by the desire for a large fortune, he had hastened to sell out when the denier had reached a million. For some months he had been planning a scheme. His wife possessed, through an uncle, the little concession of Vandame, where only two pits were open – Jean-Bart and Gaston-Marie – in such an abandoned state, and with such defective material that the output hardly covered the cost. Now he was meditating the repair of Jean-Bart, the renewal of the engine, and the enlargement of the shaft so as to facilitate the descent, keeping Gaston-Marie only for ventilation purposes. They ought to be able to shovel up gold there, he said. The idea was sound. Only the million had been spent over it, and this damnable industrial crisis broke out at the moment when large profits would have shown that he was right. Besides, he was a bad manager, with a rough kindness towards his workmen, and since his wife's death he allowed himself to be pillaged, and also gave free rein to his daughters, the elder of whom talked of going on the stage, while the younger had already had three landscapes refused at the Salon,* both of them joyous amid the downfall, and exhibiting in poverty their capacity for good household management.

'You see, Léon,' he went on, in a hesitating voice, 'you were wrong not to sell out at the same time as I did; now everything is going down. You run risk, and if you had confided your money to me you would have seen what we should have done at Vandame in our mine!'

Monsieur Grégoire finished his chocolate without haste. He replied peacefully:

'Never! You know that I don't want to speculate. I live quietly, and it would be too foolish to worry my head over business affairs. And as for Montsou, it may continue to go down, we shall always get our living out of it. It doesn't do to be so diabolically greedy! Then, listen, it is you who will bite your fingers one day, for Montsou will rise again and Cécile's grandchildren will still get their bread out of it.'

Deneulin listened with a constrained smile.

'Then,' he murmured, 'if I were to ask you to put a hundred thousand francs in my business you would refuse?'

But seeing the Grégoires' disturbed faces he regretted having gone so far; he put off his idea of a loan, reserving it until the case was desperate.

'Oh! I have not got to that! it is a joke. Good heavens! perhaps you are right; the money that other people earn for you is the best to fatten on.'

They changed the conversation. Cécile spoke again of her cousins, whose tastes interested her, while at the same time they shocked her. Madame Grégoire promised to take her daughter to see those dear little ones on the first fine day. Monsieur Grégoire, however, with a distracted air, did not follow the conversation. He added aloud:

'If I were in your shoes I wouldn't persist any more; I would do a deal with Montsou. They want it, and you will get your money back.'

He alluded to an old hatred which existed between the concession of Montsou and that of Vandame. In spite of the latter's slight importance, its powerful neighbour was enraged at seeing, enclosed within its own sixty-seven communes, this square league which did not belong to it, and after having vainly tried to kill it had plotted to buy it at a low price when in a failing condition. The war continued without truce. Each party stopped its galleries at two hundred metres from the other; it was a duel to the last drop of blood, although the managers and engineers maintained polite relations with each other.

Deneulin's eyes had lit up.

'Never!' he cried, in his turn. 'Montsou shall never have Vandame as long as I am alive. I dined on Thursday at Hennebeau's, and I saw him fluttering around me. Last autumn, when the big men came to the administration building, they made me all sorts of advances. Yes, yes, I know them – those marquises, and dukes, and generals, and ministers! Brigands who would take away even your shirt at the edge of a wood.'

He could not stop. Besides, Monsieur Grégoire did not defend the administration of Montsou – the six stewards established by the treaty of 1760, who governed the Company despotically, and the five survivors of whom on every death chose the new member among the powerful and rich shareholders. The opinion of the owner of La Piolaine, with his reasonable ideas, was that these gentlemen were sometimes rather immoderate in their exaggerated love of money.

Mélanie had come to clear away the table. Outside the dogs were again barking, and Honorine was going to the door, when Cécile, who was stifled by heat and food, left the table.

'No, never mind! it must be for my lesson.'

Deneulin had also risen. He watched the young girl go out, and asked, smiling:

'Well! and the marriage with little Négrel?'

'Nothing has been settled,' said Madame Grégoire; 'it is only an idea. We must think about it.'

'No doubt!' he went on, with a gay laugh. 'I believe that the nephew and the aunt— What baffles me is that Madame Hennebeau should be so keen on Cécile.'

But Monsieur Grégoire was indignant. So distinguished a lady, and fourteen years older than the young man! It was monstrous; he did not like joking on such subjects. Deneulin, still laughing, shook hands with him and left.

'Not yet,' said Cécile, coming back. 'It is that woman with the two children. You know, mamma, the miner's wife whom we met. Are they to come in here?'

They hesitated. Were they very dirty? No, not very; and they would leave their clogs in the porch. Already the father and mother had stretched themselves out in the depths of their large easy-chairs. They were digesting there. The fear of a change of air decided them.

'Let them come in, Honorine.'

Then la Maheude and her little ones entered, frozen and hungry, seized by fright on finding themselves in this room, which was so warm and smelled so nicely of the brioche.

CHAPTER 2

The room remained shut up and the shutters had allowed gradual streaks of daylight to form a fan on the ceiling. The confined air stupefied them so that they continued their night's slumber: Lénore and Henri in each other's arms, Alzire with her head back, lying on her hump; while old Bonnemort, having the bed of Zacharie and Jeanlin to himself, snored with open mouth. No sound came from the closet where la Maheude had gone to sleep again while suckling Estelle, her breast hanging to one side, the child lying across her belly, stuffed with milk, overcome by sleep also and stifling in the soft flesh of the bosom.

The cuckoo clock below struck six. Along the front of the settlement you could hear the sound of doors, then the clatter of clogs along the pavements; the screening women were going to the pit. And silence again fell until seven o'clock. Then shutters were drawn back, yawns and coughs were heard through the walls. For a long time a coffee-mill scraped, but no one awoke in the room.

Suddenly a sound of blows and shouts, far away, made Alzire sit up. She was conscious of the time, and ran barefooted to shake her mother.

'Mother, mother, it is late! You have to go out. Take care, you are crushing Estelle.'

And she saved the child, half-stifled beneath the enormous mass of the breasts.

'Good gracious!' stammered la Maheude, rubbing her eyes, 'I'm so knocked up I could sleep all day. Dress Lénore and Henri, I'll take them with me; and you can take care of Estelle; I don't want to drag her along for fear of hurting her, in this filthy weather.'

She hastily washed herself and put on an old blue skirt, her cleanest, and a loose jacket of grey wool in which she had made two patches the evening before.

'And the soup! Good gracious!' she muttered again.

When her mother had gone down, upsetting everything, Alzire went back into the room, taking with her Estelle, who had begun screaming. But she was used to the little one's rages; at eight she had all a woman's tender cunning in soothing and amusing her. She gently placed her in her still warm bed, and put her to sleep again, giving her a finger to suck. It was time, for now another disturbance broke out, and she had to make peace between Lénore and Henri, who at last awoke. These children could never get on together; it was only when they were asleep that they put their arms round one another's necks. The girl, who was six years old, as soon as she was awake set on the boy, her junior by two years, who received her blows without returning them. Both of them had the same kind of head, which was too large for them, as if blown out, with disorderly yellow hair. Alzire had to pull her sister by the legs, threatening to take the skin off her bottom. Then there was stamping over the washing, and over every garment that she put on to them. The shutters remained closed so as not to disturb old Bonnemort's sleep. He went on snoring amid the children's frightful clatter.

'It's ready. Are you coming, up there?' shouted la Maheude.

She had put back the blinds, and stirred up the fire, adding some coal to it. Her hope was that the old man had not swallowed all the soup. But she found the saucepan dry, and cooked a handful of vermicelli which she had been keeping for three days in reserve. They could swallow it with water, without butter, as there could not be any remaining from the day before, and she was surprised to find that Catherine in preparing the briquets had performed the miracle of leaving a piece as large as a nut. But this time the cupboard was indeed empty: nothing, not a crust, not an odd fragment, not a bone to gnaw. What was to become of them if Maigrat persisted in cutting short their credit, and if the Piolaine people would not give them the five francs? When the men and the girl returned from the pit they would want to eat, for unfortunately no one had yet found out how to live without eating.

'Come down, will you?' she cried out, getting angry. 'I ought to be gone by now.'

When Alzire and the children were there she divided the vermicelli in three small portions. She herself was not hungry, she said. Although Catherine had already poured water on the coffee-dregs of the day before, she did so over again, and swallowed two large glasses of coffee so weak that it looked like rusty water. That would keep her going all the same.

'Listen!' she repeated to Alzire. 'You must let your grandfather sleep; you must watch that Estelle does not knock her head; and if she wakes, or if she howls too much, here! take this bit of sugar and melt it and give it her in spoonfuls. I know that you are sensible and won't eat it yourself.'

'And school, mother?'

'School! well, that must be left for another day: I need you.'

'And the soup? would you like me to make it if you come back late?'

'Soup, soup: no, wait till I come.'

Alzire, with the precocious intelligence of a little invalid girl, could make soup very well. She must have understood, for she did not insist. Now the whole settlement was awake, gangs of children were going to school, and you could hear the trailing noise of their clogs. Eight o'clock struck, and a growing murmur of chatter arose on the left, from the Levaque house. The women were commencing their day around the coffee-pots, with their hands on their hips, their tongues turning without ceasing, like millstones. A faded head, with thick lips and flattened nose, was pressed against a window-pane, calling out:

'Got some news. Stop a bit.'

'No, no! later on,' replied la Maheude. 'I have to go out.'

And for fear of giving way to the offer of a glass of hot coffee she pushed Lénore and Henri, and set out with them. Up above, old Bonnemort was still snoring with a rhythmic snore which rocked the house.

Outside, la Maheude was surprised to find that the wind was no longer blowing. There had been a sudden thaw; the sky was earth-coloured, the walls were sticky with greenish moisture, and the roads were covered with pitch-like mud, a special kind of mud peculiar to the coal country, as black as diluted soot, thick and tenacious enough to pull off her clogs. Suddenly she boxed Lénore's ears, because the little one amused herself by piling the mud on her clogs as on the end of a shovel. On leaving the settlement she had gone along by the pit-bank and followed the road of the canal, making a short cut through broken-up paths, across rough country shut in by mossy palings. Sheds succeeded one another, long workshop buildings, tall chimneys spitting out soot, and soiling this ravaged suburb of an industrial district. Behind a clump of poplars the old Réquillart pit exhibited its crumbling steeple, of which the large skeleton alone stood upright. And turning to the right, la Maheude found herself on the high road.

'Stop, stop, dirty little pig! I'll teach you to make mud pies.'

Now it was Henri, who had taken a handful of mud and was moulding it. The two children had their ears impartially boxed, and resumed their orderly progress, squinting down at the tracks they were making in the mud-heaps. They draggled along, already exhausted by their efforts to unstick their shoes at every step.

On the Marchiennes side the road stretched out along its two leagues of pavement, which ran as straight as a ribbon soaked in cart grease between the reddish fields. But on the other side it went winding down through Montsou, which was built on the slope of a large undulation in the plain. These roads in the Nord, drawn like a string between manufacturing towns, with their slight curves, their slow ascents, are gradually lined with houses and tend to make the department one huge industrial city. The little brick houses, daubed over to enliven the climate, some yellow, others blue, others black – the last, no doubt, in order to reach at once their final shade – went serpentining down to right and to left to the bottom of the slope. A few large two-storied villas, the dwellings of the heads of the workshops, made gaps in the serried line of narrow façades. A church, also of brick, looked like a new model of a large furnace, with its square tower already stained by the floating coal dust. And amid the sugar works, the rope works, and the flour mills, there stood out ballrooms, bars, and beershops, which were so numerous that to every thousand houses there were more than five hundred inns.

As she approached Company's Yards, a vast series of storehouses and workshops, la Maheude decided to take Henri and Lénore by the hand, one on the right, the other on the left. Beyond was situated the house of the director, Monsieur Hennebeau, a sort of vast chalet, separated from the road by a grating, and then a garden in which some lean trees vegetated. Just then, a carriage had stopped before the door and a gentleman with decorations and a lady in a fur cloak alighted: visitors just arrived from Paris at the Marchiennes station, for Madame Hennebeau, who appeared in the shadow of the porch, was uttering exclamations of surprise and joy.

'Come along, then, dawdlers!' growled la Maheude, pulling the two little ones, who were standing in the mud.

When she arrived at Maigrat's, she was quite excited. Maigrat lived close to the manager; only a wall separated the latter's grounds from his own small house, and he had there a warehouse, a long building which opened on to the road as a shop without a front. He kept everything there, groceries, cooked meats, fruit, and sold bread, beer, and saucepans. Formerly an overseer at the Voreux, he had started with a small canteen; then, thanks to the protection of his superiors, his business had enlarged, gradually killing the Montsou retail trade. He centralized merchandise, and the considerable custom of the settlements enabled him to sell more cheaply and to give longer credit. Besides, he had remained in the Company's hands, and they had built his small house and his shop.

'Here I am again, Monsieur Maigrat,' said la Maheude humbly, finding him standing in front of his door.

He looked at her without replying. He was a stout, cold, polite man, and he prided himself on never changing his mind.

'Now you won't send me away again, like yesterday. We must have bread from now to Saturday. Sure enough, we owe you sixty francs these two years.'

She explained in short, painful phrases. It was an old debt contracted during the last strike. Twenty times over they had promised to settle it, but they had not been able; they could not even give him forty sous a fortnight. And then a misfortune had happened two days before; she had been obliged to pay twenty francs to a shoemaker who threatened to seize their things. And that was why they were without a sou. Otherwise they would have been able to go on until Saturday, like the others.

Maigrat, with protruded belly and folded arms, shook his head at every supplication.

'Only two loaves, Monsieur Maigrat. I am reasonable, I don't ask for coffee. Only two three-pound loaves a day.'

'No,' he shouted at last, at the top of his voice.

His wife had appeared, a puny creature who spent all her days over a ledger, without even daring to lift her head. She moved away, frightened at seeing this unfortunate woman turning her ardent, beseeching eyes towards her. It was said that she yielded the conjugal bed to the putter girls among the customers. It was a known fact that when a miner wished to prolong his credit, he had only to send his daughter or his wife, plain or pretty, it mattered not, provided they were compliant.

La Maheude, still imploring Maigrat with her look, felt herself uncomfortable under the pale keenness of his small eyes, which seemed to undress her. It made her angry; she could have understood it before she had had seven children, when she was young. And she went off, violently dragging Lénore and Henri who were occupied in picking up nut-shells from the gutter and examining them.

'This won't bring you luck, Monsieur Maigrat, remember!'

Now there only remained the bourgeois of La Piolaine. If these would not throw her a five-franc piece she might as well lie down and die. She had taken the Joiselle road on the left. The administration building was there at the corner of the road, a veritable brick palace, where the big-wigs from Paris, princes and generals and members of the Government, came every autumn to give large dinners. As she walked she was already spending the five francs, first bread, then coffee, afterwards a quarter of butter, a bushel of potatoes for the morning soup and the evening stew; finally, perhaps, a bit of brawn, for father needed meat.

The parish priest of Montsou, Abbé Joire, was passing by, holding up his cassock, with the delicate air of a fat, well-nourished cat afraid of wetting its fur. He was a mild man who pretended not to interest himself in anything, so as not to vex either the workers or the bosses.

'Good day, monsieur le curé.'

Without stopping he smiled at the children, and left her planted in the middle of the road. She was not religious, but she had suddenly imagined that this priest would give her something.

And the journey began again through the black, sticky mud. There were still two kilometres to walk, and the little ones dragged behind more than ever, for they were distressed, and no longer amused themselves. To right and to left of the path the same vague landscape unrolled, enclosed within mossy palings, the same factory buildings, dirty with smoke, bristling with tall chimneys. Then the flat land was spread out in immense open fields, like an ocean of brown clods, without so much as a tree-trunk, as far as the purplish line of the forest of Vandame.

'Carry me, mother.'

She carried them one after the other. Puddles made holes in the pathway, and she pulled up her clothes, fearful of arriving too dirty. Three times she nearly fell, so sticky was that confounded pavement. And as they at last arrived before the porch, two enormous dogs threw themselves upon them, barking so loudly that the little ones yelled with terror. The coachman was obliged to take a whip to them.

'Leave your clogs, and come in,' repeated Honorine.

In the dining-room the mother and children stood motionless, dazed by the sudden heat, and overawed beneath the gaze of this old lady and gentleman, who were stretched out in their easy-chairs.

'My dear,' said the old lady to her daughter, 'fulfil your little duties.

The Grégoires charged Cécile with their charities. It was part of their idea of a good education. One must be charitable. They said themselves that their house was the house of God. Besides, they flattered themselves that they performed their charity with intelligence, and they were exercised by a constant fear lest they should be deceived, and so encourage vice. So they never gave money, never! Not ten sous, not two sous, for it was a well-known fact that as soon as a poor man got two sous he drank them. Their alms were, therefore, always in kind, especially in warm clothing, distributed during the winter to needy children.

'Oh! the poor dears!' exclaimed Cécile, 'how pale they are from the cold! Honorine, go and look for the parcel in the cupboard.'

The servants were also gazing at these miserable creatures with the pity and vague uneasiness of girls who never had to worry about their own dinners. While the housemaid went upstairs, the cook forgot her duties, leaving the rest of the brioche on the table, and stood there swinging her empty hands.

'I still have two woollen dresses and some shawls,' Cécile went on; 'you will see how warm they will be, the poor dears!'

Then la Maheude found her tongue, and stammered:

'Thank you so much, mademoiselle. You are all too good.'

Tears had filled her eyes, she thought herself sure of the five francs, and was only preoccupied by the way in which she would ask for them if they were not offered to her. The housemaid did not reappear, and there was a moment of embarrassed silence. From their mother's skirts the little ones opened their eyes wide and gazed at the brioche.

'You only have these two?' asked Madame Grégoire, in order to break the silence.

'Oh, madame! I have seven.'

Monsieur Grégoire, who had gone back to his newspaper, sat up indignantly.

'Seven children! But why? good God!'

'It is imprudent,' murmured the old lady.

La Maheude made a vague gesture of apology. What can you do? You don't think about it at all, they come quite naturally. And then, when they grow up they bring something in, and that keeps the household going. Take their case, they could get on, if it was not for grandfather who was getting quite stiff, and if it was not that among the lot only two of her sons and her eldest daughter were old enough to go down into the pit. It was necessary, all the same, to feed the little ones who brought nothing in.

'Then,' said Madame Grégoire, 'you have worked for a long time at the mines?'

A silent laugh lit up la Maheude's pale face.

'Ah, yes! ah, yes! I went down till I was twenty. The doctor said that I should stay above for good after I had been confined the second time, because it seems that made something go wrong in my inside. Besides, then I got married, and I had enough to do in the house. But on my husband's side, you see, they have been down there for ages. It goes back to grandfather and to his grandfather, one doesn't know how far back, quite to the beginning when they first took the pick down there at Réquillart.'

Monsieur Grégoire thoughtfully contemplated this woman and these pitiful children, with their waxy flesh, their discoloured hair, the degeneration which stunted them, gnawed by anaemia, and with the melancholy ugliness of starvelings. There was silence again, and one only heard the burning coal as it gave out a jet of gas. The moist room had that heavy air of comfort in which our middle-class nooks of happiness slumber.

'What is she doing, then?' exclaimed Cécile impatiently. 'Mélanie, go up and tell her that the parcel is at the bottom of the cupboard, on the left.'

In the meanwhile, Monsieur Grégoire repeated aloud the reflections inspired by the sight of these starving ones.

'There is evil in this world, it is quite true; but, my good woman, it must also be said that workpeople are never prudent. Thus, instead of putting aside a few sous like our peasants, miners drink, get into debt, and end by not having enough to support their families.'

'Monsieur is right,' replied la Maheude. 'They don't thoughtfully always keep to the right path. That's what I'm always saying to the ne'er-do-wells when they complain. Now, I have been lucky; my husband doesn't drink. All the same, on feast Sundays he sometimes takes a drop too much; but it never goes farther. It is all the nicer of him, since before our marriage he drank like a hog, begging your pardon. And yet, you know, it doesn't help us much that he is so sensible. There are days like today when you might turn out all the drawers in the house and not find a farthing.'

She wished to suggest to them the idea of the five-franc piece, and went on in her low voice, explaining the fatal debt, small at first, then large and overwhelming. They paid regularly for many fortnights. But one day they got behind, and then it was all up. They could never catch up again. The gulf widened, and the men became disgusted with work which did not even allow them to pay their way. Do what they could, there was nothing but difficulties until death. Besides, it must be understood that a collier needed a glass to wash away the dust. It began there, and then he was always in the inn when worries came. Without complaining of any one it might be that the workmen did not earn as much as they ought to.

'I thought,' said Madame Grégoire, 'that the Company gave you lodging and fuel?'

La Maheude glanced sideways at the flaming coal in the fireplace.

'Yes, yes, they give us coal, not very good coal, but it burns. As to lodging, it only costs six francs a month; that sounds like nothing, but it is often pretty hard to pay. Today they might cut me up into bits without getting two sous out of me. Where there's nothing, there's nothing.'

The lady and gentleman were silent, softly stretched out, and gradually wearied and disquieted by the exhibition of this wretchedness. She feared she had offended them, and added, with the stolid and just air of a practical woman:

'Oh! I didn't want to complain. Things are like this, and one has to put up with them; all the more so that it's no good struggling, we wouldn't change anything. The best is, is it not, to try and live honestly in the place in which the good God has put us?'

Monsieur Grégoire approved of this emphatically.

'With such sentiments, my good woman, one is above misfortune.'

Honorine and Mélanie at last brought the parcel.

Cécile unfastened it and took out the two dresses. She added shawls, even stockings and mittens. They would all fit beautifully; she hastened and made the servants wrap up the chosen garments; for her music mistress had just arrived; and she pushed the mother and children towards the door.

'We are very short,' stammered la Maheude; 'if we only had a five-franc piece—'

The phrase stuck in her throat, for the Maheus were proud and never begged. Cécile looked uneasily at her father; but the latter refused decisively, with an air of duty.

'No, it is not our custom. We cannot do it.'

Then the young girl, moved by the mother's overwhelmed face, wished to do all she could for the children. They were still looking fixedly at the brioche; she cut it in two and gave it to them.

'Here! this is for you.'

Then, taking the pieces back, she asked for an old newspaper:

'Wait, you must share with your brothers and sisters.'

And beneath the tender gaze of her parents she finally pushed them out of the room. The poor urchins, who had no bread, went off, holding the brioche respectfully in their benumbed little hands.*

La Maheude dragged her children along the road, seeing neither the desert fields, nor the black mud, nor the great livid sky. As she passed through Montsou she resolutely entered Maigrat's shop, and begged so persistently that at last she carried away two loaves, coffee, butter, and even her five-franc piece, for the man also lent money by the week. It was not her that he wanted, it was Catherine; she understood that when he advised her to send her daughter for provisions. They would see about that. Catherine would box his ears if he tried any of his tricks with her.

CHAPTER 3

Eleven o'clock struck at the little church in the Deux-Cent-Quarante settlement, a brick chapel to which Abbé Joire came to say mass on Sundays. In the school beside it, also of brick, one heard the droning voices of the children, in spite of windows closed against the outside cold. The wide passages, divided into little gardens, back to back, between the four large blocks of uniform houses, were deserted; and these gardens, devastated by winter, exhibited the destitution of their marly soil, lumped and spotted by the last vegetables. People were making soup, chimneys were smoking, a woman appeared at distant intervals along the fronts, opened a door and disappeared. From one end to the other, on the pavement, the pipes dripped into tubs, although it was no longer raining, so charged was this grey sky with moisture. And the village, built all at once in the midst of the vast plain, and edged by its black roads as by a mourning border, had no touch of joyousness about it save the regular bands of its red tiles, constantly washed down by showers.

When la Maheude returned, she went out of her way to buy potatoes from a supervisor's wife whose crop was not yet exhausted. Behind a curtain of sickly poplars, the only trees in these flat regions, was a group of isolated buildings, houses placed four together, and surrounded by their gardens. As the Company reserved this new experiment for the foremen, the workpeople called this corner of the hamlet the settlement of the Bas-de-Soie, just as they called their own settlement Paie-tes-Dettes, in good-humoured irony at their wretchedness.*

'Eh! Here we are,' said la Maheude, laden with parcels, pushing in Lénore and Henri, covered with mud and quite tired out.

In front of the fire Estelle was screaming, cradled in Alzire's arms. The latter, having no more sugar and not knowing how to soothe her, had decided to pretend to give her the breast. This ruse often succeeded. But this time it was in vain for her to open her dress, and to press the mouth against the lean breast of an eight-year-old invalid; the child was enraged at biting the skin and drawing nothing.

'Pass her to me,' cried the mother as soon as she found herself free; 'she won't let us say a word.'

When she had taken from her bodice a breast as heavy as a

wineskin to the neck of which the brawling child clung, suddenly falling silent, they were at last able to talk. Otherwise everything was going on well; the little housekeeper had kept up the fire and had swept and arranged the room. And in the silence they heard upstairs grandfather's snoring, the same rhythmic snoring which had not stopped for a moment.

'What a lot of things!' murmured Alzire, smiling at the provisions. 'If you like, mother, I'll make the soup.'

The table was cluttered: a parcel of clothes, two loaves, potatoes, butter, coffee, chicory, and half a pound of brawn.

'Oh! the soup!' said la Maheude with an air of fatigue. 'We must gather some sorrel and pull up some leeks. No! I will make some for the men afterwards. Put some potatoes on to boil: we'll eat them with a little butter. And some coffee, eh? Don't forget the coffee!'

But suddenly she thought of the brioche. She looked at the empty hands of Lénore and Henri who were fighting on the floor, already rested and lively. These gluttons had slyly eaten the brioche on the road. She boxed their ears, while Alzire, who was putting the saucepan on the fire, tried to appease her.

'Let them be, mother. If it's for me, you know I don't mind a bit about brioche. They were hungry, walking so far.'

Midday struck; they heard the clogs of the children coming out of school. The potatoes were cooked, and the coffee, thickened by a good half of chicory, was passing through the percolator with a singing noise of large drops. One corner of the table was free; but only the mother was eating there. The three children were satisfied with their knees; and all the time the little boy with silent voracity looked, without saying anything, at the brawn, excited by the greasy paper.

La Maheude was drinking her coffee in little sips, with her hands round the glass to warm them, when old Bonnemort came down. Usually he rose later, and his breakfast was waiting for him on the fire. But today he began to grumble because there was no soup. Then, when his daughter-in-law said to him that you cannot always do what you like, he ate his potatoes in silence. From time to time he got up to spit in the ashes for the sake of cleanliness, and, settled in his chair, he rolled his food round in his mouth, with lowered head and dull eyes.

'Ah! I forgot, mother,' said Alzire. 'The next-door neighbour came—'

Her mother interrupted her.

'She bothers me!'

She felt a deep rancour against the Levaque woman, who had pleaded poverty the day before to avoid lending her anything; while she knew that she was well-off at the moment, since her lodger, Bouteloup, had paid his fortnight in advance. In the settlement they did not usually lend from household to household.

'Here! you remind me,' said la Maheude. 'Wrap up a millful of coffee. I will take it to la Pierronne; I owe it her from the day before yesterday.'

And when her daughter had prepared the packet she added that she would come back immediately to put the men's soup on the fire. Then she went out with Estelle in her arms, leaving old Bonnemort to chew his potatoes leisurely, while Lénore and Henri fought for the skins that dropped on the floor.

Instead of going round, la Maheude went straight across through the gardens, for fear lest Levaque's wife should call her. Her garden was just next to the Pierrons', and in the dilapidated trellis-work which separated them there was a hole through which they fraternized. The common well was there, serving four households. Beside it, behind a clump of feeble lilacs, was situated the shed, a low building full of old tools, in which the rabbits were raised which were eaten on feast days. One o'clock struck; it was time for coffee, and not a soul was to be seen at the doors or windows. Only a workman belonging to the earth-cutting shift, waiting the hour for descent, was digging up his patch of vegetable ground without raising his head. But as la Maheude arrived opposite the other block of buildings, she was surprised to see a gentleman and two ladies in front of the church. She stopped a moment and recognized them; it was Madame Hennebeau bringing her guests, the decorated gentleman and the lady in the fur mantle, to see the settlement.

'Oh! why did you take the trouble?' exclaimed la Pierronne, when la Maheude had returned the coffee. 'There was no hurry.'

She was twenty-eight, and was considered the beauty of the settlement, dark, with a low forehead, large eyes, straight mouth, and coquettish as well; with the neatness of a cat, and with a good figure, for she had no children. Her mother, la Brûlé, the widow of a pikeman who died in the mine, after having sent her daughter to work in a factory, swearing that she should never marry a collier, had never ceased to be angry since she had married, somewhat late, Pierron, a widower with a girl of eight. However, the household lived very happily, in the midst of chatter, of scandals which circulated concerning the husband's complaisance and the wife's lovers. No debts, meat twice a week, a house kept so clean that you could see yourself in the saucepans. As an additional piece of luck, thanks to favours, the Company had authorized her to sell sweets and biscuits, jars of which she exhibited, on two boards, behind the window-panes. This was six or seven sous profit a day, and sometimes twelve on Sundays. The only drawback to all this happiness was old Mother Brûlé, who screamed with all the rage of an old revolutionary, having to avenge the death of her man on the bosses, and little Lydie, who suffered in the shape of frequent blows, the passions of the family.

'How big she is already!' said la Pierronne, cooing at Estelle.

'Oh! the trouble they cause. Don't talk of it!' said la Maheude. 'You are lucky not to have any. At least you can keep clean.'

Although everything was in order in her own house, and she scrubbed every Saturday, she glanced with a jealous housekeeper's eye over such a room, in which there was even a certain coquetry, gilt vases on the sideboard, a mirror, three framed prints.

La Pierronne was about to drink her coffee alone, all her folk being at the pit.

'You'll have a glass with me?' she said.

'No, thanks; I've just had mine.'

'What does that matter?'

In fact, it mattered nothing. And both began drinking slowly. Between the jars of biscuits and sweets their eyes rested on the houses opposite, of which the little curtains in the windows formed a row, revealing by their greater or less whiteness the virtues of the housekeepers. Those of the Levaques were very dirty, veritable kitchen clouts, which seemed to have wiped the bottoms of the saucepans.

'How can they live in such dirt?' murmured la Pierronne.

Then la Maheude began and did not stop. Ah! if she only had had a lodger like Bouteloup she would have made the household go. When one knew how to do it, a lodger was an excellent thing. Only you shouldn't sleep with him. And then the husband took to drink, beat his wife, and ran after the singers at the Montsou bars.

La Pierronne assumed an air of profound disgust. These singers spread all sorts of diseases. There was one at Joiselle who had infected a whole pit.

'What surprises me is that you let your son go with their girl.'

'Ah, yes! but just try to stop it then! Their garden is next to ours. Zacharie was always there in summer with Philomène behind the lilacs, and they didn't mind what they did on the shed; you couldn't draw water at the well without surprising them.'

It was the usual story of the promiscuities of the settlement; boys and girls became corrupted together, throwing themselves on their backsides, as they said, on the low, sloping roof of the shed when twilight came on. All the putters got their first child there when they did not take the trouble to go to Réquillart or into the cornfields. It was of no consequence; they married afterwards, only the mothers were angry when their lads began too soon, for a lad who married no longer brought anything into the family.

'In your shoes I would have rather put a stop to it,' said la Pierronne, sensibly. 'Your Zacharie has already filled her up twice, and they will go on and get spliced. Anyhow, the money is gone.'

La Maheude was furious and raised her hands.

'Listen to this: I will curse them if they get spliced. Doesn't Zacharie owe us any respect? He has cost us something, hasn't he? Very well. He must return it before getting a wife to hang on him. What will become of us, eh, if our children begin at once to work for others? Might as well die!'

However, she grew calm.

'I'm speaking in a general way; we shall see later. It is fine and strong, your coffee; you make it proper.'

And after a quarter of an hour spent over other stories, she ran off, exclaiming that the men's soup was not yet made. Outside, the children were going back to school; a few women were showing themselves at their door, looking at Madame Hennebeau, who was pointing out features of the settlement to her guests. This visit began to stir up the village. The earth-cutting man stopped digging for a moment, and two hens took fright in the gardens.

As la Maheude returned, she ran into la Levaque who had come out to stop Dr Vanderhaghen, a doctor of the Company, a small hurried man, overwhelmed by work, who gave his advice as he walked.

'Sir,' she said, 'I can't sleep; I feel ill everywhere. I must tell you about it.'

He spoke to them all in a familiar tone and replied without stopping:

'Just leave me alone; you drink too much coffee.'

'And my husband, sir,' said la Maheude in her turn, 'you must come and see him. He still has those pains in his legs.'

'It is you who take too much out of him. Just leave me alone!'

The two women were left to gaze at the doctor's retreating back.

'Come in, then,' said la Levaque, when she had exchanged a despairing shrug with her neighbour. 'You know, there is something new. And you will take a little coffee. It is quite fresh.'

La Maheude refused, but without energy. Well! a drop, at all events, not to disoblige. And she entered.

The room was black with dirt, the floor and the walls spotted with grease, the sideboard and the table sticky with filth; and the stink of a badly kept house took you by the throat. Near the fire, with his elbows on the table and his nose in his plate, Bouteloup, a broad stout placid man, still young for thirty-five was finishing the remains of his boiled beef, while standing in front of him, little Achille, Philomène's first-born, who was already in his third year, was looking at him in the silent, supplicating way of a gluttonous animal. The lodger, very kind behind his big brown beard, from time to time stuffed a piece of meat into his mouth.

'Wait till I sugar it,' said la Levaque, putting some brown sugar beforehand into the coffee-pot.

Six years older than he was, she was hideous and worn out, with her bosom hanging on her belly, and her belly on her thighs, with a flattened muzzle, and greyish hair always uncombed. He had taken her naturally, without choosing, the same as he did his soup in which he found hairs, or his bed of which the sheets lasted for three months. She was part of the lodging; the husband liked repeating that good reckonings make good friends.

'I was going to tell you,' she went on, 'that la Pierronne was seen yesterday prowling about on the Bas-de-Soie side. The gentleman you know of was waiting for her behind Rasseneur's, and they went off together along the canal. Eh! that's nice, isn't it? A married woman!'

'Gracious!' said la Maheude; 'Pierron, before marrying her, used to give the overman rabbits; now it costs him less to lend his wife.'

Bouteloup began to laugh enormously, and threw a piece of bread covered in gravy into Achille's mouth. The two women went on venting their spleen at la Pierronne's expense – a flirt, no prettier than any one else, but always occupied in looking after every spot on her skin, in washing herself, and putting on face cream. Anyhow, it was the husband's affair, if he liked that sort of thing. There were men so ambitious that they would wipe the masters' behinds to hear them say thank you. And they were only interrupted by the arrival of a neighbour bringing in a little urchin of nine months, Désirée, Philomène's youngest; Philomène, taking her breakfast at the screening-shed, had arranged that they should bring her little one down there, where she suckled it, seated for a moment in the coal.

'I can't leave mine for a moment, she screams rightaway,' said la Maheude, looking at Estelle, who was asleep in her arms.

But she did not succeed in avoiding the demand to get to the domestic affair which she had read in la Levaque's eyes.

'I say, now we ought to get that settled.'

At first the two mothers, without need for talking about it, had agreed not to conclude the marriage. If Zacharie's mother wished to get her son's wages as long as possible, Philomène's mother was enraged at the idea of abandoning her daughter's wages. There was no hurry; the second mother had even preferred to keep the little one, as long as there was only one; but when it began to grow and eat and another one came, she found that she was losing, and furiously pushed for the marriage, like a woman who does not care to throw away her money.

'Zacharie has drawn his lot,' she went on, 'and there's nothing in the way. When will it be?'

'Wait till the fine weather,' replied la Maheude, constrainedly. 'They are a nuisance, these affairs! As if they couldn't wait to be married before going together! My word! I would strangle Catherine if I knew that she had done that.'

The other woman shrugged her shoulders.

'Don't worry! she'll do like the others.'

Bouteloup, with the tranquillity of a man who is at home, searched about on the dresser for bread. Vegetables for Levaque's soup, potatoes and leeks, lay about on a corner of the table, half-peeled, taken up and dropped a dozen times in the midst of continual gossiping. The woman was about to go on with them again when she dropped them anew and planted herself at the window.

'What's that there? Why, there's Madame Hennebeau with some people. They are going into la Pierronne's.'

At once both of them started again on the subject of la Pierronne. Oh! whenever the Company brought any visitors to the settlement they never failed to go straight to her place, because it was clean. No doubt they never told them stories about the overman. You can afford to be clean when you have lovers who earn three thousand francs, and are lodged and warmed, without counting the presents. If it was clean on top it was not clean underneath. And all the time that the visitors remained opposite, they went on chattering.

'There, they are coming out,' said la Levaque at last. 'They are going all around. Why, look, my dear – I believe they are going into your place.'

La Maheude was seized with fear. Who knows whether Alzire had sponged over the table? And her soup, also, which was not yet ready! She stammered a good-day, and ran off home without a single glance aside.

But everything was bright. Alzire, very seriously, with a cloth in front of her, had set about making the soup, seeing that her mother did not return. She had pulled up the last leeks from the garden, gathered the sorrel, and was just then cleaning the vegetables, while a large kettle on the fire was heating the water for the men's baths when they should return. Henri and Lénore were good for once, being absorbed in tearing up an old almanac. Old Bonnemort was smoking his pipe in silence. As la Maheude was getting her breath Madame Hennebeau knocked.

'You will allow me, will you not, my good woman?'

Tall and fair, a little heavy in her superb maturity of forty years, she smiled with an effort of affability, without showing too promi-nently her fear of soiling her bronze silk dress and black velvet mantle.

'Come in, come in,' she said to her guests. 'We are not disturbing anyone. Now, isn't this clean again! And this good woman has seven children! All our households are like this. I ought to explain to you that the Company rents them the house at six francs a month. A large room on the ground floor, two rooms above, a cellar, and a garden.'

The decorated gentleman and the lady in the fur cloak, arrived that morning by train from Paris, opened their eyes vaguely, exhibiting on their faces their astonishment at all these new things which took them out of their element.

'And a garden!' repeated the lady. 'One could live here! It is charming!'

'We give them more coal than they can burn,' went on Madame Hennebeau. 'A doctor visits them twice a week; and when they are old they receive pensions, although nothing is held back from their wages.'

'An Eldorado! a real land of milk and honey!' murmured the gentleman in delight.

La Maheude had hastened to offer chairs. The ladies refused. Madame Hennebeau was already getting tired, happy for a moment to amuse herself in the weariness of her exile by playing the part of exhibiting the beasts, but immediately disgusted by the sickly odour of wretchedness, in spite of the special cleanliness of the houses into which she ventured. Besides, she was only repeating odd phrases which she had overheard, without ever troubling herself further about this race of workpeople who were labouring and suffering beside her.

'What beautiful children!' murmured the lady, who thought them hideous, with their large heads beneath their bushy, straw-coloured hair.

And la Maheude had to tell their ages; they also asked her questions about Estelle, out of politeness. Old Bonnemort respectfully took his pipe out of his mouth; but he was none the less a subject of uneasiness, so worn out by his forty years underground, with his stiff limbs, deformed body, and earthy face; and as a violent spasm of coughing took him he preferred to go and spit outside, with the idea that his black expectoration would make people uncomfortable.

Alzire received all the compliments. What an excellent little housekeeper, with her cloth! They congratulated the mother on having a little daughter so sensible for her age. And none spoke of the hump, though looks of uneasy compassion were constantly turned towards the poor little invalid.

'Now!' concluded Madame Hennebeau, 'if they ask you about our settlements in Paris you will know what to reply. Never more noise than this, patriarchal manners, all happy and well off as you see, a place where you might come for a holiday, on account of the good air and the tranquillity.'

'It is marvellous, marvellous!' exclaimed the gentleman, in a final outburst of enthusiasm.

They left with that enchanted air with which people leave a booth in a fair, and la Maheude, who accompanied them, remained on the threshold while they went away slowly, talking very loudly. The streets were full of people, and they had to pass through several groups of women, attracted by the news of their visit, which was hawked from house to house.

Just then, la Levaque, in front of her door, had stopped la Pierronne, who was drawn by curiosity. Both of them affected a painful surprise. What now? Were these people going to bed at the Maheus'? But it was not so very delightful a place.

'Always without a sou, with all that they earn! Lord! when people have vices!'

'I have just heard that she went this morning to beg at La

Piolaine, and Maigrat, who had refused them bread, has given them something. We know how Maigrat gets paid!'

'On her? Oh, no! that would need some courage. It's Catherine that he's after.'

'Why, didn't she have the cheek to say just now that she would strangle Catherine if she were to come to that? As if big Chaval for ever so long had not put her backside on the shed!'

'Hush! here they are!'

Then la Levaque and la Pierronne, with a peaceful air and without impolite curiosity, contented themselves with watching the visitors out of the corners of their eyes. Then by a gesture they quickly called la Maheude, who was still carrying Estelle in her arms. And all three, motionless, watched the well-clad backs of Madame Hennebeau and her guests slowly disappear. When they were some thirty paces off, the gossiping recommenced with redoubled vigour.

'They carry plenty of money on their backs; worth more than themselves, perhaps.'

'Ah, for sure! I don't know the other, but the one that belongs here, I wouldn't give four sous for her, big as she is. They do tell stories—'

'Eh? What stories?'

'Why, she has men! First, the engineer.'

'That lean, little creature! Oh, he's too small! She would lose him in the sheets.'

'What does that matter, if it amuses her? I don't trust a woman who puts on such proud airs and never seems to be pleased where she is. Just look how she wiggles her rump, as if she felt contempt for us all. Not very nice, eh?'

The visitors went away at the same slow pace, still talking, when a carriage stopped in the road, in front of the church. A gentleman of about forty-eight got out of it, dressed in a black frock-coat, and with a very dark complexion and an authoritative correct expression.

'The husband,' murmured la Levaque, lowering her voice, as if he could hear her, seized by that hierarchical fear which the manager inspired in his ten thousand workpeople. 'It's true, though, that he has a cuckold's head, that man.'

Now the whole settlement was out of doors. The curiosity of the women increased. The groups approached each other, and were melted into one crowd; while bands of urchins, with snotty noses and gaping mouths, dawdled along the pavements. For a moment the schoolmaster's pale head was also seen behind the school-house hedge. In the gardens, the man who was digging stood with one foot on his spade, and stared. And the murmur of gossiping gradually increased, with a cackling sound, like a gust of wind among dry leaves.

It was especially in front of the Levaques' door that the crowd was thickest. Two women had come forward, then ten, then twenty. La Pierronne was prudently silent now that there were too many ears about. La Maheude, one of the more reasonable, also contented herself with looking on; and to calm Estelle, who was awake and screaming, she had tranquilly drawn out her breast, which hung down like an udder swaying as if pulled down by the continual flow of milk. When Monsieur Hennebeau had seated the ladies in the carriage, which went off in the direction of Marchiennes, there was a final explosion of clattering voices, all the women gesticulating and talking in each other's faces in the midst of a tumult like an ant-hill in a turmoil.

But three o'clock struck. The workers of the earth-cutting shift, Bouteloup and the others, had set out. Suddenly around the church appeared the first colliers returning from the pit with black faces and damp garments, folding their arms and arching their backs. Then there was confusion among the women: they all began to run home with the terror of housekeepers who had been led astray by too much coffee and too much tattle, and one heard nothing more than this worried cry, pregnant with the quarrels to come:

'Good Lord, and my soup! and my soup which isn't ready!'

CHAPTER 4

When Maheu came in after having left Étienne at Rasseneur's, he found Catherine, Zacharie, and Jeanlin seated at the table finishing their soup. On returning from the pit they were always so hungry that they ate in their damp clothes, without even cleaning themselves; and no one was waited for, the table was laid from morning to night; there was always someone there swallowing his portion, according to the demands of work.

As he entered the door Maheu saw the provisions. He said nothing, but his uneasy face lighted up. All the morning the emptiness of the cupboard, the thought of the house without coffee and without butter, had been troubling him; the recollection came to him painfully while he was hammering at the seam, stifled at the bottom of the cutting. What would his wife do, and what would become of them if she were to return with empty hands? And now, here was everything! She would tell him about it later on. He laughed with satisfaction.

Catherine and Jeanlin had risen, and were taking their coffee standing; while Zacharie, not filled with the soup, cut himself a large slice of bread and covered it with butter. Although he saw the brawn on a plate he did not touch it, for meat was for the father, when there was only enough for one. All of them had washed down their soup with a good swig of fresh water, the good, clear drink of the fortnight's end.

'I have no beer,' said la Maheude, when father had seated himself in his turn. 'I wanted to keep a little money. But if you would like some the little one can go and fetch a pint.'

He looked at her in astonishment. What! she had money, too!

'No, no,' he said, 'I've had a glass, it's all right.'

And Maheu began to swallow in slow spoonfuls the mixture of bread, potatoes, leeks, and sorrel piled up in the bowl which served him as a plate. La Maheude, without putting Estelle down, helped Alzire to give him all that he required, pushed near him the butter and the meat, and put his coffee on the fire to keep it quite hot.

In the meanwhile, beside the fire, they began to wash themselves in the half of a barrel transformed into a tub. Catherine, whose turn came first, had filled it with warm water; and she undressed herself calmly, took off her cap, her jacket, her breeches, and even her shirt, used to doing this since the age of eight, having grown up without seeing any harm in it. She only turned with her stomach to the fire, then rubbed herself vigorously with black soap. No one looked at her, even Lénore and Henri were no longer inquisitive to see how she was made. When she was clean she went up the stairs quite naked, leaving her damp shirt and other garments in a heap on the floor. But a quarrel broke out between the two brothers: Jeanlin had hastened to jump into the tub under the pretence that Zacharie was still eating; and the latter hustled him, claiming his turn, and calling out that he was polite enough to allow Catherine to wash herself first, but he did not wish to have the rinsings of the young urchins, especially as, when Jeanlin had been in, it would do to fill the school ink-pots. They ended by washing themselves together, also turning towards the fire, and they even helped each other, rubbing one another's backs. Then, like their sister, they disappeared up the staircase naked.

'What a mess they do make!' murmured la Maheude, taking up their garments from the floor to put them to dry. 'Alzire, just sponge up a bit.'

But a disturbance on the other side of the wall cut short her speech. They heard a man's oaths, a woman's crying, the din of a fight, with dull blows that sounded like thumps on an empty gourd.

'Levaque's wife is catching it,' Maheu peacefully stated as he scraped the bottom of his bowl with the spoon. 'It's queer; Bouteloup made out that the soup was ready.'

'Ah, yes! ready,' said la Maheude. 'I saw the vegetables on the table, not even cleaned.'

The cries grew louder, and there was a terrible push which shook the wall, followed by complete silence. Then the miner, swallowing the last spoonful, concluded, with an air of calm justice:

'If the soup is not ready, you can understand it.'

And after having drunk a glassful of water, he attacked the brawn. He cut square pieces, stuck the point of his knife into them and ate them on his bread without a fork. There was no talking when father was eating. He himself was hungry in silence; he did not recognize the usual taste of Maigrat's cold meat; this must come from somewhere else; however, he put no question to his wife. He only asked if the old man was still sleeping upstairs. No, grandfather had gone out for his usual walk. And there was silence again.

But the odour of the meat made Lénore and Henri look up, where they were amusing themselves with making rivulets with the spilt water. Both of them came and planted themselves near their father, the little one in front. Their eyes followed each morsel, full of hope when it set out from the plate and with an air of consternation when it was engulfed in the mouth. At last their father noticed the gluttonous desire which made their faces pale and their lips moist.

'Have the children had any of it?' he asked.

And as his wife hesitated:

'You know I don't like injustice. It takes away my appetite when I see them there, begging for bits.'

'But they've had some of it,' she exclaimed, angrily. 'If you were to listen to them you might give them your share and the others', too; they would fill themselves till they burst. Isn't it true, Alzire, that we have all had some brawn?'

'Sure enough, mother,' replied the little humpback, who under such circumstances could tell lies with the self-possession of a grown-up person.

Lénore and Henri stood motionless, shocked and rebellious at such lying, when they themselves were whipped if they did not tell the truth. Their little hearts began to swell, and they longed to protest, and to say that they, at all events, were not there when the others had had some.

'Get along with you,' said their mother, driving them to the other end of the room. 'You ought to be ashamed of being always in your father's plate; and even if he was the only one to have any, doesn't he work, while all you, a lot of good-for-nothings, can't do anything but spend! Yes, and the more the bigger you are.'

Maheu called them back. He seated Lénore on his left knee, Henri on the right; then he finished the brawn by playing at dinner with them. He cut small pieces, and each had his share. The children devoured with delight.

When he had finished, he said to his wife:

'No, don't give me my coffee. I'm going to wash first; and just give me a hand to throw away this dirty water.'

They took hold of the handles of the tub and emptied it into the gutter in front of the door, when Jeanlin came down in dry garments, breeches and a woollen blouse, too large for him, which were faded from wear on his brother's back. Seeing him slinking out through the open door, his mother stopped him.

'Where are you off to?'

'Out.'

'Out where? Listen to me. You go and gather a dandelion salad for this evening. Eh, do you hear? If you don't bring a salad back you'll have to deal with me.'

'All right!'

Jeanlin set out with hands in his pockets, trailing his clogs and slouching along, with the skinny hips of a ten-year-old urchin, like an old miner. Then, Zacharie came down, more carefully dressed, his body covered by a black woollen knitted jacket with blue stripes. His father called out to him not to return late; and he left, nodding his head with his pipe between his teeth, without replying. Again the tub was filled with warm water. Maheu was already slowly taking off his jacket. At a look, Alzire led Lénore and Henri outside to play. The father did not like washing with the family, as was practised in many houses in the settlement. He blamed no one, however; he simply said that it was good for the children to dabble together.

'What are you doing up there?' cried la Maheude, up the staircase.

'I'm mending my dress that I tore yesterday,' replied Catherine.

'All right. Don't come down, your father is washing.'

Then Maheu and la Maheude were left alone. The latter decided to place Estelle on a chair, and by a miracle, finding herself near the fire the child did not scream, but turned towards her parents the vague eyes of a little creature without intelligence. Maheu was crouching before the tub quite naked, having first plunged his head into it, well rubbed with the black soap the constant use of which discoloured and made yellow the hair of the race. Afterwards he got into the water, lathered his chest, belly, arms, and thighs, scrubbing them energetically with both fists. His wife, standing by, watched him.

'Well, then,' she began, 'I saw your eyes when you came in. You were bothered, eh? and the groceries cheered you up. Fancy! those Piolaine people didn't give me a sou! Oh! they are kind enough; they have dressed the little ones and I was ashamed to ask them, for it troubles me to ask for things.'

She interrupted herself a moment to wedge Estelle into the chair lest she should tip over. The father continued to work away at his skin, without hastening by a question this story which interested him, patiently waiting for an explanation.

'I must tell you that Maigrat had refused me, oh! straight! like one kicks a dog out of doors. Guess if I was on a spree! They keep you warm, woollen garments, but they don't put anything into your stomach, eh?'

He lifted his head, still silent. Nothing at La Piolaine, nothing at Maigrat's: then where? But, as usual, she was pulling up her sleeves to wash his back and those parts which he could not himself easily reach. Besides, he liked her to soap him, to rub him everywhere till she almost broke her wrists. She took soap and worked away at his shoulders while he held himself stiff so as to resist the shock.

'Then I returned to Maigrat's, and said to him, ah, I said something to him! And that it didn't do to have no heart, and that evil would happen to him if there were any justice. That bothered him; he turned his eyes and would like to have got away.'

From the back she had got down to the buttocks and was pushing into the folds, not leaving any part of the body without passing over it, making him shine like her three saucepans on Saturdays after a big clean. Only she began to sweat with this tremendous exertion of her arms, so exhausted and out of breath that her words were choked.

'At last he called me an old leech. We shall have bread until Saturday, and the best is that he has lent me a hundred sous. I have got butter, coffee, and chicory from him. I was even going to get the meat and potatoes there, only I saw that he was grumbling. Seven sous for the brawn, eighteen for the potatoes, and I've got three francs seventy-five left for a stew and some boiled beef. Eh, I don't think I've wasted my morning!'

Now she began to wipe him, dabbing with a towel the parts that would not dry. Feeling happy and without thinking of the future debt, he burst out laughing and took her in his arms.

'Leave me alone, stupid! You are damp, and wetting me. Only I'm afraid Maigrat has ideas—'

She was about to speak of Catherine, but she stopped. What was the good of disturbing him? It would only lead to endless discussion.

'What ideas?' he asked.

'Why, ideas of robbing us. Catherine will have to examine the bill carefully.'

He took her in his arms again, and this time did not let her go. The bath always finished in this way: she enlivened him by the hard rubbing, and then by the towels which tickled the hairs of his arms and chest. Besides, among all his mates of the settlement it was the hour for a bit of fun, when more children were planted than were wanted. At night all the family were about. He pushed her towards the table, jesting like a worthy man who was enjoying the only good moment of the day, calling that taking his dessert, and a dessert which cost him nothing. She, with her loose figure and breast, struggled a little for fun.

'You are silly! My Lord! you are silly! And there's Estelle looking at us. Wait till I turn her around.'

'Oh, rubbish! at three months; as if she understood!'

When he got up Maheu simply put on a dry pair of breeches. He liked, when he was clean and had taken his pleasure with his wife, to remain naked to the waist for a while. On his white skin, with the whiteness of an anaemic girl, the scratches and gashes of the coal left tattoo-marks, grafts as the miners called them; and he was proud of them, and exhibited his big arms and broad chest shining like veined marble. In summer all the miners could be seen in this condition at their doors. He even went there for a moment now, in spite of the wet weather, and shouted out a rough joke to a comrade, whose chest was also naked, on the other side of the garden. Others also appeared. And the children, trailing along the pathways, raised their heads and also laughed with delight at all this weary flesh of workers displayed in the open air.

While drinking his coffee, without yet putting on a shirt, Maheu told his wife about the engineer's anger over the planking. He was calm and relaxed, and listened with a nod of approval to the sensible advice of la Maheude, who showed much common sense in such affairs. She always repeated to him that nothing was gained by struggling against the Company. She afterwards told him about Madame Hennebeau's visit. Without saying so, both of them were proud of this.

'Can I come down yet?' asked Catherine, from the top of the staircase.

'Yes, yes; your father is drying himself.'

The young girl had put on her Sunday dress, an old frock of rough blue poplin, already faded and worn in the folds. She had on a very simple bonnet of black tulle.

'Hallo! you're dressed up. Where are you going to?'

'I'm going to Montsou to buy a ribbon for my bonnet. I've taken off the old one; it was too dirty.'

'Have you got money, then?'

'No! but la Mouquette promised to lend me ten sous.'

Her mother let her go. But at the door she called her back.

'Listen! don't go and buy that ribbon at Maigrat's. He will rob you, and he will think that we are rolling in wealth.'

The father, who was crouching down before the fire to dry his neck and shoulders more quickly, contented himself with adding:

'Try not to dawdle about at night on the road.'

In the afternoon, Maheu worked in his garden. Already he had sown there potatoes, beans, and peas; and he now set about replanting cabbage and lettuce seedlings, which he had kept fresh from the night before. This bit of garden furnished them with vegetables, except potatoes of which they never had enough. He understood gardening very well, and could even grow artichokes, which was showing off according to the neighbours. As he was preparing the bed, Levaque just then came out to smoke a pipe in his own square, looking at the cos lettuces which Bouteloup had planted in the morning; for without the lodger's energy in digging nothing would have grown there but nettles. And a conversation arose over the trellis. Levaque, refreshed and excited by thrashing his wife, vainly tried to take Maheu off to Rasseneur's. Why, was he afraid of a glass? They could have a game at skittles, lounge about for a while with the mates, and then come back to dinner. That was the way of life after leaving the pit. No doubt there was no harm in that, but Maheu was obstinate; if he did not replant his lettuces they would be withered by tomorrow. In reality he refused out of good sense, not wishing to ask a farthing from his wife out of the change from the hundred sous.

Five o'clock was striking when la Pierronne came to ask if it was with Jeanlin that her Lydie had gone off. Levaque replied that it must be something of that sort, for Bébert had also disappeared, and those rascals always went prowling about together. When Maheu had quieted them by speaking of the dandelion salad, he and his comrade set about joking at the young woman with the coarseness of good-natured devils. She was angry, but did not go away, in reality tickled by the strong words which made her scream with her hands to her sides. A lean woman came to her aid, stammering with anger like a clucking hen. Others in the distance on their doorsteps vented their indignation in support. Now the school was closed; and all the children were running about, there was a swarm of little creatures shouting and tumbling and fighting; while those fathers who were not at the public-house remained in groups of three or four, crouching on their heels as they did in the mine, smoking their pipes with an occasional word in the shelter of a wall. La Pierronne went off in a fury when Levaque wanted to feel if her thighs were firm; and he himself decided to go alone to Rasseneur's, since Maheu was still planting.

Twilight suddenly came on; la Maheude lit the lamp, irritated because neither her daughter nor the boys had come back. She could have guessed as much; they never succeeded in taking together the only meal of the day at which it was possible for them to be all round the table. Then she was waiting for the dandelion salad. What could he be gathering at this hour, in this pitch blackness, that nuisance of a child! A salad would go so well with the stew which was simmering on the fire – potatoes, leeks, sorrel, chopped up with fried onion. The whole house smelt of that fried onion, that good odour which gets stale so soon, and which penetrates the bricks of the settlements with such a stench that one perceives it far off in the country, the violent smell of the poor man's kitchen.

Maheu, when he left the garden at nightfall, at once fell into a chair with his head against the wall. As soon as he sat down in the evening he went to sleep. The cuckoo clock struck seven; Henri and Lénore had just broken a plate through insisting on helping Alzire, who was laying the table, when old Bonnemort came in first, in a hurry to have his dinner and go back to the pit. Then la Maheude woke up Maheu.

'Come and eat! So much the worse! They are big enough to find the house. The nuisance is the salad!'

CHAPTER 5

At Rasseneur's, after having eaten his soup, Étienne went back into the small room beneath the roof and facing the Voreux, which he was to occupy, and fell on to his bed dressed as he was, overcome with fatigue. In two days he had not slept four hours. When he awoke in the twilight he was dazed for a moment, not recognizing his surroundings; and he felt such uneasiness and his head was so heavy that he rose, painfully, with the idea of getting some fresh air before having his dinner and going to bed for the night.

Outside, the weather was becoming milder: the sooty sky was growing copper-coloured, laden with one of those warm rains of the Nord, the approach of which one feels by the moist warmth of the air, and the night was coming on in great mists which drowned the distant landscape of the plain. Over this immense sea of reddish earth the low sky seemed to melt into black dust, without a breath of wind now to animate the darkness. It was the wan and deathly melancholy of a funeral.

Étienne walked straight ahead at random, with no other aim but to shake off his fever. When he passed before the Voreux, already growing gloomy at the bottom of its hole and with no lantern yet shining from it, he stopped a moment to watch the departure of the day-workers. No doubt six o'clock had struck; landers, porters from the pit-eye, and grooms were going away in groups, mixed with the vague and laughing figures of the screening girls in the shade.

At first there was la Brûlé with her son-in-law, Pierron. She was abusing him because he had not supported her in a quarrel with an overseer over her reckoning of stones.

'Get along! damned good-for-nothing! Do you call yourself a man to lower yourself like that before one of these bastards who destroy us?'

Pierron followed her peacefully, without replying. At last he said:

'I suppose I should have jumped on the boss? Thanks for showing me how to get into a mess!'

'Bend your backside to him, then,' she shouted. 'By God! if my daughter had listened to me! It's not enough for them to kill the father. Perhaps you'd like me to say "thank you". No, I'll have their skins first!'

Their voices were lost. Étienne saw her disappear, with her eagle nose, her flying white hair, her long, lean arms that gesticulated furiously. But the conversation of two young people behind caused him to listen. He had recognized Zacharie, who was waiting there, and who had just been joined by his friend Mouquet.

'Are you with me?' said the latter. 'We will have something to eat, and then off to the Volcan.'

'In a while. I've something to attend to.'

'What, then?'

The lander turned and saw Philomène coming out of the screening shed. He thought he understood.

'Very well, if it's that. Then I'll go ahead.'

'Yes, I'll catch you up.'

As he went away, Mouquet met his father, old Mouque, who was also coming out of the Voreux. The two men simply wished each other good evening, the son taking the main road while the father went along by the canal.

Zacharie was already pushing Philomène in spite of her resistance into the same solitary path. She was in a hurry, another time; and the two wrangled like old housemates. There was no fun in only seeing one another out of doors, especially in winter, when the earth is moist and there are not wheatfields to lie in.

'No, no, it's not that,' he whispered impatiently. 'I've something to say to you.' He led her gently with his arm round her waist. Then, when they were in the shadow of the pit-bank he asked if she had any money.

'What for?' she demanded.

Then he became confused, spoke of a debt of two francs which had reduced his family to despair.

'Hold your tongue! I've seen Mouquet; you're going again to the Volcan with him, where those dirty women singers are.'

He defended himself, struck his chest, gave his word of honour. Then, as she shrugged her shoulders, he said suddenly:

'Come with us if it will amuse you. You see, you don't put me out. What do I want to do with the singers? Will you come?'

'And the little one?' she replied. 'How can I stir with a child that's always screaming? Let me go back, I bet they're not getting on at the house.'

But he held her and entreated. See! it was only not to look foolish before Mouquet to whom he had promised. A man could not go to bed every evening like the chickens. She was convinced, and pulled up the skirt of her gown; with her nail she cut the thread and drew out some ten-sous coins from a corner of the hem. For fear of being robbed by her mother she hid there the profit of the overtime work she did at the pit.

'I've got five, you see,' she said, 'I'll give you three. Only you must swear that you'll make your mother decide to let us marry. We've had enough of this life in the open air. And mother reproaches me for every mouthful I eat. Swear first.'

She spoke with the soft voice of a big, delicate girl, without passion, simply tired of her life. He swore, exclaimed that it was a sacred promise; then, when he had got the three coins he kissed her, tickled her, made her laugh, and would have gone all the way in this corner of the pit-bank, which was the winter bedroom of their household, if she had not again refused, saying that it would not give her any pleasure. She went back to the settlement alone, while he cut across the fields to rejoin his companion.

Étienne had followed them mechanically, from afar, without understanding, regarding it as a simple rendezvous. The girls were precocious in the pits; and he recalled the Lille work-girls whom he had waited for behind the factories, those gangs of girls, corrupted at fourteen, in the abandonment of their wretchedness. But another meeting surprised him more. He stopped.

At the bottom of the pit-bank, in a hollow into which some large stones had slipped, little Jeanlin was violently berating Lydie and Bébert, seated one at his right, the other at his left.

'What do you say? Eh? I'll slap each of you, if you want more. Who thought of it first, eh?'

In fact, Jeanlin had had an idea. After having roamed about in the meadows, along the canal, for an hour, gathering dandelions with the two others, it had occurred to him, before this pile of salad, that they would never eat all that at home; and instead of going back to the settlement he had gone to Montsou, keeping Bébert to watch, and making Lydie ring at the houses and offer the dandelions. He was experienced enough to know that, as he said, girls could sell what they liked. In the ardour of business, the entire pile had disappeared; but the girl had earned eleven sous. And now, with empty hands, the three were dividing the profits.

'That's not fair!' Bébert declared. 'Must divide into three. If you keep seven sous we shall only have two each.'

'What? not fair!' replied Jeanlin furiously. 'I gathered more first of all.'

The other usually submitted with timid admiration and a credulity which always made him the dupe. Though older and stronger, he even allowed himself to be struck. But this time the sight of all that money excited him to rebellion.

'He's robbing us, Lydie, isn't he? If he doesn't share, we'll tell his mother.'

Jeanlin at once thrust his fist beneath the other's nose.

'Say that again! I'll go and say at your house that you sold my mother's salad. And then, you silly bugger, how can I divide eleven sous into three? Just try and see, if you're so clever. Here are your two sous each. Just look sharp and take them, or I'll put them in my pocket.'

Bébert was vanquished and accepted the two sous. Lydie, who was trembling, had said nothing, for with Jeanlin she experienced the fear and the tenderness of a little beaten woman. When he held out the two sous to her she advanced her hand with a submissive laugh. But he suddenly changed his mind.

'Eh! what will you do with all that? Your mother will nab them, sure enough, if you don't know how to hide them from her. I'd better keep them for you. When you want money you can ask me for it.'

And the nine sous disappeared. To shut her mouth he had put his arms around her laughingly and was rolling with her over the pit-bank. She was his little wife, and in dark corners they used to try together the love which they heard and saw in their homes behind partitions, through the cracks of doors. They knew everything, but they were able to do nothing, being too young, fumbling and playing for hours like vicious puppies. He called that playing at papa and mamma; and when he chased her she ran away and let herself be caught with the delicious trembling of instinct, often angry, but always yielding, in the expectation of something which never came.

As Bébert was not admitted to these games and received a cuffing whenever he wanted to touch Lydie, he was always constrained, agitated by anger and uneasiness when the other two were amusing themselves, which they did not hesitate to do in his presence. His one idea, therefore, was to frighten them and disturb them, calling out that someone could see them.

'It's all up! There's a man looking.'

This time he told the truth; it was Étienne, who had decided to continue his walk. The children jumped up and ran away, and he passed by round the bank, following the canal, amused at the terror of these little rascals. No doubt it was too early at their age, but they saw and heard so much that one would have to tie them up to restrain them. Yet Étienne became sad.

A hundred paces farther on he came across more couples. He had arrived at Réquillart, and there, around the old ruined mine, all the girls of Montsou prowled about with their lovers. It was the common meeting place, the remote and deserted spot to which the putters came to get their first child when they dared not risk the shed. The broken palings opened to every one the old yard, now become a nondescript piece of ground, cluttered by the ruins of the two sheds which had fallen in, and by the skeletons of the large buttresses which were still standing. Derelict trams were lying about, and piles of old rotting wood, while a dense vegetation was reconquering this corner of the ground, displaying itself in thick grass, and springing up in young trees that were already vigorous. Every girl felt at home here; there were nooks and crannies for them; their lovers lay them over beams, behind the timber, in the trams; they even lay elbow to elbow without troubling about their neighbours. And it seemed that around this lifeless machine, near this shaft weary of disgorging coal, there was a revenge of creation in the free love which, beneath the lash of instinct, planted children in the bellies of these girls who were yet hardly women.

Yet a caretaker lived there, old Mouque, to whom the Company had given up, almost beneath the destroyed tower, two rooms which were constantly threatened by destruction from the expected fall of the last walls. He had even been obliged to shore up a part of the roof, and he lived there very comfortably with his family, he and Mouquet in one room, la Mouquette in the other. As the windows no longer possessed a single pane, he had decided to close them by nailing up boards; one could not see well, but it was warm. For the rest, this caretaker cared for nothing: he went to look after his horses at the Voreux, and never troubled himself about the ruins of Réquillart, of which the shaft only was preserved, in order to serve as a chimney for a fire which ventilated the neighbouring pit.

This was how old Mouque was ending his old age, in the midst of young love. Ever since she was ten la Mouquette had been on her back in all the corners of the ruins, not as a timid and still green little urchin like Lydie, but as a girl who was already big, and a mate for bearded lads. The father had nothing to say, for she was considerate, and never introduced a lover into the house. Besides, he was used to this sort of accident. When he went to the Voreux, when he came back, whenever he came out of his hole, he could scarcely put a foot down without treading on a couple in the grass; and it was worse if he wanted to gather wood to heat his soup or look for burdocks for his rabbit at the other end of the enclosure. Then he saw one by one the voluptuous noses of all the girls of Montsou rising up around him, while he had to be careful not to knock against the limbs stretched out level with the paths. Besides, these meetings had gradually ceased to disturb either him who was simply taking care not to stumble, or the girls whom he allowed to finish their affairs, going away with discreet little steps like a worthy man who was at peace with the ways of nature. Only just as they now knew him, he at last also knew them, as one knows the rascally magpies who got up to their tricks in the pear-trees in the garden. Ah! youth! youth! how it carries on, how it takes its fill! Sometimes he wagged his chin with silent regret, turning away from the noisy wantons who were breathing too loudly in the darkness. Only one thing put him out of temper: two lovers had acquired the bad habit of embracing outside his wall. It was not that it prevented him from sleeping, but they leaned against the wall so heavily that in the end they damaged it.

Every evening old Mouque received a visit from his friend, old Bonnemort, who regularly before dinner took the same walk. The two old men spoke little, scarcely exchanging ten words during the half-hour that they spent together. But it cheered them thus to think over the days of old, to chew their recollections over again without need to talk of them. At Réquillart they sat on a beam side by side, saying a word and then sinking into their dreams, with faces bent towards the earth. No doubt they were becoming young again. Around them lovers were turning over their sweethearts; there was a murmur of kisses and laughter; the warm odour of the girls arose in the freshness of the trodden grass. It was now forty-three years since old Bonnemort had taken his wife behind the pit; she was a putter, so slight that he had placed her on a tram to embrace her at ease. Ah! those were fine days. And the two old men, shaking their heads, at last left each other, often without saying good night.

That evening, however, as Étienne arrived, old Bonnemort, who was getting up from the beam to return to the settlement, said to Mouque:

'Good night, mate. I say, did you know Roussie?'

Mouque was silent for a moment, shrugged his shoulders; then returning to the house:

'Good night, good night, mate.'

Étienne came and sat on the beam, in his turn. His sadness was increasing, though he could not tell why. The old man, whose disappearing back he watched, reminded him of his arrival in the morning, and the flood of words which the piercing wind had dragged from his silence. What wretchedness! And all these girls, worn out with fatigue, who were still stupid enough in the evening to make little ones, more flesh for labour and suffering! It would never come to an end if they were always filling themselves with starvelings. Would it not be better if they were to shut up their bellies, and press their thighs together, as at the approach of misfortune? Perhaps these gloomy ideas only stirred confusedly in him because he was alone, while all the others at this hour were going about taking their pleasure in couples. The mild weather stifled him a little, occasional drops of rain fell on his feverish hands. Yes, all the girls had their turn; it was something stronger than reason.

Just then, as Étienne remained seated motionless in the shadows, a couple who came down from Montsou rustled against him without seeing him as they entered the uneven Réquillart ground. The girl, certainly a virgin, was struggling and resisting with low whispered supplications, while the lad in silence was pushing her towards the darkness of a corner of the shed, still upright, under which there were piles of old mouldy rope. It was Catherine and big Chaval. But Étienne had not recognized them in passing, and his eyes followed them; he was watching for the end of the story, touched by a sensuality which changed the course of his thoughts. Why should he interfere? When girls refuse it is because they like first to be forced.

On leaving the settlement of the Deux–Cent–Quarante Catherine had gone to Montsou along the road. From the age of ten, since she had earned her living at the pit, she went about the country alone in the complete liberty of the colliers' families; and if no man had possessed her at fifteen it was owing to the tardy awakening of her puberty; the crisis had not yet arrived. When she was in front of the Company's Yards she crossed the road and entered a laundress's where she was certain to find la Mouquette; for the latter stayed there from morning till night, among women who treated each other with coffee all round. But she was disappointed; la Mouquette had just then been regaling them in her turn so thoroughly that she was not able to lend the ten sous she had promised. To console her they vainly offered a glass of hot coffee. She was not even willing for her companion to borrow from another woman. A need of economy had come to her, a sort of superstitious fear, the certainty that that ribbon would bring her bad luck if she were to buy it now.

She hastened back to the road to the settlement, and had reached the last houses of Montsou when a man at the door of the Piquette bar called her:

'Eh! Catherine! where are you off to so quick?'

It was big Chaval. She was vexed, not because he displeased her, but because she was not inclined to joke.

'Come in and have a drink. A little glass of sweet wine, won't you?'

She refused politely; the night was coming on, they were expecting her home. He had advanced, and was entreating her in a low voice in the middle of the road. It had been his idea for a long time to persuade her to come up to the room which he occupied on the first storey of the Piquette, a fine room for a couple, with a large bed. Did he frighten her, that she always refused? She laughed good-naturedly, and said that she would come up some day when children didn't grow. Then, one thing leading to another, she told him, without knowing how, about the blue ribbon which she had not been able to buy.

'But I'll pay for it,' he exclaimed.

She blushed, feeling that it would be best to refuse again, but possessed by a strong desire to have the ribbon. The idea of a loan came back to her, and at last she accepted on condition that she should return to him what he spent on her. They began to joke again: it was agreed that if she did not sleep with him she should return him the money. But there was another difficulty when he talked of going to Maigrat's.

'No, not Maigrat's; mother won't let me.'

'Why? Do we have to say where we go? He has the best ribbons in Montsou.'

When Maigrat saw Chaval and Catherine coming to his shop like two lovers who are buying their engagement gifts, he became very red, and exhibited his pieces of blue ribbon with the rage of a man who is being made fun of. Then, when he had served the young people, he planted himself at the door to watch them disappear in the twilight; and when his wife came to ask him a question in a timid voice, he fell on her, abusing her, and exclaiming that he would make them repent some day, the filthy creatures, who had no gratitude, when they ought all to be on the ground licking his feet.

Chaval accompanied Catherine along the road. He walked beside her, swinging his arms; only he pushed her with his hip, leading her without seeming to do so. She suddenly perceived that he had made her leave the pavement and that they were taking the narrow Réquillart road. But she had no time to be angry; his arm was already round her waist, and he was dazing her with a constant caress of words. How stupid she was to be afraid! Did he want to hurt such a little darling, who was as soft as silk, so tender that he could have devoured her? And he breathed behind her ear, in her neck, so that a shudder passed over the skin of her whole body. She felt stifled, and had nothing to reply. It was true that he seemed to love her. On Saturday evenings, after having blown out the candle, she had asked herself what would happen if he were to take her in this way; then, on going to sleep, she had dreamed that she would no longer refuse, quite overcome by pleasure. Why, then, at the same idea to-day did she feel repugnance and something like regret? While he was tickling her neck with his moustache so softly that she closed her eyes, the shadow of another man, of the lad she had seen that morning, passed over the darkness of her closed eyelids.

Catherine suddenly looked around her. Chaval had led her into the ruins of Réquillart and she recoiled, shuddering, from the darkness of the fallen shed.

'Oh! no! oh, no!' she murmured, 'please let me go!'

The fear of the male had taken hold of her, that fear which stiffens the muscles in an impulse of defence, even when girls are willing, and feel the conquering approach of man. Her virginity which had nothing to learn took fright as at a threatening blow, a wound of which she feared the unknown pain.

'No, no! I don't want to! I tell you that I am too young. It's true! Another time, when I am properly grown up.'

He growled in a low voice:

'Stupid! There's nothing to fear. What does that matter?'

But without speaking more he had seized her firmly and pushed her beneath the shed. And she fell on her back on the old ropes; she ceased to protest, yielding to the male before her time, with that hereditary submission which from childhood had thrown down on their backs all the girls of her race. Her frightened stammering grew faint, and only the ardent breath of the man was heard.

Étienne, however, had listened without moving. Another who

was taking the leap! And now that he had seen the comedy he got up, overcome by uneasiness, by a kind of jealous excitement in which there was a touch of anger. He no longer restrained himself; he stepped over the beams, for those two were too much occupied now to be disturbed. He was surprised, therefore, when he had gone a hundred paces along the path, to find that they were already standing up, and that they appeared, like himself, to be returning to the settlement. The man again had his arm round the girl's waist, and was squeezing her, with an air of gratitude, still speaking in her neck; and it was she who seemed in a hurry, anxious to return quickly, and annoyed at the delay.

Then Étienne was tormented by the desire to see their faces. It was foolish, and he hastened his steps, so as not to yield to it; but his feet slackened of their own accord, and at the first lamp-post he concealed himself in the shade. He was petrified by surprise when he recognized Catherine and big Chaval. He hesitated at first: was it indeed she, that young girl in the coarse blue dress, with that bonnet? Was that the urchin whom he had seen in breeches, with her head in the canvas cap? That was why she could pass so near him without his recognizing her. But he no longer doubted; he had seen her eyes again, with their greenish limpidity of spring water, so clear and so deep. What a whore! And he felt a furious desire to avenge himself on her with contempt, without any motive. Besides, he did not like her dressed as a girl: she was frightful.

Catherine and Chaval had passed him slowly. They did not know that they were watched. He held her to kiss her behind the ear, and she began to slacken her steps beneath his caresses, which made her laugh. Left behind, Étienne was obliged to follow them, irritated because they barred his way and because in spite of himself he had to witness these things which exasperated him. It was true, then, what she had sworn to him in the morning: she was not yet any one's mistress; and he, who had not believed her, who had deprived himself of her in order not to act like the other! and who had let her be taken beneath his nose, taking his stupidity so far as to be dirtily amused at seeing them! It made him mad! he clenched his fists, he could have devoured that man in one of those impulses to kill which made him see red.

The walk lasted for half an hour. When Chaval and Catherine approached the Voreux they slackened their pace still more; they stopped twice beside the canal, three times along the pit-bank, very cheerful now and occupied with little tender games. Étienne was obliged to stop also when they stopped, for fear of being seen. He endeavoured to feel nothing but a brutal regret: that would teach him to treat girls with consideration through being well brought up! Then, after passing the Voreux, and at last free to go and dine at Rasseneur's, he continued to follow them, accompanying them to the settlement, where he remained standing in the shade for a quarter of an hour, waiting until Chaval left Catherine to enter her home. And when he was quite sure that they were no longer together, he set off walking afresh, going very far along the Marchiennes road, trudging along, and thinking of nothing, too choked and too sad to shut himself up in a room.

It was not until an hour later, towards nine o'clock, that Étienne again passed the settlement, saying to himself that he must eat and sleep, if he was to be up again at four o'clock in the morning. The village was already asleep, and looked quite black in the night. Not a gleam shone from the closed shutters, the house fronts slept, with the heavy sleep of snoring barracks. A solitary car ran through the empty gardens. It was the end of the day, with the workers dropping from the table to the bed, overcome with weariness and food.

At Rasseneur's, in the lighted room, an engine-man and two day-workers were drinking beer. But before going in Étienne stopped to throw one last glance into the darkness. He saw again the same black immensity as in the morning when he had arrived in the wind. Before him the Voreux was crouching, with the air of an evil beast, its dimness pricked with a few lantern lights. The three braziers on the bank were burning in the air, like bloody moons, now and then showing the vast silhouettes of old Bonnemort and his yellow horse. And beyond, on the flat plain, darkness had submerged everything, Montsou, Marchiennes, the forest of Vandame, the immense sea of beetroot and of wheat, in which there only shone, like distant lighthouses, the blue fires of the blast furnaces, and the red fires of the coke ovens. Gradually the night came on, the rain was now falling slowly, continuously, burying this void in its monotonous stream. Only one voice was still heard, the thick, slow respiration of the pumping engine, breathing both by day and by night.

PART THREE

CHAPTER I

On the next day, and the days that followed, Étienne continued his work at the pit. He grew accustomed to it; his existence became regulated by this labour and to these new habits which had seemed so hard to him at first. Only one episode interrupted the monotony of the first fortnight: a slight fever which kept him in bed for forty-eight hours with aching limbs and throbbing head, dreaming in a state of semi-delirium that he was pushing his tram in a passage that was so narrow that his body would not pass through. It was simply the exhaustion of his apprenticeship, an excess of fatigue from which he quickly recovered.

And days followed days, until weeks and months had slipped by. Now, like his mates, he got up at three o'clock, drank his coffee, and carried off the double slice of bread and butter which Madame Rasseneur had prepared for him the evening before. Regularly as he went every morning to the pit, he met old Bonnemort who was going home to sleep, and on leaving in the afternoon he crossed Bouteloup who was going to his task. He had his cap, his breeches and canvas jacket, and he shivered and warmed his back in the shed before the large fire. Then came the waiting with naked feet in the receiving-room, swept by furious currents of air. But the engine, with its great steel limbs starred with copper shining up above in the shade, no longer attracted his attention, nor the cables which flew by with the black and silent motion of a nocturnal bird, nor the cages rising and plunging unceasingly, in the midst of the noise of signals, of shouted orders, of trams shaking the metal floor. His lamp burnt badly, that confounded lamp-man could not have cleaned it; and he only woke up when Mouquet bundled them all off, roguishly smacking the girls' flanks. The cage was unfastened, and fell like a stone to the bottom of a hole without causing him even to lift his head to see the daylight vanish. He never thought of a possible fall; he felt himself at home as he sank into the darkness beneath the falling rain. Below at the loading-bay, when Pierron had unloaded them with his air of hypocritical mildness, there was always the same tramping of the herd, the yard-men each going away to his cutting with trailing steps. He now knew the mine galleries better than the streets of Montsou; he knew where he had to turn, where he had to stoop, and where he had to avoid a puddle.

He had grown so accustomed to these two kilometres beneath the earth, that he could have traversed them without a lamp, with his hands in his pockets. And every time the same meetings took place: a foreman lighting up the faces of the passing workmen, old Mouque leading a horse, Bébert conducting the snorting Bataille, Jeanlin running behind the train to close the ventilation doors, and buxom la Mouquette and lean Lydie pushing their trams.

After a time, also, Étienne suffered much less from the damp and closeness of the cutting. The chimney seemed to him more convenient for climbing up, as if he had melted and could pass through cracks where before he would not have risked a hand. He breathed the coal-dust without difficulty, saw clearly in the obscurity, and sweated tranquilly, having grown accustomed to the sensation of wet garments on his body from morning to night. Besides, he no longer spent his energy recklessly; he had gained skill so rapidly that he astonished the whole stall. In three weeks he was named among the best putters in the pit; no one pushed a tram more rapidly to the incline, nor loaded it afterwards so correctly. His small figure allowed him to slip about everywhere, and though his arms were as delicate and white as a woman's, they seemed to be made of iron beneath the smooth skin, so vigorously did they perform their task. He never complained, out of pride no doubt, even when he was panting with fatigue. The only thing they had against him was that he could not take a joke, and grew angry as soon as anyone picked on him. In all other respects he was accepted and looked upon as a real miner, reduced beneath this pressue of habit, little by little, to the state of a machine.

Maheu regarded Étienne with special friendship, for he respected work that was well done. Then, like the others, he felt that this lad had more education than himself; he saw him read, write, and draw little plans; he heard him talking of things of which he himself did not know even the existence. This caused him no astonishment, for miners are rough fellows who have harder heads than engine-men; but he was surprised at the courage of this little chap, and at the cheerful way he had tackled the coal to avoid dying of hunger. He had never met a workman who grew accustomed to it so quickly. So when hewing was urgent, and he did not wish to disturb a pikeman, he gave the timbering over to the young man, being sure of the neatness and solidity of his work. The bosses were always bothering him about that damned planking question; he feared every hour the appearance of the engineer Négrel, followed by Dansaert, shouting, discussing, ordering everything to be done over again, and he had noticed that his putter's timbering gave greater satisfaction to these gentlemen, in spite of their air of never being pleased with anything, and their repeated assertions that the Company would one day or another take radical measures. Things dragged on; a deep discontent was fomenting in the pit, and Maheu himself, in spite of his calmness, was beginning to clench his fists.

There was at first some rivalry between Zacharie and Étienne. One evening they even threatened to come to blows. But the former, a good lad though careless of everything but his own pleasure, was quickly appeased by the friendly offer of a glass, and soon on good terms with him, talking politics with the putter, who, as he said, had his own ideas. The only one of the men in whom he felt a deep hostility was big Chaval: not that they were cool towards each other, for, on the contrary, they had become companions; only when they joked their eyes seemed to devour each other. Catherine continued to move between them as a tired, resigned girl, bending her back, pushing her tram, always good-natured with her companion in the putting, who aided her in his turn, and submissive to the wishes of her lover, whose caresses she now received openly. It was an accepted situation, a recognized domestic arrangement to which the family itself closed its eyes to such a degree that Chaval every evening led away the putter behind the pit-bank, then brought her back to her parents' door, where he finally embraced her in front of the whole settlement. Étienne, who believed that he had reconciled himself to the situation, often teased her about these walks, making crude remarks by way of joke, as lads and girls will at the bottom of the cuttings; and she replied in the same tone, telling in a swaggering way what her lover had done to her, yet disturbed and growing pale when the young man's eyes chanced to meet hers. Then both would turn away their heads, not speaking again, perhaps, for an hour, looking as if they hated each other because of something buried within them and which they could never explain to each other.

The spring had come. On emerging from the pit one day Étienne had felt on his face a warm April breeze, a fresh smell of new earth, of tender greenness, of the open air; and now, every time he came up the spring smelt sweeter, warmed him more, after his ten hours of labour in the eternal winter at the bottom, in the midst of that damp darkness which no summer ever dispelled. The days grew longer and longer; at last, in May, when he went down at sunrise, a vermilion sky lit up the Voreux with a dusty dawn in which the white vapour of the pumping-engine became rose-coloured. There

was no more shivering, a warm breath blew across the plain, while
the larks sang far above. Then at three o'clock he was dazzled by
the now burning sun which set alight the horizon, and reddened the
bricks beneath the filth of the coal. In June the wheat was already
high, of a bluish green, which contrasted with the dark green of the
beetroots. It was an endless vista undulating beneath the slightest
breeze; and he saw it spread and grow from day to day, and was
sometimes surprised, as if he had found it in the evening more
swollen with verdure than it had been in the morning. The poplars
along the canal were putting on their plumes of leaves. Grass was
invading the pit-bank, flowers were covering the meadows, a whole
new life was germinating and pushing up from this earth beneath
which he was groaning in misery and fatigue.

When Étienne now went for a walk in the evening he no longer
startled lovers behind the pit-bank. He could follow their tracks in
the wheat and pick out their wanton love nests by eddies among
the yellowing blades and the great red poppies. Zacharie and
Philomène came back there out of old domestic habit; old Mother
Brûlé, always on Lydie's heels, was constantly hunting her out with
Jeanlin, buried so deeply together that one had to tread on them
before they made up their minds to get up; and as to la Mouquette,
she lay about everywhere – one could not cross a field without
seeing her head plunge down while only her feet emerged as she
was flat on her back again. But they were all quite free; the young
man found nothing guilty there except on the evenings when he met
Catherine and Chaval. Twice he saw them on his approach tumble
down in the midst of a field, where the motionless stalks afterwards
remained dead. Another time, as he was going along a narrow path,
Catherine's clear eyes appeared before him, level with the wheat,
and immediately disappeared. Then the immense plain seemed to
him too small, and he preferred to pass the evening at Rasseneur's,
in the Avantage.

'Give me a glass, Madame Rasseneur. No, I'm not going out to-
night; my legs are too tired.'

And he turned towards a comrade, who always sat at the bottom
table with his head against the wall.

'Souvarine, won't you have one?'

'No, thanks; nothing.'

Étienne had become acquainted with Souvarine* through living
there side by side. He was an engine-man at the Voreux, and
occupied the furnished room upstairs next to his own. He must
have been about thirty years old, fair and slender, with a delicate

face framed by thick hair and a slight beard. His white pointed
teeth, his thin mouth and nose, with his rosy complexion, gave him
a girlish appearance, an air of obstinate gentleness, across which
the grey reflection of his steely eyes threw savage gleams. In his
poor workman's room there was nothing but a box of papers and
books. He was a Russian, and never spoke of himself, so that many
rumours got around concerning him. The colliers, who are very
suspicious with strangers, guessing from his small bourgeois hands
that he belonged to another class, had at first imagined an adventure, some assassination, and that he was escaping punishment. But
then he had behaved in such a fraternal way with them, without
any pride, distributing to the youngsters of the settlement all the
sous in his pockets, that they now accepted him, reassured by the
term 'political refugee' which circulated about him – a vague term,
in which they saw an excuse even for crime, and, as it were, a
companionship in suffering.

During the first weeks, Étienne had found him greatly reserved,
so that he only discovered his history later on. Souvarine was the
last born of a noble family in the Government of Tula. At St
Petersburg, where he studied medicine, the socialistic enthusiasm
which then carried away all the youth in Russia had decided him to
learn a manual trade, that of a mechanic, so that he could mix with
the people, in order to know them and help them as a brother. And
it was by this trade that he was now living after having fled, in
consequence of an unsuccessful attempt against the tsar's life: for a
month he had lived in a fruiterer's cellar, hollowing out a mine
underneath the road, and charging bombs, with the constant risk of
being blown up with the house. Renounced by his family, without
money, expelled from French workshops as a foreigner who was
regarded as a spy, he was dying of starvation when the Montsou
Company had at last taken him on at a time of labour shortage.
For a year he had worked there as a good, sober, silent workman,
doing day-work one week and night-work the next week, so
regularly that the bosses referred to him as an example to the
others.

'Are you never thirsty?' said Étienne to him, laughing.

And he replied with his gentle voice, almost without an accent:

'I am thirsty when I eat.'

His companion also joked at him about girls, declaring that he
had seen him with a putter in the wheat on the Bas-de-Soie side.
Then he shrugged his shoulders with tranquil indifference, What
would he do with a putter? Woman was for him just another

fellow, a comrade, when she had the fraternal feeling and the courage of a man. Otherwise what was the good of having a possible act of cowardice on one's conscience? He wanted no ties, either woman or friend; he would be master of his own life and the lives of others.

Every evening towards nine o'clock, when the inn was emptying, Étienne remained thus talking with Souvarine. He drank his beer in small sips, while the engine-man constantly smoked cigarettes, of which the tobacco had at last stained his slender fingers. His vague mystic's eyes followed the smoke in the midst of a dream; his left hand sought occupation in nervous gropings; and he usually ended by installing a tame rabbit on his knees; a large doe, always with young, who lived at liberty in the house. This rabbit, which he had named Pologne*, had grown to worship him; she would come and smell his trousers, fawn on him and scratch him with her paws until he took her up like a child. Then, lying in a heap against him, her ears laid back, she would close her eyes; and without growing tired, with an uncosncious caressing gesture, he would pass his hand over her grey silky fur, calmed by that warm living softness.

'You know I have had a letter from Pluchart,' said Étienne one evening.

Only Rasseneur was there. The last client had departed for the settlement, which was now going to bed.

'Ah!' exclaimed the innkeeper, standing up before his two lodgers. 'How are things going with Pluchart?'

During the last two months, Étienne had kept up a constant correspondence with the Lille mechanic, whom he had told of his Montsou engagement, and who was now indoctrinating him, having been struck by the propaganda which he might carry on among the miners.

'The association is getting on very well. It seems that recruits are coming in from all sides.'

'What have you got to say, eh, about their society?' asked Rasseneur of Souvarine.

The latter, who was softly scratching Pologne's head, blew out a puff of smoke and muttered, with his tranquil air:

'More foolery!'

But Étienne grew enthusiastic. A predisposition for revolt was throwing him, in the first illusions of his ignorance, into the struggle of labour against capital. It was the International Working Men's Association that they were concerned with, that famous International which had just been founded in London.* Was not that a superb effort, a campaign in which justice would at last triumph? No more frontiers; the workers of the whole world rising and uniting to guarantee to the labourer the bread that he has earned. And what a simple and great organization! At the bottom, the section which represents the community; then the federation which groups together the sections of the same province; then the nation; and then, at last, over and above all humanity incarnated in a general council in which each nation was represented by a corresponding secretary. In six months it would conquer the world, and would be able to dictate laws to the bosses should they prove obstinate.

'Foolery!' repeated Souvarine. 'Your Karl Marx is still only thinking about letting natural forces act. No politics, no conspiracies, is it not so? Everything in the open, and simply to raise wages. Don't bother me with your evolution! Set fire to the four corners of the town, mow down the people, level everything, and when there is nothing more of this rotten world left standing, perhaps a better one will grow up in its place.'

Étienne began to laugh. He did not always take in his comrade's sayings; his theory of destruction seemed to him an affectation. Rasseneur, who was still more practical, man of solid common sense, did not condescend to get angry. He only wanted to have things clear.

'Then, what? Are you going to try and create a section at Montsou?'

This was what was desired by Pluchart, who was secretary to the Federation of the Nord. He insisted especially on the services which the association would render to the miners should they go out on strike. Étienne believed that a strike was imminent: this timbering business would turn out badly; any further demands on the part of the Company would cause rebellion in all the pits.

'It's the subscriptions that are the nuisance,' Rasseneur declared, in a judicial tone. 'Fifty centimes a year for the general fund, two francs for the section; it looks like nothing, but I bet that many will refuse to give it.'

'All the more so,' added Étienne, 'because we must first have here a provident fund, which we can use if need be as an emergency fund. No mater, it is time to think about these things. I am ready if the others are.'

There was silence. The petroleum lamp smoked on the counter. Through the open door they could distinctly hear the shovel of a stoker at the Voreux stoking the engine.

'Everything is so dear!' began Madame Rasseneur, who had entered and was listening with a gloomy air, looking as if she had grown up in her everlasting black dress. 'When I tell you that I've paid twenty-two sous for eggs! The whole thing will have to blow up.'

All three men this time were of the same opinion. They spoke one after the other in a despairing voice, giving expression to their complaints. The workers could not hold out; the Revolution had only aggravated their wretchedness; only the bourgeois had grown fat since '89,* so greedily that they had not even left the bottom of the plates to lick. Who could say that the workers had had their reasonable share in the extraordinary increase of wealth and comfort during the last hundred years? They had made fun of them by declaring them free. Yes, free to starve, a freedom of which they fully availed themselves. It put no bread into your cupboard to go and vote for fine fellows who went away and enjoyed themselves, thinking no more of the wretched voters than of their old boots. No! one way or another it would have to come to an end, either quietly by laws, by an understanding in good fellowship, or like savages by burning everything and devouring one another. Even if they never saw it, their children would certainly see it, for the century could not come to an end without another revolution, that of the workers this time, a great shake-up which would cleanse society from top to bottom, and rebuild it with more cleanliness and justice.

'It will have to blow up,' Madame Rasseneur repeated energetically.

'Yes, yes,' they all three cried. 'It will have to blow up.' Souvarine was now stroking Pologne's ears, and her nose was curling up with pleasure. He said in a low voice, with abstracted gaze, as if to himself:

'Raise wages – how can you? They're fixed by an iron law to the smallest possible sum, just the sum necessary to allow the workers to eat dry bread and have children. If they fall too low, the workers die, and the demand for new men makes them rise. If they rise too high, more men come, and they fall. It is the balance of empty bellies, a life sentence to a prison of hunger.'*

When he got carried away like this, entering into the questions that stir an educated socialist, Étienne and Rasseneur became restless, disturbed by his despairing statements which they were unable to answer.

'Do you understand?' he said again, gazing at them with his

habitual calmness; 'we must destroy everything, or hunger will reappear. Yes, anarchy and nothing more; the earth washed in blood and purified by fire! Then we shall see!'

'Monsieur is quite right,' said Madame Rasseneur, who, in her revolutionary violence, was always very polite.

Étienne, in despair at his ignorance, would argue no longer. He rose, remarking:

'Let's go to bed. All this won't save me from getting up at three o'clock.'

Souvarine, having blown away the cigarette-end which was sticking to his lips, was already gently lifting the big rabbit beneath the belly to place it on the ground. Rasseneur was shutting up the house. They separated in silence with buzzing ears, as if their heads had swollen with the grave questions they had been discussing.

And every evening there were similar conversations in the bare room around the single glass which Étienne took an hour to empty. A crowd of obscure ideas, dormant within him, were stirring and expanding. Expecially consumed by the need of knowledge, he had long hesitated to borrow books from his neighbour, who unfortunately had hardly any but German and Russian works. At last he had borrowed a French book on Co-operative Societies – mere foolery, said Souvarine; and he also regularly read a newspaper which the later received, *Combat*,* an Anarchist journal published in Geneva. In other respects, notwithstanding their daily relations, he found him as reserved as ever, with his air of camping in life, without interests or feelings or possessions of any kind.

At the beginning of July, Étienne's situation began to improve. In the midst of this monotonous life, always beginning over again, an accident had occurred. The stalls in the Guillaume seam had come across a disturbance of the strata, which certainly announced that they were approaching a fault; and, in fact, they soon came across this fault which the engineers, in spite of considerable knowledge of the soil, were still ignorant of. This upset the pit; nothing was talked of but the lost seam, which was to be found, no doubt, lower down on the other side of the fault. The old miners were already expanding their nostrils, like good dogs, in a chase for coal. But, meanwhile, the hewers could not stand with folded arms, and placards announced that the Company would put up new concessions to auction.

Maheu, on coming out one day, accompanied Étienne and offered to take him on as a pikeman in his team, in place of Levaque who had gone to another yard. The matter had already been arranged with the overman and the engineer, who were very pleased with the young man. So Étienne merely had to accept this rapid promotion, glad of the growing esteem in which Maheu held him.

In the evening they returned together to the pit to take note of the placards. The cuttings put up to auction were in the Filonnière seam in the north gallery of the Voreux. They did not seem very advantageous, and the miner shook his head when the young man read out the conditions. On the following day when they had gone down, he took him to see the seam, and showed him how far away it was from the loading-bay, the crumbly nature of the earth, the thinness and hardness of the coal. But if they were to eat they would have to work. So on the following Sunday they went to the auction, which took place in the shed and was presided over by the engineer of the pit, assisted by the overman, in the absence of the divisional engineer. From five to six hundred miners were there in front of the little platform, which was placed in the corner, and the bidding went on so rapidly that they could only hear a deep tumult of voices, of shouted figures drowned by other figures.

For a moment Maheu feared that he would not be able to obtain one of the forty concessions offered by the Company. All the rivals went lower, disquieted by the rumours of a crisis and in panic over unemployment. Négrel, the engineer, did not hurry in the face of this panic, and allowed the offers to fall to the lowest possible figures, while Dansaert, anxious to push matters still further, lied with regard to the quality of the concessions. In order to get his fifty metres, Maheu struggled with a comrade who was also obstinate; in turn they each took off a centime from the tram; and if he won in the end it was only by lowering the wage to such an extent, that the foreman, Richomme, who was standing behind him, muttered between his teeth, and nudged him with his elbow, growling angrily that he could never do it at that price.

When they came out Étienne was swearing. And he broke out before Chaval, who was returning from the wheatfields in company with Catherine, amusing himself while his father-in-law was absorbed in serious business.

'By God!' he exclaimed, 'it's simply slaughter! Now it's the worker who is forced to devour the worker!'

Chaval was furious. He would never have lowered it, he wouldn't. And Zacharie, who had come out of curiosity, declared that it was disgusting. But Étienne with a violent gesture silenced them.

'It will end some day, we shall be the masters!'

Maheu, who had been mute since the auction, appeared to wake up. He repeated:

'The masters! ah! by God it won't be too soon!'

CHAPTER 2

It was the Montsou fair, the last Sunday in July. Since Saturday evening the good housekeepers of the settlement had deluged their parlours with water, throwing bucketfuls over the flags and against the walls; and the floor was not yet dry, in spite of the white sand which had been strewn over it, an expensive luxury for the purses of the poor. But the day promised to be very warm; it was one of those heavy skies threatening storm, which in summer stifle this flat bare country of the Nord.

Sunday upset the hours for rising, even among the Maheus. While the father, after five o'clock, grew weary of his bed and dressed, the children lay in bed until nine. On this day Maheu went to smoke a pipe in his garden, and then came back to eat his bread and butter alone, while waiting. He thus passed the morning in a random manner; he mended the tub, which leaked; stuck up beneath the cuckoo clock, a portrait of the Prince Imperial* which had been given to the little ones. However, the others came down one by one. Old Bonnemort had taken a chair outside, to sit in the sun, while the mother and Alzire had at once set about cooking. Catherine appeared, pushing before her Lénore and Henri, whom she had just dressed. Eleven o'clock, and the smell of rabbit, which was boiling with potatoes, was already filling the house when Zacharie and Jeanlin came down last, still yawning and with their eyes heavy.

The settlement was now in a flutter, excited by the feast-day, and in expectation of dinner, which was being hastened for the departure in groups to Montsou. Troops of children were rushing about. Men in their shirt-sleeves were trailing their old shoes with the lazy gait of days of rest. Windows and doors, opened wide in the fine weather, gave glimpses of rows of parlours which were filled with movement and shouts and the chatter of families. And from one end to the other of the frontages, there was a smell of rabbit, a rich kitchen smell which on this day struggled with the inveterate odour of fried onion.

The Maheus dined at midday. They made little noise in the midst of the chatter from door to door, in the coming and going of women in a constant uproar of calls and replies, of objects borrowed, of youngsters chased away or brought back with a slap. Besides, they had not been on good terms during the last three weeks with their neighbours, the Levaques, on the subject of the marriage of Zacharie and Philomène. The men passed the time of day, but the women pretended not to know each other. This quarrel had strengthened the relations with la Pierronne, only la Pierronne had left Pierron and Lydie with her mother, and set out early in the morning to spend the day with a cousin at Marchiennes; and they joked, for they knew this cousin; she had a moustache, and was overman at the Voreux. La Maheude declared that it was not proper to leave one's family on a feast-day Sunday.

Beside the rabbit with potatoes, a rabbit which had been fattening in the shed for a month, the Maheus had meat soup and beef. The fortnight's wages had just fallen due the day before. They could not recollect such a spread. Even at the last Saint Barbe's Day,* the annual holiday of the miners when they do nothing for three days, the rabbit had not been so fat nor so tender. So the ten pairs of jaws, from little Estelle, whose teeth were beginning to appear, to old Bonnemort, who was losing his, worked so heartily that the bones themselves disappeared. The meat was good, but they could not digest it well; they tasted it too seldom. Everything disappeared; there only remained a piece of boiled beef for the evening. They would add bread and butter if they were hungry.

Jeanlin went out first. Bébert was waiting for him behind the school, and they prowled about for a long time before they were able to entice away Lydie, whom la Brûlé, who had decided not to to out, was trying to keep with her. When she perceived that the child had fled, she shouted and brandished her lean arms, while Pierron, annoyed at the disturbance, strolled quietly away with the air of a husband who can amuse himself with a good conscience, knowing that his wife also has her little amusements.

Old Bonnemort set out next, and Maheu decided to have a little fresh air after asking la Maheude if she would come and join him out there. No, she couldn't at all, it was nothing but drudgery with the little ones; but perhaps she would, all the same; she would think about it; they could easily find each other. When he got outside he hesitated, then he went into the neighbours' to see if Levaque was ready. There he found Zacharie, who was waiting for Philomène, and la Levaque started again on that everlasting subject of marriage, saying that she was being made fun of and that she would have an explanation with la Maheude once and for all. Was life worth living when one had to keep one's daughter's fatherless children while she went off with her lover? Philomène quietly finished putting on her bonnet, and Zacharie took her off, saying that he was quite willing if his mother was willing. As Levaque had already gone, Maheu referred his angry neighbour to his wife and hastened to depart. Bouteloup, who was finishing a fragment of cheese with both elbows on the table, obstinately refused the friendly offer of a glass. He would stay in the house like a good husband.

Gradually the settlement was emptied; all men went off one after another, while the girls, watching at the doors, set out in the opposite direction on the arms of their lovers. As her father turned the corner of the church, Catherine perceived Chaval, and, hastening to join him, they took together the Montsou road. And the mother remained alone, in the midst of her scattered children, without strength to leave her chair, where she was pouring out a second glass of boiling coffee, which she drank in little sips. In the settlement there were only the women left, inviting each other to finish the dregs of the coffee-pots, around tables that were still warm and greasy with the dinner.

Maheu had guessed that Levaque was at the Avantage, and he slowly went down to Rasseneur's. In fact, behind the bar, in the little garden shut in by a hedge, Levaque was having a game of skittles with some mates. Standing by, and not playing, old Bonnemort and old Mouque were following the ball, so absorbed that they even forgot to nudge each other with their elbows. A blazing sun was beating down on them, there was only one streak of shade by the side of the inn; and Étienne was there drinking his glass at a table, annoyed because Souvarine had just left to go up to his room. Nearly every Sunday the engine-man shut himself up to write or to read.

'Will you have a game?' asked Levaque of Maheu.

But he refused: it was too hot, he was already dying of thirst.

'Rasseneur,' called Étienne, 'bring a glass, will you?'

And turning towards Maheu:

'I'll stand it, you know.'

They now all treated each other familiarly. Rasseneur did not hurry himself, he had to be called three times; and Madame Rasseneur at last brought some lukewarm beer. The young man had lowered his voice to complain about the house: they were worthy people, certainly, people with good ideas, but the beer was worthless and the soup abominable! He would have changed his lodgings ten times over, only the thought of the walk from Montsou held him back. One day or another he would go and live with some family at the settlement.

'Of course!' said Maheu in his slow voice, 'of course you would be better in a family.'

But shouts now broke out. Levaque had knocked down all the skittles at one stroke. Mouque and Bonnemort, with their eyes towards the ground, in the midst of the tumult kept silent in deep approval. And the joy at this stroke found vent in jokes, especially when the players perceived la Mouquette's radiant face behind the hedge. She had been prowling about there for an hour, and at last ventured to come near on hearing the laughter.

'What! are you alone?' shouted Levaque. 'Where are your sweethearts?'

'My sweethearts! I've put them away,' she replied, with a fine impudent gaiety. 'I'm looking for one.'

They all offered themselves, getting her going with rude comments. She refused with a gesture and laughed louder, playing the fine lady. Besides, her father was watching the game without even taking his eyes from the fallen skittles.

'Ah!' Levaque went on, throwing a look towards Étienne: 'we know who you've got your eye on my girl! You'll have to take him by force.'

Then Étienne brightened up. The putter girl was in fact hanging around him. And he refused, amused indeed, but without having the least desire for her. She remained planted behind the hedge for some minutes longer, looking at him with large fixed eyes; then she slowly went away, and her face suddenly became serious as if she were overcome by the powerful sun.

In a low voice Étienne was again giving long explanations to Maheu regarding the necessity for the Montsou miners to establish a provident fund. 'Since the Company professes to leave us free,' he repeated, 'what is there to fear? We only have their pensions and they distribute them as they please, since they don't hold back any of our pay. Well, it will be prudent to form, independent of their good pleasure, an association of mutual help on which we can count at least in cases of immediate need.'

And he gave details, and discussed the organization, promising to undertake the work involved.

'I am willing enough,' said Maheu, at last convinced. 'But there are the others; get them to make up their minds.'

Levaque had won, and they left the skittles to empty their glasses. But Maheu refused to drink a second glass; he would see later on, the day was not yet done. He was thinking about Pierron. Where could he be? No doubt at the Lenfant bar. And, having persuaded Étienne and Levaque, the three set out for Montsou, at the same moment that a new group took possession of the skittles at the Avantage.

On the road they had to pause at the Casimir, and then at the Progrès bar. Comrades called them through the open doors, and there was no way of refusing. Each time it was a glass, two if they were polite enough to return the invitation. They remained there ten minutes, exchanging a few words, and then began again, a little farther on, knowing the beer, with which they could fill themselves without any other discomfort than having to piss it out again in the same measure, as clear as rock water. At the Lenfant bar they came right upon Pierron, who was finishing his second glass, and who in order not to refuse a toast, swallowed a third. They naturally drank theirs also. Now there were four of them, and they set out to see if Zacharie was not at the Tison bar. It was empty, and they called for a glass, in order to wait for him a moment. Then they thought of the Saint-Éloi bar and accepted there a round from Richomme. Then they rambled from bar to bar, without any pretext, simply saying that they were having a stroll.

'We must go to the Volcan!' suddenly said Levaque, who was getting excited.

The others began to laugh, and hesitated. Then they accompanied their comrade in the midst of the growing crowd at the fair. In the long narrow room of the Volcan, on a platform raised at the end, five singers, the dregs of the Lille prostitutes, were walking about, low-necked and with monstrous gestures, and the customers gave ten sous when they desired to have one behind the stage. There was especially a number of putters and landers, even trammers of fourteen, all the youth of the pit, drinking more gin than beer. A few old miners also ventured there, and the worst husbands of the settlements, those whose households were falling into ruin.

As soon as the group was seated round a little table, Étienne took possession of Levaque to explain to him his idea of the provident fund. Like all new converts who have found a mission, he had become an obstinate propagandist.

'Every member,' he repeated, 'could easily pay in twenty sous a month. As these twenty sous accumulated they would form a nice

little sum in four or five years, and when one has money one is
ready, eh, for anything that turns up? Eh, what do you say?'

'I've nothing to say against it,' replied Levaque, with an
abstracted air. 'We will talk about it.'

He was excited by an enormous blonde, and determined to
remain behind when Maheu and Pierron, after drinking their
glasses, set out without waiting for a second song.

Outside, Étienne who had gone with them came across la
Mouquette, again who seemed to be following them. She was
always there, looking at him with her large fixed eyes, laughing her
good-natured laugh, as if to say: 'Are you willing?' The young man
joked and shrugged his shoulders. Then, with a gesture of anger,
she was lost in the crowd.

'Where, then, is Chaval?' asked Pierron.

'True!' said Maheu. 'He must surely be at Piquette's. Let us go to
Piquette's.'

But as they all three arrived at the Piquette bar, sounds of a
quarrel stopped them at the door; Zacharie with his fist was
threatening a thick-set phlegmatic Walloon nail-maker, while
Chaval, with his hands in his pockets, was looking on.

'Hallo! there's Chaval,' said Maheu quietly; 'he is with
Catherine.'

For five long hours the putter and her lover had been walking
about the fair. All along the Montsou road, that wide road with
low bedaubed houses winding downhill, a crowd of people wandered up and down in the sun, like a trail of ants, lost in the flat,
bare plain. The eternal black mud had dried, a black dust was rising
and floating about like a storm-cloud.

On both sides the public-houses were crowded; there were rows
of tables out on the street, where stood a double rank of hucksters
at stalls in the open air, selling scarves and looking-glasses for the
girls, knives and caps for the lads; to say nothing of sweetmeats,
sugar-plums, and biscuits. In front of the church, archery was going
on. Opposite the Yards they were playing at bowls. At the corner
of the Joiselle road, beside the administration buildings, in a spot
enclosed by fences, crowds were watching a cock-fight, two large
red cocks, armed with steel spurs, their breasts torn and bleeding.
Farther on, at Maigrat's, aprons and trousers were being won at
billiards. And there were long silences; the crowd drank and stuffed
itself without a sound; a mute indigestion of beer and fried potatoes
was expanding in the great heat, still further increased by the frying-
pans bubbling in the open air.

Chaval bought a looking-glass for nineteen sous and a scarf for three francs, to give to Catherine. At every turn they met Mouque and Bonnemort, who had come to the fair and, in meditative mood, were plodding heavily through it side by side. But another meeting made them angry; they caught sight of Jeanlin inciting Bébert and Lydie to steal bottles of gin from a temporary bar installed at the edge of an open piece of ground. Catherine succeeded in boxing her brother's ears; the little girl had already run away with a bottle. These little devils would certainly end up in prison. Then, as they arrived at another bar, the Tête-Coupée, it occurred to Chaval to take his sweetheart in to a competition of chaffinches which had been announced on the door for the past week. Fifteen nail-makers from the Marchiennes nail works had responded to the appeal, each with a dozen cages; and the gloomy little cages in which the blinded finches sat motionless were already hung upon a paling in the inn yard. It was a question as to which, in the course of an hour, should repeat the phrase of its song the greatest number of times. Each nail-maker with a slate stood near his cages to mark, watching his neighbours and watched by them. And the chaffinches had begun, the *chichouïeux* with the deeper note, the *batisecouics* with their shriller note, all at first timid, and only risking a rare phrase, then, excited by each other's songs, increasing the pace; then at last carried away by such a rage of rivalry that they would even fall dead. The nail-makers violently whipped them on with their voices, shouting out to them in Walloon to sing more, still more, yet a little more, while the spectators, about a hundred people, stood by in mute fascination in the midst of this infernal music of a hundred and eighty chaffinches all repeating the same cadence out of time. It was a *batisecouic* that won the first prize, a metal coffee-pot.

Catherine and Chaval were there and when Zacharie and Philomène entered. They shook hands, and all stayed together. But suddenly Zacharie became angry, for he discovered that a nail-maker, who had come in with his mates out of curiosity, was pinching his sister's thigh. She blushed and tried to make him be silent, trembling at the idea that all these nail-makers would throw themselves on Chaval and kill him if he objected to her being pinched. She had felt the pinch, but said nothing out of prudence. Her lover, however, merely sniggered and as they all four now went out the affair seemed to be finished. But hardly had they entered Piquette's to drink a glass, when the nail-maker reappeared, making fun of them and coming close to them with an air of provocation.

Zacharie, insulted in his good family feelings, threw himself on the insolent intruder.

'That's my sister, you swine! Just wait a bit, and I'm damned if I don't make you respect her.'

The two men were separated, while Chaval, who was quite calm, only repeated:

'Let be! it's my concern. I tell you I don't care a damn for him.'

Maheu now arrived with his party, and quieted Catherine and Philomène who were in tears. The nail-maker had disappeared, and there was laughter in the crowd. To bring the episode to an end, Chaval, who was at home at the Piquette, called for drinks. Étienne had touched glasses with Catherine, and all drank together – the father, the daughter and her lover, the son and his mistress – saying politely: 'To your good health!' Pierron afterwards persisted in paying for more drinks. And they were all in good humour, when Zacharie grew wild again at the sight of his comrade Mouquet, and called him, as he said, to go and finish his affair with the nail-maker.

'I shall have to go and do for him! Here, Chaval, keep Philomène with Catherine. I'm coming back.'

Maheu offered drinks in his turn. After all, if the lad wished to avenge his sister it was not a bad example. But as soon as she had seen Mouquet, Philomène felt at rest, and nodded her head. Sure enough the two buggers had gone off to the Volcan!

On the evenings of feast-days the fair ended in the ball-room of the Bon-Joyeux. It was a widow, Madame Désir, who kept this ball-room, a fat matron of fifty, as round as a tub, but so fresh that she still had six lovers, one for every day of the week, she said, and the six together for Sunday. She called all the miners her children; and grew tender at the thought of the flood of beer which she had poured out for them during the last thirty years; and she boasted also that a putter never became pregnant without having first stretched her legs at her establishment. There were two rooms in the Bon-Joyeux: the bar which contained the counter and tables; then, communicating with it on the same floor by a large arch, was the ball-room, a large hall only planked in the middle, being paved with bricks round the sides. It was decorated with two garlands of paper flowers which crossed one another, and were united in the middle by a crown of the same flowers; while along the walls were rows of gilt shields bearing the names of saints – Saint Éloi, patron of the iron-workers; Saint Crispin, patron of the shoemakers; Saint Barbe, patron of the miners; the whole calendar of the guilds. The ceiling was so low that the three musicians on their platform, which was about the size of a pulpit, knocked their heads against it. When it became dark four petroleum lamps were fastened to the four corners of the room.

On this Sunday there was dancing from five o'clock with the full daylight through the windows, but it was not until towards seven that the rooms began to fill. Outside, a gale was threatening, blowing great black showers of dust which blinded people and sleeted into the frying-pans. Maheu, Étienne, and Pierron, having come in to sit down, had found Chaval at the Bon-Joyeux dancing with Catherine, while Philomène by herself was looking on. Neither Levaque nor Zacharie had reappeared. As there were no benches around the ball-room, Catherine came after each dance to rest at her father's table. They called Philomène, but she preferred to stand up. The twilight was coming on; the three musicians played furiously; you could only see in the hall the movement of hips and breasts in the midst of a confusion of arms. The appearance of the four lamps was greeted noisily, and suddenly everything was lit up – the red faces, the dishevelled hair sticking to the skin, the flying skirts spreading abroad the strong odour of perspiring couples. Maheu pointed out fat la Mouquette to Étienne: she was as round and fat as a bladder of lard, revolving violently in the arms of a tall, lean lander. She had been obliged to console herself and take another man.

At last, at eight o'clock, la Maheude appeared with Estelle at her breast, followed by her brats, Alzire, Henri, and Lénore. She had come there straight to her husband without fear of missing him. They could sup later on; as yet nobody was hungry, with their stomachs soaked in coffee and thickened with beer. Other women came in, and they whispered together when they saw, behind la Maheude, Levaque enter with Bouteloup, who led in by the hand Achille and Désirée, Philomène's little ones. The two neighbours seemed to be getting on well together, one turning round to chat with the other. On the way there had been a great explanation, and la Maheude had resigned herself to Zacharie's marriage, in despair at the loss of her eldest son's wages, but overcome by the thought that she could not hold it back any longer without injustice. She was trying, therefore, to put a good face on it, though with an anxious heart, as a housekeeper who was wondering how she could make both ends meet now that the best part of her purse was going.

'Sit yourself there, neighbour,' she said, pointing to a table near that where Maheu was drinking with Étienne and Pierron.

'Is not my husband with you?' asked la Levaque.

The others told her that he would soon come. They were all seated together in a heap, Bouteloup and the youngsters so tightly squeezed among the drinkers that the two tables merged into one. There was a call for drinks. Seeing her mother and her children Philomène had decided to come near. She accepted a chair, and seemed pleased to hear that she was at last to be married; then, as they were looking for Zacharie, she replied in her soft voice:

'I am waiting for him; he is over there.'

Maheu had exchanged a look with his wife. She had then consented? He became serious and smoked in silence. He also felt anxiety for the morrow in face of the ingratitude of these children, who got married one by one leaving their parents in wretchedness.

The dancing still went on, and the end of a quadrille drowned the ball-room in red dust; the walls cracked, a cornet produced shrill whistling sounds like a locomotive in distress; and when the dancers stopped they were smoking like horses.

'Do you remember?' said la Levaque, bending towards la Maheude's ear; 'you talked of strangling Catherine if she did anything foolish!'

Chaval brought Catherine back to the family table, and both of them standing behind the father finished their glasses.

'Bah!' murmured la Maheude, with an air of resignation, 'one says things like that— But what comforts me is that she can't have a child; I feel sure of that. What if she had a baby and I had to marry her off? What would we do for a living then?

Now the cornet was whistling a polka, and as the deafening noise began again, Maheu, in a low voice, communicated an idea to his wife. Why should they not take a lodger? Étienne, for example, who was looking out for quarters? They would have room since Zacharie was going to leave them, and the money that they would lose in that direction would be in part regained in the other. La Maheude's face brightened; certainly it was a good idea, it must be arranged. She seemed to be saved from starvation once more, and her good humour returned so quickly that she ordered a new round of drinks.

Étienne, meanwhile, was seeking to indoctrinate Pierron, to whom he was explaining his plan of a provident fund. He had made him promise to subscribe, when he was imprudent enough to reveal his real aim.

'And if we go out on strike you can see how useful that fund will be. We can snap our fingers at the Company, we shall have there a fund to fight against them. Eh? don't you think so?'

Pierron lowered his eyes and grew pale; he stammered:

'I'll think over it. Good conduct, that's the best provident fund.'

Then Maheu got Étienne's attention, and directly, like a good man, proposed to take him in as a lodger. The young man accepted at once, anxious to live in the settlement with the idea of being nearer to his mates. The matter was settled in no time, la Maheude declaring that they would wait for the marriage of the children.

Just then, Zacharie at last came back, with Mouquet and Levaque. The three brought in the odours of the Volcan, a breath of gin, a musky smell of slovenly girls. They were very tipsy and seemed well pleased with themselves, digging their elbows into each other and grinning. When he knew that he was at last to be married Zacharie began to laugh so loudly that he choked. Philomène peacefully declared that she would rather see him laugh than cry. As there were no more chairs, Bouteloup had moved so as to give up half of his to Levaque. And the latter, suddenly much affected by realizing that the whole family party was there, once more had beer served out.

'By the Lord! we don't amuse ourselves as often as all that,' he roared.

They remained there till ten o'clock. Women continued to arrive, either to join or to take away their men; gangs of children followed in rows, and the mothers no longer troubled themselves, pulling out their long pale breasts, like sacks of oats, and smearing their chubby babies with milk; while the little ones who were already able to walk, gorged with beer and on all fours beneath the table, relieved themselves without shame. It was a rising sea of beer, from Madame Désir's disembowelled barrels, the beer enlarged every belly, flowing from noses, eyes, and everywhere. So puffed out was the crowd that every one had a shoulder or knee poking into his neighbour; all were cheerful and merry in thus feeling each other's elbows. A continuous laugh kept their mouths open from ear to ear. The heat was like an oven; they were roasting and felt themselves at ease with glistening skin, gilded in a thick smoke from the pipes; the only discomfort was when one had to move away; from time to time a girl rose, went to the other end, near the pump, lifted her skirt, and then came back. Beneath the garlands of painted paper the dancers could no longer see each other, they perspired so much; this encouraged the trammers to tumble the putters over, catching them at random by the hips. But where a girl tumbled with a man over her, the cornet covered their fall with its furious music; the swirl of feet wrapped them round as if the ball had collapsed upon them.

Someone who was passing warned Pierron that his daughter Lydie was sleeping at the door, across the pavement. She had drunk her share of the stolen bottle and was tipsy. He had to carry her away in his arms while Jeanlin and Bébert, who were more sober, followed him behind, thinking it a great joke. This was the signal for departure, and several families came out of the Bon-Joyeux, the Maheus and the Levaques deciding to return to the settlement. At the same moment old Bonnemort and old Mouque also left Montsou, walking in the same somnambulistic manner, preserving the obstinate silence of their recollections. And they all went back together, passing for the last time through the fair, where the frying-pans were coagulating, and by the bars from which the last glasses were flowing in a stream towards the middle of the road. The storm was still threatening, and sounds of laughter arose as they left the lighted houses to lose themselves in the dark country around. Panting breaths arose from the ripe wheat; many children must have been conceived on that night. They arrived in confusion at the settlement. Neither the Levaques nor the Maheus supped with appetite, and the latter kept on dropping off to sleep while finishing their morning's boiled beef.

Étienne had led away Chaval for one more drink at Rasseneur's.

'I am with you!' said Chaval, when his mate had explained the matter of the provident fund. 'Put it there! you're a fine fellow!'

The beginning of drunkenness was flaming in Étienne's eyes. He exclaimed:

'Yes, let's join hands. As for me, you know I would give up everything for the sake of justice, both drink and girls. There's only one thing that warms my heart, and that is the thought that we are going to sweep away those bourgeois.'

CHAPTER 3

Towards the middle of August, Étienne settled with the Maheus, Zacharie having married and obtained from the Company a vacant house in the settlement for Philomène and the two children. During the first days, the young man experienced some constraint in the presence of Catherine. There was a constant intimacy, as he everywhere replaced the elder brother, sharing Jeanlin's bed over against the big sister's. Going to bed and getting up he had to dress and undress near her, and see her take off and put on her garments. When the last skirt fell from her, she appeared of pallid whiteness, that transparent snow of anaemic blondes; and he experienced a constant emotion in finding her, with hands and face already spoilt, as white as if dipped in milk from her heels to her neck, where the line of tan stood out sharply like a necklace of amber. He pretended to turn away; but little by little he knew her: the feet at first which his lowered eyes could see; then a glimpse of a knee when she slid beneath the coverlet; then her bosom with little rigid breasts as she leant over the bowl in the morning. She would hasten without looking at him, and in ten seconds was undressed and stretched beside Alzire, with so supple and snake-like a movement that he had scarcely taken off his shoes when she disappeared, turning her back and only showing her heavy knot of hair.

She never had any reason to be angry with him. If a sort of obsession made him watch her in spite of himself at the moment when she lay down, he avoided all practical jokes or dangerous pastimes. The parents were there, and besides he still had for her a feeling, half of friendship and half of spite, which prevented him from treating her as a girl to be desired, in the midst of the abandonment of their now common life in dressing, at meals, during work, where nothing of them remained secret, not even their most intimate needs. All the modesty of the family had taken refuge in the daily bath, for which the young girl now went upstairs alone, while the men bathed below one after the other.

At the end of the first month, Étienne and Catherine seemed no longer to see each other when in the evening, before extinguishing the candle, they moved about the room, undressed. She had ceased to hasten, and resumed her old custom of doing up her hair at the edge of her bed, while her arms, raised in the air, lifted her chemise to her thighs, and he, without his trousers, sometimes helped her, looking for the hairpins that she had lost. Custom killed the shame of being naked; they found it natural to be like this, for they were doing no harm, and it was not their fault if there was only one room for so many people. Sometimes, however, an uneasiness came over them suddenly, at moment when they had no guilty thought. After some nights when he had not seen her pale body, he suddenly saw her white all over, with a whiteness which shook him with a shiver, which obliged him to turn away for fear of yielding to the desire to take her. On other evenings, without any apparent reason, she would be overcome by a panic of modesty and hasten to slip between the sheets as if she felt the hands of this lad seizing her. Then, when the candle was out, they both knew that they were not sleeping but were thinking of each other in spite of their weariness. This made them restless and sulky all the following day; they liked best the tranquil evenings when they could behave together like comrades.

Étienne only complained of Jeanlin, who slept curled up. Alzire slept lightly, and Lénore and Henri were found in the morning, in each other's arms, exactly as they had gone to sleep. In the darkhouse there was no other sound than the snoring of Maheu and la Maheude, rolling out at regular intervals like a forge bellows. On the whole, Étienne was better off than at Rasseneur's; the bed was tolerable and the sheets were changed every month. He had better soup, too, and only suffered from the rarity of meat. But they were all in the same condition, and for forty-five francs he could not demand rabbit at every meal. These forty-five francs helped the family and enabled them to make ends meet, though always leaving some small debts and arrears; so the Maheus were grateful to their lodger; his linen was washed and mended, his buttons sewn on, and his affairs kept in order; in fact he felt all around him a woman's neatness and care.

It was at this time that Étienne began to understand the ideas that were buzzing in his brain. Up till then he had only felt an instinctive revolt in the midst of the inarticulate fermentation among his mates. All sorts of confused questions came to him: Why are some miserable? why are others rich? why are the former beneath the heel of the latter without hope of ever taking their place? And his first stage was to understand his ignorance. A secret shame, a hidden annoyance, gnawed at him from that time; he knew nothing, he dared not talk about these things which were working in him like a passion – the equality of all men, and the equity which demanded a fair division of the earth's wealth. He thus took to the methodless study of those who in ignorance feel the fascination of knowledge. He now kept up a regular correspondence with Pluchart, who was better educated than himself and very involved in the Socialist movement. He had books sent to him, and his ill-digested reading still further excited his brain, especially a medical book entitled *L'Hygiène du mineur*,* in which a Belgian doctor had summed up the evils of which the people in coal mines were dying;

without counting treatises on political economy, incomprehensible in their technical dryness, Anarchist pamphlets which upset his ideas, and old numbers of newspapers which he preserved as irrefutable arguments for possible discussions. Souvarine also lent him books, and a work on Co-operative Societies had made him dream for a month of a universal exchange association abolishing money and basing the whole of social life on work. The shame of his ignorance left him, and a certain pride came to him now that he left himself thinking.

During these first months Étienne was still at the stage of the excitement of a novice; his heart was bursting with generous indignation against the oppressors, and looking forward to the approaching triumph of the oppressed. He had not yet manufactured a system, his reading had been too vague. Rasseneur's practical demands were mixed up in his mind with Souvarine's violent and destructive methods, and when he came out of the Avantage, where he was to be found nearly every day railing with them against the Company, he walked as if in a dream, imagining a radical regeneration of nations to be effected without one broken window or a single drop of blood. The methods of execution remained obscure; he preferred to think that things would go very well, for he lost his head as soon as he tried to formulate a programme of reconstruction. He even showed himself full of illogical moderation; he often said that one must banish politics from the social question, a phrase which he had read and which seemed a useful one to repeat among the phlegmatic colliers with whom he lived.*

Every evening now, at the Maheus', they delayed half an hour before going to bed. Étienne always introduced the same subject. As his nature became more refined he found himself more and more disgusted by the promiscuity of the settlement. Were they beasts to be thus penned together in the midst of the fields, so tightly packed that you could not change your shirt without exhibiting your backside to the neighbours! And how bad it was for their health; and boys and girls were forced to grow corrupt together.

'Lord!' replied Maheu, 'if there were more money there would be more comfort. All the same it's true enough that it's good for no one to live piled up like this. It always ends with making the men drunk and the girls big-bellied.'

And the family began to talk, each having his say, while the petroleum lamp vitiated the air of the room, already stinking of fried onion. No, life was certainly not a joke. You had to work like an animal at labour which was once a punishment for convicts; you left your skin there oftener than was your turn, all that without even getting meat on the table in the evening. No doubt you had your feed; you ate, indeed, but so little, just enough to suffer without dying, overcome with debts and pursued as if you had stolen the bread. When Sunday came you slept from weariness. The only pleasures were to get drunk and to get a child with your wife; then the beer swelled your belly, and the child, later on, didn't care a damn. No, it was certainly not a joke.

Then la Maheude joined in.

'The trouble is, you see, when you have to say to yourself that it won't change. When you're young you think that happiness will come some time, you hope for things; and then the wretchedness begins always over again, and you get shut up in it. Now, I don't wish harm to any one, but there are times when this injustice makes me mad.'

There was silence; they were all breathing with the vague discomfort of this closed-in horizon. Only old Bonnemort, if he was there, opened his eyes with surprise, for in his time people used not to worry about things; they were born in the coal and they hammered at the seam, without asking for more; while now there was an air stirring which made the colliers ambitious.

'It don't do to complain,' he murmured. 'A good drink is a good drink. As to the bosses, they're often bastards; but there always will be bosses, won't there? What's the use of racking your brains over those things?'

Étienne at once became animated. What! The worker was to be forbidden to think! Why! that was just it; things would change now because the worker had begun to think. In the old man's time the miner lived in the mine like an animal, like a machine for extracting coal, always under the earth, with ears and eyes stopped to outward events. So the rich, who governed, found it easy to sell him and buy him, and to live off his flesh; he did not even know what was going on. But now the miner was waking up down there, germinating in the earth just as a seed germinates; and some fine day he would spring up in the midst of the fields: yes, men would spring up, an army of men who would re-establish justice. Is it not true that all citizens are equal since the Revolution, because they vote together? Why should the worker remain the slave of the master who pays him? The big companies with their machines were crushing every-thing, and one no longer had against them the ancient guarantees when people of the same trade, united in a body, were able to defend themselves. It was for that, by God, and for no other reason, that all would blow up one day, thanks to education. You had only to look into the settlement itself: the grandfathers could not sign their names, the fathers could do so, and as for the sons, they read and wrote like schoolmasters. Ah! it was growing, it was growing, little by little, a tough harvest of men who would ripen in the sun! From the moment when they were no longer each of them stuck to his place for his whole existence, and when they had the ambition to take their neighbour's place, why should they not hit out with their fists and try for the mastery?

Maheu was moved but remained full of doubts.

'As soon as you move they give you back your certificate,'* he said. 'The old man is right; it will always be the miner who gets all the trouble, without a chance of a leg of mutton now and then as a reward.'

La Maheude, who had been silent for a while, awoke as from a dream.

'But if what the priests tell is true, if the poor people in this world become the rich ones in the next!'

A burst of laughter interrupted her; even the children shrugged their shoulders, being incredulous in the world outside, keeping a secret fear of ghosts in the pit, but glad of the empty sky.

'Ah! bosh! the priests!' exclaimed Maheu. 'If they believed that, they'd eat less and work more, so as to reserve a better place for themselves up there. No, when you're dead, you're dead.'

La Maheude sighed deeply.

'Oh, Lord, Lord!'

Then her hands fell on to her knees with a gesture of immense dejection:

'Then if that's true, we are done for, we are.'

They all looked at one another. Old Bonnemort spat into his handkerchief, while Maheu sat with his extinguished pipe, which he had forgotten, in his mouth. Alzire listened between Lénore and Henri, who were sleeping on the edge of the table. But Catherine, with her chin in her hand, never took her large clear eyes off Étienne while he was protesting, declaring his faith, and opening out the vista of the enchanting future of his social dream. Around them the settlement was asleep; you could only hear the stray cries of a child or the complaints of a belated drunkard. In the parlour the cuckoo clock ticked slowly, and a damp freshness arose from the sanded floor in spite of the stuffy air.

'Fine ideas!' said the young man; 'why do you need a God and

His paradise to make you happy? Haven't you got it in your own power to make yourselves happy on earth?'

With his enthusiastic voice he spoke on and on. The closed horizon was bursting out; a gap of light was opening in the sombre lives of these poor people. The eternal wretchedness, beginning over and over again, the brutalizing labour, the fate of a beast who gives his wool and has his throat cut, all the misfortune disappeared, as though swept away by a great flood of sunlight; and beneath the dazzling gleam of fairyland justice descended from heaven. Since God was dead, justice would assure the happiness of men, and equality and brotherhood would reign. A new society would spring up in a day just as in dreams, an immense town with the splendour of a mirage, in which each citizen lived by his work, and took his share in the common joys. The old rotten world had fallen to dust; a young humanity purged of its crimes formed but a single nation of workers, having for their motto: 'To each according to his deserts, and to each desert according to its efforts.'* And this dream grew continually larger and more beautiful and more seductive as it mounted further into the impossible.

At first la Maheude refused to listen, possessed by a deep dread. No, no, it was too beautiful; it would not do to embark upon these ideas, for they made life seem abominable afterwards, and you would have destroyed everything in the effort to be happy. When she saw Maheu's eyes shine, and that he was troubled and won over, she became restless, and exclaimed, interrupting Étienne:

'Don't listen, my man! You can see he's only telling us fairy-tales. Do you think the bourgeois would ever consent to work as we do?'

But little by little the charm worked on her also. Her imagination was aroused and she smiled at last, entering his marvellous world of hope. It was so sweet to forget for a while the sad reality! When one lives like the beasts with face bent towards the earth, one needs a corner of falsehood where one can amuse oneself by regaling on the things one will never possess. And what made her enthusiastic and brought her into agreement with the young man was the idea of justice.

'Now, there you're right!' she exclaimed. 'When a thing's just I don't mind being cut to pieces for it. And it's true enough! it would be just for us to have a turn.'

Then Maheu ventured to become excited.

'Blast it all! I am not rich, but I would give a hundred sous to keep alive to see that. What a shake-up, eh? Will it be soon? And how can we set about it?'

Étienne began talking again. The old social system was cracking; it could not last more than a few months, he affirmed roundly. As to the methods of execution, he spoke more vaguely, mixing up his reading, and fearing before ignorant hearers to enter on explanations where he might lose himself. All the systems had their share in it, softened by the certainty of an easy triumph, a universal embrace which would bring to an end all class misunderstandings; without taking count, however, of the thick-heads among the masters and bourgeois whom it would perhaps be necessary to bring to reason by force. And the Maheus looked as if they understood, approving and accepting miraculous solutions with the blind faith of new believers, like those Christians of the early days of the Church, who awaited the coming of a perfect society on the dunghill of the ancient world. Little Alzire picked up a few words, and imagined happiness under the form of a very warm house, where children could play and eat as long as they liked. Catherine, without moving, her chin always resting in her hand, kept her eyes fixed on Étienne, and when he stopped a slight shudder passed over her, and she was quite pale as if she felt the cold.

But la Maheude looked at the clock.

'Past nine! Can it be possible? We shall never get up to-morrow.'

And the Maheus left the table with hearts ill at ease and in despair. It seemed to them that they had just been rich and that they had now suddenly fallen back into the mud. Old Bonnemort, who was setting out for the pit, growled that those sort of stories wouldn't make the soup better; while the others went upstairs in single file, noticing the dampness of the walls and the pestiferous stuffiness of the air. Upstairs, amid the heavy slumber of the settlement when Catherine had got into bed last and blown out the candle, Étienne heard her tossing feverishly before getting to sleep.

Often at these conversations the neighbours came in: Levaque, who grew excited at the idea of a general sharing; Pierron, who prudently went to bed as soon as they attacked the Company. At long intervals Zacharie came in for a moment; but politics bored him, he preferred to go off and drink a glass at the Avantage. As to Chaval, he would go to extremes and wanted to draw blood. Nearly every evening he spent an hour with the Maheus; in this assiduity there was a certain unconfessed jealousy, the fear that he would be robbed of Catherine. This girl, of whom he was already growing tired, had become precious to him now that a man slept near her and could take her at night.

Étienne's influence increased; he gradually revolutionized the settlement. His propaganda was unobtrusive, and all the more sure since he was growing in the estimation of all. La Maheude, notwithstanding the caution of a prudent housekeeper, treated him with consideration, as a young man who paid regularly and neither drank nor gambled, with his nose always in a book; she spread abroad his reputation among the neighbours as an educated lad, a reputation which they abused by asking him to write their letters. He was a sort of business man, charged with correspondence and consulted by households in affairs of difficulty. Since September he had thus at last been able to establish his famous provident fund, which was still very precarious, only including the inhabitants of the settlement; but he hoped to be able to obtain the adhesion of the miners at all the pits, especially if the Company, which had remained passive, continued not to interfere. He had been made secretary of the association and he even received a small salary for the clerking. This made him almost rich. A married miner can hardly make ends meet, but a sober lad who has no burdens can even manage to save.

From this time on a slow transformation took place in Étienne. Certain instincts of refinement and comfort which had remained during his poverty were now revealed. He began to buy cloth garments; he also bought a pair of elegant boots; he became a big man. The whole settlement grouped round him. The satisfaction of his vanity was delicious; he became intoxicated with this first enjoyment of popularity; to be at the head of others, to command, he who was so young, and but the day before had been a mere labourer, this filled him with pride, and enlarged his dream of an approaching revolution in which he was to play a part. His face changed: he became serious and put on airs, while his growing ambition inflamed his theories and pushed him to ideas of violence.

But autumn was advancing, and the October cold had blighted the little gardens of the settlement. Behind the thin lilacs the trammers no longer tumbled the putters over on the shed, and only the winter vegetables remained, the cabbages pearled with white frost, the leeks and the pickling vegetables. Once more the rains were beating down on the red tiles and flowing down into the tubs beneath the gutters with the sound of a torrent. In every house the stove piled up with coal was never cold, and poisoned the air of the closed parlours. It was the season of wretchedness beginning once more.

In October, on one of the first frosty nights, Étienne, feverish after his conversation below, could not sleep. He had seen Catherine glide beneath the coverlet and then blow out the candle. She also appeared to be quite overcome, and tormented by one of those fits of modesty which still made her hasten sometimes, and so awkwardly that she only uncovered herself more. In the darkness she lay as though dead; but he knew that she also was awake, and he felt that she was thinking of him just as he was thinking of her: this mute exchange of their beings had never before filled them with such trouble. The minutes went by and neither he nor she moved, only their breathing revealed their feelings in spite of their efforts to retain it. Twice over he was on the point of rising and taking her. It was idiotic to have such a strong desire for each other and never to satisfy it. Why should they thus deprive themselves of what they desired? The children were asleep, she was quite willing; he was certain that she was waiting for him, stifling, and that she would close her arms round him in silence with clenched teeth. Nearly an hour passed. He did not go to take her, and she did not turn round for fear of calling him. The more they lived side by side, the more a barrier was raised of shame, repugnancies, delicacies of friendship, which they could not explain even to themselves.

CHAPTER 4

'Listen,' said la Maheude to her man, 'when you go to Montsou for the pay, just bring me back a pound of coffee and a kilo of sugar.'

He was sewing one of his shoes, in order to save on the cobbling.

'Good!' he murmured, without leaving his task.

'I should like you to go to the butcher's too. A bit of veal, eh? It's so long since we had any.'

This time he raised his head.

'Do you think, then, that I've got thousands coming in? The fortnight's pay is too little as it is, with their confounded idea of always stopping work.'

They were both silent. It was after breakfast, one Saturday, at the end of October. The Company, under the pretext of the disruption caused by payment, had on this day once more suspended output in all their pits. Seized by panic at the growing industrial crisis, and not wishing to augment their already considerable stock, they

profited by the smallest pretexts to force their ten thousand workers
to rest.

'You know that Étienne is waiting for you at Rasseneur's,' began
la Maheude again. 'Take him with you; he'll be more clever than
you are in clearing up matters if they haven't counted all your
hours.'

Maheu nodded approval.

'And just talk to those gentlemen about your father's affair. The
doctor's on good terms with the directors. It's true, isn't it, old un,
that the doctor's mistaken, and that you can still work?'

For ten days old Bonnemort, with benumbed paws, as he said,
had remained nailed to his chair. She had to repeat her question,
and he growled:

'Sure enough, I can work. You're done for because your legs are
bad. All that is just stories they make up, so as not to give the
hundred-and-eighty-franc pension.'

La Maheude thought of the old man's forty sous, which he
would, perhaps, never bring in any more, and she uttered a cry of
anguish:

'My God! we shall soon be all dead if this goes on.'

'When you're dead,' said Maheu, 'you don't get hungry.'

He put some nails into his shoes, and decided to set out. The
Deux-Cent-Quarante settlement would not be paid till towards four
o'clock. The men did not hurry, therefore, but waited about, going
off one by one, beset by the women, who implored them to come
back at once. Many gave them errands to do, to prevent them going
off into public-houses.

At Rasseneur's Étienne had received news. Disquieting rumours
were flying about; it was said that the Company was more and
more discontented over the timbering. It was overwhelming the
workmen with fines, and a conflict appeared inevitable. That was,
however, only the avowed dispute; beneath it there were grave and
secret causes of complication.

Just as Étienne arrived, a comrade, who was drinking a beer on
his return from Montsou, was saying that an announcement had
been stuck up at the cashier's; but he did not quite know what was
on the announcement. A second entered, then a third, and each
brought a different story. It seemed certain however, that the
Company had taken a resolution.

'What do you say about it, eh?' asked Étienne, sitting down near
Souvarine at a table where nothing was to be seen but a packet of
tobacco.

The engine-man did not hurry, but finished rolling his cigarette.

'I say that it was easy to foresee. They want to push you to extremes.'

He alone had a sufficiently keen intelligence to analyse the situation. He explained it in his quiet way. The Company, suffering from the crisis, had been forced to reduce their expenses if they were not to succumb, and it was naturally the workers who would have to tighten their bellies; under some pretext or another the Company would nibble at their wages. For two months the coal had remained at the surface of their pits, and nearly all the workshops were idle. As the Company did not dare to rest in this way, terrified at the ruinous inaction, they were meditating a middle course, perhaps a strike, from which the miners would come out crushed and worse paid. Then the new provident fund was disturbing them, as it was a threat for the future, while a strike would relieve them of it, by exhausting it when it was still small.

Rasseneur had seated himself beside Étienne, and both of them were listening in consternation. They could talk aloud, because there was no one there by Madame Rasseneur, seated at the counter.

'What an idea!' murmured the innkeeper; 'what's the good of it? The Company has no interest in a strike, nor the men either. It would be best to come to an understanding.'

This was very sensible. He was always on the side of reasonable demands. Since the rapid popularity of his old lodger, he had even exaggerated this system of possible progress, saying they would obtain nothing if they wished to have everything at once. In his fat, good-humoured nature, nourished on beer, a secret jealousy was forming, increased by the desertion of his bar, into which the workmen from the Voreux now came more rarely to drink and to listen; and he thus sometimes even began to defend the Company, forgetting his rancour as an old miner who had been sacked.

'Then you are against the strike?' cried Madame Rasseneur, without leaving the counter.

And as he energetically replied, 'Yes!' she made him hold his tongue.

'Bah! you have no courage; let these gentlemen speak.'

Étienne was meditating, with his eyes fixed on the glass which she had served him. At last he raised his head.

'I dare say it's all true what our mate tells us, and we must get resigned to this strike if they force it on us. Pluchart has just written me some very sensible things on this matter. He's against the strike too, for the men would suffer as much as the bosses, and it wouldn't come to anything decisive. Only it seems to him a capital chance to get our men to make up their minds to go into his big organization. Here's his letter.'

In fact, Pluchart, in despair at the suspicion which the International aroused among the miners at Montsou, was hoping to see them enter in a mass if they were forced to fight against the Company. In spite of his efforts, Étienne had not been able to place a single member's card, but he had given his best efforts to his provident fund, which was much better received. Yet this fund was still so small that it would be quickly exhausted, as Souvarine said, and the strikers would then inevitably throw themselves into Working Men's Association so that their brothers in every country could come to their aid.

'How much have you in the fund?' asked Rasseneur.

'Hardly three thousand francs,' replied Étienne, 'and you know that the directors sent for me yesterday. Oh! they were very polite; they repeated that they wouldn't prevent their men from forming a reserve fund. But I quite understood that they wanted to control it. We are bound to have a struggle over that.'

The innkeeper was walking up and down, whistling contemptuously. 'Three thousand francs! what can you do with that! It wouldn't buy six days' bread; and if we counted on foreigners, such as the people in England, we might as well go to bed at once and turn up our toes. No, it was too foolish, this strike!'

Then for the first time bitter words passed between these two men who usually agreed in the end, in their common hatred of capitalism.

'We shall see! and you, what do you say about it?' repeated Étienne, turning towards Souvarine.

The latter replied with his usual phrase of habitual contempt.

'A strike? Nonsense!'

Then, in the midst of the angry silence, he added gently:

'On the whole, I shouldn't say no if it amuses you; it ruins the one side and kills the other, and that is always so much cleared away. Only in that way it will take quite a thousand years to renew the world. Just begin by blowing up this prison in which you are all being done to death!'

With his delicate hand he pointed to the Voreux, the buildings of which could be seen through the open door. But an unforeseen drama interrupted him: Pologne, the big rabbit, which had ventured outside, came bounding back, fleeing from the stones of a band of pit-boys; and in her terror, with fallen ears and raised tail, she took refuge against his legs, scratching and imploring him to take her up. When he had placed her on his knees, he sheltered her with both hands, and fell into that kind of dreamy somnolence into which the caress of this soft warm fur always plunged him.

Almost at the same time Maheu came in. He would drink nothing, in spite of the polite insistence of Madame Rasseneur, who sold her beer as though she made a present of it. Étienne had risen, and both of them set out for Montsou.

On pay-day at the Company's Yards, Montsou seemed to be in the midst of a holiday as on fine Sunday feast-days. A crowd of miners arrived from all the settlements. The cashier's office being very small, they preferred to wait at the door, stationed in groups on the pavement, barring the way in a crowd that was constantly filling up. Hucksters profited by the occasion and installed themselves with their movable stalls that sold even pottery and cooked meats. But it was especially the pubs and the bars which did a good trade, for the miners before being paid went to the counters to pass the time, and returned to them to celebrate getting their pay as soon as they had it in their pockets. But they were very sensible, except when they finished it at the Volcan. As Maheu and Étienne advanced among the groups they felt that on that day a deep resentment was rising up. It was not the ordinary indifference with which the money was taken and spent at the bars. Fists were clenched and violent words were passing from mouth to mouth.

'It is true, then,' asked Maheu of Chaval, whom he met in front of the Piquette,' 'that they've played a dirty trick on us?'

But Chaval contented himself by replying with a furious growl, throwing a sidelong look on Étienne. Since the new contracts had been made he had hired himself on with others, more and more bitten by envy against this comrade, the new-comer who posed as a boss and whose boots, as he said, were licked by the whole settlement. This was complicated by a lover's jealousy. He no longer took Catherine to Réquillart or behind the pit-bank without accusing her in abominable language of sleeping with her mother's lodger; then, seized by savage desire, he would stifle her with caresses.

Maheu asked him another question:

'Is it the Voreux's turn now?'

And when he turned his back after nodding affirmatively, both men decided to enter the Yards.

The counting-house was a small rectangular room, divided in two by a grating. On the benches along the wall five or six miners were waiting, while the cashier assisted by a clerk was paying another who stood before the wicket with his cap in his hand. Above the bench on the left, a yellow placard was stuck up, quite fresh against the smoky grey of the plaster, and it was in front of this that the men had been constantly passing all the morning. They entered two or three at a time, stood in front of it, and then went away without a word, shrugging their shoulders as if their backs were crushed.

Two colliers were just then standing in front of the announcement, a young one with a square brutish head and a very thin old one, his face dull with age. Neither of them could read; the young one spelt out the words to himself, moving his lips, the old one contented himself with gazing stupidly. Many came in thus to look, without understanding.

'Read us that there!' said Maheu, who was not very strong either in reading, to his companion.

Then Étienne began to read him the announcement. It was a notice from the Company to the miners of all the pits, informing them that in consequence of the lack of care bestowed on the timbering, and being weary of inflicting useless fines, the Company had resolved to apply a new method of payment for the extraction of coal. Henceforward they would pay for the timbering separately, by the cubic metre of wood taken down and used, based on the quantity necessary for good work. The price of the tub of coal extracted would naturally be lowered, in the proportion of fifty centimes to forty, according to the nature and distance of the cuttings, and a somewhat obscure calculation endeavoured to show that this diminution of ten centimes would be exactly compensated by the price of the timbering. The Company added also that, wishing to leave every one time to convince himself of the advantages presented by this new scheme, they did not propose to apply it till Monday, the 1st of December.

'Don't read so loud over there,' shouted the cashier. 'We can't hear what we are saying.'

Étienne finished reading without paying attention to this observation. His voice trembled, and when he had reached the end they all continued to gaze steadily at the placard. The old miner and the young one looked as though they expected something more; then they went away shoulders bent.

'Good God!' muttered Maheu.

He and his companions sat down absorbed, with lowered heads, and while files of men continued to pass before the yellow piece of paper they made calculations. Were they being made fun of? They could never make up with the timbering for the ten centimes taken of the tram. At most they could only get to eight centimes, so the Company would be robbing them of two centimes, without counting the time taken by careful work. This, then, was what this disguised lowering of wages really came to. The Company was economizing out of the miners' pockets.

'Good Lord! Good Lord!' repeated Maheu, raising his head. 'We should be bloody fools if we took that.'

But the wicket being free he went up to be paid. Only the heads of the concessions presented themselves at the desk and then divided the money between their men to save time.

'Maheu and associates,' said the clerk, 'Filonnière seam, cutting No. 7.'

He searched through the lists which were prepared from the inspection of the tickets on which the captains stated every day for each stall the number of trams extracted. Then he repeated:

'Maheu and team, Filonnière seam, cutting No. 7. One hundred and thirty-five francs.'

The cashier paid.

'Beg pardon, sir,' stammered the pikeman in surprise. 'Are you sure you have not made a mistake?'

He looked at this small sum of money without picking it up, frozen by a shudder which went to his heart. It was true he was expecting a bad payment, but it could not come to so little or he must have calculated wrong. When he had given their shares to Zacharie, Étienne, and the other mate who replaced Chaval, there would remain at most fifty francs for himself, his father, Catherine, and Jeanlin.

'No, no, I've made no mistake,' replied the clerk. 'There are two Sundays and four rest days to be taken off; that makes nine days of work.' Maheu followed this calculation in a low voice: nine days gave him about thirty francs, eighteen to Catherine, nine to Jeanlin. As for old Bonnemort, he only had three days. No matter, by adding the ninety francs of Zacharie and the two mates, that would surely make more.

'And don't forget the fines,' added the clerk. 'Twenty francs for fines for defective timbering.'

The pikeman made a gesture of despair. Twenty francs of fines, four days of rest! That was what it came to, then. To think that he had once brought back a fortnight's pay of a full hundred and fifty francs when old Bonnemort was working and Zacharie had not yet set up house for himself!

'Well, are you going to take it?' cried the cashier impatiently. 'You can see there's someone else waiting. If you don't want it, say so.'

As Maheu decided to pick up the money with his large trembling hand the clerk stopped him.

'Wait: I have your name here. Toussaint Maheu, is it not? The general secretary wishes to speak to you. Go in, he is alone.'

The dazed workman found himself in an office furnished with old mahogany, upholstered with faded green rep. And he listened for five minutes to the general secretary, a tall sallow gentleman, who spoke to him over the papers of his bureau without rising. But the buzzing in his ears prevented him from hearing. He understood vaguely that the question of his father's retirement would be taken into consideration with the pension of a hundred and fifty francs, fifty years of age and forty years' service. Then it seemed to him that the secretary's voice became harder. There was a reprimand; he was accused of involving himself with politics; an allusion was made to his lodger and the provident fund; finally he was advised not to compromise himself with these follies, he, who was one of the best workmen in the mine. He wished to protest, but could only pronounce words at random, twisting his cap between his feverish fingers, and he retired, stuttering:

'Certainly, sir – I can assure you, sir—'

Outside, when he had found Étienne who was waiting for him, he broke out:

'Well, I am a bloody fool, I ought to have replied! Not enough money to get bread, and insults as well! Yes, he has been talking against you; he told me the settlement was being poisoned. And what's to be done? Good God! bend one's back and say thank you. He's right, that's the wisest plan.'

Maheu fell silent, overcome at once by rage and fear. Étienne was gloomily thinking. Once more they went through the groups who blocked the road. The exasperation was growing, the exasperation of a calm race, the muttered warning of a storm, without violent gestures, terrible to see above this solid mass. A few men who could count had made calculations, and the two centimes gained by the Company over the wood were rumoured about, and excited the hardest heads. But it was especially the rage over his disastrous pay, the rebellion of hunger against the rest days and the fines. Already there was not enough to eat, and what would happen if wages were still further lowered? In the bars the anger grew loud, and fury so dried their throats that the little money taken went over the counters.

From Montsou to the settlement Étienne and Maheu never exchanged a word. When the latter entered, la Maheude, who was alone with the children, noticed immediately that his hands were empty.

'Well, you're a nice one!' she said. 'Where's my coffee and my sugar and the meat? A bit of veal wouldn't have ruined you.'

He made no reply, stifled by the emotion he had been keeping back. Then the coarse face of this man hardened to work in the mines became swollen with despair, and large tears broke from his eyes and fell like a warm rain. He had thrown himself into a chair, weeping like a child, and flinging the fifty francs on the table:

'Here,' he stammered. 'That's what I've brought you back. That's our work for all of us.'

La Maheude looked at Étienne, and saw that he was silent and overwhelmed. Then she also wept. How were nine people to live for a fortnight on fifty francs? Her eldest son had left them, the old man could no longer move his legs: it would soon mean death. Alzire threw herself round her mother's neck, overcome on hearing her weep. Estelle was howling, Lénore and Henri were sobbing.

And the entire settlement there soon arose the same cry of wretchedness. The men had come back, and each household was lamenting the disaster of this bad pay-day. The doors opened, women appeared, crying aloud outside, as if their complaints could not be held beneath the ceilings of their small houses. A fine rain was falling, but they did not feel it, they called one another from the pavements, they showed one another in the hollow of their hands the money they had received.

'Look! they've given him this. Do they bloody well want to make fools of people?'

'As for me, see, I haven't got enough to pay for the fortnight's bread with.'

'And just count mine! I'll have to sell the shirt off my back again!'

La Maheude had come out like the others. A group had formed around la Levaque, who was shouting loudest of all, for her drunkard of a husband had not even turned up, and she knew that, large or small, the pay would melt away at the Volcan. Philomène watched Maheu so that Zacharie should not get hold of the money. La Pierronne was the only one who seemed fairly calm, for that sneak of a Pierron always arranged things, no one knew how, so as to have more hours on the foreman's ticket than his mates. But la Brûlé thought this cowardly of her son-in-law; she was among the enraged, lean and erect in the midst of the group, with her fists stretched towards Montsou.

'To think,' she cried, without naming the Hennebeaus, 'that this morning I saw their servant go by in a carriage! Yes, the cook in a carriage with two horses, going to Marchiennes to get fish, sure enough!'

A clamour arose, and the abuse began again. That servant in a white apron taken to the market of the neighbouring town in her master's carriage aroused indignation. While the workers were dying of hunger they must have their fish, then, at all costs? Perhaps they would not always be able to eat their fish: the turn of the poor people would come. And the ideas sown by Étienne sprang up and grew in this cry of revolt. It was impatience before the promised golden age, a haste to get a share of the happiness beyond this horizon of misery, closed in like the grave. The injustice was becoming too great; at last they would demand their rights, since their bread was being taken out of their mouths. The women especially would have liked at once to take by assault this ideal city of progress, in which there was to be no more wretchedness. It was almost night, and the rain increased while they were still filling the settlement with their tears in the midst of the screaming children running about.

That evening at the Avantage the strike was decided on. Rasseneur no longer struggled against it, and Souvarine accepted it as a first step. Étienne summed up the situation in a word: if the Company really wanted a strike then the Company would have a strike.

CHAPTER 5

A week passed, and work went on suspiciously and mournfully in expectation of the conflict.

Among the Maheus the fortnight threatened to be more meagre than ever. La Maheude grew bitter, in spite of her moderation and good sense. Her daughter Catherine, too, had taken it into her head to stay out one night. On the following morning she came back so weary and ill after this adventure that she was not able to go to the pit; and she told with tears how it was not her fault, for Chaval had kept her, threatening to beat her if she ran away. He was becoming mad with jealousy, and wished to prevent her from returning to Étienne's bed, where he well knew, he said, that the family made her sleep. La Maheude was furious, and, after forbidding her daughter ever to see such a brute again, talked of going to Montsou to box his ears. But, all the same, it was a day lost, and the girl, now that she had this lover, preferred not to change him.

Two days after there was another incident. On Monday and Tuesday Jeanlin, who was supposed to be quietly engaged on his task at the Voreux, had escaped, to run away into the marshes and the forest of Vandame with Bébert and Lydie. He had put them up to it; no one knew to what plunder or to what games of precocious children they had all three given themselves up. He received a vigorous punishment, a thrashing which his mother applied to him on the pavement outside before the terrified children of the settle-ment. Who could have thought such a thing of children belonging to her, who had cost so much since their birth, and who ought now to be bringing something in? And in this cry there was the remembrance of her own hard youth, of the hereditary misery which made of each little one in the brood a bread-winner later on.

That morning, when the men and the girl set out for the pit, la Maheude sat up in her bed and said to Jeanlin:

'You know that if you begin that game again, you little beast, I'll take the skin off your bottom!'

In Maheu's new stall the work was hard. This part of the Filonnière seam was so thin that the pikemen, squeezed between the wall and the roof, grazed their elbows at their work. It was, too, becoming very damp; from hour to hour they feared a rush of water, one of those sudden torrents which burst through rocks and carry away men. The day before, as Étienne was violently driving in his pick and drawing it out, he had received a jet of water in his face; but this was only an alarm; the cutting simply became damper and more unwholesome. Besides, he now thought nothing of possible accidents; he forgot himself there with his mates, careless of peril. They lived in fire-damp without even feeling its weight on their eyelids, the spider's-web veil which it left on the eyelashes. Sometimes when the flame of the lamps grew paler and bluer than usual it attracted attention, and a miner would put his head against the seam to listen to the low noise of the gas, a noise of air-bubbles escaping from each crack. But the constant threat was of landslips;

for, besides the insufficiency of the timbering, always patched up too quickly, the soil, soaked with water, would not hold.

Three times during the day Maheu had been obliged to add to the planking. It was half-past two, and the men would soon have to ascend. Lying on his side, Étienne was finishing the cutting of a block, when a distant growl of thunder shook the whole mine.

'What's that, then?' he cried, putting down his pick to listen.

He had at first thought that the gallery was falling in behind his back.

But Maheu had already glided along the slope of the cutting, saying:

'It's a fall! Quick, quick!'

All tumbled down and hastened, carried away by an impulse of anxious fraternity. Their lamps danced at their wrists in the deathly silence which had fallen; they rushed in single file along the passages with bent backs, as though they were galloping on all fours; and without slowing this gallop they asked each other questions and gave brief replies. Where was it, then? In the cuttings, perhaps. No, it came from below; no, from the haulage. When they arrived at the chimney passage, they threw themselves into it, tumbling one over the other without troubling about bruises.

Jeanlin, with his skin still red from the thrashing of the day before, had not run away from the pit on this day. He was trotting with naked feet behind his train, closing the ventilation doors one by one; when he was not afraid of meeting a foreman he jumped on to the last tram, which he was not allowed to do for fear he should go to sleep. But his great amusement was, whenever the train was shunted to let another one pass, to go and join Bébert, who was holding the reins in front. He would come up slyly without his lamp and vigorously pinch his companion, inventing mischievous monkey tricks, with his yellow hair, his large ears, his lean muzzle, lit up by little green eyes shining in the darkness. With morbid precocity, he seemed to have the obscure intelligence and the quick skill of a human throw-back which had returned to its animal ways.

In the afternoon, Mouque brought Bataille, whose turn it was, to the trammers; and as the horse was snorting in the siding, Jeanlin, who had glided up to Bébert, asked him:

'What's the matter with the old crock to stop short like that? He'll break my legs.'

Bébert could not reply; he had to hold in Bataille, who was growing lively at the approach of the other train. The horse had smelled from afar his comrade, Trompette, for whom he had felt great tenderness ever since the day when he had seen him disembarked in the pit. It was like the affectionate pity of an old philosopher anxious to console a young friend by imparting to him his own resignation and patience; for Trompette was not getting used to it, drawing his trams without any taste for the work, standing with lowered head blinded by the darkness, and for ever regretting the sun. So every time that Bataille met him he put out his head snorting, and moistened him with an encouraging caress.

'By God!' swore Bébert, 'there they are, licking each other's hide again!'

Then, when Trompette had passed, he replied, on the subject of Bataille:

'Oh, he's a cunning old beast. When he stops like that it's because he guesses there's something in the way, a stone or a hole, and he takes care of himself; he doesn't want to break his bones. To-day I don't know what was the matter with him down there at the door. He pushed it, and stood stock-still. Did you see anything?'

'No,' said Jeanlin. 'There's water, I've got it up to my knees.

The train set out again. And, on the following journey, when he had opened the ventilation door with his head, Bataille again refused to advance, neighing and trembling. At last he made up his mind, and set off with a bound.

Jeanlin, who closed the door, had remained behind. He bent down and looked at the mud through which he was paddling, then, raising his lamp, he saw that the wood had given way beneath the continual dripping of a spring. Just then a pikeman, Berloque, who was called Chicot, had arrived from his cutting, in a hurry to go to his wife who had just been confined. He also stopped and examined the planking. And suddenly, as the boy was starting to rejoin his train, a tremendous cracking sound was heard, and a landslip engulfed the man and the child.

There was deep silence. A thick dust raised by the wind of the fall passed through the passages. Blinded and choked, the miners came from every part, even from the farthest stalls, with their bobbing lamps which feebly lighted up this gallop of black figures at the bottom of these molehills. When the first men tumbled against the landslip, they shouted out and called their mates. A second group, come from the cutting below, found themselves on the other side of the mass of earth which stopped up the gallery. It was at once seen that the roof had fallen in for a dozen metres at most. The damage was not serious. But all hearts skipped a beat when a death-rattle was heard from the ruins.

Bébert, leaving his train, ran up, repeating:

'Jeanlin is underneath! Jeanlin is underneath!'

Maheu, at this very moment, had come out of the passage with Zacharie and Étienne. He was seized with the fury of despair, and could only utter oaths:

'My God! my God! my God!'

Catherine, Lydie, and la Mouquette, who had also rushed up, began to sob and shriek with terror in the midst of the fearful disorder, which was increased by the darkness. The men tried to make them be silent, but they shrieked louder as each groan was heard.

The foreman, Richomme, had come up running, in despair that neither Négrel, the engineer, nor Dansaert was at the pit. With his ear pressed against the rocks he listened; and, at last, said that those sounds could not come from a child. A man must certainly be there. Maheu had already called Jeanlin twenty times over. Not a breath was heard. The little one must have been smashed up.

And still the groans continued monotonously. They spoke to the agonized man, asking him his name. The groaning alone replied.

'Look sharp!' repeated Richomme, who had already organized a rescue, 'we can talk afterwards.'

From each end the miners attacked the landslip with pick and shovel. Chaval worked without a word beside Maheu and Étienne, while Zacharie superintended the removal of the earth. The hour for ascent had come, and no one had touched food; but they could not go up for their soup while their mates were in peril. They realized, however, that the settlement would be disturbed if no one came back, and it was proposed to send off the women. But neither Catherine nor la Mouquette, nor even Lydie, would move, nailed to the spot with a desire to know what had happened, and to help. Levaque then accepted the commission of announcing the landslip up above – a simple accident, which was being repaired. It was nearly four o'clock; in less than an hour the men had done a day's work; half the earth would have already been removed if more rocks had not slid from the roof. Maheu persisted with such energy that he refused, with a furious gesture, when another man approached to relieve him for a moment.

'Gently!' said Richomme at last, 'we are getting near. We must not finish them off.'

In fact the groaning was becoming more and more distinct. It was a continuous rattling which guided the workers; and now it seemed to be beneath their very picks. Suddenly it stopped.

In silence they all looked at one another, and shuddered as they felt the coldness of death pass in the darkness. They dug on, soaked in sweat, their muscles tense to breaking. They came upon a foot, and then began to remove the earth with their hands, freeing the limbs one by one. The head was not hurt. They turned their lamps on it, and Chicot's name went round. He was quite warm, with his spinal column broken by a rock.

'Wrap him up in a covering, and put him in a tram,' ordered the foreman. 'Now for the lad; look sharp.'

Maheu gave a last blow, and an opening was made, communicating with the men who were clearing away the soil from the other side. They shouted out that they had just found Jeanlin, unconscious, with both legs broken, still breathing. It was the father who took up the little one in his arms, with clenched jaws constantly uttering 'My God!' to express his grief, while Catherine and the other women again began to shriek.

A procession was quickly formed. Bébert had brought back Bataille, who was harnessed to the trams. In the first lay Chicot's corpse, supported by Étienne; in the second, Maheu was seated with Jeanlin, still unconscious, on his knees, covered by a strip of wool torn from the ventilation door. They started at a walking pace. On each tram was a lamp like a red star. Then behind followed the row of miners, some fifty shadows in single file. Now that they were overcome by fatigue, they trailed their feet, slipping in the mud, with the mournful melancholy of a flock stricken by an epidemic. It took them nearly half an hour to reach the loading-bay. This procession beneath the earth, in the midst of deep darkness, seemed never to end through galleries which bifurcated and turned and unrolled.

At the loading-bay Richomme, who had gone on before, had ordered an empty cage to be reserved. Pierron immediately loaded the two trams. In the first Maheu remained with his wounded little one on his knees, while in the other Étienne kept Chicot's corpse between his arms to hold it up. When the men had piled themselves up in the other decks the cage rose. It took two minutes. The rain from the tubbing fell very cold, and the men looked up towards the air, impatient to see daylight.

Fortunately a trammer sent to Dr Vanderhaghen's had found him and brought him back. Jeanlin and the dead man were placed in the foreman's room, where, from year's end to year's end, a large fire burnt. A row of buckets with warm water was ready for washing feet; and, two mattresses having been spread on the floor, the man and the child were placed on them. Maheu and Étienne alone entered. Outside, putters, miners, and boys were running about, forming groups and talking in a low voice.

As soon as the doctor had glanced at Chicot:

'Done for! You can wash him.'

Two supervisors undressed and then washed with a sponge this corpse blackened with coal and still dirty with the sweat of work.

'Nothing wrong with the head,' said the doctor again, kneeling on Jeanlin's mattress. 'Nor the chest either. Ah! it's the legs that got it.'

He himself undressed the child, unfastening the cap, taking off the jacket, drawing off the breeches and shirt with the skill of a nurse. And the poor little body appeared, as lean as an insect, stained with black dust and yellow earth, marbled by bloody patches. Nothing could be made out, and they had to wash him also. He seemed to grow leaner beneath the sponge, the flesh so pallid and transparent that one could see the bones. It was a pity to look on this last degeneration of a wretched race, this mere nothing that was suffering and half crushed by the falling of the rocks. When he was clean they perceived the bruises on the thighs, two red patches on the white skin.

Jeanlin, awaking from his faint, moaned. Standing up at the foot of the mattress with hands hanging down, Maheu was looking at him and large tears rolled from his eyes.

'Eh, are you the father?' said the doctor, raising his eyes: 'No need to cry then, you can see he is not dead. Help me instead.'

He found two simple fractures. But the right leg gave him some anxiety, it would probably have to be cut off.

At this moment the engineer, Négrel, and Dansaert, who had been informed, came up with Richomme. The first listened to the foreman's narrative with an exasperated air. He broke out: Always this cursed timbering! Had he not repeated a hundred times that they would leave their men dead down there! and those brutes who talked about going out on strike if they were forced to timber more solidly. The worst was that now the Company would have to pay for the broken pots. Monsieur Hennebeau would be pleased!

'Who is it?' he asked of Dansaert, who was standing in silence before the corpse which was being wrapped up in a sheet.

'Chicot! one of our good workers,' replied the overman. 'He has three children. Poor bugger!'

Dr Vanderhaghen ordered Jeanlin's immediate removal to his parents'. Six o'clock struck, twilight was already coming on, and they would do well to remove the corpse also; the engineer gave orders to harness the van and to bring a stretcher. The wounded child was placed on the stretcher while the mattress and the dead body were put into the van.

Some putters were still standing at the door talking with some miners who were waiting about to look on. When the door reopened there was silence in the group. A new procession was then formed, the van in front, then the stretcher, and then the train of people. They left the mine square and went slowly up the road to the settlement. The first November cold had denuded the immense plain; the night was now slowly burying it like a shroud fallen from the livid sky.

Étienne then in a low voice advised Maheu to send Catherine on to warn la Maheude so as to soften the blow. The overwhelmed father, who was following the stretcher, agreed with a nod; and the young girl set out running, for they were now near. But the van, that gloomy well-known box, had already been seen. Women ran out wildly on to the paths; three or four rushed about in anguish, without their bonnets. Soon there were thirty of them, then fifty, all choking with the same terror. Then someone was dead? Who was it? The story told by Levaque after first reassuring them, now exaggerated their nightmare: it was not one man, it was ten who had perished, and who were now being brought back in the van one by one.

Catherine found her mother agitated by a presentiment; and after hearing the first stammered words la Maheude cried:

'Father's dead!'

The young girl protested in vain, speaking of Jeanlin. Without hearing her, la Maheude had rushed forward. And on seeing the van, which was passing before the church, she grew faint and pale. The women at their doors, mute with terror, were stretching out their necks, while others followed, trembling as they wondered before whose house the procession would stop.

The vehicle passed; and behind it la Maheude saw Maheu, who was accompanying the stretcher. Then, when they had placed the stretcher at her door and when she saw Jeanlin alive with his legs broken, there was so sudden a reaction in her that she choked with anger, stammering, without tears;

'Is this it? They cripple our little ones now! Both legs! My God! What do they want me to do with him?'

'Be quiet, then,' said Dr Vanderhaghen, who had followed to attend to Jeanlin. 'Would you rather he had remained below?'

But la Maheude grew more furious, while Alzire, Lénore and Henri were crying around her. As she helped to carry up the wounded boy and to give the doctor what he needed, she cursed fate, and asked where she was to find money to feed invalids. The old man was not then enough, now this rascal too had lost his legs! And she never ceased; while other cries, more heart-breaking lamentations, were heard from a neighbouring house: Chicot's wife and children were weeping over the body. It was now quite night, the exhausted miners were at last eating their soup, and the settlement had fallen into a melancholy silence, only disturbed by these loud cries.

Three weeks passed. It was found possible to avoid amputation; Jeanlin kept both his legs, but he remained lame. On investigation the Company had resigned itself to giving a donation of fifty francs. It had also promised to find employment for the little cripple at the surface as soon as he was well. All the same their misery was aggravated, for the father had received such a shock that he was seriously ill with fever.

Since Thursday Maheu had been back at the pit and it was now Sunday. In the evening Étienne talked of the approaching date of the 1st December, preoccupied in wondering if the Company would execute its threat. They sat up till ten o'clock waiting for Catherine, who must have been delaying with Chaval. But she did not return. La Maheude furiously bolted the door without a word. Étienne was long in going to sleep, restless at the thought of that empty bed in which Alzire occupied so little room.

Next morning she was still absent; and it was only in the afternoon, on returning from the pit, that the Maheus learnt that Chaval was keeping Catherine. He created such abominable scenes with her that she had decided to stay with him. To avoid reproaches he had suddenly left the Voreux and had been taken on at Jean-Bart, Monsieur Deneulin's mine, and she had followed him as a putter. The new couple still lived at Montsou, at Piquette's.

Maheu at first talked of going to fight the man and of bringing his daughter back with a kick in the backside. Then he made a gesture of resignation: what was the good? It always turned out like that; you could not prevent a girl from sticking to a man when she wanted to. It was much better to wait quietly for the marriage. But la Maheude did not take things so easily.

'Did I beat her when she took this Chaval?' she cried to Étienne, who listened in silence, very pale. 'See now, tell me! you, who are a sensible man. We have left her free, haven't we? because, my God!

they all come to it. Now, I was in the family way when father married me. But I didn't run away from my parents, and I should never have done so dirty a trick as to carry the money I earned to a man who had no want of it before the proper age. Ah! it's disgusting, you know. People will give up having children!'

And as Étienne still replied only by nodding his head, she insisted:

'A girl who went out every evening where she wanted to! What's got into her, then, not to be able to wait till I marry her after she has helped to get us out of difficulties? Eh? it's natural, one has a daughter to work. But there! we have been too good, we ought not to let her go and amuse herself with a man. Give them an inch and they take a mile.'

Alzire nodded approvingly. Lénore and Henri, overcome by this storm, cried quietly, while the mother now enumerated their misfortunes: first Zacharie who had had to get married; then old Bonnemort who was there on his chair with his twisted feet; then Jeanlin who could not leave the room for ten days with his badly set bones; and now, as a last blow, this bitch Catherine, who had gone away with a man! The whole family was breaking up. There was only the father left at the pit. How were they to live, seven persons without counting Estelle, on his three francs? They might as well jump into the canal all together.

'It won't do any good to worry yourself,' said Maheu in a low voice, 'perhaps we have not got to the end.'

Étienne, who was looking fixedly at the floor, raised his head, and murmured with eyes lost in a vision of the future:

'Ah! it is time! it is time!

PART FOUR

CHAPTER I

On that Monday the Hennebeaus had invited the Grégoires and their daughter Cécile to lunch. They had formed their plans: on rising from table, Paul Négrel was to take the ladies to a mine, Saint-Thomas, which was being luxuriously refitted. But this was only an amiable pretext; this party was an invention of Madame Hennebeau's to hasten the marriage of Cécile and Paul.

Suddenly, on this very Monday, at four o'clock in the morning, the strike broke out. When, on the 1st of December, the Company had adopted the new wage system, the miners remained calm. At the end of the fortnight not one made the least protest on pay-day. Everybody, from the manager down to the last supervisor, considered the tariff as accepted; and great was their surprise in the morning at this declaration of war, made with a tactical unity which seemed to indicate energetic leadership.

At five o'clock Dansaert woke Monsieur Hennebeau to inform him that not a single man had gone down at the Voreux. The settlement of the Deux-Cent-Quarante, which he had passed through, was sleeping deeply, with closed windows and doors. And as soon as the manager had jumped out of bed, his eyes still swollen with sleep, he was overwhelmed. Every quarter of an hour messengers came in, and dispatches fell on his desk as thick as hail. At first he hoped that the revolt was limited to the Voreux; but the news became more serious every minute. There was the Mirou, the Crèvecœur, the Madeleine, where only the grooms had appeared; the Victoire and Feutry-Cantel, the two best disciplined pits, where the men had been reduced by a third; Saint-Thomas alone numbered all its people, and seemed to be outside the movement. Up to nine o'clock he dictated dispatches, telegraphing in all directions, to the prefect of Lille, to the directors of the Company, warning the authorities and asking for orders. He had sent Négrel to go round the neighbouring pits to obtain precise information.

Suddenly Monsieur Hennebeau recollected the lunch; and he was about to send the coachman to tell the Grégoires that the party had been put off, when a certain hesitation and lack of will stopped him – the man who in a few brief phrases had just made military preparations for a field of battle. He went up to Madame

Hennebeau, whose hair had just been done by her lady's maid, in her dressing-room.

'Ah! They are on strike,' she said quietly, when he had told her. 'Well, what has that to do with us? We are not going to leave off eating, I suppose?'

And she was obstinate; it was vain to tell her that the lunch would be disturbed, and that the visit to Saint-Thomas could not take place. She found an answer to everything. Why waste a lunch that was already cooking? And as to visiting the pit, they could give that up afterwards if the walk was really imprudent.

'Besides,' she added, when the maid had gone out, 'you know that I am anxious to receive these good people. This marriage ought to affect you more than the follies of your men. I want to have it, don't contradict me.'

He looked at her, agitated by a slight trembling, and the hard firm face of the man of discipline expressed the secret grief of a wounded heart. She had remained with naked shoulders, already over-mature, but still imposing and desirable, with the broad bust of a Ceres gilded by the autumn. For a moment he felt a brutal desire to seize her, and to roll his head between the breasts she was exposing to this warm room, which exhibited the private luxury of a sensual woman and had about it an irritating perfume of musk, but he recoiled; for ten years they had occupied separate rooms.

'Good!' he said, leaving her. Let us leave things as planned.'

Monsieur Hennebeau had been born in the Ardennes. In his early life he had undergone the hardships of a poor boy thrown as an orphan on the Paris streets. After having painfully followed the courses of the École des Mines, at the age of twenty-four he had gone to the Grand'Combe as engineer to the Sainte-Barbe mine. Three years later he become divisional engineer in the Pas-de-Calais, at the Marles mines. It was there that he married, wedding, by one of those strokes of fortune which are the rule among the Corps des Mines, the daughter of the rich owner of a spinning factory at Arras. For fifteen years they lived in the same small provincial town, and no event broke the monotony of existence, not even the birth of a child. An increasing irritation detached Madame Hennebeau, who had been brought up to respect money, and was disdainful of this husband who gained a small salary with such difficulty, and who enabled her to gratify none of the satisfactions of vanity which she had dreamed of at school. He was a man of strict honesty, who never speculated, but stood at his post like a soldier. The lack of harmony had only increased, aggravated by one of those curious misunderstandings of the flesh which freeze the most ardent; he adored his wife, she had the sensuality of a voluptuous blonde, and already they slept apart, ill at ease and easily hurt. From that time she had a lover of whom he was ignorant. At last he left the Pas-de-Calais to occupy a situation in an office in Paris, with the idea that she would be grateful to him. But Paris only completed their separation, that Paris which she had desired since her first doll, and where she washed away her provincialism in a week, becoming a woman of fashion at once, and throwing herself into all the luxurious follies of the period. The ten years which she spent there were filled by a great passion, a public intrigue with a man whose desertion nearly killed her. This time the husband could not remain in ignorance, and after some abominable scenes he resigned himself, disarmed by the quiet unconsciousness of this woman who took her happiness where she found it. It was after the break-up, and when he saw that she was ill with grief, that he had accepted the management of the Montsou mines, still hoping that she would reform down there in that desolate black country.

The Hennebeaus, since they had lived at Montsou, returned to the irritated boredom of their early married days. At first she seemed consoled by the great quiet, soothed by the flat monotony of the immense plain; she buried herself in it as a woman who has done with the world; she affected a dead heart, so detached from life that she did not even mind growing stout. Then, beneath this indifference a final fever declared itself, the need to live once more, and she deluded herself for six months by organizing and furnishing to her taste the little villa belonging to the management. She said it was frightful, and filled it with upholstery, bric-à-brac, and all sorts of artistic luxuries which were talked of as far as Lille. Now the country exasperated her, those stupid fields spread out to infinity, those eternal black roads without a tree, swarming with a horrid population which disgusted and frightened her. Complaints of exile began; she accused her husband of having sacrificed her to a salary of forty thousand francs, a trifle which hardly sufficed to keep the house up. Why could he not imitate others, demand a part for himself, obtain shares, succeed in something at last? And she insisted with the cruelty of an heiress who had brought her own fortune. He, always restrained, and taking refuge in the deceptive coldness of a man of business, was torn by desire for this creature, one of those late desires which are so violent and which increase with age. He had never possessed her as a lover; he was haunted by a continual vision, to have her once to himself as she had given herself to another. Every morning he dreamed of winning her in the evening; then, when she looked at him with her cold eyes, and when he felt that everything within her denied itself to him, he even avoided touching her hand. It was a suffering without possible cure, hidden beneath the stiffness of his attitude, the suffering of a tender nature in secret anguish at the lack of domestic happiness. At the end of six months, when the house, being definitely furnished, no longer occupied Madame Hennebeau, she fell into the languor of boredom, a victim who was being killed by exile, and who said that she was glad to die of it.

Just then Paul Négrel arrived at Montsou. His mother, the widow of Provençal captain, living in Avignon on a slender income, had had to content herself with bread and water to enable him to reach the École Polytechnique.* He had come out low in rank, and his uncle, Monsieur Hennebeau, had enabled him to leave by offering to take him as engineer at the Voreux. From that time he was treated as one of the family; he even had his room there, his meals there, lived there, and was thus enabled to send to his mother half his salary of three thousand francs. To disguise this kindness Monsieur Hennebeau spoke of the embarrassment to a young man of setting up a household in one of those little villas reserved for the mine engineers. Madame Hennebeau had once taken the part of a good aunt, treating her nephew with familiarity and watching over his comfort. During the first months, especially, she exhibited an overwhelming maternity with her advice regarding the smallest subjects. But she remained a woman, however, and slid into personal confidences. This lad, so young and so practical, with his unscrupulous intelligence, professing a philosopher's theory of love, amused her with the vivacity of the pessimism which had sharpened his thin face and pointed nose. One evening he naturally found himself in her arms, and she seemed to give herself up out of kindness, while saying to him that she had no heart left, and wished only to be his friend. In fact, she was not jealous; she joked at him about the putters, whom he declared to be abominable, and she almost sulked because he had no young man's pranks to narrate to her. Then she was carried away by the idea of getting him married; she dreamed of sacrificing herself and of finding a rich girl for him. Their relations continued a plaything, recreation, in which she felt the last tenderness of a lazy woman who had done with the world.

Two years had passed by. One night Monsieur Hennebeau had a suspicion when he heard naked feet passing his door. But this new adventure revolted him, in his own house, as if between a mother and son! And besides, on the following day his wife spoke to him about the choice of Cécile Grégoire which she had made for her nephew. She occupied herself over this marriage with such ardour that he blushed at his own monstrous imagination. He only felt gratitude towards the young man who, since his arrival, had made the house less melancholy.

As he came down from the dressing-room, Monsieur Hennebeau found that Paul, who had just returned, was in the vestibule. He seemed to be quite amused by the story of this strike.

'Well?' asked his uncle.

'Well, I've been round the settlements. They seem to be quite sensible there. I think they will first send you a deputation.'

But at that moment Madame Hennebeau's voice called from the first story:

'Is that you, Paul? Come up, then, and tell me the news. How queer they are to make such a fuss, these people who are so happy!'

And the manager had to give up getting further information, since his wife had taken his messenger. He returned and sat at his desk, on which a new packet of dispatches was placed.

At eleven o'clock the Grégoires arrived, and were astonished when Hippolyte, the footman, who was placed as sentinel, hustled them in after an anxious glance at the two ends of the road. The drawing-room curtains were drawn, and they were taken at once into the study, where Monsieur Hennebeau apologized for the reception; but the drawing-room looked over the street and it was undesirable to seem to offer provocations.

'What! you don't know?' he went on, seeing their surprise.

Monsieur Grégoire, when he heard that the strike had at last broken out, shrugged his shoulders in his placid way. Bah! it would be nothing, the people were honest. With a movement of her chin, Madame Grégoire approved his confidence in the everlasting resignation of the colliers; while Cécile, who was very cheerful that day, feeling that she looked well in her capuchin cloth costume, smiled at the word 'strike,' which reminded her of visits to the settlements and the distribution of charities.

Madame Hennebeau now appeared in black silk, followed by Négrel.

'Ah! isn't it annoying!' she said, at the door. 'As if they couldn't wait, those men! You know that Paul refuses to take us to Saint-Thomas.'

'We can stay here,' said Monsieur Grégoire, obligingly. 'We shall be quite pleased.'

Paul had merely given Cécile and her mother a formal greeting. Angry at this lack of demonstrativeness, his aunt sent him with a look to the young girl; and when she heard them laughing together she enveloped them in a maternal glance.

Meanwhile, Monsieur Hennebeau finished reading his dispatches and prepared a few replies. They talked near him; his wife explained that she had not done anything to this study, which, in fact, retained its faded old red paper, its heavy mahogany furniture, its cardboard files, scratched by use. Three-quarters of an hour passed and they were about to seat themselves at table when the footman announced Monsieur Deneulin. He entered in an excited way and bowed to Madame Hennebeau.

'Ah! you here!' he said, seeing the Grégoires.

And he quickly spoke to the manager:

'It has come, then? I've just heard of it through my engineer. With me, all the men went down this morning. But the thing may spread. I'm not at all happy about it. How is it with you?'

He had arrived on horseback, and his anxiety betrayed itself in his loud speech and abrupt gestures, which made him resemble a retired cavalry officer.

Monsieur Hennebeau was beginning to inform him regarding the precise situation, when Hippolyte opened the dining-room door. Then he interrupted himself to say:

'Have lunch with us. I will tell you more over dessert.'

'Yes, as you please,' replied Deneulin, so full of his thoughts that he accepted without ceremony.

He was, however, conscious of his impoliteness and turned towards Madame Hennebeau with apologies. She was very charming, however. When she had a seventh plate laid she placed her guests: Madame Grégoire and Cécile by her husband, then Monsieur Grégoire and Deneulin at her own right and left; then Paul, whom she put between the young girl and her father. As they attacked the *hors-d'œuvre* she said, with a smile:

'You must excuse me; I wanted to give you oysters. On the Monday, you know, there was an arrival of Ostend oysters at Marchiennes, and I meant to send the cook with the carriage. But she was afraid of being stoned—'

They all interrupted her with a great burst of gaiety. They thought the story very funny.

'Hush!' said Monsieur Hennebeau, vexed, looking at the window, through which the road could be seen. 'We need not tell the whole country that we have company this morning.'

'Well, here is a slice of sausage which they shan't have,' Monsieur Grégoire declared.

The laughter began again, but with greater restraint. Each guest made himself comfortable, in this room upholstered with Flemish tapestry and furnished with old oak chests. The silver shone behind the panes of the sideboards; and there was a large hanging lamp of red copper, in whose polished rotundities were reflected a palm and an aspidistra growing in majolica pots. Outside, the December day was frozen by a keen north-east wind. But not a breath of it entered; a greenhouse warmth brought out the delicate odour of the pineapple, sliced in a crystal bowl.

'Suppose we were to draw the curtains,' proposed Négrel, who was amused at the idea of frightening the Grégoires.

The housemaid, who was helping the footman, treated this as an order and went and closed one of the curtains. This led to interminable jokes: not a glass or a plate could be put down without precaution; every dish was hailed as a waif escaped from the pillage in a conquered town; and behind this forced gaiety there was a certain fear which betrayed itself in involuntary glances towards the road, as though a band of starvelings were watching the table from outside.

After the scrambled eggs with truffles, came the river trout. The conversation then turned to the industrial crisis, which had become aggravated during the last eighteen months.

'It was inevitable,' said Deneulin, 'the excessive prosperity of recent years was bound to bring us to it. Think of the enormous capital which has been sunk, the railways, harbours, and canals, all the money buried in the maddest speculations. In our area alone sugar works have been set up as if the department could furnish three beetroot harvests. Good heavens! and today money is scarce, and we have to wait to catch up the interest of the expended millions; so there is a fatal overproduction and a final stagnation of business.'

Monsieur Hennebeau disputed this theory, but he agreed that the fortunate years had spoilt the workers.

'When I think,' he exclaimed, 'that these chaps in our pits used to earn six francs a day, double what they earn now! And they lived well, too, and acquired luxurious tastes. Today naturally, it seems hard to them to go back to their old frugality.'

'Monsieur Grégoire,' interrupted Madame Hennebeau, 'let me persuade you, a little more trout. They are delicious, are they not?'

The manager went on:

'But, as a matter of fact, it is our fault? We, too, are cruelly struck. Since the factories have closed, one by one, we have had a deuce of a difficulty in getting rid of our stock; and in face of the growing reduction in demand we have been forced to lower our net prices. That's what the workers won't understand.'

There was silence. The footman brought in roast partridge, while the housemaid began to pour out Chambertin for the guests.

'There has been a famine in India,' said Deneulin in a low voice, as though he were speaking to himself. 'America, by ceasing to order iron, has struck a heavy blow at our furnaces. Everything hangs together; a distant shock is enough to disturb the world. And the Empire, which was so proud of this hot industrial boom!'

He attacked his partridge wing. Then, raising his voice:

'The worst is that to lower the net prices we ought logically to produce more; otherwise the reduction affects wages, and the worker is right in saying that he has to pay the damage.'

This confession, the outcome of his frankness, raised a discussion. The ladies were not at all interested. Besides, all were occupied with their plates, in the first zest of appetite. When the footman came back, he seemed about to speak, then he hesitated.

'What is it?' asked Monsieur Hennebeau. 'If there are dispatches, give them to me. I am expecting replies.'

'No, sir. It is Monsieur Dansaert, who is in the hall. But he doesn't wish to disturb you.'

The manager excused himself, and had the overman brought in. The latter stood upright, a few paces from the table, while all turned to look at him, huge, out of breath with the news he was bringing. The settlements were quiet; only it had now been decided to send a deputation. It would, perhaps, be there in a few minutes.

'Very well; thank you,' said Monsieur Hennebeau. 'I want a report morning and evening, you understand.'

And as soon as Dansaert had gone, they began to joke again, and hastened to attack the Russian salad, declaring that not a moment was to be lost if they wished to finish it. The mirth was unbounded when Négrel, having asked the housemaid for bread, she replied, 'Yes, sir,' in a voice as low and terrified as if she had behind her a troop ready for murder and rape.

'You may speak,' said Madame Hennebeau complacently. 'They are not here yet.'

The manager, who now received a packet of letters and dispatches, wished to read one of his letters aloud. It was from Pierron, who, in respectful phrases, gave notice that he was obliged to go out on strike with his comrades, in order to avoid ill-treatment; and he added that he had not even been able to avoid taking part in the deputation, although he was against the move.

'So much for the freedom of the worker!' exclaimed Monsieur Hennebeau.

Then they returned to the subject of the strike, and asked him his opinion.

'Oh!' he replied, 'we have had them before. It will be a week, or, at most, a fortnight, of idleness, as it was last time. They will go and wallow in the public-houses, and then, when they are hungry, they will go back to the pits.'

Deneulin shook his head:

'I'm not so satisfied; this time they appear to be better organized. Have they not a provident fund?'

'Yes, scarcely three thousand francs. What do you think they can do with that? I suspect a man called Étienne Lantier of being their leader. He is a good workman; it would vex me to have to give him his certificate back, as we did before to the famous Rasseneur, who still poisons the Voreux with his ideas and his beer. No matter, in a week half the men will have gone down, and in a fortnight the ten thousand will be down below.'

He was convinced. His only anxiety was concerning his own possible disgrace should the directors put the responsibility of the strike on him. For some time he had felt that he was diminishing in favour. So leaving the spoonful of Russian salad which he had taken, he read over again the dispatches received from Paris, endeavouring to read between the lines. His guests excused him; the meal was becoming a military lunch, eaten on the field of battle before the first shots were fired.

The ladies then joined in the conversation. Madame Grégoire expressed pity for the poor people who would suffer from hunger; and Cécile was already making plans for distributing gifts of bread and meat. But Madame Hennebeau was astonished at hearing of the wretchedness of the Montsou colliers. Were they not very fortunate? People who were lodged and warmed and cared for at the expense of the Company! In her indifference for the herd, she only knew the lessons she had learnt, and with which she had surprised the Parisians who came on a visit. She ending up believing them, and was indignant at the ingratitude of the people.

Négrel, meanwhile, continued to frighten Monsieur Grégoire. Cécile did not displease him, and he was quite willing to marry her to be agreeable to his aunt, but he showed no amorous fervour; like a youth of experience, who, he said, was not easily carried away now. He professed to be a Republican, which did not prevent him from treating his men with extreme severity, or from making fun of them in the company of the ladies.

'Nor have I my uncle's optimism, either,' he continued. 'I fear there will be serious disturbances. So I should advise you, Monsieur Grégoire, to lock up La Piolaine. They may pillage you.'

Just then, still retaining the smile which illuminated his good-natured face, Monsieur Grégoire was outdoing his wife in paternal sentiments with regard to the miners.

'Pillage me!' he cried, stupefied. 'And why pillage me?'

'Are you not a shareholder in Montsou! You do nothing; you live on the work of others. In fact you are an infamous capitalist, and that is enough. You may be sure that if the revolution triumphs, it will force you to restore your fortune as stolen money.'

At once he lost his childlike tranquillity, his serene unconsciousness. He stammered:

'Stolen money, my fortune! Did not my great-grandfather earn, and by hard work, too, the sum originally invested? Have we not run all the risks of the enterprise, and do I today make a bad use of my income?'

Madame Hennebeau, alarmed at seeing the mother and daughter also white with fear, hastened to intervene, saying:

'Paul is joking, my dear sir.'

But Monsieur Grégoire was beside himself. As the servant was passing round the crayfish he took three of them without knowing what he was doing and began to break their claws with his teeth.

'Ah! I don't say but what there are shareholders who abuse their position. For instance, I have been told that ministers have received shares in Montsou for services rendered to the Company. It is like a nobleman whom I will not name, a duke, the biggest of our shareholders, whose life is a scandal of prodigality, millions thrown into the street on women, feasting, and useless luxury. But we who live quietly, like good citizens as we are, who do not speculate, who are content to live wholesomely on what we have, giving a part to the poor! Come, now! your men must be mere brigands if they came and stole a pin from us!'

Négrel himself had to calm him, though amused at his anger. The crayfish were still going round; the little crackling sound of their shells could be heard, while the conversation turned to politics. Monsieur Grégoire, in spite of everything and though still trembling, called himself a Liberal and regretted Louis Philippe.* As for

Deneulin, he was for a strong government; he declared that the Emperor was gliding down the slope of dangerous concessions.*

'Remember '89,' he said. 'It was the nobility who made the Revolution possible, by their complicity and taste for philosophic novelties. Very well! the middle class today are playing the same silly game with their furious Liberalism, their rage for destruction, their flattery of the people. Yes, yes, you are sharpening the teeth of the monster that will devour us. It will devour us, rest assured!'

The ladies bade him be silent, and tried to change the conversation by asking him news of his daughters. Lucie was at Marchiennes, where she was singing with a friend; Jeanne was painting an old beggar's head. But he said these things in a distracted way; he constantly looked at the manager, who was absorbed in the reading of his dispatches and forgetful of his guests. Behind those thin leaves he felt Paris and the directors' orders, which would decide the strike. At last he could not help yielding to his preoccupation.

'Well, what are you going to do?' he asked suddenly.

Monsieur Hennebeau started; then avoided the question with a vague phrase.

'We shall see.'

'No doubt you are solidly placed, you can wait,' Deneulin began to think aloud. 'But as for me, I shall be done for if the strike reaches Vandame. I shall have renovated Jean-Bart in vain; with a single pit, I can only get along by constant production. Ah! I am not in a very pleasant situation, I can assure you!'

This involuntary confession seemed to strike Monsieur Hennebeau. He listened and a plan formed within him: in case the strike turned out badly, why not utilize it by letting things run down until his neighbour was ruined, and then buy up his concession at a low price? That would be the surest way of regaining the good graces of the directors, who for years had dreamed of possessing Vandame.

'If Jean-Bart bothers you as much as that,' he said, laughing, 'why don't you give it up to us?'

But Deneulin was already regretting his complaints. He exclaimed:

'Never, never!'

They were amused at his vigour and had already forgotten the strike by the time the dessert appeared. An apple-charlotte meringue was overwhelmed with praise. Afterwards the ladies discussed a recipe with respect to the pineapple which was declared equally exquisite. The grapes and pears completed their happy abandonment at the end of this copious lunch. All talked excitedly at the same time, while the servant poured out Rhine wine in place of champagne which was looked upon as commonplace.

And the marriage of Paul and Cécile certainly made a forward step in the sympathy produced by the dessert. His aunt had thrown such urgent looks in his direction, that the young man showed himself very amiable, and in his wheedling way reconquered the Grégoires, who had been cast down by his stories of pillage. For a moment Monsiuer Hennebeau, seeing the close understanding between his wife and his nephew, felt that abominable suspicion again revive, as if in this exchange of looks he had surprised a physical contact. But again the idea of the marriage, put forward in his presence, reassured him.

Hippolyte was serving the coffee when the housemaid entered in a fright.

'Sir, sir, they are here!'

It was the delegates. Doors banged; a breath of terror passed through the neighbouring rooms.

Around the table the guests were looking at one another with uneasy indecision. There was silence. Then they tried to resume their jokes: they pretended to put the rest of the sugar in their pockets, and talked of hiding the plate. But the manager remained grave; and the laughter fell and their voices sank to a whisper, while the heavy feet of the delegates who were being shown in tramped over the carpet of the next room.

Madame Hennebeau said to her husband, lowering her voice:

'I hope you will drink your coffee.'

'Certainly,' he replied. 'Let them wait.'

He was nervous, listening to every sound, though apparently occupied with his cup.

Paul and Cécile got up, and he made her peep through the keyhole. They were stifling their laughter and talking in a low vouce.

'Do you see them?'

'Yes, I see a big man and two small ones behind.'

'Have they got ugly faces?'

'Not at all; they are very nice.'

Suddenly Monsieur Hennebeau left his chair, saying the coffee was too hot and he would drink it afterwards. As he went out he put a finger to his lips to recommend prudence. They all sat down again and remained at table in silence, no longer daring to move, listening from afar with intent ears jarred by these coarse male voices.

CHAPTER 2

The previous day, at a meeting held at Rasseneur's, Étienne and some comrades had chosen the delegates who were to proceed on the following day to the manager's house. When, in the evening, la Maheude learnt that her man was one of them, she was in despair, and asked him if he wanted them to be thrown on the street. Maheu himself had agreed with reluctance. Both of them, when the moment of action came, in spite of the injustice of their wretchedness fell back on the resignation of their race, trembling before the morrow, preferring still to bend their backs to the yoke. In the management of affairs he usually gave way to his wife, whose advice was sound. This time, however, he grew angry at last, all the more so since he secretly shared her fears.

'Just leave me alone, will you?' he said, going to bed and turning his back. 'A fine thing to leave the mates in the lurch now! I'm doing my duty.'

She went to bed in her turn. Neither of them spoke. Then, after a long silence, she replied:

'You're right; go. Only, poor old man, we are done for.'

Midday struck while they were at lunch, for the rendezvous was at one o'clock at the Avantage, from which they were to go together to Monsieur Hennebeau's. They were eating potatoes. As there was only a small morsel of butter left, no one touched it. They would have bread and butter in the evening.

'You know that we count on you to speak,' said Étienne suddenly to Maheu.

The latter was so overcome that he was silent from emotion.

'No, no! that's too much,' cried la Maheude. 'I'm quite willing he should go there, but I don't allow him to go as a ringleader. Why him, more than anyone else?'

Then Étienne, with his fiery eloquence, began to explain. Maheu was the best worker in the pit, the most liked, and the most respected; whose good sense was always spoken of. In his mouth the miners' claims would carry decisive weight. At first Étienne had arranged to speak, but he had been at Montsou for too short a time. Someone who belonged to the country would be better listened to. In fact, the comrades were entrusting their interests to the most worthy; he could not refuse, it would be cowardly.

La Maheude made a gesture of despair.

'Go, go, my man; go and be killed for the others. I'm willing, after all!'

'But I could never do it,' stammered Maheu. 'I'd say something stupid.'

Étienne, glad to have persuaded him, clapped him on the shoulder.

'Say what you feel, and you won't go wrong.'

Old Bonnemort, whose legs were now less swollen, was listening with his mouth full, shaking his head. There was silence. When potatoes were being eaten, the children were subdued, and behaved well. Then, having swallowed his mouthful, the old man muttered slowly:

'You can say what you like, and it will be all the same as if you said nothing. Ah! I've seen these affairs, I've seen them! Forty years ago they drove us out of the manager's house, and with sabres too! Now they may receive you, perhaps, but they won't answer you any more than that wall. Lord! they have money, why should they care?'

There was silence again; Maheu and Étienne rose, and left the family in gloom before the empty plates. On going out they called for Pierron and Levaque, and then all four went to Rasseneur's, where the delegates from the neighbouring settlements were arriving in little groups. When the twenty members of the deputation had assembled there, they settled on the terms to be opposed to the Company's, and then set out for Montsou. The keen north-east wind was sweeping the street. As they arrived, it struck two.

At first the servant told them to wait, and shut the door on them; then, when he came back, he introduced them into the drawing-room, and opened the curtains. A soft daylight entered, sifted through the lace. And the miners, when left alone, in their embarrassment did not dare to sit; all of them very clean, dressed in cloth, shaven that morning, with their yellow hair and moustaches. They twisted their caps between their fingers, and looked sideways at the furniture, which was in every variety of style, as a result of the taste for the old-fashioned: Henry II easy-chairs, Louis XV chairs, an Italian cabinet of the seventeenth century, a Spanish contador of the fifteenth century, with an altar-font serving as a chimney-piece, and ancient chasuble trimming reapplied to the portières. This old gold and these old silks, with their tawny tones, all this luxurious church furniture, had overwhelmed them with respectful discomfort. The oriental carpets with their long wool seemed to bind their feet. But what especially suffocated them was the heat, heat like that of a hot-air stove, which surprised them as they felt it with cheeks frozen from the wind outside. Five minutes passed by and their awkwardness increased in the comfort of this rich room, so pleasantly warm. At last Monsieur Hennebeau entered, buttoned up in a military manner and wearing on his frock-coat the correct little bow of his decoration. He spoke first.

'Ah! here you are! You are in rebellion, it seems.'

He interrupted himself to add with polite stiffness:

'Sit down, I desire nothing more than to talk things over.'

The miners turned round looking for seats. A few of them ventured to place themselves on chairs, while the others, disturbed by the embroidered silks, preferred to remain standing.

There was a period of silence. Monsieur Hennebeau, who had drawn his easy-chair up to the fire-place, was rapidly looking them over and endeavouring to recall their faces. He had recognized Pierron, who was hidden in the last row, and his eyes rested on Étienne who was seated in front of him.

'Well,' he asked, 'what have you to say to me?'

He had expected to hear the young man speak and he was so surprised to see Maheu come forward that he could not avoid adding:

'What! you, a good workman who have always been so sensible, one of the old Montsou people whose family has worked in the mine since the first stroke of a pick! Ah! it's a pity, I'm sorry that you are at the head of the discontented.'

Maheu listened with his eyes down. Then he began, at first in a low and hesitating voice.

'It is just because I am a quiet man, sir, whom no one has anything against, that my mates have chosen me. That ought to show you that it isn't just a rebellion of trouble, badly disposed men who want to create disorder. We only want justice, we are tired of starving, and it seems to us that the time has come when things ought to be arranged so that we can at least have bread every day.'

His voice grew stronger. He lifted his eyes and went on, while looking at the manager.

'You know quite well that we cannot agree to your new system.

They accuse us of bad timbering. It's true we don't give the necessary time to the work. But if we gave it, our day's work would be still smaller, and as it doesn't give us enough food at present, that would mean the end of everything, the clean sweep that would wipe out all your men. Pay us more and we will timber better, we will put in the necessary hours to the timbering instead of putting our strength into the hewing, which is the only work that pays. There's no other arrangement possible; if the work is to be done it must be paid for. And what have you invented instead? A thing which we can't get into our heads, don't you see? You lower the price of the tram and then you pretend to make up for it by paying for all timbering separately. If that was true we should be robbed all the same, for the timbering would still take us more time. But what makes us mad is that it isn't even true; the Company compensates for nothing at all, it simply puts two centimes a tram into its pocket, that's all.'

'Yes, yes, that's it,' murmured the other delegates, noticing Monsieur Hennebeau make a violent movement as if to interrupt.

But Maheu cut the manager short. Now that he had set out his words came by themselves. At times he listened to himself with surprise as though a stranger were speaking within him. It was the things amassed within his breast, things he did not even know were there, and which came out in an expansion of his heart. He described the wretchedness that was common to all of them, the hard toil, the brutal life, the wife and little ones crying from hunger in the house. He quoted the recent disastrous payments, the absurd fortnightly wages, eaten up by fines and rest days and brought back to their families in tears. Had they decided to destroy them?

'Then, sir,' he concluded, 'we have come to tell you that if we've got to starve we would rather starve doing nothing. It will be a little less trouble. We have left the pits and we don't go down unless the Company agrees to our terms. The Company wants to lower the price of the tram and to pay for the timbering separately. We ask for things to be left as they were, and we also ask for five centimes more per tram. Now it is for you to see if you are on the side of justice and the workers.'

Voices rose among the miners.

'That's it – he has said what we all feel – we only ask what's reasonable.'

Others, without speaking, showed their approval by nodding their heads. The luxurious room had disappeared, with its gold and its embroideries, its mysterious piling up of ancient things; and they no longer even felt the carpet which they crushed beneath their heavy boots.

'Let me reply, then,' at last exclaimed Monsieur Hennebeau, who was growing angry. 'First of all, it is not true that the Company gains two centimes a tram. Let us look at the figures.'

A confused discussion followed. The manager, trying to divide them, appealed to Pierron, who hid himself, stammering. Levaque, on the contrary, was at the head of the more aggressive elements, muddling up things and affirming facts of which he was ignorant. The loud murmurs of their voices were stifled beneath the hangings in the hot-house atmosphere.

'If you all talk at the same time,' said Monsieur Hennebeau, 'we shall never come to an understanding.'

He had regained his calmness, the rough politeness, without bitterness, of an agent who has received his instructions, and means them to be respected. From the first word he never took his eye off Étienne, and manœuvred to draw the young man out of his obstinate silence. Leaving the discussion about the two centimes, he suddenly enlarged the question.

'No, acknowledge the truth: you are yielding to abominable agitators. It is a plague which is now blowing over the workers everywhere, and corrupting the best. Oh! I have no need for anyone to confess. I can see well that you have been changed, you who used to be so quiet. Is it not so? You have been promised more butter than bread, and you have been told that now your turn has come to be masters. In fact, you have been enrolled in that famous International, that army of rogues who dream of destroying society.'

Then Étienne interrupted him.

'You are mistaken, sir. Not a single Montsou collier had yet enrolled. But if they are driven to it, all the pits will enroll. That depends on the Company.'

From that moment the struggle went on between Monsieur Hennebeau and Étienne as though the other miners were no longer there.

'The Company is a providence for the men, and you are wrong to threaten it. This year it has spent three hundred thousand francs in building settlements which only return two per cent, and I say nothing of the pensions which it pays, nor of the coal and medicines which it gives. You who seem to be intelligent and have become in a few months one of our most skilful workmen, would it not be better if you were to spread these truths, rather than ruin yourself by associating with people of bad reputation? Yes, I mean Rasseneur, whom we had to get rid of in order to save our pits from socialistic corruption. You are constantly seen with him, and it is certainly he who has induced you to form this provident fund, which we would willingly tolerate if it were merely a means of saving, but which we feel to be a weapon turned against us, a reserve fund to pay the expenses of the war. And in this connection I ought to add that the Company means to control that fund.'

Étienne allowed him to continue, fixing his eyes on him, while a slight nervous quiver moved his lips. He smiled at the last remark, and simply replied:

'Then that is a new demand, for until now, sir, you have neglected to claim that control. Unfortunately, we wish the Company to occupy itself less with us, and instead of playing the part of providence to be merely just with us, giving us our due, the profits which it appropriates. Is it honest, whenever a crisis comes, to leave the workers to die of hunger in order to save the shareholders' dividends? Whatever you may say, sir, the new system is a disguised reduction of wages, and that is what we are rebelling against, for if the Company wants to economize it acts very badly by only economizing on the workers.'

'Ah! there we are!' cried Monsieur Hennebeau. 'I was expecting that – the accusation of starving the people and living by their sweat. How can you talk such folly, you who ought to know the enormous risks which capital runs in industry – in the mines, for example? A well-equipped pit today costs from fifteen hundred thousand francs to two million; and it is difficult enough to get a moderate interest on the vast sum that is thus swallowed up. Nearly half the mining companies in France are bankrupt. Besides, it is stupid to accuse those who succeed of cruelty. When their workers suffer, they suffer themselves. Can you believe that the Company has not as much to lose as you have in the present crisis? It does not govern wages; it obeys competition under pain of ruin. Blame the facts, not the Company. But you don't wish to hear, you don't wish to understand.'

'Yes,' said the young man, 'we understand very well that our lot will never be bettered as long as things go on as they are going; and that is the reason why some day or another the workers will end by arranging that things shall go differently.'

This sentence, so moderate in form, was pronounced in a low voice, but with such conviction, tremulous in its menace, that a deep silence followed. A certain constraint, a breath of fear passed through the polite drawing-room. The other delegates, though scarcely understanding, felt that their comrade had been demanding their share of this comfort; and they began to cast sidelong looks over the warm hangings, the comfortable seats, all this luxury of which the least knick-knack would have bought them soup for a month.

At last Monsieur Hennebeau, who had remained thoughtful, rose as a sign for them to depart. All imitated him. Étienne had lightly pushed Maheu's elbow, and the latter, his voice once more thick and awkward, again spoke.

'Then, sir, that is all that you reply? We must tell the others that you reject our terms.'

'I, my good fellow!' exclaimed the manager, 'I reject nothing. I am paid just as you are. I have no more power in the matter than the smallest of your trammers. I receive my orders, and my only duty is to see that they are executed. I have told you what I thought I ought to tell you, but it is not for me to decide. You have brought me your demands. I will make them known to the directors, then I will tell you their reply.'

He spoke with the correct air of a high official avoiding any passionate interest in the matter, with the courteous dryness of a simple instrument of authority. And the miners now looked at him with distrust, asking themselves what interest he might have in lying, and what he would get by thus putting himself between them and the real masters. A schemer, perhaps, this man who was paid like a worker, and who lived so well!

Étienne ventured to intervene again.

'You see, sir, how unfortunate it is that we cannot plead our cause in person. We could explain many things, and bring forward many reasons of which you could know nothing, if we only knew where we ought to go.'

Monsieur Hennebeau was not at all angry. He even smiled.

'Ah! it gets complicated as soon as you have no confidence in me; you will have to go over there.'

The delegates had followed the vague gesture of his hand toward one of the windows. Where was it, over there? Paris, no doubt. But they did not know exactly; it seemed to fall back into a terrible distance, in an inaccessible religious country, where an unknown god sat on his throne, crouching down in the depths of his tabernacle. They would never see him; they only felt him as a force far off, which weighed on the ten thousand colliers of Montsou. And when the director spoke he had that hidden force behind him delivering oracles.

They were overwhelmed with discouragement; Étienne himself signified by a shrug of the shoulders that it would be best to go; while Monsieur Hennebeau touched Maheu's arm in a friendly way and asked after Jeanlin.

'That is a severe lesson now, and it is you who defend bad timbering. You must reflect, my friends; you must realize that a strike would be a disaster for everybody. Before a week you would die of hunger. What would you do? I count on your good sense, anyhow; and I am convinced that you will go down on Monday, at the latest.'

They all left, going out of the drawing-room with the tramping of a flock and rounded backs, without replying a word to this hope of submission. The manager, who accompanied them, was obliged to continue the conversation. The Company, on the one side, had its new tariff; the workers on the other, their demand for an increase of five centimes a tram. In order that they might have no illusions, he felt he ought to warn them that their terms would certainly be rejected by the directors.

'Reflect before committing any follies,' he repeated, disturbed at their silence.

In the porch Pierron bowed very low, while Levaque pretended to adjust his cap. Maheu was trying to find something to say before leaving, when Étienne again touched his elbow. And they all left in the midst of this threatening silence. The door closed with a loud bang.

When Monsieur Hennebeau re-entered the dining-room he found his guests motionless and silent before the liqueurs. In a few words he told his story to Deneulin, whose face grew still more gloomy. Then, as he drank his cold coffee, they tried to speak of other things. But the Grégoires themselves returned to the subject of the strike, expressing their astonishment that no laws existed to prevent workmen from leaving their work. Paul reassured Cécile, stating that they were expecting the police.

At last Madame Hennebeau called the servant:

'Hippolyte, before we go into the drawing-room just open the windows and let in a little air.

CHAPTER 3

A fortnight had passed, and on the Monday of the third week the lists sent up to the managers showed a fresh decrease in the number of the miners who had gone down. It was expected that on that morning work would be resumed, but the obstinacy of the directors in not yielding exasperated the miners. The Voreux, Crèvecœur, Mirou, and Madeleine were not the only pits idle; at the Victoire and at Feutry-Cantel only about a quarter of the men had gone down; even Saint-Thomas was affected. The strike was gradually becoming general.

At the Voreux a heavy silence hung over the pit-head. It was like a dead factory, these great empty abandoned Yards where work was abandoned. In the grey December sky, along the high foot-bridges three or four empty trains bore witness to the mute sadness of things. Underneath, between the slender posts of the platforms, the stock of coal was diminishing, leaving the earth bare and black; while the supplies of wood were mouldering beneath the rain. At the quay on the canal a barge was moored, half-laden, lying drowsily in the murky water; and on the deserted pit-bank, in which the decomposed sulphates smoked in spite of the rain, a melancholy cart thrust up its shafts. But the buildings especially were growing torpid, the screening-shed with closed shutters, the steeple in which the rumbling of the receiving-room no more arose, and the machine-room grown cold, and the giant chimney too large for the occasional smoke. The winding-engine was only heated in the morning. The grooms sent down fodder for the horses, and the foremen worked alone at the bottom, having become labourers again, watching over the damage that took place in the passages as soon as they ceased to be repaired; then, after nine o'clock the rest of the service was carried on by the ladders. And above these dead buildings, buried in their garment of black dust, there could only be heard the panting of the pumping-engine, breathing with its thick, long breath all that was left of the life of the pit, which the water would destroy if that breathing should cease.

On the plain opposite, the settlement of the Deux-Cent-Quarante seemed also to be dead. The prefect of Lille had come in haste and the police had patrolled all the roads; but in face of the calmness of the strikers, prefect and police had decided to go home again. Never had the settlement given so splended an example in the vast plain. The men, to avoid going to the public-house, slept all day long; the women while dividing the coffee became reasonable, less anxious to gossip and quarrel; and even the gangs of children seemed to understand it all, and were so good that they ran about with naked feet, smacking each other silently. The word of command had been repeated and circulated from mouth to mouth; they wished to be sensible.

There was, however, a continuous coming and going of people in the Maheus' house. Étienne, as secretary, had divided the three thousand francs of the provident fund among the needy families; afterwards from various sides several hundred francs had arrived, yielded by subscriptions and collections. But now all their resources were exhausted; the miners had no more money to keep up the strike, and hunger was there, threatening them. Maigrat, after having promised credit for a fortnight, had suddenly altered his mind at the end of a week and cut off provisions. He usually took his orders from the Company; perhaps the latter wished to bring the matter to an end by starving the settlements. He acted besides like a capricious tyrant, giving or refusing bread according to the look of the girl who was sent by her parents for provisions; and he especially closed his door spitefully to la Maheude, wishing to punish her because he had not been able to get Catherine. To complete their misery it was freezing very hard, and the women watched their piles of coal diminish, thinking anxiously that they could no longer renew them at the pits now that the men were not going down. It was not enough to die of hunger, they must also die of cold.

In the Maheu household everything was already running short. The Levaques could still eat on the strength of a twenty-franc piece lent by Bouteloup. As to the Pierrons, they always had money; but in order to appear as needy as the others, for fear of loans, they got their supplies on credit from Maigrat, who would have handed over his shop to la Pierronne if she had held out her petticoat to him. Since Saturday many families had gone to bed without supper, and in face of the terrible days that were beginning not a complaint was heard, all obeyed the word of command with quiet courage. There was an absolute confidence in spite of everything, a religious faith, the blind gift of a population of believers. Since an era of justice had been promised to them they were willing to suffer for the conquest of universal happiness. Hunger went to their heads; never had their closed horizon opened up a larger world beyond to these people in the hallucination of their misery. They saw again over there, when their eyes were dimmed by weakness, the ideal city of their dream, but now growing near and seeming to be real, with its population of brothers, its golden age of labour and meals in common. Nothing overcame their conviction that they were at last entering it. The fund was exhausted; the Company would not yield; every day would aggravate the situation; and they preserved their hope and showed a smiling contempt for facts. If the earth opened beneath them a miracle would save them. This faith replaced bread and warmed their stomachs. When the Maheus and the others had too quickly digested their soup, made with clear water, they thus rose into a state of semi-vertigo, that ecstasy of a better life which flung martyrs to the wild beasts.

Étienne was henceforth the unquestioned leader. In the evening conversations he gave forth oracles, for his studies had sharpened his mind and made him able to enter into difficult matters. He spent the nights reading, and received a large number of letters; he even subscribed to the *Vengeur*, a Belgian Socialist paper, and this, the first paper to enter the settlement, gained for him extraordinary consideration among his mates. His growing popularity excited him more every day. To carry on an extensive correspondence, to discuss the fate of the workers in the four corners of the province, to give advice to the Voreux miners, especially to become a centre and to feel the world revolving round him – continually swelled the vanity of the former engine-man, the pikeman with greasy black hands. He was climbing up the ladder, he was entering this execrated middle class, with a satisfaction to his intelligence and comfort which he did not confess to himself. He had only one concern, the awareness of his lack of education, which made him embarrassed and timid as soon as he was in the presence of a gentleman in a frock-coat. If he went on instructing himself, devouring everything, the lack of method would render assimilation very slow, and would produce such confusion that at last he would know much more than he could understand. So at certain hours of good sense he experienced a restlessness with regard to his mission – a fear that he was not the man for the task. Perhaps it required a lawyer, a learned man, able to speak and act without compromising his mates? But an outcry soon restored his assurance. No, no; no lawyers! they are all rogues; they profit by their knowledge to feed off the people. Let things turn out how they will, the workers must manage their own affairs. And his dream of the popular leadership again soothed him: Montsou at his feet, Paris in the misty distance, who knows? The elections some day, the platform in a hall, where he could thunder against the middle class in the first speech pronounced by a workman in a parliament.

During the last few days Étienne had been perplexed. Pluchart wrote letter after letter, offering to come to Montsou to quicken the zeal of the strikers. It was a question of organizing a private meeting over which the mechanic would preside; and beneath this plan lay the idea of exploiting the strike, to win over to the International these miners who so far had shown themselves suspicious. Étienne feared a disturbance, but he would, however, have allowed Pluchart to come if Rasseneur had not violently condemned this proceeding. In spite of his power, the young man had to reckon with the innkeeper, whose services were of longer standing, and who had faithful followers among his clients. So he still hesitated, not knowing what to reply.

On this very Monday, towards four o'clock, a new letter came from Lille as Étienne was alone with la Maheude in the lower room. Maheu, weary of idleness, had gone fishing; if he had the luck to catch a fine fish under the sluice of the canal, they could sell it to buy bread. Old Bonnemort and little Jeanlin had just gone off to try their legs, which were now restored; while the children had departed with Alzire, who spent hours on the pit-bank collecting cinders. Seated near the miserable fire, which they no longer dared to keep up, la Maheude, with her dress unbuttoned and one breast hanging out of her dress and falling to her belly, was suckling Estelle.

When the young man had folded the letter, she questioned him:

'Is the news good? Are they going to send us any money?'

He shook his head, and she went on:

'I don't know what we shall do this week. However, we'll hold on all the same. When one has right on one's side, don't you think, it gives you heart, and one ends always by being the strongest?'

At the present time she was, to a reasonable extent, in favour of the strike. It would have been better to force the Company to be just without leaving off work. But since they had left it they ought not to go back to it without obtaining justice. On this point she was relentless. Better to die than to show oneself in the wrong when one was right!

'Ah!' exclaimed Étienne, 'if a fine old cholera was to break out, that would free us of all these Company exploiters.'

'No, no,' she replied, 'we must not wish anyone dead. That wouldn't help us at all; plenty more would spring up. Now I only ask that they should get sensible ideas, and I expect they will, for there are worthy people everywhere. You know I'm not at all for your politics.'

In fact she always blamed his violent language, and thought him aggressive. It was good that they should want their work paid for at what was worth, but why occupy oneself with such things as the bourgeois and Government? Why mix oneself up with other people's affairs, when one would get nothing out of it but hard knocks? And she kept her esteem for him because he did not get drunk, and regularly paid his forty-five francs for board and lodging. When a man behaves well one can forgive him the rest.

Étienne then talked about the Republic, which would give bread to everybody. But la Maheude shook her head, for she remembered 1848;* an awful year, which had left them as bare as worms, she and her man, in their early years together. She forgot herself in describing its horrors, in a mournful voice, her eyes lost in space, her breast still bare; while her infant, Estelle, without letting it go, had fallen asleep on her knees. And Étienne, also absorbed in thought, had his eyes fixed on this enormous breast, of which the soft whiteness contrasted with the muddy yellowish complexion of her face.

'Not a sou,' she murmured, 'nothing to eat and all the pits stopped. Just the same destruction of poor people as today.'

But at that moment the door opened, and they remained mute with surprise at seeing Catherine come in. Since her flight with Chaval she had not reappeared at the settlement. Her emotion was so great that, trembling and silent, she forgot to shut the door. She expected to find her mother alone, and the sight of the young man put out of her head the phrases she had prepared on the way.

'What on earth have you come here for?' cried la Maheude, without even moving from her chair. 'I don't want to have anything more to do with you; get along.'

Then Catherine tried to find words:

'Mother, it's some coffee and sugar; yes, for the children. I've been thinking of them and done overtime.'

She drew out of her pockets a pound of coffee and a pound of sugar, and dared to place them on the table. The strike at the Voreux troubled her while she was working at Jean-Bart, and she had only been able to think of this way of helping her parents a little, under the pretext of caring for the little ones. But her good nature did not disarm her mother, who replied:

'Instead of bringing us sweets, you would have done better to stay and earn bread for us.'

She overwhelmed her with abuse, relieving herself by throwing in her daughter's face all that she had been saying against her for the past month. To go off with a man, to hang on to him at sixteen, when the family was in want! Only the most degraded of unnatural children could do it. She could forgive a folly, but a mother never forgot a trick like that. There might have been some excuse if they had been strict with her. Not at all; she was as free as air, and they only asked her to come in to sleep.

'Tell me, what has got into you, at your age?'

Catherine, standing beside the table, listened with lowered head. A quiver shook her thin under-developed girlish body, and she tried to reply in broken words:

'Oh! if it was only me, for what little pleasure I get! It's him. What he wants I'm obliged to want too, aren't I? because, you see, he's the strongest. How can you tell how things are going to turn out? Anyhow it's done and can't be undone; it may as well be him as another now. He'll have to marry me.'

She defended herself without a struggle, with the passive resignation of a girl who has submitted to the male at an early age. Was it not the common lot? She had never dreamed of anything else; violence behind the pit-bank, a child at sixteen, and then a wretched household if her lover married her. And she did not blush with shame; she only quivered like this at being treated like a slut before this lad, whose presence oppressed her to despair.

Étienne had risen, however, and was pretending to stir up the nearly extinct fire in order not to interrupt the explanation. But their looks met; he found her pale and exhausted; pretty, indeed, with her clear eyes in the face which had grown tanned; and he experienced a singular feeling; his spite had vanished; he simply desired that she should be happy with this man whom she had preferred to him. He felt the need to occupy himself with her still, a longing to go to Montsou and force the other man to his duty. But she only saw pity in his constant tenderness; he must feel contempt for her to gaze at her like that. Then her heart contracted so that she choked, without being able to stammer any more words of excuse.

'That's it, you'd best hold your tongue,' began the implacable la Maheude. 'If you've come back to stay, come in; else get along with you at once, and think yourself lucky that I'm not free just now, or I should have put my foot into you somewhere before now.'

As if this threat had suddenly been realized, Catherine received a vigorous kick right behind, so violent that she was stupefied with

surprise and pain. It was Chaval who had leapt in through the open
door to lunge at her like a vicious beast. For a moment he had
watched her from outside.

'Ah! slut,' he yelled, 'I've followed you. I knew well enough you
were coming back here to get him to fill you up. And it's you that
pay him, eh? You pour coffee down him with my money!'

La Maheude and Étienne were stupefied, and did not stir. With a
furious movement Chaval chased Catherine towards the door.

'Out you go, by God!'

And as she took refuge in a corner he turned on her mother.

'A nice business, keeping watch while your whore of a daughter
is kicking up her legs upstairs!'

At last he caught Catherine's wrist, shaking her and dragging her
out. At the door he again turned towards la Maheude, who was
rooted to her chair. She had forgotten to put back her breast. Estelle
had gone to sleep, and her face had slipped down into the woollen
petticoat; the enormous breast was hanging free and naked like the
udder of a great cow.

'When the daughter is not at it, it's the mother who gets herself
plugged,' cried Chaval. 'Go on, show him your meat! He isn't
disgusted – your dirty lodger!'

At this Étienne was about to strike his mate. The fear of arousing
the settlement by a fight had kept him back from snatching
Catherine from Chaval's hands. But rage was now carrying him
away, and the two men were face to face with inflamed eyes. It was
an old hatred, a jealousy long unacknowledged, which was breaking
out. One of them now must do for the other.

'Take care!' stammered Étienne, with clenched teeth. 'I'll do for
you.'

'Try!' replied Chaval.

They looked at one another for some seconds longer, so close
that their hot breath burnt each other's faces. And it was Catherine
who, begging him to go, took her lover's hand again to lead him
away. She dragged him out of the settlement, fleeing without turning
her head.

'What a brute!' muttered Étienne, banging the door, and so
shaken by anger that he was obliged to sit down.

La Maheude, in front of him, had not stirred. She made a vague
gesture, and there was silence, a silence which was painful and
heavy with unspoken things. In spite of an effort his gaze again
returned to her breast, that expanse of white flesh, the brilliance of
which now made him uncomfortable. No doubt she was forty, and

had lost her shape, like a good female who had produced too much; but many would still desire her, strong and solid, with the large long face of a woman who had once been beautiful. Slowly and quietly she was putting back her breast with both hands. A rosy corner would not go in and she pushed it back with her finger, and then buttoned herself up, and was now quite black and shapeless in her old camisole.

'He's a filthy beast,' she said at last. 'Only a filthy beast could have such nasty ideas. I don't care a hang what he says; it wasn't worth answering back.'

Then in a frank voice she added, fixing her eyes on the young man:

'I have my faults, sure enough, but not that one. Only two men have touched me – a putter, long ago, when I was fifteen, and then Maheu. If he had left me like the other, Lord! I don't quite know what would have happened; and I don't pride myself either on my good conduct with him since our marriage, because when one hasn't gone wrong, it's often because one hasn't the chance. Only I say things as they are, and I know neighbours who couldn't say as much, don't you think?'

'That's true enough,' replied Étienne.

And he rose and went out, while she decided to light the fire again, after having placed the sleeping Estelle on two chairs. If the father caught and sold a fish they could manage to have some soup.

Outside, night was already coming on, a frosty night; and with lowered head Étienne walked along, sunk in dark melancholy. It was no longer anger against the man, or pity for the poor ill-treated girl. The brutal scene was effaced and lost, and he was thrown back on to the sufferings of all, the abominations of wretchedness. He thought of the settlement without bread, these women and little ones who would not eat that evening, all this struggling race with empty bellies. And the doubt which sometimes touched him awoke again the frightful melancholy of the twilight, and tortured him with a discomfort which he had never felt so strongly before. With what a terrible responsibility he had burdened himself! Must he still push them on in obstinate resistance, now that there was neither money nor credit? And what would be the end of it all if no help arrived, and stavation came to beat down their courage? He had a sudden vision of disaster; of dying children and sobbing mothers, while the men, lean and pale, went down once more into the pits. He went on walking, his feet stumbling against the stones, and the thought that the Company would be found strongest, and that he would have brought misfortune on his comrades, filled him with insupportable anguish.

When he raised his head he saw that he was in front of the Voreux. The gloomy mass of buildings looked sombre beneath the growing darkness. The deserted square, obstructed by great motionless shadows, seemed like the corner of an abandoned fortress. As soon as the winding-engine stopped, the soul left the place. At this hour of the night nothing was alive, not a lantern, not a voice; and the sound of the pump itself was only a distant moan, coming one could not say whence, in this annihilation of the whole pit.

As Étienne gazed he took heart again. If the workers were suffering hunger, the Company was eating into its millions. Why should it prove the stronger in this war of labour against money? In any case, the victory would cost it dear. They would have their corpses to count. He felt the fury of battle again, the fierce desire to have done with misery, even at the price of death. It would be as well for the settlement to die at one stroke as to go on dying bit by bit of famine and injustice. His ill-digested reading came back to him, examples of nations who had burnt their towns to stop the enemy, vague histories of mothers who had saved their children from slavery by crushing their heads against the pavement, of men who had died of want rather than eat the bread of tyrants. He got carried away, a rosy mood of gaiety grew out of his crisis of black sadness, chasing away doubt, and making him ashamed of this passing moment of cowardice. And in this revival of his faith, gusts of pride reappeared and carried him still higher; the joy of being a leader, of seeing himself obeyed, even to the point of sacrifice, the enlarged dream of his power, the evening of triumph. Already he imagined a scene of simple grandeur, his refusal of power, authority placed in the hands of the people, when they would be the masters.

But he awoke and started at the voice of Maheu, who was narrating his luck, a superb trout which he had caught and sold for three francs.

They would have their soup. Then he left his mate to return alone to the settlement, saying that he would follow him and he entered and sat down in the Avantage, awaiting the departure of a customer to tell Rasseneur decisively that he would write to Pluchart to come at once. He had made up his mind; he would organize a private meeting, for victory seemed to him certain if the Montsou colliers joined in a mass the International.

CHAPTER 4

It was at the Bon-Joyeux, Widow Désir's place, that the private meeting was organized for Thursday at two o'clock. The widow, incensed at the miseries inflicted on her children the colliers, was in a constant state of anger, especially as her inn was emptying. Never had there been a less thirsty strike; the drunkards had shut themselves up at home for fear of disobeying the sober word of command. Thus Montsou, which swarmed with people on feast-days, now exhibited its wide street in mute and melancholy desolation. No beer flowed from counters or bellies, the gutters were dry. On the pavement at the Casimir and the Progrès bars you could only see the pale faces of the landladies, looking enquiringly into the street; then in Montsou itself the deserted doors extended from the Lenfant to the Tison bars, passing by the Piquette and the Tête-Coupée; only the Saint-Éloi, which was frequented by foremen, still served occasional glasses; the solitude even extended to the Volcan, where the ladies were resting for lack of admirers, although they had lowered their price from ten sous to five in view of the hard times. A deep mourning was breaking the heart of the entire country.

'By God!' exclaimed Widow Désir, slapping her thighs with both hands, 'it's the fault of the gendarmes! Let them run me in, devil take them, if they like, but I must cause them some trouble.'

For her, all authorities and masters were gendarmes; it was a term of general contempt in which she enveloped all the enemies of the people. She had greeted Étienne's request with delight; her whole house belonged to the miners, she would lend her ball-room for nothing, and would herself issue the invitations since the law required it. Besides, if the law was not pleased, so much the better! She would give them a bit of her mind. Since yesterday the young man had brought her some fifty letters to sign; he had them copied by neighbours in the settlement who knew how to write, and these letters were sent around among the pits to delegates and to men of whom they were sure. The avowed order of the day was a discussion regarding the continuation of the strike; but in reality they were expecting Pluchart, and reckoning on a speech from him which would cause a general recruiting to the International.

On Thursday morning Étienne was disquieted by the non-appearance of his old foreman, who had promised by letter to arrive on Wednesday evening. What, then, was happening? He was annoyed that he would not be able to come to an understanding with him before the meeting. At nine o'clock he went to Montsou, with the idea that the mechanic had, perhaps, gone there direct without stopping at the Voreux.

'No, I've not seen your friend,' replied Widow Désir. 'But everything is ready. Come and see.'

She led him into the ball-room. The decorations were the same, the garlands which supported at the ceiling a crown of painted paper flowers, and the gilt cardboard shields in a line along the wall with the names of saints, male and female. Only the musicians' platform had been replaced by a table and three chairs in one corner; and the room was furnished with benches set out across the floor.

'It's perfect,' Étienne declared.

'And you know,' said the widow, 'that you're at home here. Yell as much as you like. The gendarmes will have to pass over my dead body if they do come!'

In spite of his anxiety, he could not help smiling when he looked at her, so vast did she appear, with a pair of breasts so huge that one alone would require a man to embrace it, which now led to the saying that of her six weekday lovers she had to take two every evening on account of the work.

But Étienne was astonished to see Rasseneur and Souvarine enter; and as the widow left them all three in the large empty hall he exclaimed:

'What! you here already!'

Souvarine, who had worked all night at the Voreux, the enginemen not being on strike, had merely come out of curiosity. As to Rasseneur, he had seemed constrained during the last two days, and his fat round face had lost its good-natured laugh.

'Pluchart has not arrived, and I am very anxious,' added Étienne.

The innkeeper turned away his eyes, and replied between his teeth:

'I'm not surprised; I don't expect him.'

'What!'

Then he made up his mind, and looking the other in the face bravely:

'I, too, have sent him a letter, if you want me to tell you; and in that letter I begged him not to come. Yes, I think we ought to manage our own affairs ourselves, without turning to strangers.'

Étienne, losing his self-possession and trembling with anger, turned his eyes on his mate's and stammered:

'You've done that, you've done that?'

'I have done that, certainly! and you know that I trust Pluchart; he's a knowing fellow and reliable, one can get on with him. But you see I don't care a damn for your ideas, I don't! Politics, Government, and all that, I don't care a damn for it! What I want is for the miner to be better treated. I have worked down below for twenty years, I've sweated down there with fatigue and misery, and I've sworn to make it easier for the poor buggers who are there still; and I know well enough you'll never get anything with all your ideas, you'll only make the men's fate more miserable still. When they are forced by hunger to go down again, they will be more crushed than ever; the Company will pay them by beating them down, like a runaway dog who is brought back to his kennel. That's what I want to prevent, do you see!'

He raised his voice, protruding his belly and squarely planted on his big legs. The man's whole patient, reasonable nature was revealed in clear phrases, which flowed abundantly without an effort. Was it not absurd to believe that with one stroke they could change the world, putting the workers in the place of the bosses and sharing the money as one divides an apple? It would, perhaps, take thousands and thousands of years for that to happen. There, hold your tongue, with your miracles! The most sensible plan was, if one did not wish to take a beating, to go straight forward, to demand possible reforms, in short, to improve the lot of the workers on every occasion. He did his best, so far as he could, to bring the Company to better terms; if not, damn it all! they would only starve be being obstinate.

Étienne had let him speak, his own speech cut short by indignation. Then he cried:

'Haven't you got any blood in your veins, by God?'

At one moment he would have struck him, and to resist the temptation he rushed about the hall with long strides, venting his fury on the benches, knocking them down as he went.

'Shut the door, at all events,' Souvarine remarked. 'There is no need to be heard.'

Having himself gone to shut it, he quietly sat down in one of the office chairs. He had rolled a cigarette, and was looking at the other two men with his mild subtle eyes, his lips drawn by a slight smile.

'You won't get any farther by being angry,' said Rasseneur judiciously. 'I believed at first that you had good sense. It was sensible to recommend calmness to the mates, to force them to keep indoors, and to use your power to maintain order. And now you want to get them into a real mess!'

At each turn in his walks among the benches, Étienne returned towards the innkeeper, seizing him by the shoulders, shaking him, and shouting out his replies in his face.

'But, blast it all! I mean to be calm. Yes, I have imposed order on them! Yes, I do advise them still not to stir! only it doesn't do to be made a fool of after all! You are lucky to remain cool. Now there are times when I feel that I am losing my head.'

This was a confession on his part. He made fun of his illusions as a novice, his religious dream of a city in which justice would soon reign among the men who had become brothers. A fine method truly! to fold your arms and wait, if you wished to see men devour each other to the end of the world like wolves. No! one must interfere, or injustice would be eternal, and the rich would for ever suck the blood of the poor. Therefore he could not forgive himself the stupidity of having said formerly that politics ought to be banished from the social question. He knew nothing then; now he had read and studied, his ideas were ripe, and he boasted that he had a system. He explained it badly, however, in confused phrases which contained a little of all the theories he had successively passed through and abandoned. At the summit Karl Marx's idea remained unshakeable: capital was the result of theft, it was the duty and the privilege of labour to reconquer that stolen wealth. In practice he had at first, with Proudhon, been taken in by the dream of a mutual credit, a vast bank of exchange which eliminated middlemen; then Lassalle's co-operative societies, endowed by the State, gradually transforming the earth into a single industrial town, had aroused his enthusiasm until he grew disgusted in face of the difficulty of controlling them; and he had arrived recently at collectivism, demanding that all the instruments of production should be restored to the community. But this remained vague; he knew not how to realize this new dream, still hindered by scruples of reason and good sense, not daring to risk the sectarians' absolute affirmations. He simply said that it was a question of getting possession of the government first of all. Afterwards they would see.*

'But what has got into you? Why are you going over to the bourgeois?' he continued violently, again planting himself before the innkeeper. 'You said yourself it would have to burst up!'

Rasseneur blushed slightly.

'Yes, I said so. And if it does burst up, you will see that I am no more of a coward than anyone else. Only I refuse to be among those who increase the mess in order to carve out a position for themselves.'

Étienne blushed in his turn. The two men no longer shouted, having become bitter and spiteful, conquered by the coldness of their rivalry. It was basically what always strains systems, making one man a revolutionary in the extreme, pushing the other to an affectation of prudence, carrying them, in spite of themselves, beyond their true ideas into those fatal parts which men do not choose for themselves. And Souvarine, who was listening, exhibited on his pale, girlish face a silent contempt – the crushing contempt of the man who was willing to yield his life in obscurity without even winning the glory of martyrdom.

'Then it's to me that you're saying that?' asked Étienne; 'you're jealous!'

'Jealous of what?' replied Rasseneur. 'I don't pose as a big man; I'm not trying to create a section at Montsou for the sake of being made secretary.'

The other man wanted to interrupt him, but he added:

'Why don't you be frank? You don't care a damn for the International; you're only burning to be at our head, the gentleman who corresponds with the famous Federal Council of the Nord!'

There was silence. Étienne replied, quivering:

'Good! I don't think I have anything to reproach myself with. I always asked your advice, for I knew that you had fought here long before me. But since you can't endure anyone by your side, I'll act alone in future. And first I warn you that the meeting will take place even if Pluchart does not come, and the mates will join in spite of you.'

'Oh! join!' muttered the innkeeper; 'that's not enough. You'll have to get them to pay their subscriptions.'

'Not at all. The International grants time to workers on strike. It will at once come to our help, and we shall pay later on.'

Rasseneur completely lost his temper.

'Well, we shall see. I belong to this meeting of yours, and I shall speak. I shall not let you turn our friends' heads, I shall let them know where their real interests lie. We shall see whom they mean to follow – me, whom they have known for thirty years, or you, who have turned everything upside down among us in less than a year. No, no! damn it all! We shall see which of us is going to crush the other.'

And he went out, banging the door. The garlands of flowers

swayed from the ceiling, and the gilt shields jumped against the walls. Then the great room fell back into its heavy calm.

Souvarine was smoking in his quiet way, seated before the table. After having paced for a moment in silence, Étienne began to relieve his feelings at length. Was it his fault if they had left that fat lazy fellow to come to him? And he defended himself from having sought popularity. He knew not even how it had happened, this friendliness of the settlement, the confidence of the miners, the power which he now had over them. He was indignant at being accused of wishing to bring everything to confusion out of ambition; he struck his chest, protesting his brotherly feelings.

Suddenly he stopped before Souvarine and exclaimed:

'Do you know, if I thought I'd cost a drop of blood of a friend, I would go off at once to America!'

The engine-man shrugged his shoulders, and a smile again came on his lips.

'Oh! blood!' he murmured. 'What does that matter? The earth has need of it.'

Étienne, growing calm, took a chair, and put his elbows on the other side of the table. This fair face, with the dreamy eyes, which sometimes grew savage with a red glow, disturbed him, and exercised a singular power over his will. In spite of his comrade's silence, conquered even by that silence, he felt himself gradually absorbed.

'Well,' he asked, 'what would you do in my place? Am I not right to act as I do? Isn't it best for us to join this association?'

Souvarine, after having slowly ejected a jet of smoke, replied with his favourite word:

'Oh, foolery! but meanwhile it's good enough. Besides, their International will soon begin to work. He has taken it up.'

'Who, then?'

'He!'

He had pronounced this word in a whisper, with religious fervour, casting a glance towards the east. He was speaking of the master, Bakunin the Exterminator.*

'He alone can give the knock-out blow,' he went on, 'while your learned men, with their evolution, are mere cowards. Before three years are past, the International, under his orders, will crush the old world.'

Étienne pricked up his ears in attention. He was burning to gain knowledge, to understand this worship of destruction, regarding which the engine-man only uttered occasional obscure words, as though he kept certain mysteries to himself.

'Well, but explain to me. What is your aim?'

'To destroy everything. No more nations, no more governments, no more property, no more God nor worship.'

'I quite understand. Only what will that lead you to?'

'To the primitive formless commune, to a new world, to the renewal of everything.'

'And the means of execution? How do you reckon to set about it?'

'By fire, by poison, by the dagger. The brigand is the true hero, the popular avenger, the revolutionary in action, with no phrases drawn out of books. We need a series of tremendous outrages to frighten the powerful and to arouse the people.'

As he talked, Souvarine grew terrible. An ecstasy raised him on his chair, a mystic flame darted from his pale eyes, and his delicate hands gripped the edge of the table almost to breaking. The other man looked at him in fear, and thought of the stories of which he had received vague intimation, of mines beneath the tsar's palace, of chiefs of police struck down by knives like wild boars, of his mistress, the only woman he had loved, hanged in Moscow one rainy morning, while in the crowd he kissed her with his eyes for the last time.

'No! no!' murmured Étienne, as with a gesture he pushed away these abominable visions, 'we haven't got to that yet over here. Murder and fire, never! It is monstrous, unjust, all the mates would rise and strangle the guilty one!'

And besides, he could not understand; the instincts of his race refused to accept this sombre dream of the extermination of the world, mown level like a rye-field. Then what would they do afterwards? How would the nations spring up again? He demanded a reply.

'Tell me your programme. We like to know where we are going to.'

Then Souvarine concluded peacefully, with his gaze fixed into space:

'All reasoning about the future is criminal, because it prevents pure destruction, and interferes with the progress of revolution.'

This made Étienne laugh, in spite of the cold shiver which passed over his flesh. Besides, he willingly acknowledged that there was something in these ideas, which attracted him by their fearful simplicity. Only it would be playing into Rasseneur's hands if he were to repeat such things to his comrades. It was necessary to be practical.

Widow Désir proposed that they should have lunch. They agreed, and went into the inn parlour, which was separated from the ball-room on weekdays by a movable partition. When they had finished their omelette and cheese, the engine-man proposed to depart, and as the other tried to detain him:

'What for? To listen to you talking useless foolery? I've seen enough of it. Good day.'

He went off in his gentle, obstinate way, with a cigarette between his lips.

Étienne's anxiety increased. It was one o'clock, and Pluchart was decidedly breaking his promise. Towards half-past one the delegates began to appear, and he had to receive them, for he wished to see who entered, for fear that the Company might send its usual spies. He examined every letter of invitation, and took note of those who entered; many came in without a letter, as they were admitted provided he knew them. As two o'clock struck Rasseneur entered, finishing his pipe at the counter, and chatting without haste. This provoking calmness still further disturbed Étienne, all the more as many had come merely for fun – Zacharie, Mouquet, and others. These cared little about the strike, and found it a great joke to do nothing. Seated at tables, and spending their last two sous on drink, they grinned and bantered at their mates, the serious ones, who had come to make fools of themselves.

Another quarter of an hour passed; there was impatience in the hall. Then Étienne, in despair, made a gesture of resolution. And he decided to enter, when Widow Désir, who was looking outside, exclaimed:

'But here he is, your gentleman!'

It was, in fact, Pluchart. He came in a cab drawn by a broken-winded horse. He jumped at once on to the pavement, a thin, insipidly handsome man, with a large square head – in his black cloth frock-coat he had the Sunday air of a well-to-do workman. For five years he had not done a stroke with the file, and he took care of his appearance, especially combing his hair in a correct manner, proud of his successes on the platform; but his limbs were still stiff, and the nails of his large hands, eaten away by the iron, had not grown again. Very active, he worked out his ambitions, scouring the province unceasingly in order to promote his ideas.

'Ah! don't be angry with me,' he said, anticipating questions and reproaches. 'Yesterday, lecture at Preuilly in the morning, meeting in the evening at Valençay. Today, lunch at Marchiennes with Sauvagnat. At last I was able to take a cab. I'm worn out; you can tell by my voice. But that's nothing; I shall speak all the same.'

He was on the threshold of the Bon-Joyeux, when he stopped short.

'Heavens! I'm forgetting the cards. We should have been in a fine fix!'

He went back to the cab, which the cabman drew up again, and he pulled out a little black wooden box, which he carried off under his arm.

Étienne walked radiantly in his shadow, while Rasseneur, in consternation, did not dare to offer his hand. But the other was already pressing it, and saying a rapid word or two about the letter. What a rum idea! Why not hold this meeting? One should always hold a meeting when possible. Widow Désir asked if he would take anything, but he refused. No need; he spoke without drinking. Only he was in a hurry, because in the evening he reckoned on pushing as far as Joiselle, where he wished to come to an understanding with Legoujeux. Then they all entered the ball-room together. Maheu and Levaque, who had arrived late, followed them. The door was then locked, in order to be in privacy. This made the jokers laugh even more, Zacharie shouting to Mouquet that perhaps they were going to get them all with child in there.

About a hundred miners were waiting on the benches in the close air of the room, with the warm odours of the last ball rising from the floor. Whispers ran round and all heads turned, while the new-comers sat down in the empty places. They gazed at the Lille gentleman, and the black frock-coat caused a certain surprise and discomfort.

But on Étienne's proposition the meeting formed a committee. He suggested names, while the others approved by lifting their hands. Pluchart was nominated chairman, and Maheu and Étienne himself were voted stewards. There was a movement of chairs and the officers were installed; for a moment they watched the chairman disappear beneath the table under which he slid the box, which he had not let go. When he reappeared he struck lightly with his fist to call for attention; then he began in a hoarse voice:

'Citizens!'

A little door opened and he had to stop. It was Widow Désir who, coming round by the kitchen, brought in six glasses on a tray.

'Don't put yourselves out,' she said. 'When one talks one gets thirsty.'

Maheu relieved her of the tray and Pluchart was able to go on. He said how very touched he was at his reception by the Montsou workers, he excused himself for his delay, mentioning his fatigue and his sore throat, then he gave way to Citizen Rasseneur, who wished to speak.

Rasseneur had already planted himself beside the table near the glasses. The back of a chair served him as a rostrum. He seemed very moved, and coughed before starting in a loud voice:

'Mates!'

What gave him his influence over the workers at the pit was the facility of his speech, the good-natured way in which he could go on talking to them by the hour without ever growing weary. He never ventured to gesticulate, but stood solid and smiling, drowning them and dazing them, until they all shouted: 'Yes, yes, that's true enough, you're right!' However, on this day, from the first word, he felt that there was a sullen opposition. This made him advance prudently. He only discussed the continuation of the strike, and waited for applause before attacking the International. Certainly honour prevented them from yielding to the Company's demands; but how much misery! what a terrible future if they had to persist much longer! and without declaring himself for submission he damped their courage, he showed them the settlements dying of hunger, he asked on what resources the supporters of resistance were counting. Three or four friends tried to applaud him, but this accentuated the cold silence of the majority, and the gradually rising disapprobation which greeted his phrases. Then, despairing of winning them over, he was carried away by anger, he foretold misfortune if they allowed their heads to be turned at the instigation of strangers. Two-thirds of the audience had risen indignantly, trying to silence him, since he insulted them by treating them like children unable to act for themselves. But he went on speaking in spite of the tumult, taking repeated gulps of beer, and shouting violently that the man was not born who would prevent him from doing his duty.

Pluchart had risen. As he had no bell he struck his fist on the table, repeating in his hoarse voice:

'Citizens, citizens!'

At last he obtained a little quiet and the meeting, when consulted, brought Rasseneur's speech to an end. The delegates who had represented the pits in the interview with the manager led the others, all enraged by starvation and agitated by new ideas. The voting was decided in advance.

'You don't care a damn, you don't! you can eat!' yelled Levaque, thrusting out his fist at Rasseneur.

Étienne leaned over behind the chairman's back to appease Maheu, who was very red, and beside himself with fury at this hypocritical speech.

'Citizens!' said Pluchart, 'allow me to speak!'

There was deep silence. He spoke. His voice sounded painful and hoarse; but he was used to it on his journeys, and took his laryngitis about with him like his programme. Gradually his voice expanded and he produced pathetic effects with it. With open arms and accompanying his periods with a swaying of his shoulders, he had an eloquence which recalled the pulpit, a religious fashion of sinking the ends of his sentences whose monotonous roll at last carried conviction.

His speech entered on the greatness and the advantages of the International; he always started this way in every new locality. He explained its aim, the emancipation of the workers; he showed its imposing structure – below the commune, higher the province, still higher the nation, and at the summit humanity. His arms moved slowly, piling up the stages, preparing the immense cathedral of the future world. Then there was the internal administration: he read the statutes, spoke of the congresses, pointed out the growing importance of the work, the enlargement of the programme, which, starting from the discussion of wages, was now working towards the liquidation of society, to have done with the wage system. No more nationalities. The workers of the whole world would be united by a common need for justice, sweeping away middle-class corruption, founding, at last, a free society, in which he who did not work should not reap! He roared; his breath startled the flowers of painted paper beneath the low smoky ceiling which sent back the sound of his voice.

A wave passed through the audience. Some of them cried:

'That's it! We're with you.'

He went on. The world would be conquered within three years. And he enumerated the nations already won over. From all sides people were rushing to join. Never had a young religion counted so many disciples. Then, when they had the upper hand they would dictate terms to the bosses, who, in their turn, would have a fist at their throats.

'Yes, yes! they'll have to go down the mine!'

With a gesture he enforced silence. Now he was entering on the strike question. In principle he disapproved of strikes; it was a slow method, which aggravated the sufferings of the worker. But before better things arrived, and when they were inevitable, one must accept them, for they had the advantage of disorganizing capital. And in this case he presented the International as a provider for strikers, and quoted examples: in Paris, during the strike of the bronze-workers, the bosses had granted everything at once, terrified at the news that the International was sending help; in London it had saved the miners at a colliery, by sending back, at its own expense, a ship-load of Belgians who had been brought over by the mine-owner. It was sufficient to join and the companies trembled, for the men entered the great army of workers who were resolved to die for one another rather than to remain the slaves of a capitalistic society.

Applause interrupted him. He wiped his forehead with his handkerchief, at the same time refusing a glass which Maheu passed to him. When he was about to continue fresh applause cut short his speech.

'It's all right,' he said rapidly to Étienne. 'They've had enough. Quick! the cards!'

He had dived under the table, and reappeared with the little black wooden box.

'Citizens!' he shouted, dominating the disturbance, 'here are the membership cards. Let your delegates come up, and I will give them to them to be distributed. Later on we can arrange everything.'

Rasseneur rushed forward and again protested. Étienne was also agitated, having to make a speech. Extreme confusion followed. Levaque jumped up with his fists out, as if to fight. Maheu was up and speaking, but nobody could distinguish a single word. In the growing tumult the dust rose from the floor, a floating dust of former balls, poisoning the air with a strong odour of putters and trammers.

Suddenly the little door opened, and Widow Désir filled it with her belly and breasts, shouting in a thundering voice:

'For God's sake, silence! The gendarmes!'

It was the district commissioner, who had arrived rather late to prepare a report and to break up the meeting. Four gendarmes accompanied him. For five minutes the widow had delayed them at the door, replying that she was at home, and that she had a perfect right to entertain her friends. But they had hustled her away, and she had rushed in to warn her children.

'Must clear out through here,' she said again. 'There's a dirty gendarme guarding the courtyard. It doesn't matter; my little woodshed opens into the alley. Quick, then!'

The commissioner was already knocking with his fist, and as the door was not opened, he threatened to force it. A spy must have talked, for he cried that the meeting was illegal, a large number of miners being there without any letter of invitation.

In the hall anxiety was growing. They could not escape that way; they had not even voted either for joining or for the continuation of the strike. All persisted in talking at the same time. At last the chairman suggested a vote by acclamation. Arms were raised, and the delegates declared hastily that they would join in the name of their absent mates. And it was thus that the ten thousand colliers of Montsou became members of the International. Meanwhile, the retreat began. In order to cover it, Widow Désir had propped herself up against the door, which the butt-ends of the gendarmes' muskets were forcing at her back. The miners jumped over the benches, and escaped, one by one, through the kitchen and wood-yard. Rasseneur disappeared among the first, and Levaque followed him, forgetful of his abuse, and planning how he could get an offer of a glass to pull himself together. Étienne, after having seized the little box, waited with Pluchart and Maheu, who considered it a point of honour to emerge last. As they disappeared the lock gave, and the commissioner found himself in the presence of the widow, whose breasts and belly still formed a barricade.

'It doesn't help you much to smash everything in my house,' she said. 'You can see there's nobody here.'

The commissioner, a slow man who did not care for scenes, simply threatened to take her off to prison. And he then went away with his four gendarmes to prepare a report, to the jeers of Zacharie and Mouquet, who were full of admiration for the way in which their mates had humbugged this armed force, for which they themselves did not care a toss.

In the alley outside, Étienne, hampered by the box, was rushing along, followed by the others. He suddenly thought of Pierron, and asked why he had not turned up. Maheu, also running, replied that he was ill – a convenient illness, the fear of compromising himself. They wished to retain Pluchart, but, without stopping, he declared that he must set out at once for Joiselle, where Legoujeux was awaiting orders. Then, as they ran, they shouted out to him their wishes for a pleasant journey, and rushed through Montsou with their heels in the air. A few words were exchanged, broken by the panting of their chests. Étienne and Maheu were laughing confidently, henceforth certain of victory. When the International had sent help, it would be the Company that would beg them to resume work. And in this burst of hope, in this gallop of big boots sounding over the pavement of the streets, there was something else also, something sombre and fierce, a gust of violence which would inflame the settlements in the four corners of the region.

CHAPTER 5

Another fortnight had passed by. It was the beginning of January and cold mists benumbed the immense plain. The misery had grown still greater, and the settlements were in agony from hour to hour in the increasing famine. Four thousand francs sent by the International from London had scarcely supplied bread for three days, and then nothing had come. This great dead hope was beating down their courage. On whom could they count now since even their brothers had abandoned them? They felt themselves separated from the world and lost in the midst of this deep winter.

On Tuesday no resources were left in the Deux-Cent-Quarante settlement. Étienne and the delegates had doubled their efforts. New subscriptions were opened in neighbouring towns, and even in Paris; collections were made and lectures organized. These efforts came to nothing. Public opinion, which had at first been moved, grew indifferent now that the strike dragged on for ever, and so quietly, without any dramatic incidents. Small charities scarcely sufficed to maintain the poorer families. The others lived by pawning their clothes and selling up the household goods piece by piece. Everything went to the brokers, the wool of the mattresses, the kitchen utensils, even the furniture. For a moment they thought themselves saved, for the small retail shopkeepers of Montsou, killed off by Maigrat, had offered credit to try and get back their custom; and for a week Verdonck, the grocer, and the two bakers, Carouble and Smelten, kept open shop, but when their advances were exhausted all three stopped. The bailiffs were rejoicing; there only resulted a piling up of debts which would for a long time weigh upon the miners. There was no more credit to be had anywhere and not an old saucepan to sell; they might as well lie down in a corner to die like mangy dogs.

Étienne would have sold his flesh. He had given up his salary and had gone to Marchiennes to pawn his trousers and cloth coat, happy to set the Maheus' pot boiling once more. His boots alone remained, and he retained these to keep a firm foothold, he said. His grief was that the strike had come on too early, before the provident fund had had time to swell. He regarded this as the only cause of the disaster, for the workers would surely triumph over the masters on the day when they had saved enough money to resist. And he recalled Souvarine's words accusing the Company of pushing forward the strike to destroy the fund at the beginning.

The sight of the settlement and of these poor people without bread or fire overcame him. He preferred to go out and to weary himself with distant walks. One evening, as he was coming back and passing near Réquillart, he noticed an old woman who had fainted by the roadside. No doubt she was dying of hunger; and having raised her he began to shout to a girl whom he saw on the other side of the paling.

'Why! is it you?' he said, recognizing la Mouquette. 'Come and help me then, we must give her something to drink.'

La Mouquette, moved to tears, quickly went into the shaky hovel which her father had set up in the midst of the ruins. She came back at once with gin and a loaf. The gin revived the old woman, who without speaking bit greedily into the bread. She was the mother of a miner who lived at a settlement on the Cougny side, and she had fallen there on returning from Joiselle, where she had attempted in vain to borrow half a franc from a sister. When she had eaten she went away dazed.

Étienne stood in the open field of Réquillart, where the crumbling sheds were disappearing beneath the brambles.

'Well, won't you come in and drink a little glass?' asked la Mouquette merrily.

And as he hesitated:

'Then you're still afraid of me?'

He followed her, won over by her laughter. This bread, which she had given so willingly, moved him. She would not take him into her father's room, but led him into her own room, where she at once poured out two little glasses of gin. The room was very neat and he complimented her on it. Besides, the family seemed to want for nothing; the father continued his duties as a groom at the Voreux while she, saying that she could not live with folded arms, had become a laundress, which brought her in thirty sous a day. A girl may amuse herself with men, but she isn't lazy for all that.

'I say,' she murmured, all at once coming and putting her arms round him prettily, 'why don't you like me?'

He could not help laughing, she had done this in so charming a way.

'But I like you very much,' he replied.

'No, no, not like I mean. You know that I am dying of longing. Come, it would give me so much pleasure.'

It was true, she had desired him for six months. He still looked at her as she clung to him, pressing him with her two tremulous arms, her face raised with such supplicating love that he was deeply moved. There was nothing beautiful in her large round face, with its yellow complexion eaten by the coal; but her eyes shone with a flame, a charm rose from her skin, a trembling of desire which made her rosy and young. In face of this gift which was so humble and so ardent he no longer dared to refuse.

'Oh! you are willing,' she stammered, delighted. 'Oh! you are willing!'

And she gave herself up with the fainting awkwardness of a virgin, as if it was for the first time, and she had never before known a man. Then when he left her, it was she who was overcome with gratitude; she thanked him and kissed his hands.

Étienne remained rather ashamed of this good fortune. Nobody boasted of having had la Mouquette. As he went away he swore that it should not occur again, but he preserved a friendly remembrance of her; she was a fine girl.

When he got back to the settlement, he found serious news which made him forget the adventure. The rumour was circulating that the Company would, perhaps, agree to make a concession if the delegates made a fresh attempt with the manager. At all events some foremen had spread this rumour. The truth was, that in this struggle the mine was suffering even more than the miners. On both sides obstinacy was piling up ruin: while labour was dying of hunger, capital was being destroyed. Every day of idleness was a loss of hundreds of thousands of francs. Every machine which stops is a dead machine. Tools and material are impaired, the money that is sunk melts away like water swallowed by the sand. Since the small stock of coal at the surface of the pits was exhausted, customers talked of going to Belgium, so that in future there would be a threat from that quarter. But what especially frightened the Company, although the matter was carefully concealed, was the increasing damage to galleries and workings. The foremen could not cope with the repairs, the timber was falling everywhere, and

landslips were constantly taking place. Soon the disasters became
so serious that long months would be needed for repairs before
hewing could be resumed. Already stories were going about the
country: at Crèvecœur three hundred metres of road had subsided
in a mass, stopping up access to the Cinq-Paumes; at Madeleine the
Maugrètout seam was crumbling away and filling with water. The
management refused to accept this, but suddenly two accidents, one
after the other, had forced them to admit it. One morning, near La
Piolaine, the ground was found cracked above the north gallery of
Mirou which had fallen in the day before; and on the following day
the ground subsided within the Voreux, shaking a corner of a
suburb to such an extent that two houses nearly disappeared.

Étienne and the delegates hesitated to risk any steps without
knowing the directors' intentions. Dansaert, whom they questioned,
avoided replying: certainly, the misunderstanding was deplored,
and everything would be done to bring about an agreement; but he
could say nothing definitely. At last, they decided that they would
go to Monsieur Hennebeau in order to have reason on their side;
for they did not wish to be accused, later on, of having refused the
Company an opportunity of acknowledging that it had been in the
wrong. Only they vowed to yield nothing and to maintain, in spite
of everything, their terms, which were alone just.

The interview took place on Tuesday morning, when the settlement was sinking into desperate wretchedness. It was less cordial
than the first interview. Maheu was still the speaker, and he
explained that their mates had sent them to ask if these gentleman
had anything new to say. At first Monsieur Hennebeau affected
surprise: no order had reached him, nothing could be changed so
long as the miners persisted in their detestable rebellion; and this
official stiffness produced the worst effects, so that if the delegates
had gone out of their way to offer conciliation, the way in which
they were received would only have served to make them more
obstinate. Afterwards the manager tried to seek a basis of mutual
concession; thus, if the men would accept the separate payment for
timbering, the Company would raise that payment by the two
centimes which they were accused of profiting by. Besides, he added
that he would take the offer on himself, that nothing was settled,
but that he flattered himself he could obtain this concession from
Paris. But the delegates refused, and repeated their demands: the
retention of the old system, with a rise of five centimes a tram. Then
he acknowledged that he could treat with them at once, and urged
them to accept in the name of their wives and little ones dying of

hunger. And with eyes on the ground and stiff heads they said no, always no, with fierce vigour. They separated curtly. Monsieur Hennebeau banged the doors. Étienne, Maheu, and the others went off stamping with their great heels on the pavement in the mute rage of the vanquished pushed to extremes.

Towards two o'clock the women of the settlement, on their side approached Maigrat. There was only this hope left, to bend this man and to wrench from him another week's credit. The idea originated with la Maheude, who often counted too much on people's good nature. She persuaded la Brûlé and la Levaque to accompany her; as to la Pierronne, she excused herself, saying that she could not leave Pierron, whose illness still continued. Other women joined the group till they numbered a good twenty. When the inhabitants of Montsou saw them arrive, gloomy and wretched, occupying the whole width of the road, they shook their heads anxiously. Doors were closed, and one lady hid her silver plate. It was the first time they had been seen thus, and there could not be a worse sign: usually everything was going to ruin when the women thus took to the roads. At Maigrat's there was a violent scene. At first, he had made them go in, jeering and pretending to believe that they had come to pay their debts: that was nice of them to have agreed to come and bring the money all at once. Then, as soon as la Maheude began to speak he pretended to be enraged. Were they making fun? More credit! Then they wanted to turn him into the street? No, not a single potato, not a single crumb of bread! And he told them to be off to the grocer Verdonck, and to the bakers Carouble and Smelten, since they now dealt with them. The women listened with timid humility, apologizing, and watching his eyes to see if he would relent. He began to joke, offering his shop to la Brûlé if she would have him as a lover. They were all so cowardly that they laughed at this; and la Levaque improved on it, declaring that she was willing, she was. But he at once became abusive, and pushed them towards the door. As they insisted, suppliantly, he treated one brutally. The others on the pavement shouted that he had sold himself to the Company, while la Maheude, with her arms in the air, in a burst of avenging indignation, cried out for his death, exclaiming that such a men did not deserve to eat.

The return to the settlement was melancholy. When the women came back with empty hands, the men looked at them and then lowered their heads. There was nothing more to be done, the day would end without a spoonful of soup; and the other days extended in an icy shadow, without a ray of hope. They had made up their minds to it, and no one spoke of surrender. This excess of misery made them still more obstinate, mute as tracked beasts, resolved to die at the bottom of their hole rather than come out. Who would dare to be first to speak of submission? They had sworn with their mates to hold together, and hold together they would, as they held together at the pit when one of them was beneath a landslip. It was as it ought to be; it was a good school for resignation down there. They might well tighten their belts for a week, when they had been swallowing fire and water ever since they were twelve years of age; and their devotion was thus augmented by the pride of soldiers, of men proud of their profession, who in their daily struggle with death had gained a pride in sacrifice.

With the Maheus it was a terrible evening. They were all silent, seated before the dying fire in which the last cinders were smoking. After having emptied the mattresses, handful by handful, they had decided the day before to sell the clock for three francs; and the room seemed bare and dead now that the familiar tick-tack no longer filled it with sound. The only object of luxury now, in the middle of the sideboard, was the pink cardboard box, an old present from Maheu, which la Maheude treasured like a jewel. The two good chairs had gone; old Bonnemort and the children were squeezed together on an old mossy bench brought in from the garden. And the livid twilight now coming on seemed to increase the cold.

'What's to be done?' repeated la Maheude, crouching down in the corner by the oven.

Étienne stood up, looking at the portraits of the Emperor and Empress stuck against the wall. He would have torn them down long since if the family had not preserved them for ornament. So he murmured, with clenched teeth:

'And to think that we can't get two sous out of these damned idiots, who are watching us starve!'

'If I were to take the box?' said the woman, very pale, after some hesitation.

Maheu, seated on the edge of the table, with his legs dangling and his head on his chest, sat up.

'No! I won't have it!'

La Maheude painfully rose and walked round the room. Good God! was it possible that they were reduced to such misery? The cupboard without a crumb, nothing more to sell, no idea where to get a loaf! And the fire, which was nearly out! She became angry with Alzire, whom she had sent in the morning to glean on the pit-bank, and who had come back with empty hands, saying that the Company would not allow gleaning. Did it matter a hang what the Company wanted? As if they were robbing any one by picking up the bits of lost coal! The little girl, in despair, told how a man had threatened to hit her; then she promised to go back next day, even if she was beaten.

'And that little bugger, Jeanlin,' cried the mother; 'where is he now, I should like to know? He ought to have brought the salad; we can graze on that like beasts, at all events! You will see, he won't come back. Yesterday, too, he slept out. I don't know what he's up to; the rascal always looks as though his belly were full.'

'Perhaps,' said Étienne, 'he picks up sous on the road.'

She suddenly lifted both fists furiously.

'If I knew that! My children beg! I'd rather kill them and myself too.'

Maheu had again sunk down on the edge of the table. Lénore and Henri, astonished that they had nothing to eat, began to moan; while old Bonnemort, in silence, philosophically rolled his tongue in his mouth to deceive his hunger. No one spoke any more; all were becoming benumbed beneath this aggravation of their evils; the grandfather, coughing and spitting out the black phlegm, taken again by rheumatism which was turning to dropsy; the father asthmatic, and with knees swollen with water; the mother and the little ones scarred by scrofula and hereditary anaemia. No doubt their work made this inevitable; they only complained when the lack of food killed them off; and already they were falling like flies in the settlement. But something must be found for supper. My God! where was it to be found, what was to be done?

Then, in the twilight, which made the room more and more gloomy with its dark melancholy, Étienne, who had been hesitating for a moment, at last decided with aching heart.

'Wait for me,' he said. 'I'll go and see somewhere.'

And he went out. The idea of la Mouquette had occurred to him. She would certainly have a loaf, and would give it willingly. It annoyed him to be thus forced to return to Réquillart; this girl would kiss his hands with her air of an amorous servant; but one did not leave one's friends in trouble; he would still be kind with her if need be.

'I will go and look round, too,' said la Maheude, in her turn. 'It's too stupid.'

She reopened the door after the young man and closed it violently, leaving the others motionless and mute in the faint light of a candle-end which Alzire had just lighted. Outside she stopped and thought for a moment. Then she entered the Levaques' house.

'Now then: I lent you a loaf the other day. Could you give it me back?'

But she stopped herself. What she saw was far from encouraging; the house spoke of misery even more than her own.

La Levaque, with fixed eyes, was gazing into her burnt-out fire, while Levaque, made drunk on his empty stomach by some nail-makers, was sleeping on the table. With his back to the wall, Bouteloup was mechanically rubbing his shoulders with the amazement of a good-natured fellow who has eaten up his savings, and is astonished at having to tighten his belt.

'A loaf! ah! my dear,' replied la Levaque, 'I wanted to borrow another from you!'

Then, as her husband groaned with pain in his sleep, she pushed his face against the table.

'Hold your row, bloody beast! So much the better if it burns your guts! Instead of getting people to pay for your drinks, you ought to have asked twenty sous from a friend.'

She went on relieving herself by swearing, in the midst of this dirty household, already abandoned so long that an unbearable smell was exhaling from the floor. Everything might smash up, she didn't care a hang! Her son, that rascal Bébert, had also disappeared since morning, and she shouted that it would be a good riddance if he never came back. Then she said that she would go to bed. At least she could get warm. She hustled Bouteloup.

'Come along, up we go. The fire's out. No need to light the candle to see the empty plates. Well, are you coming, Louis? I tell you that we must go to bed. We can cuddle up together there, that's a comfort. And let this damned drunkard die here of cold by himself!'

When she found herself outside again, la Maheude struck resolutely across the gardens towards Pierron's house. She heard laughter. As she knocked there was sudden silence. It was a full minute before the door opened.

'What! is it you?' exclaimed la Pierronne with affected surprise. 'I thought it was the doctor.'

Without allowing her to speak, she went on, pointing to Pierron, who was seated before a large coal fire:

'Ah! he's not gletting any better, he's not getting any better at all. His face looks all right; it's in his belly that it takes him. Then he must have warmth. We burn all that we've got.'

Pierron, in fact, looked very well; his complexion was good and his flesh fat. It was in vain that he breathed hard in order to play the sick man. Besides, as la Maheude came in she perceived a strong smell of rabbit; they had certainly put the dish out of the way. There were crumbs strewed over the table, and in the very midst she saw a forgotten bottle of wine.

'Mother has gone to Montsou to try and get a loaf,' said Pierronne again. 'We are cooling our heels waiting for her.'

But her voice choked; she had followed her neighbour's glance, and her eyes also fell on the bottle. Immediately she began again, and narrated the story. Yes, it was wine; the Piolaine people had brought her that bottle for her man, who had been ordered by the doctor to take claret. And her thankfulness poured forth in a stream. What good people they were! The young lady especially; she was not proud, going into work-people's houses and distributing her charities herself.

'I see,' said la Maheude; 'I know them.'

Her heart ached at the idea that the good things always go to the least poor. It was always so, and these Piolaine people had carried water to the river. Why had she not seen them in the settlement? Perhaps, all the same, she might have got something out of them.

'I came,' she confessed at last, 'to know if there was more going with you than with us. Have you just a little vermicelli by way of loan?'

Pierronne expressed her grief noisily.

'Nothing at all, my dear. Not what you can call a grain of semolina. If mother hasn't come back, it's because she hasn't succeeded. We must go to bed supperless.'

At this moment crying was heard from the cellar, and she grew angry and struck her fist against the door. It was that gadabout Lydie, whom she had shut up, she said, to punish her for not having returned until five o'clock, after having been roaming about the whole day. You could no longer keep her in order; she was constantly disappearing.

La Maheude, however, remained standing; she could not make up her mind to leave. This large fire filled her with a painful sensation of comfort; the thought that they were eating there enlarged the void in her stomach. Evidently they had sent away the old woman and shut up the child, to feast themselves with their rabbit. Ah! whatever people might say, when a woman behaved ill, that brought luck to her house.

'Goodnight,' she said, suddenly.

Outside night had come on, and the moon behind the clouds was lighting up the earth with a dubious glow. Instead of crossing the gardens again, la Maheude went round, despairing, afraid to go home again. But along the dead frontages all the doors smelled of famine and sounded hollow. What was the good of knocking? There was wretchedness everywhere. For weeks since they had had nothing to eat. Even the odour of onion had gone, that strong odour which revealed the settlement from afar across the country; now there was nothing but the smell of old vaults, the dampness of holes in which nothing lives. Vague sounds were dying out, stifled tears, faded oaths; and in the silence which slowly grew heavier you could hear the sleep of hunger coming on, the collapse of bodies thrown across beds in the nightmare of empty bellies.

As she passed before the church she saw a shadow slip rapidly by. A gleam of hope made her hasten, for she had recognized the Montsou priest, Abbé Joire, who said mass on Sundays at the settlement chapel. No doubt he had just come out of the sacristy, where he had been called to settle some affair. With rounded back he moved quickly on, a fat meek man, anxious to live at peace with everybody. If he had come at night it must have been in order not to compromise himself among the miners. It was said, too, that he had just obtained promotion. He had even been seen walking about with his successor, a lean man, with eyes like live coals.

'Sir, sir!' stammered la Maheude.

But he would not stop.

'Good night, good night, my good woman.'

No one had stirred. Maheu still sat dejected on the edge of the table. Old Bonnemort and the little ones were huddled together on the bench for the sake of warmth. And they had not said a word, and the candle had burnt so low that even light would soon fail them. At the sound of the door the children turned their heads; but seeing that their mother brought nothing back, they looked down on the ground again, repressing the longing to cry, for fear of being scolded. La Maheude fell back into her place near the dying fire. They asked her no questions, and the silence continued. All had understood, and they thought it useless to weary themselves more by talking; they were now waiting, despairing and without courage, in the last expectation that perhaps Étienne would find help somewhere. The minutes went by, and at last they no longer reckoned on this.

When Étienne reappeared, he held a cloth containing a dozen potatoes, cooked but cold.

'That's all I've found,' he said.

With la Mouquette also bread was wanting; it was her dinner which she had forced him to take in this cloth, kissing him with all her heart.

'Thanks,' he said to la Maheude, who offered him his share; 'I've eaten over there.'

It was not true, and he gloomily watched the children throw themselves on the food. The father and mother also restrained themselves, in order to leave more; but the old man greedily swallowed everything. They had to take a potato away from him for Alzire.

Then Étienne said that he had heard news. The Company, irritated by the obstinacy of the strikers, talked of giving back their certificates to the compromised miners. Certainly, the Company was for war. And a more serious rumour circulated: they boasted of having persuaded a large number of men to go down again. On the next day the Victoire and Feutry-Cantel would be complete; even at Madeleine and Mirou there would be a third of the men. The Maheus were furious.

'By God!' shouted the father, 'if there are traitors, we must settle their account.'

And standing up, yielding to the fury of his suffering:

'Tomorrow evening, to the forest! Since they won't let us come to an understanding at the Bon-Joyeux, we can be at home in the forest!'

This cry had aroused old Bonnemort, who had grown drowsy after his gluttony. It was the old rallying-cry, the meeting place where the miners of old days used to plot their resistance to the king's soldiers.

'Yes, yes, to Vandame! I'm with you if you go there!'

La Maheude made an energetic gesture.

'We will all go. That will finish these injustices and treacheries.'

Étienne decided that the rendezvous should be announced to all the settlements for the following evening. But the fire was dead, as with the Levaques, and the candle suddenly went out. There was no more coal and no more oil; they had to feel their way to bed in the intense cold which contracted the skin. The little ones were crying.

CHAPTER 6

Jeanlin was now well and able to walk; but his legs had set so badly that he limped on both the right and left sides, and moved with the gait of a duck, though running as fast as formerly with the skill of a mischievous and thieving animal.

One evening, at dusk, on the Réquillart road, Jeanlin, accompanied by his inseparable friends, Bébert and Lydie, was on the watch. He had taken ambush in a vacant space, behind a paling opposite an obscure grocery shop, situated at the corner of a lane. An old woman who was nearly blind displayed there three or four sacks of lentils and beans, black with dust; and it was an ancient dried codfish, hanging by the door and stained with fly-blows, to which his eyes were directed. Twice already he had sent Bébert to unhook it. But each time someone had appeared at the bend in the road. Always intruders in the way, you could not attend to your affairs.

A gentleman went by on horseback, and the children flattened themselves at the bottom of the paling, for they recognized Monsieur Hennebeau. Since the strike he was often thus seen along the roads, riding alone amid the rebellious settlements, ascertaining, with quiet courage, the lie of the land. And never had a stone whistled by his ears; he only met men who were silent and slow to greet him; most often he came upon lovers, who cared nothing for politics and took their fill of pleasure in nooks and corners. He passed by on his trotting mare with head directed straight forward, so as to disturb nobody, while his heart was swelling with an unappeased desire amid this orgy of free love. He distinctly saw these small rascals, the little boys on the little girl in a heap. Even the youngsters were already amusing themselves in their misery! His eyes grew moist, and he disappeared, sitting stiffly on his saddle, with his frock-coat buttoned up in a military manner.

'Damned luck!' said Jeanlin. 'This will never finish. Go on, Bébert! Pull it by the tail!'

But once more two men appeared, and the child again stifled an oath when he heard the voice of his brother Zacharie narrating to Mouquet how he had discovered a two-franc piece sewn into one of his wife's petticoats. They both grinned with satisfaction, slapping each other on the shoulder. Mouquet proposed a game of

crosse for the next day; they would leave the Avantage at two
o'clock, and go to the Montoire side, near Marchiennes. Zacharie
agreed. What was the good of bothering over the strike? might as
well amuse oneself, since there's nothing to do. And they turned the
corner of the road, when Étienne, who was coming along the canal,
stopped them and began to talk.

'Are they going to bed here?' said Jeanlin, in exasperation.
'Nearly night; the old woman will be taking in her sacks.'

Another miner came down towards Réquillart. Étienne went off
with him, and as they passed the paling the child heard them speak
of the forest; they had been forced to put off the rally to the
following day, for fear of not being able to announce it in one day
to all the settlements.

'I say, there,' he whispered to his two mates, 'the big affair is for
tomorrow. We'll go, eh? We can get off in the afternoon.'

And the road being at last free, he sent Bébert off.

'Go on! pull it by the tail. And look out! the old woman's got her
broom.'

Fortunately the night had grown dark. Bébert, with a leap, hung
on to the cod so that the string broke. He ran away, waving it like
a kite, followed by the two others, all three galloping. The woman
came out of her shop in astonishment, without understanding or
being able to distinguish the gang now lost in the darkness.

These young rascals had become the terror of the country. They
gradually spread themselves over it like a horde of savages. At first
they had been satisfied with the yard at the Voreux, tumbling into
the stock of coal, from which they would emerge looking like
negroes, playing at hide-and-seek amid the supply of wood, in
which they lost themselves as in the depths of a virgin forest. Then
they had taken the pit-bank by assault; they would seat themselves
on it and slide down the bare portions still boiling with interior
fires; they glided among the briers in the older parts, hiding for the
whole day, occupied in the quiet little games of mischievous mice.
And they were constantly enlarging their conquests, scuffling among
the piles of bricks until they drew blood, running about the fields
and eating without bread all sorts of milky herbs, searching the
banks of the canals to take fish from the mud and swallow them
raw; and pushing still farther, they travelled for kilometres as far as
the thickets of Vandame, under which they gorged themselves with
strawberries in the spring, with nuts and bilberries in summer. Soon
the immense plain belonged to them.

What drove them thus from Montsou to Marchiennes, constantly on the roads with the eyes of young wolves, was a growing love of plunder. Jeanlin remained the captain of these expeditions, leading the troop on to all sorts of prey, ravaging the onion fields, pillaging the orchards, attacking shop windows. In the country, people accused the miners on strike, and talked of a vast organized gang. One day, even, he had forced Lydie to steal from her mother, and made her bring him two dozen sticks of barley-sugar, which la Pierronne kept in a bottle on one of the boards in her window; and the little girl, who was well beaten, had not betrayed him because she trembled so before his authority. The worst was that he always gave himself the lion's share. Bébert also had to bring him the booty, happy if the captain did not hit him and keep it all.

For some time Jeanlin had abused his authority. He would beat Lydie as one beats one's lawful wife, and he profited by Bébert's credulity to send him on unpleasant adventures, amused at making a fool of this big boy, who was stronger than himself, and could have knocked him over with a blow of his fist. He felt contempt for both of them and treated them as slaves, telling them that he had a princess for his mistress and that they were unworthy to appear before her. And, in fact, during the past week he would suddenly disappear at the end of a road or a turning in a path, no matter where it might be, after having ordered them with a terrible air to go back to the settlement. But first he would pocket the booty.

This was what happened on the present occasion.

'Give it up,' he said, snatching the cod from his mate's hands when they stopped, all three, at a bend in the road near Réquillart.

Bébert protested.

'I want some, you know. I took it.'

'Eh! what!' he cried. 'You'll have some if I give you some. Not tonight, sure enough; tomorrow, if there's any left.'

He pushed Lydie, and placed both of them in line like soldiers shouldering arms. Then, passing behind them:

'Now, you must stay there five minutes without turning round. By God! if you do turn round, there will be beasts that will eat you up. And then you will go straight back, and if Bébert touches Lydie on the way, I shall know it and I shall hit you.'

Then he disappeared in the shadow, so lightly that the sound of his naked feet could not be heard. The two children remained motionless for the five minutes without looking round, for fear of receiving a blow from the invisible creature. Slowly a great affection had grown up between them in their common terror. He was always thinking of taking her and pressing her very tight between his arms, as he had seen others do; and she, too, would have liked it, for it would have been a change for her to be so nicely caressed. But neither of them would have allowed themselves to disobey. When they went away, although the night was very dark, they did not even kiss each other; they walked side by side, tender and despairing, certain that if they touched one another the captain would strike them from behind.

Étienne, at the same hour, had entered Réquillart. The evening before, la Mouquette had begged him to return, and he returned, ashamed, feeling an inclination which he refused to acknowledge, for this girl who worshipped him like a saint. It was, besides, with the intention of breaking it off. He would see her; he would explain to her that she ought no longer to pursue him, on account of the mates. It was not a time for pleasure; it was dishonest to amuse oneself thus when people were dying of hunger. And not having found her at home, he had decided to wait and watch the shadows of the passers-by.

Beneath the ruined steeple the old shaft opened, half blocked up. Above the black hole a beam stood erect, and with a fragment of roof at the top it had the profile of a gallows; in the broken kerbstones stood two trees – a mountain ash and a plane – which seemed to grow from the depths of the earth. It was a corner of abandoned wildness, the grassy and fibrous entry of a gulf, cluttered with old wood, planted with hawthorns and sloe-trees, which were peopled in the spring by warblers in their nests. Wishing to avoid the great expense of keeping it up, the Company, for the last ten years, had proposed to fill up this dead pit; but they were waiting to install an air-shaft in the Voreux, for the ventilation furnace of the two pits, which communicated, was placed at the foot of Réquillart, of which the former winding-shaft served as a conduit. They were content to consolidate the tubbing by beams placed across, preventing extraction, and they had neglected the upper galleries to watch only over the lower gallery, in which blazed the furnace, the enormous coal fire, with so powerful a draught that the rush of air produced the wind of a tempest from one end to the other of the neighbouring mine. As a precaution, in order that they could still go up and down, the order had been given to furnish the shaft with ladders; only, as no one took charge of them, the ladders were rotting with dampness, and in some places had already given way. Above, a large brier stopped the entry of the passage, and, as the first ladder had lost some rungs, it was necessary, in order to reach it, to hang on to a root of the mountain ash, and then to take one's chance and drop into the blackness.

Étienne was waiting patiently, hidden behind a bush, when he heard a long rustling among the branches. He thought at first that it was the scared flight of a snake. But the sudden gleam of a match astonished him, and he was stupefied on recognizing Jeanlin, who was lighting a candle and burying himself in the earth. He was seized with curiosity, and approached the hole; the child had disappeared, and a faint gleam came from the second ladder. Étienne hesitated a moment, and then let himself go, holding on to the roots. He thought for a moment that he was about to fall down the whole five hundred and eighty metres of the mine, but at last he felt a rung, and descended gently. Jeanlin had evidently heard nothing. Étienne constantly saw the light sinking beneath him, while the little one's shadow, colossal and disturbing, danced with the deformed gait of his distorted limbs. He kicked his legs about with the skill of a monkey, catching on with hands, feet, or chin where the rungs were missing. Ladders, seven metres in length, followed one another, some still firm, others shaky, yielding and almost broken; the steps were narrow and green, so rotten that it was like walking in moss; and as you went down the heat grew suffocating, the heat of an oven proceeding from the air-shaft which was, fortunately, not very active now the strike was on, for when the furnace devoured its five thousand kilograms of coal a day, you could not have risked yourself there without scorching your hair.

'What a damned little toad!' exclaimed Étienne in a stifled voice; 'where the devil is he going to?'

Twice he had nearly fallen. His feet slid on the damp wood. If he had only had a candle like the child! but he struck himself every minute; he was only guided by the vague gleam that fled beneath him. He had already reached the twentieth ladder, and the descent still continued. Then he counted them: twenty-one, twenty-two, twenty-three, and he still went down and down. His head seemed to be swelling with the heat, and he thought that he was falling into a furnace. At last he reached a landing-place, and he saw the candle going off along a gallery. Thirty ladders, that made about two hundred and ten metres.

'Is he going to drag me about long?' he thought. 'He must be going to hide out in the stable.'

But on the left, the path which led to the stable was closed by a landslip. The journey began again, now more painful and more dangerous. Frightened bats flew about and clung to the roof of the gallery. He had to hasten so as not to lose sight of the light; only where the child passed with ease, with the suppleness of a snake, he could not glide through without bruising his limbs. This gallery, like all the older passages, was narrow, and grew narrower every day from the constant fall of soil; at certain places it was a mere tube which would eventually disappear. In this stifling passage the torn and broken wood became a peril, threatening to saw into his flesh, or to run him through with the points of splinters, sharp as swords. He could only advance with precaution, on his knees or belly, feeling in the darkness before him. Suddenly a band of rats stamped over him, running from his neck to his feet in their galloping flight.

'Blast it all! haven't we got to the end yet?' he grumbled with aching back and out of breath.

They were there. At the end of a kilometre the passageway widened out, they reached a part of the gallery which was admirably preserved. It was the end of the old haulage passage cut across the bed like a natural grotto. He was forced to stop, he saw the child afar, placing his candle between two stones, and putting himself at ease with the quiet and relieved air of a man who is glad to be at home again. This gallery-end was completely changed into a comfortable dwelling. In a corner on the ground a pile of hay made a soft couch; on some old planks, placed like a table, there were bread, potatoes, and bottles of gin already opened; it was a real smuggler's cave, with booty piled up for weeks, even useless booty like soap and blacking, stolen for the pleasure of stealing. And the child, quite alone in the midst of this plunder, was enjoying it like a selfish brigand.

'Is this, then, how you treat people?' cried Étienne, when he had breathed for a moment. 'You come and gorge yourself here, when we are dying of hunger up above?'

Jeanlin, astounded, was trembling. But recognizing the young man, he quickly grew calm.

'Will you come and dine with me?' he said at last. 'Eh? a bit of grilled cod? You shall see.'

He had not let go of his cod, and he began to scrape off the fly-blows properly with a fine new knife, one of those little dagger knives, with bone handles, on which mottoes are inscribed. This one simply bore the word 'Amour'.

'You have a fine knife,' remarked Étienne.

'It's a present from Lydie,' replied Jeanlin, who neglected to add

that Lydie had stolen it, by his orders, from a street vendor at
Montsou, stationed in front of the Tête-Coupée Bar.

Then, as he still scraped, he added proudly:

'Isn't it comfortable in my house? It's a bit warmer than up
above, and it feels a lot better!'

Étienne had seated himself, and was amused in making him talk.
He was no longer angry, he felt interested in this debauched child,
who was so brave and so industrious in his vices. And, in fact, he
enjoyed a certain comfort in the bottom of this hole; the heat was
not too great, an even temperature remained here at all seasons, the
warmth of a bath, while the rough December wind was chapping
the skins of the miserable people up above. As they grew old, the
galleries became purified from noxious gases, all the fire-damp had
gone, and you could only smell now the odour of old rotten wood,
a subtle ethereal odour, as if sharpened with a dash of cloves. This
wood, besides, had become curious to look at, with a yellowish
pallor of marble, fringed with whitish thread lace, flaky growths
which seemed to drape it with an embroidery of silk and pearls. In
other places the timber was bristling with fungus. And there were
flights of white moths, snowy flies and spiders, a colourless population for ever ignorant of the sun.

'Then you're not afraid?' asked Étienne.

Jeanlin looked at him in astonishment.

'Afraid of what? I am quite alone.'

But the cod was at last scraped. He lighted a little fire of wood,
brought out the pan, and grilled it. Then he cut a loaf into two. It
was a terribly salt feast, but exquisite all the same for strong
stomachs.

Étienne had accepted his share.

'I am not surprised you get fat, while we are all growing lean. Do
you know that it is a dirty trick to stuff yourself like this? And the
others? you don't think of them!'

'Oh! why are the others such fools?'

'Well, you're right to hide yourself, for if your father knew you
stole he would sort you out.'

'What! when the bourgeois are stealing from us! It's you who are
always saying so. If I nabbed this loaf at Maigrat's you may be
pretty sure it's a loaf he owed us.'

The young man was silent, with his mouth full, and felt troubled.
He looked at him, with his muzzle, his green eyes, his large ears, a
degenerate throw-back, with an obscure intelligence and savage

cunning, slowly slipping back into the animality of old. The mine which had fashioned him had just finished him by breaking his legs.

'And Lydie?' asked Étienne again; 'do you bring her here sometimes?'

Jeanlin laughed contemptuously.

'The little one? Ah, no, not I; women blab.'

And he went on laughing, filled with immense disdain for Lydie and Bébert. Who had ever seen such boobies? To think that they swallowed all his humbug, and went away with empty hands while he ate the cod in this warm place, tickled his sides with amusement. Then he concluded, with the gravity of a little philosopher:

'Much better to be alone, then there's no falling out.'

Étienne had finished his bread. He drank a gulp of the gin. For a moment he asked himself if he ought not to show ingratitude for Jeanlin's hospitality by bringing him up to daylight by the ear, and forbidding him to plunder any more by the threat of telling everything to his father. But as he examined this deep retreat, an idea occurred to him. Who knows if there might not be need for it, either for mates or for himself, in case things should come to the worst up above! He made the child swear not to sleep out, as had sometimes happened when he forgot himself in his hay, and taking a candle-end, he went away first, leaving him quietly to pursue his domestic affairs.

La Mouquette, seated on a beam in spite of the great cold, had grown desperate in waiting for him. When she saw him she threw her arms around his neck; and it was as though he had plunged a knife into her heart when he said that he wished to see her no more. Good God! why? Did she not love him enough? Fearing to yield to the desire to enter with her, he drew her towards the road, and explained to her as gently as possible that she was compromising him in the eyes of his mates, that she was compromising the political cause. She was astonished; what had that got to do with politics? At last the thought occurred to her that he was ashamed at being seen with her. She was not offended, however; it was quite natural, and she suggested that he should rebuff her in front of people, so as to seem to have broken with her. But he would see her just once sometimes. In a terrible state she implored him; she swore to keep out of sight; she would not keep him five minutes. He was touched, but still refused. It was necessary. Then, as he left her, he wished at least to kiss her. They had gradually reached the first houses of Montsou, and were standing with their arms round one another beneath a large round moon, when a woman passed near them with a sudden start, as though she had knocked against a stone.

'Who is that?' asked Étienne, anxiously.

'It's Catherine,' replied la Mouquette. 'She's coming back from Jean-Bart.'

The woman now was going away, with lowered head and feeble limbs, looking very tired. And the young man gazed at her, in despair at having been seen by her, his heart aching with an unreasonable remorse. Had she not been with a man? Had she not made him suffer with the same suffering here, on this Réquillart road, when she had given herself to that man? But, all the same, he was grieved to have done the same to her.

'Shall I tell you what it is?' whispered la Mouquette, in tears, as she left him. 'If you don't want me it's because you want someone else.'

On the next day the weather was superb; it was one of those clear frosty days, the beautiful winter days when the hard earth rings like crystal beneath one's feet. Jeanlin had gone off at one o'clock, but he had to wait for Bébert behind the church, and they nearly set out without Lydie, whose mother had again shut her up in the cellar, and only now liberated her to put a basket on her arm, telling her that if she did not bring it back full of dandelions she should be shut up with the rats all night long. She was frightened, therefore, and wished to go at once for salad. Jeanlin dissuaded her; they would see later on. For a long time Pologne, Rasseneur's big rabbit, had attracted his attention. He was passing in front of the Avantage when, just then, the rabbit came out on to the road. With a leap he seized her by the ears, stuffed her into the little girl's basket, and all three rushed away. They would amuse themselves a lot by making her run like a dog as far as the forest.

But they stopped to gaze at Zacharie and Mouquet, who, after having drunk a glass with two other mates, had begun their big game of crosse. The stake was a new cap and a red handkerchief, deposited with Rasseneur. The four players, two against two, were bidding for the first turn from the Voreux to the Paillot farm, nearly three kilometres; and it was Zacharie who won, with seven strokes, while Mouquet required eight. They had placed the ball, the little boxwood egg, on the pavement with one end up. Each was holding his crosse, the mallet with its bent iron, long handle, and tight-strung network. Two o'clock struck as they set out. Zacharie, in a masterly manner, at his first stroke, composed of a series of three, sent the ball more than four hundred yards across the beetroot fields; for it was forbidden to play in the villages and on the streets, where people might be killed. Mouquet, who was also a good player, sent off the ball with so vigorous an shot that his single stroke brought the ball a hundred and fifty metres behind. And the game went on, backwards and forwards, always running, their feet bruised by the frozen ridges of the ploughed fields.

At first Jeanlin, Bébert, and Lydie had trotted behind the players, delighted by their vigorous strokes. Then they remembered Polagne, whom they were shaking up in the basket; and, leaving the game in the open country, they took out the rabbit, inquisitive to see how fast she could run. She went off, and they fled after her; it was a chase lasting an hour at full speed, with constant turns, with shouts to frighten her, and arms opened and closed on thin air. If she had not been at the beginning of pregnancy they would never have caught her again.

As they were panting the sound of oaths made them turn their heads. They had just come upon the crosse party again, and Zacharie had nearly split open his brother's skull. The players were now at their fourth turn. From the Paillot farm they had gone off to the Quatre-Chemins, then from the Quatre-Chemins to Montoire; and now they were going in six strokes from Montoire to Prè-des-Vaches. That made two leagues and a half in an hour; and, besides, they had had drinks at the Vincent and at the Trois-Sages Bar. Mouquet this time was ahead. He had two more strokes to play, and his victory was certain, when Zacharie, grinning as he availed himself of his privilege, played with so much skill that the ball rolled into a deep pit. Mouquet's partner could not get it out; it was a disaster. All four shouted; the party was excited, for they were neck to neck; they had to begin again. From the Prè-des-Vaches it was not two kilometres to the point of Herbes-Rousses, in five strokes. There they would refresh themselves at Lerenard's.

But Jeanlin had an idea. He let them go on, and pulled out of his pocket a piece of string which he tied to one of Polagne's legs, the left hind leg. And it was very amusing. The rabbit ran before the three young rascals, waddling along in such an extraordinary manner that they had never laughed so much before. Afterwards they fastened it round her neck, and let her run off; and, as she grew tired, they dragged her on her belly or on her back, just like a little carriage. That lasted for more than an hour. She was moaning when they quickly put her back into the basket, near the wood at Cruchot, on hearing the players whose game they had once more come across.

Zacharie, Mouquet, and the two others were covering the kilometres, with no other rest than the time for a drink at all the inns
which they had fixed on as their goals. From the Herbes-Rousses
they had gone on to Buchy, then to Croix-de-Pierre, then to
Chamblay. The earth rang beneath the helter-skelter of their feet,
rushing untiringly after the ball, which bounded over the ice; the
weather was good, they did not fall in, they only ran the risk of
breaking their legs. In the dry air the great crosse strokes exploded
like firearms. Their muscular hands grasped the strung handle; their
entire bodies were bent forward, as though to slay an ox. And this
went on for hours, from one end of the plain to the other, over
ditches and hedges and the slopes of the road, the low walls of the
enclosures. You needed to have good bellows in your chest and iron
hinges in your knees. The pikemen thus rubbed off the rust of the
mine with impassioned zeal. There were some so enthusiastic at
twenty-five that they could do ten leagues. At forty they played no
more; they were too heavy.

Five o'clock struck; twilight was already coming on. One more
turn to the Forest of Vandame, to decide who had won the cap and
the handkerchief. And Zacharie joked with his ironic indifference
to politics; it would be fine to tumble down over there in the midst
of the mates. As to Jeanlin, ever since leaving the settlement he had
been making for the forest, though apparently only scouring the
fields. With an indignant gesture he threatened Lydie, who was full
of remorse and fear, and talked of going back to the Voreux to
gather dandelions. Were they going to miss the meeting? he wanted
to know what the old people would say. He pushed Bébert, and
wanted to enliven the end of the journey as far as the trees by
detaching Pologne and pursuing her with stones. His real idea was
to kill her; he wanted to take her off and eat her at the bottom of
his hole at Réquillart. The rabbit ran ahead, with nose in the air
and ears back; a stone grazed her back, another cut her tail, and, in
spite of the growing darkness, she would have been done for it the
young rogues had not noticed Étienne and Maheu standing in the
middle of a glade. They threw themselves on the animal in desper-
ation, and put her back in the basket. Almost at the same minute
Zacharie, Mouquet, and the two others, with their last stroke at
crosse, drove the ball within a few metres of the glade. They all
came into the midst of the meeting.

Through the whole country, by the roads and pathways of the
flat plain, ever since twilight, there had been a long procession, a
rustling of silent shadows, moving separately or in groups towards

the violet thickets of the forest. Every settlement was emptied, the women and children themselves set out as if for a walk beneath the great clear sky. Now the roads were growing dark; this walking crowd, all gliding towards the same goal, could no longer be clearly seen. But one felt it, the confused tramping moved by one soul. Between the hedges, among the bushes, there was only a light rustling, a vague rumour of the voices of the night.

Monsieur Hennebeau, who was at this hour returning home mounted on his mare, listened to these vague sounds. He had met couples, long rows of strollers, on this beautiful winter night. More lovers, who were going to take their pleasure, mouth to mouth, behind the walls. Was it not what he always met, girls tumbled over at the bottom of every ditch, beggars who crammed themselves with the only joy that cost nothing? And these fools complained of life, when they could take their supreme fill of this happiness of love! Willingly would he have starved as they did if he could begin life again with a woman who would give herself to him on a heap of stones, with all her strength and all her heart. His misfortune was without consolation, and he envied these wretches. With lowered head he went back, riding his horse at a slackened pace, rendered desperate by these long sounds, lost in the depth of the black country, in which he heard only kisses.

CHAPTER 7

The Plan-des-Dames was a vast glade just opened up by the felling of trees. It spread out in a gentle slope, surrounded by tall thickets and superb beeches with straight regular trunks, which formed a white colonnade patched with green lichens; fallen giants were also lying in the grass, while on the left a mass of logs formed a geometrical cube. The cold was sharpening with the twilight and the frozen moss crackled underfoot. There was black darkness on the earth while the tall branches showed against the pale sky, where a full moon coming above the horizon would soon extinguish the stars.

Nearly three thousand colliers had come to the meeting, a swarming crowd of men, women, and children, gradually filling the glade and spreading out afar beneath the trees. Late arrivals were still coming up, a flood of heads drowned in shadow and stretching as far as the neighbouring copses. A rumbling arose from them, like a storm, in this motionless and frozen forest.

At the top, dominating the slope, Étienne stood with Rasseneur and Maheu. A quarrel had broken out, you could hear their voices in sudden bursts. Near them some men were listening: Levaque, with clenched fists; Pierron, turning his back and much annoyed that he had no longer been able to feign a fever. There were also old Bonnemort and old Mouque, seated side by side on a stump, lost in deep meditation. Then behind were the scoffers, Zacharie, Mouquet, and others who had come to make fun of the thing; while gathered together in a very different spirit the women in a group were as serious as if at church. La Maheude silently shook her head at Levaque's muttered oaths. Philomène was coughing, her bronchitis having come back with the winter. Only la Mouquette was showing her teeth with laughter, amused at the way in which old Mother Brûlé was abusing her daughter, an unnatural creature who had sent her away so that she might gorge herself with rabbit, a creature who had sold herself and who grew fat on her man's baseness. And Jeanlin had planted himself on the pile of wood, hoisting up Lydie and making Bébert follow him, all three higher up in the air than anyone else.

The quarrel was caused by Rasseneur, who wished to proceed formally to the election of officers. He was enraged by his defeat at the Bon-Joyeux, and had sworn to have his revenge, for he flattered himself that he could regain his old authority when he was once face to face, not with the delegates, but with the miners themselves. Étienne was disgusted, and thought the idea of officers was ridiculous in this forest. They ought to act in a revolutionary fashion, like savages, since they were being tracked like wolves.

As the dispute threatened to drag on, he took possession of the crowd at once by jumping on to the trunk of a tree and shouting:

'Comrades! comrades!'

The confused roar of the crowd died down into a long sigh, while Maheu stifled Rasseneur's protestations. Étienne went on in a loud voice:

'Comrades, since they forbid us to speak, since they send the police after us as if we were robbers, we have come to talk here! Here we are free, we are at home. No one can silence us any more than they can silence the birds and beasts!'

A thunder of cries and exclamations responded to him.

'Yes, yes! the forest is ours, we can talk here. Go on.'

Then Étienne stood for a moment motionless on the tree-trunk. The moon, still beneath the horizon, only lit up the topmost branches, and the crowd, remaining in the darkness, gradually grew calm and silent. He, also in darkness, stood above them all at the top of the slope like a block of shadow.

He raised his arm with a slow movement and began. But his voice was not fierce; he spoke in the cold tones of a simple envoy of the people, who was presenting his account. He was delivering the speech which the commissioner of police had cut short at the Bon-Joyeux; and he began by a rapid history of the strike, affecting a certain scientific eloquence – facts, nothing but facts. At first he spoke of his dislike of the strike; the miners had not wished it, it was the management which had provoked it with the new timbering tariff. Then he recalled the first step taken by the delegates in going to the manager, the bad faith of the directors; and, later on, the second step, the tardy concession, the two centimes given up, after the attempt to rob them. Now he showed by figures the exhaustion of the provident fund, and pointed out the use that had been made of the help sent, briefly excusing the International, Pluchart and the others, for not being able to do more for them in the midst of the cares of their conquest of the world. So the situation was getting worse every day; the Company was giving back certificates and threatening to hire men from Belgium; besides, it was intimidating the weak, and had forced a certain number of miners to go down again. He preserved his monotonous voice, as if to insist on the bad news; he said that hunger was victorious, that hope was dead, and that the struggle had reached the last feverish efforts of courage. And then he suddenly concluded, without raising his voice:

'It is in these circumstances, mates, that you have to take a decision to-night. Do you want the strike to go on? and if so, what do you expect to do to beat the Company?'

A deep silence fell from the starry sky. The crowd, which could not be seen, was silent in the night beneath these words which choked every heart, and a sigh of despair could be heard through the trees.

But Étienne was already continuing, with a change in his voice. It was no longer the secretary of the association who was speaking; it was the leader of a multitude, the apostle who was bringing truth. Could it be that any were cowardly enough to go back on their word? What! They were to suffer in vain for a month, and then to go back to the pits, with lowered heads, so that the everlasting wretchedness might begin over again! Would it not be better to die at once in the effort to destroy the tyranny of capital, which was starving the worker? Always to submit to hunger up to the moment when hunger will again throw the calmest into revolt, was it not a foolish game which could not go on for ever? And he pointed to the exploited miners, bearing alone the disasters of every crisis, forced to go without food as soon as the necessities of competition lowered net prices. No, the timbering tariff could not be accepted; it was only a disguised effort to economize on the Company's part; they wanted to rob every man of an hour's work a day. It was too much this time; the day was coming when the miserable, pushed to extremity, would bring about justice.

He stood with his arms in the air. At the word 'justice' the crowd, shaken by a longer shudder, broke out into applause which rolled along with the sound of dry leaves. Voices cried:

'Justice! it is time! Justice!'

Gradually Étienne warmed up. He had not Rasseneur's easy flowing abundance. Words often failed him, he had to force his phrases, bringing them out with an effort which he emphasized by a movement of his shoulders. Only in these continual shocks he came upon familiar images which seized his audience by their energy; while his workman's gestures, his elbows in and then extended, with his fists thrust out, his jaw suddenly advanced as if to bite, had also an extraordinary effect on his mates. They all said that even if he was not very big he made himself heard.

'The wage system is a new form of slavery,' he began again, in a more sonorous voice. 'The mine ought to belong to the miner, as the sea belongs to the fisherman, and the earth to the peasant. Do you see? The mine belongs to you, to all of you who, for a century, have paid for it with so much blood and misery!'

He boldly entered on obscure questions of law, and lost himself in the difficulties of the special regulations concerning mines. The subsoil, like the soil, belonged to the nation: only an odious privilege gave the monopoly of it to the Companies; all the more since, at Montsou, the pretended legality of the concession was complicated by treaties formerly made with the owners of the old fiefs, according to the ancient custom of Hainault. The miners, then, had only to reconquer their property; and with extended hands he indicated the whole country beyond the forest. At this moment the moon, which had risen above the horizon, lit him up as it glided from behind the high branches. When the crowd, which was still in shadow, saw him thus, white with light, distributing fortune with his open hands, they applauded anew by prolonged clapping.

'Yes, yes, he's right. Bravo!'

Then Étienne trotted out his favourite subject, the assumption of the instruments of production by the collectivity, as he kept on saying in a phrase the pedantry of which greatly pleased him. At the present time his evolution was completed. Having set out with the sentimental fraternity of the novice and the need for reforming the wage system, he had reached the political idea of its suppression. Since the meeting at the Bon-Joyeux his collectivism, still humani-n and without formula, had stiffened into a complicated gramme which he discussed scientifically, article by article. First, ffirmed that freedom could only be obtained by the destruction he State. Then, when the people had obtained possession of the ernment, reforms would begin: return to the primitive com-ne, substitution of an equal and free family for the moral and ressive family; absolute equality, civil, political, and economic; ividual independence guaranteed, thanks to the possession of the egral product of the instruments of work; finally, free vocational acation, paid for by the collectivity. This led to the total recon-uction of the old rotten society; he attacked marriage, the right bequest, he regulated everyone's fortune, he threw down the quitous monument of the dead centuries with a great movement his arm, always the same movement, the movement of the reaper ho is cutting down a ripe harvest. And then with the other hand reconstructed; he built up the future humanity, the edifice of uth and justice rising in the dawn of the twentieth century. In this ate of mental tension reason was faltering, and only the sectarian's xed idea was left. The scruples of sensitivity and of good sense were lost; nothing seemed easier than the realization of this new world. He had foreseen everything; he spoke of it as of a machine which he could put together in two hours, and he would not stop short at neither fire nor blood.*

'Our turn is come,' he cried out in a final flourish. 'Now it is for us to have power and wealth!'

The cheering rolled up to him from the depths of the forest. The moon now whitened the whole of the glade, and cut into living waves the sea of heads, as far as the dimly visible copses in the distance between the great grey trunks. And in the icy air there was fury in the faces, in the gleaming eyes, in the open mouths, the passion of famishing men, women, and children, let loose on the just pillage of the ancient wealth they had been deprived of. They no longer felt the cold, these burning words had warmed them to the bone. Religious exaltation raised them from the earth, a fever

of hope like that of the Christians of the early Church awaiting the
near coming of justice. Many obscure phrases had escaped them,
they could not properly understand this technical and abstract
reasoning; but the very obscurity and abstraction still further
enlarged the field of promises and lifted them into a dazzling region.
What a dream! to be masters, to suffer no more, to enjoy pleasures
at last!

'That's it, by God! it's our turn now! Down with the exploiters.'

The women were delirious; la Maheude, losing her calmness, was
seized with the vertigo of hunger, la Levaque shouted, old Mother
Brûlé, beside herself, was brandishing her witch-like arms, Philomène was shaken by a spasm of coughing, and la Mouquette was
so excited that she cried out words of tenderness to the orator.
Among the men, Maheu was won over and shouted with anger,
between Pierron who was trembling and Levaque who was talking
too much; while the scoffers Zacharie and Mouquet, though trying
to make fun of things, were feeling uncomfortable and were
surprised that their mate could talk on so long without having a
drink. But on top of the pile of wood, Jeanlin was making more
noise than any one, egging on Bébert and Lydie and shaking the
basket in which Pologne lay.

The clamour began again. Étienne was enjoying the intoxication
of his popularity. He held power, as it were, materialized in these
three thousand breasts, whose hearts he could move with a word.
Souvarine, if he had cared to come, would have applauded his ideas
so far as he recognized them, pleased with his pupil's progress in
anarchism and satisfied with the programme, except the article on
education, a relic of silly sentimentality, for men needed to be
dipped in a bath of holy and salutary ignorance. As to Rasseneur,
he shrugged his shoulders with contempt and anger.

'You shall let me speak,' he shouted to Étienne.

The latter jumped from the tree-trunk.

'Speak, we shall see if they'll hear you.'

Already Rasseneur had replaced him, and with a gesture
demanded silence. But the noise did not cease, his name went round
from the first ranks, who had recognized him, to the last, lost
beneath the beeches, and they refused to hear him; he was an
overturned idol, the mere sight of him angered his old disciples. His
facile elocution, his flowing, good-natured speech, which had so
long charmed them, was now treated like warm tea made to lull
cowards to sleep. In vain he talked through the noise, trying to take
up again his discourse of conciliation, the impossibility of changing

the world by a stroke of law, the necessity of allowing social evolution time to accomplish itself; they laughed at him, they hissed at him; his defeat at the Bon-Joyeux was now beyond repair. At last they threw handfuls of frozen moss at him, and a woman cried in a shrill voice:

'Down with the traitor!'

He explained that the miner could not be the proprietor of the mine, as the weaver is of his loom, and he said that he preferred sharing in the benefits, the interested worker becoming like the child of the family.

'Down with the traitor!' repeated a thousand voices, while stones began to whistle by.

Then he turned pale, and despair filled his eyes with tears. His whole existence was crumbling down; twenty years of ambitious comradeship were breaking down beneath the ingratitude of the crowd. He came down from the tree-trunk, with no strength to go on, struck to the heart.

'That makes you laugh,' he stammered, addressing the triumphant Étienne. 'Good! I hope your turn will come. It will come, I tell you.'

And as if to reject all responsibility for the evils which he foresaw, he made a large gesture, and went away alone across the country, pale and silent.

Hoots of derision arose, and then they were surprised to see old Bonnemort standing on the trunk, and in the midst of the tumult. Up till now Mouque and he had remained absorbed, with that air that they always had of reflecting on former things. No doubt he was yielding to one of those sudden crises of garrulity which sometimes made the past stir in him so violently that recollections rose and flowed from his lips for hours at a time. There was deep silence, and they listened to this old man, who was like a pale spectre beneath the moon, and as he narrated things without any immediate relation with the discussion – long stories which no one could understand – the impression was increased. He was talking of his youth; he described the death of his two uncles who were crushed at the Voreux; then he turned to the inflammation of the lungs which had carried off his wife. He kept to his main ideas, however: things had never gone well and never would go well. Thus in the forest five hundred of them had come together because the king would not lessen the hours of work; but he stopped short, and began to tell of another strike – he had seen so many! They all broke out under these trees, here at the Plan-des-Dames, lower down at the Charbonnerie, still farther towards the Saut-du-Loup. Sometimes it was freezing cold, sometimes it was hot. One evening it had rained so much that they had gone back again without being able to say anything, and the king's soldiers came up and it finished with volleys of musketry.

'We raised our hands like this, and we swore not to go back again. Ah! I have sworn; yes, I have sworn!'

The crowd listened gapingly, feeling disturbed, when Étienne, who had watched the scene, jumped on to the fallen tree, keeping the old man at his side. He had just recognized Chaval among their friends in the first row. The idea that Catherine must be there had roused a new ardour within him, the desire to be applauded in her presence.

'Mates, you have heard; this is one of our old men, and this is what he has suffered, and what our children will suffer if we don't have done with the robbers and butchers.'

He was terrible; never had he spoken so violently. With one arm he supported old Bonnemort, exhibiting him as a banner of misery and mourning, and crying for vengeance. In a few rapid phrases he went back in time to the first Maheu. He showed the whole family worn out in the mine, devoured by the Company, hungrier than ever after a hundred years of work; and contrasting with the Maheus he pointed to the big bellies of the directors sweating money, a whole band of shareholders, going on for a century like kept women, doing nothing but enjoy their bodily pleasures. Was it not fearful? a race of men dying down below, from father to son, so that bribes could be given to ministers, and generations of great lords and bourgeois could give feasts or get fat by their firesides! He had studied the diseases of the miners. He spoke of them one by one with their awful details: anaemia, scrofula, black bronchitis, the asthma which chokes, and the rheumatism which paralyses. These wretches were thrown like fodder to the machines and penned up like beasts in the settlements. The great companies slowly absorbed them, regulating their slavery, threatening to enrol all the workers of the nation, millions of hands, to bring fortune to a thousand idlers. But the miner was no longer an ignorant brute, crushed within the bowels of the earth. An army was springing up from the depths of the pits, a harvest of citizens whose seed would germinate and burst through the earth some sunny day. And they would see then if, after forty years of service, anyone would dare to offer a pension of a hundred and fifty francs to an old man of sixty who spat out coal and whose legs were swollen with the water from the cuttings. Yes! labour would call capital to account: that impersonal god, unknown to the worker, crouching down somewhere in his mysterious sanctuary, where he sucked the life out of the starvelings who nourished him! They would go down there; they would at last succeed in seeing his face by the gleam of incendiary fires, they would drown him in blood, that filthy swine, that monstrous idol, gorged with human flesh!

He was silent, but his arm, still extended in space, indicated the enemy, over there, he knew not where, from one end of the earth to the other. This time the clamour of the crowd was so great that people at Montsou heard it, and looked towards Vandame, seized with anxiety at the thought that some terrible landslip had occurred. Night-birds rose above the trees in the clear open sky.

He now concluded his speech.

'Mates, what is your decision? Do you vote for the strike to go on?'

Their voices yelled, 'Yes! Yes!'

'And what steps do you decide on? We are sure of defeat if cowards go down tomorrow.'

Their voices rose again with the sound of a tempest:

'Kill the cowards!'

'Then you decide to call them back to duty and to their sworn word. This is what we could do: present ourselves at the pit, bring back the traitors by our presence, show the Company that we are all agreed, and that we are going to die rather than yield.'

'That's it. To the pits! To the pits!'

While he was speaking Étienne had looked for Catherine among the pale shouting heads before him. She was certainly not there, but he still saw Chaval, affecting to jeer, shrugging his shoulders, but devoured by jealousy and ready to sell himself for a little of this popularity.

'And if there are any spies among us, mates,' Étienne went on 'let them look out; they're known. Yes, I can see Vandame colliers here who have not left their pit.'

'Is that meant for me?' asked Chaval, with an air of bravado.

'For you, or for anyone else. But, since you speak, you ought to understand that those who eat have nothing to do with those who are starving. You are working at Jean-Bart.'

A mocking voice interrupted:

'Oh! He works . . . He's got a woman who works for him.'

Chaval swore, while the blood rose to his face.

'By God! is it forbidden to work, then?'

'Yes!' said Étienne, 'when your mates are enduring misery for the good of all, it is forbidden to go over, like a selfish sneaking coward, to the bosses' side. If the strike had been general we would have got the best of it long ago. Not a single man at Vandame ought to have gone down when Montsou was not working. The real blow would be if work stopped in the entire area, at Monsieur Deneulin's as well as here. Do you understand? there are only traitors in the Jean-Bart cuttings; you're all traitors!'

The crowd around Chaval grew threatening, and fists were raised and cries of 'Kill him! kill him!' began to be uttered. He had grown pale. But, in his infuriated desire to triumph over Étienne, an idea came to him.

'Listen to me, then! come tomorrow to Jean-Bart, and you shall see if I'm working. We're on your side; they've sent me to tell you so. The fires must be extinguished, and the engine-men, too, must go on strike. All the better if the pumps do stop! the water will destroy the pits and everything will be done for!'

He was furiously applauded in his turn, and now Étienne himself was outflanked. Other speakers followed on the tree-trunk, gesticulating amid the tumult, and throwing out wild propositions. It was a mad outburst of faith, the impatience of a religious sect which, tired of hoping for the expected miracle, had at last decided to provoke it. These heads, emptied by famine, saw everything red, and dreamed of fire and blood in the midst of a glorious apotheosis from which would arise universal happiness. And the tranquil moon bathed this surging sea, the deep forest encircled with its vast silence this murderous cry. The frozen moss crackled beneath the heels of the crowd, while the beeches, erect in their strength, with the delicate tracery of their black branches against the white sky, neither saw nor heard the miserable beings who writhed at their feet.

There was some pushing, and la Maheude found herself near Maheu. Both of them, driven out of their ordinary good sense, and carried away by the slow exasperation which had been working within them for months, agreed with Levaque, who went to extremes by demanding the heads of the engineers. Pierron had disappeared. Bonnemort and Mouque were both talking together, saying vague violent things which nobody heard. For a joke Zacharie demanded the demolition of the churches, while Mouquet, with his crosse in his hand, was beating it against the ground for the sake of increasing the row. The women were furious. Levaque, with her fists to her hips, was setting to with Philomène, whom she

accused of having laughed; la Mouquette talked of attacking the
gendarmes by kicking them somewhere; old Mother Brûlé, who had
just slapped Lydie on finding her without either basket or salad,
went on launching blows into space against all the masters whom
she would like to have got at. For a moment Jeanlin was in terror,
Bébert having learned through a trammer that Madame Rasseneur
had seen them steal Pologne; but when he had decided to go back
and quietly release the beast at the door of the Avantage, he shouted
louder than ever, and opened his new knife, brandishing the blade
and proud of its glitter.

'Mates! mates!' repeated the exhausted Étienne, hoarse with the
effort to obtain a moment's silence for a definite understanding.

At last they listened.

'Mates! tomorrow morning at Jean-Bart, is it agreed?'

'Yes, yes! at Jean-Bart! death to the traitors!'

The tempest of these three thousand voices filled the sky, and
died away in the pure brightness of the moon.

PART FIVE

CHAPTER I

At four o'clock the moon had set, and the night was very dark. Everything was still asleep at Deneulin's; the old brick house stood mute and gloomy, with closed doors and windows, at the end of the large ill-kept garden which separated it from the Jean-Bart mine. The other frontage faced the deserted road to Vandame, a large country town, about three kilometres off, hidden behind the forest.

Deneulin, tired after the previous day spent in part below, was snoring with his face toward the wall, when he dreamt that he had been called. At last he awoke, and really hearing a voice, hurriedly opened the window. One of his foremen was in the garden.

'What is it, then?' he asked.

'There's a rebellion, sir; half the men will not work, and are preventing the others from going down.'

He scarcely understood, with head heavy and dazed with sleep, and the bitter cold struck him like an icy shower.

'Then make them go down, by God!' he stammered.

'It's been going on an hour,' said the foreman. 'Then we thought it best to come for you. Perhaps you will be able to persuade them.'

'Very good; I'll go.'

He quickly dressed, his mind quite clear now, and very anxious. The house might have been pillaged; neither the cook nor the man-servant had stirred. But from the other side of the staircase alarmed voices were whispering; and when he came out he saw his daughters' door open, and they both appeared in white dressing-gowns, slipped on in haste.

'Father, what is it?'

Lucie, the elder, was already twenty-two, a tall dark girl, with a haughty air; while Jeanne, the younger, as yet scarcely nineteen years old, was small, with golden hair and an endearing, gracious manner.

'Nothing serious,' he replied, to reassure them. 'It seems that some troublemakers are causing a disturbance down there. I am going to see.'

But they exclaimed that they would not let him go before he had taken something warm. If not, he would come back ill, with his stomach upset, as he always did. He struggled, gave his word of honour that he was too much in a hurry.

'Listen!' said Jeanne, at last, hanging to his neck, 'you must drink a little glass of rum and eat two biscuits, or I shall remain like this, and you'll have to take me with you.'

He resigned himself, declaring that the biscuits would choke him. They had already gone down before him, each with her candlestick. In the dining-room below they hastened to serve him, one pouring out the rum, the other running to the pantry for the biscuits. Having lost their mother when very young, they had been rather badly brought up alone, spoilt by their father, the elder haunted by the dream of singing on the stage, the younger mad over painting, for which she showed a singular boldness of taste. But when they had to reduce expenses after serious business difficulties, these apparently extravagant girls had suddenly developed into very sensible and shrewd managers, with an eye for errors of centimes in accounts. Today, with their boyish and artistic demeanour, they looked after the household accounts, were careful over every sou, haggled with the tradesmen, renovated their dresses unceasingly, and in fact, succeeded in keeping up decent appearances despite the growing poverty of the house.

'Eat, papa,' repeated Lucie.

Then, noticing his silent gloomy preoccupied air, she was again frightened.

'Is it serious, then, that you look at us like this? Tell us; we will stay with you, and they can do without us at that lunch.'

She was speaking of a party which had been planned for the morning. Madame Hennebeau was to go in her carriage, first for Cécile, at the Grégoires', then to call for them, so that they could all go to Marchiennes to lunch at the Forges, where the manager's wife had invited them. It was an opportunity to visit the workshops, the blast furnaces, and the coke ovens.

'We will certainly remain,' declared Jeanne, in her turn.

But he grew angry.

'A fine idea! I tell you that it is nothing. Just be so good as to get back into your beds again, and dress for nine o'clock, as was arranged.'

He kissed them and hastened to leave. They heard the noise of his boots vanishing over the frozen earth in the garden.

Jeanne carefully placed the stopper in the rum bottle, while Lucie locked up the biscuits. The room had the cold neatness of dining-rooms where the table is but meagrely supplied. And both of them took advantage of this early descent to see if anything had been left uncared for the evening before. A serviette had been left out, the servant should be scolded. At last they were upstairs again.

While he was taking the shortest cut through the narrow paths of his kitchen garden, Deneulin was thinking of his compromised fortune, this Montsou denier, this million which he had realized, dreaming to multiply it tenfold, and which was today running such great risks. It was an uninterrupted course of ill-luck, enormous and unforeseen repairs, ruinous conditions of exploitation, then the disaster of this industrial crisis, just when the profits were beginning to come in. If the strike broke out here, he would be finished. He pushed a little door: the buildings of the pit could be made out in the black night, by the deepening of the shadow, starred by a few lanterns.

Jean-Bart was not as important as the Voreux, but its renewed installation made it a nice pit, as the engineers say. They had not been contented by enlarging the shaft one metre and a half, and deepening it to seven hundred and eight metres, they had equipped it afresh with a new engine, new cages, entirely new material, all set up according to the latest scientific improvements; and even a certain seeking for elegance was visible in the constructions, a screening-shed with carved frieze, a steeple adorned with a clock, a receiving-room and an engine-room both rounded into an apse like a Renaissance chapel, and surmounted by a chimney with a mosaic spiral made of black bricks and red bricks. The pump was placed on the other shaft of the concession, the old Gaston-Marie pit, reserved solely for this purpose. Jean-Bart, to right and left of the winding-shaft, only had two conduits, one for the steam ventilator and the other for the ladders.

In the morning, ever since three o'clock, Chaval, who had arrived first, had been corrupting his comrades, convincing them that they ought to imitate those at Montsou, and demand an increase of five centimes a tram. Soon four hundred workmen had passed from the shed into the receiving-room, in the midst of a tumult of gesticulation and shouting. Those who wished to work stood with their lamps, barefooted, with shovel or pick beneath their arms; while the others, still in their clogs, with their overcoats on their shoulders because of the great cold, were barring the way to the shaft; and the captains were growing hoarse in the effort to restore order, begging them to be reasonable and not to prevent those who wanted from going down.

But Chaval was furious when he saw Catherine in her trousers and jacket, her head tied up in the blue cap. On getting up, he had roughly told her to stay in bed. In despair at this work stoppage she had followed him all the same, for he never gave her any money; she often had to pay both for herself and him; and what was to become of her if she earned nothing? She was overcome by fear, the fear of a brothel at Marchiennes, which was the fate of putter-girls without bread and without lodging.

'By God!' cried Chaval, 'what the devil have you come here for?'

She stammered that she had no income to live on and that she wanted to work.

'Then you put yourself against me, wench? Back you go at once, or I'll kick you all the way there in the backside.'

She recoiled timidly but she did not leave, resolved to see how things would turn out. Deneulin had arrived by the screening-stairs. In spite of the weak light of the lanterns, with a quick look he took in the scene, with this crowd wrapped in shadow; he knew every face – the pikemen, the porters, the landers, the putters, even the trammers. In the nave, still new and clean, the work was waiting for them; the steam in the engine, under pressure, made slight whistling sounds; the cages were hanging motionless to the cables; the trams, abandoned on the way, were encumbering the metal floors. Scarcely eighty lamps had been taken; the others were flaming in the lamp cabin. But no doubt a word from him would suffice, and work would begin again.

'Well, what's going on then, my lads?' he asked in a loud voice. 'What are you angry about? Just explain to me and we will see if we can agree.'

He usually behaved in a paternal way towards his men, while at the same time demanding hard work. With an authoritative, rough manner, he had tried to win them over by a good-natured approach which burst out in loud blasts, and he often gained their love; the men especially respected in him his courage, always in the cuttings with them, the first in danger whenever an accident terrified the pit. Twice, after fire-damp explosions, he had been let down, fastened by a rope under his armpits, when the bravest drew back.

'Now,' he began again, 'you are not going to make me repent of having trusted you. You know that I have refused police protection. Talk quietly and I will hear you.'

All were now silent and awkward, moving away from him; and it was Chaval who at last said:

'Well, Monsieur Deneulin, we can't go on working; we must have five centimes more the tram.'

He seemed surprised.

'What! five centimes! and why this demand? I don't complain about your timbering, I don't want to impose a new tariff on you like the Montsou directors.'

'Maybe! but the Montsou mates are right, all the same. They won't have the tariff, and they want a rise of five centimes because it is not possible to work properly at the present rates. We want five centimes more, don't we, you others?'

Voices approved, and the noise began again in the midst of violent gesticulation. Gradually they drew near, forming a small circle.

A flame came into Deneulin's eyes, and his fist, that of a man who liked strong government, was clenched, for fear of yielding to the temptation of seizing one of them by the neck. He preferred to discuss on the basis of reason.

'You want five centimes, and I agree that the work is worth it. Only I can't give them. If I gave them I should simply be done for. You must understand that I have to live first in order for you to live, and I've gone as far as I can, the least rise in net prices will upset me. Two years ago, you remember, at the time of the last strike, I yielded, I was able to then. But that rise of wages was not the less ruinous, for these two years have been a struggle. Today I would rather let the whole thing go than not be able to tell next month where to get the money to pay you.'

Chaval laughed roughly in the face of this boss who told them his affairs so frankly. The others lowered their faces, obstinate and incredulous, refusing to take into their heads the idea that a boss did not earn millions out of his men.

Then Deneulin, persisting, explained his struggle with Montsou, always on the watch and ready to devour him if, some day, he had the stupidity to come to grief. It was savage competition which forced him to economize, the more so since the great depth of Jean-Bart increased the price of extraction, an unfavourable condition hardly compensated by the great thickness of the coal-beds. He would never have raised wages after the last strike if it had not been necessary for him to imitate Montsou, for fear of seeing his men leave him. And he threatened them with the future; a fine result it would be for them, if they obliged him to sell, to pass beneath the terrible yoke of the directors! He did not sit on a throne far away in an unknown sanctuary; he was not one of those shareholders who pay agents to skin the miner who has never seen them; he was an employer, he risked something besides his money, he risked his intelligence, his health, his life. Stoppage of work would simply mean death, for he had no stock, and he must fulfil orders. Besides, his standing capital could not sleep. How could he keep his commitments? Who would pay the interest on the sums his friends had entrusted to him? It would mean bankruptcy.

'That's where we are, my good fellows,' he said, in conclusion. 'I want to convince you. We don't ask a man to cut his own throat, do we? and if I give you your five centimes, or if I let you go out on strike, it's the same as if I cut my throat.'

He was silent. Grunts went round. A number among the miners seemed to hesitate. Several went back towards the shaft.

'At least,' said a foreman, 'let every one be free. Who are those who want to work?'

Catherine had advanced among the first. But Chaval fiercely pushed her back, shouting:

'We are all agreed; it's only bloody rogues who'll leave their mates!'

After that, conciliation appeared impossible. The cries began again, and men were hustled away from the shaft, at the risk of being crushed against the walls. For a moment the owner, in despair, tried to struggle alone, to force the crowd to do his will; but it was useless madness, and he had to withdraw. For a few minutes he rested, out of breath, on a chair in the receiver's office, so overcome by his powerlessness that no ideas came to him. At last he grew calm, and told an inspector to go and bring Chaval; then, when the latter had agreed to the interview, he motioned the others away.

'Leave us.'

Deneulin's idea was to see what this fellow was after. At the first words he felt that he was vain, and was devoured by passionate jealousy. Then he attacked him by flattery, affecting surprise that a workman of his merit should so compromise his future. It seemed as though he had long had his eyes on him for rapid advancement; and he ended by squarely offering to make him foreman later on. Chaval listened in silence, with his fists at first clenched, but then gradually relaxed. Something was working in the depths of his brain; if he persisted in the strike he would be nothing more than Étienne's lieutenant, while now another ambition opened, that of passing into the ranks of the bosses. The heat of pride rose to his face and intoxicated him. Besides, the band of strikers whom he had expected since the morning had not arrived; some obstacle must have stopped them, perhaps the police; it was time to submit. But all the same he shook his head; he acted the incorruptible man, striking his breast indignantly. Then, without mentioning to the owner the rendezvous he had given to the Montsou men, he promised to calm his mates, and to persuade them to go down.

Deneulin remained hidden, and the foremen themselves stood aside. For an hour they heard Chaval holding forth and discussing, standing on a tram in the receiving-room. Some of the men booed him; a hundred and twenty went off exasperated, persisting in the resolution which he had made them take. It was already past seven. The sun was rising brilliantly; it was a bright day of hard frost; and all at once movement began in the pit, and work began. First the crank of the engine plunged, rolling and unrolling the cables on the drums. Then, in the midst of the tumult of the signals, the descent took place. The cages filled and were engulfed, and rose again, the shaft swallowing its ration of trammers and putters and pikemen; while on the metal floors the landers pushed the trams with a thunderous sound.

'By God! What the devil are you doing there?' cried Chaval to Catherine, who was awaiting her turn. 'Will you just go down and not laze about!'

At nine o'clock, when Madame Hennebeau arrived in her carriage with Cécile, she found Lucie and Jeanne quite ready and very elegant, in spite of their dresses having been renovated for the twentieth time. But Deneulin was surprised to see Négrel accompanying the carriage on horseback. What! were the men also in the party? Then Madame Hennebeau explained in her maternal way that they had frightened her by saying that the streets were full of evil faces, and so she preferred to bring a defender. Négrel laughed and reassured them: nothing to cause anxiety, threats of brawlers as usual, but not one of them would dare to throw a stone at a window-pane. Still pleased with his success, Deneulin related the story of the failed rebellion at Jean-Bart. He said that he was now quite at rest. And on the Vandame road, while the young ladies got into the carriage, all congratulated themselves on the superb day, oblivious of the long swelling shudder of the marching people afar off in the country, though they might have heard the sound of it if they had pressed their ears against the earth.

'Well! it is agreed,' repeated Madame Hennebeau. 'This evening you will call for the young ladies and dine with us. Madame Grégoire has also promised to come for Cécile.'

'You may count on me,' replied Deneulin.

The carriage went off towards Vandame, Jeanne and Lucie leaning down to laugh once more to their father, who was standing by the roadside; while Négrel gallantly trotted behind the fleeing wheels.

They crossed the forest, taking the road from Vandame to Marchiennes. As they approached Tartaret, Jeanne asked Madame Hennebeau if she knew Côte-Verte, and the latter, in spite of her stay of five years in the country, acknowledged that she had never been on that side. Then they made a detour. Tartaret, on the outskirts of the forest, was an uncultivated moor, of volcanic sterility, under which for ages a coal mine had been burning. Its history was lost in legend. The miners of the place said that fire from heaven had fallen on this Sodom in the bowels of the earth, where the putter-girls had committed abominations together, so that they had not even had the time to come to the surface, and to-day were still burning at the bottom of this hell. The calcined rocks, of a sombre red, were covered by an efflorescence of alum like leprosy. Sulphur grew like a yellow flower at the edge of the fissures. At night, those who were brave enough to venture to look into these holes declared that they saw flames there, sinful souls shrivelling in the furnace within. Wandering lights moved over the soil, and hot vapours, the poisons from the devil's filth and his dirty kitchen, were constantly smoking. And like a miracle of eternal spring, in the midst of this accursed moor of Tartaret, Côte-Verte appeared, with its meadows for ever green, its beeches with leaves unceasingly renewed, its fields where no less than three harvests ripened. It was a natural hot-house, warmed by the fire in the deep strata beneath. The snow never lay on it. The enormous bouquet of verdure, beside the leafless forest trees, blossomed on this December day, and the frost had not even nipped the edge of it.*

Soon the carriage was passing over the plain. Négrel joked over the legend, and explained that a fire often occurred at the bottom of a mine from the fermentation of the coal dust; if not mastered it would burn on for ever, and he mentioned a Belgian pit which had been flooded by diverting a river and running it into the pit. But he became silent. For the last few minutes groups of miners had been constantly passing the carriage; they went by in silence, with sidelong looks at the luxurious carriage which forced them to stand aside. Their numbers went on increasing. The horses were obliged to cross the little bridge over the Scarpe at walking pace. What was going on, then, to bring all these people onto the roads? The young ladies became frightened, and Négrel began to sense trouble afoot in the animation of the country; it was a relief when they at last arrived at Marchiennes. The batteries of coke ovens and the chimneys of the blast furnaces, beneath a sun which seemed to extinguish them, were belching out smoke and raining their everlasting soot through the air.

CHAPTER 2

At Jean-Bart, Catherine had already been at work for an hour, pushing trams as far as the relays; and she was soaked in such a bath of perspiration that she stopped a moment to wipe her face.

At the bottom of the cutting, where he was hammering at the seam with his mates, Chaval was astonished when he no longer heard the rumble of the wheels. The lamps burnt badly, and the coal dust made it impossible to see.

'What's up?' he shouted.

When she answered that she was sure she would melt, and that her heart was going to stop, he replied furiously:

'Do like us, stupid! Take off your shirt.'

They were seven hundred and eight metres to the north in the first passage of the Désirée seam, which was at a distance of three kilometres from the loading-bay. When they spoke of this part of the pit, the miners of the region grew pale, and lowered their voices, as if they had spoken of hell; and most often they were content to shake their heads as men who would rather not speak of these fiery depths. As the galleries sank towards the north, they approached Tartaret, penetrating to that interior fire which calcined the rocks above. The cuttings at the point at which they had arrived had an average temperature of forty-five degrees. They were there in the accursed city, in the midst of the flames which the passers-by on the plain could see through the fissures, spitting out sulphur and poisonous vapours.

Catherine, who had already taken off her jacket, hesitated, then took off her trousers also; and with naked arms and naked thighs, her shirt tied round her hips by a cord like a blouse, she began to push again.

'Anyhow, that's better,' she said aloud.

In the stifling heat she still felt a vague fear. Ever since they began working here, five days ago, she had thought of the stories told her in childhood, of those putter-girls of the days of old who were burning beneath Tartaret, as a punishment for things which no one dared to repeat. No doubt she was too big now to believe such silly stories; but still, what would she do if she were suddenly to see coming out of the wall a girl as red as a stove, with eyes like live coals? The idea made her perspire still more.

At the relay, eighty metres from the cutting, another putter took the tram and pushed it eighty metres farther to the incline, so that the receiver could forward it with the others which came down from the upper galleries.

'Gracious! you're making yourself comfortable!' said this woman, a lean widow of thirty, when she saw Catherine in her shirt. 'I can't do it, the trammers at the brow bother me with their dirty tricks.'

'Ah, well!' replied the young girl. 'I don't care about the men! I feel too bad.'

She went off again, pushing an empty tram. The worst was that in this bottom passage another cause was added to the proximity of Tartaret to make the heat unbearable. They were by the side of old workings, a very deep abandoned gallery of Gaston-Marie, where, ten years earlier, an explosion of fire-damp had set the seam alight; and it was still burning behind the clay wall which had been built there and was kept constantly repaired, in order to limit the disaster. Deprived of air, the fire ought to have become extinct, but no doubt unknown currents kept it alive; it had gone on for ten years, and heated the clay wall like the bricks of an oven, so that those who passed felt half-roasted. It was along this wall, for a length of more than a hundred metres, that the haulage was carried on, in a temperature of sixty degrees.

After two journeys, Catherine again felt stifled. Fortunately, the passage was large and convenient in this Désirée seam, one of the thickest in the district. The bed was one metre ninety in height, and the men could work standing. But they would rather have worked with twisted necks and a little fresh air.

'Hallo, there! are you asleep?' said Chaval again, roughly, as soon as he no longer heard Catherine moving. 'How the devil did I come to get stuck with such a bitch? Will you just fill your tram and push?'

She was at the bottom of the cutting, leaning on her shovel; she was feeling ill, and she looked at them all with a foolish air without obeying. She scarcely saw them by the reddish gleam of the lamps, entirely naked like animals, so black, so encrusted in sweat and coal, that their nakedness did not frighten her. It was a confused task, the bending of ape-like backs, an infernal vision of scorched limbs, spending their strength amid dull blows and groans. But they could see her better, no doubt, for the picks left off hammering, and they joked about her taking off her trousers.

'Eh! you'll catch cold; look out!'

'It's because she's got such fine legs! I say, Chaval, there's enough there for two.'

'Oh! let's see. Lift up! Higher! higher!'

Then Chaval, without growing angry at these jokes, turned on her.

'That's it, by God! Ah! she likes dirty jokes. She'd stay there to listen till tomorrow.'

Catherine had painfully decided to fill her tram, then she pushed it. The gallery was too wide for her to get a purchase on the timber on both sides; her naked feet were twisted in the rails where they sought a point of support, while she slowly moved on, her arms stiffened in front, and her back breaking. As soon as she came up to the clay wall, the fiery torture again began, and the sweat fell from her whole body in enormous drops as from a storm-cloud. She had scarcely got a third of the way before she streamed, blinded, soiled also by the black mud. Her narrow shirt, black as though dipped in ink, was sticking to her skin, and rising up to her waist with the movement of her thighs; it hurt her so that she had once more to stop her task.

What was the matter with her, then, today? Never before had she felt as if there were wool in her bones. It must be the bad air. The ventilation did not reach to the bottom of this distant passage. One breathed there all sorts of vapours, which came out of the coal with the low bubbling sound of a spring, so abundantly sometimes that the lamps would not burn; to say nothing of fire-damp, which nobody noticed, for from one week's end to the other the men were always breathing it in throughout the seam. She knew that bad air well; dead air the miners called it; the heavy asphyxiating gases below, above them the light gases which catch fire and blow up all the stalls of a pit, with hundreds of men, in a single burst of thunder. From her childhood she had swallowed so much that she was surprised she bore it so badly, with buzzing ears and burning throat.

Unable to go farther, she felt the need of taking off her shirt. It was beginning to torture her, this garment of which the least folds cut and burnt her. She resisted the longing, and tried to push again, but was forced to stand upright. Then quickly, saying to herself that she would cover herself at the relay, she took off everything,

the cord and the shirt, so feverishly that she would have torn off
her skin if she could. And now, naked and pitiful, brought down to
the level of the female animal seeking its living in the mire of the
streets, covered with soot and mud up to the belly, she laboured on
like a cab-hack. On all fours she pushed onwards.

But a feeling of despair came over her, it gave her no relief to be
naked. What more could she take off? The buzzing in her ears
deafened her, she seemed to feel a vice gripping her temples. She fell
on her knees. The lamp, wedged into the coal in the tram, seemed
to her to be going out. The intention to turn up the wick alone
survived in the midst of her confused ideas. Twice she tried to
examine it, and both times when she placed it before her on the
earth she saw it turn pale, as though it also lacked breath. Suddenly
the lamp went out. Then everything whirled around her in the
darkness; a millstone turned in her head, her heart grew weak and
left off beating, numbed in its turn by the immense weariness which
was putting her limbs to sleep. She had fallen back in anguish amid
the asphyxiating air close to the ground.

'By God! I believe she's lazing again,' growled Chaval's voice.

He listened from the top of the cutting, and could not hear the
sound of wheels.

'Eh, Catherine! you idle bitch!'

His voice was lost afar in the black gallery, and not a sound
replied.

'I'll come and make you move, I will!'

Nothing stirred, there was only the same silence, as of death. He
came down furiously, rushing along with his lamp so violently that
he nearly fell over the putter's body which barred the way. He
looked at her in stupefaction. What was the matter, then? was it a
trick to have a bit of a sleep? But the lamp which he had lowered to
light up her face almost went out. He lifted it and lowered it afresh,
and at last understood; it must be a gust of bad air. His violence
disappeared; the devotion of the miner in face of a comrade's peril
was awaking within him. He shouted for her shirt to be brought,
and seized the naked and unconscious girl in his arms, holding her
as high as possible. When their garments had been thrown over her
shoulders he set out running, supporting his burden with one hand,
and carrying the two lamps with the other. The deep galleries
unrolled before him as he rushed along, turning to the right, then
to the left, seeking life in the frozen air of the plain which blew
down the air-shaft. At last the sound of water stopped him, a trickle
flowing from the rock. He was at a junction in the huge haulage

gallery which formerly led to Gaston-Marie. The air here blew in like a tempest, and was so fresh that a shudder went through him as he seated himself on the earth against the props; his mistress was still unconscious, with closed eyes.

'Catherine, come now, by God! no fooling around. Hold yourself up a bit while I dip this in the water.'

He was frightened to find her so limp. However, he was able to dip her shirt in the water, and to bathe her face with it. She was like a corpse, already buried in the depths of the earth, with her slender girlish body which seemed to be still hesitating before filling out to the forms of puberty. Then a shudder ran over her childish breast, over the belly and thighs of the poor little creature deflowered before her time. She opened her eyes and stammered:

'I'm cold.'

'Ah! that's better now!' cried Chaval, relieved.

He dressed her, slipped on the shirt easily, but swore over the difficulty he had in getting on the trousers, for she could not help much. She remained dazed, not understanding where she was, nor why she was naked. When she remembered she was ashamed. How had she dared to take everything off! And she questioned him; had she been seen so, without even a handkerchief around her waist to cover her? He joked, and made up stories, saying that he had just brought her there in the midst of all the mates standing in a row. What an idea, to have taken his advice and shown off her bum! Afterwards he assured her that the mates could not even know whether it was round or square, he had rushed along so swiftly.

'Hell! but I'm dying of cold,' he said, dressing himself in turn.

Never had she seen him so kind. Usually, for one good word that he said to her she received at once two bullying ones. It would have been so pleasant to live in agreement; a feeling of tenderness when through her in the languor of her fatigue. She smiled at him, and murmured:

'Kiss me.'

He embraced her, and lay down beside her, waiting till she was able to walk.

'You know,' she said again, 'you were wrong to shout at me over there, for I couldn't do more, really! Even in the cutting you're not so hot; if you only knew how it roasts you at the bottom of the passage!'

'Sure enough,' he replied, 'it would be better under the trees. You feel bad in that stall, I'm afraid, my poor girl.'

She was so touched at hearing him agree with her that she tried to be brave.

'Oh! it's a bad place. Then, today the air is poisoned. But you shall see soon if I'm lazy. When you have to work, you work; isn't it true? I'd die rather than stop.'

There was silence. He held her with one arm round her waist, pressing her against his breast to keep her from harm. Although she already felt strong enough to go back to the stall, she forgot everything in her delight.

'Only,' she went on in a very low voice, 'I should like it so much if you were kinder. Yes, it is so good when we love each other a little.'

And she began to cry softly.

'But I do love you,' he cried, 'for I've taken you with me.'

She only replied by shaking her head. There are often men who take women just in order to have them, caring mighty little about their happiness. Her tears flowed more freely; it made her despair now to think of the happy life she would have led if she had chanced to fall to another lad, whose arm she would always have felt thus round her waist. Another? and the vague image of that other arose from the depth of her emotion. But it was done with; she only desired now to live to the end with this one, if he did not push her about too much.

'Then,' she said, 'try to be like this sometimes.'

Sobs cut short her words, and he embraced her again.

'You're silly! There, I swear to be kind. I'm not worse than any one else, go on!'

She looked at him, and began to smile through her tears. Perhaps he was right; you never met women who were happy. Then, although she distrusted his oath, she gave herself up to the joy of seeing him affectionate. Good God! if only that could last! They had both embraced again, and as they were pressing each other in a long clasp they heard steps, which made them get up. Three mates who had seen them pass had come up to know how she was.

They set out together. It was nearly ten o'clock, and they took their lunch into a cool corner before going back to sweat it out at the bottom of the cutting. They were finishing the double slice of bread-and-butter, their briquet, and were about to drink the coffee from their flask, when they were disturbed by a noise coming from stalls in the distance. What was that? was it another accident? They got up and ran. Pikemen, putters, trammers kept running past them; no one knew anything; all were shouting; it must be some great misfortune. Gradually the whole mine was in terror, frightened shadows emerged from the galleries, lanterns danced and flew away in the darkness. Where was it? Why could no one say?

All at once a foreman passed by, shouting:

'They are cutting the cables! they are cutting the cables!'

Then the panic increased. There was a furious gallop through the gloomy passages. They were confused. Why cut the cables? And who was cutting them, when men were below? It seemed monstrous.

But the voice of another foreman rang out and then disappeared:

'The Montsou men are cutting the cables! Everyone up!'

When he had understood, Chaval stopped Catherine short. The idea that he would meet the Montsou men up above, should he get out, made him weak at the knees. It had come, then, that gang which he thought had fallen into the hands of the police. For a moment he thought of retracing his path and ascending through Gaston-Marie, but that was no longer possible. He swore, hesitating, hiding his fear, repeating that it was stupid to run like that. They would not, surely, leave them at the bottom.

The foreman's voice echoed anew, now approaching them:

'Everyone up! To the ladders! to the ladders!'

And Chaval was carried away with his mates. He pushed Catherine and accused her of not running fast enough. Did she want, then, to remain in the pit to die of hunger? For those Montsou rogues were capable of breaking the ladders without waiting for people to come up. This abominable suggestion ended by driving them wild. Along the galleries there was only a furious rush, helter-skelter; a race of madmen, each striving to arrive first and mount before the others. Some men shouted that the ladders were broken and that no one could get out. And then in frightened groups they began to reach the loading-bay, where they were all engulfed. They threw themselves toward the shaft, they crushed through the narrow door to the ladder passage; while an old groom who had prudently led back the horses to the stable, looked at them with an air of contemptuous indifference, accustomed to spending nights in the pit and certain that he could eventually be drawn out of it.

'By God! Climb up in front of me,' said Chaval to Catherine. 'At least I can hold you if you fall.'

Out of breath, and suffocated by this race of three kilometres which had once more bathed her in sweat, she gave herself up, without understanding, to the rushing of the crowd. Then he pulled her by the arm, almost breaking it; and she cried with pain, her tears bursting out. Already he was forgetting his oath, never would she be happy.

'Go on, then!' he roared.

But he frightened her too much. If she went first he would bully her the whole time. So she resisted, while the wild flood of their comrades pushed them to one side. The water that filtered from the shaft was falling in great drops, and the floor of the loading-bay, shaken by this tramping, was trembling over the sump, the muddy cesspool ten metres deep. At Jean-Bart, two years earlier, a terrible accident had happened just here; the breaking of a cable had sent the cage to the bottom of the sump, in which two men had been drowned. And they all thought of this; every one would be left down there if they all crowded on to the planks.

'Bloody fool!' shouted Chaval. 'Die then; I shall be rid of you!'

He climbed up and she followed.

From the bottom to daylight there were a hundred and two ladders, about seven metres in length, each placed on a narrow landing which occupied the breadth of the passage and in which a square hold scarcely allowed the shoulders to pass. It was like a flat chimney, seven hundred metres in height, between the wall of the shaft and the brattice of the winding-cage, a damp pipe, black and endless, in which the ladders were placed one above the other, almost straight, in regular stages. It took a strong man twenty-five minutes to climb up this giant column. The passage, however, was no longer used except in cases of accident.

Catherine at first climbed bravely. Her naked feet were used to the hard coal on the floors of the passages, and did not suffer from the square rungs, covered with iron rods to prevent them from wearing away. Her hands, hardened by the haulage, grasped without fatigue the uprights that were too big for her. And it even interested her and took her out of her grief, this unforeseen ascent, this long procession of men flowing on and hoisting themselves up three on a ladder, so that even when the head should emerge in daylight the tail would still be trailing over the sump. They were not there yet, the first could hardly have ascended a third of the shaft. No one spoke now, only their feet moved with a low sound; while the lamps, like travelling stars, spaced out from below upward, formed a continually increasing line.

Catherine heard a trammer behind her counting the ladders. It gave her the idea of counting them also. They had already gone up fifteen, and were arriving at a landing-place. But at that moment she collided with Chaval's legs. He swore, shouting to her to look out. Gradually the whole column stopped and became motionless. What was wrong? had something happened? and every one recovered his voice to ask questions and to express his fear. Their anxiety had increased since leaving the bottom; their ignorance as to what was going on above oppressed them more as they approached daylight. Someone shouted that they would have to go down again, that the ladders were broken. That was their worst fear, the dread of finding themselves face to face with empty space. Another explanation came down from mouth to mouth; there had been an accident, a pikeman had slipped off a rung. No one knew exactly, the shouts made it impossible to hear; were they going to spend all night there? At last, without any precise information being obtained, the ascent began again, with the same slow, painful movement, in the midst of the tread of feet and the dancing of lamps. It must certainly be higher up where the ladders were broken.

At the thirty-second ladder, as they passed a third landing-stage, Catherine felt her legs and arms grow stiff. At first she had felt a slight tingling in her skin. Now she lost the sensation of the iron and the wood beneath her feet and in her hands. A vague pain, which gradually became a burning sensation, heated her muscles. And in the dizziness which came over her, she recalled her grandfather Bonnemort's stories of the days when there was no passage, and little girls of ten used to take out the coal on their shoulders up bare ladders; so that if one of them slipped, or a fragment of coal simply rolled out of a basket, three or four children would fall down head first from the blow. The cramp in her limbs became unbearable, she would never reach the end.

Fresh stoppages allowed her to breathe. But the terror which came down every time from above dazed her still more. Above and below her, respiration became more difficult. This interminable ascent was causing giddiness, and the nausea affected her with the others. She was suffocating, intoxicated with the darkness, exasperated with the walls which crushed against her flesh, and shuddering also with the dampness, her body perspiring beneath the great drops which fell on her. They were approaching a level where so thick a rain fell that it threatened to extinguish their lamps.

Chaval twice spoke to Catherine without obtaining any reply. What the devil was she doing down there? Had she lost her tongue? She might at least tell him if she was all right. They had been climbing for half an hour, but so heavily that they had only reached the fifty-ninth ladder; there were still forty-three. Catherine at last stammered that she was getting on all right. He would have called her an idle bitch if she had acknowledged her weariness. The iron of the rungs must have cut her feet; it seemed to her that it was sawing into them to the bone. After every step she expected to see her hands slip from the uprights; they were so skinned and stiff she could not close her fingers, and she feared she would fall backward with torn shoulders and dislocated thighs in this continual effort. It was especially the defective slope of the ladders from which she suffered, the almost perpendicular position which obliged her to hoist herself up by the strength of her wrists, with her belly against the wood. The panting of many breaths now drowned the sound of the feet, forming an enormous moan, multiplied tenfold by the walls of the passage, arising from the depths and disappearing up to the light. There was a groan; word ran along that a trammer had just cut his head open against the edge of a platform.

And Catherine went on climbing. They had passed the water level. The rain had ceased; a mist made the musty air heavy, poisoned with the odour of old iron and damp wood. Mechanically she continued to count in a low voice – eighty-one, eighty-two, eighty-three; still nineteen. The repetition of these figures supported her merely by their rhythmic balance; she had no further conscious-ness of her movements. When she lifted her eyes the lamps turned in a spiral. Her blood was pounding; she felt that she was dying; the last breath would have knocked her over. The worst was that those below were now pushing, and that the entire column was pushing and shoving, yielding to the growing anger of its fatigue, the furious need to see the sun again. The first mates had emerged; there were, then, no broken ladders; but the idea that they might yet be broken to prevent the last from coming up, when others were already breathing up above, nearly drove them mad. And when a new stoppage occurred oaths broke out, and all went on climbing, hustling each other, passing over each other's bodies to arrive at all costs.

Then Catherine fell. She had cried Chaval's name in despairing appeal. He did not hear; he was struggling, digging his heels into a comrade's ribs to get up before him. And she was rolled down and trampled over. As she fainted she dreamed. It seemed to her that she was one of the little putter-girls of old days, and that a fragment of coal, fallen from the basket above her, had thrown her to the bottom of the shaft, like a sparrow struck by a flint. Five ladders only remained to climb. It had taken nearly an hour. She never knew how she reached daylight, carried up on people's shoulders, supported by the throttling narrowness of the passage. Suddenly she found herself in the dazzling sunlight, in the midst of a yelling crowd who were booing at her.

CHAPTER 3

From early morning, before daylight, a tremor had swept through the settlements, and that tremor was now swelling through the roads and over the whole country. But the departure had not taken place as arranged, for the news had spread that cavalry and police were scouring the plain. It was said that they had arrived from Douai during the night, and Rasseneur was accused of having betrayed his mates by warning Monsieur Hennebeau; a putter even swore that she had seen the servant taking a dispatch to the telegraph office. The miners clenched their fists and watched the soldiers from behind their shutters by the pale light of the early morning.

Towards half-past seven, as the sun was rising, another rumour circulated, reassuring the impatient. It was a false alarm, a simple military exercise, such as the general occasionally ordered since the strike had broken out, at the wish of the prefect of Lille. The strikers detested this official; they reproached him with deceiving them by the promise of a conciliatory intervention, which was limited to a march of troops into Montsou every week, to overawe them. So when the cavalry and police quietly took the road back to Marchiennes, after contenting themselves with deafening the settlements by the stamping of their horses over the hard earth, the miners jeered at this silly prefect and his soldiers who turned on their heels when things were beginning to get hot. Up till nine o'clock they stood peacefully about, in good humour, in front of their houses, following with their eyes up the streets the harmless backs of the last gendarmes. In the depths of their large beds the good people of Montsou were still sleeping, with their heads among the feathers. At the manager's house, Madame Hennebeau had just been seen setting out in the carriage, leaving Monsieur Hennebeau at work, no doubt, for the closed and silent villa seemed dead. Not one of the pits had any military guard; it was a fatal lack of foresight in the hour of danger, the natural stupidity which accompanies catastrophes, the fault which a government commits whenever there is need of precise knowledge of the facts. And nine o'clock was striking when the colliers at last took the Vandame road, to repair to the meeting decided on the day before in the forest.

Étienne had very quickly perceived that he would certainly not find over at Jean-Bart the three thousand comrades on whom he was counting. Many believed that the demonstration was put off, and the worst was that two or three groups, already on the way, would compromise the cause if he did not at all costs put himself at their head. Almost a hundred, who had set out before daylight, were taking refuge beneath the forest beeches, waiting for the others. Souvarine, whom the young man went up to consult, shrugged his shoulders; ten resolute fellows could do the job better than a crowd; and he turned back to the open book before him, refusing to join in. The whole thing threatened to turn into sentiment when it would have been enough to adopt the simple method of burning Montsou. As Étienne left the house he saw Rasseneur, seated before the metal stove and looking very pale, while his wife, in her everlasting black dress, was abusing him in polite and cutting terms.

Maheu was of the opinion that they ought to keep their promise. A meeting like this was sacred. However, the night had calmed their fever; he was now fearing misfortune, and he explained that it was their duty to go over there to keep their mates on the right path. La Maheude approved with a nod. Étienne repeated complacently that it was necessary to adopt revolutionary methods, without threatening any person's life. Before setting out he refused his share of a loaf that had been given him the evening before, together with a bottle of gin; but he drank three little glasses, one after the other, saying that he wanted to keep out the cold; he even went off with a flask full. Alzire would look after the children. Old Bonnemort, whose legs were suffering from yesterday's walk, remained in bed.

They did not go away together, from motives of prudence. Jeanlin had disappeared long ago. Maheu and la Maheude went off on the side sloping towards Montsou; while Étienne turned towards the forest, where he proposed to join his mates. On the way he caught up a group of women among whom he recognized old Mother Brûlé and la Levaque; as they walked they were eating chestnuts which la Mouquette had brought; they swallowed the skins so as to feel more in their stomachs. But in the forest he found no one; the

men were already at Jean-Bart. He took the same route, and arrived
at the pit at the moment when Levaque and some hundred others
were turning into the square. Miners were coming up from every
direction – the men by the main road, the women by the fields, all
at random, without leaders, without weapons, flowing naturally
thither like water which runs down a slope. Étienne spotted Jeanlin,
who had climbed up on a footbridge, installed as though at a
theatre. He ran faster, and entered among the first. There were
scarcely three hundred of them.

There was some hesitation when Deneulin showed himself at the
top of the staircase which led to the receiving-hall.

'What do you want?' he asked in a loud voice.

After having watched the departure of the carriage, from which
his daughters were still laughing and waving towards him, he had
returned to the pit overtaken by a strange anxiety. Everything,
however, was found in good order. The men had gone down; the
cage was working, and he became reassured again, and was talking
to the overman when the approach of the strikers was announced
to him. He had placed himself at a window of the screening-shed;
and in the face of this increasing flood which filled the square, he at
once felt his impotence. How could he defend these buildings, open
on every side? he could scarcely group some twenty of his workmen
round himself. He was lost.

'What do you want?' he repeated, pale with repressed anger,
making an effort to accept his disaster courageously.

There were pushes and growls amid the crowd. Étienne at last
came forward, saying:

'We do not come to injure you, sir, but work must cease
everywhere.'

Deneulin frankly treated him like a fool.

'Do you think you will do me some good if you stop work at my
place? You might just as well fire a gun off into my back. Yes, my
men are below, and they shall not come up, unless you mean to
murder me first!'

These rough words raised a clamour. Maheu had to hold back
Levaque, who was pushing forward in a threatening manner, while
Étienne went on discussing, and tried to convince Deneulin of the
lawfulness of their revolutionary conduct. But the latter replied by
invoking the right to work. Besides, he refused to discuss such folly;
he was master in his own place. His only regret was that he had not
four gendarmes here to sweep away this mob.

'To be sure, it is my fault; I deserve what has happened to me.

With fellows of your sort force is the only argument. It's like the Government that thinks it can buy you by concessions. You will overthrow it, that's all, when it has given you weapons.'

Étienne was quivering, but still restrained himself. He lowered his voice.

'I beg you, sir, give the order for your men to come up. I cannot answer for my mates. You may avoid a disaster.'

'No! leave me alone! Do I know you? You do not belong to my works, you have no quarrel with me. It is only brigands who thus scour the country to pillage houses.'

Loud vociferations now drowned his voice, the women especially abused him. But he continued to hold his own, experiencing a certain relief in this frankness with which he expressed his disciplinarian nature. Since he was ruined in any case, he thought platitudes a useless cowardice. But their numbers went on increasing; nearly five hundred were pushing towards the door, and he might have been torn to pieces if his overman had not pulled him violently back.

'For mercy's sake, sir! There will be a massacre. What is the good of letting men be killed for nothing?'

He struggled and protested in one last cry thrown at the crowd:

'You gang of brigands, you will know what for, when we are masters again!'

They led him away; the hustling of the crowd had thrown the first ranks against the staircase so that the rail was twisted. It was the women who pushed and screamed and urged on the men. The door yielded at once; it was a door without a lock, simply closed by a latch. But the staircase was too narrow for the pushing crowd, which would have taken long to get in if the rear of the besiegers had not gone off to enter by other openings. Then they poured in on all sides – by the shed, the screening-place, the boiler buildings. In less than five minutes the whole pit belonged to them; they swarmed onto every storey in the midst of furious gestures and cries, carried away by their victory over this master who resisted.

Maheu, in terror, had rushed forward among the first, saying to Étienne:

'They must not kill him!'

The latter was already running; then, when Étienne understood that Deneulin had barricaded himself in the foremen's room, he replied:

'Well, would it be our fault? such a madman!'

He was feeling anxious, however, being still too calm to yield to this outburst of anger. His pride of leadership also suffered on seeing the crowd escape from his authority and become enraged, going beyond the cold execution of the will of the people, such as he had anticipated. In vain he called for coolness, shouting that they must not put right on their enemies' side by acts of useless destruction.

'To the boilers!' shouted old Mother Brûlé. 'Put out the fires!'

Levaque, who had found a file, was brandishing it like a dagger, dominating the tumult with a terrible cry:

'Cut the cables! cut the cables!'

Soon they all repeated this; only Étienne and Maheu continued to protest, dazed, and shouting into the tumult without making themselves heard. At last the former was able to cry:

'But there are men below, mates!'

The noise increased and voices arose from all sides:

'So much the worse! – Ought not to go down! – Serve the traitors right! – Yes, yes, let them stay there! – And then, they have the ladders!'

Then, when this idea of the ladders had made them still more obstinate, Étienne saw that he would have to yield. For fear of a greater disaster he hastened towards the engine, wishing at all events to bring the cages up, so that the cables, being cut above the shaft, should not smash them by falling down with their enormous weight. The engine-man had disappeared as well as the few daytime workers; and he took hold of the starting lever, manipulating it while Levaque and two others climbed up the metal scaffold which supported the pulleys. The cages were hardly fixed on the keeps when the strident sound was heard of the file biting into the steel. There was deep silence, and this noise seemed to fill the whole pit; all raised their heads, looking and listening, seized by emotion. In the first rank Maheu felt a fierce joy possess him, as if the teeth of the file would deliver them from misfortune by eating into the cable of one of these dens of wretchedness, into which they would never descend again.

But la Brûlé had disappeared by the shed stairs still shouting:

'The fires must be put out! To the boilers! to the boilers!'

Some women followed her. La Maheude hastened to prevent them from smashing everything, just as her husband had tried to reason with the men. She was the calmest of them; you could demand your rights without making a mess in people's places. When she entered the boiler building the women were already chasing away the two stokers, and la Brûlé, armed with a large shovel, and crouching down before one of the stoves, was violently emptying it, throwing the red-hot coke on to the brick floor, where it continued to burn with black smoke. There were ten stoves for the five boilers. Soon the women warmed to the work, la Levaque manipulating her shovel with both hands, la Mouquette raising her clothes up to her thighs so as not to catch fire, all looking red in the reflection of the flames, sweating and dishevelled in this witch's kitchen. The piles of coal increased, and the burning heat cracked the ceiling of the vast hall.

'Enough, now!' cried la Maheude; 'the store-room is afire.'

'So much the better,' replied la Brûlé. 'That will do the job. Ah, by God! haven't I said that I would pay them out for the death of my man!'

At this moment Jeanlin's shrill voice was heard:

'Look out! I'll put it out, I will! Leave it to me!'

He had come in among the first, and had scurried about among the crowd, delighted at the fray and seeking out what mischief he could do; the idea had occurred to him to turn on the discharge taps and let off the steam.

The jets went off with the violence of gunshot; the five boilers were emptied with a huge blast, whistling out in an earpiercing roar of thunder. Everything had disappeared in the midst of the vapour, the hot coal grew pale, and the women were nothing more than shadows with broken gestures. The child alone appeared mounted on the gallery, behind the whirlwinds of white steam, filled with delight and grinning broadly in the joy of unleashing this hurricane.

This lasted nearly a quarter of an hour. A few buckets of water had been thrown over the heaps to complete their extinction; all danger of a fire had gone, but the anger of the crowd had not subsided; on the contrary, it had been whipped up. Men went down with hammers, even the women armed themselves with iron bars; and they talked of smashing boilers, of breaking engines, and of demolishing the mine.

Étienne, forewarned, hastened up with Maheu. He himself was becoming intoxicated and carried away by this hot fever of revenge. He struggled, however, and entreated them to be calm, now that, with cut cables, extinguished fires, and empty boilers, work was impossible. Still no one listened to him and he was again about to be carried away by the crowd, when hoots arose outside at a little low door where the ladder passage emerged.

'Down with the traitors! – Oh! look at the filthy chops of the cowards! – Down with them! down with them!'

The men were beginning to come up from below. The first arrivals, blinded by the daylight, stood there with quivering eyelids. Then they moved away, trying to reach the road and flee.

'Down with the cowards! down with the traitors!'

The whole gang of strikers had run up. In less than three minutes there was not a man left in the buildings; the five hundred Montsou men were ranged in two rows, and the Vandame men, who had had the treachery to go down, were forced to pass between this double line. And as every fresh miner appeared at the door of the passage, covered with the black mùd of work and with garments in rags, the hooting increased, and ferocious jokes arose. Oh! look at that one! – three inches of legs and then his arse! and this one with his nose eaten by those Volcan girls! and this other, with eyes pissing out enough wax to furnish ten cathedrals! and this other, the tall fellow without a bum and as long as Lent! An enormous putter-woman, who rolled out with her breast to her belly and her belly to her backside, raised a furious laugh. They wanted to handle them, the joking increased and was turning to cruelty, blows would be raining down; while the row of poor devils came out shivering and silent beneath the abuse, with sidelong looks in expectation of blows, glad when they could at last rush away out of the mine.

'Hey! how many are there in there?' asked Étienne.

He was astonished to see them still coming out, and irritated at the idea that it was not a mere handful of workers, urged by hunger, terrorized by the foremen. They had lied to him, then, in the forest; nearly all Jean-Bart had gone down. But a cry escaped from him and he rushed forward when he saw Chaval standing on the threshold. 'By God! is this the meeting you called us to?'

Curses broke out and there was a movement of the crowd towards the traitor. What! he had sworn with them the day before, and now they found him down below with the others! Was he, then, making fools of people?

'Off with him! To the shaft! to the shaft!'

Chaval, white with fear, stammered and tried to explain. But Étienne cut him short, beside himself with anger and sharing the fury of the crowd.

'You wanted to be in it with us, and you'll be in it. Come on! get a move on, you pig!'

Another cry drowned his voice. Catherine, in her turn, had just appeared, dazzled by the bright sunlight, and frightened at falling into the midst of these savages. She was panting, with legs aching from the hundred and two ladders, and with bleeding palms, when la Maheude, seeing her, rushed forward with her hand up.

'Ah! slut! you, too! When your mother is dying of hunger you betray her for that pimp of yours!'

Maheu held back her arm, and stopped the blow. But he shook his daughter; he was enraged, like his wife; he threw her behaviour in her face, and both lost their heads, shouting louder than their mates.

The sight of Catherine had completed Étienne's exasperation. He repeated:

'On we go to the other pits, and you come with us, you swine!'

Chaval had scarcely time to get his clogs from the shed and to throw his woollen jacket over his frozen shoulders. They all dragged him on, forcing him to run in the midst of them. Catherine, bewildered, also put on her clogs, buttoning at her neck her man's old jacket, with which she kept off the cold; and she ran behind her lover, she would not leave him, for surely they were going to murder him.

Then in two minutes Jean-Bart was emptied. Jeanlin had found a horn and was blowing it, producing strident sounds, as though he were gathering oxen together. The women – la Brûlé, la Levaque, and la Mouquette – raised their skirts to run, while Levaque, with an axe in his hand, waved it about like a drum-major's stick. Other men continued to arrive; there were nearly a thousand, without order, again flowing on to the road like a torrent let loose. The gates were too narrow, and the palings were broken down.

'To the pits! – Down with the traitors! – No more work!'

And Jean-Bart fell suddenly into a great silence. Not a man was left, not a breath was heard. Deneulin came out of the foremen's room, and quite alone, with a gesture forbidding any one to follow him, he inspected the pit. He was pale and very calm.

At first he stopped in front of the shaft, lifting his eyes to look at the cut cables; the steel ends hung useless, the bite of the file had left a bleeding sore, a fresh wound which gleamed in the black grease. Afterwards he went up to the engine, and looked at the crank, which was motionless, like the joint of a colossal limb struck by paralysis. He touched the metal, which had already cooled, and the cold made him shudder as though he had touched a corpse. Then he went down to the boiler-room, walked slowly in front of the extinguished stoves, yawning and inundated, and struck his foot against the boilers, which sounded hollow. Well then! it was the end; his ruin was complete. Even if he mended the cables and lit the fires, where would he find men? Another fortnight's strike and he would be bankrupt. And in this certainty of disaster he no longer felt any hatred of the Montsou bandits; he felt that all had a hand in it, that it was a general agelong fault. They were brutes, no doubt, but brutes who could not read, and who were dying of hunger.

CHAPTER 4

And the troop went off over the flat plain, white with frost beneath the pale winter sun, and overflowed the path as they passed through the beetroot fields.

From the Fourche-aux-Boeufs, Étienne had assumed command. He cried his orders while the crowd moved on, and organized the march. Jeanlin galloped at the head, performing barbarous music on his horn. Then the women came in the first ranks, some of them armed with sticks: la Maheude, with wild eyes seemed to be seeking afar for the promised city of justice, la Brûlé, la Levaque, la Mouquette, striding along beneath their rags, like soldiers setting out for war. If they ran into trouble, they would see if the police dared to strike women. And the men followed in a confused flock, a stream that grew larger and larger, bristling with iron bars and dominated by Levaque's single axe, with its blade glistening in the sun. Étienne, in the middle, kept Chaval in sight, forcing him to walk ahead of him; while Maheu, behind, gloomily kept an eye on Catherine, the only woman among these men, obstinately trotting near her lover for fear that he would be hurt. Bare heads were dishevelled in the open air; only the clatter of clogs could be heard, like the movement of released cattle, carried away by Jeanlin's wild trumpeting.

But suddenly a new cry arose:

'Bread! bread! bread!'

It was midday; the hunger of six weeks on strike was awaking in these empty stomachs, whipped up by this race across the fields. The few crusts of the morning and la Mouquette's chestnuts had long been forgotten; their stomachs were crying out, and this suffering was added to their fury against the traitors.

'To the pits! No more work! Bread!'

Étienne, who had refused to eat his share at the settlement, felt an unbearable tearing sensation in his chest. He made no complaint, but mechanically took his flask from time to time and swallowed a gulp of gin, shaking so much that he thought he needed it to carry him to the end. His cheeks were heated and his eyes inflamed. He kept his head, however, and still wished to avoid needless destruction.

As they arrived at the Joiselle road a Vandame pikeman, who had joined the band for revenge on his master, urged the men towards the right, shouting:

'To Gaston-Marie! Must stop the pump! Let the water destroy Jean-Bart!'

The mob was already turning, in spite of the protests of Étienne, who begged them to let the pumping continue. What was the good of destroying the galleries? It offended his workman's heart, in spite of his resentment. Maheu also thought it unjust to take revenge on a machine. But the pikeman still shouted his cry of vengeance, and Étienne had to shout still louder:

'To Mirou! There are traitors down there! To Mirou! to Mirou!'

With a gesture, he had turned the crowd towards the left road; while Jeanlin, going ahead, was blowing louder than ever. A great commotion was produced in the crowd; this time Gaston-Marie was saved.

And the four kilometres which separated them from Mirou were covered in half an hour, almost at running pace, across the interminable plain. The canal on this side cut across it with a long icy ribbon. The leafless trees on the banks, changed by the frost into giant candelabra, alone broke this pale uniformity, prolonged and lost in the sky at the horizon as on a sea. An undulation of the ground hid Montsou and Marchiennes; there was nothing but bare immensity.

They reached the pit, and found a foreman standing on a footbridge at the screening-shed to receive them. They all well knew old Quandieu, the doyen of the Montsou foremen, an old man whose skin and hair were quite white, and who was in his seventies, a miracle of fine health in the mines.

'What have you come after here, you pack of meddlers?' he shouted.

The crowd stopped. It was no longer a master, it was a mate; and a certain respect held them back before this old workman.

'There are men down below,' said Étienne. 'Make them come up.'

'Yes, there are men there,' said old Quandieu, 'some six dozen; the others were afraid of you evil buggers! But I warn you that not one comes up, or you will have to deal with me!'

Exclamations arose, the men pushed, the women advanced. Quickly coming down from the footbridge, the foreman now barred the door.

Then Maheu tried to intervene.

'It is our right, old man. How can we make the strike general if we don't force all the mates to be on our side?'

The old man was silent a moment. Evidently his ignorance on the subject of solidarity equalled the pikeman's. At last he replied:

'It may be your right, I can't say. But I only know my orders. I am alone here; the men are down till three, and they shall stay there till three.'

The last words were lost in booing. Fists were threateningly advanced, the women deafened him, and their hot breath blew in his face. But he still held out, his head erect, and his beard and hair white as snow; his courage had so swollen his voice that he could be heard distinctly over the tumult.

'By God! you shall not pass! As true as the sun shines, I would rather die than let you touch the cables. Don't push any more, or I'm damned if I don't fling myself down the shaft in front of you!'

The crowd drew back shuddering and impressed. He went on:

'Where is the swine who does not understand that? I am only a workman like you others. I have been told to guard here, and I'm guarding.'

That was as far as old Quandieu's intelligence went, stiffened by the obstinacy of his military duty, his narrow brain, and his eyes dimmed by the black melancholy of half a century spent underground. The men looked at him moved, feeling within them an echo of what he said, this military obedience, the sense of fraternity and resignation in danger. He saw that they were hesitating still, and repeated:

'I'm damned if I don't fling myself down the shaft before your eyes!'

A great shudder ran through the mob. They all turned, and in the rush took the right-hand road, which stretched far away through the fields. Again cries arose:

'To Madeleine! to Crèvecoeur! no more work! Bread! bread!'

But in the centre, as they went on, there was a disturbance. It was Chaval, they said, who was trying to take advantage of an opportunity to escape. Étienne had seized him by the arm, threatening to do for him if he was planning some treachery. And the other struggled and protested furiously:

'What's all this for? Isn't a man free? I've been freezing the last hour. I want to clean myself. Let me go!'

He was, in fact, suffering from the coal glued to his skin by sweat, and his woollen jersey was no protection.

'On you go, or we'll clean you up,' replied Étienne. 'It's your fault for going on about asking for blood.'

They were still running, and he turned towards Catherine, who was keeping up well. It annoyed him to feel her so near him, so miserable, shivering beneath her man's old jacket and her muddy trousers. She must be nearly dead of fatigue, she was running all the same.

'You can go off, you can,' he said at last.

Catherine seemed not to hear. Her eyes, on meeting Étienne's, only flickered with reproach for a moment. She did not stop. Why did he want her to leave her man? Chaval was not at all kind, it was true; he would even beat her sometimes. But he was her man, the one who had had her first; and it enraged her that they should throw themselves on him – more than a thousand of them. She would have defended him without any tenderness at all, out of pride.

'Off you go!' repeated Maheu, violently.

Her father's order slackened her pace for a moment. She trembled, and her eyelids swelled with tears. Then, in spite of her fear, she came back to the same place again, still running. Then they let her be.

The mob crossed the Joiselle road, went a short distance along the Cron road and then went up towards Cougny. On this side, factory chimneys striped the flat horizon; wooden sheds, brick workshops with large dusty windows, appeared along the street. They passed one after another the low buildings of two settlements – the Cent-Quatre-Vingts, then the Soixante-Seize; and from each of them, at the sound of the horn and the clamour arising from every mouth, whole families came out – men, women, and children – running to join their mates in the rear. When they came up to Madeleine there were at least fifteen hundred. The road descended in a gentle slope; the rumbling flood of strikers had to turn round the pit-bank before they could spread over the yards.

It was now not more than two o'clock. But the foremen had been warned and were hastening the ascent as the mob arrived. The men were all up, only some twenty remained and were now disembarking from the cage. They fled and were pursued with stones. Two were struck, another left the sleeve of his jacket behind. This man-hunt saved the material, and neither the cables nor the boilers were touched. The flood was already moving away, rolling on towards the next pit.

This one, Crèvecoeur, was only five hundred metres away from Madeleine. There, also, the mob arrived in the midst of the ascent. A putter-girl was taken and whipped by the women with her breeches split open and her buttocks exposed before the laughing men. The trammer-boys had their ears boxed, the pikemen got away, their sides blue from blows and their noses bleeding. And in this growing ferocity, in this age-old need of revenge which was turning every head with madness, the choked cries went on, death to traitors, hatred against ill-paid work, the roaring of bellies after bread. They began to cut the cables, but the file would not bite, and the task was too long now that the fever was on them for moving onward, for ever onward. At the boilers a tap was broken; while the water, thrown by bucketsful into the stoves, made the metal gratings burst.

Outside they were talking of marching on Saint-Thomas. This was the best disciplined pit. The strike had not touched it, nearly seven hundred men must have gone down there. This exasperated them; they would wait for these men with sticks, ranged for battle, just to see who would get the best of it. But the rumour spread that there were gendarmes at Saint-Thomas, the gendarmes of the morning whom they had made fun of. How was this known? nobody could say. No matter! they were seized by fear and decided on Feutry-Cantel. Their giddiness carried them on, all were on the road, clanking their clogs, rushing forward. To Feutry-Cantel! to Feutry-Cantel! The cowards there were certainly four hundred in number and there would be fun! Situated three kilometres away, this pit lay in a fold of the ground near the Scarpe. They were already climbing the slope of the Plâtrières, beyond the road to Beaugnies, when a voice, no one knew from whom, started the rumour that the soldiers were, perhaps, down there at Feutry-Cantel. Then from one end to the other of the column it was repeated that the soldiers were there. They slackened their pace, panic gradually spread across this land made idle from lack of work, which they had been scouring for hours. Why had they not come across any soldiers? This impunity troubled them, at the thought of the repression which they felt to be coming.

Without any one knowing where it came from, a new word of command turned them towards another pit.

'To the Victoire! to the Victoire!'

Were there, then, neither soldiers nor police at the Victoire? Nobody knew. All seemed reassured. And turning round they descended from the Beaumont side and cut across the fields to reach the Joiselle road. The railway line barred their passage, and they crossed it, pulling down the palings. Now they were approaching Montsou, the gradual undulation of the landscape grew less, the sea of beetroot fields enlarged, reaching far away to the black houses at Marchiennes.

This time it was a march of five good kilometres. So strong an impulse pushed them on that they had no feeling of their terrible fatigue, or of their bruised and aching feet. The rear continued to lengthen, increased by mates enlisted on the roads and in the settlements. When they had passed the canal at the Magache bridge, and appeared before the Victoire, there were two thousand of them. But three o'clock had struck, the ascent was completed, not a man remained below. Their disappointment was spent in vain threats; they could only heave broken bricks at the workmen who had arrived to take their duty at the earth-cutting. There was a rush, and the deserted pit belonged to them. And in their rage at not finding a traitor's face to strike, they attacked things. A rankling abscess was bursting within them, a poisoned boil of slow growth. Years and years of hunger tortured them with a thirst for massacre and destruction.

Behind a shed Étienne saw some porters filling a wagon with coal.

'Just clear out of the bloody place!' he shouted. 'Not a bit of coal goes out!'

At his orders some hundred strikers ran up, and the porters only just had time to escape. Men unharnessed the horses, which were frightened and set off, struck in the haunches; while others, over-turning the wagon, broke the shafts.

Levaque, with violent blows of his axe, had thrown himself on the platforms to break down the footbridges. They resisted, and it occurred to him to tear up the rails, destroying the line from one end of the square to the other. Soon the whole mob set to this task. Maheu pulled up the metal chairs, armed with his iron bar which he used as a lever. During this time la Brûlé led away the women and invaded the lamp cabin, where their sticks covered the soil with the debris of lamps. La Maheude, in a frenzy, was smashing things

as vigorously as la Levaque. All were soaked in oil, and la
Mouquette dried her hands on her skirt, laughing to find herself so
dirty. Jeanlin, for a joke, had emptied a lamp down her neck. But
all this revenge produced nothing to eat. Stomachs were crying out
louder than ever. And the great lamentation dominated still:

'Bread! bread! bread!'

A foreman who used to be at the Victoire kept a stall near by.
No doubt he had fled in fear, for his shed was abandoned. When
the women came back, and the men had finished destroying the
railway, they besieged the stall, the shutters of which yielded at
once. They found no bread there; there were only two pieces of raw
flesh and a sack of potatoes. But in the pillage they discovered some
fifty bottles of gin, which disappeared like a drop of water drunk
up by the sand.

Étienne, having emptied his flask, was able to refill it. Little by
little a terrible drunkenness, the drunkenness of the starved, was
inflaming his eyes and baring his teeth like a wolf's between his
pallid lips. Suddenly he noticed that Chaval had gone off in the
midst of the tumult. He swore, and men ran to seize the fugitive,
who was hiding with Catherine behind the timber supply.

'Ah! you dirty swine; you are afraid of getting into trouble!'
shouted Étienne. 'It was you in the forest who called for a strike of
the engine-men, to stop the pumps, and now you want to play a
filthy trick on us! Very well! By God! we will go back to Gaston-
Marie. I will have you smash the pump; yes, by God! you shall
smash it!'

He was drunk; he was urging his men against this pump which
he had saved a few hours earlier.

'To Gaston-Marie! to Gaston-Marie!'

They all cheered, and rushed on, while Chaval, seized by the
shoulders, was drawn and pushed violently along, while he constantly asked to be allowed to wash.

'Just clear off?' cried Maheu to Catherine who had also begun to
run again.

This time she did not even draw back, but turned her burning
eyes on her father, and went on running.

Once more the mob ploughed through the flat plain. They were
retracing their steps over the long straight paths, by the fields
endlessly spread out. It was four o'clock; the setting sun lengthened
the shadows of this horde with their furious gestures over the frozen
soil.

They avoided Montsou, and farther on rejoined the Joiselle road;

to spare the journey round Fourche-aux-Boeufs, they passed beneath the walls of La Piolaine. The Grégoires had just gone out, having to visit a lawyer before going to dine with the Hennebeaus, where they would find Cécile. The estate seemed asleep, with its avenue of deserted limes, its kitchen garden and its orchard bared by the winter. Nothing was stirring in the house, and the closed windows were misty from the condensation within. Out of the profound silence an impression of good-natured comfort arose, the patriarchal sensation of good beds and a good table, the wise happiness of the proprietor's existence.

Without stopping, the mob cast gloomy looks through the grating and at the length of protecting walls, bristling with broken bottles. The cry arose again:

'Bread! bread! bread!'

The dogs alone replied, by barking ferociously, a pair of Great Danes, with rough coats, who stood with open jaws. And behind the closed blind there were only the servants, Mélanie the cook and Honorine the housemaid, attracted by this cry, pale and perspiring with fear at seeing these savages go by. They fell on their knees, and thought themselves killed on hearing a single stone breaking a pane of a neighbouring window. It was a joke of Jeanlin's; he had made a sling with a piece of cord, and had just sent a little passing greeting to the Grégoires. Already he was again blowing his horn, the mob was lost in the distance, and the cry grew fainter:

'Bread! bread! bread!'

They arrived at Gaston-Marie in still greater numbers, more than two thousand five hundred madmen, breaking everything, sweeping away everything, with the force of a raging torrent. Some gendarmes had passed here an hour earlier, and had gone off towards Saint-Thomas, led astray by some peasants; in their haste they had not even taken the precaution of leaving a few men behind to guard the pit. In less than a quarter of an hour the fires were overturned, the boilers emptied, the buildings torn down and devastated. But it was the pump which they specially threatened. It was not enough to stop it in the last expiring breath of its steam; they threw themselves on it as on a living person whose life they required.

'The first blow is yours!' repeated Étienne, putting a hammer into Chaval's hand. 'Come! you have sworn with the others!'

Chaval drew back trembling, and in the hustling the hammer fell; while other men, without waiting, battered the pump with blows from iron bars, blows from bricks, blows from anything they could lay their hands on. Some even broke sticks over it. The nuts leapt off, the pieces of steel and copper were dislocated like torn limbs. The blow of a shovel, delivered with full force, fractured the metal body; the water escaped and emptied out, and there was a supreme gurgle like an agonizing death-rattle.

That was the end, and the mob found itself outside again, madly pushing on behind Étienne, who would not let Chaval go.

'Kill him! the traitor! To the shaft! to the shaft!'

The livid wretch, clinging with imbecile obstinacy to his fixed idea, continued to stammer his need of cleaning himself.

'Wait, if that bothers you,' said la Levaque. 'Here! here's a bucket!'

There was a pool there, formed by the water from the pump. It was white with a thick layer of ice; and they struck it and broke the ice, forcing him to dip his head in this cold water.

'Down you go, then,' repeated la Brûlé. 'By God! if you don't dip your head in, we'll shove you in. And now you shall have a drink; yes, yes, like a beast, with your snout in the trough!'

He had to drink on all fours. They all laughed, with cruel laughter. One woman pulled his ears, another woman threw in his face a handful of dung found fresh on the road. His old woollen jacket in tatters no longer held together. He was haggard, stumbling, and lurched about trying to flee.

Maheu had pushed him, and la Maheude was among those who grew furious, both of them satisfying an old grudge; even la Mouquette, who generally remained such good friends with her old lovers, was wild with this one, treating him as a good-for-nothing, and talking of taking his breeches down to see if he was still a man.

Étienne made her hold her tongue.

'That's enough. There's no need for all to set to it. If you like, you, we will just settle it together.'

His fists closed and his eyes were lit up with homicidal fury; his intoxication was turning into the desire to kill.

'Are you ready? It's you or me. Give him a knife; I've got mine.'

Catherine, exhausted and terrified, gazed at him. She remembered what he had told her about his desire to destroy a man when he had drunk, poisoned after the third glass, to such an extent had his drunkards of parents put this beastliness into his body. Suddenly she leapt forward, struck him with both hands, and choking with indignation shouted into his face:

'Coward! coward! coward! Isn't it enough, then, all the vile

things you've done? You want to kill him now that he can't stand
up any longer!'

She turned towards her father and her mother; she turned
towards the others.

'You are cowards! cowards! Kill me, then, with him! I will tear
your eyes out, I will, if you touch him again. Oh! the cowards!'

And she planted herself in front of her man to defend him,
forgetting the beatings, forgetting the life of misery, lifted up by the
idea that she belonged to him since he had taken her, and that it
brought her shame when they so crushed him.

Étienne had grown pale beneath the girl's blows. At first he had
been about to knock her down; then, after having wiped his face
with the movement of a man who is coming out of a drunken state,
he said to Chaval, in the midst of deep silence:

'She is right; that's enough. Off you go.'

Immediately Chaval was away, and Catherine galloped behind
him. The crowd gazed at them as they disappeared round a corner
of the road; but la Maheude muttered:

'You were wrong; ought to have kept him. He is sure to be up to
some treachery.'

But the mob began to march on again. Five o'clock was about to
strike. The sun, as red as a furnace on the edge of the horizon,
seemed to set fire to the whole plain. A pedlar who was passing
informed them that the military were descending from the Crèvecoeur side. Then they turned. An order rang out:

'To Montsou! To the manager's place! – Bread! bread! bread!'

CHAPTER 5

Monsieur Hennebeau had placed himself in front of his study
window to watch the departure of the carriage which was taking
away his wife to lunch at Marchiennes. His eyes followed Négrel
for a moment, as he trotted beside the carriage door. Then he
quietly returned and seated himself at his desk. When neither his
wife nor his nephew animated the place with their presence the
house seemed empty. On this day the coachman was driving his
wife; Rose, the new housemaid, had leave to go out till five o'clock;
there only remained Hippolyte, the valet de chambre, trailing about

the rooms in slippers, and the cook, who had been occupied since dawn in struggling with her saucepans, entirely absorbed in the dinner which was to be given in the evening. So Monsieur Hennebeau promised himself a day of serious work in this deep calm of the deserted house.

Towards nine o'clock, although he had received orders to send every one away, Hippolyte took the liberty of announcing Dansaert, who was bringing news. The manager then heard, for the first time, of the meeting in the forest the evening before; the details were very precise, and he listened while thinking of the affair with la Pierronne, so well known that two or three anonymous letters every week denounced the licentiousness of the overman. Evidently the husband had talked, and no doubt the wife had, too. He even took advantage of the occasion; he let the overman know that he was aware of everything, contenting himself with recommending prudence for fear of a scandal. Startled by these reproaches in the midst of his report, Dansaert denied, stammered excuses, while his great nose confessed the crime by its sudden redness. He did not insist, however, glad to get off so easily; for, as a rule, the manager displayed the implacable severity of the virtuous man whenever an employee allowed himself the indulgence of a pretty girl in the pit. The conversation continued concerning the strike; that meeting in the forest was only the swagger of blusterers; nothing serious threatened. In any case, the settlements would surely not stir for some days, beneath the impression of respectful fear which must have been produced by the military manoeuvres of the morning.

When Monsieur Hennebeau was alone again he was, however, on the point of sending a telegram to the prefect. Only the fear of uselessly showing a sign of anxiety held him back. Already he could not forgive himself his lack of insight in saying everwhere, and even writing to the directors, that the strike would last at most a fortnight. It had been going on and on for nearly two months, to his great surprise, and he was in despair over it; he felt himself every day to be losing face and compromised, and was forced to imagine some brilliant achievement which would bring him back into favour with the directors. He had just asked them for orders in the case of a skirmish. There was delay over the reply, and he was expecting it by the afternoon post. He said to himself that there would be time then to send out telegrams, and to obtain the military occupation of the pits, if such was the desire of those gentlemen. In his own opinion there would certainly be a battle, bloodshed and deaths. This responsibility troubled him in spite of his usual energy.

Up to eleven o'clock he worked peacefully; there was no sound in the dead house except Hippolyte's waxing-stick, which was rubbing a floor far away on the first floor. Then, one after the other, he received two messages, the first announcing the attack on Jean-Bart by the Montsou mob, the second telling of the cut cables, the overturned fires, and all the destruction. He could not understand. Why had the strikers gone to Deneulin instead of attacking one of the Company's pits? Besides, they were quite welcome to sack Vandame; that would merely ripen the plan of conquest which he was meditating. And at midday he lunched alone in the large dining-room, served so quietly by the servant that he could not even hear his slippers. This solitude made his preoccupations more gloomy; he was feeling sick at the heart when a foreman, who had arrived running, was shown in, and told him of the mob's march on Mirou. Almost immediately, as he was finishing his coffee, a telegram informed him that Madeleine and Crèvecoeur were in their turn threatened. Then his perplexity became extreme. He was expecting the postman at two o'clock; ought he at once to ask for troops? or would it be better to wait patiently, and not to act until he had received the directors' orders? He went back into his study; he wished to read a report which he had asked Négrel to prepare the day before for the prefect. But he could not put his hand on it: he reflected that perhaps the young man had left it in his room, where he often wrote at night, and without taking any decision, pursued by the idea of this report, he went upstairs to look for it in the room.

As he entered, Monsieur Hennebeau was surprised: the room had not been done, no doubt through Hippolyte's forgetfulness or laziness. There was a moist heat there, the close heat of the past night, made heavier from the mouth of the hot-air stove being left open; and he was suffocated, too, with a penetrating perfume, which he thought must be the odour of the water with which the washbasin was full. There was great disorder in the room – garments scattered about, damp towels thrown on the backs of chairs, the bed left unmade, with a sheet drawn back and draggling on the carpet. But at first he only glanced round with an abstracted look as he went towards a table covered with papers to look for the missing report. Twice he examined the papers one by one, but it was certainly not there. Where the devil could that madcap Paul have stuffed it?

And as Monsieur Hennebeau went back into the middle of the room, glancing at each article of furniture, he noticed in the open bed a bright point which shone like a star. He approached mechanically and put out his hand. It was a little gold scent-bottle lying between two folds of the sheet. He at once recognized a scent-bottle belonging to Madame Hennebeau, the little ether bottle which was always with her. But he could not understand its presence here: how could it have got into Paul's bed? And suddenly he grew terribly pale. His wife had slept there.

'Beg your pardon, sir,' murmured Hippolyte's voice through the door. 'I saw you going up.'

The servant entered and was thrown into consternation by the disorder.

'Lord! Why, the room is not done! So Rose has gone out, leaving all the housework to me!'

Monsieur Hennebeau had hidden the bottle in his hand and was pressing it almost to breaking point.

'What do you want?'

'It's another man, sir; he has come from Crèvecoeur with a letter.'

'Good! Leave me alone; tell him to wait.'

His wife had slept there! When he had bolted the door he opened his hand again and looked at the little bottle which had left its imprint in red on his flesh. Suddenly he saw and understood; this filthiness had been going on in his house for months. He recalled his old suspicion, the rustling against the doors, the naked feet at night through the silent house. Yes, it was his wife who went up to sleep there!

Falling into a chair opposite the bed, which he gazed at fixedly, he remained some minutes as though crushed. A noise aroused him; someone was knocking at the door, trying to open it. He recognized the servant's voice.

'Sir – Ah! you are shut in, sir.'

'What is it now?'

'There seems to be a hurry; the men are breaking everything. There are two more messengers below. There are also some telegrams.'

'Just leave me alone! I am coming directly.'

The idea that Hippolyte would himself have discovered the scent-bottle, had he done the room in the morning, had just sent a chill through him. And besides, this man must know; he must have found the bed still hot with adultery twenty times over, with madame's hairs trailing on the pillow, and abominable traces staining the linen. The man kept interrupting him, and it could only be out of malice. Perhaps he had stayed with his ear to the door, excited by the debauchery of his masters.

Monsieur Hennebeau did not move. He still gazed at the bed. His long past of suffering unfolded before him: his marriage with this woman, their immediate misunderstanding of the heart and of the flesh, the lovers whom she had had unknown to him, and the lover whom he had tolerated for ten years, as one tolerates an impure taste in a sick woman. Then came their arrival at Montsou, the mad hope of curing her, months of languor, of sleepy exile, the approach of old age which would, perhaps, at last give her back to him. Then their nephew arrived, this Paul to whom she became a mother, and to whom she spoke of her dead heart buried for ever beneath the ashes. And he, the foolish husband, foresaw nothing; he adored this woman who was his wife, whom other men had possessed, but whom he alone could not possess! He adored her with shameful passion, so that he would have fallen on his knees if she had but given him the leavings of other men! The leavings of the others she gave to this boy.

The sound of a distant bell at this moment made Monsieur Hennebeau start. He recognized it; it was struck, by his orders, when the postman arrived. He rose and spoke aloud, breaking into the flood of coarseness which he painfully could not contain.

'Ah! I don't care a bloody hang for their telegrams and their letters! not a bloody hang!'

Now he was carried away by rage, the need of some sewer in which to stamp down all this filthiness with his heels. This woman was a bitch; he sought for crude words and buffeted her image with them. The sudden idea of the marriage between Cécile and Paul, which she was arranging with so quiet a smile, completed his exasperation. There was, then, not even passion, not even jealousy at the bottom of this persistent sensuality? It was now a perverse plaything, the habit of the woman, a recreation taken like a favourite dessert. And he put all the responsibility on her, he regarded as almost innocent the lad at whom she had bitten in this reawakening of appetite, just as one bites at an early green fruit, stolen by the wayside. Whom would she devour, on whom would she fall, when she no longer had complaisant nephews, sufficiently practical to accept in their own family the table, the bed, and the wife?

There was a timid scratch at the door, and Hippolyte allowed himself to whisper through the keyhole:

'The postman, sir. And Monsieur Dansaert, too, has come back, saying that they are killing one another.'

'I'm coming down, good God!'

What should he do to them? Chase them away on their return from Marchiennes, like stinking animals whom he would no longer have beneath his roof? He would take a stick to them, and would tell them to carry on elsewhere their poisonous fornication. It was with their sighs, with their mingled breaths, that the damp warmth of this room had grown heavy; the penetrating odour which had suffocated him was the odour of musk which his wife's skin exhaled, another perverse taste, a fleshly need of violent perfumes; and he seemed to feel also the heat and odour of fornication, of living adultery, in the pots which lay about, in the basins still full, in the disorder of the linen, of the furniture, of the entire room tainted with vice. The fury of impotence threw him on to the bed, which he struck with his fists, belabouring the places where he saw the imprint of their two bodies, enraged with the disordered coverlets and the crumpled sheets, soft and inert beneath his blows, as though exhausted themselves by the embraces of the whole night.

But suddenly he thought he heard Hippolyte coming up again. He was stopped by shame. For a moment he stood panting, wiping his forehead, calming the bounds of his heart. Standing before a mirror he looked at his face, so changed that he did not recognize himself. Then, when he had watched it gradually grow calmer by an effort of supreme will, he went downstairs.

Five messengers were standing below, not counting Dansaert. All brought him news of increasing gravity concerning the march of the strikers among the pits; and the overman told him at length what had gone on at Mirou and the fine behaviour of old Quandieu. He listened, nodding his head, but he did not hear; his thoughts were in the room upstairs. At last he sent them away, saying that he would take due measures. When he was alone again, seated before his desk, he seemed to grow drowsy, with his head between his hands, covering his eyes. His mail was there, and he decided to look for the expected letter, the directors' reply. The lines at first danced before him, but he understood at last that these gentlemen desired a fight; certainly they did not order him to make things worse, but they intimated that disturbances would hasten the conclusion of the strike by provoking energetic repression. After this, he no longer hesitated, but sent off telegrams on all sides – to the prefect of Lille, to the military headquarters at Douai, to the police at Marchiennes. It was a relief; he had nothing to do but shut himself in; he even spread the report that he was suffering from gout. And all the afternoon he hid himself in his study, receiving no one, contenting himself with reading the telegrams and letters which continued to rain in. He thus followed the mob from afar, from Madeleine to Crèvecoeur, from Crèvecoeur to the Victoire, from the Victoire to Gaston-Marie. Information also reached him of the bewilderment of the police and the troops, wandering along the roads, and always with their backs to the pits being attacked. They might kill one another, and destroy everything! He put his head between his hands again, with his fingers over his eyes, and buried himself in the deep silence of the empty house, where he only heard now and then the noise of the cook's saucepans as she bustled about preparing the evening's dinner.

The twilight was already darkening the room; it was five o'clock when a disturbance made Monsieur Hennebeau jump, as he sat dazed and inert with his elbows in his papers. He thought that it was the two wretches coming back. But the tumult increased, and a terrible cry broke out just as he was going to the window:

'Bread! bread! bread!'

It was the strikers, now invading Montsou, while the gendarmes, expecting an attack on the Voreux, were galloping off in the opposite direction, to occupy that pit.

Just then, two kilometres away from the first houses, a little beyond the crossways where the main road cut the Vandame road, Madame Hennebeau and the young ladies had witnessed the passing of the mob. The day had been spent pleasantly at Marchiennes; there had been a delightful lunch with the manager of the Forges, then an interesting visit to the workshops and to the neighbouring glass works to occupy the afternoon; and as they were now going home in the limpid air of the beautiful winter day, Cécile had had the whim to drink a glass of milk, as she noticed a little farm near the edge of the road. They all then got down from the carriage, and Négrel gallantly leapt off his horse; while the peasant-woman, alarmed by all these fine people, rushed about, and spoke of laying a cloth before serving the milk. But Lucie and Jeanne wanted to see the cow milked, and they went into the cattle-shed with their cups, making a little rural party, and laughing greatly at the straw in which their feet sank.

Madame Hennebeau, with her indulgent maternal air, was sipping her drink, when a strange roaring noise outside disturbed her.

'What is that, then?'

The cattle-shed, built at the edge of the road, had a large door for carts, for it was also used as a barn for hay. The young girls, who had put out their heads, were astonished to see on the left a black flood, a shouting mob which was moving along the Vandame road.

'Heavens!' muttered Négrel, who had also gone out. 'Are our noisy devils getting angry at last?'

'It is perhaps the colliers again,' said the peasant woman. 'This is twice they've passed. Seems things are not going well; they're masters of the country.'

She uttered every word prudently, watching the effect on their faces; and when she noticed the fright of all of them, and their deep anxiety at this encounter, she hastened to conclude:

'Oh, the rascals! the rascals!'

Négrel, seeing that it was too late to get into their carriage and reach Montsou, ordered the coachman to bring the vehicle into the farmyard, where it would remain hidden behind a shed. He himself fastened his horse, which a lad had been holding, beneath the shed. When he came back he found his aunt and the young girls in a panic, and ready to follow the peasant-woman, who suggested that they should take refuge in her house. But he was of the opinion that they would be safer where they were, for certainly no one would come and look for them in the hay. The door, however, shut very badly, and had such large chinks in it, that the road could be seen between the worm-eaten planks.

'Come now, courage!' he said. 'We will sell our lives dearly.'

This joke increased their fear. The noise grew louder, but nothing could yet be seen; along the vacant road the wind of a tempest seemed to be blowing, like those sudden gusts which precede great storms

'No, no! I don't want to look,' said Cécile, going to hide herself in the hay.

Madame Hennebeau, who was very pale and felt angry with these people who had spoilt her pleasure, stood in the background with a sidelong look of repugnance; while Lucie and Jeanne, though trembling, had placed their eyes at a crack, anxious to lose nothing of the spectacle.

A sound of thunder came near, the earth was shaken, and Jeanlin galloped up first, blowing his horn.

'Take out your scent-bottles, the sweat of the people is passing by!' murmured Négrel, who, in spite of his republican convictions, liked to make fun of the populace when he was with ladies.

But this witticism was carried away in the hurricane of gestures and cries. The women had appeared, nearly a thousand of them, with outspread hair dishevelled by running, their naked skin appearing through their rags, the nakedness of females weary with giving birth to starvelings. A few held their little ones in their arms, raising them and shaking them like banners of mourning and vengeance. Others, who were younger, with the swollen breasts of amazons, brandished sticks; while frightful old women were yelling so loudly that the cords of their fleshless necks seemed to be breaking. And then the men came up, two thousand frenzied men – trammers, pikemen, menders – a compact mass which rolled along like a single block in confused serried rank so that it was impossible to distinguish their faded trousers or ragged woollen jerseys, all effaced in the same earthy uniformity. Their eyes were burning, and one could only distinguish the holes of black mouths singing the *Marseillaise*;* the stanzas were lost in a confused roar, accompanied by the clatter of clogs over the hard earth. Above their heads, amid the bristling iron bars, an axe passed by, carried erect; and this single axe, which seemed to be the banner of the mob, showed in the clear air the sharp profile of a guillotine-blade.*

'What horrible faces!' stammered Madame Hennebeau.

Négrel said between his teeth:

'Devil take me if I can recognize one of them! Where did all those bandits spring from?'

And in fact anger, hunger, these two months of suffering and this enraged helter-skelter through the pits had lengthened the placid faces of the Montsou colliers into the muzzles of wild beasts. At this moment the sun was setting; its last rays of sombre purple cast a gleam of blood over the plain. The road seemed to be full of blood; men and women continued to rush by, bloody as butchers in the midst of slaughter.

'Oh! superb!' whispered Lucie and Jeanne, stirred in their artistic tastes by the beautiful horror of it all.

They were frightened, however, and drew back close to Madame Hennebeau, who was leaning on a trough. She was frozen at the thought that a glance between the planks of that disjointed door might suffice to get them slaughtered. Négrel also, who was usually very brave, felt himself grow pale, seized by a terror that was superior to his will, the terror which comes from the unknown. Cécile, in the hay, no longer stirred; and the others, in spite of the wish to turn away their eyes, could not do so: they carried on watching.

It was the red vision of the revolution, which would one day inevitably carry them all away, on some bloody evening at the end of the century. Yes, some evening the people, unbridled at last, would thus gallop along the roads, making the blood of the bourgeoisie flow, parading severed heads and sprinkling gold from disembowelled coffers. The women would yell, the men would have those wolf-like jaws open to bite. Yes, there would be the same rags, the same thunderous tramping of clogs, the same terrible rabble, with dirty skins and tainted breath, sweeping away the old world beneath an overflowing flood of barbarians. Fires would blaze out; they would not leave standing a single stone of the towns; they would return to the savage life of the woods, after the great orgy, the great feast-day, when the poor in a single night would tear the women apart and empty the cellars of the rich. There would be nothing left, not a sou of the great fortunes, not a title-deed of properties acquired; until the day dawned when a new earth would perhaps spring up once more. Yes, it was these things which were passing along the road like a force of nature herself, and they were receiving the terrible wind of it in their faces.

A great cry arose, dominating the *Marseillaise*:

'Bread! bread! bread!'

Lucie and Jeanne pressed themselves against Madame Hennebeau, who was almost fainting; while Négrel placed himself before them as though to protect them with his body. Was the old social order cracking this very evening? And what they saw immediately after completed their stupefaction. The mob had nearly passed by, there were only a few stragglers left, when la Mouquette came up. She was taking her time, watching the bourgeois at their garden gates or the windows of their houses; and whenever she saw them, as she was not able to spit in their faces, she showed them what for her was the supreme sign of contempt. Doubtless she spotted someone now, for suddenly she raised her skirts, bent her back, and showed her enormous buttocks, naked beneath the last rays of the setting sun. There was nothing obscene about those buttocks, and nothing comic in this wild gesture.

Everything disappeared: the flood rolled on to Montsou along the turns of the road, between the low houses streaked with bright colours. The carriage was drawn out of the yard, but the coachman dared not take it upon him to drive back madame and the young ladies without delay; the strikers occupied the street. And the problem was, there was no other road.

'We must go back, however, for dinner will be ready,' said Madame Hennebeau, exasperated by annoyance and fear. 'These

dirty workpeople have again chosen a day when I have visitors.
How can you do good to such creatures?'

Lucie and Jeanne were occupied in pulling Cécile out of the hay.
She was struggling, believing that those savages were still passing
by, and repeating that she did not want to see them. At last they all
took their places in the carriage again. It then occurred to Négrel,
who had remounted, that they might go through the back streets of
Réquillart.

'Go gently,' he said to the coachman, 'for the road is atrocious.
If any groups prevent you from returning to the road over there,
you can stop behind the old pit, and we will return on foot through
the little garden door, while you can put up the carriage and horses
anywhere, in some inn outhouse.'

They set out. The mob, far away, was streaming into Montsou.
As they had twice seen gendarmes and dragoons, the inhabitants
were agitated and seized by panic. Abominable stories were circulating; it was said that written placards had been set up threatening
to rip open the bellies of the bourgeois. Nobody had read them, but
all the same they were able to quote the exact words. At the
lawyer's especially the terror was at its height, for he had just
received by post an anonymous letter warning him that a barrel of
powder was buried in his cellar, and that it would be blown up if
he did not declare himself on the side of the people. Just then the
Grégoires, delayed in their visit on the arrival of this letter, were
discussing it, and decided that it must be the work of a joker, when
the invasion of the mob completed the terror of the house. They,
however, smiled, drawing back a corner of the curtain to look out,
and refused to admit that there was any danger, certain, they said,
that all would finish up well. Five o'clock struck, and they had time
to wait until the street was free for them to cross the road to dine
with the Hennebeau's, where Cécile, who had surely returned, must
be waiting for them. But no one in Montsou seemed to share their
confidence. People were wildly running about; doors and windows
were banged to. They saw Maigrat, on the other side of the road,
barricading his shop with a large supply of iron bars, and looking
so pale and trembling that his feeble little wife was obliged to fasten
the screws. The mob had come to a halt in front of the manager's
house, and the cry echoed:

'Bread! bread! bread!'

Monsieur Hennebeau was standing at the window when Hippolyte came in to close the shutters, for fear the windows would be
broken by stones. He closed all of them on the ground floor, and

then went up to the first floor; the creak of the window-catches was heard and the clack of the shutters one by one. Unfortunately, it was not possible to shut the kitchen window in the area in the same way, a window unfortunately lit up by the gleams from the saucepans and the spit.

Mechanically, Monsieur Hennebeau, who wished to look out, went up to Paul's room on the second floor: it was on the left, the best situated, for it overlooked the road as far as the Company's Yards. And he stood behind the blinds looking down on the crowd. But this room had again overcome him, the toilet table sponged and in order, the cold bed with neat and well-drawn sheets. All his rage of the afternoon, that furious battle in the depths of his silent solitude, had now turned to an immense fatigue. His whole being was now like this room, grown cold, swept of the filth of the morning, returned to its habitual correctness. What was the good of a scandal? had anything really changed in his house? His wife had simply taken another lover; that she had chosen him in the family scarcely aggravated the fact; perhaps even it was an advantage, for she thus preserved appearances. He pitied himself when he thought of his mad jealousy. How ridiculous to have struck that bed with his fists! Since he had tolerated another man, he could certainly tolerate this one. It was only a matter of a little more contempt. A terrible bitterness filled his mouth, the uselessness of everything, the eternal pain of existence, shame for himself who always adored and desired this woman in the dirt in which he had abandoned her.

Beneath the window the yells broke out with increased violence:

'Bread! bread! bread!'

'Idiots!' said Monsieur Hennebeau between his clenched teeth.

He heard them abusing him for his large salary, calling him a bloated idler, a filthy pig who stuffed himself with good things, while the workers were dying of hunger. The women had noticed the kitchen, and there was an outburst of insults against the pheasant roasting there, against the sauces that with fat odours irritated their empty stomachs. Ah! the stinking bourgeois, they would be stuffed with champagne and truffles till their guts burst.

'Bread! bread! bread!'

'Idiots!' repeated Monsieur Hennebeau; 'am I happy?'

Anger arose in him against these people who could not understand. He would willingly have made them a present of his large salary to possess their tough skin and their easy copulation without regret. Why could he not seat them at his table and stuff them with his pheasant, while he went to fornicate behind the hedges, to tumble the girls, making fun of those who had tumbled them before him! He would have given everything, his education, his comfort, his luxury, his power as manager, if he could be for one day the vilest of the wretches who obeyed him, free in his flesh, enough of a blackguard to beat his wife and to take his pleasure with his neighbours' wives. And he longed also to be dying of hunger, to have an empty belly, a stomach twisted by cramps that would make his head turn with giddiness: perhaps that would have eased his endless suffering. Ah! to live like a brute, to possess nothing, to scour the fields with the ugliest and dirtiest putter, and to be able to be happy!

'Bread! bread! bread!'

Then he grew angry and shouted furiously in the tumult:

'Bread! is that enough, idiots!'

He could eat, and all the same he was groaning with torment. His devastated household, his whole painful life, choked him like a death agony. Things were not all for the best because one had bread. Who was the fool who placed earthly happiness in the sharing of wealth? These revolutionary dreamers might demolish society and rebuild another society; they would not add one joy to humanity, they would not take away one pain, by giving everyone a share of the bread and butter. They would even enlarge the unhappiness of the world; they would one day make the very dogs howl with despair when they had taken them out of the simple satisfaction of their instincts, to raise them to the unappeasable suffering of their passions. No, the one good thing was not to exist, and if one existed, to be a tree, a stone, less still, a grain of sand, which cannot bleed under the heel of passers-by.

And in this exasperation of his torment, tears welled up in Monsieur Hennebeau's eyes, and fell in burning drops on his cheeks. Twilight was enveloping the road when stones began to riddle the front of the house. With no anger now against these starving people, only enraged by the burning wound in his heart he continued to stammer in the midst of his tears:

'Idiots! idiots!'

But the cry of the belly dominated, and a roar blew like a tempest, sweeping everything before it:

'Bread! bread! bread!'

CHAPTER 6

Sobered by Catherine's blows, Étienne had remained at the head of his mates. But while he was hoarsely urging them on to Montsou, he heard another voice within him, the voice of reason, asking, in astonishment, the meaning of all this. He had not intended any of these things; how had it happened that, having set out for Jean-Bart with the object of acting calmly and preventing disaster, he had finished this day of increasing violence by besieging the manager's house?

He it certainly was, however, who had just cried, 'Halt!' Only at first his sole idea had been to protect the Company's Yards, which there had been talk of destroying. And now that stones were already grazing the façade of the house, he sought in vain for some lawful prey on which to throw the mob, so as to avoid greater misfortunes. As he thus stood alone, powerless, in the middle of the road, he was called by a man standing on the threshold of the Tison bar, where the landlady had just put up the shutters in haste, leaving only the door free.

'Yes, it's me. Will you listen?'

It was Rasseneur. Some thirty men and women, nearly all belonging to the settlement of the Deux-Cent-Quarante, who had remained at home in the morning and had come in the evening for news, had rushed into this bar on the approach of the strikers. Zacharie occupied a table with his wife, Philomène. Farther on, Pierron and la Pierronne, with their backs turned, were hiding their faces. No one was drinking, they had simply taken shelter.

Étienne recognized Rasseneur and was turning away, when the latter added:

'You don't want to see me, eh? I warned you, things are getting awkward. Now you can ask for bread, they'll give you bullets.'

Then Étienne came back and replied:

'What troubles me is, the cowards who fold their arms and watch us risking our skins.'

'Your plan, then, is to pillage over there?' asked Rasseneur.

'My plan is to remain to the last with our friends, even if it means dying together.'

In despair, Étienne went back into the crowd, ready to die. On the road, three children were throwing stones, and he gave them a good kick, shouting out to his comrades that it was no good breaking windows.

Bébert and Lydie, who had joined Jeanlin, were learning from him how to work the sling. They each threw a pebble, playing at who could do the most damage. Lydie had awkwardly cracked the head of a woman in the crowd, and the two boys were loudly laughing. Bonnemort and Mouque, seated on a bench, were gazing at them behind. Bonnemort's swollen legs bore him so badly, that he had great difficulty in dragging himself so far; no one knew what curiosity impelled him, for his face had the earthy look of those days when he never spoke a word.

Nobody, however, any longer obeyed Étienne. The stones, in spite of his orders, went on hailing, and he was astonished and terrified by these brutes he had unmuzzled, who were so slow to move and then so terrible, so ferociously tenacious in their rage. All the old Flemish blood was there, heavy and placid, taking months to get heated, and then giving itself up to abominable savagery, listening to nothing until the beast was glutted by atrocities. In his southern land crowds flared up more quickly, but they did far less damage. He had to struggle with Levaque to obtain possession of his axe, and he knew not how to keep back the Maheus, who were throwing stones with both hands. The women, especially, terrified him – la Levaque, la Mouquette, and the others – who were agitated by murderous fury, with teeth and nails out, barking like bitches, and driven on by la Brûlé, whose lean figure dominated them all.

But there was a sudden stop; a moment's surprise brought a little of that calmness which Étienne's supplications could not obtain. It was simply the Grégoires, who had decided to bid farewell to the lawyer, and to cross the road to the manager's house; and they looked so peaceful, they so clearly seemed to believe that the whole thing was a joke on the part of their worthy miners, whose resignation had nourished them for a century, that the latter, in fact, left off throwing stones, for fear of hitting this old gentleman and old lady who had come out of the blue. They allowed them to enter the garden, mount the steps, and ring at the barricaded door, which was by no means opened in a hurry. Just then, Rose, the housemaid, was returning, laughing at the furious workmen, all of whom she knew, for she belonged to Montsou. And it was she who, by striking her fists against the door, at last forced Hippolyte to half open it. It was time, for as the Grégoires disappeared, the hail of stones began again. Recovering from its astonishment, the crowd was shouting louder than ever:

'Death to the bourgeois! Long live the people!'

Rose went on laughing, in the hall of the house, as though amused by the adventure, and repeated to the terrified manservant:

'They're not bad-hearted; I know them.'

Monsieur Grégoire methodically hung up his hat. Then, when he had assisted Madame Grégoire out of her thick winter wrap, he said, in his turn:

'Of course, they don't basically mean any harm. When they have shouted well they will go home to supper with more of an appetite.'

At this moment Monsieur Hennebeau came down from the second floor. He had seen the scene, and came to receive his guests in his usual cold and polite manner. The pallor of his face alone revealed the grief which had shaken him. The man in him was tamed; there only remained in him the correct administrator resolved to do his duty.

'You know,' he said, 'the ladies have not yet come back.'

For the first time anxiety disturbed the Grégoires. Cécile not come back! How could she get back now if the miners were to prolong their joking?

'I thought of having the place cleared,' added Monsieur Hennebeau. 'But the problem is that I'm alone here, and, besides, I do not know where to send my servant to bring me four men and a corporal to clear away this mob.'

Rose, who had remained there, ventured to murmur anew:

'Oh, sir! they are not bad-hearted!'

The manager shook his head, while the tumult increased outside, and they could hear the dull crash of the stones against the house.

'I don't wish to be hard on them, I can even excuse them; one must be as foolish as they are to believe that we are anxious to injure them. But it is my duty to prevent disturbance. To think that there are gendarmes all along the roads, as I am told, and that I have not been able to see a single man since the morning!'

He interrupted himself, and drew back before Madame Grégoire, saying:

'Please, madame, do not stay here, come into the drawing-room.'

But the cook, coming up from below in exasperation, kept them in the hall a few minutes longer. She declared that she could no longer accept any responsibility for the dinner, for she was expecting from the Marchiennes pastrycook some vol-au-vent crusts which she had ordered for four o'clock. The pastrycook had evidently turned aside on the road for fear of these bandits. Perhaps they had even pillaged his hampers. She saw the vol-au-vent blockaded behind a bush, besieged, going to swell the bellies of the three thousand wretches who were asking for bread. In any case, monsieur was warned; she would rather pitch her dinner into the fire if it was to be spoilt because of the revolt.

'Patience, patience,' said Monsieur Hennebeau. 'All is not lost, the pastrycook may come.'

And as he turned toward Madame Grégoire, opening the drawing-room door himself, he was much surprised to observe, seated on the hall bench, a man whom he had not noticed before in the deepening shade.

'What! you, Maigrat! what is it, then?'

Maigrat arose; his fat, pale face was changed by terror. He no longer possessed his usual calm stolidity; he humbly explained that he had slipped into the manager's house to ask for aid and protection should the brigands attack his shop.

'You see that I am threatened myself, and that I have no one,' replied Monsieur Hennebeau. 'You would have done better to stay at home and guard your property.'

'Oh! I have put up iron bars and left my wife there.'

The manager showed impatience, and did not conceal his contempt. A fine guard, that skinny creature worn out by beatings!

'Well, I can do nothing; you must try to defend yourself. I advise you to go back at once, for there they are again demanding bread. Listen!'

In fact, the tumult began again, and Maigrat thought he heard his own name in the midst of the cries. To go back was no longer possible, they would have torn him to pieces. Besides, the idea of his ruin overwhelmed him. He pressed his face to the glass panel of the door, perspiring and trembling in anticipation of the disaster, while the Grégoires decided to go into the drawing-room.

Monsieur Hennebeau quietly endeavoured to do the honours of his house. But in vain he begged his guests to sit down; the close, barricaded room, lighted by two lamps in the daytime, was filled with terror at each new clamour from without. Amid the stuffy hangings the fury of the mob rolled more disturbingly, with vague and terrible menace. They talked, however, constantly brought back to this inconceivable revolt. He was astonished at having foreseen nothing; and his information was so defective that he specially talked against Rasseneur, whose detestable influence, he said, he was able to recognize. Besides, the gendarmes would come; it was impossible that he should be thus abandoned. As to the Grégoires, they only thought about their daughter, the poor darling who was so quickly frightened! Perhaps, in face of the peril, the carriage had returned to Marchiennes. They waited on for another quarter of an hour, worn out by the noise in the street, and by the sound of the stones from time to time striking the closed shutters which resounded like drums. The situation was no longer bearable. Monsieur Hennebeau spoke of going out to chase away the braggarts by himself, and to meet the carriage, when Hippolyte appeared, exclaiming:

'Sir! sir, here is madame! They are killing madame!'

The carriage had not been able to pass through the threatening groups in the Réquillart lane. Négrel had carried out his idea, walking the hundred metres which separated them from the house, and knocking at the little door which led to the garden, near the outbuildings. The gardener would hear them, for there was always someone there to open up. And, at first, things had gone perfectly; Madame Hennebeau and the young ladies were already knocking when some women, who had been warned, rushed into the lane. Then everything was spoilt. The door was not opened, and Négrel in vain sought to burst it open with his shoulder. The rush of women increased, and fearing they would be carried away, he adopted the desperate method of pushing his aunt and the girls before him, in order to reach the front steps, by passing through the besiegers. But this manoeuvre led to a hustling. They were not left free, a shouting mob followed them, while the crowd drifted up to right and to left, without understanding, simply astonished at these dressed-up ladies lost in the midst of the battle. At this moment the confusion was so great that it led to one of those curious misunderstandings which can never be explained. Lucie and Jeanne reached the steps, and slipped in through the door, which the housemaid opened; Madame Hennebeau had succeeded in following them, and behind them Négrel at last came in, and then bolted the door, feeling sure that he had seen Cécile go in first. She was no longer there, having disappeared on the way, so carried away by fear, that she had turned her back to the house, and had moved of her own accord into the thick of the danger.

At once the cry arose:

'Long live the people! Death to the bourgeois! To death with them!'

A few of them in the distance, beneath the veil which hid her face, mistook her for Madame Hennebeau; others said she was a friend of the manager's wife, the young wife of a neighbouring manufacturer who was hated by his men. And besides it mattered little, it was her silk dress, her fur mantle, even the white feather in her hat, which exasperated them. She smelled of perfume, she wore a watch, she had the delicate skin of a lazy woman who had never touched coal.

'Stop!' shouted old Mother Brûlé, 'we'll stuff it up your arse, that lace!'

'The lazy sluts steal it from us,' said la Levaque. 'They stick fur on to their skins while we are dying of cold. Just strip her naked, to show her how to live!'

At once la Mouquette rushed forward.

'Yes, yes! whip her!'

And the women, in this savage rivalry, struggled and stretched out their rags, as though each were trying to get a morsel of this rich girl. No doubt her backside was not better made than any one else's. More than one of them were rotten beneath their gewgaws. This injustice had lasted quite long enough; they should be forced to dress themselves like workwomen, these harlots who dared to spend fifty sous on the washing of a single petticoat.

In the midst of these furies Cécile was shaking with paralysed legs, stammering over and over again the same phrase:

'Ladies! please! please! Ladies, please don't hurt me!'

But she suddenly uttered a shrill cry; cold hands had seized her by the neck. The rush had brought her near old Bonnemort, who had taken hold of her. He seemed drunk from hunger, stupefied by his long misery, suddenly arousing himself from the resignation of half a century, under the influence of some unknown malicious impulse. After having in the course of his life saved a dozen mates from death, risking his bones in fire-damps and landslips, he was yielding to things which he would not have been able to express, compelled to do thus, fascinated by this young girl's white neck. And as on this day he had lost his tongue, he clenched his fingers, with his air of an old infirm animal ruminating over his recollections.

'No! no!' yelled the woman. 'Uncover her arse! out with her arse!'

In the house, as soon as they had realized the mishap, Négrel and Monsieur Hennebeau bravely reopened the door to run to Cécile's help. But the crowd was now pressing against the garden railings, and it was not easy to go out. A struggle took place here, while the Grégoires in terror stood on the steps.

'Let her be then, old man! It's the Piolaine young lady,' cried la

Maheude to the grandfather, recognizing Cécile, whose veil had been torn off by one of the women.

For his part, Étienne, overwhelmed at this retaliation on a child, was trying to force the mob to let go of their prey. An inspiration came to him; he brandished the axe, which he had snatched from Levaque's hands.

'To Maigrat's house, by God! there's bread in there! Down with Maigrat's damned shack!'

And at random he struck the first blow of the axe against the shop door. Some comrades had followed him – Levaque, Maheu, and a few others. But the women were furious, and Cécile had fallen from Bonnemort's fingers into la Brûlé's hands. Lydie and Bébert, led by Jeanlin, had slipped on all fours between her petticoats to see the lady's bottom. Already the women were pulling her about; her clothes were beginning to split, when a man on horseback appeared, pushing on his animal, and using his riding-whip on those who would not stand back quick enough.

'Ah! scum! You are going to flog our daughters, are you?'

It was Deneulin who had come for the dinner engagement. He quickly jumped on to the road, took Cécile by the waist, and, with the other hand manipulating his horse with remarkable skill and strength, he used it as a living wedge to split the crowd, which drew back before the rush. At the railing the battle continued. He passed through, however, with some bruises. This unforeseen assistance delivered Négrel and Monsieur Hennebeau, who were in great danger amid the oaths and blows. And while the young man at last led in the fainting Cécile, Deneulin protected the manager with his tall body, and at the top of the steps was hit by a stone which nearly put his shoulder out.

'That's it,' he cried; 'break my bones now you've broken my machines!'

He promptly pushed the door to, and a volley of stones fell against it.

'What madmen!' he exclaimed. 'Two seconds more, and they would have broken my skull like an empty marrow. There is nothing to say to them; what could you do? They know nothing, you can only knock them down.'

In the drawing-room, the Grégoires were weeping as they watched Cécile recover. She was not hurt, there was not even a scratch to be seen, only her veil was lost. But their fright increased when they saw before them their cook, Mélanie, who described how the mob had demolished la Piolaine. Mad with fear she had run to warn her masters. She had come in when the door was ajar at the moment of the fray, without anyone noticing her; and in her endless narrative the single stone with which Jeanlin had broken one window-pane became a regular cannonade which had crushed through the walls. Then Monsieur Grégoire's ideas were altogether upset: they were murdering his daughter, they were razing his house to the ground; it was, then, true that these miners could bear him ill will, because he lived like a worthy man on their labour?

The housemaid, who had brought in a towel and some eau-de-Cologne, repeated:

'All the same it's queer, they're not bad-hearted.'

Madame Hennebeau, seated and very pale, had not recovered from the shock of the upset; and she was only able to smile when Négrel was complimented. Cécile's parents especially thanked the young man, and the marriage might now be regarded as settled. Monsieur Hennebeau looked on in silence, turning from his wife to this lover whom in the morning he had been swearing to kill, then to this young girl by whom he would, no doubt, soon be freed from him. There was no haste, only the fear remained with him of seeing his wife fall lower, perhaps to some lackey.

'And you, my little darlings,' asked Deneulin of his daughters; 'have they broken any of your bones?'

Lucie and Jeanne had been much afraid, but they were pleased to have seen it all. They were now laughing.

'By George!' the father went on, 'we've had a fine day! If you want a dowry, you would do well to earn it yourselves, and you may also expect to have to support me.'

He was joking, but his voice trembled. His eyes swelled with tears as his two daughters threw themselves into his arms.

Monsieur Hennebeau had heard this confession of his ruin. A quick thought lit up his face. Vandame would now belong to Montsou; this was the hoped-for compensation, the stroke of fortune which would bring him back to favour with the gentlemen on the directorate. At every crisis of his existence, he took refuge in the strict execution of the orders he had received; in the military discipline in which he lived he found his small share of happiness.

But they grew calm; the drawing-room fell back into a weary peacefulness, with the quiet light of its two lamps, and the warm stuffiness of the hangings. What, then, was going on outside? The troublemakers were silent, and stones no longer struck the house; one only heard deep, dull blows, the blows of a hatchet which one hears in distant woods. They wished to find out, and went back into the hall to venture a glance through the glass panel of the door. Even the ladies went upstairs to post themselves behind the blinds on the first floor.

'Do you see that scoundrel, Rasseneur, over there on the threshold of the public-house?' said Monsieur Hennebeau to Deneulin. 'I had guessed as much; he must be in it.'

It was not Rasseneur, however, it was Étienne, who was striking blows from his axe at Maigrat's shop. And he went on calling to the men; did not the goods in there belong to the colliers? Had they not the right to take back their property from this thief who had exploited them so long, who was starving them on the orders of the Company? Gradually they all left the manager's house, and ran up to pillage the neighbouring shop. The cry 'Bread! bread! bread!' broke out anew. They would find bread behind that door. The rage of hunger carried them away, as if they suddenly felt that they could wait no longer without expiring on the road. Such furious thrusts were made at the door that at every stroke of the axe Étienne feared he would wound someone.

Meanwhile Maigrat, who had left the hall of the manager's house, had at first taken refuge in the kitchen; but, hearing nothing there, he imagined some abominable attempt against his shop, and came up again to hide behind the pump outside, when he distinctly heard the cracking of the door and shouts of pillage in which his own name was mixed. It was not a nightmare, then. If he could not see, he could now hear, and he followed the attack with ringing ears; every blow struck him in the heart. A hinge must have given way; five minutes more and the shop would be taken. The thing was stamped on his brain in real and terrible images – the brigands rushing forward, then the drawers broken open, the sacks emptied, everything eaten, everything drunk, the house itself carried away, nothing left, not even a stick with which he might go and beg through the villages. No, he would never allow them to complete his ruin; he would rather leave his life there. Since he had been there he noticed at a window of his house his wife's thin silhouette, pale and confused, behind the panes; no doubt she was watching the blows with her usual silent air like a poor beaten creature. Beneath there was a shed, so placed that from the garden of the large house one could climb on it from the palings; then it was easy to get on to the tiles up to the window. And the idea of thus returning home now pursued him in his remorse at having left. Perhaps he would have time to barricade the shop with furniture; he even invented other and more heroic defences – boiling oil, lighted petroleum, poured out from above. But this love of his property struggled against his fear, and he groaned in the struggle against his cowardice. Suddenly, on hearing a deeper blow of the axe, he made up his mind. Avarice won the day; he and his wife would cover the sacks with their bodies rather than abandon a single loaf.

Almost immediately the jeering broke out:

'Look! look! – The tom-cat's up there! After the cat! after the cat!'

The mob had just seen Maigrat on the roof of the shed. In his fever of anxiety he had climbed the palings with agility in spite of his weight, and without worrying about the breaking wood; and now he was flattening himself along the tiles, and endeavouring to reach the window. But the slope was very steep; he was hampered by his stoutness, and his nails were torn. He would have dragged himself up, however, if he had not begun to tremble with the fear of being hit by stones; for the crowd, which he could not see, continued to cry beneath him:

'After the cat! after the cat! – Do for him!'

And suddenly both his hands let go at once, and he rolled down like a ball, leapt at the gutter, and fell across the middle wall in such a way that, by ill chance, he rebounded on the side of the road, where his skull was broken open on the corner of a stone post. His brains had spurted out. He was dead. His wife up above, pale and confused behind the window-panes, still looked out.

They were stupefied at first. Étienne stopped short, and the axe slipped from his hands. Maheu, Levaque, and the others forgot the shop, with their eyes fixed on the wall along which a thin red streak was slowly flowing down. And the cries ceased, and silence spread over the growing darkness.

All at once the yelling began again. It was the women, who rushed forward overcome by a thirst for blood.

'Then there is a God, after all! Ah! the bloody beast, he's done for!'

They surrounded the still warm body. They insulted it with jeers, abusing his shattered head, calling him dirty chops, yelling in the face of death the pent-up rancour of their starved lives.

'I owed you sixty francs, now you're paid, thief!' said la Maheude, mad with rage like the others. 'You won't refuse me credit any more. Wait! wait! I must fatten you once more!'

With her fingers she scratched up some earth, took two handfuls and stuffed it violently into his mouth.

'There! eat that! There! eat! eat! you used to eat us!'

The abuse increased, while the dead man, stretched on his back, gazed motionless with his large fixed eyes at the immense sky where night was falling. This earth heaped in his mouth was the bread he had refused to give. And henceforth he would eat of no other bread. It had not brought him luck to starve poor people.

But the women had another revenge to wreak on him. They moved around, smelling him like she-wolves. They were all seeking for some outrage, some savagery that would relieve them.

La Brûlé's shrill voice was heard: 'Cut him like a tom-cat!'

'Yes, yes, get the tom-cat! get the tom-cat! He's done it too often, the dirty beast!'

La Mouquette was already unfastening and pulling off his trousers, while la Levaque raised his legs. And old Mother Brûlé with her dry old hands separated his naked thighs and seized his dead virility. She took hold of everything, tearing with an effort which bent her lean spine and made her long arms crack. The soft skin resisted; she had to try again, and at last carried away the fragment, a lump of hairy and bleeding flesh, which she brandished with a laugh of triumph.

'I've got it! I've got it!'

Shrill voices saluted the abominable trophy with curses.

'Ah! swine! you won't fill our daughters any more!'

'Yes! we've done with paying on your beastly body; we shan't any more have to offer a backside in return for a loaf.'

'Here, I owe you six francs; would you like to settle it? I'm quite willing, if you can do it still!'

This joke shook them all with terrible gaiety. They showed each other the bleeding piece of flesh as an evil beast from which each of them had suffered, and which they had at last crushed, and saw before them there, inert, in their power. They spat on it, they thrust out their jaws, saying over and over again, with furious bursts of contempt:

'He can do it no more! he can do it no more! – It's not even a man that they'll put away in the earth. Go and rot then, good-for-nothing!'

La Brûlé then planted the whole lump on the end of her stick, and holding it in the air, bore it about like a flag, rushing along the road, followed, helter-skelter, by the yelling mob of women. Drops of blood rained down, and that pitiful flesh hung like a waste piece of meat on a butcher's stall. Up above, at the window, Madame Maigrat still stood motionless; but beneath the last gleams of the setting sun, the confused flaws of the window-panes distorted her white face which looked as though it were laughing. Beaten and deceived at every hour, with shoulders bent from morning to night over a ledger, perhaps she was laughing, while the band of woman rushed along with that evil beast, that crushed beast, at the end of the stick.

This frightful mutilation was accomplished in a state of horrified silence. Neither Étienne nor Maheu nor the others had had time to interfere; they stood motionless before this gallop of furies. At the door of the Tison bar appeared a few heads – Rasseneur pale with disgust, Zacharie and Philomène stupefied at what they had seen. The two old men, Bonnemort and Mouque, were gravely shaking their heads. Only Jeanlin was making fun, nudging Bébert with his elbow, and forcing Lydie to look up. But the women were already coming back, turning round and passing beneath the manager's windows. Behind the blinds the ladies were stretching out their necks. They had not been able to observe the scene, which was hidden from them by the wall, and they could not see clearly in the growing darkness.

'What is it they have at the end of that stick?' asked Cécile, who had grown bold enough to look out.

Lucie and Jeanne declared that it must be a rabbit-skin.

'No, no,' murmured Madame Hennebeau, 'they must have been pillaging a pork butcher's, it looks like a piece of pork.'

At this moment she shuddered and was silent. Madame Grégoire had nudged her with her knee. They both remained stupefied. The young ladies, who were very pale, asked no more questions, but with large eyes followed this red vision through the darkness.

Étienne once more brandished the axe. But the feeling of anxiety did not disappear; this corpse now barred the road and protected the shop. Many had drawn back. Satiety seemed to have appeased them all. Maheu was standing by gloomily, when he heard a voice whisper in his ear to escape. He turned round and recognized Catherine, still in her old overcoat, black and panting. With a movement he repelled her. He would not listen to her, he threatened to strike her. With a gesture of despair she hesitated, and then ran towards Étienne.

'Run away! run away! the gendarmes are coming!'

He also pushed her away and abused her, feeling the blood of the blows she had given him mounting to his cheeks. But she would not be repelled; she forced him to throw down the axe, and drew him away by both arms, with irresistible strength.

'I tell you the gendarmes are coming! Listen to me. Chaval has gone for them and is bringing them, if you want to know. It's too much for me, and I've come. Run away, I don't want them to take you.'

And Catherine drew him away, while, at the same instant, a heavy gallop shook the pavement from afar. Immediately a voice arose: 'The gendarmes! the gendarmes!' There was a general panic, so mad a rush for life that in two minutes the road was free, absolutely clear, as though swept by a hurricane. Maigrat's corpse alone made a patch of shadow on the white earth. In front of the Tison bar, only Rasseneur remained, feeling relieved, and openly applauding the easy victory of the sabres; while in dim and deserted Montsou, in the silence of the closed houses, the bourgeois remained with perspiring bodies and chattering teeth, not daring to look out. The plain was shrouded beneath the thick night, only the blast furnaces and the coke furnaces were burning against the tragic sky. The heavy gallop of the gendarmes approached; they came up in an indistinguishable sombre mass. And behind them the Marchiennes pastrycook's vehicle, a little covered cart which had been confided to their care, at last arrived, and a small drudge of a boy jumped down and quietly unpacked the crusts for the *vol-au-vent*.

PART SIX

The first fortnight of February passed and a black cold prolonged the hard winter without pity for the poor. Once more the authorities had scoured the roads; the prefect of Lille, an attorney, a general. And the police were not sufficient, the military had come to occupy Montsou; a whole regiment of men were camped between Beaugnies and Marchiennes. Armed pickets guarded the pits, and there were soldiers in front of every machine. The manager's house, the Company's Yards, even the houses of certain residents, were bristling with bayonets. Nothing was heard along the streets but the slow movement of patrols. On the pit-bank of the Voreux a sentinel was always placed in the frozen wind that blew up there, like a look-out man above the flat plain; and every two hours, as though in an enemy's country, were heard the sentry's cries:

'Who goes there? – Advance and give the password!'

Nowhere had work been resumed. On the contrary, the strike had spread; Crèvecoeur, Mirou, Madeleine, like the Voreux, were producing nothing; at Feutry-Cantel and the Victoire there were fewer men every morning; even at Saint-Thomas, which had been hitherto exempt, there was a shortage of men. There was now a silent persistence in the face of this exhibition of force which exasperated the miners' pride. The settlements looked deserted in the midst of the beetroot fields. Not a workman stirred, only at rare intervals was one to be met by chance, isolated, with sidelong looks, lowering his head before the red trousers. And in this deep melancholy calm, in this passive opposition to the guns, there was a deceptive gentleness, a forced and patient obedience of wild beasts in a cage, with their eyes on the tamer, ready to spring at his neck if he turned his back. The Company, who were being ruined by this lack of work, talked of hiring miners from the Borinage, on the Belgian frontier, but did not dare; so the battle continued as before between the colliers, who were shut up at home, and the dead pits guarded by soldiery.

On the morrow of that terrible day this calm had come about all at once, hiding such a panic that the greatest silence possible was kept concerning the damage and the atrocities. The inquiry which had been opened showed that Maigrat had died from his fall, and the frightful mutilation of the corpse remained vague, already surrounded by a legend. For its part, the Company did not acknowledge the disasters it had suffered, any more than the Grégoires cared to compromise their daughter in the scandal of a trial in which she would have to give evidence. However, some arrests took place, mere supernumeraries as usual, silly and frightened, knowing nothing. By mistake, Pierron was taken off with handcuffs on his wrists as far as Marchiennes, to the great amusement of his mates. Rasseneur, also, was nearly arrested by two gendarmes. The management was content with preparing lists of names and giving back certificates in large numbers. Maheu had received his, Levaque also, as well as thirty-four of their mates in the settlement of the Deux-Cent-Quarante alone. And all the severity was directed against Étienne, who had disappeared on the evening of the fray, and who was being sought, although no trace of him could be found. Chaval, in his hatred, had denounced him, refusing to name the others at Catherine's appeal, for she wished to save her parents. The days passed, everyone felt that nothing was yet concluded; and with oppressed hearts everyone was awaiting the end.

At Montsou, during this period, the inhabitants awoke with a start every night, their ears buzzing with an imaginary alarm-bell and their nostrils haunted by the smell of powder. But what completed their discomfiture was a sermon by the new curé, Abbé Ranvier, that lean priest with eyes like red-hot coals who had succeeded Abbé Joire. He was indeed unlike the smiling discreet man, so fat and gentle, whose only anxiety was to live at peace with everybody. Abbé Ranvier went so far as to defend these abominable brigands who had dishonoured the district. He found excuses for the atrocities of the strikers; he violently attacked the bourgeoisie, throwing on them the whole of the responsibility. It was the bourgeoisie that, by dispossessing the Church of its ancient liberties in order to misuse them itself, had turned this world into a cursed place of injustice and suffering; it was the middle class that prolonged misunderstandings, that was pushing on towards a terrible catastrophe by its atheism, by its refusal to return to the old beliefs, to the fraternity of the early Christians. And he dared to threaten the rich. He warned them that if they obstinately persisted in refusing to listen to the voice of God, God would surely put Himself on the side of the poor. He would take back their fortunes from those who faithlessly enjoyed them, and would distribute them to the humble of the earth for the triumph of His glory. The devout trembled at this; the lawyer declared that it was Socialism of the worst kind; all saw the curé at the head of a mob, brandishing a cross, and with vigorous blows demolishing the bourgeois society of '89.*

Monsieur Hennebeau, when informed, contented himself with saying, as he shrugged his shoulders:

'If he troubles us too much the bishop will free us from him.'

And while the breath of panic was thus blowing from one end of the plain to the other, Étienne was dwelling beneath the earth, in Jeanlin's burrow at the bottom of Réquillart. He was in hiding there; no one believed him so near; the quiet audacity of that refuge, in the very mine, in that abandoned passage of the old pit, had baffled his pursuers. Above, the sloes and hawthorns growing among the fallen scaffolding of the belfry filled up the mouth of the hole. No one ventured down; you had to know the trick – how to hang on to the roots of the mountain ash and to let go fearlessly, to catch hold of the rungs that were still solid. Other obstacles also protected him, the suffocating heat of the passage, a hundred and twenty metres of dangerous descent, then the painful gliding on all fours for a quarter of a league between the narrowed walls of the gallery before discovering the brigand's cave full of plunder. He lived there in the midst of abundance, finding gin there, the rest of the dried cod, and provisions of all sorts. The large hay bed was excellent, and not a current of air could be felt in this equal temperature, as warm as a bath. Light, however, was in short supply. Jeanlin, who had made himself provider, with the prudence and discretion of a savage and delighted to make fun of the gendarmes, had even brought him pomade, but could not succeed in putting his hands on a packet of candles.

After the fifth day Étienne never lighted up except to eat. He could not swallow in the dark. This complete and interminable night, always of the same blackness, was his chief torment. It was in vain that he was able to sleep in safety, that he was warm and provided with bread, the night had never weighed so heavily on his soul. It seemed to him even to crush his thoughts. Now he was living on stolen goods. In spite of his communistic theories, old scruples of his upbringing arose, and he contented himself with gnawing his share of dry bread. But what was to be done? One must live, and his task was not yet accomplished. Another shame overcame him: remorse for that savage drunkenness from the gin, drunk in the great cold on an empty stomach, which had thrown him, armed with a knife, on Chaval. This stirred in him the whole of that unknown terror, the hereditary ill, the long ancestry of drunkenness, no longer tolerating a drop of alcohol without falling into homicidal mania. Would he then end up as a murderer? When he found himself in shelter, in this profound calm of the earth, his violent instincts sated, he had slept for two days the sleep of a beast, gorged and overcome; and the depression continued, he lived in a bruised state with bitter mouth and aching head, as after some tremendous spree. A week passed by; the Maheus, who had been warned, were not able to send a candle; he had to give up seeing clearly, even when eating.

Now Étienne remained for hours stretched out on his hay. Vague ideas were working within him for the first time: a feeling of superiority, which placed him apart from his mates, an exaltation of his person as he grew more educated. Never had he reflected so much; he asked himself the reason for his disgust on the morrow of that furious rampage among the pits; and he did not dare to reply to himself, his recollections were repulsive to him, the ignoble desires, the coarse instincts, the odour of all that wretchedness shaken out to the wind. In spite of the torment of the darkness, he came to dread the hour for returning to the settlement. How nauseous were all these wretches in a heap, living at the common trough! There was not one with whom he could seriously talk politics; it was a bestial existence, always the same air tainted by onion, in which one choked! He wished to enlarge their horizons, to raise them to the comfort and good manners of the middle class, by making them masters; but how long it would take! and he no longer felt the courage to await victory, in this prison of hunger. By slow degrees the vanity he derived from leadership, his constant preoccupation with thinking in their place, left him free, breathing into him the soul of one of those bourgeois whom he despised.

Jeanlin one evening brought a candle-end, stolen from a carter's lantern, and this was a great relief for Étienne. When the darkness began to stupefy him, weighing on his brain almost to madness, he would light up for a moment; then, as soon as he had chased away the nightmare, he extinguished the candle, miserly of this brightness which was as necessary to his life as bread. The silence buzzed in his ears, he only heard the flight of a band of rats, the cracking of the old timber, the tiny sound of a spider weaving her web. And with eyes open, in this warm nothingness, he returned to his fixed idea – the thought of what his mates were doing above. Desertion on his part would have seemed to him the worst cowardice. If he thus hid himself, it was to remain free, to give counsel or to act. His long meditations had fixed his ambition. While awaiting something better, he would like to be Pluchart, leaving manual work in order to work only at politics, but alone, in a clean room, under the pretext that brain work absorbs the entire life and needs quiet.

At the beginning of the second week, the child having told him that the gendarmes thought he had gone to Belgium, Étienne ventured out of his hole at nightfall. He wished to ascertain the situation, and to decide if it was still advisable to persist. He himself considered the risk doubtful. Before the strike he felt uncertain of the result, and had simply yielded to the facts; and now, after having been intoxicated with rebellion, he came back to this first doubt, despairing of making the Company yield. But he would not yet confess this to himself; he was tortured when he thought of the miseries of defeat, and the heavy responsibility of suffering which would weigh upon him. The end of the strike: was it not the end of his part, the overthrow of his ambitions, his life falling back into the brutishness of the mine and the horrors of the settlement? And honestly, without any base calculation or falsehood, he endeavoured to find his faith again, to prove to himself that resistance was still possible, that Capital was about to destroy itself in face of the heroic suicide of Labour.

Throughout the entire country, in fact, there was nothing but ruin. At night, when he wandered through the black country, like a wolf who has come out of his wood, he seemed to hear the financial crashes from one end of the plain to the other. He now passed by the roadside nothing but closed dead workshops, becoming rotten beneath the dull sky. The sugar works had especially suffered: the Hoton sugar works, the Fauvelle works, after having reduced the number of their hands, had come to grief one after the other. At the Dutilleul flour works the last mill had stopped on the second Saturday of the month, and the Bleuze rope works, for mine cables, had been quite ruined by the strike. On the Marchiennes side the situation was growing worse every day. All the fires were out at the Gagebois glass works, men were continually being sent away from the Sonneville workshops, only one of the three blast furnaces of the Forges was alight, and not one battery of coke ovens was burning on the horizon. The strike of the Montsou colliers, born of the industrial crisis which had been growing worse for two years, had increased it and precipitated the downfall. To the other causes of suffering – the stoppage of orders from America, and the accumulation of invested capital in excessive production – was now added the unforeseen lack of coal for the few furnaces which were still kept up; and that was the supreme agony, this bread for machines which the pits no longer furnished. Frightened by the general unrest, the Company, by diminishing its output and starving its miners, inevitably found itself at the end of December without a fragment of coal at the surface of its pits. Everything held together, the plague blew from afar, one fall led to another; industries tumbled over each other as they fell, in so rapid a series of catastrophes that the shocks echoed as far as the neighbouring cities, Lille, Douai, Valenciennes, where absconding bankers were bringing ruin on whole families.

At the turn of a road Étienne often stopped in the frozen night to hear the ruins falling down. He breathed deeply in the darkness, the joy of annihilation seized him, the hope that the day would dawn on the extermination of the old world, with not a single fortune left standing, the scythe of equality levelling everything to the ground. But in this massacre it was the Company's pits that especially interested him. He would continue his walk, blinded by the darkness, visiting them one after the other, glad to discover some new disaster. Landslips of increasing gravity continued to occur on account of the prolonged abandonment of the passages. Above the north gallery of Mirou the ground sank in to such an extent, that the Joiselle road, for the distance of a hundred metres, had been swallowed up as though by the shock of an earthquake; and the Company, disturbed at the rumours raised by these accidents, paid the owners for their vanished fields without bargaining. Crèvecoeur and Madeleine, which lay in very shifting rock, were becoming stopped up more and more. It was said that two captains had been buried at the Victoire; there was an inundation at Feutry-Cantel, it had been necessary to wall up a gallery for the length of a kilometre at Saint-Thomas, where the ill-kept timbering was breaking down everywhere. Thus every hour enormous sums were spent, making great breaches in the shareholders' dividends; a rapid destruction of the pits was going on, which must end at last by eating up the famous Montsou deniers which had multiplied a hundred times in a century.

In the face of these repeated blows, hope was again born in Étienne; he came to believe that a third month of resistance would crush the monster – the weary, sated beast, crouching down there like an idol in his unknown tabernacle. He knew that after the Montsou troubles there had been great excitement in the Paris newspapers, quite a violent controversy between the official newspapers and the opposition newspapers, terrible narratives, which were especially directed against the International, of which the

Empire was becoming afraid after having first encouraged it; and the directors not daring to turn a deaf ear any longer, two of them had condescended to come and hold an inquiry, but with an air of regret, not appearing to care about the upshot; so disinterested, that in three days they went away again, declaring that everything was proceeding as well as possible. He was told, however, from other quarters that during their stay these gentlemen had worked non-stop, displaying feverish activity, and absorbed in transactions of which no one about them uttered a word. And he charged them with affecting confidence they did not feel, and came to look upon their departure as a nervous flight, feeling now certain of triumph since these terrible men were letting everything go.

But on the following night Étienne despaired again. The Company's back was too robust to be so easily broken; they might lose millions, but later on they would get them back again by gnawing at their men's bread. On that night, having pushed as far as Jean-Bart, he guessed the truth when an overseer told him that there was talk of yielding Vandame to Montsou. At Deneulin's house, it was said, the wretchedness was pitiful, the wretchedness of the rich; the father made ill by his powerlessness, aged by his anxiety over money, the daughters struggling to fend off tradesmen, trying to save the clothes on their backs. There was less suffering in the famished settlements than in this middle-class house where they shut themselves up to drink water. Work had not been resumed at Jean-Bart, and it had been necessary to replace the pump at Gaston-Marie; while, in spite of all the hasty measures a flood had already begun which made great expenses necessary. Deneulin had at last risked his request for a loan of one hundred thousand francs from the Grégoires, and the refusal, though he had expected it, completed his dejection: if they refused, it was for his sake, in order to save him from an impossible struggle; and they advised him to sell. He, as usual, violently refused. It enraged him to have to pay the expenses of the strike; he hoped at first to die of it, with a rush of blood to the head, or strangled by apoplexy. Then what was to be done? He had listened to the directors' offers. They wrangled with him, they depreciated this superb prey, this repaired pit, equipped anew, where the lack of capital alone paralysed the output. He would be lucky if he got enough out of it to satisfy his creditors. For two days he had struggled against the directors at Montsou, furious at the quiet way with which they took advantage of his embarrassment and shouting his refusals at them in his loud voice. And there the affair remained, and they had returned to Paris to await patiently his last groans. Étienne could see this compensation for the disasters, and was again seized by discouragement before the invincible power of the great capitalists, so strong in battle that they fattened themselves in defeat by eating the corpses of the small capitalists who fell at their side.

The next day, fortunately, Jeanlin brought him a piece of good news. At the Voreux the lining of the shaft was threatening to break, and water was filtering in from all the joints; in great haste a gang of carpenters had been set on to repair it.

Up to now Étienne had avoided the Voreux, warned by the everlasting black silhouette of the sentinel stationed on the pit-bank above the plain. He could not be avoided, he stood out in the air, like the flag of the regiment. Towards three o'clock in the morning the sky became overcast, and he went to the pit, where some mates explained to him the bad condition of the lining; they even thought that it would have to be done entirely over again, which would stop the output of coal for three months. For a long time he prowled around, listening to the carpenters' mallets hammering in the shaft. That wound which had to be dressed rejoiced his heart.

As he went back in the early daylight, he saw the sentinel still on the pit-bank. This time he would certainly be seen. As he walked he thought about those soldiers who were taken from the people, to be armed against the people. How easy the triumph of the revolution would be if the army were suddenly to declare itself in favour! It would be enough if the workman and the peasant in the barracks were to remember their origins. That was the supreme peril, the great terror, which made the teeth of the middle class chatter when they thought of a possible defection of the troops. In two hours they would be swept away and exterminated with all the delights and abominations of their iniquitous life. It was already said that whole regiments were tainted with socialism. Was it true? When justice came, would it be thanks to the cartridges distributed by the bourgeoisie? And snatching at another hope, the young man dreamed that the regiment, with its posts, now guarding the pits, would come over to the side of the strikers, shoot down the Company to a man, and at last give the mine to the miners.

He then noticed that he was mounting the pit-bank, his head filled with these reflections. Why should he not talk with this soldier? He would get to know what his ideas were. With an air of indifference, he continued to come nearer, as though he were gleaning old wood among the rubbish. The sentinel remained motionless.

'Eh, mate! terrible weather,' said Étienne, at last. 'I think we shall have snow.'

He was a small soldier, very fair, with a pale, gentle face covered with red freckles. He wore his military great-coat with the awkwardness of a recruit.

'Yes, perhaps we shall, I think,' he murmured.

And with his blue eyes he gazed at the livid sky, the smoky dawn, with soot weighing like lead afar over the plain.

'What idiots they are to put you here to freeze!' Étienne went on. 'You would think the Cossacks were coming! And then there's always wind here.'

The little soldier shivered without complaining. There was certainly a little cabin of dry stones there, where old Bonnemort used to take shelter when it blew a hurricane, but the order being not to leave the summit of the pit-bank, the soldier did not stir from it, his hands so stiffened by cold that he could no longer feel his weapon. He belonged to the guard of sixty men who were protecting the Voreux, and as this cruel sentry-duty frequently came round, he had already nearly stayed there for good with frozen feet. His work demanded it; a passive obedience finished the benumbing process, and he replied to these questions with the stammered words of a sleepy child.

Étienne in vain endeavoured during a quarter of an hour to make him talk about politics. He replied 'yes' or 'no' without seeming to understand. Some of his comrades said that the captain was a republican; as far as he was concerned, he had no idea – it was all the same to him. If he was ordered to fire, he would fire, so as not to be punished. The workman listened, seized with the popular hatred against the army – against these brothers whose hearts were changed by sticking a pair of red pantaloons on to their buttocks.

'Then what's your name?'

'Jules.'

'And where do you come from?'

'From Plogof, over there.'

He stretched out his arm at random. It was in Britanny, he knew no more. His small pale face grew animated. He began to laugh, and felt warmer.

'I have a mother and a sister. They are waiting for me, sure enough. Ah! it won't be for tomorrow. When I left, they came with me as far as Pont-l'Abbé. We had borrowed the Lepalmecs' horse: it nearly broke its legs at the bottom of the Audierne Hill. Cousin Charles was waiting for us with sausages, but the women were crying too much, and they stuck in our throats. God! what a long way off our home is!'

His eyes grew moist, though he was still laughing. The desert moorland of Plogof, that wild storm-beaten extremity of the Raz, appeared to him beneath a dazzling sunny vision in the rosy season of heather.

'Do you think,' he asked, 'if I'm not punished, that they'll give me a month's leave in two years?'

Then Étienne talked about Provence, which he had left when he was quite small. The daylight was growing, and flakes of snow began to fly in the earthy sky. And at last he felt anxious on noticing Jeanlin, who was prowling about in the midst of the bushes, looking amazed to see him up there. The child was beckoning to him. What was the good of this dream of fraternizing with the soldiers? It would take years and years, and his useless attempt depressed him as though he had expected to succeed. But suddenly he understood Jeanlin's gesture. The sentinel was about to be relieved, and he went away, running off to bury himself at Réquillart, his heart crushed once more by the certainty of defeat; while the little scamp who ran beside him was accusing that dirty beast of a trooper of having called out the guard to fire at them.

On the summit of the pit-bank Jules stood motionless, with eyes vacantly gazing at the falling snow. The sergeant was approaching with his men, and the regulation cries were exchanged.

'Who goes there? – Advance and give the password!'

And they heard the heavy steps begin again, ringing as though in an occupied country. In spite of the growing daylight, nothing stirred in the settlements; the colliers remained in silent rage beneath the military boot.

CHAPTER 2

Snow had been falling for two days; since the morning it had ceased, and an intense frost had frozen the immense sheet. This black country, with its inky roads and walls and trees powdered with coal dust, was now white, a single whiteness stretching out without end. The Deux-Cent-Quarante settlement lay beneath the snow as though it had disappeared. No smoke came out of the chimneys; the houses, without fire and as cold as the stones in the street, did not melt the thick layer on the tiles. It was nothing more than a quarry of white slabs in the white plain, a vision of a dead village wrapped in its shroud. Along the roads the passing patrols alone made a muddy mess with their stamping.

At the Maheus' the last shovelful of coalchips had been burnt the evening before, and it was no use any longer to think of gleaning on the pit-bank in this terrible weather, when the sparrows themselves could not find a blade of grass. Alzire, from the obstinacy with which her poor hands had dug in the snow, was dying. La Maheude had to wrap her up in the fragment of a coverlet while waiting for Dr. Vanderhaghen, for whom she had twice gone out without being able to find him. The servant had, however, promised that he would come to the settlement before night, and the mother was standing at the window watching, while the little invalid, who had wished to be downstairs, was shivering on a chair, having the illusion that it was better there near the cold grate. Old Bonnemort opposite, his legs bad once more, seemed to be sleeping; neither Lénore nor Henri had come back from scouring the roads, in company with Jeanlin, to beg for some sous. Maheu alone was walking heavily up and down the bare room, stumbling against the wall at every turn, with the stupid air of an animal which can no longer see its cage. The oil had also run out; but the reflection of the snow from outside was so bright that it vaguely lit up the room, in spite of the deepening night.

There was a noise of clogs, and la Levaque pushed open the door like a gale of wind, beside herself, shouting furiously from the threshold at la Maheude:

'You're the one then who said that I force my lodger to give me twenty sous when he sleeps with me?'

The other shrugged her shoulders.

'Don't bother me. I said nothing; and who told you so?'

'They tell me you said so; it doesn't concern you who it was. You even said you could hear us at our dirty tricks behind the wall, and that the filth gets into our house because I'm always on my back. Just tell me you didn't say so, eh?'

Every day quarrels broke out as a result of the constant gossiping of the women. Especially between those households which lived door to door, squabbles and reconciliations took place every day. But never before had such bitterness thrown them one against the other. Since the strike hunger exasperated their rancour, so that they felt the need to strike out; an altercation between two gossiping women would finish up with a murderous fight between their two men.

Just then Levaque arrived in his turn, dragging Bouteloup.

'Here's our mate; let him just say if he has given my wife twenty sous to sleep with her.'

The lodger, hiding his timid gentleness in his great beard, protested and stammered:

'Oh! that? No! Never anything! never!'

At once Levaque became threatening, and thrust his fist beneath Maheu's nose.

'You know that won't do for me. If a man's got a wife like that, he ought to beat her up. If not, then you believe what she says.'

'By God!' exclaimed Maheu, furious at being dragged out of his dejection, 'what is all this clatter again? Haven't we got enough to do with our misery? Just leave me alone, damn you! or I'll let you have it! Anyway, who says that my wife said so?'

'Who says so? La Pierronne said so.'

La Maheude broke into a sharp laugh, and turning towards La Levaque:

'Ah! la Pierronne, is it? Well! I can tell you what she told me. Yes, she told me that you sleep with both your men – the one underneath and the other on top!'

After that it was no longer possible to come to an understanding. They all grew angry, and the Levaques, as a reply to the Maheus, asserted that la Pierronne had said a good many other things on their account; that they had sold Catherine, that they were all rotten together, even to the little ones, with a dirty disease caught by Étienne at the Volcan.

'She said that! She said that!' yelled Maheu. 'Good! I'll go to her, I will, and if she says that she said that, she'll feel my hand on her chops!'

He dashed out, and the Levaques followed him to see what would happen, while Bouteloup, who hated disputes, furtively returned home. Excited by the altercation, la Maheude was also going out, when a cry from Alzire held her back. She crossed the ends of the coverlet over the little one's quivering body, and placed herself before the window, looking out vaguely. And that doctor, who still hadn't come!

At the Pierrons' door Maheu and the Levaques met Lydie, who was stamping in the snow. The house was closed, and a thread of light came through a crack in the shutter. The child replied at first to their questions with constraint: no, her father was not there, he had gone to the wash-house to join la Brûlé and bring back the bundle of linen. Then she was confused, and would not say what her mother was doing. At last she let out everything with a sly, spiteful laugh: her mother had pushed her out of the door because Monsieur Dansaert was there, and she prevented them from talking. Since the morning he had been going about the settlement with two policemen, trying to pick up workmen, browbeating the weak ones, and announcing everwhere that if the descent did not take place on Monday at the Voreux, the Company had decided to hire men from the Borinage. And as night came on he sent away the policemen, finding la Pierronne alone; then he had remained with her to drink a glass of gin before a good fire.

'Hush! hold your tongue! We must see them,' said Levaque, with a lewd laugh. 'We'll explain everything directly. Get off with you, youngster.'

Lydie drew back a few steps while he put his eye to a crack in the shutter. He stifled a low cry and his back bent with a quiver. In her turn his wife looked through, but she said, as though taken by a fit of colic, that it was disgusting. Maheu, who had pushed her, wishing also to see, then declared that he had had enough for his money. And they began again, in a row, each taking a look as at a peep-show. The parlour, glittering with cleanliness, was enlivened by a large fire; there were cakes on the table with a bottle and glasses, in fact quite a feast. What they saw going on in there at last exasperated the two men, who under other circumstances would have laughed over it for six months. That she should let herself be stuffed up to the neck, with her skirts in the air, was funny. But, good God! was it not disgusting to do that in front of a great fire, and to get up one's strength with biscuits, when the mates had neither a slice of bread nor a bit of coal?

'Here's father!' cried Lydie, running away.

Pierron was quietly coming back from the wash-house with the bundle of linen on his shoulder. Maheu immediately addressed him:

'Here! they tell me that your wife says that I sold Catherine, and that we are all rotten at home. And what do they pay you in your house, your wife and the gentleman who is this minute wearing her out?'

The astonished Pierron could not understand, and la Pierronne, seized with fear on hearing the tumult of voices, lost her head and half opened the door to see what was the matter. They could see her, looking very red, with her dress open and her skirt tucked up at her waist; while Dansaert, in the background, was wildly buttoning up his trousers. The overman rushed away and disappeared, trembling with fear that this story would reach the manager's ears. Then there would be an awful scandal, laughter, and jeers and abuse.

'You, who are always saying that other people are dirty!' shouted la Levaque to la Pierronne; 'it's not surprising that you're clean when you get the bosses to scour you.'

'Ah! it's fine for her to talk!' said Levaque again. 'Here's a trollop who says that my wife sleeps with me and the lodger, one below and the other above! Yes! yes! that's what they tell me you say.'

But la Pierronne, grown calm, held her own against this abuse, very contemptuous in the assurance that she was the best looking and the richest.

'I've said what I've said; just leave me alone, will you! What have my affairs got to do with you, a pack of jealous creatures who resent it because we are able to save up money! Go away! Go away! You can say what you like; my husband knows well enough why Monsieur Dansaert was here.'

Pierron, in fact, was furiously defending his wife. The quarrel turned. They accused him of having sold himself, of being a spy, the Company's watch dog; they charged him with shutting himself up, to gorge himself with the good things with which the bosses paid him for his treachery. In defence, he pretended that Maheu had slipped beneath his door a threatening paper with two cross-bones and a dagger above. And this necessarily ended in a struggle between the men, as the quarrels of the women always did now that famine was enraging the mildest. Maheu and Levaque rushed on Pierron with their fists, and had to be pulled off.

Blood was flowing from her son-in-law's nose, when la Brûlé, in her turn, arrived from the wash-house. When informed of what had been going on, she merely said:

'The swine dishonours me!'

The road was becoming deserted, not a shadow spotted the naked whiteness of the snow, and the settlement, falling back into its death-like immobility, went on starving beneath the intense cold.

'And the doctor?' asked Maheu, as he shut the door.

'Not come,' replied la Maheude, still standing at the window.

'Are the little ones back?'

'No, not back.'

Maheu again began his heavy walk from one wall to the other, looking like a stricken ox. Old Bonnemort, seated stiffly on his chair, had not even lifted his head. Alzire also had said nothing, and was trying not to shiver, so as to avoid giving them pain; but in spite of her courage in suffering, she sometimes trembled so much that you could hear against the coverlet the quivering of the little invalid girl's lean body, while with her large open eyes she stared at the ceiling, from which the pale reflection of the white gardens lit up the room like moonshine.

The emptied house was now in its last agony, having reached a final stage of destitution. The mattress covers had followed the wool to the second-hand dealers; then the sheets had gone, the linen, everything that could be sold. One evening they had sold a handkerchief belonging to grandfather for two sous. Tears fell over each object of the poor household which had to go, and the mother was still lamenting that one day she had carried away in her skirt the pink cardboard box, her man's present from days gone by, as one would carry away a child to get rid of it on some doorstep. They were bare; they had only their skins left to sell, so worn-out and injured that no one would have given a farthing for them. They no longer even took the trouble to search, they knew that there was nothing left, that they had come to the end of everything, that they must not hope even for a candle, or a bit of coal, or a potato, and they were waiting to die, only grieved about the children, and revolted by the useless cruelty that gave the little one a disease before starving it.

'At last! here he is!' said la Maheude.

A dark figure passed before the window. The door opened. But it was not Dr Vanderhaghen; they recognized the new priest, Abbé Ranvier, who did not seem at all surprised at coming into this dead house, without light, without fire, without bread. He had already been to three neighbouring houses, going from family to family, seeking willing listeners, like Dansaert with his two gendarmes; and at once he exclaimed, in his feverish fanatic's voice:

'Why were you not at mass on Sunday, my children? You are wrong, the Church alone can save you. Now promise me to come next Sunday.'

Maheu, after staring at him, went on pacing heavily, without a word. It was la Maheude who replied:

'To mass, sir? What for? Isn't the good Lord making fun of us? Look here! what has my little girl there done to Him, to be shaking with fever? Hadn't we enough misery, that He had to make her ill too, just when I can't even give her a cup of warm tea.'

Then the priest stood and talked at length. He spoke of the strike, this terrible wretchedness, this exasperated rancour of famine, with the ardour of a missionary who is preaching to savages for the glory of his religion. He said that the Church was with the poor, that she would one day cause justice to triumph by calling down the anger of God on the iniquities of the rich. And that day would come soon, for the rich had taken the place of God, and were governing without God, in their impious theft of power. But if the workers desired the fair division of the goods of the earth, they ought at once to put themselves in the hands of the priests, just as on the death of Jesus the poor and the humble grouped themselves around the apostles. What strength the pope would have, what an army the clergy would have under them, when they were able to command the numberless crowd of workers! In one week they would purge the world of the wicked, they would chase away the unworthy masters. Then, indeed, there would be a real kingdom of God, every one recompensed according to his merits, and the law of labour as the foundation for universal happiness.

La Maheude, who was listening to him, seemed to hear Étienne, in those autumn evenings when he announced to them the end of their evils. Only she had always distrusted the cloth.

'That's all very well, what you say there, sir,' she replied, 'but that's because you no longer agree with the bourgeois. All our other priests dined at the manager's, and threatened us with the devil as soon as we asked for bread.'

He began again, and spoke of the deplorable misunderstanding between the Church and the people. Now, in veiled phrases, he hit at the town priests, at the bishops, at the highly placed clergy, sated with enjoyment, gorged with domination, making pacts with the liberal bourgeoisie, in the imbecility of their blindness, not seeing that it was this bourgeoisie which had dispossessed them of the rule of the world. Deliverance would come from the country priests, who would all rise to re-establish the kingdom of Christ, with the help of the poor; and already he seemed to be at their head; he raised his bony form to his full height like the chief of a band, a revolutionary of the gospel, his eyes so filled with light that they illuminated the gloomy room. This enthusiastic sermon lifted him to mystic heights, and the poor people had long ceased to understand him.

'No need for so many words,' growled Maheu suddenly. 'You'd best begin by bringing us a loaf.'

'Come on Sunday to mass,' cried the priest. 'God will provide for everything.'

And he went off to catechize the Levaques in their turn, so carried away by his dream of the final triumph of the Church, and so contemptuous of facts, that he would thus go through the settlements without charity, with empty hands amid this army dying of hunger, being a poor devil himself who looked upon suffering as the spur to salvation.

Maheu continued his pacing, and nothing was heard but his regular tramp which made the floor tremble. There was the sound of a rust-eaten pulley; old Bonnemort was spitting into the cold grate. Then the rhythm of the feet began again. Alzire, weakened by fever, was rambling in a low voice, laughing, thinking that it was warm and that she was playing in the sun.

'Good God!' muttered la Maheude, after having touched her cheeks, 'how she burns! I don't expect that damned beast now, the brigands must have stopped him from coming.'

She meant the doctor and the Company. She uttered a joyous exclamation, however, when the door once more opened. But her arms fell back and she remained standing still with a gloomy face.

'Good evening,' whispered Étienne, when he had carefully closed the door.

He often came thus at night-time. The Maheus learnt of his retreat after the second day. But they kept the secret and no one in the settlement knew exactly what had become of the young man. A legend had grown up around him. People still believed in him and mysterious rumours circulated: he would reappear with an army and chests full of gold; and there was always the religious expectation of a miracle, the realized ideal, a sudden entry into that city of justice which he had promised them. Some said they had seen him lying back in a carriage, with three other gentlemen, on the Marchiennes road; others affirmed that he was in England for a few days. At length, however, suspicions began to arise and jokers accused him of hiding in a cellar, where la Mouquette kept him warm; for this relationship, when known, had done him harm. There was a growing disaffection in the midst of his popularity, a gradual increase of the despairing among the faithful, and their number was certain, little by little, to grow.

'What brutal weather!' he added. 'And you – nothing new, always from bad to worse? They tell me that little Négrel has been to Belgium to recruit workers in Le Borinage. Good God! we are done for if that is true!'

He shuddered as he entered this dark icy room, where it was some time before his eyes were able to see the unfortunate people whose presence he guessed by the deepening of the shadows. He was experiencing the repugnance and discomfort of the workman who has risen above his class, refined by study and stimulated by ambition. What wretchedness! and odours! and the bodies in a heap! And a terrible pity caught him by the throat. The spectacle of this agony so overcame him that he tried to find words to advise submission.

But Maheu came violently up to him, shouting:

'Belgians! They won't dare, the buggers! Let the Belgians go down, then, if they want us to destroy the pits!'

With an embarrassed air, Étienne explained that it was not possible to move, that the soldiers who guarded the pits would protect the descent of the Belgian workmen. And Maheu clenched his fists, irritated especially, as he said, by having bayonets in his back. Then the colliers were no longer masters in their own place? They were treated, then, like convicts, forced to work by a loaded musket! He loved his pit, it was a great grief to him not to have been down for two months. He was driven wild, therefore, at the idea of this insult, these strangers whom they threatened to introduce. Then the recollection that his certificate had been given back to him struck him to the heart.

'I don't know why I'm angry,' he muttered. 'I don't belong to their dump any longer. When they have turned me out from here, I may as well die on the road.'

'Come now,' said Étienne, 'if you like, they'll take your certificate back tomorrow. They don't sack good workmen.'

He interrupted himself, surprised to hear Alzire, who was laughing softly in the delirium of her fever. So far he had only made out old Bonnemort's stiff shadow, and the gaiety of the sick child frightened him. It was indeed too much if the little ones were going to die of it. With trembling voice he made up his mind.

'Look here! this can't go on, we are done for. We must give up.'

La Maheude, who had been motionless and silent up to now, suddenly broke out, and swearing like a man, she shouted in his face:

'What's that you say? You're the one saying that, by God!'

He was about to give reasons, but she would not let him speak.

'Don't repeat that, by God! or, woman as I am, I'll put my fist into your face. Then we have been dying for two months, and I have sold my household, and my little ones have fallen ill, and there is to be nothing done, and the injustice is to begin again! Ah! do you know! when I think of that my blood stands still. No, no, I would burn everything, I would kill everything, rather than give up.'

She pointed at Maheu in the darkness, with a vague, threatening gesture.

'Listen to this! If any man goes back to the pit, he'll find me waiting for him on the road to spit in his face and cry coward!

Étienne could not see her, but he felt a heat like the breath of a barking animal. He had drawn back, astonished at this fury which was his doing. She was so changed that he could no longer recognize the woman who was once so sensible, reproaching him for his violent schemes, saying that we ought not to wish anyone dead, and who was now refusing to listen to reason and talking of killing people. Instead of him, it was she who talked politics, who dreamed of sweeping away the bourgeois at a stroke, who demanded the republic and the guillotine to free the earth of these rich robbers who fattened themselves on the labour of starvelings.

'Yes, I could flay them with my fingers. We've had enough of them! Our turn is come now; you used to say so yourself. When I think of father, grandfather, grandfather's father, what all of them who went before have suffered, what we are suffering, and that our sons and our sons' sons will suffer over again, it makes me mad – I could take a knife. The other day we didn't do enough at Montsou; we ought to have pulled the bloody place to the ground, down to the last brick. And do you know I've only one regret, that we didn't let the old man strangle the Piolaine girl. Hunger may strangle my little ones for all they care!'

Her words fell like the blows of an axe in the night. The closed horizon would not open, and the impossible ideal was turning to poison in the depths of this mind which had been crushed by grief.

'You have misunderstood me,' Étienne was able to say at last, beating a retreat. 'We ought to come to an understanding with the Company. I know that the pits are suffering much, so that they would probably consent to an arrangement.'

'No, never!' she shouted.

Just then Lénore and Henri came back with their hands empty. A gentleman had given them two sous, but the girl kept kicking her little brother, and the two sous fell into the snow, and as Jeanlin had joined in the search they had not been able to find them.

'Where is Jeanlin?'

'He's gone away, mother; he said he had business.'

Étienne was listening with an aching heart. Once she had threatened to kill them if they ever held out their hands to beg.

Now she sent them herself on to the roads, and suggested that all of them – the ten thousand colliers of Montsou – should take stick and wallet, like beggars of old, and scour the terrified country.

The anguish continued to increase in the black room. The little urchins came back hungry, they wanted to eat; why could they not have something to eat? And they grumbled, flung themselves about, and at last trod on the feet of their dying sister, who groaned. The mother furiously boxed their ears in the darkness at random. Then, as they cried still louder, asking for bread, she burst into tears, and dropped on to the floor, seizing them in one embrace with the little invalid; then, for a long time, her tears fell in a nervous spasm which left her limp and worn out, stammering over and over again the same phrase, calling out for death:

'O God! why do You not take us? O God! for pity's sake take us, to have done with it!'

The grandfather didn't move, like an old tree twisted by the rain and wind; while the father continued walking between the fireplace and the cupboard, without turning his head.

But the door opened, and this time it was Doctor Vanderhaghen.

'The devil!' he said. 'This light won't spoil your eyes. Look sharp! I'm in a hurry.'

As usual, he scolded, exhausted by work. Fortunately, he had matches with him, and the father had to strike six, one by one, and to hold them while he examined the invalid. Uncovered, she shivered beneath this flickering light, as lean as a bird dying in the snow, so small that you could only see her hump. But she smiled with the wandering smile of the dying, and her eyes were very large; while her poor hands contracted over her hollow breast. And as the half-choked mother asked if it was right to take away from her the only child who helped in the household, so intelligent and gentle, the doctor grew annoyed.

'Ah! she is going. Dead of hunger, your blessed child. And not the only one, either; I've just seen another one over there. You all send for me, but I can't do anything; it's meat that you want to cure you.'

Maheu, with burnt fingers, had dropped the match, and the darkness closed over the little corpse, which was still warm. The doctor had gone away in a hurry. Étienne heard nothing more in the black room but la Maheude's sobs, repeating her cry for death, that melancholy and endless lamentation:

'O God! it is my turn, take me! O God! take my man, take the others, for pity's sake, to have done with it!'

CHAPTER 3

On that Sunday, ever since eight o'clock, Souvarine had been sitting alone in the parlour of the Avantage, at his accustomed place, with his head against the wall. Not a single collier knew where to get two sous for a drink, and never had the bars had fewer customers. So Madame Rasseneur, motionless at the counter, preserved an irritated silence; while Rasseneur, standing before the iron fireplace, seemed to be gazing with a reflective air at the brown smoke from the coal.

Suddenly, in the heavy silence of this over-heated room, three light quick blows struck against one of the window-panes made Souvarine turn his head. He rose, for he recognized the signal which Étienne had already used several times before, in order to call him, when he saw him from without, smoking his cigarette at an empty table. But before the engine-man could reach the door, Rasseneur had opened it, and, recognizing the man who stood there in the light from the window, he said to him:

'Are you afraid that I shall give you away? You can talk better here than on the road.'

Étienne entered. Madame Rasseneur politely offered him a glass, which he refused, with a gesture. The innkeeper added:

'I guessed long ago where you hide yourself. If I was a spy, as your friends say, I would have sent the police after you a week ago.'

'There is no need for you to defend yourself,' replied the young man. 'I know that you have never eaten that sort of bread. People may have different ideas and respect each other all the same.'

And there was silence once more. Souvarine had gone back to his chair, with his back to the wall and his eyes fixed on the smoke from his cigarette, but his feverish fingers were moving restlessly, and he ran them over his knees, seeking the warm fur of Pologne, who was absent this evening; he was in a state of unconscious discomfort, something was lacking, he could not exactly say what.

Seated on the other side of the table, Étienne at last said:

'Tomorrow work begins again at the Voreux. The Belgians have come with little Négrel.'

'Yes, they landed them at nightfall,' muttered Rasseneur, who remained standing. 'As long as people don't kill each other again!'

Then raising his voice:

'No, you know, I don't want to begin our disputes over again, but this will end badly if you hold out any longer. Why, your story is just like what's happened to your International. I met Pluchart the day before yesterday, at Lille, where I went on business. It's going wrong, that set-up of his.'

He gave details. The association, after having conquered the workers of the whole world, in an outburst of propaganda which had left the bourgeoisie still shuddering, was now being devoured and slowly destroyed by an internal struggle between vanities and ambitions. Since the anarchists had got the upper hand in it, chasing out the earlier evolutionists, everything was breaking up; the original aim, the reform of the wage-system, was lost in the midst of the squabbling of sects; the scientific framework was disorganized by the hatred of discipline. And already it was possible to foresee the final collapse of this general revolt which for a moment had threatened to carry away in a breath the old rotten society.

'Pluchart is ill over it,' Rasseneur went on. 'And he has no voice at all now. All the same, he talks on in spite of everything and wants to go to Paris. And he told me three times over that our strike was done for.'

Étienne with his eyes on the ground let him talk on without interruption. The evening before he had chatted with some mates, and he felt that hints of spite and suspicion were directed at him, those first hints of unpopularity which precede defeat. And he remained gloomy, he would not confess dejection in the presence of a man who had foretold to him that the crowd would jeer at him too on the day when they had to avenge themselves for a miscalculation.

'No doubt the strike is done for, I know that as well as Pluchart,' he said. 'But we foresaw that. We accepted this strike against our wishes, we didn't count on finishing up with the Company. Only you get carried away, you begin to expect things, and when it turns out badly you forget that you ought to have expected that, instead of lamenting and quarrelling as if it were a catastrophe from heaven.'

'Then if you think the game's lost,' asked Rasseneur, 'why don't you make the mates listen to reason?'

The young man looked at him fixedly.

'Listen! enough of this. You have your ideas, I have mine. I came in here to show you that I feel respect for you in spite of everything. But I still think that if we come to grief over this trouble, our starved carcasses will do more for the people's cause than all your common-sense politics. Ah! if one of those bloody soldiers would just put a bullet in my heart, that would be a fine way of ending it all!'

His eyes were moist, as in this cry he betrayed the secret desire of the vanquished for a refuge in which he could lose his torment for ever.

'Well said!' declared Madame Rasseneur, casting on her husband a look which was full of all the contempt of her radical opinions.

Souvarine, with a vague gaze, feeling about with his nervous hands, did not appear to hear. His fair girlish face, with the thin nose and small pointed teeth, seemed to be growing savage in some mystic dream full of bloody visions. And he began to dream aloud, replying to a remark of Rasseneur's about the International which had been let fall in the course of the conversation.

'They are all cowards; there is only one man who can turn their set-up into a terrible instrument of destruction. It requires will, and none of them have will; and that's why the revolution will miscarry once more.'

He went on in a voice of disgust, lamenting the imbecility of men, while the other two felt like intruders on the confessions of a sleepwalker made in the darkness of night. In Russia there was nothing going on well, and he was in despair over the news he had received. His old companions were all turning into politicians; the famous Nihilists who made Europe tremble – sons of village priests, of the lower middle class, of tradesmen – could not rise above the idea of national liberation, and seemed to believe that the world would be delivered when they had killed their despot. As soon as he spoke to them of razing society to the ground like a ripe harvest – as soon as he even pronounced the infantile word 'republic' – he felt that he was misunderstood and a disturber, henceforth uprooted, enrolled among the lost leaders of cosmopolitan revolution. His patriotic heart struggled, however, and it was with painful bitterness that he repeated his favourite expression:

'Foolery! They'll never get out of it with their foolery.'

Then, lowering his voice still more, in a few bitter words he described his old dream of fraternity. He had given up his rank and his fortune; he had gone among workmen, only in the hope of seeing at last the foundation of a new society of labour in common. All the sous in his pockets had long gone to the urchins of the settlement; he had been as tender as a brother with the colliers, smiling at their suspicions, winning them over by his quiet work-manlike ways and his dislike of chattering. But decidedly the fusion had not taken place; he remained a stranger, with his contempt of all bonds, his desire to keep himself free of all petty vanities and enjoyments. And since this morning he had been especially exasperated by reading an incident in the newspapers.

His voice changed, his eyes grew bright, he fixed them on Étienne, directly addressing him:

'Now, do you understand that? These hatworkers in Marseilles who have won the great lottery prize of a hundred thousand francs have gone off at once and invested it, declaring that they are going to live without doing anything! Yes, that is your idea, all of you French workmen; you want to unearth a treasure in order to consume it alone afterwards in some lazy, selfish corner. You may cry out as much as you like against the rich, you haven't got courage enough to give back to the poor the money that luck brings you. You will never be worthy of happiness as long as you own anything, and your hatred of the bourgeois proceeds solely from an angry desire to be bourgeois yourselves in their place.'

Rasseneur burst out laughing. The idea that the two Marseilles workmen ought to give up the big prize seemed to him absurd. But Souvarine grew pale; his face changed and became terrible in one of those religious rages which exterminate nations. He cried:

'You will all be mown down, overthrown, cast on the dung-heap. Someone will be born who will annihilate your race of cowards and pleasure-seekers. And look here! you see my hands; if my hands were able they would take up the earth, like that, and shake it until it was smashed to fragments, and you were all buried beneath the rubbish.'

'Well said,' declared Madame Rasseneur, with her polite and convinced air.

There was silence again. Then Étienne spoke once more of the Borinage men. He questioned Souvarine concerning the steps that had been taken at the Voreux. But the engine-man was still preoccupied, and scarcely replied. He only knew that bullets would be distributed to the soldiers who were guarding the pit; and the nervous restlessness of his fingers over his knees increased to such an extent that, at last, he became conscious of what was lacking – the soft and soothing fur of the tame rabbit.

'Where is Pologne, then?' he asked.

The innkeeper laughed again as he looked at his wife. After an awkward silence he made up his mind:

'Pologne? She is nice and warm.'

Since her adventure with Jeanlin the pregnant rabbit, no doubt wounded, had only brought forth dead young ones; and to avoid feeding a useless mouth they had resigned themselves that very day to serve her up with potatoes.

'Yes, you ate one of her legs this evening. Eh! You licked your fingers after it!'

Souvarine had not understood at first. Then he became very pale, and his face contracted with nausea; while, in spite of his stoicism, two large tears were swelling beneath his eyelids.

But no one had time to notice this emotion, for the door had opened roughly and Chaval had appeared, pushing Catherine before him. After having made himself drunk with beer and bluster in all the public-houses of Montsou, the idea had occurred to him to go to the Avantage to show his old friends that he was not afraid. As he came in, he said to his mistress:

'By God! I tell you you'll drink a glass in here; I'll break the jaws of the first man who gives me a funny look!'

Catherine, moved at the sight of Étienne, had become very pale. When Chaval in his turn noticed him, he grinned in his evil fashion.

'Two glasses, Madame Rasseneur! We're celebrating the new start of work.'

Without a word she poured out, as a woman who never refused her beer to any one. There was silence, and neither the landlord nor the two others stirred from their places.

'I know people who've said that I was a spy,' Chaval went on swaggeringly, 'and I'm waiting for them just to say it again to my face, so that we can have it out.'

No one replied, and the men turned their heads and gazed vaguely at the walls.

'There are some who sham, and there are some who don't sham,' he went on louder. 'I've nothing to hide. I've left Deneulin's dump, and tomorrow I'm going down to the Voreux with a dozen Belgians, who have been given me to lead because I'm held in esteem; and if anyone doesn't like that, he can just say so, and we'll talk it over.'

Then, as the same contemptuous silence greeted his provocations, he turned furiously on Catherine.

'Will you drink, by God? Drink with me to the death of all the dirty bastards who refuse to work?'

She raised her glass, but with so trembling a hand that the two glasses struck together with a tinkling sound. He had now pulled out of his pocket a handful of silver, which he exhibited with drunken ostentation, saying that he had earned that with his sweat, and that he defied the shammers to show ten sous. The attitude of his mates exasperated him, and he turned to direct insults.

'Then it is at night that the moles come out? The gendarmes have to be asleep before we meet the brigands.'

Étienne had risen, very calm and resolute.

'Listen! You are getting on my nerves. Yes, you are a spy; your money still stinks of some treachery. You've sold yourself, and it disgusts me to touch your skin. No matter; I'm your man. It is quite time that one of us did for the other.'

Chaval clenched his fists.

'Come along, then, cowardly dog! It takes a lot of talk to get you going. You all alone – I'm quite willing; and you shall pay for all the bloody tricks that have been played on me.'

With a pleading gesture Catherine advanced between them. But they had no need to repel her; she felt the necessity of the battle, and slowly drew back of her own accord. Standing against the wall, she remained silent, so paralysed with anguish that she no longer shivered, her large eyes gazing at these two men who were going to kill each other over her.

Madame Rasseneur simply removed the glasses from the counter for fear that they might be broken. Then she sat down again on the bench, without showing any improper curiosity. But two old mates could not be left to murder each other like this. Rasseneur persisted in interfering, and Souvarine had to take him by the shoulder and lead him back to the table, saying:

'It doesn't concern you. There is one of them too many, and the stronger must live.'

Without waiting for the attack, Chaval's fists were already throwing punches into empty space. He was the taller of the two, and his blows swung about, aiming at the face, with furious cutting movements of both arms one after the other, as though he were handling a couple of sabres. And he went on talking, playing to the gallery with volleys of abuse, which served to excite him.

'Ah! you filthy pimp, I'll have your nose! I'll stuff your bloody nose somewhere! Just let me get at your chops, you whores' delight; I'll make a hash of it for the pigs and then we shall see if the strumpets will run after you!'

In silence, and with clenched teeth, Étienne gathered up his small frame, according to the rules of the game, protecting his chest and face with both fists; and he watched and let them fly like springs released, with terrible straight blows.

At first they did each other little damage. The whirling and blustering blows of the one, the cool watchfulness of the other, prolonged the struggle. A chair was overthrown; their heavy boots crushed the white sand scattered on the floor. But at last they were out of breath, their panting respiration was heard, while their faces became red and swollen as from an interior fire which flamed out in their flashing eyes.

'Got ya!' yelled Chaval; 'a hit on your carcass!'

In fact his fist, working like a flail, had struck his adversary's shoulder. Étienne restrained a groan of pain and the only sound that was heard was the dull bruising of the muscles. Étienne replied with a straight blow to Chaval's chest, which would have knocked him out, had he had not saved himself by one of his constant goat-like leaps. The blow, however, caught him on the left flank with such effect that he tottered, momentarily winded. He became furious on feeling his arm grow limp with pain, and kicked out like a wild beast, aiming at Étienne's groin with his heel.

'I'll get your guts!' he stammered in a choked voice. 'I'll pull them out and unwind them for you!'

Étienne avoided the blow, so indignant at this infraction of the laws of fair fighting that he broke his silence.

'Hold your tongue, brute! And no feet, by God! or I'll take a chair and bash you with it!'

Then the struggle became serious. Rasseneur was disgusted, and would again have interfered, but a severe look from his wife held him back: had not two customers a right to settle a score in the house? He simply placed himself in front of the fireplace, for fear lest they should tumble over into it. Souvarine, in his quiet way, had rolled a cigarette, but he forgot to light it. Catherine was motionless against the wall; only her hands had unconsciously risen to her waist, and with constant fidgeting movements were twisting and tearing at the stuff of her dress. She was striving as hard as possible not to cry out, and so, perhaps, kill one of them by declaring her preference; but she was, too, so distraught that she did not even know which she preferred.

Chaval, who was bathed in sweat and striking at random, soon became exhausted. In spite of his anger, Étienne continued to cover himself, parrying nearly all the blows, a few of which grazed him. His ear was split, a finger nail had torn at his neck, and this so smarted that he swore in his turn as he threw one of his terrible straight punches. Once more Chaval saved his chest by a leap, but he had lowered himself, and the fist reached his face, smashing his nose and crushing an eye. Immediately a spurt of blood came from his nostrils, and his eye became swollen and bluish. Blinded by this red flood, and dazed by the shock to his skull, the wretch was beating the air with his arms at random, when another blow, striking him at last full in the chest, finished him. There was a crunching sound; he fell on his back with a heavy thud, like a sack of plaster being unloaded.

Étienne waited.

'Get up! If you want some more, we'll begin again.'

Without replying, Chaval, after a few minutes' stupefaction, moved on the ground and stretched his limbs. He picked himself up with difficulty, resting for a moment curled up on his knees, doing something with his hand in the bottom of his pocket which could not be observed. Then, when he was up, he rushed forward again, his throat swelling with a savage yell.

But Catherine had seen it, and in spite of herself a loud cry came from her heart, astonishing her like the avowal of a preference she had herself been ignorant of:

'Watch out! he's got his knife!'

Étienne had only time to parry the first blow with his arm. His woollen jacket was cut by the thick blade, one of those blades fastened by a copper clasp into a boxwood handle. He had already seized Chaval's wrist, and a terrible struggle began; for he felt that he would be lost if he let go, while the other shook his arm in an effort to free it and strike. The weapon was gradually lowered as their stiffened limbs grew fatigued. Étienne twice felt the cold sensation of the steel against his skin; and he had to make a supreme effort, crushing the other's wrist so that the knife slipped from his hand. Both of them had fallen to the earth, and it was Étienne who snatched it up, brandishing it in his turn. He held Chaval down beneath his knee and threatened to slit his throat.

'Ah, traitor! by God! you've got it coming to you now!'

He felt an awful voice within, deafening him. It arose from the depths of his being and was beating in his head like a hammer, a sudden mania for murder, a need to taste blood.* Never before had the crisis so shaken him. He was not drunk, however, and he struggled against the hereditary disease with the despairing shudder of a man who is mad with lust and struggles on the verge of rape. At last he controlled himself; he threw the knife behind him, stammering in a hoarse voice:

'Get up – off with you!'

This time Rasseneur had rushed forward, but without quite daring to venture between them, for fear of catching a nasty blow.

He did not want any one to be murdered in his house, and was so angry that his wife, sitting erect at the counter, remarked to him that he always cried out too soon. Souvarine, who had nearly caught the knife in his legs, decided to light his cigarette. Was it, then, all over? Catherine was looking on stupidly at the two men, who were unexpectedly both living.

'Off you go!' repeated Étienne. 'Off you go, or I'll do for you!'

Chaval arose, and with the back of his hand wiped away the blood which continued to flow from his nose; with his jaw smeared red and his bruised eye, he went away trailing his feet, furious at his defeat. Catherine mechanically followed him. Then he turned round, and his hatred broke out in a flood of filth.

'No, no! since you want him, sleep with him, dirty slut! and don't put your bloody feet in my place again if you value your life!'

He violently banged the door. There was deep silence in the warm room, only the low crackling of the coal was heard. On the ground there only remained the overturned chair and a pool of blood which the sand on the floor was soaking up.

CHAPTER 4

When they came out of Rasseneur's, Étienne and Catherine walked on in silence. The thaw was beginning, a slow cold thaw which dirtied the snow without melting it. In the livid sky a full moon could be faintly seen behind great clouds, black rags driven furiously by a tempestuous wind far above; and on the earth not a single breath was stirring, nothing could be heard but drippings from the roofs from which fell white lumps with a soft thud.

Étienne felt awkward with this woman who had been given to him, and in his disquiet he could find nothing to say. The idea of taking her with him to hide at Réquillart seemed absurd. He had offered to lead her back to the settlement, to her parents' house, but she had refused in terror. No, no! anything rather than be a burden on them once more after having behaved so badly to them! And neither of them spoke any more; they tramped on at random through the roads which were becoming rivers of mud. At first they went down towards the Voreux; then they turned to the right and passed between the pit-bank and the canal.

'But you'll have to sleep somewhere,' he said at last. 'Now, if I only had a room, I could easily take you—'

But a curious attack of timidity interrupted him. The past came back to him, their old longings for each other, and the delicacies and the shame which had prevented them from coming together. Did he still desire her, that he felt so troubled, gradually warmed at the heart by a fresh longing? The recollection of the blows she had dealt him at Gaston-Marie now attracted him instead of filling him with spite. And he was surprised; the idea of taking her to Réquillart was becoming quite natural and easy to do.

'Now, come on, decide; where would you like me to take you? You must hate me very much to refuse to come with me!'

She was following him slowly, delayed by the painful slipping of her clogs into the ruts; and without raising her head she murmured:

'I have enough trouble, good God! don't give me any more. What good would it do us, what you ask, now that I have a lover and you have a woman yourself?'

She meant la Mouquette. She believed that he still went with this girl, as the rumour ran for the last fortnight; and when he swore to her that it was not so she shook her head, for she remembered the evening when she had seen them eagerly kissing each other.

'Isn't it a pity, all this nonsense?' he whispered, stopping. 'We might have got on so well.'

She shuddered slightly and replied:

'Never mind, you've nothing to be sorry for; you've not lost much. If you knew what a weakling I am – no bigger than two sous of butter, so ill made that I shall never become a woman, sure enough!'

And she went on freely accusing herself, as though the long delay of her puberty had been her own fault. In spite of the man whom she had had, this lessened her, placed her among the urchins. You have some excuse, at any rate, when you can produce a child.

'My poor thing!' said Étienne, with deep pity, in a very low voice.

They were at the foot of the pit-bank, hidden in the shadow of the enormous pile. An inky cloud was just then passing over the moon; they could no longer even distinguish their faces, their breaths were mingled, their lips were seeking each other for that kiss which had tormented them with desire for months. But suddenly the moon reappeared, and they saw the sentinel above them, at the top of the rocks white with light, standing out erect on the Voreux. And before they had kissed a sense of shame separated them, that old modesty in which there was something of anger, a vague repugnance, and much friendship. They set out again painfully, up to their ankles in mud.

'Then it's settled. You don't want to have anything to do with me?' asked Étienne.

'No,' she said. 'You after Chaval; and after you another, eh? No, that disgusts me; it doesn't give me any pleasure. What's the use of doing it?'

They were silent, and walked some hundred paces without exchanging a word.

'But, anyhow, do you know where to go to?' he said again. 'I can't leave you out on a night like this.'

She replied, simply:

'I'm going back. Chaval is my man. I have nowhere else to sleep but with him.'

'But he will beat you to death.'

There was silence again. She had shrugged her shoulders in resignation. He would beat her, and when he was tired of beating her he would stop. Wasn't that better than to roam the streets like a whore? Then she was used to beatings; she said, to console herself, that eight out of ten girls were no better off than she was. If her lover married her some day it would, all the same, be very nice of him.

Étienne and Catherine were moving instinctively towards Montsou, and as they came nearer their silences grew longer. It was as though they had never before been together. He could find no argument to convince her, in spite of the deep vexation which he felt at seeing her go back to Chaval. His heart was breaking, he had nothing better to offer than an existence of wretchedness and flight, a night with no tomorrow should a soldier's bullet blow out his brains. Perhaps, after all, it was wiser to suffer what he was suffering rather than risk a fresh suffering. So he led her back to her lover's, with sunken head, and made no protest when she stopped him on the main road, at the corner of the Yards, twenty metres from the Piquette bar, saying:

'Don't come any farther. If he sees you it will only make things worse.'

Eleven o'clock struck at the church clock. The bar was closed, but gleams came through the cracks in the shutters.

'Good-bye,' she murmured.

She had given him her hand; he kept it, and she had to draw it away painfully, with a slow effort, to leave him. Without turning her head, she went in through the little latched door. But he did not turn away, standing at the same place with his eyes on the house, anxious as to what was happening within. He listened, trembling lest he should hear the cries of a beaten woman. The house remained black and silent; he only saw a light appear at a first-floor window, and as this window opened, and he recognized the thin shadow that was leaning over the road, he came near.

Catherine then whispered very low:

'He's not come back. I'm going to bed. Please go away.'

Étienne went off. The thaw was increasing; a regular shower was falling from the roofs, humidity flowed down the walls, the palings, the whole confused mass of this industrial district lost in the night. At first he turned towards Réquillart, sick with fatigue and sadness, having no other desire except to disappear under the earth and to be annihilated there. Then the idea of the Voreux occurred to him again. He thought of the Belgian workmen who were going down, of his mates at the settlement, exasperated against the soldiers and resolved not to tolerate strangers in their pit. And he passed again along the canal through the puddles of melted snow.

As he stood once more near the pit-bank the moon was shining brightly. He raised his eyes and gazed at the sky. The clouds were galloping by, whipped on by the strong wind which was blowing up there; but they were growing white, and ravelling out thinly with the misty transparency of troubled water over the moon's face. They succeeded each other so rapidly that the moon, veiled at moments, constantly reappeared in limpid clearness.

With his gaze full of this pure brightness. Étienne was lowering his head, when a sight on the summit of the pit-bank attracted his attention. The sentinel, stiffened by cold, was walking up and down, taking twenty-five paces towards Marchiennes, and then returning towards Montsou. The white glitter of his bayonet could be seen above his black silhouette, which stood out clearly against the pale sky. But what interested the young man, behind the cabin where Bonnemort used to take shelter on stormy nights, was a moving shadow – a crouching beast in ambush – which he immediately recognized as Jeanlin, with his long thin spine like a weasel's. The sentinel could not see him. That devil of a child was certainly preparing some practical joke, for he was still furious against the soldiers, and asking when they were going to be freed from these murderers who had been sent here with guns to kill people.

For a moment Étienne thought of calling him to prevent him from doing some stupid trick. The moon was hidden. He had seen him draw himself up ready to spring; but the moon reappeared, and the child remained crouching. At every turn the sentinel came as far as the cabin, then turned his back and walked in the opposite direction. And suddenly, as a cloud threw its shadow, Jeanlin leapt on to the soldier's shoulders with the great bound of a wild cat, and gripping him with his claws buried his large open knife in his throat. The horse-hair collar resisted; he had to apply both hands to the handle and hang on with all the weight of his body. He had often bled fowls which he had found behind farms. It was so rapid that there was only a stifled cry in the night, while the musket fell with the sound of old iron. Already the moon was shining again.

Motionless with stupor, Étienne was still looking on. The soldier's shout had been choked in his chest. Above, the pit-bank was empty; no shadow was visible against the wild flight of clouds. He ran up and found Jeanlin on all fours in front of the corpse, which was lying back with extended arms. Beneath the limpid light the red trousers and grey overcoat contrasted harshly with the snow. Not a drop of blood had flowed, the knife was still in the throat up to the handle. With a furious, unreasoning blow of the fist he knocked the child down beside the body.

'What have you done that for?' he stammered wildly.

Jeanlin picked himself up and rested on his hands, with a feline movement of his thin spine; his large ears, his green eyes, his prominent jaws were quivering and aflame with the shock of his deadly blow.

'By God! why have you done this?'

'I don't know; I wanted to.'

He persisted in this reply. For three days he had wanted to. It tormented him, it made his head ache behind his ears, because he thought about it so much. Why worry about these damned soldiers who were bullying the miners in their own homes? Of the violent speeches he had heard in the forest, the cries of destruction and death shouted among the pits, five or six words had remained with him, and these he repeated like a street urchin playing at revolution. And he knew no more; no one had urged him on, it had come to him of itself, just as the desire to steal onions from a field came to him.

Startled at this obscure growth of crime in the recesses of this childish brain, Étienne again pushed him away with a kick, like a dumb animal. He trembled lest the guard at the Voreux had heard the sentinel's stifled cry, and looked towards the pit every time the moon was uncovered. But nothing stirred, and he bent down, felt the hands that were gradually becoming icy, and listened to the heart, which had stopped beneath the overcoat. Only the bone handle of the knife could be seen with the gallant motto on it, the simple word 'Amour', engraved in black letters.*

His eyes went from the throat to the face. Suddenly he recognized the little soldier; it was Jules, the recruit with whom he had talked one morning. And deep pity came over him in front of this fair gentle face, marked with freckles. The blue eyes, wide open, were gazing at the sky with that fixed look with which he had before seen him searching the horizon for the country of his birth. Where was it, that Plogof which had appeared to him beneath the dazzling sun? Over there, over there! The sea was moaning afar on this tempestuous night. That wind passing above had perhaps swept over the moors. Two women perhaps were standing there, the mother and the sister, clutching their wind-blown coifs, gazing as if they could see what was now happening to the little fellow across the leagues which separated them. They would always be waiting for him now. What an abominable thing it is for poor devils to kill each other for the sake of the rich!

But this corpse had to be disposed of. Étienne at first thought of throwing it into the canal, but was deterred from this by the certainty that it would be found there. His anxiety became extreme, every minute was of importance; what decision should he take? He had a sudden inspiration: if he could carry the body as far as Réquillart, he would be able to bury it there for ever.

'Come here,' he said to Jeanlin.

The child was suspicious.

'No, you want to beat me. And then I have business. Good night.'

In fact, he had arranged to meet Bébert and Lydie in a hiding-place, a hole made under the wood supply at the Voreux. They had planned to sleep out, so as to be there if the Belgians' bones were to be broken by stoning when they went down the pit.

'Listen!' repeated Étienne. 'Come here, or I shall call the soldiers, who will cut your head off.'

And as Jeanlin was making up his mind, he rolled his handkerchief, and bound the soldier's neck tightly, without drawing out the knife, so as to prevent the blood from flowing. The snow was melting; on the soil there was neither a red patch nor the footmarks of a struggle.

'Take the legs!'

Jeanlin took the legs, while Étienne seized the shoulders, after having fastened the gun behind his back, and then they both slowly descended the pit-bank, trying to avoid rolling any rocks down.

Fortunately the moon was hidden. But as they passed along the canal it reappeared brightly, and it was a miracle that the guard did not see them. Silently they hastened on, hindered by the swinging of the corpse, and obliged to place it on the ground every hundred metres. At the corner of the Réquillart lane they heard a sound which froze them with terror, and they only had time to hide behind a wall to avoid a patrol. Farther on, a man came across them, but he was drunk, and moved away abusing them. At last they reached the old pit, bathed in perspiration, and so exhausted that their teeth were chattering.

Étienne had guessed that it would not be easy to get the soldier down the ladder shaft. It was an awful task. First of all Jeanlin, standing above, had to let the body slide down, while Étienne, hanging on to the bushes, had to accompany it to enable it to pass the first two ladders where the rungs were broken. Afterwards, at every ladder, he had to perform the same manoeuvre over again, going down first, then receiving the body in his arms; and he had to descend thirty ladders, two hundred and ten metres, feeling the body constantly falling over him. The gun scraped his spine; he had not allowed the child to go for the candle-end, which he preserved avariciously. What was the use? The light would only embarrass them in this narrow passageway. When they arrived at the pit-eye, however, out of breath, he sent the youngster for the candle. He then sat down and waited for him in the darkness, near the body, with heart beating violently. As soon as Jeanlin reappeared with the light, Étienne consulted with him, for the child had explored these old workings, even to the cracks through which men could not pass. They set out again, dragging the dead body for nearly a kilometre, through a maze of ruined galleries. At last the roof became low, and they found themselves kneeling beneath a sandy rock supported by half-broken planks. It was a sort of long chest in which they laid the little soldier as in a coffin; they placed his gun by his side; then with vigorous blows of their heels they broke the timber at the risk of being buried themselves. Immediately the rock gave way, and they scarcely had time to crawl back on their elbows and knees. When Étienne returned, seized by the desire to look once more, the roof was still falling in, slowly crushing the body beneath its enormous weight. And then there was nothing more left, nothing but the vast mass of the earth.

Jeanlin, having returned to his own corner, his robbers' cave, was stretching himself out on the hay, overcome by weariness, and murmuring:

'Damn it! the brats will have to wait for me; I'm going to have an hour's sleep.'

Étienne had blown out the candle, of which there was only a small end left. He also was worn out, but he was not sleepy; painful nightmarish thoughts were beating like hammers in his skull. Only one at last remained, torturing him and fatiguing him with a question to which he could not reply: Why had he not killed Chaval when he held him beneath the knife? and why had this child just killed a soldier whose very name he did not know? It upset his revolutionary beliefs, the courage to kill, the right to kill. Was he, then, a coward? In the hay the child had begun snoring, the snoring of a drunken man, as if he were sleeping off the intoxication of his murder. Étienne was disgusted and irritated; it hurt him to know that the boy was there and to hear him. Suddenly he started, a wave of fear passed over his face. A light rustling, a sob, seemed to him to have come out of the depths of the earth. The image of the little soldier, lying over there with his gun beneath the rocks, sent a shiver down his spine and made his hair stand up. It was idiotic, the whole mine seemed to be filled with voices; he had to light the candle again, and only grew calm on seeing the emptiness of the galleries by this pale light.

For another quarter of an hour he reflected, still absorbed in the same struggle, his eyes fixed on the burning wick. But there was a spluttering, the wick was going out, and everything fell back into darkness. He shuddered again; he could have boxed Jeanlin's ears, to keep him from snoring so loudly. The proximity of the child became so unbearable that he escaped, tormented by the need for fresh air, hastening through the galleries and up the passage, as though he could hear a shadow, panting, at his heels.

Up above, in the midst of the ruins of Réquillart, Étienne was at last able to breathe freely. Since he dared not kill, it was for him to die; and this idea of death, which had already touched him, came again and fixed itself in his head, as a last hope. To die bravely, to die for the revolution, that would end everything, would settle his account, good or bad, and prevent him from thinking more. If his mates attacked the Belgians, he would be in the first rank, and would have a good chance of getting shot. It was with a firmer step that he returned to prowl around the Voreux. Two o'clock struck, and the loud noise of voices was coming from the foremen's room, where the guards who watched over the pit were posted. The disappearance of the sentinel had taken the guards by surprise; they had gone to arouse the captain, and after a careful examination of the place, they concluded that it must be a case of desertion. Hiding in the shade, Étienne remembered the republican captain of whom the little soldier had spoken. Who knows if he might not be persuaded to pass over to the people's side! The troops would raise their rifles, and that would be the signal for a massacre of the bourgeois. A new dream took possession of him; he thought no more of dying, but remained for hours with his feet in the mud, and a drizzle from the thaw falling on his shoulders, filled by the feverish hope that victory was still possible.

Up to five o'clock he watched out for the Belgians. Then he saw that the Company had cunningly arranged that they should sleep at the Voreux. The descent had begun, and the few strikers from the Deux-Cent-Quarante settlement who had been posted as scouts had not yet warned their mates. It was he who told them of the trick, and they set out running, while he waited behind the pit-bank, on the towing-path. Six o'clock struck, and the earthy sky was growing pale and lighting up with a reddish dawn, when Abbé Ranvier came along a path, holding up his cassock and showing his thin legs. Every Monday he went to say an early mass at a convent chapel on the other side of the pit.

'Good morning, my friend,' he shouted in a loud voice, after staring at the young man with his flaming eyes.

But Étienne did not reply. Far away between the Voreux platforms he had just seen a woman pass by, and he rushed forward anxiously, for he thought he recognized Catherine. Since midnight, Catherine had been walking about the thawing roads. Chaval, on coming back and finding her there, had knocked her out of bed with a blow. He shouted to her to go at once by the door if she did not wish to go by the window; and scarcely dressed, in tears, and bruised by kicks in her legs, she had been forced to go down, pushed outside by a final blow. This sudden separation dazed her, and she sat down on a stone, looking up at the house, still expecting that he would call her back. It was not possible; he would surely look for her and tell her to come back when he saw her thus shivering and abandoned, with no one to take her in.

After two hours she made up her mind, dying of cold and as motionless as a dog thrown into the street. She left Montsou, then retraced her steps, but dared neither to call from the pathway nor to knock at the door. At last she went off by the main road to the right with the idea of going to the settlement, to her parents' house. But when she reached it she was seized by such shame that she rushed away along the gardens for fear of being recognized by

someone, in spite of the heavy sleep which weighed on all behind
the closed shutters. And after that she wandered about, frightened
at the slightest noise, trembling lest she should be seized and led
away as a strumpet to that house at Marchiennes, the threat of
which had haunted her like a nightmare for months. Twice she
stumbled against the Voreux, but terrified at the loud voices of the
guard, she ran away out of breath, looking behind her to see if she
was being pursued. The Réquillart lane was always full of drunken
men; she went back to it, however, with the vague hope of meeting
there the man she had repelled a few hours earlier.

Chaval had to go down the mine that morning, and this thought
brought Catherine again towards the pit, though she felt that it
would be useless to speak to him: all was over between them. There
was no work going on at Jean-Bart, and he had sworn to kill her if
she worked again at the Voreux, where he feared that she would
compromise him. So what was to be done? – to go elsewhere, to die
of hunger, to yield beneath the blows of every man who might pass?
She dragged herself along, tottering amid the ruts, with aching legs
and mud up to her waist. The thaw had now filled the streets with
a flood of mire. She waded through it, still walking, not daring to
look for a stone to sit on.

Daylight appeared. Catherine had just recognized the back of
Chaval, who was cautiously going round the pit-bank, when she
noticed Lydie and Bébert putting their noses out of their hiding-
place beneath the wood supply. They had spent the night there on
the look-out, without going home, since Jeanlin's order was to
await him; and while he was sleeping off the drunkenness of his
murder at Réquillart, the two children were lying in each other's
arms to keep warm. The wind was blowing between the poles of
chestnut and oak, and they rolled themselves up as in some wood-
cutter's abandoned hut. Lydie did not dare complain about her
sufferings, the woes of the small beaten woman that she was, any
more than Bébert found courage to complain of the leader's blows
which made his cheeks swell up; but the leader was really abusing
his power, risking their bones in mad marauding expeditions while
refusing to share the booty. Their hearts rose in revolt, and they
had at last kissed each other in spite of his orders, risking a box of
the ears from the invisible hand with which he had threatened them.
It never came, so they went on kissing each other softly, with no
thought of anything else, putting into that caress the passion they
had long struggled against – the whole of their martyred and tender
natures. All night through they had thus kept each other warm, so

happy, at the bottom of this secret hole, that they could not remember that they had ever been so happy before – not even on Saint-Barbe's day, when they had eaten fritters and drunk wine.

The sudden sound of a bugle made Catherine start. She raised herself, and saw the Voreux guards taking up their arms. Étienne arrived running; Bébert and Lydie jumped out of their hiding-place with a leap. And beneath the growing daylight, a gang of men and women were coming from the settlement, gesticulating wildly with anger.

CHAPTER 5

All the entrances to the Voreux had been closed, and the sixty soldiers, with grounded arms, were barring the only door left free, the one leading to the receiving-room by a narrow staircase into which opened the foremen's room and the shed. The men had been drawn up in two lines by the captain against the brick wall, so that they could not be attacked from behind.

At first the gang of miners from the settlement kept at a distance. They were some thirty at most, and talked together in a violent and confused way.

La Maheude, who had arrived first, with dishevelled hair beneath a handkerchief knotted on in haste and with Estelle asleep in her arms, repeated in feverish tones:

'Don't let anyone in or anyone out! Shut them all in there!'

Maheu approved, and just then old Mouque arrived from Réquillart. They wanted to prevent him from going. But he protested; he said that his horses had to eat their hay all the same, and cared precious little about the revolution. Besides, there was a horse dead, and they were waiting for him to draw it up. Étienne freed the old groom, and the soldiers allowed him to go to the shaft. A quarter of an hour later, as the gang of strikers, which had gradually grown larger, was becoming threatening, a large door opened on the ground floor and some men appeared drawing out the dead beast, a miserable mass of flesh still fastened in the rope net; they left it in the midst of the puddles of melting snow. The surprise was so great that no one prevented the men from returning and barricading the door afresh. They all recognized the horse, with his head bent back and stiff against his side. Whispers ran around:

'It's Trompette, isn't it? it's Trompette.'

It was, in fact, Trompette. Since his descent he had never become acclimatized. He had remained melancholy, with no taste for his job, as though tortured by a regret for daylight. In vain Bataille, the doyen of the mine, would rub him with his ribs in his friendly way, softly biting his neck to impart to him a little of the resignation gained in his ten years beneath the earth. These caresses increased his melancholy, his skin quivered beneath the confidences of the comrade who had grown old in darkness; and both of them, whenever they met and snorted together, seemed to be grieving, the old one that he could no longer remember, the young one that he could not forget. In the stable they were neighbours at the manger, and lived with lowered heads, breathing in each other's nostrils, exchanging a constant dream of daylight, visions of green grass, of white roads, of infinite yellow light. Then, when Trompette, bathed in sweat, lay in agony in his litter, Bataille had smelled at him despairingly with short sniffs like sobs. He felt that he was growing cold, the mine was taking from him his last joy, that friend fallen from above, fresh with good odours, who recalled to him his youth in the open air. And he had broken his tether, neighing with fear, when he perceived that the other no longer stirred.

Mouque had indeed warned the overman a week ago. But who bothered about a sick horse at such a time as this! These gentlemen did not at all like moving the horses. Now, however, they had to make up their minds to take him out. The evening before, the groom had spent an hour with two men tying up Trompette. They harnessed Bataille to bring him to the shaft. The old horse slowly pulled, dragging his dead comrade through so narrow a gallery that he had to keep shaking his way through at the risk of taking the skin off. And he tossed his head in distress, listening to the grazing sound of the carcass on its way to the knacker's yard. At the loading-bay, when he was unharnessed, he followed with his melancholy eye the preparations for the ascent – the body pushed on to the cross-bars over the sump, the net fastened beneath a cage. At last the porters rang for the meat; he lifted his neck to see it go up, at first softly, then at once lost in the darkness, flying up for ever to the top of that black hole. And he remained with neck stretched out, his vague beast's memory perhaps recalling the things of the earth. But it was all over; he would never see his comrade again, and he himself would thus be tied up in a pitiful bundle on the day when he too would ascend up there. His legs began to tremble, the fresh air which came from the distant country choked him, and he seemed intoxicated when he went heavily back to the stable.

At the surface the colliers stood gloomily before Trompette's carcass. A woman said in a low voice:

'At least a man can go down if he wants to!'

But a new flood of people arrived from the settlement, and Levaque, who was at the head followed by his wife and Bouteloup, shouted:

'Kill them, those Belgians! No blacklegs here! Kill them! Kill them!'

All rushed forward, and Étienne had to stop them. He went up to the captain, a tall thin young man of scarcely twenty-eight years, with a despairing, resolute face. He explained things to him; he tried to win him over, watching the effect of his words. What was the good of risking a useless massacre? Was not justice on the side of the miners? They were all brothers, and they ought to understand one another. When he came to use the word 'republic' the captain made a nervous movement; but he preserved his military stiffness, and said suddenly:

'Keep off! Do not force me to do my duty.'

Three times over Étienne tried again. Behind him his mates were growling. The report ran that Monsieur Hennebeau was at the pit, and they talked of letting him down by the neck, to see if he would hew his coal himself. But it was a false rumour; only Négrel and Dansaert were there. They both showed themselves for a moment at a window of the receiving-room; the overman stood in the background, rather out of countenance since his adventure with la Pierronne, while the engineer bravely looked round on the crowd with his bright little eyes, smiling with that sneering contempt in which he enveloped men and things generally. Jeers arose, and they disappeared. And in their place only Souvarine's pale face was seen. He was just then on duty; he had not left his machine for a single day since the strike began, no longer talking, more and more absorbed by a fixed idea, which seemed to be shining like steel in the depths of his pale eyes.

'Keep off!' repeated the captain loudly. 'I don't want to hear anything. My orders are to guard the pit, and I shall guard it. And do not press on to my men, or I shall have to drive you back.'

In spite of his firm voice, he was growing pale with increasing anxiety, as the flood of miners continued to swell. He would be relieved at midday; but fearing that he would not be able to hold out until then, he had sent a trammer from the pit to Montsou to ask for reinforcements.

He was answered by a volley of shouts:

'Down with the foreigners! Kill the Belgians! We mean to be masters in our own place!'

Étienne drew back in despair. The end had come; there was nothing more except to fight and to die. And he ceased to hold back his mates. The mob moved up to the little troop. There were nearly four hundred of them, and the people from the neighbouring settlements were all running up. They all shouted the same cry. Maheu and Levaque said furiously to the soldiers:

'Get off with you! We have nothing against you! Get off with you!'

'This doesn't concern you,' said La Maheude. 'Let us attend to our own affairs.'

And from behind, la Levaque added, more violently:

'Must we kill you to get through? Just bugger off!'

Even Lydie's shrill voice was heard. She had crammed herself in more closely, with Bébert, and was saying, in a high voice:

'Oh, the white-livered pigs!'

Catherine, a few paces off, was gazing and listening, stupefied by new scenes of violence, into the midst of which ill luck seemed to be always throwing her. Had she not suffered too much already? What fault had she committed, then, that misfortune would never give her any rest? The day before she had understood nothing of the fury of the strike; she thought that when one has one's share of beatings it is useless to go and seek for more. And now her heart was swelling with hatred; she remembered what Étienne had often told her when they used to sit up; she tried to hear what he was now saying to the soldiers. He was treating them as mates; he reminded them that they also belonged to the people, and that they ought to be on the side of the people against those who took advantage of their wretchedness.

But a tremor ran through the crowd, and an old woman rushed up. It was old Mother Brûlé, terrible in her leanness, with her neck and arms in the air, coming up at such a pace that the wisps of her grey hair blinded her.

'Ah! by God! here I am,' she stammered, out of breath; 'that traitor Pierron shut me up in the cellar!'

And without waiting she fell on the soldiers, her black mouth belching abuse.

'Pack of scoundrels! dirty scum! ready to lick their masters' boots, and only brave against poor people!'

Then the others joined her, and there were volleys of insults. A few, indeed, cried: 'Long live the soldiers! down the mines with the officer!' but soon there was only one clamour: 'Down with the red-breeches!' These men, who had listened quietly, with motionless mute faces, to the fraternal appeals and the friendly attempts to win them over, preserved the same stiff passivity beneath this hail of abuse. Behind them the captain had drawn his sword, and as the crowd pressed in on them more and more, threatening to crush them against the wall, he ordered them to present bayonets. They obeyed, and a double row of steel points was placed in front of the strikers' breasts.

'Ah! the bloody swine!' yelled la Brûlé, drawing back.

But already they were coming on again, in excited contempt of death. The women were throwing themselves forward, la Maheude and la Levaque shouting:

'Kill us! Kill us, then! We want our rights!'

Levaque, at the risk of getting cut, had seized three bayonets in his hands, shaking and pulling them in an effort to snatch them away. He twisted them in the strength of his fury; while Bouteloup, standing aside, and annoyed at having followed his mate, quietly watched him.

'Just come on then and try it,' said Maheu; 'come on then if you are brave enough!'

And he opened his jacket and drew aside his shirt, showing his naked chest, with his hairy skin tattooed by coal. He pressed on the bayonets, compelling the soldiers to draw back, terrible in his insolence and bravado. One of them had pricked him in the chest, and he became like a madman, trying to make it enter deeper and to hear his ribs crack.

'Cowards, you don't dare! There are ten thousand behind us. Yes, you can kill us; there are ten thousand more of us to kill yet.'

The position of the soldiers was becoming critical, for they had received strict orders not to make use of their weapons until the last extremity. And how were they to prevent these furious people from impaling themselves? Besides, the space was getting less; they were now pushed back against the wall, and it was impossible to draw further back. Their little troop – a mere handful of men – opposed to the rising flood of miners, still held its own, however, and calmly executed the brief orders given by the captain. He, with his keen eyes and nervously compressed lips, only feared lest they should get carried away by this abuse. Already a young sergeant, a tall lean fellow whose thin moustache was bristling up, was blinking his eyes in a disquieting manner. Near him an old soldier, with tanned skin and stripes won in twenty campaigns, had grown pale when he saw his bayonet twisted like a straw. Another, doubtless a recruit still smelling of the fields, became very red every time he heard himself called 'scum' and 'riff-raff.' And the violence did not cease, the outstretched fists, the abominable words, the shovelfuls of accusations and threats which buffeted their faces. It required all the force of order to keep them thus, with mute faces, in the proud, gloomy silence of military discipline.

A collision seemed inevitable, when Richomme, the foreman, appeared from behind the troop with his benevolent white head, overwhelmed by emotion. He spoke out loudly:

'By God! this is idiotic! such nonsense can't go on!'

And he threw himself between the bayonets and the miners.

'Mates, listen to me. You know that I am an old workman, and that I have always been one of you. Well, by God! I promise you, that if they're not just with you, I'm the man to go and say to the bosses how things lie. But this is too much, it does no good at all to howl bad names at these good fellows, and try and get your bellies ripped up.'

They listened, hesitating. But up above, unfortunately, little Négrel's short profile reappeared. He feared, no doubt, that he would be accused of sending a foreman in place of venturing out himself; and he tried to speak. But his voice was lost in the midst of so frightful a tumult that he had to leave the window again, simply shrugging his shoulders. Richomme then found it useless to entreat them in his own name, and to repeat that the thing must be arranged between mates; they repelled him, suspicious of him. But he was obstinate and remained amongst them.

'By God! let them break my head as well as yours, for I don't leave you while you are so foolish!'

Étienne, whom he begged to help him in making them hear reason, made a gesture of powerlessness. It was too late, there were now more than five hundred of them. And besides the madmen who were rushing up to chase away the Belgians some came out of inquisitiveness, or to joke and amuse themselves over the battle. In the midst of one group, at some distance, Zacharie and Philomène were looking on as if at a theatre so peacefully that they had brought their two children, Achille and Désirée. Another stream was arriving from Réquillart, including Mouquet and la Mouquette.

The former at once went on, grinning, to slap his friend Zacharie on the back; while la Mouquette, in a very excited condition, rushed to the first rank of the wildest group.

Meanwhile, every minute, the captain looked down the Montsou road. The desired reinforcements had not arrived, and his sixty men could hold out no longer. At last it occurred to him to strike the imagination of the crowd, and he ordered his men to load their guns. The soldiers executed the order, but the disturbance increased, the blustering, and the mockery.

'Ah! these shammers, they're going off to target practice!' jeered the women, la Brûlé, la Levaque, and the others.

La Maheude, with her breast covered by the little body of Estelle, who was awake and crying, came so near that the sergeant asked her what she was going to do with that poor little brat.

'What the devil's that to do with you?' she replied. 'Fire at it if you dare!'

The men shook their heads with contempt. None believed that they would fire on them.

'There are no bullets in their cartridges,' said Levaque.

'Are we Cossacks?' cried Maheu. 'You don't fire against Frenchmen, by God!'

Others said that when people had been through the Crimean campaign they were not afraid of lead. And all continued to thrust themselves on to the rifles. If firing had begun at this moment the crowd would have been mown down.

In the front rank la Mouquette was choking with fury, thinking that the soldiers were going to gash the women's skins. She had spat out all her coarse words at them, and could find no vulgarity low enough, when suddenly, having nothing left but that mortal offence with which to bombard the faces of the troop, she showed her backside. With both hands she raised her skirts, bent her back, and stuck out her huge round buttocks.

'Here, that's for you! and it's a lot too clean, you dirty blackguards!'

She ducked and butted so that each might have his share, repeating after each thrust:

'There's for the officer! there's for the sergeant! there's for the soldiers!'

A tempest of laughter arose; Bébert and Lydie were in convulsions; Étienne himself, in spite of his sombre fears, applauded this insulting nudity. All of them, the banterers as well as the infuriated, were now jeering at the soldiers as though they had seen them spattered with filth; only Catherine, standing aside on some old timber, remained silent, her heart pounding, slowly carried away by the hatred that was rising within her.

But there was a scuffle. To calm the excitement of his men, the captain decided to take prisoners. With a leap la Mouquette escaped, saving herself between the legs of her comrades. Three miners, Levaque and two others, were seized among the more violent, and kept in sight at the other end of the foremen's room. Négrel and Dansaert, above, were shouting to the captain to come in and take refuge with them. He refused; he felt that these buildings with their doors without locks would be taken by assault, and that he would undergo the shame of being disarmed. His little troop was already growling with impatience; it was impossible to flee before these wretches in clogs. The sixty, with their backs to the wall and their rifles loaded, again faced the mob.

At first the strikers drew back and there was a deep silence; they were astonished at this energetic measure. Then a cry arose calling for the prisoners, demanding their immediate release. Some said that they were being murdered in there. And without any attempt at concerted action, carried away by the same impulse, by the same desire for revenge, they all ran to the piles of bricks which stood nearby, those bricks for which the marly soil supplied the clay, and which were baked on the premises. The children brought them one by one, and the women filled their skirts with them. Every one soon had ammunition at his feet, and the battle of stones began.

It was la Brûlé who set to first. She broke the bricks on the sharp edge of her knee, and with both hands she hurled the two fragments. La Levaque was almost putting her shoulders out, being so large and soft that she had to come near to get her aim, in spite of Bouteloup's entreaties, and he dragged her back in the hope of being able to lead her away now that her husband had been taken off. They all grew excited, and la Mouquette, tired of making herself bleed by breaking the bricks on her over fat thighs, preferred to throw them whole. Even the youngsters came into line, and Bébert showed Lydie how the brick ought to be sent from under the elbow. There was a shower of enormous hailstones, producing low thuds. And suddenly, in the midst of these furies, Catherine was observed with her fists in the air also brandishing half-bricks and throwing them with all the force of her little arms. She could not have said why she was so choked up, she was dying of the desire to kill. Would it not soon be done with, this cursed life of misfortune? She had had enough of it, beaten and driven away by her man, wandering about like a lost dog in the mud of the roads, without being able to ask a crust from her father, who was starving like herself. Things never seemed to get better; they were getting worse ever since she could remember. And she broke the bricks and threw them before her with the one idea of sweeping everything away, her eyes so blinded that she could not even see whose jaws she might be crushing.

Étienne, who had remained in front of the soldiers, nearly had his skull broken. His ear was grazed, and turning round he started when he realized that the brick had come from Catherine's feverish hands; but at the risk of being killed he remained where he was, gazing at her. Many others also forgot themselves there, absorbed in the battle, with empty hands. Mouquet criticized the blows as though he were looking on at a game of skittles. Oh, good shot! and that other, no luck! He joked, and with his elbow pushed Zacharie, who was squabbling with Philomène because he had boxed Achille's and Désirée's ears, refusing to put them on his back so that they could see. There were spectators crowded all along the road. And at the top of the slope near the entrance to the settlement, old Bonnemort appeared, resting on his stick,motionless against the rust-coloured sky.

As soon as the first bricks were thrown, Richomme had again placed himself between the soldiers and the miners. He was entreating one group, exhorting the other, careless of danger, in such despair that large tears were flowing from his eyes. It was impossible to hear his words in the midst of the tumult; only his large grey moustache could be seen moving.

But the hail of bricks came faster; the men were joining in, following the example of the women.

Then la Maheude noticed that Maheu was standing behind with empty hands and sombre air.

'What's up with you?' she shouted. 'Are you a coward? Are you going to let your mates be carried off to prison? Ah! if only I hadn't got this child, you'd see!'

Estelle, who was clinging to her neck, screaming, prevented her from joining la Brûlé and the others. And as her man did not seem to hear, she kicked some bricks against his legs.

'By God! will you take that? Must I spit in your face in front of people to get you worked up?'

Becoming very red, he broke some bricks and threw them. She urged him on, dazing him, shouting behind him cries of death, stifling her daughter against her breast with her arms; and he moved further forward until he was opposite the guns.

Beneath this shower of stones the little troop almost disappeared. Fortunately they struck too high, and the wall was riddled. What was to be done? The idea of going in, of turning their backs for a moment turned the captain's pale face purple; but it was no longer possible, they would be torn to pieces at the least movement. A brick had just broken the peak of his cap, drops of blood were running down his forehead. Several of his men were wounded; and he felt that they were losing self-control in that unbridled instinct of self-defence when obedience to leaders ceases. The sergeant had uttered a 'By God!' for his left shoulder had nearly been put out, and his flesh bruised by a shock like the blow of a washerwoman's paddle on her linen. Grazed twice over, the recruit had his thumb smashed, while his right knee was smarting. How much longer did they have to put up with this? A stone having bounded back and struck the old soldier with the stripes beneath the belly, his cheeks turned green, and his weapon trembled as he stretched it out at the end of his lean arms. Three times the captain was on the point of ordering them to fire. He was choked by anguish; an endless struggle for several seconds set at odds in his mind all ideas and duties, all his beliefs as a man and as a soldier. The rain of bricks increased, and he opened his mouth and was about to shout 'Fire!' when the guns went off by themselves, three shots at first, then five, then the roll of a volley, then one by itself, some time afterwards, in the deep silence.

There was a moment of stupefaction. They had fired, and the gaping crowd stood motionless, as yet unable to believe it. But heart-rending cries arose while the bugle was sounding to cease firing. And there was a mad panic, the rush of cattle filled with grapeshot, a wild flight through the mud. Bébert and Lydie had fallen one on top of the other at the first three shots, the little girl struck in the face, the boy wounded beneath the left shoulder. She was killed outright, and never stirred again. But he moved, seized her with both arms in the convulsion of his agony, as if he wanted to take her again, as he had taken her at the bottom of their dark hiding-place where they had spent the past night. And Jeanlin, who just then ran up from Réquillart still half asleep, skipping about in the midst of the smoke, saw him embrace his little wife and die.

The five other shots had brought down la Brûlé and Richomme. Struck in the back as he was entreating his mates, he had fallen on to his knees, and slipping on to one hip he was groaning on the ground with eyes still full of tears. The old woman, whose breast had been torn open, had fallen back stiff and crackling, like a bundle of dry faggots, stammering one last oath in the gurgling of blood.

But then the volley had swept the whole area, mowing down the inquisitive groups who were laughing at the battle a hundred paces off. A bullet entered Mouquet's mouth and threw him down with a fractured skull at the feet of Zacharie and Philomène, whose two youngsters were splashed with red drops. At the same moment, la Mouquette received two bullets in the belly. She had seen the soldiers take aim, and in an instinctive movement of her good nature she had thrown herself in front of Catherine, shouting out to her to take care; she uttered a loud cry and fell on to her back overturned by the shock. Étienne ran up, wishing to raise her and take her away; but with a gesture she said it was all over. Then she choked, but without ceasing to smile at both of them, as though she were glad to see them together now that she was going away.

All seemed to be over, and the hurricane of bullets had been lost in the distance as far as the frontages of the settlement, when the last shot, isolated and delayed, had been fired.

Maheu, struck in the heart, turned round and fell with his face down into a puddle black with coal. La Maheude leant down in stupefaction.

'Eh! old man, get up. It's nothing, is it?'

Her hands were encumbered with Estelle, whom she had to put under one arm in order to turn her man's head.

'Say something! where are you hurt?'

His eyes were vacant, and his mouth was dribbling with a bloody foam. She understood: he was dead. Then she remained seated in the mud with her daughter under her arm like a bundle, gazing at her old man with a besotted air.

The pit was free. With a nervous movement the captain had taken off and then put on his cap, struck by a stone; he preserved his pallid stiffness in face of the disaster of his life, while his men with mute faces were reloading. The frightened faces of Négrel and Dansaert could be seen at the window of the receiving-room. Souvarine was behind them with a deep wrinkle on his forehead, as though his fixed idea had printed itself there threateningly. On the other side of the horizon, at the edge of the plain, Bonnemort had not moved, supported by one hand on his stick, the other hand up to his brow to see better the murder of his people below. The wounded were howling, the dead were growing cold in twisted postures, spattered with the liquid mud of the thaw, here and there forming puddles among the inky patches of coal which reappeared beneath the tattered snow. And in the midst of these human corpses, all small, poor and lean in their wretchedness, lay Trompette's carcass, a monstrous and pitiful mass of dead flesh.

Étienne had not been killed. He was still waiting beside Catherine, who had fallen down with fatigue and anguish, when a sonorous voice made him start. It was Abbé Ranvier, who was coming back after saying mass, and who, with both arms in the air, with the inspired fury of a prophet, was calling the wrath of God down on the murderers. He foretold the era of justice, the approaching extermination of the bourgeoisie by fire from heaven, since it was bringing its crimes to a climax by massacring the workers and the disinherited of the world.

PART SEVEN

The shots fired at Montsou had reached as far as Paris with a formidable echo. For four days all the opposition papers had been indignant, printing atrocious narratives on their front pages: twenty-five wounded, fourteen dead, including three women and two children. And there were prisoners taken as well; Levaque had become a sort of hero, and was credited with a reply of antique sublimity to the examining magistrate. The Empire, taking a direct hit from these few bullets, affected the calm of omnipotence, without itself realizing the gravity of its wound. It was simply an unfortunate incident, something lost over there in the black country, very far from the Parisian boulevards which formed public opinion; it would soon be forgotten. The Company had received official instructions to hush up the affair, and to put an end to a strike which from its irritating duration was becoming a social danger.

So on Wednesday morning three of the directors appeared at Montsou. The little town, sick at heart, which had not dared hitherto to rejoice over the massacre, now breathed again, and tasted the joy of being saved. The weather, too, had become fine; there was a bright sun – one of those first February days which, with their moist warmth, tip the lilac shoots with green. All the shutters had been flung back at the administration building, the vast structure seemed alive again. And cheering rumours were circulating; it was said that the directors, deeply moved by the catastrophe, had rushed down to open their paternal arms to the wayward inhabitants of the settlements. Now that the blow had fallen – a more vigorous one doubtless than they had wished for – they were generous in their task of relief, and decreed measures that were excellent though tardy. First of all they sent away the Belgians, and made much of this extreme concession to their workmen. Then they put an end to the military occupation of the pits, which were no longer threatened by the defeated strikers. They also hushed up the case of the sentinel which had disappeared from the Voreux; the district had been searched without finding either the gun or the corpse, and although there was a suspicion of crime, it was decided to consider the soldier a deserter. In every way they thus tried to attenuate matters, trembling with fear for the morrow, judging it dangerous to acknowledge the irresistible savagery of a crowd set free amid the falling structure of the old world. And besides, this work of conciliation did not prevent them from bringing purely administration affairs to a satisfactory conclusion; for Deneulin had been seen to return to the administration buildings, where he met Monsieur Hennebeau. The negotiations for the purchase of Vandame continued, and it was considered certain that Deneulin would accept the Company's offers.

But what particularly stirred the locals were the great yellow posters which the directors had stuck up in profusion on the walls. On them were to be read these few lines, in very large letters: 'Workers of Montsou! We do not wish that the errors of which you have lately seen the sad effects should deprive sensible and willing workmen of their livelihood. We shall therefore reopen all the pits on Monday morning, and when work is resumed we shall examine with care and consideration those cases in which there may be room for improvement. We shall, in fact, do all that is just or possible to do.' In one morning the ten thousand colliers passed before these placards. Not one of them spoke, many shook their heads, others went away with trailing steps, without changing one line in their motionless faces.

Up till now the settlement of the Deux-Cent-Quarante had persisted in its fierce resistance. It seemed that the blood of their mates, which had reddened the mud of the pit, was barricading the road against the others. Scarcely a dozen had gone down, merely Pierron and some sneaks of his sort, whose departure and arrival were gloomily watched without a gesture or a threat. Therefore a deep suspicion greeted the placard stuck on to the church door. Nothing was said about the returned certificates in it. Would the Company refuse to take them on again? and the fear of retaliation, the fraternal idea of protesting against the dismissal of the more compromised men, made them all obstinate still. It was dubious; they would see. They would return to the pit when these gentlemen were good enough to put things plainly. Silence reigned in the little low houses. Hunger itself seemed nothing; all might die now that violent death had passed over their roofs.

But one house, the Maheus', remained especially black and mute in its overwhelming grief. Since she had followed her man to the cemetery, la Maheude had never said a word. After the battle, she had allowed Étienne to bring back Catherine muddy and half dead; and as she was undressing her, before the young man, in order to put her to bed, she thought for a moment that her daughter also had received a bullet in the belly for her shirt was stained with larges patches of blood. But she soon understood that it was the flow of puberty, which was at last breaking out in the shock of this abominable day. Ah! another piece of luck, that wound! A fine present, to be able to make children for the gendarmes to kill; and she never spoke to Catherine, nor did she, indeed, talk to Étienne. The latter slept with Jeanlin, at the risk of being arrested, seized by such horror at the idea of going back to the darkness of Réquillart that he would have preferred a prison. A shudder shook him, the horror of the night after all those deaths, an unacknowledged fear of the little soldier who slept down there underneath the rocks. Besides, he dreamed of a prison as of a refuge in the midst of the torment of his defeat; but they did not trouble him, and he dragged on his wretched hours, not knowing how to tire out his body. Only at times la Maheude looked at both of them, at him and her daughter, with a spiteful air, as though she were asking them what they were doing in her house.

Once more they all slept in a heap. Old Bonnemort occupied the former bed of the two youngsters, who slept with Catherine now that poor Alzire no longer dug her hump into her big sister's ribs. It was when going to bed that the mother felt the emptiness of the house by the coldness of her bed, which was now too large. In vain she took Estelle to fill the vacancy; that did not replace her man, and she wept quietly for hours. Then the days began to pass by as before, always without bread, but without the luck to die outright; odd things picked up here and there did the wretches the dubious favour of keeping them alive. Nothing had changed in their existence, only her man was gone.

On the afternoon of the fifth day, Étienne, made miserable by the sight of this silent woman, left the room, and walked slowly along the paved street of the settlement. The inaction which weighed on him impelled him to take constant walks, with arms swinging idly and lowered head, always tortured by the same thought. He tramped thus for half an hour, when he felt, with an uneasy sense, that his mates were coming to their doors to look at him. His little remaining popularity had been driven to the winds by the shooting, and he never passed now without meeting fiery looks which pursued him. When he raised his head there were threatening men there, women drawing aside the curtains from their windows; and beneath their still silent accusation and the restrained anger of these eyes, enlarged by hunger and tears, he became awkward and could scarcely walk straight. These dumb reproaches seemed to be always increasing behind him. He became so terrified, lest he should hear the entire settlement come out to shout its wretchedness at him, that he returned shuddering. But at the Maheus' the scene which awaited him still further disturbed him. Old Bonnemort was near the cold fireplace, glued to his chair ever since two neighbours, on the day of the slaughter, had found him on the ground, with his stick broken, struck down like an old tree hit by lightening. And while Lénore and Henri, to deceive their hunger, were scraping, with deafening noise, an old saucepan in which cabbages had been boiled the day before, la Maheude, after having placed Estelle on the table, was standing up, threatening Catherine with her fist.

'Say that again, by God! Just dare to say that again!'

Catherine had declared her intention to go back to the Voreux. The idea of not earning her bread, of being thus tolerated in her mother's house, like a useless animal that is in the way, was becoming every day more unbearable; and if it had not been for the fear of Chaval she would have gone down on Tuesday.

She said again, stammering:

'What do you want? We can't go on doing nothing. We should get some bread at least.'

La Maheude interrupted her.

'Listen to me: the first one of you who goes to work, I'll strangle. No, that would be too much to kill the father and go on exploiting the children! I've had enough of it; I'd rather see you all put in your coffins, like him that's gone already.'

And her long silence broke out into a furious flood of words. A fine sum Catherine would bring her! hardly thirty sous, to which they might add twenty sous if the bosses were good enough to find work for that scoundrel Jeanlin. Fifty sous, and seven mouths to feed! The kids were only good for swallowing soup. As for grandfather, he must have busted something in his brain when he fell, for he seemed imbecile; unless it had turned his blood to see the soldiers firing at his mates.

'That's it, old man, isn't it? They've quite done for you. It's no good having your hands still strong; you're done for.'

Bonnemort looked at her with his dim eyes without understanding. He remained for hours with a fixed gaze, having no intelligence now except to spit into a plate filled with ashes, which was put beside him for cleanliness.

'And they've not settled his pension, either,' she went on. 'And I'm sure they won't give it to him, because of our ideas. No! I tell you that we've had enough of those people who bring ill luck.'

'But,' Catherine ventured to say, 'they promise on the placard—'

'Just leave me alone with your damned placard! More bird-lime for catching us and doing us in. They can be mighty kind now that they have torn us apart.'

'But where shall we go, mother? They won't keep us at the settlement, sure enough.'

La Maheude made a vague, terrible gesture. Where should they go to? She did not know at all; she avoided thinking, it made her mad. They would go elsewhere – somewhere. And as the noise of the saucepan was becoming unbearable, she turned round on Léonore and Henri and boxed their ears. Estelle, who had been crawling on all fours, fell down and increased the disturbance. The mother quieted her with a clout – a good thing if it had killed her! She spoke of Alzire; she wished the others might have that child's luck. Then suddenly she burst out into loud sobs, with her head against the wall.

Étienne, who was standing by, did not dare to interfere. He no longer counted for anything in the house, and even the children drew back from him suspiciously. But the unfortunate woman's tears went to his heart, and he murmured:

'Come, come! courage! we must try to get by.'

She did not seem to hear him, and was pouring out her grief now in a low continuous lament.

'Ah! the wretchedness! is it possible? Things did go on before these horrors. We ate our dry bread, but we were all together; and what has happened, good God! What have we done, then, that we should have such troubles – some dead and buried, and the others with nothing left but to long to join them? It's true enough that they harnessed us like horses to work, and it's not at all a just sharing of things to be always getting the stick and making rich people's fortunes bigger without hope of ever enjoying the good things of life. There's no pleasure in life when hope goes. Yes, that couldn't have gone on longer; we had to breathe a bit. If we had only known! Is it possible to make oneself so wretched through wanting justice?'

Sighs swelled her breast, and her voice choked with immense sadness.

'Then there are always some clever people there who promise you that everything can be arranged by just taking a little trouble. Then you lose your head, and you suffer so much from things as they are that you ask for things that can't be. Now, I was dreaming like a fool; I seemed to see a life of good friendship with everybody; I went off into the air, my faith! into the clouds. And then you break your back when you tumble down into the mud again. It's not true; there's nothing there of the things that people tell of. What there is, is only wretchedness, ah! wretchedness, as much as you like of it, and bullets into the bargain.'

Étienne listened to this lamentation, and every tear struck him with remorse. He knew not what to say to calm la Maheude, broken by her terrible fall from the heights of the ideal. She had come back to the middle of the room, and was now looking at him; she addressed him with contemptuous familiarity in a last cry of rage:

'And you, do you talk of going back to the pit, too, after driving us out of the bloody place! I've nothing to reproach you with; but if I were in your shoes I should be dead of grief by now after causing such harm to your mates.'

He was about to reply, but then shrugged his shoulders in despair. What was the good of explaining, for she would not understand in her grief? And he went away, for he was suffering too much, and resumed his desperate walk outside.

There again he found the settlement apparently waiting for him, the men at their doors, the women at their windows. As soon as he appeared growls could be heard, and the crowd increased. The breath of gossip, which had been swelling for four days, was breaking out in a universal malediction. Fists were raised towards him, mothers spitefully pointed him out to their boys, old men spat as they looked at him. It was the change which follows on the morrow of defeat, the fatal reverse of popularity, an execration exasperated by all the suffering endured without result. He had to pay the price for famine and death.

Zacharie, who came up with Philomène, hustled Étienne as he went out, grinning maliciously.

'Well, he's getting fatter. It's filling, then, to thrive on other people's deaths?'

La Levaque had already come to her door with Bouteloup. She spoke of Bébert, her youngster, killed by a bullet, and cried:

'Yes, there are cowards who get children murdered! Let him go and look for mine underground if he wants to give it me back!'

She was forgetting her man in prison, for the household was going on since Bouteloup remained; but she thought of him, however, and went on in a shrill voice:

'Clear off! there are rogues that are free to walk about while good men are locked away!'

In trying to avoid her, Étienne had come across La Pierronne,

who was running up across the gardens. She had regarded her
mother's death as a deliverance, for the old woman's violence
threatened to get them hanged; nor did she weep over Pierron's
little girl, that little minx Lydie – good riddance! But she joined in
with her neighbours with the idea of getting reconciled with them.

'And my mother, eh, and the little girl? You were seen; you were
hiding yourself behind them when they stopped the bullets instead
of you!'

What was to be done? Strangle la Pierronne and the others, and
fight the whole settlement? Étienne wanted to do so for a moment.
The blood was throbbing in his head, he now looked upon his
mates as savages, he was irritated to see them so unintelligent and
barbarous that they wanted to revenge themselves on him for the
logic of events. How stupid it all was! and he felt disgust at his
powerlessness to tame them again; and he just hastened his steps as
though he were deaf to abuse. Soon it became a flight; every house
jeered at him as he passed, they dogged his steps, it was a whole
community cursing him with a voice that was becoming like thunder
in its overwhelming hatred. It was he, the exploiter, the murderer,
who was the sole cause of their misfortune. He rushed out of the
settlement, pale and terrified, with this yelling crowd behind his
back. When he at last reached the main road most of them left him;
but a few persisted, until at the bottom of the slope before the
Avantage he met another group coming from the Voreux.

Old Mouque and Chaval were there. Since the death of his
daughter la Mouquette, and of his son Mouquet, the old man had
continued his job as groom without a word of regret or complaint.
Suddenly, when he saw Étienne, he was shaken by fury, tears broke
out from his eyes, and a flood of coarse words burst from his
mouth, black and bleeding from his habit of chewing tobacco.

'You devil! you bloody swine! you filthy bastard! Wait, you've
got to pay me for my poor children; you won't get away with it!'

He picked up a brick, broke it, and threw both pieces.

'Yes! yes! clear him off!' shouted Chaval, who was grinning in
excitement, delighted at this vengeance. 'Every one gets his turn;
now you're up against the wall, you dirty bastard!'

And he also attacked Étienne with stones. A savage clamour
arose; they all took up bricks, broke them, and threw them, to rip
him open, as they would like to have done to the soldiers.* He was
dazed and cold and could not flee; he faced them, trying to calm
them with words. His old speeches, once so warmly received, came
back to his lips. He repeated the words with which he had

intoxicated them at the time when he could keep them in hand like a faithful flock; but his power was dead, and only stones replied to him. He had just been struck on the left arm, and was drawing back, in great peril, when he found himself hemmed in against the front of the Avantage.

For the last few moments Rasseneur had been at his door.

'Come in,' he said simply.

Étienne hesitated; it choked him to take refuge there.

'Come in; then I'll speak to them.'

He resigned himself, and took refuge at the other end of the parlour, while the innkeeper filled up the doorway with his broad shoulders.

'Look here, my friends, just be reasonable. You know very well that I've never deceived you. I've always been in favour of calm, and if you had listened to me, you certainly wouldn't be where you are now.'

Rolling his shoulders and belly, he went on at length, allowing his facile eloquence to flow with the lulling gentleness of warm water. And all his old success came back; as he regained his popularity, naturally and without an effort, as if he had never been jeered and called a coward a month before. Voices arose in approval: 'Very good! we are with you! that is the way to put it!' Thundering applause broke out.

Étienne, in the background, grew faint, and there was bitterness at his heart. He recalled Rasseneur's prediction in the forest, threatening him with the ingratitude of the mob. What imbecile brutality! What an abominable forgetfulness for all he had done! It was a blind force which constantly destroyed itself. And beneath his anger at seeing these brutes spoil their own cause, there was despair at his own fall and the tragic end of his ambition. What! was he already done for! He remembered hearing beneath the beeches three thousand hearts beating to the echo of his own. On that day he had held his popularity in both hands. Those people had belonged to him; he had felt that he was their master. Mad dreams had then intoxicated him. Montsou at his feet, Paris beyond, becoming a deputy perhaps, crushing the bourgeois in a speech, the first speech ever made by a workman in a parliament. And it was all over! He awakened, miserable and detested; his people were dismissing him by flinging bricks.

Rasseneur's voice rose higher:

'Never will violence succeed; the world can't be remade in a day.

Those who have promised you to change it all at one stroke are either making fun of you or they are rascals!'

'Bravo! bravo!' shouted the crowd.

Who then was the guilty one? And this question which Étienne put to himself overwhelmed him more than ever. Was it in fact his fault, this misfortune which was consuming him, the wretchedness of some, the murdering of others, these women, these children, lean, and without bread? He had had that lamentable vision one evening before the catastrophe. But then an unknown force was sweeping him along, he was carried away with his mates. Besides, he had never led them, it was they who had led him, who obliged him to do things which he would never have done if it were not for the shock of that crowd pushing him on. At each new act of violence he had been stupefied by the course of events, for he had neither foreseen nor desired any of them. Could he anticipate, for instance, that his followers in the settlement would one day stone him? These infuriated people lied when they accused him of having promised them an existence all fine food and idleness. And in this justification, in this reasoning, in which he tried to fight against his remorse, lurked the fear that he had not risen to the height of his task; it was the doubt of the half-cultured man still perplexing him. But he felt himself at the end of his courage, he was no longer in tune with his mates; he feared this enormous mass of the people, blind and irresistible, moving like a force of nature, sweeping away everything, outside rules and theories. A certain repugnance was detaching him from them – the discomfort of his new tastes, the slow movement of all his being towards a superior class.

At this moment Rasseneur's voice was lost in the midst of enthusiastic shouts:

'Hurrah for Rasseneur! he's right! Bravo, bravo!'

The innkeeper shut the door, while the mob dispersed; and the two men looked at each other in silence. They both shrugged their shoulders. They finished up by having a drink together.

On the same day there was a great dinner at La Piolaine; they were celebrating the engagement of Négrel and Cécile. Since the previous evening the Grégoires had had the dining-room waxed and the drawing-room dusted. Mélanie reigned in the kitchen, watching over the roasts and stirring the sauces, the odour of which rose up to the attics. It had been decided that Francis, the coachman, would help Honorine to wait at table. The gardener's wife would wash up, and the gardener would open the gate. Never had the comfortable, patriarchal old house been in such a state of gaiety.

Everything went off beautifully. Madame Hennebeau was charming with Cécile, and she smiled at Négrel when the Montsou lawyer gallantly proposed the health of the future household. Monsieur Hennebeau was also very amiable. His smiling face impressed the guests. The rumour was that he was rising in favour with the directors, and that he would soon be made an officer of the Legion of Honour, on account of the energetic manner in which he had put down the strike. Nothing was said about recent events; but there was an air of triumph in the general joy, and the dinner became the official celebration of a victory. At last, then, they were saved, and once more they could begin to eat and sleep in peace. A discreet allusion was made to those dead whose blood the Voreux mud had yet scarcely drunk up. It was a necessary lesson; and they were all affected when the Grégoires added that it was now the duty of all to go and heal the wounds in the settlements. They had regained their benevolent placidity, excusing their brave miners, whom they could already see again at the bottom of the mines, giving a good example of everlasting resignation. The Montsou notables, who had now ceased trembling, agreed that the question of the wage system ought to be studied, cautiously. The roasts came on; and the victory became complete when Monsieur Hennebeau read a letter from the bishop announcing Abbé Ranvier's removal. The bourgeois throughout the province had been roused to anger by the story of this priest who treated the soldiers as murderers. And when the dessert appeared the lawyer resolutely declared that he was a free-thinker. Deneulin was there with his two daughters. In the midst of the joy, he forced himself to hide the melancholy of his ruin. That very morning he had signed the sale of his Vandame concession to the Montsou Company. With the knife at his throat he had submitted to the directors' demands, at last giving up to them that prey they had coveted for so long, scarcely obtaining from them the money necessary to pay off his creditors. He had even accepted, as a lucky chance, at the last moment, their offer to keep him as divisional engineer, thus resigning himself to watch, as a simple salaried employee, over the pit which had swallowed up his fortune. It was the death of the proprietors, eaten up, one by one, by the ever-hungry ogre of capital, drowned in the rising flood of great companies. He alone paid the full price of the strike; he understood that they were drinking to his disaster when they drank to Monsieur Hennebeau's rosette. And he only consoled himself a little when he saw the fine courage of Lucie and Jeanne, who looked charming in their mended clothes, laughing in the face of misfortune, like happy tomboys disdainful of money.

When they went into the drawing-room for coffee, Monsieur Grégoire drew his cousin aside and congratulated him on the courage of his decision.

'What do you expect? Your real mistake was to risk the million of your Montsou share over Vandame. You gave yourself a terrible time, and it has disappeared in that dreadful life of labour, while mine, which has not stirred from my drawer, still keeps me comfortably doing nothing, as it will keep my grandchildren's children.

CHAPTER 2

On Sunday Étienne escaped from the settlement at nightfall. A very clear sky, sprinkled with stars, lit up the earth with the blue haze of twilight. He went down towards the canal, and followed the bank slowly, in the direction of Marchiennes. It was his favourite walk, a grass-covered path two leagues long, passing straight beside this geometrical water-way, which unrolled itself like an endless ingot of molten silver. He never met anyone there. But on this day he was vexed to see a man come up to him. Beneath the pale starlight, the two solitary walkers only recognized each other when they were face to face.

'What! is it you?' said Étienne.

Souvarine nodded his head without replying. For a moment they remained motionless, then side by side they set out towards Marchiennes. Each of them seemed to be lost in thought, as though they were far away from each other.

'Have you seen in the paper about Pluchart's success in Paris?' asked Étienne, at length. 'After that meeting at Belleville, they waited for him on the pavement, and gave him an ovation. Oh! he's set up now, in spite of his sore throat. He can do what he likes in the future.'

The engine-man shrugged his shoulders. He felt contempt for fine talkers, fellows who go into politics as one goes into a bar, to make money out of fine phrases.

Étienne was now onto studying Darwin.* He had read fragments, summarized and popularized in a five-sous volume; and out of this ill-understood reading he had gained for himself a revolutionary idea of the struggle for existence, the lean eating the fat, the strong people devouring the effete bourgeoisie. Souvarine furiously attacked the stupidity of the Socialists who accept Darwin, that apostle of scientific inequality, whose famous selection was only good for aristocratic philosophers. His mate persisted, however, wishing to reason out the matter, and expressing his doubts with a hypothesis: supposing the old society were no longer to exist, swept away with every last crumb; well, was there not a fear that the new world would grow up again, slowly corrupted by the same injustices, some sick and others flourishing, some more skilful and intelligent, profiting from everything, and others stupid and lazy, becoming slaves again? But before this vision of eternal wretchedness, the engine-man shouted out fiercely that if justice was not possible with mankind then mankind must disappear. For every rotten society there must be a massacre, until the last creature is exterminated. And there was silence again.

For a long time, with sunken head, Souvarine walked over the short grass, so absorbed that he kept to the extreme edge, by the water, with the quiet assurance of a sleep-walker on a roof. Then he shuddered without any apparent reason, as though he had stumbled against a shadow. His eyes lifted and his face was very pale; he said softly to his companion;

'Did I ever tell you how she died?'

'Whom do you mean?'

'My woman, back there, in Russia.'

Étienne made a vague gesture, astonished at the tremor in his voice and at the sudden desire for confidence in this lad, who was usually so impassive in his stoical detachment from others and from himself. He only knew that the woman was his mistress, and that she had been hanged in Moscow.

'The affair hadn't gone well,' Souvarine said, with eyes still vacantly following the white stream of the canal between the bluish colonnades of tall trees. 'We had been a fortnight at the bottom of a hole mining the railway, and it was not the imperial train that was blown up, it was a passenger train. Then they arrested Anoushka. She brought us bread every evening, disguised as a peasant woman. She lit the fuse, too, because a man might have attracted attention. I followed the trial, hidden in the crowd, for six days.'*

His voice faltered and he coughed as though he were choking.

'Twice I wanted to cry out, and to rush over the people's heads to join her. But what was the good? One man less would be one soldier less; and I could see that she was telling me not to come, when her large eyes met mine.'

He coughed again.

'On the last day in the square I was there. It was raining; they stupidly bungled the job, put off by the falling rain. It took twenty minutes to hang the other four; the rope broke, they could not finish the fourth. Anoushka was standing up waiting. She could not see me, she was looking for me in the crowd. I got on to a post and she saw me, and our eyes never left each other. When she was dead, she was still looking at me. I waved my hat; I walked away.'

There was silence again. The white road of the canal unrolled to the far distance, and they both walked with the same quiet step as though each had fallen back into his isolation. At the horizon, the pale water seemed to pierce the sky with a little shaft of light.

'It was our punishment,' Souvarine went on harshly. 'We were guilty of loving each other. Yes, it is well that she is dead; heroes will be born from her blood, and I no longer have any cowardice in my heart. Ah! nothing, no family, no wife, no friend! Nothing to make your hand tremble on the day when you must take others' lives or give up your own.'

Étienne had stopped, shuddering in the cool night. He discussed no more, he simply said:

'We have gone far; shall we go back?'

They went back towards the Voreux slowly, and he added, after a few paces:

'Have you seen the new placards?'

The Company had that morning put up some more large yellow posters. They were clearer and more conciliatory, and the Company undertook to take back the certificates of those miners who went down on the following day. Everything would be forgotten, and pardon was offered even to those who were most implicated.

'Yes, I've seen then,' replied the engine-man.

'Well, what do you think of it?'

'I think that it's all over. The flock will go down again. You are all too cowardly.'

Étienne feverishly excused his mates: a man may be brave, a mob which is dying of hunger has no strength. Step by step they were returning to the Voreux; and before the black mass of the pit he continued swearing that he, at least, would never go down; but he could forgive those who did. Then, as the rumour ran that the carpenters had not had time to repair the tubbing, he asked for information. Was it true? Had the weight of the soil against the timber which formed the lining of scaffolding in the shaft pushed it in so far that the winding-cages rubbed as they went down for over fifty metres?

Souvarine, who once more became uncommunicative, replied briefly. He had been working the day before, and the cage did, in fact, jar; the engine-men had even had to double the speed to pass that spot. But all the bosses received any observations with the same irritating remark: it was coal they wanted; that could be repaired later on.

'What if it caves in?' Étienne murmured. 'It will be a fine mess.'

With eyes vaguely fixed on the pit in the shadow, Souvarine quietly concluded:

'If it does smash up, the mates will know all about it, since you've advised them to go down again.'

Nine o'clock struck at the Montsou steeple; and his companion having said that he was going to bed, he added, without putting out his hand:

'Well, good-bye. I'm going away.'

'What! you're going away?'

'Yes, I've asked for my certificate back. I'm going elsewhere.'

Étienne, astonished and moved, looked at him. After walking for two hours he said that to him! And in so calm a voice, while the mere announcement of this sudden separation made his own heart ache. They had got to know each other, they had toiled together; that always makes one sad, the idea of not seeing a person again.

'You're going away! And where are you going?'

'Somewhere – I don't know at all.'

'But I shall see you again?'

'No, I think not.'

They were silent and remained for a moment facing each other without finding anything to say.

'Then good-bye.'

'Good-bye.'

While Étienne walked up towards this settlement, Souvarine turned and again went along the canal bank; and there, now alone, he continued to walk, with sunken head, so lost in the darkness that he seemed merely a moving shadow of the night. Now and then he stopped, he counted the hours that struck afar. When he heard midnight strike he left the bank and turned towards the Voreux.

At that time the pit was empty, and he only came across a sleepy-eyed foreman. It was not until two o'clock that they would begin to get up steam to resume work. First he went to take from a cupboard a jacket which he pretended to have forgotten. Various tools – a brace fitted with a bit, a small but very strong saw, a hammer, and a chisel – were rolled up in his jacket. Then he left. But instead of going out through the shed he passed through the narrow corridor which led to the escape shaft. With his jacket under his arm he quietly went down without a lamp, measuring the depth by counting the ladders. He knew that the cage jarred at three hundred and seventy-four metres against the fifth section of the lower tubbing. When he had counted fifty-four ladders he put out his hand and was able to feel the bulge in the planking. It was there. Then, with the skill and coolness of a good workman who has been reflecting over his task for a long time, he set to work. He began by sawing a panel out of the partition so as to communicate with the winding-shaft. With the help of matches, which quickly lighted up and died out, he was then able to ascertain the condition of the tubbing and of the recent repairs.

Between Calais and Valenciennes the sinking of mine shafts was surrounded by immense difficulties on account of the masses of subterranean water in great tables at the level of the lowest valleys. Only the construction of tubbings, frameworks jointed like the stays of a barrel, could keep out the springs which flow in and isolate the shafts in the midst of the lakes, which with deep obscure waves beat against the walls. It had been necessary in sinking the Voreux to establish two tubbings: on the upper level, in the shifting sands and white clays bordering the chalky stratum, and fissured in every part, swollen with water like a sponge; then at the lower level, immediately above the coal stratum, in a yellow sand as fine as flour, flowing with liquid fluidity; it was here that the Torrent was to be found, that subterranean sea so dreaded in the coal pits of the Nord, a sea with its storms and its shipwrecks, an unknown and unfathomable sea, rolling its dark floods more than three hundred metres beneath the daylight. Usually the tubbings resisted the enormous pressure; the only thing to be dreaded was the piling up of the neighbouring soil, shaken by the constant movement of the old galleries which were filling up. When the rocks sank this way, lines of fracture were sometimes produced which slowly extended as far as the scaffolding, perforating it and pushing it into the shaft; and finally the great danger was of a landslip and a flood filling the pit with an avalanche of earth and a deluge of water.

Souvarine, sitting astride in the opening he had made, discovered a very serious defect in the fifth row of tubbing. The wood was bellied out from the framework; several planks had even come out of their shouldering. Huge leaks, *pichoux* as the miners call them, were jetting out of the joints through the tow and pitch with which they were caulked. The carpenters, pressed for time, had been content to place iron squares at the angles, so carelessly that not all the screws were put in. A considerable movement was evidently going on behind in the sand of the Torrent.

Then with his brace he unscrewed the squares so that another push would tear them all off. It was a foolhardy task, during which he frequently only just escaped from falling headlong down the hundred and eighty metres which separated him from the bottom. He had been obliged to seize the oak guides, the joists along which the cages slid; and suspended over the void he crossed the length of the cross-beams with which they were joined from point to point, slipping along, sitting down, turning over, simply buttressing himself on an elbow or a knee, with a calm contempt of death. A mere breath of wind would have sent him over, and three times he caught himself in time without so much as a shudder. First he felt around with his hand and then got to work, only lighting a match when he lost his bearings in the midst of these slimy beams. After loosening the screws he attacked the wood itself, and the peril became still greater. He had been looking for the linchpin, the piece which held the others; he attacked it furiously, making holes in it, sawing it, thinning it so that it lost its resistance; while through the holes and the cracks the water which escaped in small jets blinded him and soaked him in icy rain. Two matches were extinguished. They all became damp and then there was night, the bottomless depth of darkness.

From this moment he was seized by rage. The breath of the invisible intoxicated him, the black horror of this rain-beaten hole urged him to mad destruction. He wreaked his fury at random against the tubbing, striking where he could with his brace, with his saw, seized by the desire to bring the whole thing at once down on his head. He brought as much ferocity to the task as though he had been digging a knife into the body of some hated living creature. He would kill the Voreux at last, that evil beast with ever-open jaws which had swallowed so much human flesh! The bite of his tools could be heard, he stretched out, he crawled, climbed down, then up again, holding on by a miracle, in continual movement, like some night bird flitting amid the scaffolding of a belfry.

But he grew calm, dissatisfied with himself. Why could not things be done coolly? Without haste he took a deep breath, and then went back into the ladder passage, stopping up the hole by replacing the panel which he had sawn off. That was enough; he did not wish to raise the alarm by excessive damage which they would have tried to repair immediately. The beast was wounded in the belly; we should see if it was still alive that night. And he had left his mark; the frightened world would know that the beast had not died a natural death. He took his time in methodically rolling up his tools in his jacket, and slowly climbed up the ladders. Then, when he had emerged from the pit without being seen, it did not even occur to him to go and change his clothes. Three o'clock struck. He remained standing on the road waiting.

At the same hour Étienne, who was not asleep, was disturbed by a slight sound in the thick night of the bedroom. He distinguished the low breathing of the children, and the snoring of Bonnemort and la Maheude; while Jeanlin near him was breathing with a prolonged flute-like whistle. No doubt he had dreamed, and he was settling back down when the noise began again. It was the creaking of a mattress, the stifled effort of someone who was getting up. Then he imagined that Catherine must be ill.

'Is it you? What is the matter?' he asked in a low voice.

No one replied, and the snoring of the others continued. For five minutes nothing stirred. Then there was fresh creaking. Feeling certain this time that he was not mistaken, he crossed the room, putting his hands out into the darkness to feel the opposite bed. He was surprised to find the young girl sitting up, holding in her breath, awake and on the watch.

'Well! why don't you reply? What are you doing, then?'

At last she said:

'I'm getting up.'

'Getting up at this hour?'

'Yes, I'm going back to work at the pit.'

Étienne felt deeply moved, and sat down on the edge of the mattress, while Catherine explained her reasons to him. She suffered too much by living thus in idleness, feeling continual looks of reproach weighing on her; she would rather run the risk of being knocked about down there by Chaval. And if her mother refused to take her money when she brought it, well! she was big enough to fend for herself and make her own soup.

'Go away; I want to dress. And don't say anything, will you, please?'

But he remained near her; he had put his arms round her waist in a caress of grief and pity. Pressed one against the other in their nightshirts, they could feel the warmth of each other's naked flesh, at the edge of this bed, still warm with the night's sleep. She had at first tried to free herself; then she began to cry quietly, in her turn taking him by the neck to press him against her in a despairing embrace. And they remained, without any further desires, with the past of their unfortunate love, which they had not been able to satisfy. Was it, then, done with for ever? Would they never dare to love each other some day, now that they were free? It only needed a little happiness to dissipate their shame – that awkwardness which prevented them from coming together because of all sorts of ideas which they themselves could not understand clearly.

'Go to bed again,' she whispered. 'I don't want to light up, it would wake mother. It is time; leave me.'

He would not listen to her; he was pressing her wildly, his heart full of an overwhelming sadness. The need for peace, an irresistible need for happiness, came over him; and he imagined himself married, in a neat little house, with no other ambition than to live and to die there, both of them together. He would be satisfied with bread; and if there were only enough for one, she should have it. What was the good of anything else? Was there anything in life worth more?

But she was unfolding her naked arms.

'Please, leave me.'

Then, in a sudden impulse, he said in her ear:

'Wait, I'm coming with you.'

And he was himself surprised at what he had said. He had sworn never to go down again; where then did this sudden decision come from, arising from his lips without any deliberation, without even a moment's discussion? There was now such calm within him, so complete a cure of his doubts, that he persisted like a man saved by chance, who has at last found the only harbour from his torment. So he refused to listen to her when she became alarmed, understanding that he was devoting himself for her and fearing the harsh words which would greet him at the pit. He laughed at everything; the placards promising pardon and that was enough.

'I want to work; that's my idea. Let us dress and make no noise.'

They dressed in the darkness, taking every precaution. She had secretly prepared her miner's clothes the evening before; he took a jacket and breeches from the cupboard; and they did not wash themselves for fear of rattling the bowl. All the others were asleep, but they had to cross the narrow passage where the mother slept. When they started, as ill luck would have it, they stumbled against a chair. She work up and asked drowsily:

'Eh! what is it?'

Catherine had stopped, trembling, and violently pressing Étienne's hand.

'It's me; don't trouble yourself,' he said. 'I feel stifled and am going outside to breathe a bit.'

'Very well.'

And la Maheude fell asleep again. Catherine dared not stir. At last she went down into the parlour and divided a slice of bread-and-butter which she had kept from a loaf given by a Montsou lady. Then they gently closed the door and went away.

Souvarine had remained standing near the Avantage, at the corner of the road. For half an hour he had been looking at the colliers who were returning to work in the darkness, passing by with the dull tramp of a herd. He was counting them, as a butcher counts his beasts at the entrance to the slaughter-house, and he was surprised at their number; even his pessimism had not foreseen that the number of cowards would have been so great. The stream continued to pass by, and he grew stiff, very cold, with clenched teeth and bright eyes.

But he trembled. Among the men passing by, whose faces he could not distinguish, he had just recognized one by his walk. He came forward and stopped him.

'Where are you going to?'

Étienne, in surprise, instead of replying, stammered:

'What! you've not set out yet!'

Then he confessed he was going back to the pit. No doubt he had sworn not to do so; only it was no life to wait with folded arms for things which would perhaps happen in a hundred years; and, besides, reasons of his own had decided him.

Souvarine had listened to him, shuddering. He seized him by the shoulder, and pushed him towards the settlement.

'Go home again; I want you to. Do you understand?'

But Catherine having approached, he recognized her also. Étienne protested, declaring that he allowed no one to judge his conduct. And the engine-man's eyes went from the young girl to her companion, while he stepped back with a sudden gesture of surrender. When there was a woman in a man's heart, that man was done for; he might as well die. Perhaps he saw again in a rapid vision his mistress hanging over there in Moscow, that last link cut from his flesh, which had rendered him free of the lives of others and of his own life. He said simply:

'Go.'

Étienne, feeling awkward, was delaying, and trying to find some friendly word, so as not to separate in this manner.

'Then you're still going?'

'Yes.'

'Well, give me your hand, mate. A pleasant journey and no ill feeling.'

The other stretched out an icy hand. Neither friend nor woman.

'Good-bye for good this time.'

'Yes, good-bye.'

And Souvarine, standing motionless in the darkness, watched Étienne and Catherine entering the Voreux.

CHAPTER 3

At four o'clock the descent began. Dansaert, who was personally installed in the controller's office in the lamp cabin, wrote down the name of each worker who presented himself and had a lamp given to him. He took them all, without comment, keeping to the promise of the placards. When, however, he noticed Étienne and Catherine at the wicket, he started and became very red, and was opening his mouth to refuse their names; then, he contented himself with a sneer of triumph, and a jeer. Ah! Ah! so the big strong man has been thrown down? The Company was, then, in luck since the terrible Montsou prize-fighter had come back to it to ask for bread? Étienne silently took his lamp and went towards the shaft with the putter.

But it was in the receiving-room that Catherine feared the mates' worst insults. At the very entrance she recognized Chaval, in the midst of some twenty miners, waiting till a cage was free. He came furiously towards her, but the sight of Étienne stopped him. Then he affected to sneer with an offensive shrug of the shoulders. Very good! he didn't care a hang, since the other had come to occupy the place that was still warm; good riddance! It only concerned the gentleman if he liked other people's leftovers; and beneath this exhibition of contempt he was again seized by a tremor of jealousy, and his eyes flashed. For the rest, the mates did not stir, standing silent, with eyes lowered. They contented themselves with casting a sidelong look at the new-comers; then, dejected and without anger, they again stared fixedly at the mouth of the shaft, with their lamps in their hands, shivering beneath their thin jackets in the constant draughts of this large room. At last the cage was wedged on to the keeps, and they were ordered to get in. Catherine and Étienne were squeezed in one tram, already containing Pierron and two pikemen. Beside them, in the other tram, Chaval was loudly saying to old Mouque that the directors had made a mistake in not taking advantage of the opportunity to free the pits of the blackguards who were corrupting them; but the old groom, who had already fallen back into the dog-like resignation of his existence, no longer grew angry over the death of his children, and simply replied by a gesture of conciliation.

The cage freed itself and slipped down into the darkness. No one spoke. Suddenly, when they were in the middle third of the descent, there was a terrible jarring. The iron creaked, and the men were thrown on to each other.

'By God!' growled Étienne, 'are they going to flatten us? We'll end up by being left here for good, with their bloody tubbing. And they talk about having repaired it!'

The cage had, however, cleared the obstacle. It was now descending beneath so violent a fall of rain, like a storm, that the workmen anxiously listened to the water pouring down. A number of leaks must then have appeared in the caulking of the joints.

Pierron, who had been working for several days, when asked about it, did not like to show his fear, which might be considered as an attack on the management, so he only replied:

'Oh, no danger! it's always like that. No doubt they've not had time to caulk the leaks.'

The torrent was roaring over their heads, and they at last reached the loading-bay beneath a rush of water. Not one of the foremen had thought of climbing up the ladders to investigate the matter. The pump would be enough, the carpenters would examine the joints the following night. The reorganization of work in the galleries was enough trouble. Before allowing the pikemen to return to the coal face, the engineer had decided that for the first five days all the men should do certain maintenance jobs which were extremely urgent. Landslips were threatening everywhere; the passages had suffered to such an extent that the timbering had to be repaired along a length of several hundred metres. Gangs of ten men were were therefore formed below, each under the control of a foreman. Then they were set to work at the most damaged spots. When the descent was complete, it was found that three hundred and twenty-two miners had gone down, about half of those who worked there when the pit was in full swing.

It turned out that Chaval was in the same gang as Catherine and Étienne. This was not by chance; he had at first hidden behind his mates, and had then forced the foreman's hand. This gang went to the end of the north gallery, nearly three kilometres away, to clear out a landslip which was stopping up a gallery in the Dix-Huit-Pouces seam. They attacked the fallen rocks with shovel and pick. Étienne, Chaval and five others cleared away the rubble while Catherine, with two trammers, wheeled the earth up to the incline. They seldom spoke, and the foreman never left them. The putter's two lovers, however, were on the point of coming to blows. While growling that he had had enough of this trollop, Chaval was still thinking of her, and slyly hustling her about, so that Étienne had threatened to settle him if he did not leave her alone. They eyed each other fiercely, and had to be separated.

Towards eight o'clock Dansaert passed by to have a look at the work. He appeared to be in a very bad humour, and was furious with the foreman; nothing had gone well, what was the meaning of such work, the planking would everywhere have to be done over again! And he went away declaring that he would come back with the engineer. He had been waiting for Négrel since morning, and could not understand the cause of this delay.

Another hour passed by. The foreman had stopped the removal of the rubble to employ all his people in supporting the roof. Even the putter and the two trammers left off tramming to prepare and bring pieces of timber. At this end of the gallery the gang formed a sort of advance guard at the very extremity of the mine, now without communication with the other stalls. Three or four times strange noises, distant rushes, made the workers turn their heads to listen. What was it, then? It was as if the passages were being emptied and the mates already returning at a running pace. But the sound was lost in the deep silence, and they set to wedging their wood again, dazed by the loud blows of the hammer. At last they returned to clearing the rubble, and the tramming began once more. Catherine came back from her first journey in terror, saying that no one was to be found at the incline.

'I called, but there was no reply. They've all cleared out of the place.'

The bewilderment was so great that the ten men threw down their tools to rush away. The idea that they were abandoned, left alone at the bottom of the mine, so far from the loading-bay, drove them wild. They only kept their lamps and ran in single file – the men, the boys, the putter; the foreman himself lost his head and shouted out, more and more frightened at the silence in this endless wilderness of galleries. What then had happened that they did not meet a soul? What accident could thus have driven away their mates? Their terror was increased by the uncertainty of the danger, the threat which they felt there without knowing what it was.

When they at last came near the loading-bay, a flood barred their way. They were at once in water up to the knees, and were no longer able to run, laboriously fording the flood with the thought that one minute's delay might mean death.

'By God! it's the tubbing that's given way,' cried Étienne. 'I said we'd be left here for good.'

Since the descent Pierron had anxiously observed the increase of the deluge which fell from the shaft. As he loaded the trams with the help of two other men he raised his head, his face covered with large drops, and his ears ringing with the roar of the tempest above. But he trembled especially when he noticed that the sump beneath him, ten metres deep, was filling up; the water was already spurting through the floor and covering the metal plates. This showed that the pump was no longer sufficient to cope with the leaks. He heard it panting with the groan of fatigue. Then he warned Dansaert, who swore angrily, replying that they must wait for the engineer. Twice he returned to the attack without extracting anything else but exasperated shrugs of the shoulder. Well! the water was rising; what could he do?

Mouque appeared with Bataille, whom he was leading to work, and he had to hold him with both hands, for the sleepy old horse had suddenly reared up, and, with a shrill neigh, was stretching his head towards the shaft.

'Well, philosopher, what's bothering you? Ah! it's because it's raining. Come along, that doesn't concern you.'

But the beast quivered all over his body, and Mouque forcibly drew him to the haulage gallery.

Almost at the same moment as Mouque and Bataille were disappearing at the end of a gallery, there was a crackling in the air, followed by the prolonged noise of a fall. It was a piece of tubbing which had got loose and was falling a hundred and eighty metres down, rebounding against the walls. Pierron and the other loaders were able to get out of the way, and the oak plank only smashed an empty tram. At the same time, a mass of water, the leaping flood of a broken dyke, rushed down. Dansaert wanted to go up and examine it; but, while he was still speaking, another piece rolled down. And in terror at the threatening catastrophe, he no longer hesitated, but gave the order to go back up, sending the foreman to warn the men in their stalls.

Then a terrible stampede began. From every gallery rows of workers came rushing up, trying to take the cages by assault. They crushed madly against each other in order to be taken up at once. Some who had thought of trying the ladder passage came down again shouting that it was already blocked. The terror they all felt each time that the cage rose was that this time it was able to get past, but who knew if it would be able to pass again in the midst of the obstacles obstructing the shaft? The collapse must be continuing above, for a series of low detonations was heard, the planks were splitting and bursting amid the continuous and increasing roar of a storm. One cage soon became useless, broken in and no longer sliding between the guides, which were doubtless broken. The other jarred to such a degree that the cable would certainly break soon. And there remained a hundred men to be taken up, all panting, clinging to one another, bleeding and half drowned. Two were killed by falls of planking. A third, who had seized the cage, fell back fifty metres up and disappeared in the sump.

Dansaert, however, was trying to arrange matters in an orderly manner. Armed with a pick he threatened to open the skull of the first man who refused to obey; and he tried to arrange them in file, shouting that the loaders were to go up last after having sent up their mates. He was not listened to, and he had to prevent the pale and cowardly Pierron from entering among the first. At each departure he pushed him aside with a blow. But his own teeth were chattering, a minute more and he would be swallowed up; everything was smashing up there, a flood had broken loose, a murderous rain of scaffolding. A few men were still running up when, mad with fear, he jumped into a tram, allowing Pierron to jump in behind him. The cage rose.

At this moment the gang to which Étienne and Chaval belonged had just reached the pit-eye. They saw the cage disappear and rushed forward, but they had to draw back under the final downfall of the tubbing; the shaft was blocked up and the cage would not come down again. Catherine was sobbing, and Chaval was choked with shouting oaths. There were twenty of them; were those bloody bosses going to abandon them like this? Old Mouque, who had brought back Bataille without hurrying, was still holding him by the bridle, both of them stupefied, the man and the beast, in the face of this rapidly mounting flood. The water was already rising to their thighs. Étienne in silence, with clenched teeth, supported Catherine between his arms. And the twenty yelled with their faces turned up, obstinately gazing at the shaft like imbeciles, staring into the shifting hole which was belching out a flood and from which no help could henceforth come to them.

At the surface, Dansaert, on arriving, saw Négrel running up. By chance Madame Hennebeau had that morning delayed him on rising, as they looked through catalogues for the purchase of wedding presents. It was ten o'clock.

'Well! what's happening, then?' he shouted from afar.

'The pit is ruined,' replied the overman.

And he described the catastrophe in a few stammered words, while the engineer incredulously shrugged his shoulders. What! could tubbing be demolished just like that? They were exaggerating; it had to be looked into.

'I suppose no one has been left down below?'

Dansaert was confused. No, no one; at least, so he hoped. But some of the men might have been delayed.

'But,' said Négrel, 'what in the name of creation have you come up for, then? You can't leave your men!'

He immediately gave orders to count the lamps. In the morning three hundred and twenty-two had been distributed, and now only two hundred and fifty-five could be found; but several men acknowledged that in the panic they had dropped theirs and left them behind. An attempt was made to have a roll-call, but it was impossible to establish the exact number. Some of the miners had gone away, others did not hear their names. No one was agreed as to the number of missing mates. It might be twenty, perhaps forty. And the engineer could only make out one thing with certainty: there were men down below, for their yells could be distinguished through the sound of the water and the fallen scaffolding, on leaning over the mouth of the shaft.

Négrel's first concern was to send for Monsieur Hennebeau, and to try to close the pit; but it was already too late. The colliers who had rushed to the Deux-Cent-Quarante settlement, as though pursued by the cracking tubbing, had frightened the families; and bands of women, old men, and little ones came running up, shaken by cries and sobs. They had to be pushed back, and a line of overseers was formed to keep them off, for they would have interfered with the operations. Many of the men who had come up from the shaft remained there stupidly without thinking of changing their clothes, riveted by fear in front of this terrible hole in which they had nearly remained for ever. The women, rushing wildly around them, implored them for names. Was So-and-so among them? and that one? and this one? They did not know, they stammered; they shuddered terribly, and made gestures like madmen, gestures which seemed to be pushing away some abominable vision which was still present in their minds. The crowd rapidly increased, and the lamentations arose from the roads. And up there on the pit-bank, in Bonnemort's cabin, a man was seated on the ground, Souvarine, who had not gone away, who was looking on.

'The names! the names!' cried the women, with voices choked by tears.

Négrel appeared for a moment, and said hurriedly:

'As soon as we know the names they shall be given out, but nothing is lost so far: everyone will be saved. I am going down.'

Then, silent with anguish, the crowd waited. The engineer, in fact, with quiet courage was preparing to go down. He had had the cage unfastened, giving orders to replace it at the end of the cable by a tub; and as he feared that the water would extinguish his lamp, he had another fastened beneath the tub, to protect it.

Several foremen, trembling and with white, troubled faces, helped in these preparations.

'You will come with me, Dansaert,' said Négrel, abruptly.

Then, when he saw them all without courage, and that the overman was tottering, giddy with terror, he pushed him aside with a movement of contempt.

'No, you will be in my way. I would rather go alone.'

He was already in the narrow bucket, which swayed at the end of the cable; and holding his lamp in one hand and the signal-cord in the other, he shouted to the engine-man:

'Gently!'

The engine set the drums in motion, and Négrel disappeared in the abyss, from which the yells of the wretches trapped below could still be heard.

At the upper part nothing had moved. He found that the tubbing here was in good condition. Balanced in the middle of the shaft he lighted up the walls as he turned round; the leaks between the joints were so slight that his lamp did not go out. But at three hundred metres, when he reached the lower tubbing, the lamp was extinguished, as he expected, for a jet had filled the tub. After that he was only able to see by the hanging lamp which preceded him in the darkness, and, in spite of his courage, he shuddered and turned pale in the face of the horror of the disaster. A few pieces of timber alone remained; the others had fallen in with their frames. Behind, enormous cavities had been hollowed out, and the yellow sand, as fine as flour, was flowing in massive quantities; while the waters of the Torrent, that subterranean sea with its unknown tempests and shipwrecks, were discharging in a flow like a weir. He went down lower, lost in the midst of these chasms which continued to multiply, beaten and turned round by the water sprouting from the springs, so badly lighted by the red star of the lamp moving on below, that he seemed to see the roads and squares of some destroyed town far away in the play of the great moving shadows. No human work was any longer possible. His only remaining hope was to attempt to save the men in peril. As he sank down he heard the cries becoming louder, and he was obliged to stop; an impassable obstacle barred the shaft – a mass of scaffolding, the broken beams of the guides, the split partitions entangled with the metal-work torn from the pump. As he looked on for a long time with aching heart, the yelling suddenly ceased. No doubt, the rapid rise of the water had forced the wretches to flee into the galleries, if, indeed, the flood had not already engulfed them.

Négrel had to resign himself to pulling the signal-cord as a sign to draw up. Then he had himself stopped again. He could not imagine the cause of this sudden accident. He wished to investigate it, and examined the pieces of the tubbing which were still in place. At a distance the tears and cuts in the wood had surprised him. His lamp, drowned in dampness, was going out, and, touching with his fingers, he clearly recognized the marks of the saw and of the brace – the whole abominable labour of destruction. Evidently this catastrophe had been intentionally produced. He was stupefied, and the pieces of timber, cracking and falling down with their frames in a last slide, nearly carried him with them. His courage vanished. The thought of the man who had done that made his hair stand on end, and froze him with a supernatural fear of evil, as though, mixed with the darkness, the man were still there paying for his immeasurable crime. He shouted and shook the cord furiously; and it was, indeed, time, for he perceived that the upper tubbing, a hundred metres higher, was in its turn beginning to move. The joints were opening, losing their caulking, and streams were rushing through. It was now only a question of hours before the tubbing would all fall down.

At the surface Monsieur Hennebeau was anxiously waiting for Négrel.

'Well, what?' he asked.

But the engineer was choked, and could not speak; he felt faint.

'It is not possible; such a thing is unheard of. Did you get a good look?'

He nodded with a cautious air. He refused to talk in the presence of some foremen who were listening, and led his uncle ten metres away, and not thinking this far enough, drew still farther back; then, in a low whisper, he at last told of the outrage, the torn and sawn planks, the pit bleeding at the throat and dying. Turning pale, the manager also lowered his voice, with that instinctive need of silence in face of the monstrosity of great orgies and great crimes. It was useless to look as though they were trembling before the ten thousand Montsou men; later on they would see. And they both continued whispering, overcome at the thought that a man had had the courage to go down, to hang in the midst of space, to risk his life twenty times over in his terrible task. They could not even understand this mad courage in destruction; they refused to believe, in spite of the evidence, just as we doubt those stories of celebrated escapes of prisoners who fly through windows thirty metres above the ground.

When Monsieur Hennebeau came back to the foreman a nervous spasm was drawing his face. He made a gesture of despair, and gave orders that the mine should be evacuated at once. It was a kind of funeral procession, in silent abandonment, with glances thrown back at those great masses of bricks, empty and still standing, but which nothing henceforth could save.

And as the manager and the engineer came down last from the receiving-room, the crowd met them with its clamour, repeating obstinately:

'The names! the names! Tell us the names!'

La Maheude was now there, among the women. She remembered the noise in the night; her daughter and the lodger must have gone away together, and they were certainly down at the bottom. And after having cried that it was a good thing, that they deserved to stay there, the heartless cowards, she had run up, and was standing in the first row, trembling with anguish. Besides, she no longer dared to doubt; the discussion going on around her informed her as to the names of those who were down. Yes, yes, Catherine was among them, Étienne also – a mate had seen them. But there was not always agreement with regard to the others. No, not this one; on the contrary, that one, perhaps Chaval, with whom, however, a trammer declared that he had come up. La Levaque and La Pierronne, although none of their people were in danger, cried out and lamented as loudly as the others. Zacharie, who had come up among the first, in spite of his inclination to make fun of everything, had weepingly kissed his wife and mother, and remained near the latter, quivering, and showing an unexpected degree of affection for his sister, refusing to believe that she was below as long as the bosses had made no official statement.

'The names! the names! For pity's sake, the names!'

Négrel, who was exhausted, shouted to the overseers:

'Can't you make them be still? It's enough to drive you insane! We don't know the names!'

Two hours had already gone by. In the first terror no one had thought of the other shaft at the old Réquillart mine. Monsieur Hennebeau was about to announce that the rescue would be attempted from that side, when a rumour ran round: five men had just escaped the flood by climbing up the rotten ladders of the old unused passage, and old Mouque was named. This caused surprise, for no one knew he was below. But the narrative of the five who had escaped increased the weeping; fifteen mates had not been able to follow them, having gone astray, and been walled up by falls. And it was no longer possible to assist them, for there were already ten metres of water in Réquillart. All the names were known, and the air was filled with the groans of a slaughtered people.

'Will you make them be quiet?' Négrel repeated furiously. 'Make them draw back! Yes, yes, to a hundred metres! There is danger; push them back, push them back!'

It was necessary to struggle against these poor people. They were imagining all sorts of disasters, and they had to be driven away so that the deaths might be concealed; the foremen explained to them that the shaft would destroy the whole mine. This idea rendered them mute with terror, and they at last allowed themselves to be driven back step by step; the guards, however, who kept them back had to be doubled, for they were fascinated by the spot and continually moved back. Thousands of people were hustling each other along the road; they were running up from all the settlements, and even from Montsou. And the man above, on the pit-bank, the fair man with the girlish face, smoked cigarettes to occupy himself, keeping his clear eyes fixed on the pit.

Then the wait began. It was midday; no one had eaten, but no one moved away. In the misty sky, of a dirty grey colour, rusty clouds were slowly passing by. A big dog, behind Rasseneur's hedge, was barking furiously without stopping, irritated by the living breath of the crowd. And the crowd had gradually spread over the neighbouring ground, forming a circle at a hundred metres round the pit. The Voreux arose in the centre of the great space. There was not a soul there, not a sound; it was a desert. The windows and the doors, left open, showed the abandonment within; a forgotten ginger cat, sensing danger in this solitude, jumped from a staircase and disappeared. No doubt the furnaces were not yet extinguished, for the tall brick chimney gave out a light smoke beneath the dark clouds; while the weathercock on the steeple creaked in the wind with a short, shrill cry, the only melancholy voice of these vast buildings condemned to die.

At two o'clock nothing had moved. Monsieur Hennebeau, Négrel and other engineers who had hastened up, formed a group in black coats and hats standing in front of the crowd; and they, too, did not move away, though their legs were aching with fatigue, and they were feverish and ill at their impotence in the face of such a disaster, only whispering occasional words as though at a dying person's bedside. The upper tubbing must nearly all have fallen in, for sudden echoing sounds could be heard like deep broken falls, succeeded by silence. The wound was constantly enlarging; the landslip which had begun below was rising and approaching the surface. Négrel was seized by nervous impatience; he wanted to see, and he was already advancing alone into this awful void when he was seized by the shoulders. What was the good? he could prevent nothing. An old miner, however, circumventing the overseers, rushed into the shed; but he quietly reappeared, he had gone for his clogs.

Three o'clock struck. Still nothing. A falling shower had soaked the crowd, but they had not withdrawn a step. Rasseneur's dog had begun to bark again. And it was at twenty minutes past three only that the first shock was felt. The Voreux trembled, but continued solid and upright. Then a second shock followed immediately, and a long cry came from open mouths; the tarred screening-shed, after having tottered twice, had fallen down with a terrible crash. Beneath the enormous pressure the structures broke and jarred each other so powerfully that sparks leapt out. From this moment the earth continued to tremble, the shocks succeeded one another, subterranean downfalls, the rumbling of a volcano in eruption. Afar the dog was no longer barking, but he howled plaintively as though announcing the earthquakes which he felt coming; and the women, the children, all these people who were looking on, could not keep back a clamour of distress at each of these tremors which shook them. In less than ten minutes the slate roof of the steeple fell in, the receiving-room and the engine-rooms were split open, leaving a huge breach. Then the sounds ceased, the collapse stopped, and there was again deep silence.

For an hour the Voreux remained thus, breached, as though bombarded by an army of barbarians. There was no more crying out; the enlarged circle of spectators merely looked on. Beneath the piled-up beams of the sifting-shed, fractured tipping cradles could be made out with their broken and twisted hoppers. But the debris had especially accumulated at the receiving-room, where there had been a rain of bricks, and large portions of wall and masses of plaster had fallen in. The iron scaffold which bore the pulleys had bent, half buried in the pit; a cage was still suspended, a torn cable-end was hanging; then there was a pile of trams, metal plates, and ladders. By chance the lamp cabin remained standing, exhibiting on the left its bright rows of little lamps. And at the end of its disembowelled chamber, the engine could be seen seated squarely on its massive foundation of masonry; its copper was shining and its huge steel limbs seemed to possess indestructible muscles. The enormous crank, bent in the air, looked like the powerful knee of some giant quietly reposing in his strength.

After this hour of respite, Monsieur Hennebeau's hopes began to rise. The movement of the soil must have come to an end, and there would be some chance of saving the engine and the remainder of the buildings. But he would not yet allow anyone to approach, considering another half-hour's patience desirable. This waiting became unbearable; the hope increased the anguish and all hearts were beating quickly. A dark cloud, growing at the horizon, hastened the twilight, a sinister nightfall over this wreck destroyed by the earth's tempests. Since seven o'clock they had been there without moving or eating.

And suddenly, as the engineers were cautiously advancing, a supreme convulsion of the soil put them to flight. Subterranean detonations broke out; a whole monstrous artillery was cannonading in the abyss below. At the surface, the last buildings were tipped over and crushed. At first a sort of whirlpool carried away the rubble from the sifting-shed and the receiving room. Next, the boiler building burst and disappeared. Then it was the low square tower, where the pumping-engine was groaning, which fell on its face like a man mown down by a bullet. And then a terrible thing was seen; the engine, dislocated from its massive foundation, with broken limbs, was struggling against death; it moved, it straightened its crank, its giant's knee, as though to rise; but, crushed and swallowed up, it was dying. The chimney alone, thirty metres high, still remained standing, though shaken, like a mast in a storm. They thought that it would be crushed to fragments and crumble to dust, when suddenly it sank in one block, swallowed up by the earth, melted like a colossal candle; and nothing was left, not even the point of the lightning conductor. It was done for; the evil beast crouching in this hole, gorged with human flesh, was no longer breathing with its thick, long respiration. The Voreux had been swallowed whole by the abyss.

The crowd rushed away yelling. The women hid their eyes as they ran. Terror drove the men along like a pile of dry leaves. They tried not to shout and they shouted, with bursting lungs, and arms in the air, before the immense hole which had opened up. This crater, like an extinct volcano, fifteen metres deep, extended from the road to the canal for a space of at least forty metres. The whole square of the mine had followed the buildings, the gigantic platforms, the footbridges with their rails, a complete train of trams, three wagons; without counting the wood supply, a forest of cut timber, gulped down like straw. At the bottom it was only possible to distinguish a confused mass of beams, bricks, iron, plaster, frightful remains, piled up, entangled, blackened in the fury of the catastrophe. And the hole became larger, cracks started to appear from the edges, reaching afar, across the fields. A fissure reached as far as Rasseneur's bar, and his front wall had cracked. Would the settlement itself be swallowed up? How far ought they to flee to reach shelter at the end of this abominable day, beneath this leaden cloud which also seemed about to crush the earth.

Négrel uttered a cry of pain. Monsieur Hennebeau, who had drawn back, was in tears. The disaster was not complete; one bank of the canal gave way, and the canal emptied itself like a bubbling stream through one of the cracks. It disappeared there, falling like a cataract down a deep valley. The mine drank up this river; the galleries would now be submerged for years. Soon the crater was filled and a lake of muddy water occupied the place where once stood the Voreux, like one of those lakes beneath which lie cursed evil cities. There was a terrified silence, and nothing now could be heard but the fall of this water rumbling in the bowels of the earth.

Then on the shaken pit-bank Souvarine rose up. He had recognized la Maheude and Zacharie sobbing before this destruction, the weight of which was so heavy on the heads of the wretches who were in agony beneath. And he threw down his last cigarette; he went away, without looking back, into the now dark night. In the distance his shadow diminished and mingled with the darkness. He was going away, to the unknown. He was going tranquilly to wreak destruction, wherever there might be dynamite to blow up towns and men. He will be there, without doubt, when the bourgeoisie in its dying moments, shall hear the very paving stones in the streets bursting up beneath their feet.

CHAPTER 4

On the night that followed the collapse of the Voreux Monsieur Hennebeau had left for Paris, wishing to inform the directors in person before the newspapers published the news. And when he returned on the following day he appeared to be quite calm, with his usual correct administrative air. He had evidently freed himself from responsibility; he did not appear to have decreased in favour. On the contrary, the decree appointing him officer of the Legion of Honour was signed twenty-four hours afterwards.

But if the manager remained safe, the Company was reeling beneath the terrible blow. It was not the few million francs that had been lost, it was the wound in the side, the deep incessant fear of the morrow in face of this massacre of one of their mines. The Company was so impressed that once more it felt the need of silence. What was the good of stirring up this abomination? If the villain were discovered, why make a martyr of him in order that his awful heroism might turn other heads, and give birth to a long line of incendiaries and murderers? Besides, the real culprit was not suspected. The Company came to think that there was an army of accomplices, not being able to believe that a single man could have had courage and strength for such a task; and it was precisely this thought which weighed on them, the thought of an ever-increasing threat to the existence of their mines. The manager had received orders to organize a vast system of espionage, and then to dismiss quietly, one by one, the dangerous men who were suspected of having had a hand in the crime. They contented themselves with this method of purification – a prudent and politic method.

There was only one immediate dismissal, that of Dansaert, the overman. Ever since the scandal at la Pierronne's house he had become impossible. A pretext was made of his attitude in face of danger, the cowardice of a foreman abandoning his men. This was also a prudent sop thrown to the miners, who hated him.

Among the general public, however, many rumours had circulated, and the directors had to send a letter of correction to one newspaper, contradicting a story in which mention was made of a barrel of powder lighted by the strikers. After a rapid inquiry the Government inspector had concluded that there had been a natural rupture of the tubbing, occasioned by the piling up of the soil; and the Company had preferred to be silent, and to accept the blame of a lack of proper inspection. In the Paris press, after the third day, the catastrophe had become a topical news item; people talked of nothing else but the men perishing at the bottom of the mine, and the telegrams published every morning were eagerly read. At Montsou the bourgeois grew pale and speechless at the very name of the Voreux, and a legend had formed which made the boldest tremble as they whispered it. The whole country showed great pity for the victims; visits were organized to the destroyed pit, and whole families hastened up to shudder at the ruins which lay so heavily over the heads of the buried wretches.

Deneulin, who had been appointed divisional engineer, was plunged into the midst of the disaster on beginning his duties; and his first care was to turn the canal back into its bed, for this torrent increased the damage every hour. Extensive works were necessary, and he at once set a hundred men to construct a dyke. Twice over the impetuosity of the stream carried away the first dams. Now pumps were set up and a furious struggle was going on; step by step the vanished soil was being violently reconquered.

But the rescue of the buried miners was a still more absorbing task. Négrel was appointed to attempt a supreme effort, and hands were not lacking to help him; all the colliers rushed to offer themselves in an outburst of brotherhood. They forgot the strike, they did not trouble themselves at all about payment; they might get nothing, they only asked to risk their lives as soon as there were mates in danger of death. They were all there with their tools, waiting to know where they ought to start work. Many of them, sick with fright after the accident, shaken by nervous tremors, soaked in cold sweats, and the prey of continual nightmares, got up in spite of everything, and were as eager as any in their desire to fight against the earth, as though they had revenge to take on it. Unfortunately, the difficulty began when the question arose, What could be done? how could they go down? from what side could they attack the rocks?

Négrel's opinion was that not one of the unfortunate people was alive; the fifteen had surely perished, drowned or suffocated. But in these mine catastrophes the rule is always to assume that buried men are alive, and he acted on this supposition. The first problem to which he set his mind was to decide where they could have taken refuge. The foremen and old miners whom he consulted were agreed on one point: in face of the rising water the men had certainly come up from gallery to gallery to the highest cuttings, so that they were, without doubt, driven to the end of some upper passages. This agreed with old Mouque's information, and his confused narrative even gave reason to suppose that in the wild flight the group had separated into smaller groups, leaving fugitives at every level. But the foremen were not unanimous when the discussion of possible attempts at rescue arose. As the passages nearest to the surfaces were a hundred and fifty metres down, there could be no question of sinking a shaft. Réquillart remained the one means of access, the only point by which they could approach. The worst was that the old pit, now also inundated, no longer communicated with the Voreux; and above the level of the water only a few ends of galleries belonging to the first level were left free. The pumping process would require years, and the best plan would be to visit these galleries and ascertain if any of them approached the submerged passages at the end of which the distressed miners were thought to be. Before logically arriving at this point, much discussion had been necessary to dispose of a crowd of impracticable plans.

Négrel now began to stir up the dust of the archives; he discovered the old plans of the two pits, studied them, and decided on the points at which their investigations ought to be carried on. Gradually this hunt excited him; he was, in his turn, seized by a fever of devotion, in spite of his ironical indifference to men and things. The first difficulty was in going down at the Réquillart; it was necessary to clear out the rubble from the mouth of the shaft, to cut down the mountain ash, and clear away the sloes and the hawthorns; they had also to repair the ladders. Then they began to feel around. The engineer, having gone down with ten workmen, made them strike the iron of their tools against certain parts of the seam which he pointed out to them; and in deep silence they each placed an ear to the coal, listening for any distant blows in reply. But they went in vain through every practicable gallery; there was no reply. Their confusion increased. At what spot should they cut into the bed? Towards whom should they go, since no one appeared to be there? They went on searching, becoming more and more anxious and nervous.

From the first day, la Maheude came in the morning to Réquillart. She sat down on a beam in front of the shaft, and did not stir till evening. When a man came up, she rose and questioned him with her eyes: Nothing? No, nothing! And she sat down again, and waited still, without a word, with a hard, fixed gaze. Jeanlin also, seeing that his den was invaded, prowled around with the frightened air of a beast of prey whose burrow will betray his spoils. He thought of the little soldier lying beneath the rocks, fearing lest they should trouble his sound sleep; but that side of the mine was beneath the water, and, besides, their investigations were directed more to the left, in the west gallery. At first, Philomène had also come, accompanying Zacharie, who was one of the gang; then she became wearied at catching cold, for no reason, and went back to the settlement, dragging through her days, a limp, indifferent woman, occupied from morning to night in coughing. Zacharie, on the contrary, lived for nothing else; he would have devoured the soil to get back to his sister. At night he shouted out that he saw her, he heard her, very lean from hunger, her chest sore with calling for help. Twice he had tried to dig without orders, saying that it was there, that he was sure of it. The engineer would not let him go down any more, and he would not go away from the pit, from which he was driven off; he could not even sit down and wait near his mother, he was so deeply stirred by the need to act, which drove him constantly on.

It was the third day. Négrel, in despair, had resolved to aban the attempt in the evening. At midday, after lunch, when he c back with his men to make one last effort, he was surprised to Zacharie, red and gesticulating, come out of the mine shouting:

'She's there! She's replied to me! Come along, quickly!'

He had slid down the ladders, in spite of the watchman, and was claiming that he had heard hammering over there, in the first passage of the Guillaume seam.

'But we have already been twice in that direction,' Négrel observed, sceptically. 'Anyhow, we'll go and see.'

La Maheude had risen, and had to be prevented from going

down. She waited, standing at the edge of the shaft, gazing down into the darkness of the hole.

Négrel, down below, struck three blows, at long intervals. He then applied his ear to the coal, cautioning the workers to be very silent. Not a sound reached him, and he shook his head; evidently the poor lad was dreaming. In a fury Zacharie struck in his turn, and listened anew with bright eyes, and limbs trembling with joy. Then the other workmen tried the experiment, one after the other, and all grew animated, hearing the distant reply quite clearly. The engineer was astonished; he again applied his ear, and was at last able to catch a sound of aerial softness, a rhythmical roll scarcely audible, the well-known cadence beaten by the miners when they are fighting against the coal in the midst of danger. The coal transmits the sound with crystalline limpidity for a very great distance. A foreman who was there estimated that the thickness of the block which separated them from their mates could not be less than fifty metres. But it seemed as if they could already stretch out a hand to them, and joy broke out. Négrel decided to begin at once the approach work.

When Zacharie, up above, saw la Maheude again, they embraced each other.

'It won't do to get excited,' la Pierronne, who had come for a visit out of inquisitiveness, was cruel enough to say. 'If Catherine isn't there, it would be such grief for you afterwards!'

That was true; Catherine might be somewhere else.

'Just leave me alone, will you? Damn it!' cried Zacharie in a rage. 'She's there; I know it!'

La Maheude sat down again in silence, with motionless face, continuing to wait.

As soon as the story had spread to Montsou, a new crowd arrived. Nothing was to be seen; but they remained there all the same, and had to be kept at a distance. Down below, the work went on day and night. For fear of meeting an obstacle, the engineer had had three descending galleries opened in the seam, converging to the point where the enclosed miners were supposed to be. Only one pikeman could hew at the coal on the narrow face of the tunnel; he was relieved every two hours, and the coal piled in baskets was passed up, from hand to hand, by a chain of men, increased as the hole was hollowed out. The work at first proceeded very quickly; they did six metres a day.

Zacharie had secured a place among the workers chosen for the hewing. It was a position of honour which was disputed over, and he became furious when they wished to relieve him after his regulation two hours of labour. He robbed his mates of their turn, and refused to let go of the pick. His gallery was soon in advance of the others. He fought against the coal so fiercely that his breath could be heard coming from the tunnel like the roar of a forge. When he came out, black and muddy, dizzy with fatigue, he fell to the ground and had to be wrapped up in a covering. Then, still tottering, he plunged back again, and the struggle began anew – the low, deep blows, the stifled groans, the victorious frenzy of destruction. The worst was that the coal now became harder; he twice broke his tool, and was exasperated that he could not advance as fast. He suffered also from the heat, which increased with every metre of progress, and was unbearable at the end of this narrow hole where the air could not circulate. A hand ventilator worked well, but aeration was so inadequate that on three occasions it was necessary to take out fainting hewers who were being asphyxiated.

Négrel lived below with his men. His meals were sent down to him, and he sometimes slept for a couple of hours on a bale of straw, rolled in a coat. The one thing that kept them going was the pleas of the wretches beyond, the call which was sounded ever more distinctly to hasten on the rescue. It now rang very clearly with a musical sonority, as though struck on the plates of a harmonica. It drove them on; they advanced to this crystalline sound as men advance to the sound of cannon in battle. Every time that a pikeman was relieved, Négrel went down and struck, then applied his ear; and every time, so far, the reply had come, rapid and urgent. He had no doubt remaining; they were advancing in the right direction, but with what fatal slowness! They would never arrive soon enough. On the first two days they had indeed hewn through thirteen metres; but on the third day they fell to five, and then on the fourth to three. The coal was becoming denser and harder, to such an extent that they now had difficulty in hacking through two metres. On the ninth day, after superhuman efforts, they had advanced thirty-two metres, and calculated that some twenty must still be left ahead of them. For the prisoners it was the beginning of the twelfth day; twelve times over they had spent twenty-four hours without bread, without fire, in that icy darkness! This awful idea filled the workers eyes with tears and stiffened their arms. It seemed impossible that Christian folk could live any longer. The distant blows had become weaker since the previous day, and every moment they trembled lest they should stop.

La Maheude came regularly every morning to sit at the mouth of the shaft. In her arms she brought Estelle, who could not remain alone from morning to night. Hour by hour she followed the workers, sharing their hopes and fears. There was feverish expectation among the groups standing around, and even as far as Montsou, with endless discussions. Every heart in the district was beating down there beneath the earth.

On the ninth day, at the breakfast hour, no reply came from Zacharie when he was called for the relay. He was like a madman, working on furiously with oaths. Négrel, who had come up for a moment, was not there to make him obey, and only a foreman and three miners were below. No doubt Zacharie, infuriated with the feeble vacillating light, which delayed his work, committed the folly of opening his lamp, although severe orders had been given, for leakages of fire-damp had taken place, and the gas remained in enormous masses in these narrow, unventilated passages. Suddenly, a roar of thunder was heard, and a spout of fire darted out of the tunnel as from the mouth of a cannon charged with grapeshot. Everything flamed up and the air caught fire like powder, from one end of the galleries to the other. This torrent of flame carried away the foreman and three workers, ran up the shaft, and leapt up to the daylight in an eruption which split the rocks and the ruins around. The inquisitive fled, and la Maheude arose, pressing the frightened Estelle to her breast.

When Négrel and the men came back they were seized by a terrible rage. They stamped their heels on the earth as on a stepmother who was killing her children at random in the imbecile whims of her cruelty. They were devoting themselves, they were coming to the help of their mates, and still they must lose some of their men! After three long hours of effort and danger they reached the galleries once more, and the melancholy ascent of the victims took place. Neither the foreman nor the workers were dead, but they were covered by awful wounds which gave out an odour of charred flesh; they had drunk of fire, the burns had got into their throats, and they constantly moaned and prayed to be finished off. One of the three miners was the man who had smashed the pump at Gaston-Marie with a final blow of the shovel during the strike; the two others still had scars on their hands, and grazed, torn fingers from the energy with which they had thrown bricks at the soldiers. The pale and shuddering crowd took off their hats when they were carried by.

La Maheude stood waiting. Zacharie's body at last appeared. His clothes were burnt, his body was nothing but black charcoal, calcined and unrecognizable. His head had been smashed by the explosion and was no longer there. And when these awful remains were placed on a stretcher, la Maheude followed them mechanically, her burning eyelids without a tear. With Estelle drowsily lying in her arms, she went along, a tragic figure, her hair lashed by the wind. At the settlement Philomène seemed stupid; then she wept a flood of tears and was quickly relieved. But the mother had already returned with the same step to Réquillart; she had accompanied her son, she was returning to wait for her daughter.

Three more days passed by. The rescue work had been resumed amid incredible difficulties. The approach galleries had fortunately not fallen in after the fire-damp explosion; but the air was so heavy and so vitiated that more ventilators had to be installed. Every twenty minutes the pikemen relieved one another. They were advancing; scarcely two metres separated them from their mates. But now they worked feeling cold at their hearts, striking hard only out of vengeance; for the noises had ceased, and the low, clear cadence of the call no longer sounded. It was the twelfth day of their labours, the fifteenth since the catastrophe; and since the morning there had been a death-like silence.

The new accident increased the curiosity at Montsou, and the inhabitants organized excursions with such spirit that the Grégoires decided to follow the fashion. They arranged a party, and it was agreed that they should go to the Voreux in their carriage, while Madame Hennebeau took Lucie and Jeanne there in hers. Deneulin would show them over his yards, and then they would return by Réquillart, where Négrel would tell them the exact state of things in the galleries, and if there was still hope. Finally, they would dine together in the evening.

When the Grégoires and their daughter Cécile arrived at the ruined mine, toward three o'clock, they found Madame Hennebeau already there, in a sea-blue dress, protecting herself under her parasol from the pale February sun. The warmth of spring was in the clear sky. Monsieur Hennebeau was there with Deneulin, and she was listening, distractedly, to the account which the latter gave her of the efforts which had been made to dam up the canal. Jeanne, who always carried a sketch-book with her, began to draw, carried away by the horror of the subject; while Lucie, seated beside her on the remains of a wagon, was crying out with pleasure, and finding it awfully jolly. The incomplete dam allowed numerous leaks, and frothy streams fell in a cascade down the enormous hole of the engulfed mine. The crater was being emptied, however, and the water, soaked up by the earth, was sinking, and revealing the fearful ruin at the bottom. Beneath the tender azure of this beautiful day there lay a cesspool, the ruins of a town drowned and melted in mud.

'And people come out of their way to see that!' exclaimed Monsieur Grégoire, disillusioned.

Cecile, rosy with health and glad to breathe such pure air, was cheerfully joking, while Madame Hennebeau made a little grimace of repugnance as she murmured:

'The fact is, this is not pretty at all.'

The two engineers laughed. They tried to interest the visitors, taking them round and explaining to them the workings of the pumps and the piledriver which drove in the stakes. But the ladies became anxious. They shuddered when they knew that the pumps would have to work for six or seven years before the shaft was reconstructed and all the water drained from the mine. No, they would rather think of something else; this destruction only gave you bad dreams.

'Let us go,' said Madame Hennebeau, turning towards her carriage.

Lucie and Jeanne protested. What! so soon! and the drawing which was not finished! They wanted to remain; their father would bring them to dinner in the evening. Monsieur Hennebeau alone took his place with his wife in the carriage, for he wished to question Négrel.

'Very well! go on ahead,' said Monsieur Grégoire. 'We will follow you; we have a little visit of five minutes to make over there at the settlement. Go on, go on! we shall be at Réquillart as soon as you.'

He got in behind Madame Grégoire and Cécile, and while the other carriage went along by the canal, theirs gently ascended the slope.

Their excursion was to be completed by a charity visit. Zacharie's death had filled them with pity for this tragic Maheu family, about whom the whole country was talking. They had no pity for the father, the rogue, the slayer of soldiers, who had to be struck down like a wolf. But the mother touched their hearts, that poor woman who had just lost her son after having lost her husband, and whose daughter was perhaps a corpse beneath the earth to say nothing of an invalid grandfather, a child who was lame as the result of a landslip, and a little girl who died of starvation during the strike. So that, though this family had in part deserved its misfortunes by the detestable spirit it had shown, they had resolved to assert the breadth of their charity, their desire for forgetfulness and conciliation, by themselves bringing alms. Two parcels, carefully wrapped up, had been placed beneath a seat of the carriage.

An old woman pointed out to the coachman la Maheude's house, No. 16 in the second block. But when the Grégoires alighted with the parcels, they knocked in vain; at last they struck their fists against the door, still without reply; the house echoed mournfully, like a house emptied by grief, frozen and dark, long since abandoned.

'There's no one there,' said Cécile, disappointed. 'What a nuisance! What shall we do with all this?'

Suddenly the door of the next house opened, and la Levaque appeared.

'Oh, sir! I beg pardon, ma'am. Excuse me, miss. It's the neighbour that you want? She's not there; she's at Réquillart.'

With a flow of words she told them the story, repeating to them that people must help one another, and that she was keeping Lénore and Henri in her house to allow the mother to go and wait over there. Her eyes had fallen on the parcels, and she began to talk about her poor daughter, who had become a widow, displaying her own wretchedness, while her eyes shone with covetousness. Then, in a hesitating way, she muttered:

'I've got the key. If the lady and gentleman would really like — The grandfather is there.'

The Grégories looked at her in stupefaction. What! The grandfather was there! But no one had replied. He was sleeping, then? And when la Levaque made up her mind to open the door, what they saw stopped them on the threshold. Bonnemort was there alone, with large fixed eyes, glued to his chair in front of the cold fireplace. Around him the room appeared larger without the clock or the polished deal furniture which formerly animated it; there only remained against the green crudity of the walls the portraits of the Emperor and Empress, whose rosy lips were smiling with official benevolence. The old man did not stir nor bat an eyelid at the sudden light from the door; he seemed imbecile, as though he had not seen all these people come in. At his feet lay his plate of ashes, like a cat's litter tray.

'Don't mind if he's not very polite,' said la Levaque obligingly. 'Seems he's broken something in his brain. It's a fortnight since he left off speaking.'

But Bonnemort was shaken by some agitation, a deep scraping which seemed to arise from his belly, and he spat into the plate a thick black gobbet of phlegm. The ashes were soaked into a coaly mud, all the coal of the mine which he drew from his chest. He had already fallen back into immobility. He moved no more, except at intervals, to spit.

Uneasy, and with stomachs turned, the Grégoires endeavoured to utter a few friendly and encouraging words.

'Well, my good man,' said the father, 'you have a cold, then?'

The old man, with his eyes to the wall, did not turn his head. And a heavy silence fell once more.

'They ought to make you a little tea,' added the mother.

He preserved his mute stiffness.

'I say, papa,' murmured Cécile, 'they certainly told us he was an invalid; only we did not think of it afterwards—'

She interrupted herself, much embarrassed. After having placed on the table some stew and two bottles of wine, she undid the second parcel and drew from it a pair of enormous shoes. It was the present intended for the grandfather, and she held one boot in each hand, in confusion, contemplating the poor man's swollen feet, which would never walk again.

'Oh they come a little late, don't they, my worthy fellow?' said Monsieur Grégoire again, to enliven the situation. 'It doesn't matter, they're always useful.'

Bonnemort neither heard nor replied, with his terrifying face as cold and as hard as a stone.

Then Cécile furtively placed the shoes against the wall. But in spite of her precautions the nails clanked; and those enormous boots were totally out of place in the room.

'He won't say thank you,' said la Levaque, who had cast a look of deep envy on the shoes. 'Might as well give a pair of spectacles to a duck, asking your pardon.'

She went on; she was trying to draw the Grégoires into her own house, where she hoped to move them to pity. At last she thought of a pretext; she praised Henri and Lénore, who were so good, so gentle, and so intelligent, answering like angels the questions they were asked. They would tell the lady and gentleman all that they wished to know.

'Will you come for a moment, my child?' asked the father, glad to get away.

'Yes, I'll follow you in a while,' she replied.

Cécile remained alone with Bonnemort. What kept her there trembling and fascinated, was the thought that she seemed to recognize this old man: where then had she met this square livid

face, tattooed with coal? Suddenly she remembered; she saw again a
mob of shouting people who surrounded her, and she felt cold
hands pressing her neck. It was he; she saw the man again; she
looked at his hands placed on his knees, the hands of an invalid
workman whose whole strength is in his wrists, still firm in spite of
his age. Gradually Bonnemort seemed to awake, he noticed her and
examined her in turn. A flame rose to his cheeks, a nervous spasm
twisted his mouth, from which flowed a thin streak of black saliva.
Fascinated, they remained opposite each other – she healthy, plump,
and fresh from the long idleness and sated comfort of her race; he
swollen with water, with the pitiful ugliness of a worn-out beast,
destroyed from father to son by a century of work and hunger.

After ten minutes, when the Grégoires, surprised at not seeing
Cécile, came back into the Maheus' house, they uttered a terrible
cry. Their daughter was lying on the ground, blue in the face,
strangled. At her neck fingers had left the red imprint of a giant's
hand. Bonnemort, tottering on his dead legs, had fallen beside her
without the strength to rise. His hands were still hooked, and he
looked round with his imbecile air and large open eyes. In his fall
he had broken his plate, the ashes were spread round, the mud of
the black phlegm had stained the floor; while the great pair of
shoes, safe and sound, stood side by side against the wall.

It was never possible to establish the exact facts. Why had Cécile
come near? How could Bonnemort, stuck in his chair, have been
able to seize her throat? Evidently, when he held her, he must have
become furious, constantly pressing, falling over with her, and
stifling her cries to the last groan. Not a sound, not a moan had
traversed the thin partition to the neighbouring house. It seemed to
be an outbreak of sudden madness, a longing to murder on seeing
this white young neck. Such a savagery was stupefying in an old
invalid, who had lived like a worthy man, an obedient brute,
opposed to new ideas. What rancour, unknown even to himself, by
some slow process of poisoning, had risen from his innermost being
to his brain? The horror of it led to the conclusion that he was
unaware of what he was doing, that it was the crime of an idiot.

The Grégoires, meanwhile on their knees, were sobbing, choked
with grief. Their beloved daughter, that daughter desired so long,
on whom they had lavished all their possessions, whom they used
to watch sleeping, on tiptoe, whom they never thought sufficiently
well nourished, never sufficiently plump! It was the collapse of their
very life; what was the good of living now that they would have to
live without her?

La Levaque cried out wildly.

'Ah, the old bugger! what's he done there? Who would have expected such a thing? And la Maheude, who won't come back till evening! Shall I go and fetch her?'

The father and mother were crushed, and did not reply.

'Eh? I'd better. I'll go.'

But, before going, la Levaque looked at the shoes. The whole settlement was excited, and a crowd was already bustling around. Perhaps they would get stolen. And then the Maheus had no man, now, to put them on. She quietly carried them away. They would just fit Bouteloup's feet.

At Réquillart the Hennebeaus, with Négrel, waited a long time for the Grégoires. Négrel, who had come up from the pit, gave a detailed account. They hoped to communicate that very evening with the prisoners, but they would certainly find nothing but corpses, for the death-like silence continued. Behind the engineer, la Maheude, seated on the beam, was listening whitefaced, when la Levaque came up and told her about the old man's strange deed. And she only made a sweeping gesture of impatience and irritation. She followed her, however.

Madame Hennebeau was much affected. What an abomination! That poor Cécile, so merry that very day, so full of life an hour before! Monsieur Hennebeau had to lead his wife for a moment into old Mouque's hovel. With his awkward hands he unfastened her dress, troubled by the scent of musk which her open bodice exhaled. And as with streaming tears she clasped Négrel, terrified at this death which cut short the marriage, the husband watched them lamenting together, and was delivered from one anxiety. This misfortune would arrange everything; he preferred to keep his nephew for fear of his coachman.

CHAPTER 5

At the bottom of the shaft the abandoned wretches were yelling with terror. The water now came up to their waists. The noise of the torrent dazed them, the final falling in of the tubbing sounded like the last crack of doom; and their bewilderment was completed by the neighing of the horses shut up in the stable, the terrible, unforgettable death-cry of an animal that is being slaughtered.

Mouque had let Bataille loose. The old horse was there, trembling, with its dilated eyes fixed on this water which was constantly rising. The loading-bay was rapidly filling; the greenish flood slowly mounted under the red gleam of the three lamps which were still burning under the roof. And suddenly, when he felt the icy water soaking his coat, he set out in a furious gallop, and was engulfed and lost at the end of one of the haulage galleries.

Then there was a general rush, the men following the beast.

'Nothing more to be done in this damned hole!' shouted Mouque. 'We must try Réquillart.'

The idea that they might get out by the old neighbouring pit if they arrived before the passage was cut off, now carried them along. The twenty hustled one another as they went in single file, holding their lamps in the air so that the water should not extinguish them. Fortunately, the gallery rose in an imperceptible slope, and they proceeded for two hundred metres, struggling against the flood, which was not now gaining on them. Long-buried superstitions reawakened in these distracted souls; they called upon mother earth, for it was the earth that was avenging herself, discharging blood from her veins because they had cut one of her arteries. An old man stammered forgotten prayers, bending his thumbs backwards to appease the evil spirits of the mine.

But at the first turning disagreement broke out; the groom proposed turning to the left, others declared that they could make a short cut by going to the right. A minute was lost.

'Well, die there! what the devil does it matter to me?' Chaval brutally exclaimed. 'I go this way.'

He turned to the right, and two mates followed him. The others continued to rush behind old Mouque, who had grown up at the bottom of Réquillart. He himself hesitated, however, not knowing where to turn. They lost their heads; even the old men could no longer recognize the passages, which lay like a tangled skein before them. At every bifurcation they were pulled up short by uncertainty, and yet they had to decide.

Étienne was running in the rear, delayed by Catherine, who was paralysed by fatique and fear. He would have gone to the right with Chaval, for he thought that the better road; but he had not, preferring to part company with Chaval. The rush continued, however; some of the mates had gone from their side, and only seven were left behind old Mouque.

'Hang on to my neck and I will carry you,' said Étienne to the young girl, seeing her grow weak.

'No, let me be,' she murmured. 'I can't do more; I would rather die straightaway.'

They delayed and were left fifty metres behind; he was lifting her, in spite of her resistance, when the gallery was suddenly stopped up; an enormous block fell in and separated them from the others. The inundation was already soaking the soil, which was shifting on every side. They had to retrace their steps; then they no longer knew in what direction they were going. There was an end of all hope of escaping by Réquillart. Their only remaining hope was to reach the upper workings, from which they might perhaps be delivered if the water subsided.

Étienne at last recognized the Guillaume seam.

'Good!' he exclaimed. 'Now I know where we are. By God! we were on the right road; but we might as well go to the devil now! Here, let us go straight on; we will climb up the chimney.'

The flood was beating against their breasts, and they walked very slowly. As long as they had light they did not despair, and they blew out one of the lamps to save oil, meaning to empty it into the other lamp. They had reached the chimney passage, when a noise behind made them turn. Was it some mates, then, who had also found the road barred and were returning? A roaring sound came from afar; they could not understand this tempest which approached them, spattering foam. And they cried out when they saw a gigantic whitish mass coming out of the shadow and trying to rejoin them between the narrow timbering in which it was being crushed.

It was Bataille. On leaving the loading-bay he had wildly galloped along the dark galleries. He seemed to know his road in this subterranean town which he had inhabited for eleven years, and his eyes saw clearly in the depths of the eternal night in which he had lived. He galloped on and on, bending his head, drawing up his feet, passing through these narrow passages in the earth, filled by his huge body. Road came after road, and the forked turnings were taken without any hesitation. Where was he going? Over there, perhaps, towards that vision of his youth, to the mill where he had been born on the bank of the Scarpe, to the confused recollection of the sun burning in the air like a great lamp. He desired to live, his beast's memory awoke; the longing to breathe once more the air of the plains drove him straight onwards to the discovery of that hole, the exit beneath the warm sun leading into daylight. Revolt drove away his lifelong resignation; this pit was murdering him after having blinded him. The water which pursued him was lashing him on the flanks and biting him on the rump. But as he went deeper in, the galleries became narrower, the roofs lower, and the walls jutted out. He galloped on in spite of everything, grazing himself, leaving shreds of his limbs on the timber. From every side the mine seemed to be pressing in on him to get him and to stifle him.

Then Étienne and Catherine, as he came near them, saw that he was wedged and strangling between the rocks. He had stumbled and broken his two front legs. With a last effort, he dragged himself a few metres, but his flanks could not pass through; he remained hemmed in and garrotted by the earth. With his bleeding head stretched out, he still looked for some crack with his great troubled eyes. The water was rapidly covering him; he began to neigh with that terrible prolonged death-rattle with which the other horses had already died in the stable. It was a sight of fearful agony, this old beast shattered and motionless, struggling at this depth, far from the daylight. The flood was over his mane, and his cry of distress never ceased; he uttered it more hoarsely, with his large open mouth stretched out. There was a last rumble, a hollow sound like a barrel which is being filled; then deep silence fell.

'Oh, my God! take me away!' Catherine sobbed. 'Ah, my God! I'm afraid; I don't want to die. Take me away! take me away!'

She had seen death. The fallen shaft, the inundated mine, nothing had seized her with such terror as the death-cry of Bataille. And she went on hearing it; her ears were ringing with it; all her flesh was shuddering with it.

'Take me away! take me away!'

Étienne had seized her and carried her off; it was, indeed, time. They began to climb up the chimney passage, in water up to the shoulders. He was obliged to help her, for she had no strength to cling to the timber. Three times over he thought that she was slipping from him and falling back into that deep sea of which the tide was roaring beneath them. However, they were able to breathe for a few minutes when they reached the first gallery, which was still free. The water reappeared, and they had to hoist themselves up again. And for hours this ascent continued, the flood chasing them from passage to passage, and constantly forcing them to climb up. At the sixth level a respite made them feverish with hope, and it seemed that the waters were remaining stationary. But a more rapid rise took place, and they had to climb to the seventh and then to the eighth level. Only one remained, and when they had reached it they anxiously watched each centimetre by which the water gained on them. If it did not stop they would then die like the old horse, crushed against the roof, and their lungs filled by the flood.

Landslips echoed out at every moment. The whole mine was shaken, and its distended bowels burst with the enormous flood which gorged them. At the end of the galleries pockets of air, driven back, pressed together and crushed, exploding terribly, splitting rocks and spilling mounds of earth. There was a terrifying uproar of interior cataclysms, a remnant of prehistoric upheavals when deluges overthrew the earth, burying the mountains beneath the plains.

And Catherine, shaken and dazed by this continuous avalanche, joined her hands, stammering out the same words in a ceaseless refrain.

'I don't want to die! I don't want to die!'

To reassure her, Étienne swore that the water was not now moving. Their flight had lasted for fully six hours, and they would soon be rescued. He said six hours without knowing, for they had lost all sense of time. In reality, a whole day had already passed in their climb up through the Guillaume seam.

Drenched and shivering, they settled themselves down. She undressed without shame and wrung out her clothes. Then she put on her jacket and breeches again and let them finish drying on her. As her feet were bare, he made her take his own clogs. They could wait patiently now; they had lowered the wick of the lamp, leaving only the feeble gleam of a night-light. But their stomachs were torn by cramps, and they both realized that they were dying of hunger. Up till now they had not felt that they were living. The catastrophe had occurred before breakfast, and now they found their bread-and-butter soaked through with water and changed into a sop. She had to become angry before he would accept his share. As soon as she had eaten she fell asleep from weariness, on the cold earth. He was tormented by insomnia, and watched over her with a fixed gaze and his head in his hands.

How many hours passed like this? He would have been unable to say. All that he knew was that in front of him, through the hole in the chimney, he had seen the flood reappear, black and moving, the beast whose back was ceaselessly swelling out to reach them. At first it was only a thin line, a slippery serpent stretching itself out; then it grew into a crawling, crouching creature; and soon it reached them, and the sleeping girl's feet were touched by it. In his anxiety he hesitated to wake her. Was it not cruel to snatch her from the repose of the unconscious ignorance, which was, perhaps, lulling her with a dream of the open air and of life beneath the sun? Besides, where could they escape? And he thought and remembered that the incline at this part of the seam communicated end to end with the incline extending to the upper level. That would be a way out. He let her sleep as long as possible, watching the flood gain on them, waiting for it to chase them away. At last he lifted her gently, and a great shudder passed over her.

'Ah, my God! it's true! it's beginning again, my God!'

She remembered, she cried out, again seeing death so near.

'No! calm down,' he whispered. 'We can get through, believe me!'

To reach the incline they had to walk doubled up, again soaked to the shoulders. And the climbing began anew, now more dangerous, through the hole entirely lined with timber, a hundred metres long. At first they tried to pull the cable so as to anchor one of the carts at the bottom, for if the other should come down during their ascent, they would be crushed. But nothing moved, some obstacle interfered with the mechanism. They ventured in, not daring to make use of the cable which was in their way, and tearing their nails against the smooth timbers. He walked behind, supporting her with his head when she slipped with torn hands. Suddenly they came across the splinters of a beam which barred the way. A portion of the soil had fallen down and prevented them from going any higher. Fortunately a door opened here and they came out into a passageway. They were astonished to see the flicker of a lamp in front of them. A man cried wildly to them:

'More silly fools with the same idea!'

They recognized Chaval, who had found himself blocked by the landslip which filled the upbrow; his two mates who had set out with him had been left on the way with fractured skulls. He was injured in the elbow, but had had the courage to go back on his knees, take their lamps, and search them to steal their bread-and-butter. As he escaped, a final landslide behind his back had closed the gallery.

His first thought was that he would not share his provisions with these people who came up out of the earth. He would sooner knock their brains out. Then he, too, recognized them; his anger died away and he began to laugh with a laugh of evil joy.

'Ah! it's you Catherine! you've come a cropper, and you want to come back to your man again. Well, well! we'll have a merry dance together.'

He pretended not to see Étienne. The latter, overwhelmed by this encounter, made a gesture as though to protect the girl, who was pressing herself against him. However, he had to accept the situation. Speaking as though they had left each other good friends an hour before, he simply asked:

'Have you looked down below? We can't pass through the cuttings, then?'

Chaval was still sniggering.

'Ah, nonsense! the cuttings! They've fallen in too; we are between two walls, a real rat-trap. But you can go back by the brow if you are a good diver.'

The water, in fact, was rising; they could hear it rippling. Their retreat was already cut off. And he was right; it was a rat-trap, a stretch of gallery obstructed at both ends by great falls of earth. There was no way out; all three were walled up.

'Then you'll stay?' Chaval added, jeeringly. 'Well, it's the best you can do, and if you'll just leave me alone, I shan't even speak to you. There's still room here for two men. We shall soon see which will die first, provided they don't reach us, which seems too much to expect.'

The young man said:

'If we were to tap they would hear us, perhaps.'

'I'm tired of tapping. Here, try yourself with this stone.'

Étienne picked up the fragment of sandstone which the other had already broken off, and against the seam at the end he struck the miner's call, the prolonged roll by which workmen in peril signal their presence. Then he placed his ear to listen. Twenty times over he persisted; no sound replied.

During this time Chaval affected to be coolly attending to his affairs. First he arranged the three lamps against the wall; only one was burning, the others could be used later on. Afterwards, he placed on a piece of timber the two slices of bread-and-butter which were still left. That was the side-board; he could last quite two days with that, if he were careful. He turned round saying:

'You know, Catherine, there will be half for you when you are famished.'

The young girl was silent. It was her final torment to find herself again between these two men.

And their awful life began. Neither Chaval nor Étienne opened his mouth, seated on the earth a few paces from each other. At a hint from the former the latter extinguished his lamp, a piece of useless luxury; then they sank back into silence. Catherine was lying down near Étienne, ill-at-ease under the glances of her former lover. The hours passed by; they heard the low murmur of the water still rising; while from time to time deep shocks and distant echoes announced the final settling down of the mine. When the lamp was empty and they had to open another to light it, they were, for a moment, disturbed by the fear of fire-damp; but they would rather have been blown up at once than live on in darkness. Nothing exploded, however; there was no fire-damp. They stretched themselves out again, and the hours continued to pass by.

A noise aroused Étienne and Catherine, and they raised their heads. Chaval had decided to eat; he had cut off half a slice of bread-and-butter, and was chewing it slowly, to avoid the temptation of swallowing it all. They gazed at him, tortured by hunger.

'Well, do you refuse?' he said to the girl, in his provoking way. 'You're wrong.'

She had lowered her eyes, fearing to yield; her stomach was torn by such cramps that tears were swelling beneath her eye-lids. But she understood what he was asking; in the morning he had breathed down her neck; he was seized again by one of his old fits of desire on seeing her near the other man. The looks with which he called her had a passion in them which she knew well, the flame of his crises of jealousy when he would fall on her with his fists, accusing her of committing abominations with her mother's lodger. And she was not willing; she trembled lest, by returning to him, she should throw these two men on to each other in this narrow cave, where they were all facing death together. Good God! why could they not end together in comradeship!

Étienne would have died of starvation rather than beg a mouthful of bread from Chaval. The silence became heavy; an eternity seemed to stretch out before them with the slowness of monotonous minutes which passed by, one by one, without hope. They had now been shut up together for a day. The second lamp was growing pale, and they lighted the third.

Chaval started on his second slice of bread-and-butter, and growled:

'Come on, stupid!'

Catherine shivered. Étienne had turned away in order to leave her free. Then, as she did not stir, he said to her in a low voice:

'Go on, my child.'

The tears which she was stifling then gushed forth. She wept for a long time, without even strength to rise, no longer knowing if she was hungry, suffering with pain which she felt all over her body. He was standing up, going backwards and forwards, vainly beating the miners' call, enraged at this remainder of life which he was obliged to live here tied to a rival whom he detested. Not even enough space to die away from each other! As soon as he had gone ten paces he had to come back and run up against this man. And this wretched girl whom they were fighting over even in the depths of the earth! She would belong to the one who lived longest; he would steal her from him should he go first. There was no end to it; the hours followed the hours; the revolting promiscuity became worse, with their foul breaths and the filth of their bodily needs satisfied in common. Twice he rushed against the rocks as though to open them with his fists.

Another day was done, and Chaval had seated himself near Catherine, sharing with her his last half-slice. She was chewing the mouthfuls painfully; he made her pay for each with a caress, in his jealous obstinacy not willing to die until he had had her again in the other man's presence. She abandoned herself in exhaustion. But when he tried to take her she complained.

'Oh, let me be! you're crushing me.'

Étienne, with a shudder, had turned his face against the props so as not to see. He turned round with a wild leap.

'Let her be, by God!'

'Does it concern you?' said Chaval. 'She's my woman; she belongs to me!'

And he grabbed her again and held her tight, out of bravado, crushing his red moustache against her mouth, and adding:

'Will you leave us alone, eh? Will you be good enough to look over there if we are at it?'

But Étienne, with white lips, shouted:

'If you don't let her go, I'll throttle you!'

The other quickly stood up, for he had understood by the hiss of the voice that his mate was in earnest. Death seemed to them too slow; it was necessary that one of them should immediately make way for the other. It was the old battle beginning over again, down in the earth where they would soon sleep side by side; and they had so little room that they could not swing their fists without grazing them.

'Watch out!' growled Chaval. 'This time I'll have you.'

From that moment Étienne became mad. His eyes clouded over in a red haze, his chest was congested by the flow of blood. The need to kill seized him irresistibly, a physical need, like the irritation of mucus which causes a violent spasm of coughing. It rose and broke out beyond his will, under the pressure of the hereditary disease. He had seized a slab of shale from the wall and he shook it and tore it out, a very large, heavy piece. Then with both hands and with superhuman strength he brought it down on Chaval's skull.

Chaval had not time to jump backwards. He fell, his face crushed, his skull broken. The brains had bespattered the roof of the gallery, and a purple jet flowed from the wound, like the continuous jet of a spring. Immediately there was a pool, which reflected the smoky star of the lamp. Darkness was invading the walled-up cave, and this body, lying on the earth, looked like a black heap of slag.

Leaning over, with wide eyes, Étienne looked at him. It was done, then; he had killed a man. All his struggles came back to mind confusedly, that useless fight against the poison which lay dormant in his muscles, the slowly accumulated alcohol of his race. He was, however, only intoxicated by hunger; the remote intoxication of his parents had been enough. His hair stood up before the horror of this murder; and yet, in spite of the repulsion which came from his education, a certain joy made his heart beat, the animal joy of an appetite finally satisfied. He felt pride, too, the pride of the stronger man. The little soldier came to mind, with his throat opened up by a knife, killed by a child. Now he, too, had killed.

But Catherine, standing upright, uttered a loud cry:

'My God! he is dead!'

'Are you sorry?' asked Étienne, wildly.

She was choking, she stammered. Then, tottering, she threw herself into his arms.

'Ah, kill me too! Ah, let us both die!'

She clasped him, hanging to his shoulders, and he clasped her; and they wished that they would die. But death was in no hurry, and they unlocked their arms. Then, while she hid her eyes, he dragged away the wretch, and threw him down the incline, to remove him from the narrow space in which they still had to live. Life would no longer have been possible with that corpse beneath their feet. And they were terrified when they heard it plunge into the midst of the foam which leapt up. The water had already filled the hole, then? They saw it; it was entering the gallery.

Then there was a new struggle. They had lighted the last lamp; as it burnt out, it lit up the flood, with its regular, obstinate rise which never ceased. At first the water came up to their ankles; then it wetted their knees. The passage sloped up, and they took refuge at the end. This gave them a respite for some hours. But the flood caught them up, and engulfed them to the waist. Standing up, brought to bay, with their backs up against the rock, they watched it ever and ever rising. When it reached their mouths, all would be over. The lamp, which they had fastened up, threw a yellow light on the rapid surge of the little waves. It was becoming pale; they could make out no more than a constantly diminishing semicircle, as though eaten away by the darkness which seemed to grow with the flood; and suddenly the darkness enveloped them. The lamp had gone out, after having spat forth its last drop of oil. There was now complete and absolute night, that night of the earth which they would have to sleep through without ever again opening their eyes to the brightness of the sun.

'By God!' Étienne swore, in a low voice.

Catherine, as though she had felt the darkness seize her, sheltered herself against him. She repeated, in a whisper, the miner's saying:

'Death blows out the lamp.'

Yet in the face of this threat their instincts struggled, the will to live animated them. He violently set himself to hollow out the slate with the hook of the lamp, while she helped him with her nails. They formed a sort of elevated bench, and when they had both hoisted themselves up to it, they found themselves seated with hanging legs and bent backs, for the vault forced them to lower their heads. They now only felt the icy water at their heels; but before long the cold was at their ankles, their calves, their knees, with its invincible, inexorable movement. The bench, not properly smoothed, was soaked in moisture, and so slippery that they had to cling on to avoid slipping off. It was the end; what could they expect, reduced to this niche where they dared not move, exhausted, starving, having neither bread nor light? and they suffered especially from the darkness, which would not allow them to see the coming of death. There was deep silence; the mine, being gorged with water, no longer stirred. They had nothing beneath them now but the sensation of that sea, swelling out its silent tide from the depths of the galleries.

The hours went by, all equally black; but they were not able to measure their exact duration, becoming more and more vague in their calculation of time. Their torment, which might have been expected to lengthen the minutes, rapidly bore them away. They thought that they had only been shut up for two days and a night, when in reality the third day had already come to an end. All hope of help had gone; no one knew they were there, no one could come down to them. And hunger would finish them off if the flood spared them. For one last time it occurred to them to beat the call, but the stone was lying beneath the water. Besides, who would hear them?

Catherine was leaning her aching head against the seam, when she sat up with a start.

'Listen!' she said.

At first Étienne thought she was speaking of the lapping of the ever-rising water. He lied in order to quiet her.

'It's me you hear; I'm moving my legs.'

'No, no; not that! Over there, listen!'

And she placed her ear to the coal. He understood, and did likewise. They waited for some seconds, with stifled breath. Then, very far away and very weak, they heard three blows at long intervals. But they still doubted; their ears were ringing; perhaps it was the cracking of the soil. And they knew not what to strike with in answer.

Étienne had an idea.

'You have the clogs. Take them off and strike with the heels.'

She struck, beating the miner's call; and they listened and again distinguished the three blows far off. Twenty times over they did it, and twenty times the blows replied. They wept and embraced each other, at the risk of losing their balance. At last the mates were there, they were coming. An overflowing joy and love carried away the torments of waiting and the rage of their vain appeals, as though their rescuers had only to split the rock with a finger to deliver them.

'Eh!' she cried merrily; 'wasn't it lucky that I leant my head?'

'Oh, you've got an ear!' he said in his turn. 'I didn't hear a thing.'

From that moment they relieved each other, one of them always listening, ready to answer at the least signal. They soon caught the sounds of the pick; the work of approaching them was beginning, a gallery was being opened. Not a sound escaped them. But their joy sank. In vain they laughed to deceive each other; despair was gradually seizing them. At first they entered into long explanations; evidently they were being approached from Réquillart. The gallery ran down into the seam; perhaps several were being opened, for there were always three men hewing. Then they talked less, and were at last silent when they came to calculate the enormous mass which separated them from their mates. They continued their reflections in silence, counting the days and days that a workman would take to penetrate such a block. They would never be reached soon enough; they would have time to die twenty times over. And no longer venturing to exchange a word in their increased anguish, they gloomily replied to the appeals by a roll of the clogs without hope, only retaining the mechanical need to tell the others that they were still alive.

Thus passed a day, two days. They had been at the bottom six days. The water had stopped at their knees, neither rising nor falling, and their legs seemed to be melting away in this icy bath. They could keep them out of the water for an hour or so, but their position then became so uncomfortable that they were twisted by horrible cramps, and were obliged to let their feet fall in again. Every ten minutes they hoisted themselves back by a jerk on the slippery rock. Jagged edges of the coal face struck into their spines, and they felt at the back of their necks a ceaseless intense pain, through having to keep constantly bent in order to avoid striking their heads. And their suffocation increased; the air, driven back by the water, was compressed into a sort of diving bell, in which they were shut up. Their voices were muffled, and seemed to come from afar. Their ears began to buzz, they heard the wild peals of bells, the tramp of a herd of animals beneath a storm of hail, going on unceasingly.

At first Catherine suffered horribly from hunger. She pressed her poor shrivelled hands against her breasts, her breathing was deep and hollow, a continuous tearing moan, as though pincers were tearing at her stomach.

Étienne, choked by the same torment, was feeling feverishly round him in the darkness, when his fingers came upon a half-rotten piece of timber, which his nails could crumble. He gave a handful of it to the girl, who swallowed it greedily. For two days they lived on this worm-eaten wood, devouring it all, in despair when it was finished, grazing their hands in the effort to crush the other planks which were still solid with resisting fibres. Their torture increased, and they were enraged that they could not chew the cloth of their clothes. A leather belt, which he wore round the waist, relieved them a little. He bit small pieces from it with his teeth, and she chewed them, and endeavoured to swallow them. This occupied their jaws, and gave them the illusion of eating. Then, when the belt was finished, they went back to their clothes, sucking them for hours.

But soon these violent crises subsided; hunger became only a low deep ache with the slow progressive waning of their strength. No doubt they would have succumbed if they had not had as much water as they desired. They merely bent down and drank from the hollow of the hand, and this they did very frequently, parched by a thirst which all this water could not quench.

On the seventh day Catherine was bending down to drink, when her hand struck a floating body before her.

'I say, look! What's this?'

Étienne felt in the darkness.

'I can't make it out; it seems like the cover of a ventilation door.'

She drank, but as she was drawing up a second mouthful the body came back, striking her hand. And she uttered a terrible cry.

'My God! it's him!'

'Who?'

'Him! You know well enough. I felt his moustache.'

It was Chaval's corpse, risen from the incline and pushed on to them by the flow. Étienne stretched out his arm; he, too, felt the moustache and the crushed nose, and shuddered with disgust and fear. Seized by horrible nausea, Catherine had spat out the water which was still in her mouth. It seemed to her that she had been drinking blood, and that all the deep water before her was now that man's blood.

'Wait!' stammered Étienne. 'I'll push it away!'

He kicked the corpse, which moved off. But soon they felt it again striking against their legs.

'By God! Go away!'

And the third time Étienne had to leave it. The current always brought it back. Chaval would not go; he wanted to be with them, against them. This awful companion was poisoning the air. All that day they never drank, struggling, preferring to die. It was not until the next day that their suffering decided them: they pushed away the body at each mouthful and drank in spite of it. It had not been worth while to knock his brains out, for he came back between him and her, obstinate in his jealousy. To the very end he would be there, even though he was dead, preventing them from coming together.

A day passed, and again another day. At every shiver of the water Étienne received a slight blow from the man he had killed, the simple elbowing of a neighbour who is reminding you of his presence. And every time it came he shuddered. He continually saw it there, swollen, greenish, with the red moustache and the crushed face. Then he no longer remembered; he had not killed him; the other man was swimming and trying to bite him.

Catherine was now shaken by long endless fits of crying, after which she was completely prostrated. She fell at last into a condition of irresistible drowsiness. He would arouse her, but she stammered a few words and at once fell asleep again without even raising her eyelids; and fearing lest she should be drowned, he put his arm round her waist. It was he now who replied to the mates. The blows of the pick were now approaching, he could hear them behind his back. But his strength, too, was diminishing; he had lost all courage to strike. They knew they were there; why weary oneself more? It no longer interested him whether they came or not. In the stupefaction of waiting he would forget for hours at a time what he was waiting for.

One relief comforted them a little: the water receded, and Chaval's body moved off. For nine days the work of their deliverance had been going on, and they were for the first time taking a few steps in the gallery when a fearful commotion threw them to the ground. They felt for each other and remained in each other's arms like mad people, not understanding, thinking the catastrophe was beginning over again. Nothing more stirred, the sound of the picks had ceased.

In the corner where they were seated holding each other, side by side, a low laugh from Catherine.

'It must be good outside. Come, let's go out of here.'

Étienne at first struggled against this madness. But the contagion was shaking his stronger head, and he lost the exact sensation of reality. All their senses seemed to go astray, especially Catherine's. She was shaken by fever, tormented now by the need to talk and move. The ringing in her ears had become the murmur of flowing water, the song of birds; she smelled the strong odour of crushed grass, and could see clearly great patches floating before her eyes, so large that she thought she was out of doors, near the canal, in the meadows on a fine summer day.

'Eh? how warm it is! Take me, then; let us stay together. Oh, always, always!'

He pressed her, and she rubbed herself against him for a long time, continuing to chatter like a happy girl:

'How silly we have been to wait so long! I would have liked you at once, and you did not understand; you sulked. Then, do you remember, at our house at night, when we could not sleep, with our faces out listening to each other's breathing, with such a longing to come together?'

He was won over by her gaiety, and joked over the recollection of their silent tenderness.

'You struck me once. Yes, yes, blows on both cheeks!'

'It was because I loved you,' she murmured. 'You see, I prevented myself from thinking of you. I said to myself that it was quite done with, and all the time I knew that one day or another we should get together. It only needed an opportunity – some lucky chance. Wasn't it so?'

A shudder froze him. He tried to shake off this dream; then he repeated slowly:

'Nothing is ever done with; a little happiness is enough to make everything begin again.'

'Then you'll keep me, and it will be all right this time?'

And she slipped down fainting. She was so weak that her low voice died out. In terror he kept her against his heart.

'Are you in pain?'

She sat up surprised.

'No, not at all. Why?'

But this question aroused her from her dream. She gazed at the darkness with distraction, wringing her hands in another fit of sobbing.

'My God, my God, how black it is!'

Gone were the meadows, the smell of the grass, the song of larks, the great yellow sun; it was the fallen, inundated mine, the stinking gloom, the melancholy dripping of this cellar where they had been groaning for so many days. Her warped senses all now increased the horror of it all; her childish superstitions came back to her; she saw the Black Man, the old dead miner who returns to the pit to wring naughty girls' necks.

'Listen! did you hear?'

'No, nothing; I heard nothing.'

'Yes, the Man – you know? Look! he is there. The earth has let all the blood out of her veins to avenge herself for being cut into; and he is there – you can see him – look! blacker than night. Oh, I'm so afraid, I'm so afraid!'

She became silent, shivering. Then in a very low voice she whispered:

'No, it's still the other one.'

'What other one?'

'The one who is with us; who is dead.'

The image of Chaval haunted her, she talked of him confusedly, she described the dog's life she had led with him, the only day when he had been kind to her at Jean-Bart, the other days of embraces and blows, when he would kill her with caresses after having covered her with kicks.

'I tell you that he's coming, that he will still keep us from being together! His jealousy is coming on him again. Oh, push him off! Oh, keep me close!'

With a sudden impulse she hung on to him, seeking his mouth and pressing her own passionately against it. The darkness lighted up, she saw the sun again, and she laughed a quiet laugh of love. He shuddered to feel her thus against his flesh, half naked beneath the tattered jacket and trousers, and he seized her with a reawakening of his virility. This was at last their wedding night, at the bottom of this tomb, on this bed of mud, the longing not to die before they had had their happiness, the obstinate longing to live and make life one last time. They loved each other in despair of everything, in death.

After that there was nothing more. Étienne was seated on the ground, still in the same corner, and Catherine was lying motionless on his knees. Hours and hours passed by. For a long time he thought she was sleeping; then he touched her; she was very cold, she was dead. He did not move, however, for fear of arousing her. The idea that he was the first who had possessed her as a woman, and that she might be pregnant, filled him with tenderness. Other ideas, the desire to go away with her, joy at what they would both do later on, came to him at moments, but so vaguely that it seemed only as though they had touched his brow like the breath of sleep. He grew weaker, he only had strength to make a little gesture, a slow movement of the hand, to assure himself that she was there, like a sleeping child in her frozen stiffness. Everything was being destroyed; the night itself had disappeared, and he was nowhere, out of space, out of time. Something was certainly striking beside his head, violent blows were approaching him; but he had been too lazy to reply, benumbed by immense fatigue; and now he knew nothing, he only dreamed that she was walking before him, and that he heard the gentle tapping of her clogs. Two days passed; she had not stirred; he touched her with the same mechanical gesture, reassured to find her so quiet.

Étienne felt a shock. Voices were sounding, rocks were rolling at his feet. When he saw a lamp he wept. His blinking eyes followed the light, he was never tired of looking at it, enraptured by this reddish point which scarcely penetrated the darkness. But some mates carried him away, and he allowed them to introduce spoonfuls of soup between his clenched teeth. It was only in the Réquillart gallery that he recognized someone standing before him, the engineer, Négrel; and these two men, with their contempt for each other

– the rebellious workman and the sceptical master – threw themselves into each other's arms, sobbing loudly from the deep stirrings of all the humanity within them. They felt an immense sadness, the misery of generations, the extremity of grief that life can bring.

At the surface, la Maheude, stricken down near Catherine's body, uttered a cry, then another, then another – very long, deep, incessant moans. Several corpses had already been brought up, and placed in a row on the ground: Chaval, who was thought to have been crushed beneath a landslip, a trammer, and two hewers, also crushed, with brainless skulls and bellies swollen with water. Women in the crowd went out of their minds tearing their skirts and scratching their faces. When Étienne was at last taken out, after having been accustomed to the lamps and fed a little, he was like a skeleton, and his hair was quite white. People turned away and shuddered at the sight of this old man. La Maheude left off crying to stare at him stupidly with her gaping eyes.

CHAPTER 6

It was four o'clock in the morning, and the fresh April night was growing warm at the approach of day. In the limpid sky the stars were twinkling, while the east grew purple with dawn. And a slight shudder passed over the drowsy black country, the vague rumour which precedes awakening.

Étienne, with long strides, was following the Vandame road. He had just spent six weeks at Montsou, in bed at the hospital. Though very thin and yellow, he felt strong enough to go, and he went. The Company, still trembling for its pits, was constantly sending men away, and had given him notice that he could not be kept on. He was offered the sum of one hundred francs, with the paternal advice to leave off working in mines, as it would now be too hard for him. But he refused the hundred francs. He had already received a letter from Pluchart, calling him to Paris, and enclosing money for the journey. His old dream would be realized. The night before, on leaving the hospital, he had slept at the Bon-Joyeux, Widow Désir's place. And he rose early; only one wish was left, to bid his mates farewell before taking the eight o'clock train at Marchiennes.

For a moment Étienne stopped on the road, which was now

becoming rose-coloured in the light of dawn. It was good to breathe that pure air of the precocious spring. It would turn out to be a superb day. The sun was slowly rising, and the lift of the earth was rising with it. And he set out walking again, vigorously striking with his dogwood stick, watching the plain afar, as it rose from the vapours of the night. He had seen no one; la Maheude had come once to the hospital, and, probably, had not been able to come again. But he knew that the whole settlement of the Deux-Cent-Quarante was now going down to work at Jean-Bart, and that she too had taken work there. Little by little the deserted roads were full of people, and colliers constantly passed Étienne with pallid, silent faces. The Company, people said, was taking advantage of its victory. After two and a half months of strike, when they had returned to the pits, conquered by hunger, they had been forced to accept the timbering tariff, that disguised decrease in wages, now the more hateful because stained with the blood of their mates. They were being robbed of an hour's work, they were being made to break their oath never to submit; and this imposed perjury stuck in their throats like gall. Work was beginning again everywhere, at Mirou, at Madeleine, at Crèvecœur, at the Victoire. Everywhere, in the morning haze, along the roads lost in darkness, the herd was tramping on, rows of men trotting with faces bent towards the earth, like cattle led to the slaughter-house. They shivered beneath their thin garments, folding their arms, rolling their hips, bending their backs with the humps formed by the 'briquet' between the shirt and the jacket. And in this wholesale return to work, in these mute shadows, all black, without a laugh, without a look aside, one felt the teeth clenched with rage, the hearts swollen with hatred, a resignation brought about by the needs of the belly.

The nearer Étienne approached the pit the more their number increased. They nearly all walked alone; those who came in groups were in single file, already exhausted, tired of one another and of themselves. He noticed one who was very old, with eyes that shone like hot coals beneath his livid forehead. Another, a young man, was panting with the restrained fury of a storm. Many had their clogs in their hands; you could scarcely hear the soft sound of their coarse woollen stockings on the ground. It was an endless flow, a defeated band, the forced march of a beaten army, moving on with lowered heads, sullenly absorbed in the desire to renew the struggle and achieve revenge.

When Étienne arrived, Jean-Bart was emerging from the shadows; the lanterns, hooked on to the platform, were still burning in the nascent dawn. Above the obscure buildings a trail of steam arose like a white plume delicately tinted with carmine. He passed up the sifting-staircase to go to the receiving-room.

The descent was beginning, and the men were coming from the shed. For a moment he stood by, motionless amid the noise and movement. The rolling of the trams shook the metal floor, the drums were turning, unrolling the cables in the midst of cries from the trumpet, the ringing of bells, blows of the mallet on the signal block; he saw the monster again swallowing his daily ration of human flesh, the cages rising and plunging down, engulfing their burden of men, without ceasing, with the facile gulp of a voracious giant. Since his accident he had a nervous dread of the mine. The cages, as they sank down, turned his stomach. He had to turn away his head; the pit exasperated him.

But in the vast and still sombre hall, feebly lighted up by the exhausted lanterns, he could not see a friendly face. The miners, who were waiting there with bare feet and their lamps in their hands, looked at him with large restless eyes, and then lowered their faces, drawing back with an air of shame. No doubt they knew him and no longer had any resentment against him; they seemed, on the contrary, to fear him, blushing at the thought that he would reproach them with cowardice. This attitude made his heart swell; he forgot that these wretches had stoned him, he again began to dream of changing them into heroes, of directing a whole people, of saving this force of nature which was destroying itself. A cage was filling up with men, and the batch disappeared; as others arrived he saw at last one of his stalwarts in the strike, a worthy fellow who had sworn to die before giving up.

'You too!' he murmured, with aching heart.

The other turned pale and his lips trembled; then, with a movement of excuse:

'What else can I do? I've got a wife.'

Now in the new crowd coming from the shed he recognized them all.

'You too! – you too! – you too!'

And all shrank back, stammering in choked voices:

'I have a mother.' – 'I have children.' – 'We must get bread.'

The cage did not reappear; they waited for it mournfully, with such sorrow at their defeat that they avoided meeting each other's eyes, obstinately gazing at the shaft.

'And la Maheude?' Étienne asked.

They made no reply. One made a sign that she was coming.

Others raised their arms, trembling with pity. Ah, poor woman! what wretchedness! The silence continued, and when Étienne stretched out his hand to bid them farewell, they all pressed it vigorously, putting into the silent handshake their rage at having yielded, their feverish hope of revenge. The cage was there; they got into it and disappeared, devoured by the abyss.

Pierron had appeared with his open foreman's lamp fixed into the leather of his cap. For the past week he had been chief of the gang at the loading-bay, and the men moved away, for promotion had rendered him bossy. The sight of Étienne annoyed him; he came up, however, and was at last reassured when the young man announced his departure. They talked. His wife now kept the Progrès bar, thanks to the support of all those gentlemen, who had been so good to her. But he interrupted himself and turned furiously on to old Mouque, whom he accused of not sending up the dung-heap from his stable at the regulation hour. The old man listened with bent shoulders. Then, before going down, suffering from this reprimand, he, too, gave his hand to Étienne, with the same long pressure as the others, warm with restrained anger and quivering with future rebellion. And this old hand which trembled in his, this old man who was forgiving him for the loss of his dead children, affected Étienne to such a degree that he watched him disappear without saying a word.

'Then la Maheude is not coming this morning?' he asked Pierron after a time.

At first the latter pretended not to understand, for there was ill luck even in speaking of her. Then, as he moved away, under the pretext of giving an order, he said at last:

'Eh! la Maheude? There she is.'

In fact, la Maheude had reached the shed with her lamp in her hand, dressed in trousers and jacket, with her head covered by her cap. It was by a charitable exception that the Company, pitying the fate of this unhappy woman, so cruelly afflicted, had allowed her to go down again at the age of forty; and as it seemed difficult to set her again at haulage work, she was employed to work a small ventilator which had been installed in the north gallery, in those infernal regions beneath Tartaret, where there was no movement of air. For ten hours, with aching back, she turned her wheel at the bottom of a burning hot tunnel, baked by forty degrees of heat. She earned thirty sous.

When Étienne saw her, a pitiful sight in her male garments – her breasts and belly seeming to be swollen by the dampness of the cuttings – he stammered with surprise, trying to find words to explain that he was going away and that he wished to say good-bye to her.

She looked at him without listening, and said at last, in a familiar tone:

'Eh? it surprises you to see me here. It's true enough that I threatened to wring the neck of the first of my children who went down again; and now that I'm going down I ought to wring my own, ought I not? Ah, well! I should have done it by now if it hadn't been for the old man and the little ones at the house.'

And she went on in her low, fatigued voice. She did not excuse herself, she simply told things as they were – that they had been nearly starved, and that she had made up her mind to do it, so that they might not be sent away from the settlement.

'How is the old man?' asked Étienne.

'He is always very gentle and very clean. But he is quite off his nut. He was not sentenced for that business, you know. There was talk of shutting him up with the madmen, but I was not willing; they would have slipped something in his soup. His story has, all the same, been very bad for us, for he'll never get his pension; one of those gentlemen told me that it would be immoral to give him one.'

'Is Jeanlin working?'

'Yes, those gentlemen found something for him to do at the top. He gets twenty sous. Oh! I don't complain; the bosses have been very good, as they told me themselves. The brat's twenty sous and my thirty, that makes fifty. If there were not six of us we would get enough to eat. Estelle eats a lot now, and the worst is that it will be four or five years before Lénore and Henri are old enough to come to the pit.'

Étienne could not withhold an expression of grief.

'They, too!'

La Maheude's pale cheeks turned red, and her eyes flamed. But her shoulders sank as if beneath the weight of destiny.

'What can we do? They have to follow the others. They have all been done for down there; now it's their turn.'

She was silent; some landers, who were rolling trams, disturbed them. Through the large dusty windows the early sun was entering, drowning the lanterns in grey light; and the engine moved every three minutes, the cables unrolled, the cages continued to swallow down men.

'Come along, you idlers, look sharp!' shouted Pierron. 'Get in; we shall never get done today.'

La Maheude, whom he was looking at, did not stir. She had already allowed three cages to pass, and she said, as though arousing herself and remembering Étienne's first words.

'Then you're going away?'

'Yes, this morning.'

'You're right; better be somewhere else if you can. And I'm glad to have seen you, because you can know now, anyhow, that I've nothing against you. For a moment I could have killed you, after all that slaughter. But one thinks, doesn't one? One sees that when all's reckoned up it's nobody's fault. No, no! it's not your fault; it's the fault of everybody.'

Now she talked with tranquillity of her dead, of her man, of Zacharie, of Catherine; and tears only came into her eyes when she uttered Alzire's name. She had resumed her calm reasonableness, and judged things sensibly. It would bring no luck to the bourgeois to have killed so many poor people. Sure enough, they would be punished for it one day, for everything has to be paid for. There would even be no need to interfere; the whole thing would blow up by itself. The soldiers would fire on the masters just as they had fired on the men. And in her everlasting resignation, in that hereditary discipline under which she was again bowing, a conviction had established itself, the certainty that injustice could not last any longer, and that, if there were no God left, another would spring up to avenge the wretched.

She spoke in a low voice, with suspicious glances round. Then, as Pierron was approaching, she added, aloud:

'Well, if you're going, you must take your things from our house. There are still two shirts, three handkerchiefs, and an old pair of trousers.'

Étienne, with a gesture, refused these few things that had been saved from the dealers.

'No, it's not worth it; they can be for the children. In Paris I can look after myself.'

Two more cages had gone down, and Pierron decided to speak straight to la Maheude.

'Look, you, over there, they are waiting for you! Is that little chat nearly done?'

But she turned her back. Why should he be so zealous, this man who had sold himself? The descent didn't concern him. His men hated him enough already on his level. And she persisted, with her lamp in her hand, frozen amid the draughts in spite of the mildness of the season. Neither Étienne nor she found anything more to say.

They remained facing each other with hearts so full that they would have liked to speak once more.

At last she spoke for the sake of speaking.

'La Levaque is in the family way. Levaque is still in prison; Bouteloup is taking his place meanwhile.'

'Ah, yes! Bouteloup.'

'And, listen! did I tell you? Philomène has gone away.'

'What! gone away?'

'Yes, gone away with a Pas-de-Calais miner. I was afraid she would leave the two brats to me. But no, she took them with her. Eh? A woman who spits blood and always looks as if she were on the point of death!'

She mused for a moment, and then went on in a slow voice: 'There's been talk on my account. You remember they used to say I slept with you. Lord! After my man's death that might very well have happened if I had been younger. But now I'm glad it wasn't so, for we would have regretted it, sure enough.'

'Yes, we would have regretted it,' Étienne repeated, simply.

That was all; they spoke no more. A cage was waiting for her; she was being called angrily, threatened with a fine. Then she made up her mind, and pressed his hand. Deeply moved, he still looked at her, so worn and old, with her livid face, her discoloured hair escaping from the blue cap, her body sagging from all her confinements, deformed beneath the jacket and trousers. And in this last handshake he felt again the long, silent grip of his mates, the promise to be there on the day when they would begin again. He understood perfectly. There was a tranquil faith in the depths of her eyes. It would be soon, and this time it would be the final blow.

'What an idle creature!' exclaimed Pierron.

Pushed and hustled, la Maheude squeezed into a tram with four others. The signal-cord was drawn to call for the meat, the cage was unhooked and fell into the night, and there was nothing more but the rapid flight of the cable.

Then Étienne left the pit. Below, beneath the screening-shed, he noticed a creature seated on the earth, with legs stretched out, in the midst of a thick pile of coal. It was Jeanlin, who was employed there to clean the large lumps of coal. He held a block of coal between his thighs, and freed it with a hammer from the fragments of slate. A fine powder drowned him in such a flood of soot that the young man would never have recognized him if the child had not lifted his ape-like face, with the protruding ears and small greenish eyes. He laughed, with a joking air, and, giving a final blow to the block, disappeared in the black dust which arose.

Outside Étienne followed the road for a while, absorbed in his thoughts. All sorts of ideas were buzzing in his head. But he felt the open air, the free sky, and he breathed deeply. The sun was appearing in glory on the horizon, there was a reawakening of gladness over the whole country. A flood of gold rolled from the east to the west on the immense plain. This heat of life was expanding and extending in a tremor of youth, in which vibrated the sighs of the earth, the song of birds, all the murmuring sounds of the waters and the woods. It was good to be alive, and the old world wanted to live through one more spring.

And filled by that hope, Étienne slackened his pace, his eyes wandering to right and to left amid the gaiety of the new season. He thought about himself, he felt himself strong, seasoned by his hard experiences at the bottom of the mine. His education was complete, he was going away armed, a rational soldier of the revolution, having declared war against society as he saw it and as he condemned it. The joy of rejoining Pluchart and of being, like Pluchart, a leader who was listened to, inspired him with speeches, and he began to form the phrases. He was considering an expanded programme; that bourgeois refinement, which had raised him above his class, had deepened his hatred of the bourgeois. He felt the need of glorifying these workers, whose odour of wretchedness was now unpleasant to him; he would show that they alone were great and pure, the only nobility and the only strength in which humanity could be renewed. He already saw himself on the rostrum, triumphing with the people, if the people did not destroy him.

The loud song of a lark made him look up towards the sky. Little red clouds, the last vapours of the night, were melting in the limpid blue; and the vague faces of Souvarine and Rasseneur came to his memory. Decidedly, all was spoilt when each man tried to get power for himself. Thus that famous International which was to have renewed the world had aborted, and its formidable army had been cut up and crumbled away from internal dissensions. Was Darwin right, then, and the world only a battlefield, where the strong devoured the weak for the sake of the beauty and continuance of the race?* This question troubled him, although he settled it like a man who is satisfied with his knowledge. But one idea dissipated his doubts and enchanted him – that of taking up his old explanation of the theory the first time that he should speak. If any class must be devoured, would not the people, still new and full of life, devour the bourgeoisie, exhausted by enjoyment? The new society would arise from new blood. And in this expectation of an invasion of barbarians, regenerating the old decayed nations, reappeared his absolute faith in an approaching revolution, the real one – that of the workers – the fire of which would inflame this century's end with that purple of the rising sun which he saw like blood on the sky. He walked on, dreaming, striking his dogwood stick against the stones on the road, and when he glanced around him he saw again familiar places. Over there, at the Fourche-aux-Bœufs, he remembered that he had taken command of the mob that morning when the pits were sacked. Today the brutish, deathly, ill-paid work was beginning over again. Beneath the earth, down there at seven hundred metres, it seemed to him he heard low, regular, continuous blows of the picks; it was the men he had just seen go down, the black army of workers, who were hammering in their silent rage. No doubt they were beaten. They had left behind their dead and their money; but Paris would not forget the volleys fired at the Voreux, and the blood of the Empire, too, would flow from that incurable wound. And if the industrial crisis was drawing to an end, if the workshops were opening again one by one, a state of war was no less declared, and peace was henceforth impossible. The colliers had reckoned up their men; they had tried their strength, with their cry for justice arousing the workers all over France. Their defeat, therefore, reassured no one. The Montsou bourgeois, in their victory, felt the vague uneasiness that arises on the morrow of a strike, looking behind them to see if their end did not lie inevitably over there, in spite of all, beyond that great silence. They understood that the revolution would be born again unceasingly, perhaps tomorrow, with a general strike – the common understanding of all workers having general funds, and so able to hold out for months, eating their own bread. This time only a push had been given to a rotten society, but they had heard the rumbling beneath their feet, and they felt more shocks arising, and still more, until the old edifice would be crushed, fallen in and swallowed up, going down like the Voreux into the abyss.

Étienne took the Joiselle road, to the left. He remembered that he had prevented the mob from rushing on to Gaston-Marie. Afar, in the clear sky he saw the headgear of several pits – Mirou to the right, Madeleine and Crèvecœur side by side. Work was going on everywhere; he seemed to hear the blows of the picks at the bottom of the earth, striking now from one end of the plain to the other, one blow, and another blow, and yet more blows, beneath the fields and roads and villages which were laughing in the sunlight, all the obscure labour of an underground prison, so crushed by the enormous mass of the rocks that one had to know it was underneath there to distinguish its great painful sigh. And he now thought that, perhaps, violence did not hasten things. Cutting cables, tearing up rails, breaking lamps, what a useless task it was! It was not worth while for three thousand men to rush about in a devastating mob doing that. He vaguely divined that lawful methods might one day be more terrible. His reason was ripening, he had sown the wild oats of his anger. Yes, la Maheude was right, with her good sense, when she said that that would be the real weapon – to organize quietly, to know one another, to unite in associations when the laws would permit it; then, on the morning when they felt their strength, and millions of workers would be face to face with a few thousand idlers, to take the power into their own hands and become the masters. Ah! what a reawakening of truth and justice! Then the sated and crouching god would receive his death-blow, the monstrous idol hidden in the depths of his sanctuary, in that unknown distance where poor wretches fed him with their flesh without ever having seen him.

But Étienne, leaving the Vandame road, now came on to the paved highway. On the right he saw Montsou, which was lost in the valley. Opposite were the ruins of the Voreux, the accursed hole where three pumps were working unceasingly. Then there were the other pits on the horizon, the Victoire, Saint-Thomas, Feutry-Cantel; while, towards the north, the smoke of the tall chimneys of the blast furnaces and of the batteries of coke ovens was rising in the transparent morning air. If he was not to miss the eight o'clock train he had to hurry, for he still had six kilometres before him.

And beneath his feet, the deep blows, those obstinate blows of the pick, continued. His mates were all there; he heard them following him at every stride. Was that not la Maheude beneath the beetroots, with her bent back and her hoarse breathing accompanying the rumble of the ventilator? To left, to right, farther on, he seemed to recognize others beneath the wheatfields, the hedges, the young trees. Now the April sun, in the open sky, was shining forth in all its glory, and warming the pregnant earth. From her fertile womb life was springing forth, buds were bursting into green leaves, and the fields were quivering with the growth of the grass. On every side seeds were swelling, stretching out, cracking through the plain, filled by the need of heat and light. The rising sap was mixed with whispering voices, the sound of the seeds of life expanding in a great kiss. Again and again, more and more distinctly, as though they were approaching the soil, his mates were hammering. In the fiery rays of the sun on this youthful morning the country seemed full of that sound. Men were springing forth, a black avenging army, germinating slowly in the furrows, growing towards the harvests of the next century, and their germination would soon burst open the earth.

NOTES

---

p. 5 Marchiennes: a small town in the Nord department of northern France, situated between Valenciennes to the east and Douai to the west. Montsou is a fictitious place, based on the mining community of Anzin, which Zola visited in 1884 to prepare the novel. The name suggests ironically 'mont de sous', mountain of money.

p. 5 March: though it is never indicated clearly in the text, one can deduce that the action of *Germinal* begins in March 1866 and ends in April 1867.

p. 6 Étienne Lantier: born in 1846, he is one of the illegitimate sons of Gervaise Macquart, the heroine of *L'Assommoir* (1877), and Auguste Lantier, the villain of the same novel.

p. 7 The Voreux: the name of the pit introduces the theme of the voracious monster swallowing its daily ration of human flesh.

p. 7 ... the people: the character alludes to: (1) the industrial and financial crisis of 1866, brought about by reckless speculation during the middle years of the Second Empire; (2) Napoleon III's expedition to Mexico and the Mexican war, an attempt to establish and secure the rule of the archduke Ferdinand Maximilian of Austria as Emperor of Mexico. Having begun in 1861, fighting was continuing in 1866 and would do so until, at the insistence of the United States, the French troops withdrew the following year; (3) an epidemic of cholera which broke out in the Valenciennes region, in fact, later in the year 1866.

p. 9 Bonnemort: another ironic name, meaning 'Good Death'.

p. 19 the Emperor and the Empress: Louis Napoleon Bonaparte (1808–73), having been elected President of the Second Republic in December 1848 and having taken full powers after the *coup d'état* of December 1851, was proclaimed Emperor on 2 December 1852. He married a Spanish countess, Eugénie de Montijo, in 1853.

p. 24 la Mouquette: this hearty and lusty character contrasts significantly with the slight, submissive and sexually retarded Catherine.

p. 37 poison to him: the first reference to the tainted blood of the Macquart branch of the Rougon-Macquart family. The fatal flaw of inherited alcoholism, despite Étienne's attempts to hold it in check, will manifest itself at several points in the novel.

p. 38 Rue de la Goutte-d'Or: the setting of *L'Assommoir* (1877), Zola's novel dealing with the fate of Étienne's mother, Gervaise Macquart, and her hopeless struggle against poverty and degradation in a slum of Paris.

p. 41 a game of crosse: Zola's notes on his stay in Anzin contain details of the rules of this game, a rudimentary form of golf, played with an egg-shaped ball over long distances with two teams of two players. Confusingly there was a game for two players, also called 'crosse' (or 'jeu du criquet'), seemingly a simple form of cricket, in which the players took turns to defend a goal and to hit the ball in order to score runs.

p. 64 in a century: despite the severe economic depression of 1866, the Second Empire was generally a period of considerable prosperity, during which even the wages of some workers rose and huge fortunes were made amongst the upper classes.

p. 67 the Salon: the official annual art exhibition in Paris, dating back to 1791, which by 1866 exhibited over 3,000 paintings. In 1863 Napoleon III instituted the 'Salon des Refusés' for works, including many early Impressionist paintings, rejected by the conservative judges of the official salon.

p. 78 ... little hands: this episode recalls Marie Antoinette's legendary reply when told of the lack of bread amongst the starving people of Paris: 'Qu'ils mangent donc de la brioche!', usually rendered as 'Let them eat cake!' 'Brioche' is a slightly sweet, light bread.

p. 79 ... wretchedness: 'Bas-de-Soie' means 'Silk Stockings' and 'Paie-tes-Dettes' 'Pay-Your-Debts'.

p. 114 Souvarine: Zola's preliminary notes indicate his intention to make of this character 'a frightening figure'. This somewhat anachronistic and out-of-place character may have emerged to some degree from Zola's conversations with the Russian novelist Turgenev. He inherits certain characteristics of the Russian revolutionary Peter Kropotkin, an exponent of 'propaganda by the deed', who similarly renounced his noble origins. Souvarine's ideas, however, are closer to Bakunin's, the fiery Russian anarchist whom he evokes later in the novel.

p. 116 Pologne: 'Poland'. If the name of the rabbit has any political significance, it may refer to the long history of martyrdom and repression of Poland, particularly at the hands of the Russians. The Polish insurrection of 1863-4 had recently been crushed, ending hopes of establishing an independent national state.

p. 116 ... in London: The International Working Men's Association, known as the First International, was founded at a mass meeting in London on 28 September 1864. Though he had no direct role in organizing the meeting, Karl Marx soon became the leader of the General Council of the Association. Members were organized in local groups that were integrated into a national federation. The headquarters of the General Council were in London, with the annual congress meeting in different cities. Zola indirectly depicts in *Germinal* the dissensions within the First International, having consulted Émile de Laveleye's study *Le Socialisme contemporain*, 2nd ed. (Paris, 1883). Contending factions included reformist followers of Proudhon's ideas and radical disciples of Blanqui, but the main struggle was between Marxists and Bakuninists, leading to a split in the International at the congress in The Hague in 1872.

p. 118 '89: that is, 1789, the date of the (first) French Revolution.

p. 118 prison of hunger: Souvarine is referring to the 'iron law of wages' outlined by the British economist David Ricardo (1772–1823), according to which the wages of workers inevitably stabilize around the subsistence level. Any rise in wage rates above the subsistence level leads the working population to increase, bringing about more competition for work. This glut of labour causes wages to fall back to the subsistence level.

p. 119 *Combat*: the titles of the newspapers that Étienne reads, *Le Combat* [*Struggle*] and *Le Vengeur* [*The Avenger*], mentioned later, are based on real, left-wing publications of the period following the events of *Germinal*: *L'Égalité* [*Equality*] and *La Bataille* [*The Battle*]. Two newspapers with the names that Zola uses did, however, briefly exist in 1870.

p. 121 the Prince Imperial: Eugène Louis Napoleon, born in 1856. Such gifts of portraits of the Imperial family were not only an attempt to promote family values during the Second Empire, but also a part of the highly developed propaganda of the regime, a way of forming and perpetuating the image of the Napoleonic dynasty. After the fall of the Second Empire, the Prince was destined to die fighting in the British army against the Zulus in 1879.

p. 122 St Barbe's Day: (or **St Barbara's Day**): 4 December, the day of the 'patron' saint of miners.

p. 134 *L'Hygiène du mineur*: not a known source. Zola took copious notes on a number of works dealing with the occupational hazards of mining and incorporated the information into his novel.

p. 135 ... with whom he lived: Zola took this expression from one of his documentary sources: Georges Stell, *Les Cahiers de doléances des mineurs français* (Paris, Bureaux du capitaliste, 1883).

p. 137 your certificate: the practice of giving industrial workers a 'certificate' (*livret* in French), which bore the individual's name, a physical description, details of past employment and of outstanding debts, dated back to Napoleonic times. The document was returned to the worker when he left the job or was fired. Under the Second Empire the procedure was reinforced and applied to women. Though, as in the case of Étienne, employers did not always respect the law, they were required to keep the *livrets* of their workers and, in certain places, have them stamped by the police. The practice was officially abolished in 1890.

p. 138 to its efforts: Zola came across this saying by Saint-Simon, the French philosopher, economist and utopian political thinker (1760–1825), in one of his sources, Laveleye's study, *Le Socialisme contemporain*.

p. 166 École Polytechnique: This élite 'school' was founded in 1794 and was given a military status in 1804 by Napoleon. Responsible to the Ministry of Defence, it educates future high-ranking civil servants and military officers and has as its motto: 'Pour la Patrie, les Sciences, la Gloire' ['For Country, Science, Glory'].

p. 172 Louis-Philippe: he ruled France from 1830 until he was deposed in the 1848 revolution, which ushered in the short-lived Second Republic. The constitutional monarchy, despite its repressions, seemed to Monsieur Grégoire more liberal than the dictatorship of Napoleon III.

p. 173 dangerous concessions: despite the Emperor's avowed sympathy for the working classes, the Second Empire was a repressive regime. After 1860, however, significant concessions were made under pressure from Orleanist liberals and, to a lesser degree, republicans seeking a restoration of the parliamentary system. These mild reforms anticipated the so-called 'Liberal Empire' of 1870.

p. 187 1848: La Maheude remembers the events of 1848 when the February Revolution ousted Louis-Philippe but was unable to prevent widespread unemployment and famine. The government of the new Republic brutally put down a second revolt of the workers in June of the same year.

p. 195 ... they would see: Étienne's views are taken from sections of laveleye's book and evoke the following thinkers and theories:

– Karl Marx (1818–23), German social philosopher and the main theorist of modern socialism and communism, author of the monumental *Das Kapital* (vol. I, 1867) and, with Friedrich Engels, of the famous *Communist Manifesto* (1848). Marx asserted that an inexorable class struggle determines the course of the history of society, that the bourgeoisie had inevitably outlived its worth as the most productive force of society, having flourished out of the exploitation of the proletariat, and that it was due to be overthrown by revolutionary action.

– Pierre Joseph Proudhon (1809–65), French social theorist, author of *What Is Property?* (1840) – to which he replied 'Property is theft' – a work in which he most famously outlined his anarchist views. He later sought to establish a national bank that would redistribute credit to the advantage of the working class and advocated a system of 'mutualism' whereby small federated groups would negotiate with one another on economic and political matters on the basis of consensus.

– Ferdinand Lassalle (1825–64), German socialist who, influenced to some degree by Marx, elaborated a theory of state socialism according to which the state would provide capital outlays to enable the workers to establish cooperatives.

– collectivism: in general terms, any political theory according to which the individual only acquires significance by membership of a social entity such as a race, class or nation. In economic terms, as here, any theory that favours the abolition of private property and advocates the collective ownership of the means of production, distribution and exchange.

p. 197 Bakunin the Exterminator: Mikhail Bakunin (1814–76), Russian revolutionary, political writer and one of the chief propagators of anarchist theories, took an active part in subversive movements in a number of European countries. He held to a doctrine of extreme individualism and was opposed to Marx's philosophy of impersonal historical forces. He put his trust in the revolutionary capacities of the peasants whereas Marx saw the industrial proletariat as the source of revolutionary change. His differences with Marx, who had him expelled from the International in 1872, caused a deep split in the European revolutionary movement for several years. But, like Marx, Bakunin was uncompromising in his views and vigorously advocated the overthrow of the present order by violent methods.

p. 231 ... at neither fire nor blood: Étienne's views expressed here are a confused mixture of anarchist ideas taken largely from Bakunin and collectivist ideas from Marx and Guesde.

p. 248 ... the edge of it: Tartaret, the burning mine, is based upon fact, for Zola read about such cases in one of his sources: *La Vie souterraine, ou les mines et les mineurs* (Paris, Hachette, 1866) by Louis Laurent Simonin. Though the known examples did not occur in the Nord region, Zola incorporated the phenomenon into his novel to show the superstitious nature of the miners, but also to create a kind of symbolic topography relating to a main theme of the text: the Utopia of an eternal spring emerging from the hell of the mine below.

p. 284 the *Marseillaise*: this revolutionary battle song, which was composed by Claude Rouget de l'Isle, was commonly sung by striking miners. Banned during the Second Empire, as it had been during previous reactionary régimes, it became the national anthem in 1879.

p. 284 a guillotine-blade: like the singing of 'la Marseillaise', an evident reference to the French Revolution.

p. 307 ... demolishing the bourgeois society of '89: the Abbé Ranvier's views are representative of the militant Catholic socialism of the time, which attempted to rally the working classes to the cause of the church.

p. 332 a need to taste blood: homicidal mania, which was originally to be a far more prominent feature of Étienne's character, was passed on to and fully developed in the character of Jacques Lantier, invented for the purpose in *La Bête humaine* [*The Human Beast*] (1890).

p. 338 'Amour', engraved in black letters: the inscription 'Love' gives an ironic twist to the knifing episode, which will become a source of obsession in Étienne's mind.

p. 363 ... to the soldiers: this incident recalls the stoning of Saint Étienne, the first Christian martyr, giving a biblical resonance to the character's mission to save the people.

p. 367 Darwin: Charles Darwin (1809–82), renowned English naturalist, famous for his theory of evolution, author of *On the Origin of Species by means of Natural Selection* (1859). The 'struggle for existence' and the 'survival of the fittest' are key notions in Darwin's system of natural selection, creating the conditions which favour the survival and continuation of certain species. Darwinism, as Souvarine points out, does not sit well with socialism, but can more easily be used to justify the advantages of those in power who can claim to have flourished in the struggle for existence.

p. 368 ... for six days': Zola seems to combine in this episode two real incidents from the history of assassination attempts on the life of Alexander II: on 1 December 1879, the German nihilist Leo Hartmann, with the help of Sophia Perovskaïa, tried unsuccessfully to blow up his train near Moscow; on 15 April 1881, Sophia Perovskaïa was executed, along with four accomplices, after the assassination of the Tsar on 13 March 1881.

p. 425 ... continuance of the race?: Étienne's persistence in evoking Darwin's views to justify his belief in the natural emancipation of the workers reflects Zola's own growing conviction, evident in a number of the later novels of the Rougon-Macquart series, that social progress would emerge, not from the activities of politicians or from the application of intellectual schemes, but from the very struggles of life itself.

CONCISE GLOSSARY OF MINING TERMS

brakesman: the engine-man who attended to the winding machine and directed the movement of cars and cages.

carman: a driver.

cutting: an area of the coal-face.

earth-cutting: in the afternoons the rippers or stonemen would clear away in the earth-cutting the rubble left after the pikemen had finished hewing the coal and fill in the trenches in the seam.

engine-man: a mechanic employed to service the machines of the mine.

exhaustion pump: the drainage pump for drawing up water infiltrating into the shaft and the galleries.

lander: a worker who loaded the cages with trams or miners and operated the descent and the rise of the cages.

patching: doing repair work in the mine.

pikeman: the cutter, i.e. the miner who hewed the coal with a pickaxe.

pit-frame: the headgear of the pit, the structure supporting the pulleys.

pit-bank: the slag heap or the raised ground or platform at the surface where the coal was screened and sorted.

pit-eye: the loading-bay.

platform: the slag heap.

putter (or **putter girl**): the haulier who pushed the trams from the junction to the working face and returned with the loaded trams.

receiving room: the hall at the top of the landing stage or pithead where the coal was received.

screen: a large sieve for grading or sizing the coal.

screener: the worker who sifted and loaded the coal at the pit-bank.

screening shed: the building in which the coal was sorted.

shaft: the deep pit sunk from the surface by means of which a mine was worked.

sifter: another name for the screener or sorter who worked at the surface.

siftings: the products of the sifting process whereby the coal was separated according to size.

stalls: sections of the working space at the coal face for one or two miners.

timbering: the use of wooden supports in the working area to prevent the rock from caving in.

tipping cradle: a device for tilting over the tubs to unload the contents.

tram: the tub in which the putter transported the coal.

trammer: another name for the putter.

tubbing: the lining of a pit shaft or tunnel with watertight casing.

winding machine (or **engine**): the equipment for lowering and raising loads through the shaft.

ZOLA AND HIS CRITICS

By the time *Germinal* appeared in March 1885 the publication of a new Zola novel was a major literary event and there was a growing awareness of the writer's importance as a major literary figure in France and abroad. Previous novels, notably *L'Assommoir*, *Nana* and *Pot-Bouille*, had provoked scandalized reactions and led to vehement denunciations from mainly conservative critics outraged by what they considered to be a crude and immoral form of literature. Though he was a shy and retiring man, controversy was not entirely unwelcome to the novelist who, more afraid of indifference than of dispute and disrepute, saw such denunciations as a sign of his vitality. Nor were the controversies entirely unprovoked. In his preliminary notes for *Germinal*, for example, Zola had written about one particular scene, that 'the bourgeois reader must be made to feel a shudder of terror'. Zola's publisher, too, Georges Charpentier, was far from unhappy about the stir caused by the works of his friend and most successful writer. After the windfall of *L'Assommoir*, each novel was launched by a carefully planned publicity campaign. So too with *Germinal*. Even though, as was the convention, the novels had already appeared in instalments in a newspaper – *Germinal* in *Gil Blas* from 26 November 1884 to 25 February 1885 – thousands of copies of a Zola novel were snapped up on the first day of publication.

The immediate reaction to *Germinal* in the Parisian press was predictable, with the usual objections about the inaccuracy of certain details of content and protests about the crudity of certain scenes. When criticized, for example, for having his miners from the Nord region speak like Parisian workers, Zola patiently replied that, if he had used their patois, he doubted if anyone would have bothered to read the novel (*Le Matin*, 7 March 1885). To the charge that he had disparagingly misrepresented and bestialized the noble, hard-working and virtuous miners of the north, he replied that sentimental arguments were irrelevant and that, if anything, he had attenuated the truth (*Le Figaro*, 5 April 1885). To the accusation that his novel was crude and 'sensual', he responded that, whereas his critics defined 'man' by his brain, he defined him by all of his organs and that his depiction of the lower classes would have been false and incomplete if he had not taken into account 'all the consequences of the ignorance and deprivation in which they had to live' (*Le Figaro*, 27 April 1885).

More discerning critics of *Germinal* tended to concentrate on the artistic merits of the novel, drawing comparisons between the descriptions of life in the mines and Dante's *Inferno*, between the epic sweep of the novel and Homer's works, between the descriptions of the plight of the starving workers and Hugo's *Les Misérables*. Like other critics of the day, Louis Desprez, a young naturalist writer, was moved by the lyricism of *Germinal*, writing to its author (on 8 March 1885):

> *L'Assommoir* was more a 'novel'; *Germinal* is more a 'poem', with Romantic settings, like the forest bathed in moonlight in which the miners' meeting is held, [. . .]. In you the lyricist and the observer are mixed; everything is 'seen' and becomes enormous [. . .].
>
> Decidedly, I think like you that strict observation is not enough, and that one cannot write a novel as one draws up an account in a register, coldly, with fine bourgeois indifference. Anger and pity have to breathe through the pages. You have expressed better than anyone the joys and the miseries of the human animal. In your work the flesh takes its pleasures and endures its suffering: that is your great glory. [. . .] In *Germinal* there are painful pages which cause a physical malaise in the reader. If Catherine's climb up the perpendicular ladders or the tortures of the last days are tragic, it is because you bleed, you suffer with your characters.

Similarly, the writer Gustave Geffroy, having evoked the teeming life, the energy, the movement, sounds and smells of the novel (in *La Justice*, 14 July 1885), is led to wonder:

> These hallucinations in face of the material world, this creation of living objects, these violent interpretations of the unconscious forces of life, these cadences that run through a whole volume, these rhythmic repetitions, is all this not enough to reveal in Émile Zola the poet that people generally refuse to see in him, the poet who can superbly magnify and idealize the world of things?

Octave Mirbeau, another writer sympathetic to Zola, was struck, on reading critical reactions to *Germinal*, by 'the hate that the distinguished bourgeois harbour against Mr Zola' (*Le Matin*, 6 November 1885). This hate, he adds, has changed in its forms of expression, but it is no less ferocious than in the more violent responses to earlier novels:

> It is no longer at the stage of representing Mr Zola as a wild and dangerous being, an anarchist of art, writing on top of a barricade, with dynamite. No! He is now depicted with a tow-like tuft of hair on his head, a large cash-box between his legs, and bawling out to show off his wares and to invite gawking passers-by into his booth.

Henry Céard, a fellow naturalist writer, writing in a Buenos Aires newspaper, *Sud América* (17–18 April 1885), defends Zola against charges of indecency and, like other critics of *Germinal*, emphasizes the novel's poetic qualities:

> Yes, his literature is above all a literature of resonance. [...] Facts only exist for him as springboards on which his imagination, always in both a tranquil and excited state in his solitude, takes infinite leaps and bounds. Consequently, he sees less what he looks at than what he imagines. The workings of his mind take over from reality, and the truth to which he devotes himself is always a subjective truth; he sees, but in himself, like mystics and visionaries. These qualities are essentially poetic. He proceeds always either by accumulation or by exaggeration. The most ordinary of sights, as he describes them, take on an unforgettable intensity.

Céard goes on, in his long article, to observe that Zola's characters all have a 'symbolic' function, like Bonnemort, the resigned miner, Maheu, the miner waking to new ideas, Chaval, the traitor, Lantier, the socialist revolutionary, and so on. Indeed, the real subject of the novel is, according to Céard, the crowd, 'the immense sob of humanity from which rises the echo, the clamour of universal suffering'. He even suggests that Zola would have done better to have dispensed with individual characters altogether. In a famous reply (a letter to Céard of 22 March 1885), Zola objects to the view that his characters have no individual life and points out that the main protagonists, like Étienne and la Maheude, develop during the course of the novel and are an essential part of his scheme: 'My subject is the reciprocal action and reaction of the individual and the crowd, the one upon the other.' As for his exaggerations, he makes the much-quoted claim that they are integral to the rendering of truth: 'Now – I am perhaps wrong on this point – I still believe that, for my part, I distort in the direction of the truth. I have a tendency to expand true details, leaping up to the stars on the springboard of exact observation. Truth wings its way up to the symbol.'

A measure of the general approval with which *Germinal* was met by some of the most talented critics of the time in France is the important article by Jules Lemaitre, in the *Revue politique et littéraire* (14 March 1885), then in his book *Les Contemporains* (Paris, 1886; trans. by A. W. Evans in *Literary Impressions*, London, Daniel O'Connor, 1921). This article is not only a significant contribution to the discussion of the merits of Zola's novel but also, in view of the eminence of the critic himself, a landmark study in the reception and acceptance of the novelist's works in his own country. Lemaitre too underlines the importance of the crowd in the novel:

> It is thus the story, not of a man or of some men, but of a multitude. I do not know of any novel in which such masses are made to live and move, at one moment it crawls and swarms, at another it is carried along in a dizzy movement by the urge of blind instincts. The poet, with his robust patience, with his gloomy brutality, with his power of evocation, unrolls a series of vast and lamentable pictures, composed of monochrome details which pile up, pile up, ascend and spread out like a tide – a day in the mine, a day in the workmen's dwellings, a meeting of the strikers in a clearing of the woods, the furious rush of three thousand unhappy souls over the flat country, the impact of this mass against the soldiers, ten days of lingering death in the flooded mine. . . .

Whilst defining briefly the role of each character in the novel, Lemaitre also argues that Zola had no intention of writing a 'psychological tragedy', but produced a 'drama of the sensations' with its 'holocausts of flesh' and, amongst the novel's symbolic evocations, 'its monstrous invisible idol, crouching somewhere, one knows not where, like the God Mithra in his sanctuary'. Zola, he adds, leaves it to the psychologists to write the monograph of each character, for he 'has only an imagination for vast material wholes and infinite external details'. Lemaitre's much-quoted conclusion situates Zola's talent in a long-standing epic tradition:

> The characters in epic poetry are not less general than the subject, and, as they represent vast groups, they appear to be larger than in nature. It is the same with M. Zola's characters, although this is reached by a contrary method. Whilst the old poets endeavour to deify their figures, we have seen that he animalizes his. But this even adds to the epic appearance; for he manages, through the falsehood of this reduction, to give to modern figures the simplicity of primitive types. He sets masses in motion, as in epic poetry. And the *Rougon-Macquart* series has also its

marvels. In epic poetry the gods were originally the personifications of natural forces. M. Zola lends to those forces, either freely let loose or disciplined by human industry, a terrifying life, the beginnings of a soul, an obscure and monstrous will.

There is an artless and rudimentary philosophy in epic poetry. It is the same with the *Rougon-Macquart* series. The only difference is that the wisdom of the old poets is generally optimistic, and consoles and ennobles man as much as it can, whilst that of M. Zola is black and desperate. But in both there is the same simplicity, the same artlessness of conception. Finally and especially, the procedure of M. Zola's novels is, I know not how, that of the ancient epics, by the slow power, the broad sweep, the tranquil accumulation of details, the absolute frankness of the narrator's methods. He no more hurries than Homer does.

Lemaitre then sums up his study with a single formula to characterize Zola's series, one with which the novelist was not entirely in agreement because of its negative implications: 'a pessimist epic of human animality'.

Significantly missing from these often eloquent assessments is any consideration of the political message of *Germinal*. The major critics clearly fought shy of committing themselves on such dangerous terrain and preferred to focus on the literary aspects of the novel, particularly in view of the ambiguity of its implications. Not that others refrained from such commentary. A left-wing deputy, Clovis Hughes, for example, gave a lecture on the socialist value of *Germinal*, whilst, at the other extreme, there were denunciations of what was perceived as the novel's subversive and treacherous attack on the order of French society. But most of his contemporary readers would, no doubt, have agreed with the novelist's own assessment of the political purpose of the work in a letter to D. Dautresme (mid-December 1885), when he was accused of being a socialist or a revolutionary by his more dismissive conservative critics:

> *Germinal* is a work of pity, and not a work of revolution. What I wanted was to cry out to the happy people of this world, to those who are the masters:
>
>> Take care, look below ground, look at these wretches who work and suffer. There is still perhaps time to avoid the final catastrophes. But hurry and be just, otherwise there is a danger: the earth will open up and nations will be swallowed up in one of the most terrible upheavals of History.

Yes, a cry of pity, a cry for justice, that is all I wish for. If the ground continues to crack, if tomorrow the disasters that have been predicted terrify the world, it will be because I will not have been heard.

Despite the commercial success of the novel, the large number of reviews and the laudatory pronouncements by certain important critics, *Germinal* did not, however, have as much impact and certainly not the same shock effect as *L'Assommoir*, *Nana* or *Pot-Bouille*, even taking into account its own controversial themes. As Alain Pagès puts it in his study of the novel's reception (*La Bataille littéraire*, Paris, Séguier, 1989, p. 243), *Germinal* 'did not have its legend, like the other popular Zola novels'. The fact is that the novelist's war with the critics was largely over; only occasional skirmishes remained. In any case, he seemed uncommitted to either side in the political struggles that he depicted. One could even argue that, though critics made comparisons with ancient literature, his novel was ahead of its time, dealing with the problems of the class struggle and of industrial strife, which later generations would be better able to interpret in the light of *post-factum* ideological considerations and political awareness.

British and American critics of the nineteenth century were either too affected by Anglo-Saxon attitudes of morality and taste or only had access to the highly bowdlerized English translations to be able to produce significant assessments of *Germinal*. An important exception was Havelock Ellis, who, as we know, was totally familiar with the full French text and who, two years after doing the translation, wrote about the novel in a general article on 'Zola: The Man and His Work', published in *The Savoy* (of January 1896, pp. 67–80), then in his book *Affirmations* (London, Constable, 1898, pp. 131–57). Ellis pays due attention to Zola's visionary qualities: 'Whatever is robust, whatever is wholesomely exuberant, whatever, wholesomely or not, is possessed by the devouring fury of life – of such things Zola can never have enough. [. . .] All the forces of Nature, it seems to him, are raging in the fury of generative desire or reposing in the fullness of swelling maturity.' But, in contrast to Desprez's view, the English critic sees irony and impartiality as the most distinctive features of Zola's vision:

Irony may be called the soul of Zola's work, the embodiment of his moral attitude towards life. It has its source, doubtless, like so much else that is characteristic, in his early days of poverty and aloofness from the experiences of life. There is a fierce impartiality – the impartiality of one who is outside and shut off – in this manner of presenting the brutalities and egoisms and pettiness of men. [...] Zola believes, undoubtedly, in a reformed, even perhaps a revolutionised, future of society, but he has no illusions. He has no tenderness for the working-classes, no pictures of rough diamonds. We may see this very clearly in *Germinal*. Here every side of the problem of modern capitalism is presented: the gentle-natured shareholding class unable to realise a state of society in which people should not live on dividends and give charity; the official class with their correct authoritative views, very sure that they will always be needed to control labour and maintain social order; and the workers, some brutalised, some suffering like dumb beasts, some cringing to the bosses, some rebelling madly, a few striving blindly for justice.

[...] His pity for men and women is boundless; his disdain is equally boundless. It is only towards animals that his tenderness is untouched by contempt; some of his most memorable passages are concerned with the sufferings of animals. The New Jerusalem may be fitted up, but the Montsou miners will never reach it; they will fight for the first small, stuffy, middle-class villa they meet on the way. And Zola pours out the stream of his pitiful, pitiless irony on the weak, helpless, erring children of men. It is this moral energy, combined with his volcanic exuberance, which lifts him to a position of influence above the greater artists with whom we may compare him.

For Ellis, Zola's works will be of inestimable value to future historians:

What would we not give for a thirteenth-century Zola! [...] The abbeys and churches of those days have in part come down to us, but no *Germinal* remains to tell of the lives and thoughts of the men who hewed these stones, and piled them, and carved them. How precious such a record would have been we may realise when we recall the incomparable charm of Chaucer's prologue to *The Canterbury Tales*. But our children's children, with the same passions alive in their hearts under incalculably different circumstances, will in the pages of the Rougon-Macquart series find themselves back again among all the strange remote details of a vanished world. What a fantastic and terrible page of old-world romance!

During the first half of the twentieth century, *Germinal* continued to be widely read throughout the world as one of Zola's most popular works and emerged, alongside *L'Assommoir*, as his greatest achievement in the novel form. Yet this period, the familiar limbo period of neglect after a writer's death, is characterized in general by an almost total disregard for Zola's works by professional critics. Certain prominent writers during these years deplored this neglect, amongst them André Gide, hardly a disciple of naturalism, who, in his diary, considered it a 'monstrous injustice' and ranked *Germinal* as one of the ten best novels written in French. Nevertheless, in that age of contending political systems, Zola's social novels attracted comment from critics, mainly of the left, preoccupied with the ideology of literary texts. There is, in fact, a long tradition, from Lafargue to Lukács, of Marxist views on Zola that are highly critical of his naturalist worldview, of his tendency to assimilate society to a biological model, of his failure to depict the class struggle in other than Darwinian terms, of his fatalism and his preference for reformist solutions to social injustices. Thus Lukács, who has come to represent the orthodox Marxist view of the period, argues in his study 'The Zola Centenary' in *Studies in European Realism*, trans. Edith Bone (London, Hillway, 1950), that, even though the novelist 'fought a courageous battle against the reactionary evolution of French capitalism', the ideology of his own class was 'too deeply ingrained in his thinking' and his novels are too Romantic, rhetorical, descriptive, merely painting the 'outer trappings of modern life'. For Lukács, Zola's fate is to be 'one of the literary tragedies of the nineteenth century', that of a writer destined for great things, but inhibited by capitalism from accomplishing his true destiny:

> Zola's resolute struggle for the cause of progress will survive many of his one-time fashionable novels, and will place his name in history side by side with that of Voltaire who defended Calas as Zola defended Dreyfus. Surrounded by the fake democracy and corruption of the Third Republic, by the false so-called democrats who let no day pass without betraying the traditions of the great French revolution, Zola stands head and shoulders above them as the model of the courageous and high-principled *bourgeois* who – even if he failed to understand the essence of socialism – did not abandon democracy even when behind it the Socialist demands of the working class were already voiced.

Other Marxist critics, however, saw more in Zola's works than good intentions, like the militant communist writer Henri Barbusse, who, in his biography *Zola* (1932), translated by M. B. and F. C. Green (London, Dent, 1932), admires the novelist as a 'force of nature', as a fighter for truth, a writer who was 'instinctively right', a 'socialist without knowing it' (pp. 249–64):

> For Zola's books, and notably *Germinal*, fell like meteors amidst the dull and affected books featuring the modern worker.

Germinal, a great book, is, as much as *L'Assommoir*, drawn from life. It cast into the midst of foggy public opinion a terrible cargo of pictures of poverty and of sombre strugglings that seemed to come from another world.

It made the ghosts of the damned of the earth walk the streets of the capitals. It revealed to every passer-by their physical shapes with eerie frightfulness, and their existence – if not their destiny – to the marrow. And thus it spread an uneasiness that is the nightmare of revolutionary truth (pp. 172–3).

Germinal is, in fact, the one novel by Zola that left-wing critics have singled out for admiration, whatever their reservations about his stated views and his art in general. Thus in his *Zola, semeur d'orages* (Paris, Éditions sociales, 1952), the commentator on and translator of the works of Marx, Engels and Lenin, Jean Fréville, though he systematically takes up the usual Marxist criticisms of Zola's naturalist views and defines him as a 'bourgeois democrat, the prisoner of his class prejudices', hails him as 'the gatherer of storms, raining fire and brimstone on bourgeois society' and singles out *Germinal* for particular praise as an atonement for the errors of *L'Assommoir*:

That Zola's socialism, even in *Germinal*, does not derive from revolutionary Marxism and that his socialism remains impregnated with petit-bourgeois sentimentality, no one will deny. But whoever seeks to make a general assessment on Zola the novelist must start from this essential observation: it was by delving into the reality of the class struggle and by remaining faithful to it that he wrote his masterpiece.

Realism triumphs in *Germinal*. The true picture of the life of the miners forces Zola to condemn capitalism. [. . .]

[. . .] After the lyricism of *L'Assommoir*, after the sad poetry of the still, a symbol of fatal decline, there follows the somber epic of the mine and the strike, the glorification of the struggles of the workers, the burning breath of the storm that will carry away the old world . . . (pp. 103–5).

The fiftieth anniversary of Zola's death, in 1952, signaled the start of an upsurge of interest amongst literary critics in the novelist and his works. Since then there are few French writers, if any, on whom more critical attention has been lavished, with a constant stream of books, articles, editions, translations, adaptations, conferences, research projects and programmes. *Germinal* has acquired a central place in this massive reassessment of Zola's works as a key text to which modern critics apply their various modes of interpretation.

Whereas most critics in the early part of this period tended to concentrate on the historical and biographical sources of Zola's novel, Marcel Girard broke new ground in an important article on the 'universe' of *Germinal* ('L'univers de *Germinal*', in the *Revue des Sciences humaines*, January–March 1953), presenting a coherent thematic study of the material landscape, the colours, the 'monsters' of the mine, the evasions of the miners into dreaming, sexual pleasure, rebellion, from the oppressive, weighty hell of their fate:

> All these themes come together in the episode of the soldier, Jules, whose corpse is taken down into the depths of Réquillart by Étienne and Jeanlin. There, he is crushed slowly by the collapse of the gallery that Étienne destroys behind him. [...] If Zola has often represented the earth, in the novel of that name [*La Terre*], and even in the last pages of *Germinal*, as the source of all life and as the mother of all men, he also tends to consider it as the shroud of men. Between these two myths, the one as primitive as the other, Zola hesitates throughout all of his works. The optimistic myth – with a few exceptions – will generally dominate after *Germinal*, as if the writer had exorcized in this novel all the demons of the night and freed himself from the oppressive weight of the material world (p. 67).

British and North American critics have been particularly active in this wave of renewed interest in Zola's life and works. The distinguished critic Irving Howe, for instance, wrote an incisive study of *Germinal* in the afterword to an American edition of the novel (New York, New American Library, 1970). Casting aside his own inherited prejudices against the author, he was 'overwhelmed' on rereading the novel 'by its magnitude of structure, its fertility of imagination, its reenactment of a central experience in modern life'. He defines its main theme as the release of 'one of the central myths of the modern era: the story of how the dumb acquire speech' and sees Zola transcending in this novel the limitations of his deterministic beliefs:

> The nineteenth-century novelist – Dickens or Balzac, Hardy or Zola – enacts in his own career the vitalism about which the thought of his age drives him to a growing skepticism. Zola's three or four great novels are anything but inert or foredoomed. He may start with notions of inevitability, but the current of his narrative boils with energy and

novelty. *Germinal* ends with the gloom of defeat, but not a gloom predestined. There is simply too much appetite for experience in Zola, too much sympathy and solidarity with the struggles by which men try to declare themselves, too much hope for the generations always on the horizon and always promising to undo the wrongs of the past, for *Germinal* to become a mere reflex of a system of causality. Somehow – we have every reason to believe – Zola's gropings into the philosophy of determinism freed him to become a writer of energy, rebellion, and creation.

In general, as was already evident in the earlier studies of the novel, overall assessments tend to be divided between discussions of its political significance and appreciations of its artistic effects. The skilfully crafted opening scene is frequently evoked, as in Colin Smethurst's brief introduction to the novel (*Zola: 'Germinal'*, London, Edward Arnold, 1974):

Before touching on questions of social description and conflict, ideologies and themes, *Germinal* hits us as an atmosphere: blackness, bleakness, earth more liquid than solid, a sort of cosmic broth gone dead; the only defining element the straight-line road drawing along it a man. The man's first observations to emerge from this shadowy world are a sense of numbness, then of fear. The three fires which appear, disappear, reappear, the gigantic and fantastic set of buildings – not yet perceived as a mine – animated with breathings from an invisible source, have much in common with the blasted heath of *Macbeth* as a place of doubt and uncertainty, fear, monstrosity and blackness (p. 26).

F. W. J. Hemmings also admires Zola's Balzacian ability to envelop the reader initially, before the main conflict begins, in the atmosphere of the sinister mine and the life of the mining community. This novel, which the author made into 'the vessel for the darkest poetry of [his] maturity', is remarkable also, according to the same critic, who is the author of the standard study of Zola in English – *Emile Zola*, 2nd ed. (Oxford, Clarendon Press, 1966) – for its crowd-scenes, 'instances of the type-phenomena of mass-psychology', crowds at play, at work, at meetings, in rebellion, in a panic: 'Nearly all these scenes illustrate the truth that Zola intuitively grasped, that people in the aggregate are more ferocious, but also more cowardly, than each separate component of the group.' As for the novel's political message, F. W. J. Hemmings concludes his chapter on this novel with a balanced view:

Germinal, in short, is neither a revolutionary nor a reactionary work; remaining carefully and intentionally neutral, Zola left unexamined the full political significance of the social issues that he raised, while he made their existence, and gravity, blindingly clear. It is arguable, however, that in 1885 the mere exposure and graphic portrayal of social injustice constituted in itself a revolutionary act. [...] In publishing this novel Zola was surely fulfilling what Sartre had defined as 'the writer's function': 'to ensure that no one may remain in ignorance of the world and that no one may call himself guiltless of what goes on in it' (p. 209).

Discussion continues on the ideological implications of *Germinal*, with sharp divisions amongst left-wing critics in particular. At one extreme, Paule Lejeune has devoted a whole book to a (rare) virulent attack on *Germinal* as an anti-working-class novel: *'Germinal': un roman antipeuple* (Paris, Nizet, 1978). The author denounces Zola as a 'petit-bourgeois' writer, a self-made man, ambitious, accumulating wealth and possessions, yet writing about the poor, revealing the fear of his own class at the prospect of social revolution, reducing the workers to the level of a horde of barbarians. Referring to an early criticism of *L'Assommoir*, she writes:

And this is what we have seen in every chapter of *Germinal*: a distrust with regard to the masses, a constant denial of their capacities for thought and for organisation, a display of their vulgarity, of their uncontrolled bestial, blood-thirsty violence, as well as, running through the novel, a lesson in resignation presented to the workers through the tragic and demoralising example of the Maheu family. As Ranc said of *L'Assommoir*, it is with 'a bourgeois scorn' that Zola elaborates his naturalist product on the world of the workers (pp. 218–19).

An opposite (and far more typical) view is expressed by another left-wing critic, André Wurmser, who, recognizing the limitations of Zola's socialism, writes (in a collection of articles under the title *Zola*: Paris, Hachette, 1969) of the positive impact of *Germinal* and compares it to the novelist's dramatic intervention in the Dreyfus Affair:

One cannot reread *Germinal*, however much one admires it, without a little irritation. But by virtue of his frank and controlled denunciation of working-class conditions, his depiction of the heroism of the workers, of their misery and, this time, of its causes, by virtue of his picture of the grandeur of la Maheude in revolt and of the misfortunes of la Maheude in defeat, Zola is, even more than he will be at the time of the Affair, a

moment of human conscience. For it is to save millions and millions of
innocent people unjustly condemned by an insolent and parasitical caste
that *Germinal* 'accuses' (p. 225).

More revealing than the sometimes rhetorical statements for or
against *Germinal* are the attempts to define the ideological tensions
inherent in Zola's novel. André Marc Vial, for example, concludes
his study of *'Germinal' et le socialisme de Zola* (Paris, Éditions
sociales, 1975) with what he perceives as being a fundamental
division at the heart of the text:

> Ideology and literature: one can certainly detect two ideologies at work
> in *Germinal*: the one, which the author inherited, mechanistic determin-
> ism, the arm of the bourgeoisie in its militant period; the other, dialectic,
> which emerges in the very struggles of the fourth estate, of the working
> classes. Precisely, *two* ideologies that are contradictory. And not one, a
> systematised view. And this is one of the strengths of the novel, because
> they embrace the contradictory complexity of Zola's *living* vision. A
> great work does not set out to present a codified ideology, but a vision
> of this kind. And it becomes in turn an element of the reality on which
> ideologies function (p. 110).

Such contradictions have been thoroughly explored by the detailed
and perceptive analyses of representatives of the modern tendency
of 'sociocriticism', notably in the incisive studies of Henri Mitterand. In an article on 'Knowledge and Imagination: *Germinal* and
Ideology', in his *Le Discours du roman* (Paris, PUF, 1980), he
writes:

> A sharp divide runs through *Germinal*: the methodologically acquired
> knowledge is split, eroded by the mythical imagery, thus by ideology.
> Hence the novel's literary richness. Paradoxically, it is out of this internal
> discord that the work achieves its best effects. [...] The ideology is not
> fully present, nor fully ambiguous – both mystifying and instructive –
> only because it is woven into the thread of a narrative, of a literary
> structure, and because, in this way, its substance takes shape to the
> extent that the text, in a final paradox, acquires an inexhaustible
> openness of meaning and of effects, and transcends the very social
> structures that inspired the writer's dream (p. 139).

In another article in the same volume, 'Idéologie et mythe: *Germinal*
et les fantasmes de la révolte' ['Ideology and Myth: *Germinal* and
the Fantasies of Revolt', trans. Janice Best], Mitterand again studies
how the workers' rebellion is presented in a 'mythical mode', for

example, in scenes of ritual, propitiatory sacrifice: the castration of Maigrat, the murder of the little soldier, the strangulation of Cécile Grégoire by Bonnemort, scenes in which only marginal figures (women, children, old men) take part and in which the real power of the bourgeoisie is unaffected. The novel employs, furthermore, imagery deriving from the world of nature to denote the miners' revolt:

> In all of these comparisons, the author makes use of a-historical and non-rational concepts which are borrowed sometimes from the order of instinctual behaviour (passionate anger, violence, the thirst for rape, fire and blood).
>
> A type of magical transformation occurs here as well, but it is the author's doing: human actions are naturalised, treated as if they formed an integral part of physical determinism. Historical and social denotation is overwhelmed, submerged by biological and natural connotation. The narrative leaves history behind to inject social tragedy into the series of cataclysms which periodically affect the order of the world and are constituent elements of this order.

Clearly the notion of myth is a key concept in the interpretation of *Germinal* by modern critics, recalling one of the most influential studies dealing with the novel, by Philip Walker, 'Prophetic Myths in Zola' (*PMLA*, September 1959), which explores the mythical dimensions of the novel in a more traditional sense of the term, relating certain events and features to classical mythology. Taking up a similar perspective in his more recent book *'Germinal' and Zola's Philosophical and Religious Thought* (Amsterdam–Philadelphia, John Benjamins, 1984), Walker writes:

> A careful reading of the novel will also show that nearly all the explicit classical mythological allusions scattered throughout its text – the comparison of the women mutilating Maigrat's corpse to Furies, of Mme Hennebeau to Ceres, the naming of the burning mine, Tartaret, after Tartarus, the obvious parallels between the Dieu Inconnu [the Unknown God] and Cronus, or, to mention another example, between the new society prophesied in the conclusion and the Golden Age – suggest particularly Greco-Roman stories of the Creation and the War of the Gods: the cosmic struggles between Uranus and Cronus, Cronus and Jupiter (p. 61).

The ending of the novel, in particular, invites such comparisons:

In some respects, the novel's concluding vision, a new generation of men rising up with the wheat out of the earth after the inundation of Le Voreux, may remind us of the myth of Deucalion and Pyrrha. There are, in addition, such an impressive number of analogies between the Greco-Roman mythical cosmos and the setting of *Germinal* (Oceanus and the Torrent, the Elysian Fields and Catherine's dying hallucinations, the Vale of Enna and Côte-Verte) that it is almost impossible not to believe that Zola had classical mythology, which he knew well, more or less in mind when he wrote the novel and that consciously or unconsciously he was tempted to conceive of the modern social cataclysm that he recounts in it in terms of these ancient myths treating of the succession of the primordial ages, the metamorphoses of primitive gods, and the origins of man (p. 62).

In a chapter of his massive study *Réalité et mythe chez Zola* (Paris, Champion, 1981), Roger Ripoll also dwells upon the mythical dimensions of *Germinal*, though carefully relating them to the subjective points of view of the characters themselves: the myth of capital through the eyes of Étienne and Bonnemort, the visions of hell through the fears of Catherine, all lending a relative significance to their interpretation. But, above all, he emphasizes the dynamic nature of the novel's mythical developments:

There exists therefore a tightly formed interrelationship amongst the elements that go to make up the mythology of *Germinal*. No myth is isolated or gratuitous. A system of classification which would distinguish amongst the myths of fatality (capital, the devouring pit, hell, the earth), the myths of violence (animality and destruction), and the optimistic myth of germination could not submit to rigorous scrutiny. This is, no doubt, because of the relationships of opposition that exist amongst these different myths, but, more than that, it is because of the double role that some of them play: the myth of animality links up submission to fatality and the destructive instinct, whilst the myth of the earth indicates both crushing oppression and renewal. In this world, all is conflict, all is movement, and it is important to note that the novel does not end with an affirmation of the unity of life, in which all the temporary convulsions would be absorbed, but with the prediction of a future which will manifest itself as a disruptive power (p. 748).

SUGGESTIONS FOR FURTHER READING

The standard study of Zola's life and works in English is still F. W. J. Hemmings, *Emile Zola*, 2nd ed. (Oxford, Clarendon Press, 1966), with the same critic's *The Life and Times of Emile Zola* (London, Elek; New York, Scribner's, 1977) providing an immensely readable biographical supplement with excellent illustrations. Also to be strongly recommended is Philip Walker's informative and elegantly written biography, *Zola* (London, Routledge & Kegan Paul, 1985). For more information there are Frederick Brown's recent massive *Zola. A Life* (New York, Farrar Straus Giroux, 1995) and Graham King's *Garden of Zola: Emile Zola and his Novels for English Readers* (London, Barrie & Jenkins; New York, Barnes & Noble, 1978). The collection of essays *Zola and the Craft of Fiction* (Leicester, Leicester University Press, 1990), ed. Robert Lethbridge and Terry Keefe, contains a number of modern interpretations written in English of Zola's art as a novelist. *Critical Essays on Emile Zola* (Boston, Mass., G. K. Hall, 1986), ed. David Baguley, presents a selection of significant studies, some translated from the French, that date from 1868 to the present and includes a stimulating essay on *Germinal* by the American critic Irving Howe and by the leading authority on Zola, Henri Mitterand, as well as a general assessment of the novelist by Havelock Ellis, the author of the present translation.

A number of books written in English deal specifically with *Germinal*. E. M. Grant's *Zola's 'Germinal': a Critical and Historical Study* (Leicester, Leicester University Press, 1962) and Richard H. Zakarian's *Zola's 'Germinal': a Critical Study of Its Primary Sources* (Geneva, Droz, 1972) are informative traditional studies. Philip Walker's *'Germinal' and Zola's Philosophical and Religious Thought* (Amsterdam. John Benjamins, 1984) deals incisively with Zola's ideas as they are manifested in the novel. Colin Smethurst's *Zola: 'Germinal'* (London, Edward Arnold, 1974) is a short but excellent introduction to the background and themes of the novel in the series 'Studies in French Literature'.

Bibliographical information on Zola criticism may be found in

Brian Nelson, *Emile Zola: A Selective Analytical Bibliography* (London, Grant & Cutler, 1982), and, with more detailed annotations, in the chapter on Zola by Philip Walker and David Baguley in *Critical Bibliography of French Literature. The Nineteenth Century*, ed. David Baguley (Syracuse, N.Y., Syracuse University Press, 1994). For more extensive coverage, see the listings in the two volumes of *Bibliographie de la critique sur Emile Zola: vol. I – 1864–1970; vol. II – 1971–1980* (Toronto, University of Toronto Press, 1976 and 1982) by David Baguley, with supplement in *Les Cahiers naturalistes*, a journal devoted to the study of Zola and naturalism, edited by Alain Pagès. Numbers 50 (1976) and 59 (1985) deal extensively with *Germinal*.

Naturalism by Lilian R. Furst and Peter N. Skrine (London, Methuen, 1971) is a brief introduction to the broader field of naturalist literature. George J. Becker's anthology, *Documents of Modern Literary Realism* (Princeton, N.J., Princeton University Press, 1963), contains a number of important texts by naturalist writers translated into English. A useful collection of modern views is provided by Brian Nelson (ed.), *Naturalism in the European Novel. New Critical Perspectives* (New York–Oxford, Berg, 1992). David Baguley's *Naturalist Fiction: The Entropic Vision* (Cambridge, Cambridge University Press, 1990) applies genre theory to the themes, techniques and strategies of naturalist literature. Historical, social and political background information is to be found in abundance in Theodore Zeldin's two volumes on *France 1848–1945* (Oxford, Clarendon Press, 1973), and in a more concise form in Roger Magraw, *France 1815–1914. The Bourgeois Century* (London, Fontana, 1983, with corrections 1987).

Studies on naturalism, Zola and *Germinal* written in French are legion. Only a very few titles can be listed here. The standard edition of Zola's complete works is edited by Henri Mitterand. *Émile Zola: Œuvres complètes* (Paris, Cercle du Livre Précieux, 1966–9). The main critical editions of *Germinal* are by Henri Mitterand in vol. 3 of the Bibliothèque de la Pléiade edition of the *Rougon-Macquart* (Paris, Gallimard, 1964) and by Colette Becker in the Classiques Garnier edition (Paris, Bordas, 1989). For recent general introductions to Zola and his works, see Colette Becker, *Zola en toutes lettres* (Paris, Bordas, 1990), and Marc Bernard, *Zola* (Paris, Seuil, 1988), originally published in 1952 but updated by Jean-Pierre Leduc-Adine. A highly selective list of the most significant modern interpretations of Zola's works would include Jean Borie's psychoanalytical study, *Zola et les mythes* (Paris, Seuil,

1971), Philippe Hamon's study of characters and their functions in *Le Personnel du roman: le système des personnages dans les 'Rougon-Macquart' d'Emile Zola* (Geneva, Droz, 1983), thematic studies such as Auguste Dezalay's *L'Opéra des 'Rougon-Macquart'* (Paris, Champion, 1981) Roger Ripoll's *Réalité et mythe chez Zola* (Paris, Champion, 1981) and *Feux et signaux de brume. Zola* (Paris, Grasset, 1975) by Michel Serres. On Zola and the naturalist movement, excellent surveys are provided by Yves Chevrel, *Le Naturalisme* (Paris, P.U.F., 1982), then, in the 'Que sais-je?' series, by Henri Mitterand, *Zola et le naturalisme* (Paris, P.U.F., 1986), and Alain Pagès, *Le Naturalisme* (Paris, P.U.F., 1989). Of special note amongst books in French on *Germinal* are: Colette Becker, *Emile Zola: 'Germinal'* (Paris, P.U.F., 1984), and *La Fabrique de 'Germinal'* (Paris, SEDES, 1986) by the same critic, which reproduces Zola's preparatory dossier; Henri Marel, *'Germinal': une documentation intégrale* (Glasgow, University of Glasgow French and German Publications, 1989); and Alain Pagès, *La Bataille littéraire* (Paris, Séguier, 1989), on the critical reception of *Germinal* and naturalism. The *Dictionnaire d'Emile Zola* (Paris, Robert Laffont, 1993), compiled by Colette Becker, Gina Gourdin-Servenière and Véronique Lavielle, is a very valuable reference work.

TEXT SUMMARY

Part One

(1) Étienne Lantier, an out-of-work mechanic, arrives by chance one night at the Montsou mine. He meets Vincent Maheu, nicknamed Bonnemort, an elderly miner who is working a night shift at the surface and who informs Lantier about the owners of the mine, the Anzin Company, about his own lifetime of toil in the mine and about his family's situation. (2) At four o'clock that morning, the other working members of the Maheu family are described rising and preparing for their shift. (3) With the news that one of his team of workers has died in the night, Maheu (Bonnemort's son) takes on Étienne as a putter to haul the coal with Catherine, his young daughter. The frightening descent into the pit is evoked through Étienne's reactions. (4) The backbreaking hard labour of the miners at the coalface is described. Étienne and Catherine strike up a friendship during the break, provoking the jealousy of the brutish pikeman, Chaval, who has designs on Catherine. (5) Paul Négrel, the chief engineer of the mine, during a tour of inspection, fines Maheu's team for neglect of the timbering, causing them to leave off early in anger and giving Catherine and Étienne the opportunity to watch a horse, Trompette, being lowered down into the mine. (6) On their return to the surface, Maheu finds lodgings for Étienne at the inn run by Rasseneur, a former miner dismissed for his political activities.

Part Two

(1) On the morning of the same day, the family of Léon Grégoire, a shareholder in the mining company living comfortably off his ancestors' investments, takes breakfast in their cosy house, pampering their daughter, Cécile, then receiving Deneulin, owner of the small Vandame mine, which the Montsou company wishes to acquire. (2) Earlier that morning, Maheu's wife, la Maheude, rises with their three youngest children and embarks upon a desperate search for food and money at the Grégoires' house and at the shop of the lecherous grocer, Maigrat. (3) The daily activities of the women of the miners' settlement are described and Madame Hennebeau, the wife of the mine director, shows visitors from Paris around selected homes in the settlement. (4) The working members of the Maheu family return that afternoon to eat and wash. Maheu makes love to his wife.

(5) Étienne goes for a walk that evening and witnesses on the waste land around the mines the love-making of the young people of the mining community, including to his dismay Chaval forcing his attentions on Catherine.

Part Three

(1) During the spring, Étienne grows accustomed to work in the pit and holds political discussions in the inn with Rasseneur, the moderate reformer, and Souvarine, the anarchist, which, along with his readings, further his political education. (2) On the last Sunday in July, the miners hold their annual feast day. Étienne has begun to organize the workers, seeking subscriptions for a provident fund in case of a strike. (3) Étienne moves in with the Maheu household as a lodger, continuing his political education, beguiling the family with his visions of a better future and extending his influence throughout the whole settlement. He curbs his feelings of love for Catherine. (4) When the company announces a new system for remunerating the workers at the coalface separately for the timbering, thereby reducing their rate of pay, the miners, urged on by Étienne, decide to go on strike. (5) One of the Maheu children, Jeanlin, is injured in a mine accident. Chaval keeps Catherine with him and Étienne calls for the strike to start.

Part Four

(1) On the first day of the strike, Monsieur and Madame Hennebeau are entertaining the Grégoire family for lunch to promote the prospect of marriage between Cécile Grégoire and Paul Négrel, who is Hennebeau's nephew. A delegation of striking miners arrives at the house. (2) In his discussion with the delegation Hennebeau is paternalistic and unyielding. (3) By the end of December the strike has spread and Étienne has become the undisputed leader. There is widespread hunger in the settlement. When Catherine tries to deliver some food supplies to the Maheu household, Chaval brutally drags her away after a confrontation with Étienne. (4) In their discussions at a secret meeting of delegates Étienne clashes with Rasseneur, who is more moderate than the newcomer. Pluchart, secretary of the Nord branch of the International, arrives to speak in support of the strike and of Étienne's position, seeking to recruit members for the organization. The police break up the meeting. (5) Despite the growing problem of starvation in their families, the hardened miners refuse the company's moderate concessions, which fall short of their demands, and the strike continues. Étienne and la Mouquette make love. (6) Étienne discovers Jeanlin's hideaway and his stock of supplies in the depths of the mine. Three thousand miners, men, women, children, meet one January night in the Vandame forest. Étienne, in a long speech, urges them to continue the strike, defeating Rasseneur, who advocates conciliation.

Chaval, to outdo Étienne, his rival, incites the miners to force the workers at the Jean-Bart mine to join them on strike.

Part Five

(1) The next morning Deneulin persuades his miners to continue working. Chaval agrees, betraying the promise made in the forest meeting. (2) Down in the Jean-Bart mine, Catherine succumbs to heat and exhaustion just as the news breaks out that the Montsou miners have cut the cables, leading to a desperate rush to leave the mine by the escape ladders. (3) Earlier that morning the mob of striking miners angrily sets off to Jean-Bart where they take control, cut the cables and manhandle the blacklegs. (4) The mob goes on a rampage of destruction from mine to mine, crying out for bread. Catherine prevents the intoxicated Étienne from killing Chaval. (5) In the midst of these events, Hennebeau discovers his wife's infidelity with his nephew, Négrel, as the rampaging mob of strikers arrives at the Montsou director's house, singing 'La Marseillaise' and demanding bread. (6) As the Grégoire family arrives at Hennebeau's house, Cécile, accidently left outside, is saved from the attentions of the mob by Deneulin. The bourgeois characters look on as the frenzied women in the mob castrate the grocer, Maigrat, who has fallen from his roof, and then parade their 'trophy' along the street. The arrival of the gendarmes disperses the crowd.

Part Six

(1) By the beginning of February, troops have moved in to protect the mines, there have been arrests and Étienne has taken refuge in Jeanlin's hideaway. Despite the cold and hunger, the strike continues. (2) Alzire, the fourth Maheu child, dies of starvation in the general destitution of the mining community. (3) In the Avantage inn, Étienne, Rasseneur and Souvarine hold further animated political discussions that are interrupted one night by the arrival of Chaval, who provokes a fight with Étienne. Humiliated and defeated, Chaval abandons Catherine. (4) Étienne and Catherine walk together until she decides to try to return to Chaval. Étienne, alone, sees Jeanlin stab a sentry in the moonlight. They bury the body in the mine to leave no trace. (5) A battalion of soldiers confronts a crowd of strikers at the Montsou mine and, under provocation, opens fire, killing, amongst others, Maheu and la Mouquette.

Part Seven

(1) The shooting and its repercussions plunge the strikers into despair and confusion. Étienne loses all influence over the miners and is chased out of the settlement with stones. Rasseneur returns to favour. There is a dinner at the Grégoires' house to celebrate Cécile's engagement to Négrel. (2) The company makes certain concessions and many of the miners, including

Catherine and Étienne, return to work. But Souvarine has sabotaged the mine. (3) During the first shift, the Montsou mine collapses and is flooded, trapping Étienne, Catherine and other miners below. (4) Rescue work begins. Zacharie Maheu, a member of the rescue squad, is killed in an explosion. When the Grégoire family makes a charitable visit to la Maheude's house, Cécile is left alone with Bonnemort, who strangles her. (5) Étienne and Catherine are trapped together for days in the flooded mine, where Étienne kills Chaval in a fight. He and Catherine finally consummate their love as the girl dies of hunger and exhaustion. Étienne is rescued. (6) On a fine April morning, Étienne leaves the mining area to join Pluchart in Paris. He bids farewell to his former comrades, including la Maheude, all cowed into submission by the failure of the strike but silently resolved to rise again against injustice. As he leaves the scene, Étienne is filled with hope for the future and senses the violent upheavals that lie ahead.

FOREIGN LITERATURE IN TRANSLATION
IN EVERYMAN

A Hero of Our Time
MIKHAIL LERMONTOV
*The Byronic adventures of
a Russian army officer*
£5.99

L'Assommoir
ÉMILE ZOLA
*One of the most successful novels
of the nineteenth century and one
of the most scandalous*
£6.99

Poor Folk and **The Gambler**
FYODOR DOSTOYEVSKY
*These two short works of doomed
passion are among Dostoyevsky's
quintessential best. Combination
unique to Everyman*
£4.99

Yevgeny Onegin
ALEXANDER PUSHKIN
*Pushkin's novel in verse is Russia's
best-loved literary work. It contains some of the loveliest Russian
poetry ever written*
£5.99

The Three-Cornered Hat
ANTONIO PEDRO DE ALARCÓN
*A rollicking farce and one of
the world's greatest masterpieces
of humour. Available only in
Everyman*
£4.99

Notes from Underground
and **A Confession**
FYODOR DOSTOYEVSKY *and*
LEV TOLSTOY
*Russia's greatest novelists ruthlessly
tackle the subject of their mid-life
crises. Combination unique to
Everyman*
£4.99

Selected Stories
ANTON CHEKHOV
edited and revised by Donald
Rayfield
*Masterpieces of compression and
precision. Selection unique to
Everyman*
£7.99

Selected Writings
VOLTAIRE
*A comprehensive edition of
Voltaire's best writings. Selection
unique to Everyman*
£6.99

Fontamara
IGNAZIO SILONE
*'A beautifully composed tragedy.
Fontamara is as fresh now, and as
moving, as it must have been when
first published.' London Standard.
Available only in Everyman*
£4.99

All books are available from your local bookshop or direct from:
Littlehampton Book Services Cash Sales, 14 Eldon Way, Lineside Estate,
Littlehampton, West Sussex BN17 7HE (*prices are subject to change*)

To order any of the books, please enclose a cheque (in sterling) made payable to
Littlehampton Book Services, or phone your order through with credit card details (Access,
Visa or Mastercard) on 01903 721596 (24 hour answering service) stating card number
and expiry date. (*Please add £1.25 for package and postage to the total of your order.*)

In the USA, for further information and a complete catalogue call 1-800-526-2778

CLASSIC NOVELS
IN EVERYMAN

The Time Machine
H. G. WELLS
*One of the books which defined
'science fiction' – a compelling
and tragic story of a brilliant
and driven scientist*
£3.99

Oliver Twist
CHARLES DICKENS
*Arguably the best-loved of
Dickens's novels. With all the
original illustrations*
£4.99

Barchester Towers
ANTHONY TROLLOPE
*The second of Trollope's
Chronicles of Barsetshire,
and one of the funniest of all
Victorian novels*
£4.99

The Heart of Darkness
JOSEPH CONRAD
*Conrad's most intense, subtle,
compressed, profound and
proleptic work*
£3.99

Tess of the d'Urbervilles
THOMAS HARDY
*The powerful, poetic classic
of wronged innocence*
£3.99

Wuthering Heights and Poems
EMILY BRONTË
*A powerful work of genius – one of
the great masterpieces of literature*
£3.99

Pride and Prejudice
JANE AUSTEN
*Proposals, rejections, infidelities,
elopements, happy marriages –
Jane Austen's most popular novel*
£2.99

North and South
ELIZABETH GASKELL
*A novel of hardship, passion
and hard-won wisdom amidst the
conflicts of the industrial revolution*
£4.99

The Newcomes
W. M. THACKERAY
*An exposé of Victorian polite
society by one of the nineteenth-
century's finest novelists*
£6.99

Adam Bede
GEORGE ELIOT
*A passionate rural drama enacted
at the turn of the eighteenth
century*
£5.99

All books are available from your local bookshop or direct from:
Littlehampton Book Services Cash Sales, 14 Eldon Way, Lineside Estate,
Littlehampton, West Sussex BN17 7HE (*prices are subject to change*)

To order any of the books, please enclose a cheque (in sterling) made payable to
Littlehampton Book Services, or phone your order through with credit card details (Access,
Visa or Mastercard) on 01903 721596 (24 hour answering service) stating card number
and expiry date. (*Please add £1.25 for package and postage to the total of your order.*)

In the USA, for further information and a complete catalogue call 1-800-526-2778